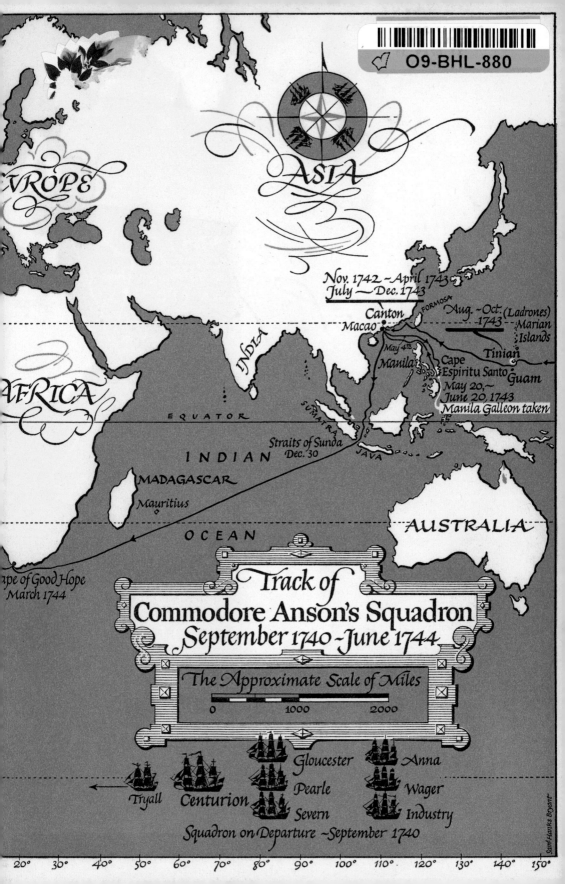

EUROPE

ASIA

AFRICA

INDIA

FORMOSA

Nov. 1742 – April 1743
July — Dec. 1743

Aug. ~ Oct.
1743

(Ladrones)
Marian
Islands

Canton
Macao

May 4th

Manila

Cape
Espiritu Santo

Tinian

Guam

May 20, ~
June 20, 1743
Manila Galleon taken

EQUATOR

SUMATRA

JAVA

Straits of Sunda
Dec. 30

INDIAN

MADAGASCAR

Mauritius

AUSTRALIA

OCEAN

Cape of Good Hope
March 1744

Track of
Commodore Anson's Squadron
September 1740 - June 1744

The Approximate Scale of Miles

0   1000   2000

Gloucester

Anna

Tryall   Centurion

Pearle

Wager

Severn

Industry

Squadron on Departure ~ September 1740

Sant-Hanks Bryant

20°   30°   40°   50°   60°   70°   80°   90°   100°   110°   120°   130°   140°   150°

By F. van Wyck Mason

VALLEY FORGE, 1777

PROUD NEW FLAGS

THREE HARBOURS

RIVERS OF GLORY

GOLDEN ADMIRAL

CUTLASS EMPIRE

BLUE HURRICANE

EAGLE IN THE SKY

SILVER LEOPARD

OUR VALIANT FEW

STARS ON THE SEA

THE YOUNG TITAN

THE COLONEL NORTH STORIES

MANILA GALLEON

Manila Galleon

Manila Galleon

F. van Wyck Mason
Illustrated by John Alan Maxwell

LITTLE, BROWN AND COMPANY · BOSTON · TORONTO

Published simultaneously in Canada
by Little, Brown & Company (Canada) Limited

PRINTED IN THE UNITED STATES OF AMERICA

This Book Is Affectionately Dedicated
to
Eric and Hope Parker
of Scopwick House, Lincolnshire,
Whose Friendship and Generosity
Have Been Unfailing
in War and in Peace

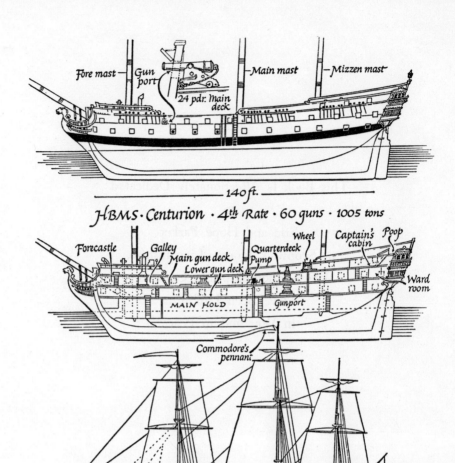

Fore mast — Gun port — Main mast — Mizzen mast

24 pdr. Main deck

140 ft.

HBMS · Centurion · 4th Rate · 60 guns · 1005 tons

Forecastle — Galley — Main gun deck — Lower gun deck — Quarterdeck — Pump — Wheel — Captain's cabin — Poop

MAIN HOLD — Gunport — Ward room

Commodore's pennant

HBMS Centurion

Foreword

I T WAS IN LONDON, 1946, while I was occupying a bed in the
Station Hospital, that I chanced upon a copy of Thomas Pascoe's
Journal and became irrevocably intrigued by Commodore George
Anson's epic voyage. Then and there, I resolved, for better or for
worse, to attempt to describe this modern Odyssey.

Unfortunately it was necessary to omit, or merely to refer in passing,
to much fascinating incident. The mutiny on the *Wager* in itself is
deserving of a long and exciting novel. The almost incredible smallboat voyages made by Captain Cheap and the mutinous seamen also
are replete with examples of incredible suffering, of unyielding te-
nacity of purpose and of villainy or devotion to duty.

Alas, that, in the interests of story length, it was necessary to gloss
over the Commodore's second visit to Canton and his historic nego-
tiations with the Chantuck, or Viceroy, for it was on that occasion that
George Anson's diplomatic genius manifested itself to secure, in China,
rights and privileges for the navies of the world which were enjoyed
until the Red Star became ascendant over what once had been the
Celestial Empire.

It is to John Masefield's incomparable *Sea Life in Nelson's Time*
that I owe so many details concerning the plan, the discipline, the
duties, the customs and the food — such as it was — aboard a British
ship-of-the-line. After conducting a considerable research on the subject I feel reasonably safe in assuming that, after Anson had effected

[ix]

his reforms, the passage of a little more than a hundred years would have brought relatively few changes in life — and death — aboard ships of the Royal Navy.

To touch with one's own hands the log so meticulously kept by Lieutenant Peircy Brett lent a rare thrill, while to read some of George Anson's few official reports — he loathed paperwork — became a supreme moment when I reflected upon the terrible conditions under which he must have penned them.

Throughout, I have referred constantly — aside from Pascoe's *Journal* — to the Reverend Richard Walter's scholarly *Account* abrim as it is with useful and colorful detail.

For details of the *Wager*'s loss I relied largely on the lively, if somewhat naïve, observations of Midshipman John Byron, who was serving aboard that unfortunate vessel when she was lost.

It has always appeared curious to me that while almost every English-speaking person has heard of Horatio Nelson, very few indeed know anything at all about George Anson, who, in fact, made possible Nelson's historic career some forty to fifty years later.

Justly, Anson has been termed — if not remembered — as the "Father of the Modern Royal Navy." As such, is he not then to be considered the "Grandfather of the United States Navy"?

It was he who, in 1748, finally persuaded the Lords Commissioners of the Admiralty for the first time to put the officers and men of the Royal Navy into uniform — in uniforms designed by Anson himself. Until that time, all naval personnel had been forced to wear civilian garb — to their vast disadvantage when on foreign duty.

When appointed to the Board of Admiralty, 1745, he at once instituted reforms and set about rooting out that corruption and incompetence in the Admiralty and at the Royal Victualing and Dockyards which had subjected him and his men to some of the most appalling sufferings ever recorded in the history of seafaring.

Among this brilliant and well-loved officer's accomplishments is the fact that, in 1755, he organized the celebrated Corps of Royal Marines on a permanent basis, i.e., composed of soldiers especially trained for service at sea.

Not only was George Anson an excellent organizer and diplomat, he was a fighting Admiral as well. In 1747, after a hard, cleverly fought action with the Marquis de la Jonquière, he captured nineteen of the Frenchman's thirty-eight ships.

He was, moreover, a supreme judge of human nature: of the officers and midshipmen, who accompanied him on the epic voyage, nine later achieved flag rank. Of these, nine became Rear Admirals, seven Vice-Admirals, three were appointed full Admirals and three eventually won the highest of Naval honors — First Lord of the Admiralty.

In this book I have departed from a long-established practice by adding an appendix, in order to list these above-mentioned flag officers and to indicate the few purely fictional characters.

On those several occasions when Anson is described as addressing the Ship's Company, I have reproduced his remarks *verbatim,* as recorded by men present and have not attempted to edit his sometimes quaint phraseology.

Needless to say, all incidents, even trivial ones, described in this book — with the exception of the obviously personal activities of fictional characters — are based on fact. Excerpts from various journals, accounts, narratives, diaries, etc., written by Anson's companions on this voyage are reproduced just as they appear.

It has been no easy matter to attempt to present an account of conditions prevalent aboard the expedition's ships without overloading the narrative with nautical terms or dwelling in too much detail upon the frightful sufferings of Anson and his men over a period of almost four years.

Since this is a story of combat, courage and survival, it is possible that some of my readers may have been similarly tested, almost two hundred years later, on Tinian, Guam, Taiwan and off Cape Espiritu Santo — all of which were well known to Anson's men.

To Mrs. W. A. Anson of Ronan's Lea, Brailes, Oxfordshire, I owe many thanks for having kindly granted permission to reproduce on the book jacket that splendid portrait of the Commodore which now graces her home.

Those who were most responsible for aiding me in the preparation of this book are: Jeanne Hand Mason — "Incidentally" of *The Young Titan* foreword — who has worked long, hard and intelligently as my principal secretary, and Mrs. Neville Burnett-Herkes who, years ago, assisted me with *Three Harbours.*

My sincere appreciation goes also to Miss Margaret Franklin, who, in London, spared me much tedious basic research in the Public Records Office and in the British Museum.

Finally, I wish once again to thank Mr. Robert H. Haynes, Assistant

Librarian of Widener Library, Harvard College, Cambridge, Massachusetts, for his able and judicious assistance.

F. VAN WYCK MASON

Hampton Head
Southampton, Bermuda

[xii]

Contents

[xv]

Manila Galleon

Prologue

BY THE BRIEF unearthly glare of lightning flashes which steadily were becoming more vivid, Peter Vesey — Doctor of Medicine by virtue of degrees hard-earned at Oxford and Edinburgh Universities — could glimpse through a ragged pattern of trees a faint sheen created by the Upper Thames. Although riffled by the storm's first warning puffs, it yet wound slowly, serenely towards the village of Henley and the home which recently he'd constructed on its southern bank.

The young physician — he was only twenty-nine — felt sure rain must begin to fall at any moment. The fitful wind, rising, stirred a nearby orchard and sent apple blossom petals drifting across the rutted road like the delicate ghosts of snowflakes.

His mount, a strong young mare, seemed to sense the impending downpour as well as he, for she pointed delicate ears downstream, in which direction forage and a dry stall were awaiting her. Gradually she quickened her trot.

Now thunder began to reverberate down the river valley creating a rumble like that of bowling balls rolling along some Titan's alley. The rhythmic *clink-clinking* of instruments and medicine bottles crammed into Peter Vesey's saddlebags quickened when, riding with the ease of one reared in a hunting saddle, he spurred his increasingly nervous mount to an easy canter.

The time, on this warm late spring night, Vesey judged to be near eleven, so, of course, houses without exception were shuttered and dark. Watchdogs, however, clamored fiercely at the mare's dainty hoofbeats.

What a surprise that Granny Swinden, so sorely stricken with calentures, had taken that wholly unexpected turn for the better. The

[3]

tough old woman had begun to rally from the minute he'd entered her cottage, soberly prepared to ease her passing. In fact, Mrs. Swinden got so much better and had begun to chatter so garrulously he hadn't seen any necessity for lingering until daylight.

A sudden crackling peal of thunder caused the mare to shy violently, to stand half-crouched with quivering legs gathered under her. A reassuring pressure on the reins and a few soothing words served to set her moving forward again an instant before the night became filled with a wet confusion which quickly drenched Dr. Vesey to his smallclothes.

The wind increased and blew so hard that a succession of twigs, wet leaves and even small branches were dashed into the rider's face. Swiftly, the dirt road degenerated into a quagmire intermittently revealed by the lightning's blue-white throbbing. He glimpsed a family of ghostly-looking swans, cowering in a reed bed on the Thames's farther bank. When the thundering approached an ear-shattering crescendo the mare, stung by hard-driven drops, began to plunge and rear, so, to steady her, Dr. Vesey reined to a walk.

Splashing slowly on through the downpour, Vesey wished the hour weren't so advanced, but he encouraged himself by thinking that Pamela probably wouldn't have gone to bed. She wasn't in the least frightened by lightning. On the contrary she so greatly enjoyed a thunderstorm's noise and vivid majesty that she might very well still be up to brew a cup of tea.

Rain began to pelt his eyelids so hard that he had to shield them behind a raised forearm. A good thing, he reflected, that his mount could sense where she was going; he hadn't the least notion.

The worst of the storm's fury seemed to have exhausted itself when, with cold trickles running down his back and chest, Dr. Vesey splashed into an avenue of majestic oaks at the end of which lay Minden — his home. For all that the house was small, it was of neatly dressed gray stone, comfortable and smart architecturally. How fortunate he'd been to be able to construct this dwelling for his bride upon the site of an ancient manor house which had burnt down a few years ago: otherwise, he never could have boasted of such venerable trees lining Minden's driveway.

To his vast relief a light, warm and cheery, *was* glowing through lessening rain, which undoubtedly meant that Pamela had remained awake to view this terrifying display of lightning.

He made no effort to check the mare when she began to trot.

[4]

What incredible luck. In a very few minutes now, Pamela would be brewing tea. He visualized her, dark and slim, fetching brandy in a cut-glass decanter. Lord knew he could use such refreshment. Since quitting Minden, late in the afternoon, he must easily have covered fifteen miles and that after having stayed up the whole of the previous night delivering his sister of a squalling, beet-red daughter.

Vesey's streaming features formed a stiff smile on recalling the way the midwife had glowered at him. Undoubtedly she, like the rest of England, never had heard of Dr. William Hunter — the "male midwife" — behind whom he had "walked" to learn the "Paris Method." He'd come eventually to agree that it was *not* beneath a physician's dignity, but rather his duty, to assist at childbirth.

Chilled and weary as he was, Vesey took time to rub down the mare thoroughly once he'd unsaddled and unbridled her. Next he made sure there was a generous bait of grain in her feedbox and pitchforked plenty of hay into the manger.

Slinging sodden saddlebags over one shoulder, Dr. Vesey splashed through a succession of puddles and, smiling, turned his front door's silvered knob. The smile faded when, on calling a greeting, he got no response.

Vaguely uneasy, he hung the heavy leather bags to a staghorn rack and sought Pamela in the pantry. Perhaps she'd heard the mare's hoofs and had gone out to put the kettle on? Although his wife wasn't there he forebore to rouse the servants. Lord knew the poor creatures were required to remain on call from early morning until he returned from his rounds which, sometimes, was very late at night.

Nor was Pamela in the library, which puzzled him, since a decanter of sherry and a half-filled wineglass stood on a table. The young physician's alarm mounted because he recalled seeing a similar partially filled glass on the living room mantelpiece.

The storm appeared to be gathering fresh fury; lightning again blazed very nearby and heart-stilling thunderclaps caused windowpanes and shutters to rattle. Dripping dark spots along the carpets, Vesey hurriedly ranged through the upper floor and observed that although the four-poster's covers had been turned down there was no trace of Pamela.

Now thoroughly alarmed, the doctor had started below when he halted on the staircase and began softly to laugh. The summerhouse! Of course Pamela had gone out there; from which vantage point she could see the river and more fully enjoy the storm's vivid fury. Why hadn't he recalled before that she was given to doing this?

His muddied riding boots crunched loudly upon the driveway's wet gravel, but the thundering effectively concealed his progress.

Urged on by an especially vicious squall, Vesey covered the last few yards to the summerhouse at a run and dashed inside. As he was flinging open the door a very brilliant flash of lightning illuminated the interior in such detail that he could have read titles on a series of flower prints gracing the summerhouse's far wall.

The sudden glare also revealed, in pitiless clarity, two figures extended upon the rattan settee on which Pamela often reposed during pleasant weather. The person above showed dark, while the one beneath shone vividly white. This, Vesey realized, was because the woman's dress had been pulled so high as to expose the entire length of long, slim legs which glimmered pale as those of an alabaster statue.

A roaring which made the thunder's crash pale to insignificance commenced in Peter Vesey's head. Emitting a strangled growl, he bounded forward.

BOOK I

"A Particular Service—"

~I~

HBMS *Centurion*

A RADIANT FULL MOON flooded the lofty poopdeck of the Fourth Rate line-of-battleship, HBMS *Centurion*. It sketched the mizzen shrouds as a neat pattern of black rectangles across a deck that gleamed white as a field covered by new-fallen snow. The moonlight also drew faint flashes from the buttons and sword hilts of four officers gathered below HBMS *Centurion*'s three stern lights — massive fixed lanterns of wrought-iron elaborately gilded.

Commodore George Anson, tallest of the group, held himself very erect and yet, somehow, not stiffly. Even by moonlight the clear, bright blueness of his widely spaced eyes and the strength and straightness of a rather strong nose easily was discernible. Now in his forty-third year, Anson's stature was slightly above the average, but being wide-shouldered and otherwise muscular, he appeared to be much larger than he really was.

Deliberately — Anson's movements were seldom abrupt — he turned to a tall, craggy-faced individual wearing a long-skirted scarlet tunic laced in tarnished gold, a yellow waistcoat and white knee breeches and stockings. Lieutenant Colonel Mordaunt Cratcherode's was the only uniform visible, for, to their grief, the officers and men of King George II's Navy as yet wore civilian dress wherever they went.

For a long moment Commodore Anson regarded the quarterdeck immediately below and a Marine sentry who was shambling along it with his musket canted awkwardly across one shoulder. Said he presently in deep measured tones, "I trust, Colonel Cratcherode, you will quickly smarten up your Jollies. The ones I have noticed thus far on my flagship appear to be deplorably raw and ill-trained."

[9]

The gaunt Lieutenant Colonel commanding all land troops assigned to the squadron jerked a stiff nod. "Of that, sir, I assure you I am most painfully aware." The moon's serene brilliance picked out a puckered, purplish scar slanting across the Army officer's jutting right cheekbone. "Only explanation I can offer, sir, is that thus far the only drafts my officers and I have received are a mixed bag of sickly green recruits and hardened troublemakers."

Brusquely, Colonel Cratcherode cleared his throat, stood glaring down at that slovenly, red-coated figure walking sentry post beside the *Centurion*'s main hatch, then rasped, " 'Pon my word, sir, what they're sending us nowadays are rejects and misfits culled from second-rate regiments. But never fear, sir, I'll have them in shape by sailing day — if I have to flog every rascal among 'em. 'Twill help me immeasurably when the draft from Colonel Bland's fine regiment arrives. To a man, his are well-seasoned troops — many of 'em veterans."

"Let us hope they appear without loss of time," remarked round-faced Captain Richard Norris in command of HBMS *Gloucester,* 50 guns. "Only land troops *I've* received in my ship are the worst lot of gallows bait ever to disgrace the King's scarlet."

Captain Norris glanced at his new command across the sparkling jet and silver waters of Portsmouth Harbor and barely suppressed a sigh. By this kindly light the squadron's other Fourth Rate appeared to be what he knew she was not — a taut, sound man-of-war, ready and able to sail anywhere the Lords of Admiralty might send her.

To Anson he said uncomfortably, "Please be good enough to refresh my memory, sir. Did you not at dinner state that I am expected to take on board one hundred land troops?"

"I did, Captain. Why do you ask?"

"Why, sir, that means I — will have to accommodate *four hundred* bodies in a ship of only eight hundred and sixty-six tons burthen!"

"No, Captain, you will have only three hundred and ninety-six officers and men to find room for," came the imperturbable correction. "I appreciate that you will be badly crowded, but then so will all the ships. There's no help for it." Anson's manner changed. "Are you still short of seamen?"

"Aye, sir — very. I have sent my pressgangs ashore, but they keep returning empty-handed — or nearly so. The countryside seems to have been swept bare."

"It appears to have been," came the Commodore's equable admission. "Therefore I am, tonight, sending my first lieutenant, Mr. Cheap, far inland to secure men. How many hands do you require?"

Briefly, Captain Norris's gaze sought the towering loom of the great First Class, St. *Albans*, 120 guns, and the multitude of lights sparkling aboard her. Would he ever command so magnificent a man-of-war?

"Why, I cannot do with less than ninety hands." Again Norris hesitated. "Sir, there's another matter —"

"— Yes?"

As in search of support, Richard Norris directed a quick glance at thick-bodied Captain Dandy Kidd. "Under the great number of stores taken on for so long a cruise as seems to be indicated, my command now rides so deep in the water that, out of common caution, I have had to order my lower gundeck ports caulked and nailed shut. Were they not, *Gloucester* most certainly would founder in half a sea."

George Anson's shoulders squared themselves a trifle. "You are quite justified in taking such a precaution. I already have ordered that lower deck gunports shall be sealed throughout the squadron. Have any of you gentlemen further comments?"

Although wary of a certain ominous hardening of the Commodore's jaw line, Captain Norris doggedly continued. "Yes, sir, I trust you'll not deem me unduly complaining, but only doing my duty, when I report that most of the sails and some of the cordage issued to *Gloucester* are either very sea-worn or fashioned from inferior canvas. Furthermore, many spars sent me by the dockyard authorities are not of Establishment quality. In fact, sir, they are deficient as to quality, length and thickness. Further, sir, my carpenter suspects that my mainmast is not quite sound."

"You have mentioned this in a Report of Survey?"

"Aye, sir. Earlier this evening I entrusted it to your secretary."

"Then, Captain, you have done all that you can to remedy these deficiencies," Anson observed, sternly suppressing his misery over the fact that Norris's complaints were well founded. Most of his other Captains, at one time or another, had reported similar defects. Worst of the situation was they'd all have to put up and shut up if, after more than three months' delay and uncertainty, the squadron was ever to go to sea.

Thought George Anson, only the good Lord knows how anxious I am over these interminable delays. Why, 'twas last January that Sir Charles Wager summoned me and said I'd been selected as Commander in Chief over an expedition to the South Sea. Today is September the tenth — and in all that time what's been accomplished? Little save to assemble and half-man the six men-of-war and two merchant victualers I'm supposed to lead on a secret "Particular Service for the Lords of Admiralty." Wonder just how well that supposed secret has been kept? God help us all if it's leaked out and the Spaniards have learned about what we intend.

He glanced at bony, hawk-nosed Lieutenant Colonel Cratcherode, saw him scowling at a corporal's guard of Marines who, in badly fitting uniforms, were shuffling on deck to relieve sentries on guard.

"Is there anything else you wish to speak of, Captain Norris?"

"No, sir." The plump officer belched — he was suffering from an acute distemper of the stomach. "May I thank you, sir, for a most excellent repast?"

The Commodore's smile was bleak, but his tone sounded cordial. "It was indeed a pleasure to have you on board. When the new hands arrive at dockside you will be signaled to that effect."

Captain Norris lifted his hat to the Commodore, then bade the others good night before descending to the upper gundeck. When he called out, "*Gloucester's* boat, please," sideboys raced to form a double rank facing inward towards the gangway. The Officer of the Deck ordered Marines to present arms as Captain Norris's barge was brought alongside. Boatswain's pipes shrilled until the visiting Captain descended the gangway ladder and had seated himself. They fell silent when, presently, with oars rhythmically dipping, the barge headed for *Gloucester* lying to her anchor, moon-bathed, beyond two other ships belonging to Anson's squadron: *Severn,* a Fourth Rate of 50 guns, and the smaller *Pearle,* which mounted 40 cannon.

Ashore, lights winked and blinked like a hundred sleepy cats, in Portsmouth, also in Gosport across the harbor. As Captain Norris sat back on his barge's hard and lumpy cushions he caught the lively sound of concertinas and the squeaking of fiddle music played aboard *St. Albans;* also raucous singing interspersed with high-pitched feminine laughter. Her crew, he knew, must be attempting with "sea wives" and red-eye rum to forget their desperation over being denied shore leave and being kept virtual prisoners at the end of a six months' cruise. This was grossly unfair — and illegal — but, as a professional naval officer, he knew there was nothing else to be done. Granted shore leave, they'd desert to a man. And where would replacements be found?

[12]

After *Gloucester*'s barge had pulled off into the night, Lieutenant Colonel Cratcherode saluted, asked to be excused and then clumped down to his tiny cabin situated just forward of the wardroom. He limped a little because of a knee wound taken in India. Besides, his malaria had begun to bother him again.

Once the Army officer had disappeared below, Anson turned to his last guest and smiled. Only in Dandy Kidd's presence could he permit himself to relax and feel freed, in a measure, from that dreadful isolation which is the penalty of becoming a Commander in Chief. He and Captain Kidd had been good friends ever since serving in HBMS *Scarborough*. He felt at once pleased and uncomfortable that he'd been instrumental in securing for that able, though rather unimaginative, individual a deserved promotion.

"Well, Captain," said he, smiling, "I must admit I find great pleasure at long last in addressing you as such. When do you plan to hoist your pendant aboard the *Wager?*"

Captain Kidd's blunt, red-brown features softened in a rare display of emotion. "Why, tomorrow morning, sir — if all goes well." Nervously he cleared his throat. "Please believe, sir, that I intend doing my utmost to justify the confidence you have placed in me."

In a happy mood Dandy Kidd then regarded the dozens of lantern-lit men-of-war swinging dark and impressive to their moorings. As usual, a flotilla of white-painted gigs and launches could be seen pulling between them, busily returning visiting officers to their own ships. And to think that now Dandy Kidd would have a boat of his own! The realization seemed almost too good to be true.

Commodore Anson observed, "The advancement was long overdue. Ahem. I presume that you have examined your command?"

Captain Kidd's happy expression faded in the moonlight. "Aye, sir. My carpenter, the bosun and I several times have surveyed the *Wager* from stem to stern and from truck to keelson."

"— And you found?"

"Why, sir, with regard to my ship's hull, cordage, sails and spars, they're better than I expected. Not of the best, or of the worst, by any means," he added hastily. "It's concerning the quality of the provisions that have been sent me that I'm worried."

"They're worse than average?" The Commodore's tricorne, trimmed in salt-greened gold braid, loomed black against the stars.

"I fear so, sir," came the reluctant admission. "Most of the salt meat that's been sent aboard is, to say the least, ancient. This morn-

[13]

ing I chanced to pass downwind from a row of salt horse — er, salted beef — casks and they positively stank! When I flatly refused to sign for 'em the victualing contractors grumbled but finally carted 'em back to the warehouse where they may have driven 'em around the court before they brought 'em back. I know because I recognized the markings on 'em. What am I to do, sir?"

"Accept them," came the curt advice. "Protests will avail you nothing. Those rascals are too well entrenched."

A desperate note entered Kidd's voice, he so wanted to make good. "Sir, it wouldn't be so bad about the beef if only the ship's bread wasn't equally uneatable — like most of the salted pork issue. Please tell me, what am I to feed my crew?"

Speaking in flat, succinct accents, Anson said, "Once we are at sea I will arrange for you to draw better provisions from the victualers which will accompany us."

"Victualers, sir?"

"Yes, two merchantmen. The *Anna* and the *Industry* have been chartered to accompany us as far as the twelfth degree of latitude, north. I have seen to it, personally, that the stores they carry are of reasonable quality."

Anson did not add that that would be possible only because he'd given the victualing officers a substantial bribe, which he could ill-afford, from his own slender resources.

George Anson's untroubled expression in no way betrayed the depth of his resentment against peculations committed by the Commissioners for Victuals and Supply. Now that His Grace the Duke of Newcastle had succeeded in having himself appointed Principal Secretary of State, the administration of the Royal Navy was descending to the nadir of corruption and inefficiency.

He was recalled to more present anxieties by Captain Kidd's asking, "I trust the *Wager* is not to carry much more field artillery? She already rides so dangerously low in the water I fear that heavy seas may swamp her."

"You will receive no more artillery, Captain, unless the Admiralty alters their present plan. You will, however, be required to load ammunition and small arms for our land troops."

Captain Kidd peered steadily into his superior's broad, moon-silvered features. "May I inquire, sir, where we have been ordered to attack the Dons?"

"You may not. I can only inform you that this squadron is 'to annoy and distress' certain territories belonging to the Spanish Crown." The Commander in Chief's expression suddenly relaxed. "'Twill be fun to find ourselves fighting the Papists once more, eh, Captain?"

"Rare fun indeed, sir, and you may rest assured that the *Wager* will enjoy taking part in the merriment." Kidd's assurance was almost pathetically fervent.

"Permission to leave the flagship, sir?"

"Of course — and good luck, Captain."

"Thank you, sir." Dandy Kidd lifted his hat and hurried below; secretly he thrilled to see *Centurion*'s gangway being manned in his honor.

Captain Kidd, however, wasn't at all thrilled over the awkward way his barge's crew tossed their oars on arriving alongside. Being a new Post Captain he hadn't been able to bring along well-trained people from a former command and so had to select his coxswain and oarsmen by guess and by God from among *Wager*'s motley complement.

～ 2 ～

"– To Annoy and Distress the Spaniards"

COMMODORE GEORGE ANSON, standing solitary on *Centurion*'s poop, watched the flagship's quartermaster strike two brisk notes on a brass bell fixed beneath the forecastle's break. All over the harbor other bells began to dispute the exact moment of nine o'clock.

Immediately the master-at-arms and his corporals tramped below roaring, "Dim the glims! Lights out! Lights out!" and used rattan canes on men who were slow about complying. Within minutes the myriad lanterns which had illumined the ships blinked out, leaving only riding lights and reflections of countless stars to keep the moon company. Only in Portsmouth and over in Gosport did lamps still glow.

Commodore George Anson, broad-shouldered second son of William Anson, Squire of Shugborough in Staffordshire, automatically checked the ships he was to command for illegal lights, then descended to the blessed privacy of the great cabin's stern gallery.

Assailed by anxieties, he paced slowly back and forth, then entered his cabin by a door at one end of the gallery — the other opened into his private head — and got his flute from its case. Astonishing how effective the playing of a few tunes could be in dispelling doubts and anxieties. Removing the slim wooden instrument in its battered velvet-lined case, he set up a rack, selected a sheet of music from a portfolio of country dances, and seated himself. But, to his surprise, he wasn't able to fix his attention on music, so let his mind run back over the years.

So, at forty-three I'm a commander of a squadron of His Majesty's ships of war and so far I've never commanded more than a single ship. Now I've eight — counting the victualers. Perhaps I'll succeed, *if* I prove to be lucky. Say what they will, I know the element of luck goes far towards shaping a flag officer's career; no matter how able, he can't go far without it.

Wonder how many actions have been lost simply because an unfavorable slant of wind came along at the wrong moment? It would be interesting to learn the number of rich prizes which have missed capture because of a passing snow squall or rainstorm.

Anson listened to the slow pacing of the Marine on duty outside his door, then continued his self-examination. Am I fashioned of the stuff that can bear high command? Am I wise enough? Sufficiently experienced? I know how to handle and fight a single ship; I proved that several times off the American coast and in the Mediterranean — but what about correctly coordinating the maneuvers of *six* men-of-war in battle? Eh? What about that, George Anson, for all that you've read your eyes out on the tactics of Drake, Howard, Hawkins and the rest? Too bad those great captains should have won their victories so long ago.

Absently Anson's broad but sensitive fingers trilled upon the holes of his flute. Can I inspire such loyalty in my captains that they will, even in the heat of battle, promptly and unquestioningly execute my orders? God only knows.

One thing, at least, ought to stand in my favor. The captains know that I wasn't made Commander in Chief through graft or influence; only got it because I understand my job. In that connection, how will the Honorable Edward Legge and George Murray shape up? Maybe they'll do all right, even if they've had their captain's commissions presented on a golden plate. Some have. A long sigh escaped the figure seated before the music rack.

[16]

Jerking loose the ribbon of crimson grosgrain with which he had secured his shoulder-length light-brown hair, George Anson continued to make a critical appraisal of his situation. He put down the moistened flute and knelt before a small, iron-bound chest to which only he had a key. From it he removed "Instructions" prepared by the Lords Commissioners, signed by the King, and given him *eight long months earlier!* He could have recited certain passages by heart but all the same read:

> You are to Sail around Cape Horn into the South Seas to Annoy and Distress the Spaniards there, whether on the Sea or on the Land to the Utmost of your Power.

He paused to smooth the well-fingered document before him.

> You are to Take, Sink, Burn or Destroy all their Vessels and Ships that you shall meet with. In case you shall find it Practicable to Seize, Surprise, or Take any of the Towns or Places belonging to the Spaniards on that Coast, you are to Attempt it.

This passage, of course, explained the presence of land troops and field artillery aboard his ships.

> — Or if you Judge it Best to go North as far as Acapulcho (in Mexico) to look for the Acapulcho Ship (a richly-laden Spanish Galeon) which Sails to that Place from Manilla (in the Philippines) at a certain Time of the Year, You may possibly, in that Case, think it more Desirable to return Home by the way of China.

The Acapulco ship! When first he'd gone to sea as a sturdy fourteen-year-old he'd been thrilled by tales and legends concerning these fabulous treasure ships. How many British seamen had not dreamed of capturing such a "Prize of All the Oceans" and becoming rich for life?

⤙ 3 ⤚
To Fill Up the Muster Book

TICHFIELD, a small but ancient market town lying over a dozen miles to the west of Portsmouth, was distinguished by neatly thatched cottages and many half-timbered structures dating from the reign of Elizabeth Tudor. Tonight it lay somnolent, drenched under the light of a full moon. Ghostly tendrils of woodsmoke spiraled lazily out of blackened chimney pots, then merged and flattened out as a gossamer pall above the shaggy rooftops. The environs of Tichfield lay silent and peaceful until a pair of cats, in the throes of love, emitted such a series of diabolical wails that watchdogs raised howls of protest.

By eight o'clock hardly a light showed in any of the dwellings enclosing a small market place still littered with the manure and refuse of the day's trading. Tichfield's inhabitants, Lieutenant David Cheap decided, had retired early, no doubt wearied by trafficking and subsequent indulgence in rude pleasures.

Some plow horses drowsing in a well-grazed pasture to the east of Tichfield lifted blunt heads and cocked furry ears when, a quarter mile outside the village, a number of farm carts were pulled to a halt. In stealthy silence then dismounted a swarm of men in baggy breeches and varicolored shirts or jerseys. Some wore brass-hilted cutlasses; others carried cudgels. Short lengths of stout cord dangled from many belts. The only firearms in evidence, however, was a brace of boarding pistols *Centurion's* first lieutenant had jammed into a wide leather belt. His square, usually taciturn features had assumed a measure of animation, if not of anticipation.

Once his party, numbering thirty in all, had formed up along the dusty, moonlit road, Lieutenant Cheap raised a hand and in a hoarse undertone warned, "No noise now, lads, and remember this well — should you be forced to draw cutlass don't you dare use its edge!" Harshly he added, "I'll see the skin off the back of anyone who disobeys."

Shaggy, shadowy heads inclined. "Aye, aye, sir. We'll remember."

"When we enter the village you will surround the inn, first off. I'm told it's full-up tonight. Anyone know its name?"

"Aye, sir, 'tis called the Sheaf of Wheat," someone muttered. "Many's the dram I've downed in its taproom. Maggie the scullery maid will do, cheerful-like, like them cats —"

"Belay that!" snapped the lieutenant, heavy undershot jaw tightening under his tricorne's battered rim. "You've leave to knock out any man you have to, but take care not to strike too hard! Cripples or men with addled wits are of no use to me."

"How young are we to take 'em, sir?"

"Fourteen and up," Cheap announced, large round eyes gleaming white in the moonlight. "Or maybe a year younger, provided the lad's big and strong. There's plenty of use for boys aboard ship."

A snigger sounded from the pressgang's rear. "Sure, a chicken for everyone, says I."

"Silence, you dirty dog! Now, when we move off, I want you all to walk along each side of the road lest the tramp of our feet alarm the yokels."

Nathaniel Wade turned onto his side and, propped on an elbow, sleepily surveyed his bride's dark and lustrous hair. How excitingly disordered it had become as a result of their recent ecstasies. Like ink spilled from Peggy's small head it spread over the pillowcase, then dripped onto the sheet. Young Wade thought, how odd, till now I've never noticed what a cute little nose Peggy has.

Moonlight, striking boldly through the window's leaded and lozenge-shaped panes, drew a high light from her bare shoulder and silvered the marble-white roundness of a generous but firm young breast which had escaped the bedclothes.

Lord's love! He still couldn't believe that this entrancing vision belonged to him. It was no longer Margaret Trusdale who lay by his side sleeping so sweetly, but Peggy Wade.

He guessed he'd never know just what had induced Goodman Trusdale, prosperous miller of Romsey, to bestow his favorite daughter on a nearly penniless young harness-maker. Maybe Mr. Trusdale somewhere had learned that, in due course, he likely would inherit childless Uncle Harold's tannery? It didn't really matter, so the bridegroom settled back, brown-stained fingers laced behind head, and stared unseeing at the ceiling's cracked and water-stained plaster.

Come tomorrow morning, he'd hire a nag with a pillion attached to the back of its saddle and convey Peggy to her new home. Which side of the family would the first child favor? Would it be fairhaired and big-boned like the Wades, or small, dark and wiry like the Trusdales? The baby was bound to be a boy; for, time out of mind, the Wades had been strongly inclined to beget male children. He himself was one of nine boys. There'd be other children, too. How many? Ten, maybe —

Nat fell into a deep sleep which he wasn't destined to enjoy for long; only minutes later, stealthy feet climbed the inn's staircase, then the bedroom's door was burst open and a number of dark figures rushed into the bridal chamber.

[19]

"Wha — wha's this?" Nat roused, only to be grabbed by the arms and pinned flat against the mattress. Powerfully, he heaved and almost had shaken off his assailants when a cudgel descended on his crown. All the stars in the universe whirled crazily before his eyes and there began such a roaring in his ears that only dimly did he recognize Peggy's ear-piercing shrieks.

When Wade regained a measure of consciousness he found himself lying face down and stark naked on the floor. Men were lashing his hands cruelly tight behind him.

A voice panted, "Lie still, ye bloody clod. Want me to bash yer again?"

Tichfield, meanwhile, was rousing to the jangling tinkle of broken glass, to the crackle of splintering wood and to the frenzied yelping of many dogs. Women's shrill screams commenced to beat down the moonlit street, mingled with shouting of men, "The pressgangsters are here! 'Ware the press! Turn out! Arm yerselves!"

"Where are they?"

"They's some of 'em raiding 'e inn right now! They's more in 'e market place."

"Where's my blunderbuss?"

"No! No! Don't you dast take my Joey, he's only a lad!"

Through blood trickling freely from his split scalp, Nat caught a glimpse of Peggy. She was backed against the wall beyond the bed and trying to hide her young body behind a sheet. Her eyes had become white-ringed with terror and her sable hair streamed wildly over sturdy shoulders as she kept screaming, "Help! Murder! Help! For God's sake, help!" Then a seaman with a tar-stiffened pigtail slapped her into a corner where she slumped, shivering violently.

"Come on, mates, find this cockerel's duds," growled a bandy-legged fellow in a torn jersey. "His fun's over for tonight."

A 'gangster flung Nat's wedding shirt over his shoulders but because the prisoner's hands were lashed together its sleeves couldn't be used. After they'd jerked up Wade's new duroy breeches they jammed on his brogans and hauled him, swaying, to his feet.

Wade, abruptly recovering the power of speech, commenced to yell, "Lemme loose, damn you! I — freeborn Englishman — You've no right!"

Encouraged by his clamor, Peggy got up and resumed her ear-piercing pleas for assistance.

"Hush that wench!" ordered a tall, black-bearded fellow.

He in the striped jersey ran over, snatched away the sheet Peggy was clutching and waggled a fist under the pert little nose Nat so recently had been admiring and snarled, "One more yip out o' ye, and ye'll lose a lot of them pretty teeth."

"Cor!" gasped a voice in the background. "Now *ain't* she the little beauty? Pity we can't fetch her along. She'd sure fill some hammocks with fun."

"Hell!" rumbled Blackbeard. "We got time to tumble 'er right now! Grab 'er ankles, Tom, and heave 'er onto 'e bed."

Nat's shoulders made a sudden violent circular motion which didn't quite free him. A fist snapped his head suddenly backwards, loosened some teeth and filled his mouth with musty-tasting blood.

Someone hailed from below, "Come down out o' there, ye mangy whoresons! Lootenant's fair frothing to get away."

While he was being hauled away Wade managed to choke, "Peggy! I — come back! Still law 'n' justice — England! Remember, I — *come back soon!*"

Not for a long time would he forget Peggy's pallid body and distorted limbs writhing towards him across their bridal bed.

The sound of blows, weeping and grunting met Wade's ears on the stairs. "Stow that jabber and line up, damn you!" The Sheaf of Wheat's brick-floored taproom was thronged by cursing 'gangsters and their struggling, desperate prisoners.

By a whale oil lamp's reddish-yellow glare, Nat was thrust into a rank of disheveled, bleeding half-naked figures surrounded by seamen carrying gleaming cutlasses.

"Well, Bosun, and how many have you caught?" Lieutenant Cheap demanded, round gray eyes bright with excitement and pleasure.

"Eight, sir."

"All bedrooms been searched?"

"Aye, aye, sir."

"That's not enough! Send these rascals to the carts."

The Sheaf of Wheat's landlord appeared still in his nightgown and tasseled nightcap. He was tearing his wispy white hair. "Last year and now again!" he wailed. "The devil take you for cruel dogs! You're ruining my custom!"

Lieutenant Cheap smiled thinly, "Don't take on so, old gaffer! We're only doing our duty." Once he had stepped out into the cobbled square he directed, "Leech, take four men and search the stables. Haycox, take three and see who you can find in yonder big house across the square. Rest of you search among the cottages along the road out of here." Grimly he added, "Don't let anyone get away, else you'll hear from me — *and* the cat!"

Leech's party discovered a brawny young fellow busy in the hayloft with Maggie, the Sheaf of Wheat's ever-obliging scullery maid. As fine a topman as had ever laid out on a royal yard, Able Seaman Tom Ramster hastily burrowed deep into dusty, sweet-smelling hay and hauled her after him. When he'd crawled as far as he could, Tom clapped a horny hand over the girl's loose mouth, hissing, "Keep mum, else I'll surely kill you."

Tom meant it. Only the day before he'd been paid off following a long, hard cruise to the Baltic. Nothing in life — or death, either — did he fear so much as a return to the 'tween decks of one of His Majesty's men-of-war.

His hands tightened so convulsively that the girl gasped, "Leave be! Yer chokin' me! I won't yell. Ye ain't paid me."

He could sense the blowsy creature's terror, could even feel her heart pounding under her damp and unbuttoned blouse.

His own heart sank when boots grated on the loft's ladder.

"Bring up yon pitchfork, Jarge," he heard someone say. "Might be a rat or two hiding here. Stand ready!"

As luck would have it the pitchfork's first tentative jab stung the scullery maid's ample bottom so shrewdly that she couldn't suppress a convulsive yelp.

"Ah! And wot do we 'ave 'ere? Ha! Curse me, Jarge, if we ain't bagged a brace o' lovebirds. Rouse out o' there!"

Tom felt a hand close over his ankle and haul him towards the loft's edge. Lean and wiry at twenty-eight, A.B. Tom Ramster surged to his feet, hurled an armful of hay at the nearest 'gangster and then drove his fist hard into the other face looming above him. He didn't realize that a third man had climbed the loft ladder.

"Look out!" the maid squalled.

From the corner of his eye Tom glimpsed the dull gleam of a cutlass blade. He'd handled one often enough to recognize it. The blade's flat smacked down so hard on Tom Ramster's red head that the next thing he knew he was lying trussed on the stable's ammonia-tinctured floor with a horse peering curiously at him over the edge of a box stall.

The pressgang might never have found old Joe Utting had he

burrowed just a little deeper into the strawpile in which he'd elected to sleep off his liquor. Joe really couldn't be blamed for having got a bit tipsy. A hard-working farmer, he'd sold his wain load of turnips for a far better price than he'd dared to expect. After the long trip over to Tichfield, Joe, quite naturally, had decided to toss a pot or two before returning to his smoky, overcrowded cottage, nine children and nagging wife.

Boatswain's Mate Leech, while reconnoitering the inn's stable-yard, tripped over the farmer's boot, then pounced like a falcon upon a terrified old hare.

"Ahoy, lads, here's a real bawcock!" he laughed, pulling the scrawny, straw-covered figure to its feet.

"Methusalem's Pa, b' God!"

"He *may* look a mite long in the tooth," admitted Leech, "but he's still plenty young enough to stop a bullet in the King's service."

In the moonlight Utting's gray hair looked whiter than it really was. He was lacking both front teeth so sprayed the air with spittle as he quavered, "For God's sake, don't take me, kind friends. I be too old and feeble." He raised knobby joined hands. "I've yet the oats to harvest and my boy Toby's down wi' a broken leg."

"Nah, then. Do we 'ave to tie ye up?"

"Oh, no! But ye mustn't take me. Have mercy — I-I've nine young uns to feed."

"Nine? Haw! Haw! Then it's high time ye gave yer old 'ooman a nice long rest — which is just what yer about to do."

Scarcely thirty minutes after the raid had been launched, the pressgang headed their newest prisoners towards carts where Cheap stood waiting on the moon-brightened highway.

"How many?" demanded the lieutenant.

Leech grinned, "Nineteen, maybe twenty, sir."

"That's not a bad haul from such a stinking little place," grunted the thick-bodied lieutenant, then pushed his unused pistols back into a brass-buckled belt. "Load these rogues into the carts. Smartly now. If they struggle or call out, club 'em! We've another three villages to visit before sunup."

At that moment, Wade, for the first time, fully appreciated the awfulness of the fate in store for him. Peggy — warm, loving Peggy, was about to be lost to him — perhaps for years! If he didn't manage to escape pretty soon his leather-working custom would be taken over by Will Jonson. He'd hated Will since boyhood. His whole being in revolt, Wade lunged towards the lieutenant, awkwardly, because of his tied hands.

"Let me go, sir! You know you've no right to arrest me without a warrant! Let me go or I'll —"

Leech dealt Nat a blow that snapped his already aching head violently to one side. He heard Lieutenant Cheap drawl, "Why, you damned unpatriotic rascal! Once you're aboard the *Centurion* you'll soon enough learn where your duty lies."

~ 4 ~

Volunteers

IN BEAULIEU, a village situated comfortably remote from Gosport, King Parmer, lantern-jawed South Carolinian coxswain of Commodore Anson's barge and veteran of seven years' service under him, with low cunning had arranged to open his recruiting office in a spirit dealer's shop. The store's odors, Parmer calculated, might furnish subtle inducements to prospective volunteers — if, indeed, any were so deluded as to appear.

As was the custom for the men detailed to a flag officer's personal craft, Coxswain Parmer and his mates were uniformly, but not handsomely, dressed; George Anson's strictly limited private funds had permitted no extravagance in such a direction. Accordingly, *Centurion*'s bargemen wore coarse red flannel shirts, black scarves and pantaloons of white duck. Purely out of vanity, the recruiting party, before setting out for Beaulieu, had dressed one another's hair. Their queues, braided as tightly as possible, had been stuffed into oiled eelskins. These, ornamented with red and white striped ribbons, stood out stiffly behind the wearer's head like a misplaced tail.

A pasty-faced drummer boy, sweating under an overlarge scarlet tunic and spotted black breeches, had "beat the town" and now was standing before the spirit shop listlessly banging on his drum. Finally a small crowd of apprentices, tramps and other idlers collected. These weren't fearful about doing so, because Coxswain Parmer's party in no way suggested a pressgang in operation. They numbered only seven in all and nowhere were handcuffs, cudgels or cutlasses to be seen.

"Well, I allow that's about the most we c'n hope for," drawled the Carolinian. "Let's go." He stepped out into the sunlight, climbed onto an overturned brewing tub and, grinning, held up both hands.

"Hear ye, friends, hear ye! Who's ready for a cruise to the tropics aboard a spandy-new man-o'-war? Who's ready to frolic wi' beautiful and willing women in warm and wonderful lands?"

No one in the gawping group evinced the least interest. They only spat or dug at the street with dusty feet.

Parmer paused, and shifted his quid. "All the rum ye c'n drink is there for the taking. I know — I been there and got drunk every night 'thout it costing me a farthing."

Still no reaction.

Shrewdly he lowered his voice, forcing his listeners to pay attention to his most telling argument. "Only the smart fellers amongst you will pay attention when I say a man c'n win enough prize money on *this* cruise to live like a Injun Nabob for rest o' his days!"

"Where yer ship's headed?" a voice called.

King Parmer hesitated only an instant before recalling a remark passed between the Commodore and his secretary, a fellow Carolinian. Said he glibly, "Why, friend, to the balmy and beautiful South Sea." Warming to his theme, the coxswain threw back his narrow head and, in seeming ecstasy, rolled his eyes. "Ah! 'Tis only in the South Sea can a common sailor feed on the fat o' the land! Why, mates, when his ship's in port out there all a feller does is lay under flowering trees," loudly he smacked his lips, "drink palm wine and bed a different brown wench every night." He leered. "Come inside, boys, and I'll tell you more about that."

His appeal apparently completed, Parmer beckoned. "And now to prove our Commodore's fine spirit he offers a full jack of prime Jamaica to any hearty who'll sign the Muster Book! His Honor wants only willing volunteers, not jailbirds, to sail on his fine new ship."

The drummer beat a long roll which fortunately drowned out Parmer's final remark, "If *that* don't serve to cozen these ox-heads, nuthin' will!"

The Carolinian then swaggered indoors and plunked himself down behind a wide board supported by two wine barrels and ostentatiously shuffled some smudged enlistment forms.

Although the drummer kept on beating, the crowd dissipated until only three men remained. One, a slim, intense-looking, young fellow with curly coal-black hair, Parmer decided, could hardly have reached his seventeenth year. Through the grog shop's dusty window panes the coxswain watched the youth try to square sloping shoulders, then, with pathetic determination, start for the shop's entrance. Once inside, he halted before Parmer's improvised desk and came to rigid attention, obviously in imitation of soldiers standing in the presence of an officer.

"Well, sir?" Parmer drawled, leathery features devoid of expression. "And what might be your pleasure?"

"Why, sir, I wish to enroll," the youth announced in an eager, high-pitched voice. "I mean to fight for my King against the murdering Papists who seize our ships and torture our seamen — like poor Captain Jenkins, whose ear they cut off."

King Parmer, while reaching for a quill, barely suppressed a guffaw. He stood ready to bet that this romantic numskull had never even sighted salt water.

"Good for you, young master. Wish they was more like you. Name?"

"Will — that is, William Pallister, sir."

"Age?"

"Twenty-one, sir."

A well-polished brass ringlet in Parmer's left ear trembled to his silent mirth. "To be sure, young master, to be sure. Now what's it, really? Sixteen? Seventeen?"

The would-be volunteer's smooth cheeks flushed as delicately as any girl's. "Why, sir, I — I guess I'm only seventeen. But I'm strong and eager to serve the King."

"Occupation?"

"Student of Divinity."

A bargeman snickered, whereupon Parmer glared over his shoulder. "Hush yo' fuss, you! Father?"

"The Reverend Richard Pallister. Vicar of Woking."

"Where's Woking?"

"— In Surrey, ye Colonial lack-wit," muttered another of his boat's crew.

"Stow that!" Parmer growled. "Yer Pa know you've gone for a sailor?"

The luminous black eyes wavered. "Why — why, no, sir. I felt sure he'd not consent."

[26]

"Ever been to sea?"

The boy's features lit. "No, sir. But I've read ever so much about the voyages of our great admirals — Hawkins, Drake, Frobisher, Dampier and the rest. Really I have!"

Parmer scratched at a cheek deeply pitted by smallpox, said quite seriously, "Well, now, shouldn't wonder but such learning will come in real handy. Make your mark here."

"Mark, sir? I can write my name." Which Will Pallister did with a very neat flourish. "See? And thank you, sir, for granting me this privilege."

A flat smile creasing his weather-beaten countenance, King Parmer shoved a bright silver shilling across the board. "Now, Bub, you can draw your rum."

"Oh, no, sir, I don't drink."

Then indeed did the Commodore's bargemen explode into raucous peals of laughter. One gap-toothed fellow clapped Will so hard on the back that he swayed. "In that case, lad, we'll drink to yer good luck. Ye'll need it, plenty!"

The recruit said, "What shall I do now, sir?"

Not unkindly Parmer told him, "That's up to you, only be here come high noon. Certain-sure. Understand?"

"Yes, sir."

"Sailors say 'Aye, aye,' not 'yes.' "

"Aye, aye, sir."

"Stow it! You only need say 'sir' to a commissioned officer."

"Well, I'll be blowed," cackled a bargeman once Will Pallister had wandered back into the sunlight. "Wot a chicken! Stand by, King, 'ere comes another noddy."

The second man who had been lingering nervously outside shambled over the grog shop's worn stone threshold. The prospective recruit's eyes somehow reminded Parmer of a misused dog's.

Peter Dobey was thin and weedy and so round-shouldered he appeared to be hunchbacked. Haltingly, the applicant stated that he was forty-three years of age, and a master tailor. Until a few days ago, Dobey said, he'd earned his living in Portsmouth cutting and stitching for the gentry and senior naval officers. Yes. He was married, had three living children.

Raising a quizzical brow, the Commodore's coxswain inquired, "What can have driven a respectable family man into volunteering?"

"Why, to be truthful, sir," explained the ex-tailor, casting a nervous look out of the door, "I reckon I'm only a few minutes ahead of a sheriff's deputy who carries a warrant for my arrest."

"Oh, so that's it."

Dobey looked apprehensively about. "Yes, that's it and only so because a parcel of high and mighty nobles, Admirals and Post Captains won't pay what they've owed sometimes for years. *My* creditors got tired of waiting and swore out a warrant." Helplessly he spread small, shiny hands. "Please, sir, won't you please sign me on? I couldn't bear for my family to suffer the shame of seeing me go to prison."

Anson's bargemen looked almost pitying. Apparently this poor frightened fool didn't in the least realize what he was letting himself in for.

Parmer nodded. "All right, mister, I'll enroll you. This Service won't refuse anything mortal that's got eyes, hands and feet."

The bent little tailor was straightening from signing the enlistment form when the sudden clatter of running feet diverted the coxswain's attention.

"There, I told you! It's the sheriff's men — but they can't touch me now, can they?"

"No. They can't."

It turned out, however, that Dobey was in error.

A tall, well-built young fellow came bounding towards the spirit shop with three obviously angry men in hot pursuit. One of them was brandishing a butcher's knife, the other two carried cudgels.

"Halt, ye damned whoreson!" panted the foremost, a brown-bearded man. "Stand like a man and take what's comin', ye dirty lecher."

One of the bargees suddenly burst out, "Damn' if it ain't 'Randy' Harry Cozens!"

"Who's he?"

"A feller wot served along o' me in the old *Winchester*. We're in luck, King. Harry's as prime a foretopman as ye'll ever spy. Even got to be made master's mate once, but he got caught drinking on watch. Court sentenced 'im to four dozen wi' the cat and broke him back to A.B."

The fugitive rushed inside, long yellow hair flying. He was hot and wheezing but wearing a wide grin all the same. "Quick, where's yer bloody pen?"

He just managed to sign before a beefy individual wearing a sher-

[28]

iff's silver badge burst in shouting, "I arrest you, Harry Cozens, in the name of the law!" He snatched a paper from his belt. "This here's a warrant fer yer arrest. Come along!"

"Arrest? Hell, just lemme at 'im," snarled the man with the knife.

Panting loudly, the constable tramped over to the improvised table, shook his fist under Parmer's pockmarked nose. "I'll take this man! The law is the law!"

"So it is, mister!" The coxswain jumped belligerently to his feet while his bargemen pulled out hitherto concealed cutlasses. "He's a King's man now! Law says you can't touch him."

It turned out that the other two pursuers were the husband and brother of some wench Cozens had seduced earlier in the day. Although the three threatened and raved, Parmer and his mates remained unmoved. At length the baffled trio went back out into the street and began to yell for help so loudly that a crowd gathered — and in an ugly mood.

Coxswain Parmer and his men might have fared badly had not a detachment of Marines, on the march to join Anson's squadron, trudged into Beaulieu. One glimpse of muskets, bayonets and red coats advancing down the street was enough for the mob. It dispersed hurriedly; Marines had been known suddenly to improvise a pressgang of their own with the object of earning the usual reward paid for every wretch delivered on shipboard.

⟨ 5 ⟩

The Pensioners

COMMODORE GEORGE ANSON had been glad of Sir Charles Wager's invitation to dine ashore, for, by regulation, he was required to live, or at least sleep, aboard his flagship so long as she remained in commission.

Swinging along on his way to the landing float at which his barge lay waiting, he overtook one of his captains, lanky and dyspeptic-looking Matthew Mitchell, who was commanding HBMS *Pearle*. Together they sauntered along the Royal Dockyard's cobbled waterfront past an impressive collection of naval vessels which were undergoing repairs.

The afternoon was uncommonly fine, with a wind blowing sufficient to send tenders, lighters and bumboats bowling about the harbor's slate-gray water.

Captain Mitchell glanced at the figure strolling sedately beside him. "May I observe, sir, that when it comes to running a pressgang your Lieutenant Cheap is past master." He frowned at a cloud of gulls wheeling above a bit of garbage. "I could wish my 'spark' even half so capable."

The taller officer commented, "I have not yet learned how many hands Mr. Cheap er-er — obtained."

"Around forty or so, I heard, sir." When Mitchell looked hopefully at his superior a slight cast affecting his left eye became noticeable. Pointedly he added, "*Pearle* remains eighty hands short, sir."

Every captain in the squadron had heard that although the Admiralty had promised Commodore Anson a draft of three hundred and fifty experienced seamen to bring his crews to the required minimum, not a one as yet had appeared and, by rumor, the squadron was due to sail very soon.

The two officers were nearing their destination when the sound of many feet, marching out of cadence, became audible — also a strange, sad undertone of voices.

Anson and his companion halted, turned about and realized that, from between a group of weather-beaten warehouses, a column of troops in red and black uniforms was debouching onto the quay. The Commodore's heart surged. At long last his land troops had arrived! His elation quickly faded on noticing that sunlight was glancing off only a few musket barrels shouldered by a Marine detachment from HBMS *St. Albans*.

Anson said, "Would you care to review my land troops, Captain?"

" 'Twould be a pleasure, sir."

Mechanically, both officers set straight tricorne hats bound in gold braid.

In the column's van marched a double rank of Marines in scarlet tunics, black breeches and pipe-clayed white crossbelts. Small brass plates set in the front of low caps shone bravely as they marched to the uninspired *flam-flamming* of a solitary drum. A few paces in advance of the column strode a young lieutenant who, when he drew near, appeared mortified by the nature of his assignment.

"Good God, sir," Matthew Mitchell burst out when, for the first time, he got a good look at the files immediately behind the Marines. "Those can't be *your* men!"

[30]

"Halt your column!" Anson called sharply, then beckoned over the lieutenant. "What are those — those poor old things doing here?"

The sea soldier considered this grave, blue-eyed gentleman somewhat truculently, but nonetheless obeyed his command. He'd no idea whom he might be addressing, since the Royal Navy wore no uniforms. "Why, these are some troops sent to serve aboard Commodore Anson's squadron."

"Say 'sir' when you address me! From whose regiment are they?"

There was that in Anson's tone which stiffened the subaltern to rigid attention.

"Why, sir, they're from no regiment. For the most part they're Out-Pensioners from Chelsea Hospital."

"Thank you. You may continue your march," Anson directed in a flat monotone which effectively concealed his sense of sickened desperation.

So these were the "seasoned and disciplined troops" promised by Lord Newcastle? God above! Like a mordant acid bitterness and outrage welled into his being while he watched pass by him the most pitiable imaginable array of limping, semi-crippled and gray-haired Invalid-Pensioners.

Under the filthy, long-skirted scarlet tunics, Anson and his incredulous companion recognized men sixty and seventy years of age. Many had bodies so warped by wounds and disease that they were forced to lean on sticks to keep from falling. Others swung bent and stiffened legs between battered crutches or stumped sullenly along on peglegs! Horrified beyond expression, George Anson noticed many a missing eye and vanished hand; he heard others, sunken-eyed and cadaverous, racked by the tearing cough of advanced consumption.

A few of the poor old creatures were weeping in dreary silence, but many more steadily cursed the ungrateful country which had routed them out of well-earned retirement and the bleak comforts of Chelsea College.

Matthew Mitchell's long, sallow features quivered as he burst out, "You must protest this damned, contemptible outrage, sir! For God's sake, lodge an immediate protest! How can they be so mad as to expect you to fight the Spaniards with such worthless wrecks?"

Just then a graybeard collapsed at Anson's feet, groaning, "Don't cane me, sir! I — I've kept up this far, but I can't go no farther! God 'elp me, I just can't."

[31]

Abruptly, Anson stooped to help the fallen Invalid-Pensioner to rise, then, wide cheeks suffused, he snapped, "Who commands this escort?"

"Who the devil wants to know?" A burly, red-faced Major of Marines strode up.

"I, Commodore Anson, wish to know." A baleful light shone in his bright blue eyes. "Who are you?"

"Major Clark, sir, off the *St. Albans*. How can I be of service?"

"Halt that column! Bring to me the Pensioner officers in command of these unhappy wretches."

"Yes, sir." Major Clark, looking anxious, called out, "Captains Arnand and Colley, report here!"

Being so crippled by rheumatism that he had to use a pair of canes, Captain Arnand slowly quitted the column. Captain Colley's wrinkled skin was the color of dirty parchment and liberally blotched by chocolate-brown liver spots. Fearfully, his red-rimmed eyes peered from sunken sockets. He was gasping painfully for breath.

Flushed with embarrassment, George Anson identified himself. "I scarce know what to say to you, gentlemen, except that I hope you will credit me with having had no part in this — this monstrous business!"

"Nor have I — or any officer in the squadron," hastily interjected Captain Mitchell.

"I've little doubt of that, sir," Captain Arnand quavered. "I feel confident that you will put a stop to this abuse of loyal old soldiers."

Captain Colley gasped, "On my honor, sir, there ain't thirty men among the lot of us fit to shoulder a musket."

Major Clark looked daggers, attempted to bluster. "Pay no heed to these old croakers, sir. For the most part they're malingering."

"I can best judge that for myself, sir," snapped Anson. "Go back to your men."

Suddenly Captain Colley sank onto his knees and raised trembling hands. "For God's sake, gentlemen, spare me. Like the most of us, I'd not survive a week on shipboard." The Pensioner officer's speech was slurred, which was not strange, considering that only the blackened stumps of a few teeth remained in a mouth framed in snow-white bristles.

Captain Arnand swayed over his canes. "As you hope for God's mercy, gentlemen, put a halt to this crime! Look at that poor fellow. Can't you see how close he is to death?"

[32]

Even dour Captain Mitchell frowned when he noticed a veteran whose unbuttoned tunic, flapping open, disclosed a long, suppurating wound. From it pus was draining onto his sagging black pantaloons.

Croaked Captain Colley, "If that ain't enough — take a look at him."

A marcher, wearing a corporal's worsted knot on one shoulder, was so nearly blind that he had to be guided over the waterfront's uneven cobbles.

Stony-faced, the Commodore strode over to the old man who'd fallen before him and now sat slumped on the curb.

"Oh, God," he was sobbing drearily. "Why weren't I strong enough in me legs to run off —"

"Some of you escaped?" Anson queried in a voice he didn't recognize.

The invalid stared dully up at the ruddy face and clear blue eyes above. "Aye, zur. 'Tis only the feeblest of us is 'ere."

"Did many men — er — desert?"

"Nearly the half of us, zur, Sergeant Dineen among 'em." The ancient wiped red, heavily granulated eyes on his cuff. "Damn escort fetched him twice back, but the third time Tom really got away — pegleg and all. He's a lucky bastid — if he ain't got caught again and hanged up for a deserter."

"Take courage," Anson said gently. "Inform your mates that I am about to do everything possible to stop this outrage."

He beckoned the Marine Major. "You may proceed, but slowly, mind you, to Number Three Warehouse. Make these men as comfortable as possible there."

Numbed, the two Naval officers listened to the Marine guards shouting, "On yer feet! On yer feet!" From the column arose a sad sound like the lowing of thirsty cattle.

At the head of the column the beefy Major roared, "Form ranks! Briskly now!"

[33]

~~~ 6 ~~~

"The Lord Mayor's Men"

AT THE OFFSHORE END of a wharf in His Majesty's Dockyard in Southampton lay several smallboats from various ships belonging to Commodore Anson's squadron. Near the wharf's land end waited a trio of lieutenants, the oldest of whom was not yet thirty: Charles Saunders from *Centurion*, Peircy Brett of *Gloucester* and Marine Lieutenant Hamilton out of *Wager*. In undisguised disgust they were listening to the clank and rattle of chains drawing near.

Some ragged small boys left off playing among a pile of rusty anchor chain and, whooping gleefully, ran out to line the wharf. "Here come the Lord Mayor's men! The Lord Mayor's men! The Lord Mayor's men!"

A slattern came out of a nearby tavern and grabbed an urchin by his ear. "Come along 'ome, ye little barstard. Ye'll learn nothin' good watchin' another pack o' thieves, cut-purses and murderers pass by."

Morosely, Saunders, second lieutenant of the flagship, watched six, tough-looking bailiffs who, carrying blunderbusses, led the straggling column. It further was guarded on either flank by constables. These proved ready, overeager to use heavy staves or clubs.

Three abreast, the convicts came clanking along the quay. Some stared incuriously at the shipping, grim gray warehouses, gull-whitened pilings. Most kept their eyes lowered. All wore manacles, Saunders observed, but a few — probably dangerous or extra slippery characters — also wore gyves or leg-irons, which consisted of heavy iron rings locked about their ankles and connected by a short length of chain, the center of which was supported through being tied to the prisoner's belt.

Wager's Marine lieutenant described the criminal types usually to be found in such a draft: hardened, out-and-out felons, vicious and depraved to a man; sneak-thieves and others of that kidney; recaptured deserters who already could feel a cat peeling the skin off their backs.

Superior types of prisoners, Hamilton explained, were to be found

[34]

in the embezzler; the absconding debtor; the hot-tempered gentleman who, lacking influence, had been too quick with his dueling rapier; and the vice-ridden rakehell.

"Good God," Lieutenant Saunders muttered, "with such riffraff manning our ships what sort of cruise can be in store for us?"

Tall, long-faced Peircy Brett, ever the optimist, kept his eye out for less villainous convicts who might possibly be secured for service aboard *Gloucester*.

After a considerable wait he noticed an unusual figure. Although slightly built, this felon stood taller than the average and apparently was in his early thirties. He attracted Brett because, despite the degradation of chains, he held himself proud and erect. His pointed face, although dirty and long unshaven, was sensitive, cleanly modeled and framed in greasy, white-blond ringlets. It further interested Brett to note that this prisoner was wearing the remains of a lace-trimmed shirt and knee breeches of stained sky-blue satin. For all the attention this remarkable figure was paying his companions he might have been enjoying a morning stroll through Hyde Park.

In fact, the convict, in the depths of his misery, was attempting, without much success, to pretend that such was the case. Alas, the drag of ten-pound manacles shattered even the most determined efforts at self-delusion. He simply could not blink the fact that, at this moment, the sixth Earl of Burfurd was walking between a rapist and a swaggering murderer. What pseudonym should he give to the enrolling officer? Ought to use one; hadn't he blackened an ancient and honored title badly enough already? Surely, Lady Sophia Pangborne deserved to be spared futher embarrassment. What about the name of his ex-valet, Ted Waxter? Why not? Hadn't the rascal run off with the last of his few rings and fobs?

"Oi, chum, lend me an 'and, will yer? Me jooelry's such a bother." The double-ironed murderer to Lord Burfurd's left was panting and stumbling in his effort to keep pace with this doleful column.

"A pleasure, sir. A vast pleasure, indeed," Burfurd grinned, then slipped chained hands under the other's elbow. "One, two, three — *there's* the brave little man."

What might the dainty and exquisite Sophia now be thinking of her erstwhile betrothed — if indeed she was thinking of him at all? Closing his eyes, Lawrence Burfurd visualized her, tearful and utterly dumfounded at that moment when the Bow Street Runners had cornered him at her father's town house in Berkeley Square.

[35]

Lud! How piteously her features had quivered while the Runners were snapping on the manacles.

"Oh, Larry! Larry, darling," she'd wailed. "Tell me this is but a nightmare — some dreadful error —"

He recalled having managed a faint laugh, "Aye, my love, to be sure 'tis an error, but one of my own making. Seems your humble admirer makes a wretched bad highwayman."

"*Highwayman!*" Sophia had come close to fainting. "But why? *Why?* WHY?"

"Alas, my dear, I could devise no other means of satisfying certain pressing debts of honor."

Probably certain connections of the late Lord Burfurd's friends were to be thanked for having prevailed upon the Lord Mayor of London to commute his death sentence — mandatory for highway robbery — to service in His Majesty's Navy. Or were these anonymous gentlemen entitled to thanks? Lord Burfurd was beginning to doubt it.

Only one other face attracted Lieutenant Brett's favorable consideration. This fellow was handsome save for a huge, high-bridged nose and jutting jaw. Yet the way the convict held up his head and stared straight ahead from wide-set, bright brown eyes invited speculation.

Lieutenant Saunders emitted short and mirthless laughter. "Can sailors actually be fashioned out of such human offal? Mr. Brett, what's your opinion?"

"It's been done in the past, Mr. Saunders, so I expect we can do it again. Mr. Hamilton, how many of these charming creatures is the *Gloucester* to receive?"

The Marine ran his finger down a list. "Seventy, sir. The *Centurion*'s to take eighty. The *Severn*, *Pearle* and *Wager* twenty-five each."

⟭ 7 ⟬

'Tween Decks

SEAMEN pulling *Centurion*'s longboat, riding deep under its cargo of human misery, sweated because a stiff breeze, blowing directly across the harbor, was raising a chop which kept wave tops licking over the thwarts.

[36]

Acutely aware of rusty manacles biting coldly into his wrists, Nathaniel Wade glowered at HBMS *Centurion* lying trim and taut to her anchor. So this was the vessel on which he would be forced to serve; for how long and where? Only God knew.

The former leather-worker sat huddled on a bench between a convicted forger and a terrified, despairing middle-aged seaman by the name of Buckle who was endlessly and sulphurously cursing the day he'd deserted HBMS *Dreadnought* — "They'll flay me alive — they'll kill me!"

While the longboat threshed along the flagship's counter Wade noted that her waterline was painted white, with a two-foot band of black showing above it. The rest of this line-of-battle-ship's sides were of highly varnished natural wood, while her topsides were of a glistening white.

Two tiers of gunports ran almost the whole length of *Centurion*'s side; a third but much shorter line of ports pierced her forecastle and quarterdeck on both beams. Although he had yet to know it, they numbered sixty in all.

Gunport lids, painted scarlet on their undersides, showed as so many regularly spaced, brilliant red squares. Into the red-ringed muzzle of each cannon had been inserted a blue-and-gold tampion intended to protect its bore from salt water.

A puff of wind swung the trig Fourth Rate to her anchor and displayed effectively her lofty and brightly gilded stern. Up there two elaborately carved stern walks or galleries ran, superimposed, all the way across the ship's bulging stern.

"The upper one," Buckle was explaining to a strangely curious fellow prisoner, "is the Captain's walk. One below's the wardroom's; that's where the quarterdeck officers eat and live."

Centurion's three yellow-painted masts towered against the azure sky. Supported by newly tarred shrouds, they centered a bewildering tracery of pale brown stays, braces and halyards.

All at once Bill Buckle knuckled away his tears and spat into dirty water sloshing under the longboat's floor gratings. "Well, at least we're lucky in one thing," he told Wade. "The flagship's fairly new and her lines is sweeter than most o' the bloody floating barns built in the King's shipyards."

" 'Floating barns'?" demanded the forger in dull curiosity.

"Aye. Us can't touch 'e French or even 'e damn' Spanish when it comes to building fast and comfortable ships."

[37]

"What's wrong with the ships we build in England?" Wade queried.

"As you'll damn' soon learn, our vessels is pierced below decks fer too many guns to be readily handled. Another fault is that a lot of men-o'-war are so designed they'll roll out their masts, given half a chance, and are so tender that their lower deck guns can't be fought in half a heavy sea. Worst of all, British-built ships are turrible slow sailers."

Uneasily the deserter eased his manacles away from a ring of raw and festering sores. "Wonder how many they'll give me?"

"Give you what?" inquired the forger, a nervous, sparrow-like fellow.

"Lashes wi' the cat."

"What's a 'cat'?"

"Just you pray God you don't never find out, firsthand," Buckle said, tears again filling his eyes. " 'Tis the cat-o'-nine-tails that's used to flog sailors."

Wade felt an icy current start to trickle down his back. Hoarsely he asked, "A sailor can — can get *whipped?*"

"God, yes! He gets beat all the time with a bosun's cane, or a colt, or a starter. But they don't hurt nothing like the cat." A trifle proudly he added, "Me, I c'n easy eat three dozen 'thout squeaking; have, twice. But I know I can't stand more."

A prisoner on the seat behind bent forward, "Niver worry, frind. They'll not flay ye — this time!"

"Why not?"

" 'Tis so disperate shorthanded are all the ships, the officers'll not risk the disabling of a single man."

When the longboat neared the flagship's steep side Wade glimpsed a group of men standing about *Centurion*'s quarterdeck. He guessed they must be officers, but wasn't sure, for, to his astonishment, the only uniform visible up there was a scarlet tunic worn by a tall, hawk-faced officer who'd a mean look about him.

Peering aloft, Wade wondered, how can anyone make sense out of all those hundreds of ropes? Well, I won't have to because I'm going to get away somehow, even if I can't swim.

Although a huge Blue Ensign fluttering grandly from *Centurion*'s stern staff provoked few, if any, patriotic emotions in most of her cutter's passengers, Will Pallister felt stirred to the depths of his being.

[38]

Did not yonder piece of bunting represent the King's majesty and England's glory on the high seas?

"Oh, she's so beautiful!" young Pallister burst out. Like the other volunteers, he'd been privileged to sit, unshackled, near the cutter's stern.

The sun was drawing dazzling flashes off the gilded stern galleries and from *Centurion's* figurehead consisting of a large golden lion rampant which clutched between its forepaws a shield bearing the royal coat of arms.

Will's sensitive features flushed. At last this looked like the Navy he'd read so much about. He winced, however, when bearded and unshaven faces were thrust out of nearby gunports and began to call obscenities and degenerate invitations. Deeply shocked, young Pallister turned aside, scarlet to his collar.

Tom Ramster, who'd been wise enough to accept the inevitable and had "volunteered" on arrival in Portsmouth, slapped him on the shoulder. "Don't pay them buggers no heed, mate," the veteran advised, then considered casually the youth's immature figure and smooth skin. "I've taken a liking to ye, lad, so never fear but Tom will look out for ye once we're aboard."

"Oh, thank you. Thank you so much, Mr. Ramster. I appreciate your kindness."

"Ye don't have to 'mister' me; that's only for officers and snotties."

"— Er — 'snotties'?"

"Midshipmen," Ramster grunted. "They'll fair make life a hell fer ye, never fear."

"Tell me, do you recognize any of the boats hereabouts?"

"They're ships, not boats, Willie boy. Aye, I know most of 'em, worse luck. That one wi' the green hull and white topsides is the *Gloucester*. Heard tell her hull's rotten in places. She's a Fourth Rate — like the *Severn* — she's that blue and white craft lyin' just beyond."

The veteran's black-nailed forefinger indicated other vessels composing George Anson's squadron. "That black and orange sloop's the *Tryall*. She's the smallest and fastest of our fighting ships — only two hundred tons burthen."

Pallister's eyes widened. "Can a tiny boat — er, ship like that sail the open ocean?"

"Aye. Why not? Many smaller have crossed the ocean time and again. Now off to port lays the *Pearle*; she's painted yellow and green. She's a Fifth Rate, though I'll admit she don't much look like one. Look at her damn' bulging bows, tumble-home sides; you can lay yer last farthin' she'll prove slower running nor cold tar."

Ramster spat moodily. "See them redcoats movin' about on her deck, Willie boy? Them's Marines. You'll come to hate the very sight of 'em."

Because the longboat had not yet completed unloading her cargo of felons, the cutter's coxswain ordered its crew to toss oars, which allowed her to rock a few yards short of the gangway.

In open-mouthed dismay, the minister's son then watched convicts and impressed men, badly hampered by their manacles, being driven up a set of battens, or wooden steps, permanently nailed to the ship's side. Two prisoners lost their balance and fell back into the longboat to be roundly cursed and punished by the coxswain's colt, a length of thick, knotted rope.

When, finally, the last chained man had clanked up the battens, the longboat shoved off, leaving room for the cutter to be rowed alongside.

A Marine's red face appeared above, bellowed, "Step lively, you dumb oxes! Don't miss them 'and 'olds."

Will Pallister's last doubts concerning the wisdom of his decision dissipated when, after scrambling lightly up the side, he stepped onto a broad deck, white and spotless under the sun. Along each side showed a long row of dull black guns and red carriages with their tackle neatly spaced.

"Keep moving, ye unlicked pup!" Without warning, a boatswain's mate brought a cane smacking across Will's shoulder with sufficient force to send him lurching past a double rank of wooden-faced figures in red coats and white crossbelts.

"But, but — I didn't *do* anything," gasped the youth when Ramster's hand steadied him and they were driven down a broad ladder-stair into malodorous semidarkness.

"Ye don't have to. Now stay close whilst I look about."

In the lower gundeck's crepuscular gloom the newcomers immediately were engulfed by a dense throng of shouting, and often drunken seamen. Immediately the youth became hopelessly confused by the intolerable pressing of bodies against him. He could hardly move, so great was the crush of people. Eyes filling with tears, Will clung to Ramster's hairy wrist and tried to accustom himself to the 'tween deck's poisonous atmosphere.

[40]

The veteran braced legs apart and, glaring about, growled, "Christ's mercy! How many men are they trying to cram into this bloody hooker?"

Someone sang out, "As if we ain't packed tighter'n herrings in a barrel, they aim to jam a hundred and more soljers in on top o' us!"

～ 8 ～

The Quarter Bill

UNDER HEAVY GUARD the recruits were lined up along both sides of *Centurion*'s broad and sunlit deck. Anxiously, all three groups, volunteers, 'pressed men and felons, stood awaiting a moment of vast importance. Every new hand was about to have his duty and station listed in the ship's Quarter Bill.

Complete silence descended when big-jawed Lieutenant Cheap appeared in a fusty, bottle-green frock coat and a turkey-red waistcoat which flapped almost down to his thick knees, and made his way to a plain wooden table which, with three straight chairs, had been placed at the foot of the mainmast.

From the side of his mouth Ramster whispered, "Now look alive, Willie boy. If yer offered a choice of station speak up for the afterguard. Ye're slight enough to make a good topman, but a damn' sight too green; ye'd soon fall and get killed."

Will stole a glance at the tough, brutally handsome young man standing very straight beside him. "Where will you go?"

"To the tops. A.B.s always get sent there or onto the fo'c'sle. Old A.B.s and the smart-looking landlubbers wind up in the afterguard. Weak, stupid and known troublemakers generally serve in the waist, where they'll get killed off quick."

"Why?"

"Enemy gunners always aim for 'midships — Spanishers especially."

Although silence prevailed on the upper gundeck, from below arose an ugly undertone pierced by high-pitched wails from boys beginning to understand the hideous fate in store for some of them.

After staring deliberately about the deck, Lieutenant Cheap seated himself, carefully placed his sword across his knees, commenced to scan a thick sheaf of documents handed him by Mr. Weldon, the purser.

Cheap turned to a scared-looking clerk at his left. "I'll look at the volunteers first."

The clerk nodded, called in a loud, carrying voice, "Albert Adams, stand forth!"

As each man came to stand before the table he was required to give his name, home and occupation, and, without further ado, was assigned a station.

Presently Coxswain Parmer smiled wryly. Yonder came the fugitive tailor who, too readily, had exchanged the frying pan of a debtor's prison for the fire of service aboard a King's ship.

"Name?" rasped Lieutenant Cheap, heavy brows joined.

"Peter Dobey," quavered the stoop-shouldered volunteer.

The master-at-arms, standing a step behind, growled, "Say 'sir' when you address an officer, you scurvy dog!"

"Profession?"

"Master tailor, sir."

"Ever been to sea?"

"No, sir."

"Any distinguishing marks, Mr. Waller?"

The ship's surgeon made a cursory examination and ended by prodding the meager figure's abdomen. "— Minor hernia, left side."

"Got teeth enough?"

"Yes, sir. Eleven."

The clerk's pen scraped loudly before he glanced at Lieutenant Cheap. "Where is he to serve, sir?"

"Put him in the fo'c'sle under the sailmaker."

Without looking up, the purser announced, "As a landsman, Dobey, your monthly pay will be twenty-three shillin', sixpence."

As Tom Ramster had predicted, he was assigned to the foretopmast and granted an able seaman's pay, which amounted to twenty-six shillings each month.

"Thankee kindly, sir." Ramster knuckled a reddish forelock and, grinning, disappeared down the main ladder.

"We could do with more of that rascal's kidney," grunted the first lieutenant. "Well, get on with it."

A raucous voice greeted Ramster's descent. "Well, blow me down if 'tain't 'Rowley Red' hisself! How'd a old hand like you get 'pressed?"

"Reckon I was too busy poppin' yer sister's maidenhead," laughed

[42]

Ramster. Then his grin faded. "Whew! I've slung my hammock in some gamey berthdecks but this is the worst *ever!* If the stink's this bad here on the maindeck, what's it like down in the orlop?"

Wild-eyed landsmen piteously were asking, "Where's a feller go to piss?" "What am I supposed to do?" "God, I'm hungry. When do we get fed?" "Where do I sleep?"

Hammering in the orlop attracted Ramster's attention. On investigation the veteran discovered the flagship's carpenter and his mates sullenly nailing hammock hooks into the orlop deck's red-painted beams.

When Tom noticed how closely together these were being spaced, he scowled. "Cock's bones! You can't berth men that close together! What's the space ye're allowing?"

Sourly, the carpenter glared over a sweaty shoulder; it was stifling hot in the 'tween decks. "Twelve inches. Them's the orders."

"The hell you say! Least apart *I* ever see on any ship was twenty. Fellow any real size will have to lie on his side all night."

Said he to himself, B' God, here's one lad who ain't going to try it. He hurried to the purser's storeroom, drew and was charged with a hammock and blanket and fought his way along the main gundeck until he reached the end of a line of hooks. Boldly, he detached and flung away two hammocks already slung but unwisely deserted. He'd fight their owners later. Then, remembering the minister's boy, he freed two more.

This done, he filled his chest and roared, "Now listen to me, all you whoresons! This here set of hooks belong to 'Rowley Red' Ramster! Lay a finger on 'em and ye'll find yerself short some teeth!"

When no one seemed disposed to object, Ramster slung his hammock, then wondered why his head had begun to swim. Why? Cock's bones! He'd not had a drink in a long while. Suddenly he realized that the atmosphere below was so noxious because all gunports along the entire lower tier not only had been closed and barred, but also caulked with pitch and oakum! What a nightmare *this* cruise promised to be.

He made his way aft and, purely by chance, discovered Will Pallister cowering between Numbers 12 and 14 guns. "Come on, get up. No one's going to harm you, Willie boy. Did you get posted to the afterguard?"

Utterly bewildered, the youth could only goggle at Ramster as if he were a fearsome apparition. There had been nothing like this somber, foul-smelling inferno described in any of the books he'd read.

"Get up, don't squat there sniveling like a ruined virgin."

"Oh! Mr. Ramster, what's to become of me?"

"You'll find out. Now tell me, *did* you get posted aft? Dammit, answer me, boy."

"Why, why I don't know. I — I couldn't understand a word of what the officer said. Oh — h!"

A hand had slipped into Pallister's pocket, had begun fumbling for the few coins it contained. A breath rank with rum fanned his face, yelled, "Ha! Fresh fish! Here's a fresh fish!"

A knot of men closed in and, before Ramster could intervene, threw young Pallister onto the deck and had torn off his shoes, belt and cap. They even stole the red silk neckerchief his sister had given him on his seventeenth birthday.

"Get back, ye slimy swine!" Viciously, Ramster drove huge fists at the crowd. "Leave him be! This one's 'Rowley Red's' chicken!"

"What in blazes is going on here?" The thieves recoiled from a narrow-faced individual in black tricorne and scarlet jacket. He was forcing a passage through the shadowy throng by the liberal use of a rattan cane tipped with a rawhide lash.

"I — I've been robbed," sobbed Pallister. "Please, kind sir, make them restore my shoes. I — I've no others."

"Go barefoot then!" rasped the Marine corporal, then continued to drive the snarling crowd before him.

Because Nathaniel Wade's name began with a "W" his was among the last to be listed on *Centurion*'s Quarter Bill.

"You'll serve as apprentice seaman on the fo'c'sle," the clerk informed. "Below wid yez! Next man."

A slash across the shoulders from a colt wielded by a bearded boatswain's mate sent Wade below in a murderous rage. What right had they to treat a freeborn Englishman like this? He'd committed no crime.

"Fresh fish! Fresh fish!"

The first hand placed upon Nat Wade released that storm which had seethed within him for two infernal nights and days. Always clever with his fists — as anyone around Tichfield could testify — the leather-worker lashed out so hard he sent a hulking fellow spinning. Next he clipped on the jaw a shaggy ruffian who, in falling, banged

[44]

his head so hard against a 32-pound cannon's pommel that he sprawled in shuddering unconsciousness on the deck.

A strange, scarlet haze shimmering before his eyes, Wade looked about for another target but found none. The thieves had pounced on their senseless accomplice and were tearing off his shoes, stockings and shirt so dexterously that, in a few instants, he lay stripped naked as a newborn babe.

Wade panted, "Come on, ye thieving cowards. What holds you heroes back? Maybe I'd best come to you."

Head lowered, fists driving, Wade charged and felt better every time his knuckles impacted upon some half-seen body.

The press of cursing men suddenly fell back. All at once he stood alone, panting, in the center of a widening circle.

9

Retrospections

ONCE OLDHAM, the Commodore's red-nosed steward, had cleared away a supper of cold mutton, boiled cabbage and potatoes, George Anson, in critical deliberation, savored claret from a case recently delivered for his private use. Um. This time, his wine and spirit merchants had made no mistake. Secretly he deemed himself something of a connoisseur — especially with regard to the vintages of Bordeaux and Beaujolais — but would have died cheerfully rather than confess the fact.

Seated under the brass whale-oil lamp which alone illumined *Centurion's* great cabin, the big, full-blooded figure pondered certain vital decisions. Why couldn't he learn more rapidly to cope with his new and complex responsibilities? Possibly he lacked the capacity to command a squadron?

He saw himself again hurrying through a light snow falling on that unforgettable evening of November 18, 1739, to keep an appointment at the Admiralty. Even now Anson could recall exactly how the famous Board Room — nerve center of the Royal Navy — had appeared. Its ceiling had been very high and white and, at geometric intervals, ornamented with Tudor roses done in gold leaf.

There had been a fire roaring in the chimney place bright enough to reveal the arms of Charles II on its cast-iron fireback and to draw rich tones from the chamber's heavy oak paneling. To the paneling had hung a profusion of charts on rollers and a circular map of Western Europe from Scandinavia to Gibraltar. From the center of this radiated thin gold lines indicating the points of the compass. A golden needle with its axis on Vienna was geared, Anson later learned, to a vane on the Admiralty's roof which enabled the Board Room's occupants to determine in which direction the wind was blowing. Often the position of this needle had determined whether a fleet should be ordered to sail or not.

At a long and ponderous mahogany table had sat four figures, their glittering frock coats bright against Grinling Gibbons's intricate pear wood carvings of navigational instruments: parallel rulers, astrolabes, dividers, compasses and the like.

Two of the four waiting men Anson immediately had recognized: seventy-eight-year-old Sir Charles Wager and Lord Hardwicke, Elizabeth's beetle-browed father. The others proved to be the Secretary of the Admiralty and the Duke of Devonshire.

How loud had sounded the ticking of a stately but curiously designed grandfather's clock standing in a far corner. Subconsciously, Anson had noticed that a mirror set in its pendulum door reflected the flames of a silver candelabrum flaring upon the conference table.

It was there and then that he'd first learned of the honor — and enormous responsibility — about to be bestowed upon him.

Quite clearly, he recalled how loudly the Secretary had coughed and cleared his throat before beginning to read:

"Instructions for our trusty and well-beloved George Anson, Esquire, Commander-in-Chief —"

How his heart had leaped at that!

"— of our ships designed to be sent into the South Seas in America. Given at Court at Saint James's —"

Anson put down his empty wineglass and settled back into an uncomfortable oak armchair to stare unseeingly at a rack of brass-mounted muskets which encircled the mizzenmast where it passed through his cabin.

Briefly, he recalled his first command: How inspired to great things he'd felt on that rainy June day of 1722 when, with the ink scarcely dry on his lieutenant's commission, he'd boarded HBMS *Weasel*. What a sweet-sailing little sloop she'd been. In her he'd thrown the fear of God — and the law — into quite a few smugglers operating out of Dutch ports.

A reminiscent smile curving his wide, thin-lipped mouth, the Commodore refilled his glass. *Scarborough* was my second command. Guess the seven years I spent in her were by far the happiest of my career. No, I'll never forget the fun I had chasing and taking pirates off the Carolinas in North America. Suppose I must have done reasonably well on patrol duty or the Colonial Authorities wouldn't have waxed so fulsome in their reports to the Admiralty.

The North Carolinians especially had been grateful for *Scarborough*'s work. Lord, how embarrassed I was, back in 1735, when they told me they'd named an area in the wilderness, "Anson County," and a hamlet, "Ansonville." Even now I can't fathom why those touchy and quick-tempered Colonials and I got on so satisfactorily.

Through the stern gallery's leaded windows drifted a multitude of familiar, comforting sounds such as the steady *clunk-clunk* of oars pulling a passing smallboat; the tinny twitter of a boatswain's pipe being sounded aboard *Severn;* a chorus of variously toned ships' bells marking the hour all over Portsmouth Harbor.

I believe pretty, sleepy little Charles Town will remain my favorite American town — it seemed more sophisticated, more like home than other American ports. Besides, it was in Charles Town that I met Andrew Menzies.

What a supercilious young rake he'd been! Reckon he deserved that nickname of "Hotspur." He was reputed to ride his foxes — and women — right into the ground.

How clearly I can recall details of my final visit to Chartwell. Take for instance, the tea-colored Ashley slipping smoothly past the great house; white egrets roosting among trees on the far bank; fireflies dancing like live sparks among ghostly beards of Spanish moss; night birds trilling melodiously under a honey-hued moon.

All these things I still associate with that dreadful session at the card table. Certainly, I never suspected that Andrew Menzies was so much further gone in drink than he appeared. I suppose I should have suspected his condition. How else would one account for such recklessness in the face of persistent bad luck?

Let's see, just about when did the game end? Um. Must have been shortly before dawn when Andrew insisted on trying to recoup his losses by staking Chartwell on a single, simple cut of the cards.

I did my best to get out of it, but he threatened to call me out if I refused. I'll never forget how my hand shook, how his black eyes blazed in triumph when I cut the five of clubs. Then he cut — the trey of hearts! Nor will I ever forget Andrew's ghastly smile when he rose from the card table, mumbling, "Mr. Anson, the deeds to Chartwell will be delivered aboard your vessel before noon."

Sure enough, while *Scarborough*'s bell was sounding eight strokes to summon the Afternoon Watch, a wherry appeared alongside and discharged a patently embarrassed old gentleman.

In his mind's eye Anson could see himself as the dull-eyed victim of a monumental hang-over, receiving the barrister in his cabin.

"Kindly read these deeds, sir," the lawyer had invited. "Should you find them in order, please sign this receipt and Chartwell will become your property."

The temptation to an impecunious Naval lieutenant had been great. Chartwell was huge and its rice fields among the most productive in South Carolina; why, in only a few years he could have grown rich.

Anson, slowly revolving his wineglass, recalled having insisted that only a friendly game had taken place with all the players drunk past discretion. In short, under such conditions he did not feel justified in accepting Chartwell.

"Yours, sir, is a most generous, and may I say, most unusual attitude," Andy Menzies's lawyer dryly had observed. "I shall endeavor to persuade my young client to accept your refusal."

But next day the barrister had reappeared. "Mr. Menzies deems his honor affronted. I fear, sir, you must accept the payment."

"But I cannot do so. My conscience forbids me to take advantage of so charming a host. Please assure Mr. Menzies that his honor is not in any way impugned. His prompt offer to settle the debt, to me is sufficient and satisfactory. Please reassure my friend on that point, sir."

That same day a pirate vessel had been reported prowling off Cape Fear; so HBMS *Scarborough* had sailed at once and never again had returned to Charles Town.

He'd almost forgotten the Andrew Menzies affair, Anson mused, when, six months later, the young planter, pale and with a haunted expression in his large black eyes, had appeared aboard His Majesty's cruiser as she lay to her anchor in the port of Wilmington in the Colony of North Carolina.

While he was downing the last of his good new claret Anson's mind raced on. "Sir," Menzies had said, "since you have refused payment of your winnings in property I beg to be allowed to repay my debt with service. If I understand your nature, Mr. Anson — and I believe I do — you will not deny me the opportunity."

"Very well, Andrew, I won't."

Accordingly, the somber young Carolinian had become Anson's private secretary, without pay, since a first lieutenant, lacking private means, couldn't possibly afford so useful a luxury.

Long afterwards, he'd heard that, shortly after HBMS *Scarborough* had sailed to chase pirates, Andrew Menzies had become involved in a scandal so appalling that its very nature had had to be suppressed. In any case, "Hotspur Andrew" had made over his estates to a younger fellow named Daingerfield and, all but penniless, had sailed northward in hopes of coming up with *Scarborough* at her base port.

Anson roused to the sound of footsteps in the passage leading to his cabin — an easy matter since only flimsy wooden partitions formed its forward bulkhead. He heard his Marine sentry's challenge answered by the very person he'd been thinking about.

When Andrew Menzies appeared he was carrying a thick portfolio under a threadbare black arm and his writing stand under the other. Although he didn't say so, the secretary was a little surprised not to find the music rack and flute in evidence, the Commodore having been alone since supper. "Dispatches from the Admiralty have just come aboard, sir. I imagine you will wish to examine them?"

Anson treated his secretary to a warm smile. "Of course, Andrew. Thank you. Let's hope that you fetch good news."

Fervently, he hoped that the Lords Justices, acting for George II during the monarch's voyage to Germany in quest of a bride, had reconsidered the matter of the Invalid-Pensioners. Surely those noble lords, venal and stupid as they were, *couldn't* be so purblind as to force on him such pathetic counterfeits of seasoned troops?

In silence Menzies placed the dispatches before the Commander in Chief, then seated himself upon a hard settee which ran across the stern under the great glazed windows. Slight of build, but tall above the average, the Carolinian appeared to be easily ten years older than his actual age of thirty. Thin, olive-hued features taut, he watched Anson's bright blue eyes flit back and forth over the topmost document. His apprehension increased when a deep flush appeared above the Commodore's plain white linen stock and spread out over his bold cheekbones.

Although George Anson yearned to rant and rage, submission to authority was too deeply ingrained in his nature and he only muttered, "Incredible! How utterly monstrous!"

"I take it, sir, that you are being forced to ship the Invalids?"

"The Lords Justices, in their infinite wisdom, have so determined. However, the news is not altogether bad. To replace those Pensioners who deserted on the way down from Chelsea they're sending me a draft of two hundred and ten recruits selected from various line regiments — which likely will prove more fit than the deserters."

Anson turned up the overhead lamp's wick and standing, continued to read.

"Also I have been given a tentative departure date. Once the land troops are aboard I'm to proceed to a rendezvous off the Isle of Wight with a convoy for Gibraltar and the Mediterranean."

"And when, sir, is this convoy to sail?"

"Within a week's time — if all goes well."

"Sir, has anything been said about replacing the Invalid officers you wrote specially about?"

For all that George Anson was renowned for an equable disposition he flushed angrily. "Nothing whatever, except that Lord Newcastle insists I take them along. Damme, Andrew, that's inhuman to them and most unfair to me!"

"I know, sir. I've learned that Captain Colley is sixty-five years old. He took his wounds at Oudenarde, which I believe was fought *thirty-two years ago!* Never since has the poor devil been free of pain. As for Captain Arnand, he was crippled even longer ago."

"Where?"

"At the Siege of Gibraltar in '04."

Angrily Anson snapped a scarlet wax seal securing another document. Again the Commodore's expression hardened but in a different way.

"More bad news, sir?"

"As the politicians would say — 'in a way yes, in a way no.' Seems that, some time ago, the Dons caught wind of my expedition against Western South America and have sent out a powerful fleet under General Don José Pizarro to intercept me. Here, read for yourself."

Word has been Received from our Agents in Madrid that the Vessels being sent against You are the Flagship *Asia* of 66 guns, 700 Men; the *Hermiona* of 54 guns, 700 men; *Esperanza* of 50 guns, 450 Men; *San Estéban* of 50 guns, 350 Men. Accompanying General Pizarro are several Pataches each of which is Reported to Mount around 20 Guns. This Spanish Fleet is also Reported to be Transporting a compleat Regiment of Foot.

Menzies's thin lips compressed themselves as he read on:

Two other Line-of-Battle-Ships of the Second Rate are expected to join Don José but it is not Known When or Where.

"Granted sufficient time to train my crews, Andrew," Anson said gravely, "I shall welcome an action — if Pizarro comes my way."

"But, sir, is not your squadron much inferior in force?"

"It is. Nevertheless, if a battle offers, I will not seek to avoid it."

"But you will not hunt for Pizarro's squadron?"

"Certainly not. My first duty is to attack the King's enemies in South America."

Once his secretary had withdrawn Anson decided to relieve his anxiety by blowing a few tunes on his flute. Softly, of course. Why should he feel ashamed to confess this weakness for music? Only Menzies and Elizabeth, Lord Hardwicke's daughter, openly, at least, were aware of this deplorable weakness.

Briefly he thought once more about "Betts," so lovely, so cool, so terribly self-possessed.

Did her affection run deeper than that for a childhood friend and neighbor? Maybe, maybe not. When this cruise was over he intended to find out. Certainly, in his inarticulate, awkward way he craved her love — had for a long time.

Should he have spoken out, disclosed his love, that last evening when they'd strolled through the twilit gardens of Shugborough? No. Elizabeth Hardwicke was an earl's daughter and he but a nearly penniless and still unproven Commodore.

∽ I O ∽

Morituri Te Salutamus

ON A COLD, DRIZZLY mid-September day the squadron's smallboats were called away to fetch out the last of the land forces. Already, wheeled artillery, ammunition and caissons destined for their use had been stowed deep in *Wager*'s holds.

Lieutenant Colonel Cratcherode standing, wind-whipped, on a broad stone quay was in an uncommonly savage mood as he gathered a faded gray watch cloak tighter about bony shoulders. He was suffering acutely from a recurrence of malaria contracted years earlier in the steamy jungles of Bengal.

Cratcherode's companions, Captain Crowden and Lieutenant Gordon, appeared to be in no happier frame of mind.

Growled Crowden, "Wonder how much those bloody fat-cats in Whitehall have pocketed on this little transaction?"

Gordon shivered. "Plenty. They're no novices."

Captain Arnand limped up on his two sticks, thin red nose dripping. Then he looked Colonel Cratcherode full in the face and cried in a quavering voice, "Captain Arnand reporting for duty, sir. And may I add, '*Morituri te salutamus*'!"

Cratcherode snarled, "Be damned for your impudence! What kind of gibberish is that?"

"Means, 'We who are about to die salute thee,' " explained Captain Crowden. Himself an Invalid, he understood the bitterness behind Arnand's remark. "Old Roman gladiators' sayin', I believe."

Cratcherode, face gone scarlet behind his bristling white mustache, barked, "Stand straight when you salute a superior, you slovenly dog!"

"I haven't stood straight in near forty years, my dear Colonel, but I'll attempt it," stated Arnand, then, with a hideous gap-toothed grimace, dropped his sticks and promptly fell so heavily that muddy water spurted over Colonel Cratcherode's glossy boots. His rusty black tricorne wavered over the muddy cobbles and fell into the harbor.

A gaunt little sergeant, retaining only part of his lower jaw,

[52]

stumped forward, slipped hands beneath the fallen officer's armpits. "Damn 'e for a heartless dog!" he shrilled.

"Arrest that man!" Cratcherode raged. "I'll see him flogged for this!"

"Whyn't ye have the both of us shot, kind sir?" the sergeant sneered while his scarecrow companions cursed and snuffled. " 'Twould be a quicker, cleaner death than we'll meet aboard His bloody Majesty's ships. But maybe that's too much to ask."

～～ I I ～～

To Serve the King

A COLD WIND BLOWING across HBMS *Gloucester* set to chattering the teeth of ex-convicts — "ex" because on signing the muster book they automatically had become free men. Grouped about a deck hose, scrubbed with strong soap and with heads freshly shaven, they were clutching old blankets about them while waiting for their clothes to be boiled in the galley.

Peter Vesey noticed how, stripped down like this, most of the former felons appeared even more terribly emaciated and diseased. Many gaunt bodies were splotched with angry red rashes, new scars, running sores and very often scabs and buboes symptomatic of syphilis in its secondary stage.

The former physician glanced at his hands and winced. Dirt had been ground so deep into their roughened skin that his recent ablutions had had small effect. Infected pustules marked the place where manacles had chafed his wrists. His fingernails remained cracked, jagged and black despite efforts to clean them with a splinter.

He was finding it remarkable that, aside from being forced to scrub and to have their heads shaved to rid them of vermin, the former convicts were being treated no worse than the luckless wretches caught by some pressgang.

Shivering violently in the galley's lee, Vesey took occasion to consider more closely the only ex-felon in whom he'd noticed signs of of breeding and intelligence. He'd overheard this slightly built but muscular young fellow give the name of "Ted Waxter" to First Lieutenant Brett, in charge of *Gloucester*'s Quarter Bill.

With an air of sardonic amusement Waxter was considering a file of slovenly Marines on their way to change the guard. Absently he passed a hand over his shaven scalp, then his large and wideset dark brown eyes sought a heap of lank, white-blond locks under his bare feet. He thought, if only dear Sophia could see her former intended right now she'd likely faint for a second time — fashionably and prettily, of course.

Becoming aware of Vesey's interest, he summoned a wry grin. "Ecod, for the first time I'd really enjoy donning a wig — usually can't abide the smelly, crawly things."

Vesey hugged his blanket closer and said through chattering teeth, "H-hated 'em m-myself. N-never c-could get my man to k-keep 'em neat and c-combed."

" 'Your man,' eh? Well, I'm demmed! I'd one, too. Amusin' rascal, but he stole me blind. Why are you —?" Waxter broke off and, in his embarrassment, began to whistle "Lillibullero" between his teeth. To inquire into a fellow prisoner's misfortune simply was not done in the best jailbird circles.

"Look alive there!" the cook's helpers warned as they used sticks to lift clothes from a great copper cauldron and drop them, steaming sourly, onto the deck. A barrel-chested boatswain's mate used his colt to indicate garments which, disintegrated beyond further use, were to be set aside for cleaning rags.

Scowling, he confronted the blanket-draped group. "Nah listen to me, ye bloody mothers' mistakes. You will naw march down to the purser's store and draw what ye're short. Ye must all wear britches, shirt, stockings and shoes. Understand?"

"S'ye, guv'nor," squeaked a beady-eyed ex-convict, " 'ow in 'ell are we to pay for these fawncy court clothes?"

"Stow that, ye ugly yelping dog!" The boatswain's mate struck the speaker across the face with his colt. "That'll teach you address a ship's officer 'thout being spoken to." He glared about. "Whatever ye draw from the slop chest will be deducted from yer pay — if any — at the end o' this cruise. You 'Mayor's men' are more likely to end up in a hammock with a stitch in yer nose and roundshot at yer stinking feet."

While buttoning the stained remains of his frilled lawn shirt Waxter turned to Vesey. "Where did they assign you?"

"Don't know. Heard something about the afterguard — whatever that may be."

"That mean serving among the Marines?"

"No."

"I've been assigned there, too. Heard it means duty in the ship's hind-end, which apparently is an honor for us Knights of the Ball and Chain."

Vesey pulled on breeches — bought last winter for the county ball — but was angered to see the remains of his shirt reposing among the condemned garments. "Can't make head or tail of this ship talk. 'Tis worse even than learning the elements of physic."

"Then you're one of those physickers?"

"Past tense."

The advantages of being assigned to the afterguard neither man perceived at the moment. It meant that they would berth aft, just forward of the Marines. In fair weather they might enjoy a measure of light and fresh air and would be spared the orlop's crowded and pestilential gloom.

～ 1 2 ～

"Spanish Ladies"

ON THE 18th of September, 1740, *Centurion* at seven-thirty A.M. fired a gun. At the same moment, Midshipman Francis Drake obeyed George Anson's command to break out his bright red and swallow-tailed Commodore's pendant. Next, he ordered hoisted the "get under weigh" flag.

Immediately, Royal Jacks and Blue Ensigns appeared on all eight vessels belonging to the squadron. Fifes and drums struck up "Spanish Ladies," the traditional sailing day tune, whereupon men in the 'tween decks leaned against the capstan's bars and started to walk up the anchor.

Red-faced with embarrassment, Anson watched his half-trained seamen clamber uncertainly out along the yards and clumsily shake out topsails and gallants. Sailing masters and their mates bawled and shouted. Boatswains cursed and used their colts with merciless impartiality, but the squadron's getting under way remained a dreadful exhibition of seamanship.

By the dozen, upper sails filled under a stiff breeze which sent the

[55]

squadron lumbering down the harbor towards Spithead and St. Helen's on the Isle of Wight.

Only Andrew Menzies, standing respectfully to leeward, could sense the acuteness of Anson's professional shame.

Sailing Master Justinian Nutt, gray-faced and anxious, watched *Centurion's* snowy gallants suddenly fill and begin to tug at their braces. Gradually, the flagship heeled, commenced to feel alive. Aloft sounded the creaking of topgallant yards being braced about and the staccato rattling of blocks. Topmen, mostly veterans, scrambled nimbly about, prepared to set the royals.

Nat Wade, lying out on *Centurion's* ponderous mainyard, not knowing what was expected of him, swayed, shivering and frightened, with bare toes hooked tight over the foot-ropes. Red-faced men were shouting furiously from the deck, but they served only to bewilder him.

With a boat cloak whipping briskly about him, George Anson mused: Can it be that finally I'm sailing? Lord, what an interminable wait it's been; wonder if I've endured it without too greatly annoying the Admiralty?

How many of the two thousand and twenty-three of us sailing today will ever see England again? Not many of those poor old Pensioners; that's certain.

Pray God I don't encounter Don José Pizarro off Portugal or Madeira. If I do, I've no choice but to engage him, no matter what the risk. Worse still — thanks to all these unmitigated delays — I'll have to weather the Horn in wintertime. Can the storms there be as terrible as everyone reports?

A few feet away, Andrew Menzies also stood lost in thought. How many of Anson's captains would prove capable of surmounting the responsibilities, problems and handicaps which already were being thrust upon them? Could they successfully navigate dangerous and almost unknown waters relying, as they must, on charts little corrected since Sir Francis Drake and that quasi-pirate, Captain Dampier, had braved the Horn to enter the vast Pacific?

Only Menzies was aware that the new Commodore's chief concern lay in the fact that, although latitude could be determined with fair accuracy, he could estimate longitude only through the use of "dead reckoning." What a pity he'd failed to secure from Greenwich Observatory even one of those newly invented Harrison chronometers which, by all accounts, were able to keep absolutely correct time.

[56]

Captain Arnand's Prophecy

WHEN, OFF PORTUGAL, on the 29th of September, His Majesty's ships *St. Albans, Dragon* and other men-of-war guarding the Mediterranean convoy exchanged salutes, then squared away for the Straits of Gibraltar, George Anson heaved a sigh eloquent of relief.

Finally, he was on his own! No more catering to the vagaries of superior officers, no more apprehension over the possible arrival of asinine instructions from the Admiralty!

Centurion's second and third lieutenants, standing to leeward of the Commodore's chunky figure, read his relief.

In an undertone young Philip de Saumarez commented, "I warrant this is the Commodore's happiest moment since he received his orders."

Charles Saunders, tall, black-haired and with a faint cleft dividing his bluish chin, nodded solemnly. "— And for us all, I venture.

"I'll never cease to marvel," he continued *sotto voce*, "how patiently the Commodore suffers fools in high places. Have you noticed that, in attaining his ends, he displays the patience of Job and the subtlety of an Italian diplomat?"

A sailor, baggy brown breeches whipping in the breeze, climbed to the quarterdeck and, removing his hat, stood awaiting permission to speak. But Anson failed to notice him. He was much too preoccupied in noting the dilatory fashion in which his ships were being maneuvered toward their daytime Order-of-Sailing stations.

This called for swift little *Tryall* to sail as scout ship well out in front. Next came *Centurion*, with *Gloucester, Severn* and *Pearle* cruising abreast. Then came *Wager*, deep with military supplies, and, a few cables' lengths astern of her, followed the victualers, *Anna* and *Industry*. Respectively of 110 and 120 tons burthen, how pathetically tiny they appeared!

At length Lieutenant de Saumarez crossed to the waiting seaman. "Well, what is it you want?"

The brown-faced fellow knuckled his forelock as he ducked his head, "Why, sir, Mr. Waller's compliments and will one o' the quarterdeck gentlemen please come to the after cockpit? Mr. Waller says Captain Arnand ain't long for this world."

"Wait here, my man." De Saumarez's sensitive olive-hued features contracted. He strode over to salute the Commodore standing lonely by the weather rail. "Sir, there's a message from Mr. Waller —"

"— Not again!" Anson's eyes of piercing blue swung inboard to meet the younger man's intense black ones. "Pray go ascertain what the complaint is this time."

For some reason suddenly ill at ease, de Saumarez followed the barefooted messenger down to the orlop where his narrow nostrils pinched themselves against the mephitic stench prevailing in that dim place.

Only with difficulty did the lieutenant force his way between laden hammocks jammed so thickly together that they reminded him of a colony of giant bats roosting under Cyclopean eaves. In the cockpit it was so infernally hot and airless that patients and the untrained loblolly boys detailed to care for them had stripped to the waist and were gasping like newly caught fish.

At length de Saumarez located Captain Arnand in a tiny cubicle created by the slinging of old sails.

Sweating profusely, Surgeon Thomas Waller said, "You have barely come in time, sir." A "purser's glim" faintly gilded Waller's large and bulbous nose and thick, loose lips, the linings of which protruded unattractively in a perceptible double fold.

"Commodore's compliments, sir. What seems to be wrong?" de Saumarez demanded impatiently; like all quarterdeck officers he loathed the necessity of spending time below decks.

Behind square-lensed spectacles Mr. Waller's eyes narrowed. "Sir, Captain Arnand wishes to convey a message to the Commodore; he no longer responds to any treatment I can devise."

It was unmistakable that Captain Arnand was *in extremis* and about to die, so, when he began to mumble, de Saumarez bent low to listen and discovered that the veteran was babbling incoherently about the Duke of Marlborough's victories at Ramillies and Blenheim.

Conquering a sudden nausea, de Saumarez bent lower still above the frail, white-haired figure. "Sir, is there anything you wish done to ease your suffering?"

The patient stopped his mumbling, stared vacantly upwards a moment, then cried weakly, "Eh? Who? Wha's that — Major? Rest

[58]

easy, says Brigadier Rowe? Good. My men — exhausted. French cavalry's testing our flank near the Nebel River. Don't send Lambert — too badly hit. I'll go." A thin wail escaped the old man. "Oh God, Harry, my legs won't work. Who — you?"

From a nearby cubicle Captain Colley croaked, "Come off it, Arthur. This Navy bastard's just come down to gloat over your misery."

Over the slow creak and whine of timbers above his head de Saumarez burst out, "That's a damned lie! The Commodore, all of us, did our utmost to prevent your being shipped aboard!"

"Then who is responsible?" railed Colley.

"Those precious swine, the Lords Justices. They refused even to consider the Commodore's protests."

"Eh?" choked Arnand. "Wha's that?"

"You'll have to bend lower, sir," Centurion's surgeon advised. "I can no longer feel the old fool's pulse."

Surprisingly, Arnand raised a disheveled skull-like head, glared about and cried, "I'm not dead yet — not just yet, damn your eyes!"

Profoundly moved, de Saumarez slipped a hand beneath the dying officer's chill and nearly fleshless shoulders. "Please, sir, believe that this outrageous treatment of you old soldiers is none of the Navy's doing."

From deep in their sockets Arthur Arnand's eyes glinted in the feeble lamp light. De Saumarez saw the vital spark in them waver, then flare, savagely bright. "Perhaps it's as you say," admitted the veteran. Then in a ringing voice he continued, "Now hear the fate a wrathful God has in store for you! I see the most of you shot-mangled, drowning, freezing, dying by inches of hunger, thirst and disease! You'll meet with treachery, cannibals and mutinies. I see your proud ships storm-tossed, burning, wrecked on a pitiless coast."

Arthur Arnand's voice swelled until it penetrated to the cockpit's farthest recesses, even carried into the orlop. "Many's the man who'll wish he'd died with me. You dream of taking the Manila ship? Bah! You never will — she'll prove only a golden will-o'-the-wisp luring you to your deaths. I see — I —"

Arnand's voice halted as abruptly as if a knife had been drawn across his throat; his body slumped back onto the filthy blankets.

The few Catholics among the sick hurriedly crossed themselves, while Philip de Saumarez drew a great, convulsive breath of poisoned air, aware that icy fingers seemed to be closing over his heart.

Less than an hour after Captain Arnand died *Centurion* fired a gun, half-masted her ensign and signaled her consorts to heave to. Once topsails had been backed and the ships had begun to lose way, George Anson, his lieutenants and warrant officers on duty lined the quarterdeck's break. Below, Marines and the Watch on Deck, facing inwards, formed double ranks across *Centurion*'s waist.

Solemnly, the Reverend Richard Walter, chaplain to the squadron, took his place beside Captain Arnand's body, which had been sewn into a clean hammock. Covered by a faded Blue Ensign and with a ten-pound shot at its feet the corpse rested upon a plank supported by two trestles.

George Anson's hands, held clasped behind him, gradually tightened until their knuckles shone white. No matter where the true responsibility might lie, experience warned that, eventually, he would be held accountable for Captain Arnand's death — and for those which were certain to follow.

While wind hummed softly through the rigging and yards creaked high above, the ship's company followed the Commodore's example, and bared and bent their heads while the Reverend Walter solemnly read the Service for the Dead. When he had done, a pair of fairly able-bodied Invalid-Pensioners raised the plank's inboard end; an audible sigh arose when Captain Arnand's remains slipped over the side, splashed and then went spiraling, bubbling down into the Atlantic's dark blue. Quickly, the white canvas oblong became lost to sight.

It was all very impressive — and depressing.

In no time at all Captain Arnand's dying words sped throughout the flagship, losing nothing with each repetition. Soon not a soul in Anson's squadron but was shuddering, openly or privately, over some version of the Invalid Captain's awful prophecy.

When Peter Vesey heard what had been said he surveyed *Gloucester*'s sweltering and all but lightless 'tween decks, then commented, "A dying man's prescience isn't required to predict what's obvious. Discounting battle, shipwreck, starvation and the other charming possibilities mentioned by the late Captain, disease alone won't leave one in ten alive."

"It's as bad as that?"

"Certainly. You can't pack men together like lice, give 'em bad air to breathe, feed 'em on swill, and expect them to live very long."

Ted Waxter laughed a little. "That's as may be, friend Peter, but I'll give you the same ten-to-one odds that *I'll* survive! And so should you. We're clever enough to contrive and outlast the stupid brutes about us."

Aboard *Centurion* Will Pallister was terribly frightened until he recited to Tom Ramster: " 'I will say of the Lord, He is my refuge and my fortress: my God; in him will I trust. Thou shalt not be afraid for the terror by night; nor for the arrow that flieth by day; nor for the pestilence that walketh in darkness; nor for the destruction that wasteth at noonday.' "

Ramster guffawed, then sobered. "Say, that's real pretty — but me, I don't like this business. When a feller's dying he likely sees the truth of what's coming — heard that said plenty of times."

Said Nat Wade to the ex-tailor Dobey, "Some of us are going to die sure enough, but *I'm* going to pull through and get back to my wife."

Joe Utting said nothing when Arnand's prophecy was discussed by his messmates. He was too busy worrying about whether Jimmie and John could complete the harvest — they were only twelve and thirteen — and Toby must still be laid up with his broken leg.

From then on death struck the squadron so often that soon the Reverend Walter and the Captains of the other ships were forced to abbreviate their funeral services, it not being desirable in any way to delay the squadron's alarmingly slow progress towards Madeira.

Men already were commenting on an ominous coincidence: only a few hours after Captain Arnand had given up the ghost a steady northeast wind, usually to be depended on at this season, unaccountably faltered and all but died out as Captain Colley was following his old companion-in-arms over the side.

~~~ 14 ~~~

Funchal Passage

BECAUSE NATHANIEL WADE was young, strong and intelligent, he developed a new alertness, copied the tactics of experienced sailors

[61]

and stood ready to use his fists on the least provocation. In the fearfully crowded 'tween decks he found plenty of occasion.

Among other things, he taught himself to wake the instant his watch was called — even at four in the morning. Only once did Wade get doused by a bucket of water through not having turned out smartly enough. Far more quickly than any of the other impressed landsmen he learned the proper method of striking and lashing his hammock with the requisite seven turns and then finding his way on deck through the mass of men sleeping in the insufferably crowded semidarkness.

Shrewdly he studied the ways of veteran A.B.s, learned how to escape extra duty and how to avoid trouble with the always short-tempered corporals and Marines. A burly redheaded A.B. named Ramster became so tickled by the serious way Wade copied his every move in the tops that he invited the leather-worker to join the mess of which he was captain. With one exception, it otherwise was composed of sea-wise veterans.

Each mess included eight men who ate, standing, from a long narrow tableboard slung between the carriage guns. When not in use these tableboards were hoisted to the deck beams above by means of pulleys; there, they'd be out of the way.

To each messman the purser's mate had issued, in addition to a wooden trencher, a spoon, a tin pint pot with a handle and an earthenware bowl. Every man carried a clasp knife slung to a lanyard about his neck — once its point had been broken off by the master-at-arms, lest it be used for settling arguments.

After meals the messes scraped their eating utensils as clean as possible before stowing them in their mess kid, that shallow tub which each mess "cook," or captain, carried to the galley to draw his and his messmates' rations. When not in use, such rancid-smelling kids were secured to the ship's side.

The only other landsman in Tom Ramster's mess was Will Pallister, the minister's young son. Everybody, Wade included, at first took him to be the powerful A.B.'s "chicken." But it wasn't so. For, to that lusty veteran's surprise, when he'd crawled into Will's hammock one night off the Isle of Wight and had commenced to explore the youth's smooth and trembling body, something had stung his ribs hard enough to start a hot blood trickle running over his side. He'd left off fumbling then, had whispered into the youth's ear, "Just what the hell are ye up to, Willie boy?"

[62]

"You've b-been awfully k-kind to me, Mr. Ramster," the youth had breathed, "but if — if y-you don't l-leave me alone — I fear I will be forced t-to drive this knife into you — all the way."

For a moment Ramster had deliberated — it would have been child's play to have disarmed Pallister — but he'd ended by grunting, "Ye damn' ungrateful little devil," and by returning to his own hammock. Had his life depended upon it, Ramster couldn't have explained why he took the minister's gentle-eyed son into his mess after selecting his "chicken," a big-eyed twelve-year-old cockney reputed to be very adept in the vice of Sodom.

Thrice a day Ramster would report to the purser's storeroom to draw each man's food and wine — or liquor allowance — for his mess. Then as mess captain, or "cook," he would seek the ship's brick-floored galley situated just abaft *Centurion's* forecastle where he would draw his perquisite, the "cook's ration," a double allowance of grog, before carrying the communal rations below.

Although George Anson kept an increasingly anxious eye on his barometer and old salts whistled for wind, the squadron made painfully slow progress towards the Madeira Islands.

Because, when warmed with wine, the captain of a homeward bound French Indiaman let drop that a Spanish squadron recently had sailed from Corruna with the express intention of intercepting him, Anson ordered intensified gun drills and doubled lookouts posted throughout the squadron. Officers and midshipmen of the Watch on Deck carried spyglasses into the fighting tops and scanned the horizon day and night. Daily the tension mounted.

As Captain Legge observed to his second, " 'Twon't do to get caught with green crews and our lower gundecks sealed. The Commodore will have no choice but to cut and try to run for it."

It was during this period that Pallister discovered that, try as he would, he'd make no part of a topman; when sent aloft he invariably vomited and earned a caning.

Swarthy Lieutenant de Saumarez chanced to note his clumsiness aloft and called him down from the rigging.

"You're so infernal awkward aloft you'll soon fall and get killed, which isn't desirable, being as shorthanded as we are," de Saumarez observed dispassionately. "Can you read?"

"Y-yes, sir, — I mean, aye, aye, sir."

"Write? Understand arithmetic? Grammar? Syntax?"

"Aye, aye, sir. My father's a schoolmaster as well as a minister."

The young lieutenant's dark eyes narrowed. "Ha! Now I remember. You were one of the idiots who volunteered, free-willing." Some of his severity disappeared. "Why'd you do it? Girl break your heart?"

"No, sir. I've never had aught to do with girls."

"That's fortunate because you'll have to do without them for quite a while longer. Meantime, go report yourself to Mr. Pascoe. He's the schoolmaster. Tell him I believe you can assist him in drilling some knowledge into those blockheads at present occupying the midshipmen's berth."

As was expected, the feebler Invalid-Pensioners continued to die off at an alarming rate; also the weakest or most diseased among the impressed hands and Lord Mayor's men.

Not until dawn of October the 27th, thirty-five days after quitting St. Helen's, did *Tryall*, scouting as usual in advance of her consorts, fire a gun and make signal that land had been sighted.

"And the Lord's name be praised." George Anson felt a crushing load fall from his shoulders. He felt so cheered he went to his cabin, where he and Lieutenant Saunders solemnly toasted those pale blue peaks on the horizon. "Now if only those damn' Spaniards aren't lying off Funchal."

His luck held and sundown found the squadron shortening sail off Funchal's beautiful and capacious harbor.

Anson felt absurdly pleased when a pair of British privateers lying in the roadstead dutifully fired eleven guns and dipped their colors in honor of his broad red pendant. Smiling, he ordered *Centurion's* saluting battery to return this courtesy with five guns.

Barely had the squadron dropped anchor than a boat put out from the nearer privateer and was pulled hard over to the flagship. The privateer captain, a tough-looking little Scot, swarmed lightly up the gangway ladder and asked to be conducted immediately to *Centurion's* lantern-lit quarterdeck.

Narrowly, the Commodore considered this gray-whiskered visitor and, for a long instant, delayed in acknowledging the other's lifted cap; it might be well to remind this privateer that he found himself aboard a King's ship. Carefully suppressing any trace of anxiety,

[64]

Anson said pleasantly, "Well, Captain, and to what do I owe the promptness of this courtesy?"

The Scot, who said his name was Grant, slowly revolved a round wool cap between gnarled fingers. "I take it you'd no sight of them?"

"No sight of whom?" demanded Lieutenant Cheap curtly. "What *are* you babbling about?"

With calm indifference Captain Grant considered the speaker, then readdressed the Commodore.

"Sir-r, there's a fleet o' seven great Spanish ships-o'-the-line been laying in wait for ye. Has been, a fortni't, now."

"Thank you for the information," Anson said, "but I've seen nothing of them." He almost added "fortunately," but didn't.

The Scot's gray and bloodshot eyes narrowed themselves. "Nevertheless, sir-r, they've been cruising to the westward of Madeira these past ten days. Generally, they hide below the horizon, but every morning their Admiral sends a swift *patache* to spy out the harbor here."

"I thank you for the warning, Captain Grant. In what strength is the enemy?"

The Scottish Captain shrugged, spread horny hands. "Why, sir-r, like I just said, the Don has seven ships-o'-the-line wi' him, and a number of lesser craft."

The Commodore's expression remained imperturbable for all that he was thinking: so there are seven ships-of-the-line out there to my four; fair enough odds. If it comes to a fight I'll land the superfluous supplies, ready my lower-tier guns and go out and see what this fellow Pizarro has to offer. Why not? Seems wiser to engage near home, so I can send the prizes in safely and repair damages there.

But is my first duty to fight here, or to evade action and proceed into the Pacific?

Even when Captain Grant's gig put off, George Anson had not yet reached a decision.

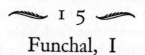

1 5

Funchal, I

IF THE OVERCROWDING aboard *Centurion* was frightful, conditions in *Gloucester* were infinitely worse. Her main gundeck was ten feet shorter than the flagship's and two precious feet less in the beam.

Ordinary Seaman Peter Vesey, after standing the Mid-Watch — midnight to four A.M. — went below and, by dint of much shoving between tight-wedged hammocks, struggled to his own sleeping place, but he ached so in his every joint and muscle that, exhausted as he was, he couldn't sleep in this hot and airless inferno. He squirmed in the narrow canvas until he could face away from his right-hand neighbor, who kept coughing heavily. Even though he couldn't see him, the former physician guessed that the consumptive was spraying his surroundings with scarlet droplets.

Great drops of sweat continued to break out over Vesey's body even after he had unbuttoned his sour-smelling shirt down to his belt. He yearned to strip it off but didn't; removed, it was sure to be stolen.

To refrain from falling over the verge of despair, Peter Vesey stared into the darkness. He'd had a glimpse of *Gloucester's* captain at close range, had noted that his skin and the whites of his eyes were yellow and that chocolate-brown blotches were speckling his thick neck and backs of his hands. Undoubtedly Captain Norris was suffering from a very bad liver; probably his kidneys were also infected.

The ex-doctor stifled a moan. Could it be that a few short months ago Peter Vesey had been a respected physician with a flourishing practice centered on Henley-on-Thames? Could it be that Peter Vesey had ever lived with a lovely wife in a handsome home?

How very proud and surprised he'd been to win the hand of the Honorable Pamela Gresham, daughter of one of the most distinguished and powerful families in Oxford County. The only shadow on three years of otherwise happy marriage had been their childlessness. Had they been able to produce offspring might things have turned out not so tragically? Only God in his high Heaven could answer that.

Grunting snores from nearby hammocks, the consumptive's coughing, and the monotonous moaning of fever-stricken seamen continued to deprive him of sleep. How black it was in here; quite as lightless as it had been on that fatal night when, amid a furious thunderstorm, he'd returned so unexpectedly from attending Granny Swinden. How vastly relieved he'd been to see lamps still glowing in his home.

He recalled how surprised he'd been when, on stepping indoors, he'd received no reply to his call, "Pamela, I'm home!"

Even now, lying sweat-bathed and half-suffocated, he could recall how hard wind-driven raindrops had stung his face when, on inspiration, he'd hurried out to search the gazebo. It must have been while he was running towards the summerhouse that, to his ultimate undoing, he'd discovered a cased lancet forgotten in his riding cloak's pocket.

The thunder and the wind's wild booming had been so deafening that neither Pamela nor Sir Arthur Markham had heard him run over the gravel. Just as he'd flung himself indoors, an especially vivid flash of lightning had illuminated the interior to disclose two figures upon a settee entwined in the throes of love.

Grinding his teeth, Peter Vesey recalled how the slim and pallid outline of Pamela's body had gleamed, uninterrupted, from her stockings' tops to her armpits. Sir Arthur's fingers had shown, dark and spider-like, against his wife's cheeks as they immobilized her face the better to receive his kisses.

So lost in ecstasy had been the recumbent figures that neither had noticed his presence. Gripped by the paralysis of utter astonishment he'd watched his neighbor and close friend bend to kiss a nipple exposed by Pamela's dishabille, had heard her moan as her arms rose to encircle Sir Arthur's neck and draw him down so that she might crush her mouth against his. It must have been when they had begun softly, triumphantly to laugh that he'd gone berserk and his hand had snatched the lancet from its case.

When he'd been able once more to think rationally, Sir Arthur was lying stretched out on the gazebo's tiled floor with both hands seeking to suppress blood spurting from his neck.

Pamela, having pulled down her garments, had stared at him, huge-eyed. "See what you've done, you stupid, ill-bred clod," she'd cried in a frozen voice. "I expect you've killed poor Arthur."

Unfortunately for Peter Vesey, he'd succeeded in checking the hemorrhage long enough to permit the half-dressed servants to hear, and remember, that amazing tissue of lies Sir Arthur had managed to improvise. Baseless, overpowering jealousy on Dr. Vesey's part, alone, had prompted the attack. Markham had gasped that, as God was his witness, he and Mrs. Vesey had been sheltering from the storm and conversing of commonplaces when the doctor had burst in.

A moment later, Ordinary Seaman Vesey recalled, Sir Arthur had lapsed into unconsciousness and had died.

At the trial Sir Arthur's dying statement had been repeated, under oath, by the servants and solemnly substantiated by the Honorable Lady Pamela. Such had been her icy composure that the jury had lost little time in bringing in the verdict which everybody had anticipated.

What a fool he'd been to entertain the least hope of avoiding the gallows. Socially, Peter Vesey had been acceptable but unimportant, coming as he had from another county, whereas the Gresham and Markham families had been prominent in Oxfordshire for generations.

How strange, mused the ex-felon, it's little more than a month ago that the bailiff placed a black kerchief, folded into a triangle, on Sir Hubert Worley's head. I'll never forget how grotesque it looked there. What were his exact words? Oh, yes. "Peter Vesey, hear the sentence of this Court. On the tenth day of August next you shall be taken from the prison in which you are now confined and conducted to the place of execution, there to be hanged by the neck until you are dead, dead, dead. And may God have mercy upon your soul."

Ordinary Seaman Vesey had not been surprised to hear from his anguished sister that Pamela, when she'd learned of his reprieve from the gallows, had instituted proceedings for divorce, with an eye towards espousing the late Sir Arthur's handsome brother, Paul.

Even now, the wretched seaman had no idea who had been responsible for his having been allowed to serve in the Navy as an alternative to having his neck stretched.

All of a sudden the consumptive burst into a paroxysm of coughing so violent that when it ended Vesey groped for the fellow's wrist. He could detect no pulsing in it. Should he get up and notify a ship's corporal? Before he could make up his mind, an ear-piercing blast on a boatswain's pipe sounded from above.

A hoarse voice bellowed, "Starboard Watch, ahoy! Out and down!"

Lanterns glimmered in the orlop. "Hit the deck, ye sluggards!"

Curses and the resounding *whack! whack!* of colts and starters descending sent the men tumbling out of their hammocks.

"There's a dead man in that hammock," Vesey informed a gap-toothed boatswain's mate.

"What of it? Let the bugger rot and get to hell on deck, you lead-footed ape!"

HBMS *Gloucester*'s night lights were drawing faint yellow streaks across the Fourth Rate's streaming deck when, at four o'clock of a warm, rainy morning, the new Watch ran, coughing and spitting, to their stations.

Lights and the dim outline of white-painted houses in Funchal showed faintly beneath the silhouette of a semicircle of steep hills rising immediately behind the port.

"Ah-h! That's better," sighed Waxter, after drawing a series of deep breaths. "Below, I always feel poisoned."

Moving slowly, silently, like drugged men, the cook and his heavy-eyed helpers appeared and set about kindling fires in the galley.

"Look alive, you lazy dogs!" a midshipman's thin voice shrilled out of the darkness. "Clean the deck!"

Buckets, mops, brooms and holystones were brought out and put to use. By means of short ropes they would drag the stones back and forth across the deck that continually was sprinkled with sand. Because they'd been quick to learn, Waxter and Vesey ran to claim a holystone which was a heavy slab of sandstone with a ring set in its center, otherwise they would have had to use "bibles" — small, individual holystones employed by men who, on hands and knees, had to scour areas unattainable to a two-man holystone. Such work quickly raised abcesses on a man's knees that were painful and slow to heal.

The *clack! clack!* of head pumps at work resounded dully through the gray downpour. The hoses they supplied writhed about the deck like sable serpents after seamen engaged in sluicing off freshly holy-stoned areas.

A tall and pimply midshipman supervised the work; made liberal use of a rattan cane whenever he fancied some bible or holystone was not being employed with sufficient vigor.

Once the bible men and holystoners had completed their work, swabs were used to dry the decking despite the drumming rain. Next the Watch turned its attention to the Fourth Rate's brasswork.

"You, there!" The midshipman pointed his cane at Waxter. "Brighten that deadlight!"

"Aye, aye, sir." His overfine features expressionless as those of an effigy on some Crusader's sarcophagus, Lord Burfurd caught up a rag.

Vesey was sent to burnish the brass caps on a pair of bitts. A vacant-eyed seaman, emaciated as a hermit, was sent over to work on a deadlight beside Waxter. In kneeling he swayed and groaned as he dropped onto knees raw and bloody from contact with a sanded deck. Waxter saw the other's polishing rag move slowly about the salt-stained brass frame. Finally, the skeletonic figure emitted a choked sigh and collapsed on the streaming deck.

Snarling, the midshipman strode over and dealt the unconscious man a shrewd kick. "Get up! Try to malinger, would you, you lazy dog!"

But the inert figure lay still, whereupon a pair of seamen were detailed to carry the senseless man down to sick bay.

It wasn't the smartest method of attracting favorable attention, but it was worth a try, Waxter decided, so, having shined his own frame to perfection, he set about completing the stricken seaman's job. He'd been working only a few minutes when a figure loomed above him, unfortunately that of Robert Robinson, one of *Gloucester*'s supernumerary lieutenants who was reported to disguise sadistic impulses behind a pleasant expression.

"What's the meaning of this, you scurvy dog? In half an hour's time you've not even begun to clean that frame."

Scurvy dog? Acid currents commenced to surge through Lord Burfurd's being, but he held onto his temper. Thin cheek pulsing, he straightened and looked Lieutenant Robinson straight in the eye. "Your pardon, sir, I was only trying to help —"

"Damn your ugly eyes, how dare you to answer back an officer! Gag this man!"

A pair of Marines, their red jackets dark with rain, promptly pinioned Waxter.

A third held an iron marlinespike horizontally across the prisoner's mouth, growled, "Open up, ye bloody waister, else ye'll lose some teeth!"

The spike then was jammed like a horse's bit between Waxter's jaws and a length of spun yarn knotted behind his head so tightly that the corners of his mouth were drawn back in an anguished grimace.

Rasped Lieutenant Robinson, "Stand to attention, you insolent dog, till I order your release."

So Lord Burfurd, crimson with humiliation and outrage at such injustice, stood barefoot in the pelting rain with a heavy metal rod jammed between his teeth. Murderous impulses surged through him when blood dripped over his chin and, mingling with the rain, stained his shirt. To avoid strangling he was forced to swallow continuously. Soon his lower jaw commenced to ache like a huge bad tooth, but he dared not relax from attention, let alone attempt to ease the gag, because a Marine was standing behind with bayonet ready to jab him.

Balefully, the anguished seaman's eyes followed Lieutenant Robinson's erect figure as, almost gracefully, he inspected various pieces of brasswork. Silently he swore, "Someday — someday I'll make that swine pay through the nose."

An age seemed to have elapsed before a Marine corporal came up and ordered, "Stand easy." When he used a clasp knife to slash the spun yarn, the marlinespike, falling, scattered blood drops across the spotless deck.

～ 1 6 ～
Funchal, II

No ONE, saving possibly Andrew Menzies, suspected the intensity of the anxiety which kept gnawing, ratlike, at George Anson's peace of mind. Would the Board of Admiralty approve his conduct? Probably not. Few of those noble lords had ever set foot aboard a man-of-war.

He took a quick turn along his private stern walk. Could any of them, Winchelsea, Devonshire, Lennox or even Lord Hardwicke — Elizabeth's father — be made to understand the reasoning behind his decision to partially unload the squadron in Funchal and so enable him and his captains to use their lower deck guns? But what would they say if Don José Pizarro elected to ignore Portugal's neutrality, sailed in and caught the King's ships denied the use of most of their heavy guns?

In the meantime he was doing everything possible to improve the squadron's chances. All day, gun drills were being conducted throughout the squadron; green topmen were being kept aloft to learn the art of swiftly making and reducing canvas.

It was too bad that a number of landlubbers, threatened beyond caution, had missed their hold and had fallen. Some crashed onto the deck and were killed outright. Others, more fortunate, landed in the harbor's refuse-littered water and generally were pulled out, half-drowned, by boats working alongside. Several were drowned because not one man in fifty was able to swim.

Lieutenant Cheap appeared and touched his hat with an air of concern. "Sir, shall I start breaking out the extra stores?"

Anson treated his heavy-jawed subordinate to a searching glance. Did he appreciate the nature of the terrible dilemma confronting his Commander in Chief? "Not just yet, Mr. Cheap. First I wish to receive the scout ship's report."

Suffering from inner turmoil, Anson, outwardly impassive, received Captain Grant, who, surprisingly, had volunteered to search the sea west of Madeira and ascertain the enemy's strength and position.

A lowering sun was gilding the façades of the forts guarding Funchal when, her topsails glowing red in the sunset, Captain Grant's sloop, responding to the signal, "Pass within hail," ran saucily past *Centurion*'s stern galleries.

"I've fair news, sir-r!" the Scot bellowed above a rattling of blocks and the slatting of canvas caused by having let fly his topsail sheets. "I've sighted never a sail oot yonder!"

Through a leather speaking trumpet Anson shouted down, "Thank you, Captain. I'm vastly in your debt. Was there any indication of direction taken by the Spaniards?"

"None, sir-r. Howsomever, I spoke a Basque feesherman offshore who'd talked wi' one o' their *pataches* and heard that when your ships proved so tardy in touching Funchal their Admiral decided ye must have elected to ignore Madeira and sailed direct for the Americas. Mayhap they've turned that way, too."

Conscious of crushing responsibilities, George Anson ordered *Tryall* to conduct a final reconnaissance of the ocean around Madeira before ordering the sick to be set ashore and his ships cleaned as thoroughly as they could be without landing stores. Finally, he ordered that the wretched Invalid-Pensioners should be allowed to bask in the hot sun as long as they pleased.

Water casks were refilled while agent-victualers roamed the island's countryside in search of poultry, fruits, vegetables, goats, swine and bullocks. Few, if any of these, proved to be of good quality.

In succession Anson sent his men-of-war out to sea for practice in firing on drifting targets. Lieutenant Colonel Cratcherode landed such of his troops as were fit for duty — which were precious few —

and drilled them mercilessly, a necessary step since most of them had never previously loaded a musket.

For a week the squadron lingered in warm and beautiful Funchal, then *Centurion* made signal: "All lieutenants and captains will report immediately aboard the flagship." Wearing dress swords and apprehensive expressions, they saluted the quarterdeck and promptly were directed to the great cabin. The Commodore received them in a crisp white wig, Mechlin lace jabot, scarlet knee breeches and a bottle-green frock coat laced with gold braid.

Once all the officers were assembled his deep voice filled the cabin. "I regret to inform you, gentlemen, that the precarious state of Captain Norris's health renders it imperative that he return to England. By consequence, I am pleased to make the following promotions.

"Gentlemen, as of today Captain Mitchell of *Pearle* will assume command of *Gloucester*. Captain Kidd" — Anson glanced at that solid little man and enjoyed his wide grin — "is hereby promoted from the *Wager* to be commander and master of the *Pearle*. In his room, the Honorable George Murray is hereby promoted from the *Tryall*, sloop, to be captain and master of the *Wager*, storeship. By virtue of the authority vested in me as Commander in Chief I am promoting Mr. David Cheap to the rank of Post Captain. Henceforward he will command and be master of the *Tryall*."

Lieutenants Saunders and de Saumarez looked as pleased as they felt. True, Cheap's promotion must mean a step up for them, but, principally, they were happy to see Cheap leave the flagship. Undoubtedly a capable officer and a most excellent seaman, David Cheap was also harsh and capricious when it came to maintaining discipline.

At six A.M. on the fourth of November, 1740, the squadron saluted the port, weighed anchor and, breaking out a smother of sail, headed for South America.

I 7

In the Orlop

THE SQUADRON'S STORESHIP, HBMS *Wager,* was an old East India-man and therefore very round-bowed and slow in the water. Dis-placing a mere 559 tons, she was carried on the Navy List as a Fifth Rate, but, on quitting England, she somehow had packed on board 521 suffering, sweltering human beings.

Named after Sir Charles Wager, Anson's friend and benefactor, she sailed extra sluggishly because of the great supply of ship's stores she was carrying for the rest of the squadron against the long voyage in prospect. There were in her holds small arms, field guns and caissons for fighting the Spaniards on land — if, indeed, any troops existed by the time Anson's ships arrived off the west coast of South America.

If, for a seasoned seaman like Harry Cozens, service afloat was merely the repetition of unpleasant experiences, for farmer Joe Ut-ting it was undiluted hell.

At first Utting had been so hopelessly confused that not even the brutal application of colts and canes could drive him towards the execution of even the simplest of duties. To his slow wits everything pertaining to guns or rigging remained a dreadful, insoluble mystery.

Perhaps it was this helplessness which caused reckless, yellow-haired Harry Cozens suddenly to befriend him. Poor Joe was such a complete "Jimmy Dux" — the age-old sea term for a farmer — that, inevitably, he became a "waister" and was assigned to such lowly tasks as cleaning gratings from the heads — latrine sheds over-hanging the ship's side at her cutwater. Often he was driven with curses and blows down to swamp out the orlop into which the bulk of the Invalids and recruits had been crammed. These luckless wretches were forced, when too far gone to reach the heads, to defecate or vomit on the deck.

Utting's only halfway agreeable duty was that of feeding livestock confined in the ship's manger.

"Poor beasties, ye be e'en worse off than I," he'd mutter and his farmer's heart would mourn for the familiar creatures condemned to sway in the dark, bawling for water, food and fresh air.

The manger, Utting discovered, was a sort of broad trough designed to carry off water which kept spurting endlessly in through the ship's poorly stopped hawseholes. Joe would linger in the ammonia-tinctured gloom as long as he dared, scratching a pig's back or allowing a terrified sheep to muzzle his hand. "Ye poor patient creatures, were it up to Joe Utting he would pen you on deck — or else cut yer throats. 'Tain't right for you, who know green grass and open sky, to suffer so."

He lingered longest over watering and feeding, talking farm language to the bullocks bought in Funchal. They had been jammed so tight together that the ship's ceaseless motion rubbed raw and bleeding patches off their hides. That they could understand only Portuguese seemed to make no difference; the cattle quieted as soon as the ex-farmer appeared.

As a last duty Utting slopped the swine from heavy wooden buckets brimming with "Burgoo" — that villainous-tasting oatmeal gruel which, with "Scotch coffee" — scorched bread — and a single sea-biscuit, invariably constituted breakfast aboard ship.

Longingly, he thought of the clean, stone barn back home which sheltered his milch cows, Brindle and Bess. About now I reckon Bess must ha' dropped her calf; should prove good and sturdy, or else I got cheated when I paid a pound to have her served by Squire Benbow's fine red bull. Did she get a heifer or a bull calf? Guess I'll never know.

The farmer's stomach heaved whenever he neared the pigpens. Faugh! he told himself, the muck in them must be easy a foot deep. After he'd done slopping the hogs he conversed gravely with a black and white sow he'd named Emily after a sister he didn't much care for.

"God's mercy, Emily, you don't know what I'd give for just one home-cooked meal! Ain't et decent food ever since that danged press-gang found me. Tell me, Emily, why did I have to go and get stupid drunk on that partic'lar night?"

For over a week dinner and supper allowance had been "junk" — tough beef so heavily encrusted with salt that, if consumed, the eater suffered tortures from thirst.

"Only allowance I c'n keep down is pea soup — especially when the cooks mix some rice in it. Too bad the small-beer they used to give us is finished. Don't take much to *mistela*, that sour Spanish wine. Harry Cozens and the rest call it 'Miss Taylor.' I wonder why?

[75]

Wonder how long it'll be before they start serving grog? Can't be so bad as this 'Miss Taylor' wine we've been drinking. My friend Cozens says every man will draw a gill of grog with dinner and supper. He says grog's good — one part rum mixed in three parts water. Maybe so, but I'd liefer swill a tankard of ale at the Sheaf of Wheat."

A voice bellowed, "Hey, you dead down there, Jimmy Dux? Shake a leg on deck!"

"Comin', sir!" Heavy swill buckets bumping against his legs, Joe Utting lurched down a passage between a double row of fieldpieces. Time and again the motion sent him banging into gun barrels, wheels or a caisson's corner. Discordantly, lashings securing this mass of freight creaked and squealed under *Wager's* endless rolling.

It was fine to get back on deck and flush the buckets under a deck pump. As he worked he watched the chartered victualers, *Anna* and *Industry*, plow along astern. How very tiny they looked — kind of like gulls resting on a stormy day in a big, empty field.

A cane's lash descending on his shoulders made Joe gasp. "Now then," rasped a midshipman, "go down to the Marines' berth and help muck it out!"

"Yes, yer Honor, I — I'll go right away. Faster 'n fast, sir."

On his way Utting encountered a gap-toothed sailmaker's mate. "Please, friend, which way's the Marines' berth?"

"By God, Jimmy Dux, ye've only to follow yer nose to find it. 'Tis like a hog-wallow today."

"What's wrong with a hog-wallow? 'Tis the only place the critters c'n cool off. They can't sweat, ye know."

The deeper Utting penetrated into *Wager's* 'tween decks the more fetid grew the atmosphere. He gasped. Whew! By comparison the ship's manger smelt like a violet patch!

"Lot o' deaders this morning," grunted a fellow waister. "Nine — so far."

Joe, carrying bucket and swab, was forced to bend double in order to pass under rows of close-packed hammocks. There was no way of forcing a passage through them.

Since *Wager* had run into heavy weather, many flux-stricken soldiers, unable to rise, had been forced to urinate and move their bowels where they lay.

When, hopelessly, Joe began to ply his swab, whiskered, nightmarish faces peered over hammock edges, gasped, "Water! Water! I'm burning up. Just a little mouthful of water!"

"Ah, will ye stow that?" snarled a bearded loblolly boy. "No parlor maids down 'ere to coddle yer lordships."

Sweating, forever losing his balance on the slimy decking, the ex-farmer glimpsed fellow waisters listlessly attempting to scrape up filth which had collected under the gun carriages.

"Attention, ye swabs! Here comes 'e surgeon," someone shouted over ship's noises.

Mr. Henry Ettrick, borrowed from *Centurion* at Funchal, appeared at the bottom of the main ladder, held up a lantern, looked briefly about, then hurriedly returned on deck observing, "There's nothing I can accomplish down there," which was no less than the truth since his experience, heretofore, had been confined to physicking and amputating shattered limbs from healthy seamen.

"This old bugger's dead at last," announced a nearby waister. He turned to Utting, "Nah, then, lend me an 'and." Together they tilted the hammock enough to permit a terribly emaciated body to thump onto the deck.

"Un'ook 'is 'ammock," directed the chief loblolly, "and pile it with them's what's to be washed. Good. Nah then, Jimmy Dux, grab 'old of the blighter's feet; lucky 'e don't weigh much."

Nevertheless, it proved hard work to transport even this slight burden to a small place cleared among the tightly lashed stores. In it the sailmaker and a brace of mates were busy sewing into clean white hammocks a number of cadavers which no one had bothered to cleanse.

"A bloomin' record," cackled Utting's companion. "Makes ten deaders in one dye!"

Two of the sailmaker's gang dropped the still-warm body onto a hammock spread flat on the deck. Immediately a third placed a ten-pound shot between the bony, unwashed feet, then flipped over the hammock's ends and began to sew them closed.

The sailmaker, a morose-looking individual whom nothing seemed to feaze, grunted, "Not so fast." Sinking onto his heels, he ran a strong curved needle and a length of sailmaker's thread through the corpse's nostrils. "He's dead, all right," he remarked. "No quiver, never a blink." Next he drew the ends together and tied them into a neat reef knot.

The sailmaker chuckled as he pulled canvas over the staring eyes and horribly grinning mouth. "How's that, me lad? Now yer all neat, ready and shipshape for yer visit with Davy Jones."

[77]

Joe Utting and the other waister were told to lug the dead on deck and leave them in the gangway until somebody got around to heaving them overboard.

~ 18 ~
Latitude 12° 20′

HENRY COZENS, recently promoted to quartermaster's mate and ever alert to the unusual, guessed what was about to happen when *Anna*, the larger victualer, fired a gun and raised a faded red flag to her forepeak. Interest rising, Cozens watched an acknowledgment fired by the saluting battery on *Centurion*'s forecastle. Next, a string of bright, varicolored signal flags climbed leisurely into the flagship's rigging.

Cozens, his long, straw-blond hair whipping in the breeze, overheard Mr. Clark, *Wager*'s sailing master, growl, "Now why the hell must we all heave to because Mr. Gerard wants to speak the flagship?"

As the Watch swarmed aloft to reduce canvas and otherwise prepare to bring the old Indiaman into the wind, Cozens, while spinning the Fifth Rate's wheel, asked Quartermaster Cummins, "What's afoot?"

"Reckon them victualers have reached their charter's westward limit."

"Charter limit?"

"To be sure," grunted Cummins. "Those victualers aren't King's ships — they're only merchantmen chartered to carry some of our extra supplies. Lay you three to one the victualers will go home and the Commodore will order more stores crammed into us."

Presently *Anna* worked up alongside the flagship, whereupon her master shouted a request for permission to board.

Once the squadron lay in the wind, rocking idly to the Atlantic's long and dark blue swells, both merchant captains clambered up *Centurion*'s gangway ladder carrying their contracts under their arms. Immediately they were conducted to the great cabin, which, to their surprise, proved to be sparsely furnished and as bleak as a Spartan barracks.

Mr. Gerard removed his hat, said very respectfully, "By our calculations, sir, we have now reached latitude twelve degrees twenty minutes. Does this agree with your officers' reckonings?"

Sunlight, glancing off a wave, flashed through the great glazed stern windows and revealed in detail the sunburnt faces assembled about George Anson's table-desk.

Lieutenant de Saumarez inclined his narrow head. "Aye, Mr. Gerard, it does. We lie in the latitude of twelve degrees and twenty minutes."

Mr. Gerard shifted his gaze to the Commodore. "Then, yer Honor, under the terms of these charters we are not required to accompany you any farther."

"That is true, Mr. Gerard," came the quiet admission.

"Then, sir, weather being fair, will you be pleased to send your boats for the stores we've carried for you?"

"I would gladly comply," Anson said slowly, "save for one consideration. Because of the length of this voyage, my vessels were very heavily laden at the outset — and remain so. It will be next to impossible to provide storage space for what you now carry in your bottoms.

"I trust, gentlemen, that you appreciate my position?" Anson queried, head barely missing the slowly swinging cabin lamp. "Will you consider accepting a further charter?"

To the surprise of *Centurion*'s officers, Mr. Gerard spoke up promptly, "Why, yer Honor, I'd be pleased to keep the *Anna* on in yer company, if she ain't too little, that is."

"She'll do," Anson smiled. "May I ask why you seem so ready to pursue this voyage?"

"Why, yer Honor, I — I've always had a taste to visit the west coast of America." Then, more honestly, he added, "Mayhap me and my lads hope to earn shares in the treasures ye'll be taking out there."

Greatly pleased, Anson swung bright blue eyes to rest on Gerard's companion. "Well, Captain, what have you to say about keeping on with me?"

Unhappily the merchant skipper stared at his feet. "I'd like to, yer Honor, really I would, but it can't be done. The balance of my lading is for Barbados, where my agents have a cargo waiting."

"Forget Barbados," Saunders advised. "You'll do better for yourself by keeping on with us. Think of all the gold and glory we'll win in the Pacific."

[79]

Abruptly the second skipper's manner altered. He almost snarled, " 'Gold and glory' say you, sir? Be that as it may, I ain't forgetting what that old Captain Arnand promised. As far as I know, what a dying man sees is like to be truth." He turned away from Saunders, who had flushed, and addressed the imperturbable Commodore. "So, begging yer Honor's pardon, I'll stick to me owners' instructions. Always have."

For three days the squadron rocked and tossed under a cloudless sky while their smallboats removed from *Industry* each vessel's share of hard bread, rum, sugar and brandy, a difficult task even in fair weather. To George Anson's profound relief the transfers were accomplished without a single casualty. At the rate his people were perishing, the life of every man was of increasing value.

~~~ I 9 ~~~

Doldrums

THE DAY AFTER *Industry* dipped her colors and disappeared to the southwest the squadron picked up the northeast trade winds and, for five glorious days, the ships were hurried along their course. Perfect visibility quieted some of the Commodore's never-ending anxieties; now lookouts should spy Don José Pizarro's topmasts the instant they lifted above the horizon.

On those rare occasions when an officer permitted the Watch on deck to "take a caulk" — sun-softened tar in the deck's caulking often striped a sleeper's shirt — Will Pallister clambered out onto the ship's carved and gilded beak, just aft of her lion figurehead. Ecstatically, he then admired the diamantine sparkle of sunlit spray, the gorgeous sapphire hues this vast ocean was commencing to assume.

Now the ships were plowing through vast patches of yellow-gold Sargasso weed upon which rested quantities of those dainty little gray-black birds called "sea chickens" by old hands. The youth especially loved to follow the play of porpoises which, a week ago, had appeared to escort George Anson's seven ships.

Best of all, Will enjoyed watching the fairy-fragile flying fish. Like flashes of light, they would burst from a wave top and go skittering over a succession of sparkling whitecaps. Sometimes the lustrous, big-eyed creatures became entangled in the rigging and fell onto the deck. Will was sickened to see them devoured, raw and still wriggling, by semistarved deckhands. Half-famished though he was, he couldn't bring himself to eat them — they were too lovely. Rather he wished he could preserve them with a paintbox and brush or sketch those flitting sea chickens which seemed so effortlessly to dance over waves and weed.

The flagship signaled that during this fine weather any dubious top hamper should be inspected and replaced; also that gun crews should be drilled as often as possible. These precautions stemmed from the lonely Commander in Chief's dread that he might suddenly be forced to engage Pizarro's squadron.

Gradually, the men's spirit commenced to revive; soon they began to brag about the terrible things they were going to do to the Papists.

All went well until the wind faltered and then died out, leaving Anson's squadron in the grip of the doldrums. Day after day the ships drifted with slack sails over an ocean distorted by shimmering heat rays. Below decks the atmosphere grew so insufferably polluted that even healthy hands began to die. The Invalid-Pensioners expired like lice dropped into a fire.

Every morning, *Centurion*'s consorts — with the curious exception of *Tryall* and *Anna* — signaled the number of men who had perished. Finally, five weeks out of Funchal, the aggregate became so appalling that Anson, in desperation, sent for his chief surgeon.

"Mr. Waller, something must be done. Soon my ships will not be even half-manned."

In pained tones the big-bellied surgeon protested, "I assure you, sir, my mates and I are doing all that we can —"

"I'm confident of that, but the fact remains my men are perishing at a rate which endangers this expedition. I intend to conduct an inspection of the lower decks."

An expression of incredulous astonishment appeared on Waller's red and glistening countenance. "*You* go 'tween decks, sir? Why, why — isn't that unusual?"

Anson understood the other's consternation; save in the stress of storm or battle, it was almost unprecedented for a Captain of the Royal Navy ever to descend into the body of his ship.

George Anson grimly ranged *Centurion*'s reeking main and orlop decks. Although hardened to human suffering through long service in the King's ships, Anson's broad features grew rigid, then paled beneath his sunburn. He was utterly shaken to discover many gaunt wrecks of men gasping, helpless and often stark-naked, in filthy hammocks; some were dying, quite ignored by the few indifferent loblolly boys on duty.

"Sir," gasped Waller, "I — I am most unwell — I feel so dizzy I fear I — I will faint. May I —"

One glance at the chief surgeon brought conviction that Waller wasn't shamming. His eyes were congested, his complexion red-gray and his breath very short.

"You may retire," Anson said, blotting sweat from his face, "but report to me the instant you feel sufficiently restored."

"Mr. Saunders, signal all medical officers to come aboard the flagship."

When the medical officers congregated, harried and anxious, Anson snapped, "What do you suggest be done to remedy the situation?"

" 'Fore God, there isn't much, sir," gloomily admitted Andrew Kerr of *Gloucester*. "But I am of the opinion that the rigging of windsails and the cutting of ventilating ports in the ship's side might serve to better conditions."

Anson turned to Mr. Ettrick of *Wager*. "D'you agree?"

"Aye, sir, the atmosphere below decks in my ship is pestilential. The circulation of fresh air through the 'tween decks may help."

"Very well," said Anson crisply, "tell your captains that I desire them to rig larger air-sails. Also they will at once order cut as many ventilating ports as is consistent with safety." Briefly Anson debated ordering the lower gunports unsealed, but reluctantly decided not to. His ships were too dangerously overloaded, rode too deep in the sea.

For three weeks the squadron wallowed, helpless to proceed, in the doldrums until, on the morning of December 7, 1740, at long last a steady breeze began to blow, but perversely, *out of the southwest,* forcing the square-rigged men-of-war endlessly to tack and wear.

Three days later, *Tryall,* sailing as usual in advance of her consorts, fired a gun and signaled the electrifying news: *Soundings have been reached at sixty fathoms.*

Said Sailing Master Nutt, "Sixty fathoms, eh? Unless my dead-reckoning is in error, that means we're nearing Abrolhos Bank off Brazil."

In the privacy of the great cabin, Anson knelt and mumbled a brief but heartfelt prayer of thanksgiving. Surely South America could not lie far off?

One afternoon *Tryall* came running back to report that Chief Surgeon Waller, lent to her a few days back, had died of heat apoplexy.

Next day Anson suffered the loss of another loyal friend when Robert Weldon, *Centurion*'s purser, died of the bloody flux.

Six days passed after soundings had been reached and still no land was in sight!

Anson for a long while paced the stern walk, his flute forgotten. What had gone wrong with Justinian Nutt's dead reckoning? Heretofore, almost invariably they'd proved reasonably accurate, had coincided with his own findings. If *only* he'd been granted one of those precious new chronometers and *accurately* been able to determine longitude. Probably those soundings had not been Abrolhos Bank at all, only an unchartered marine ridge.

One could almost smell the black depression which, gradually, had come to settle upon even the most optimistic officers and men. No wonder the weaker despaired. Land, fresh food and water *must* lie somewhere nearby or why had green boughs been seen or so many land birds come to perch in the rigging?

When he thought of the soaring death rate Anson paused, placed hands on the gallery's rail and fought to stifle expression of his anguish.

About noon of the following day *Tryall* fired a gun and showed a green flag which meant that land was in sight! Sure enough, towards evening a row of blunt, blue-gray triangles appeared on the horizon. Salutes were fired, flags broken out on all seven ships. Ragged cheers followed when it became known that the Commodore had ordered all hands to "splice the main brace."

Baffled by contrary winds, two days dragged by before the sunbleached squadron finally came to anchor off the islands of Santa Catharina and Alvoredo. Not far beyond them, the lush green coast of Brazil stretched interminable distances.

"Sir!" called Lieutenant Saunders. "Seems to be some panicking ashore."

"So I observe," came Anson's reply as he surveyed the shore through a battered telescope.

Alarm guns boomed in a pair of yellow-brown forts guarding the entrance to the port of Santa Catharina. Roads and trails leading away from the port were growing darker with fleeing figures.

"Idiots must take us for buccaneers, sir," remarked Saunders.

"Is it any wonder, considering our appearances?" laughed de Saumarez.

Commodore Anson turned to his signal officer, Passed Midshipman Foley. "I want ensigns shown at all mastheads. Mr. Saunders, you will take my barge and reassure the authorites that they have nothing to fear from Portugal's oldest ally."

Once *Centurion's* lieutenant, clad in his best, hastily shaven, and carrying a copy of George Anson's commission, had reached shore, the forts, to the Commodore's vast but unspoken relief, dipped their colors and fired eleven guns each. *Centurion* promptly acknowledged these courtesies with an equal number of salutes.

Soon a flotilla of sailing canoes, pirogues and barcas put out; their dark-skinned occupants waved bright cloths, held up flowers and fruits as they drew near.

～ 2 0 ～
The Beach

HARDLY HAD ANSON'S ships anchored in Santa Catharina's harbor, under the guns of Forts San Juan and Santa Cruz, than the Commodore dispatched Second Lieutenant de Saumarez to reconnoiter a low, sandy island shaded by dense groves of coconut palms.

Quite correctly, George Anson reasoned that on whatever wind blew, this island should remain as cool as was possible upon a coast so humid and torrid.

Young de Saumarez reported jubilantly, "Sir, not only is this island's sand hard and dry but also it boasts a great spring of cool, sweet water which rises in the middle of the beach!"

"Good enough. Now, Mr. Foley, signal all captains to send parties ashore at once to rig shelters for their sick and disabled."

By sundown of arrival day crude pavilions contrived from light spars and old sails had sprung, mushroom-like, into existence. That this hospital lay within effective range of the forts enforcing the authority of Governor Dom José Silva da Paz seemed the site's only drawback.

Governor Silva da Paz proved to be plump, effusive and mahogany-faced. Short of stature, Dom José had twinkling eyes and a smile so ready that, at mess in the wardroom, Saunders remarked to the second lieutenant, "Aye, the fellow *seems* friendly, but, Philip my lad, I'd not trust him farther than I can heave an eel with buttered hands."

"I presume the Commodore shares your misgivings?"

"No telling. Poor devil's said hardly a word since reading the strength returns."

"Bad?"

"Incredibly bad." Saunders flapped his serviette at a halo of small but persistent black flies which were whining by the millions on board. "We've thirty dead of our own and around eighty sick, of whom many are going to die — or so the learned Mr. Kerr declares."

"What about the others?"

"The *Gloucester*'s report is the worst. Since Funchal they've dropped forty-two men overboard."

The odor of death must have been strong in the air, for while the sick were being landed flocks of black buzzards abandoned their accustomed perches on the thatched or red-tiled roofs of Santa Catharina to settle on dead trees near the island's sandy beach.

When Captain the Honorable George Murray ordered *Wager*'s sick set ashore, Joe Utting, pallid and ghost-thin, was among those lowered over the storeship's side. All he could think about was, have 'e lads stooked the corn as they should?

While pouring a tot of French brandy in his lonely cabin George Anson asked himself, What could I have done to prevent these losses? What will the Admiralty think of me when they read that I've already lost a quarter of my forces even before rounding the Horn? Will it now be possible to carry out my orders?

In a savage, self-critical mood he stared out of *Centurion*'s stern windows at Santa Catharina's placid, sunset-hued harbor and saw its surface dotted with the expedition's smallboats, pirogues, catamarans and log canoes, all gunwale-deep under cargoes of fowls, fruits and vegetables.

At an informal conclave preceding their twice-a-day tour of the hospital, Mr. Ettrick, the flagship's surgeon since Waller's death, thoughtfully stroked his chin. "Strange, the men have an universal

[85]

craving for vegetables and unsalted meat," he mused. "Mark you, these rogues will plead for a melon harder than eternal redemption."

"Can't blame 'em. Redemption's a very chancy business," was the dry comment of Mr. Kerr of *Gloucester*. "Ah, here come the rest of us sawbones."

Mr. Vincent Oakley of *Wager* and his mates, James Hall and Robert Elliott, appeared plowing over the sand towards the improvised hospital.

In their wake tramped Peter Vesey, now chief of *Centurion*'s loblolly boys. He was wondering, why is it that so many Invalid-Pensioners are complaining about the reopening of wounds which had been closed for years?

Torrid sunlight, beating through thin, old sails, lent the sick a spurious healthy look.

Vesey offered watered wine to an old man whose withered leg was discharging through a reopened wound. "And where were you wounded?" Vesey couldn't help asking.

"Why, sir, 'twas at the battle of the Boyne."

"The Boyne! Wasn't that fought fifty years ago?"

"Aye, sir, that it was, to be sure."

Obedient to explicit orders from the Commodore, the medical officers finally moved off among the shelters.

To Peter Vesey it had long been apparent that most of these pompous ignoramuses were serving at sea only because they had failed in practice ashore. They were only ignorant and often brutal surgeons and not physicians who, owning a medical degree and a smattering of Latin, were allowed to call themselves "doctor."

Whenever he found opportunity, Vesey never ceased to conjecture why the shortest casualty lists should have been those of *Anna* and *Tryall*, the smallest and least comfortable vessels. Why? Gradually he came to the conclusion that the ratio of disease and death must be in direct proportion to the number of men aboard per tun burthen — even though a small crew consumed the same vile food and suffered under the same iron discipline.

Plodding barefoot over the trampled sand after the surgeons, the graduate of Oxford and the Royal School of Medicine in Edinburgh was hard-pressed to keep a straight face over some of the diagnoses he was forced to overhear. Patients variously were said to be suffering from strangury, flux, the gravels, the purples and/or the megrims. On the other hand, these fellows in rusty black didn't go far wrong

[86]

in prescribing treatments for a multitude of ulcers, bedsores and hideously painful boils.

Self-important, the somber group wandered about, waving leafy branches in a futile attempt to thwart swarms of mosquitoes and sandflies.

Before long the ex-convict, bringing up the rear, decided that a bespectacled, cleaver-faced surgeon's mate called James Allen, a former horse doctor, possessed more practical knowledge than the rest of these smug medicos put together. Just possibly he might have read a treatise on shipboard diseases and the treatment thereof written, after nine years at sea, by a naval physician called James Land?

At length Mr. Ettrick paused by Joe Utting's hammock, pursed his lips and rumbled, "Stick out your tongue, fellow. Um. 'Tis obvious you've become gravely stricken with — ahem — calentures and the purples."

Pettishly Mr. Ettrick shook his head and moved on. "No use wasting time on him. He's too far gone."

Vacantly Joe stared after him, thought dully: so this high-and-mighty sawbones won't waste time on old Joe? Well, Joe's going to make a liar out of him. Joe ain't going to croak 'cause he *won't!* Got to add that milk shed to the barn. Needed one the longest time.

Ordinary seaman Peter Dobey lay writhing in delirium. His ravings indicated that once he'd been a gentleman's tailor.

"This man," pronounced Mr. Oakley of *Wager*, "obviously is *in extremis*. Wager he won't see tomorrow's sunrise."

"Take you," grunted Mr. Kerr of *Gloucester*. "Six shillings on it. Fellow's only suffering a morbidity of the bowels."

Mr. Kerr lost because the ex-tailor quit raving and gasped his last just as a half-moon saw itself reflected in the harbor's black and placid water, and the high, thin voices of sentries in the forts commenced, ironically enough, to call, "All is well."

Will Pallister rejoiced in his duties as assistant schoolmaster because they afforded him ample time to observe the beautiful forests, bold, blue-green mountains of the Brazilian mainland. From the heights several delicate, veil-like waterfalls could be seen tumbling towards their death in the sea. It oughtn't to be difficult in his new capacity to obtain pen, ink and paper. Then he'd make an attempt at sketching. Whether he'd prove to be any good at drawing or not, he'd no idea.

[87]

It came as considerable encouragement that, when sent ashore with a message for the Governor, he observed one of *Gloucester's* lieutenants busily sketching the harbor — and, incidentally, the forts. So it *wasn't* unmanly to draw pictures! Good!

Will began to see Santa Catharina not as a collection of humble white-washed mud-brick and palm-thatched huts, but as a strange and deliciously picturesque foreign place. He found vast entertainment in the naked brown children, the scrawny pigs and chickens which wandered unmolested where they would. The variety of pets, bright-eyed monkeys, flaming macaws and parrots of various hues made his fingers itch for a paintbrush.

After observing the inhabitants, almost universally clad in dirty white rags, it was easy to credit reports that the founders of Santa Catharina had been mostly buccaneers, military deserters and fugitives from justice. A great majority of the population consisted of languid, undersized Indians and *mestizos*.

The Portuguese garrison proved to be mostly European barely kept up to strength by a stream of replacements sent up from Maldonado which, Will ascertained, was an important port lying on the River Plate some eight hundred miles farther south.

Near the edge of a palm- and acacia-lined central plaza young Pallister entered a street in which slatternly brown women displayed themselves altogether nude in doorways or leaned out of barred windows to make obscene gestures and call invitations that often were mocked by screeching parrots which seemed to be everywhere. Flushing, Will hurried on, wishing that Ramster or Buckle had been here in his stead.

Aside from a patrol of red-jacketed Marines, the only Englishmen Pallister encountered were a pair of purser's mates sent ashore to purchase provisions, and Mr. Menzies, whom the Commodore had sent to keep an eye on their transactions.

Diffidently, young Pallister strode up to the Governor's mildewed yellow mansion. On handing his letter to a fat Negro butler, he was instructed to wait for a reply.

To the youth's surprised discomfiture Governor Dom José Silva da Paz himself appeared and said in remarkably clear English, "Present my most distinguished compliments to your gallant Admiral and say to him that I am delightful to accept his invitation to dine aboard his ship."

Beady black eyes intent, he added, "Say also that I offer to my

[88]

gallant English friend whatever assistance it is possibly. Say that I will ordering runners into the back countries to fetching in many goats, swine and oxes."

Concerned by a loss of men so great that it was threatening the expedition's success, George Anson risked desertions by granting the crews shore leave, much to the delight of local pimps, whores, pet dealers and merchants.

For pets Peter Vesey, Bill Buckle and Coxswain Parmer selected tufted marmosets because they were small, clean and easy to control. Andrew Menzies, Pallister and Schoolmaster Pascoe bought yellow and green parrots which screamed Portuguese obscenities on the least provocation — fortunately they were not understood by the last two owners.

As for Tom Ramster and Ted Waxter, they purchased half a dozen gamecocks apiece — and turned a pretty penny by first fighting them and then selling the fallen warriors for food.

Not a few sailors purchased agoutis, queer-looking creatures that resembled huge guinea pigs and were reputed to make an excellent stew.

In the meantime the Commodore ordered all vessels to be thoroughly cleansed below decks, but in succession, lest General Pizarro's fleet suddenly appear.

Under guard, woodcutting parties were sent into steaming forests where monstrous serpents and man-eating "tygers" were reported to lurk.

Watering parties, too, were detailed to the mainland to fill casks at a waterfall. When their task was completed, men lucky enough to have been detailed to this duty fell to gorging themselves on the abundant wild fruit or, romping like schoolboys, bathed grimy bodies under the thundering waterfall.

Nat Wade, however, quietly drifted out of sight in search of a trail that might lead inland. Cost what it might, he wasn't going to return to the misery of existence aboard HBMS *Centurion* — or any man-of-war. He would start back to Peggy, his wife. Dear, lovely Peggy. Nothing was going to shake him from this mortal determination.

Chattered at by furry black and white monkeys and a variety of brilliant and often outlandish birds, the ex-leather-worker struggled into the rain forest's humid gloom. Here he was slowed, panting, by

[89]

an endless succession of entangling and tenacious creepers, vines and lianas. Giant leeches immediately attached themselves to his neck and arms while thorns lacerated his limbs.

Sick with disappointment, Wade at length was forced to halt. It was no use. Lacking a cutlass or a blade of some sort, a man simply couldn't force a way through this almost solid wall of vegetation. Sunk in despair, he turned back.

Under the critical eyes of tyrannical lieutenants and midshipmen, men toiled from dawn to dusk. Aboard *Gloucester* and *Pearle* corpses were discovered behind cargo. Some must have been there a long time; they had been completely devoured by rats which, during the voyage across from Funchal, had multiplied beyond belief.

Once the worst of the filth had been scraped off, all 'tween decks were scrubbed with that best of all disinfectants, strong vinegar; next, hatches were battened down and the still-reeking hulls fumigated with sulphur and gunpowder dried in vinegar.

As a finishing measure, smudge fires of sassafras and other sweet-smelling woods smoldered in a battery of braziers. So for hours smoke oozed through supposedly sealed gunports and climbed into the humid breathless air off Santa Catharina. Even the most discouraged agreed that everything possible was being done to restore the squadron to a healthful condition.

A fresh problem joined the legion of anxieties besieging George Anson's peace of mind when Captain Cheap requested, and was granted, permission to board the flagship.

"Well, Captain, and what brings you here? Some agreeable errand, I trust. I could welcome one," he added quietly.

Cheap's blunt features formed a look of apology. "I fear not, sir. Just now my carpenter reported that both of *Tryall*'s masts have sprung!"

"Sprung?" queried the Commodore. "How can that be? They are brand-new!"

"Aye, sir," Cheap agreed uncomfortably, "the masts they put into her *were* new, but on inspection I found them to be both of inferior quality and imperfectly seasoned. You know how it goes, sir? Somebody has pocketed the difference."

"Yes. I know," sighed Anson, "all too well."

Although this entailed exasperating delay, *Tryall* was laid alongside *Gloucester* to have the defective masts "fished" — a process of supporting the faulty spars by splints very like those applied to a man's broken limb.

To accomplish this under the equatorial heat required such exertions that work gangs often had to be replaced. But for sudden brief thundershowers, of which several descended every day, many men must have succumbed to heat exhaustion alone. These cool intervals also benefited the sick, slowly recovering from the ravages of dysentery, typhus and assorted other ailments. Everyone agreed it was a major miracle that scurvy had not appeared during that interminable, miserable voyage from Madeira.

~~~ 2 1 ~~~

The Deserters

ONCE THE SHIPS had been as thoroughly disinfected as possible and no reports of Pizarro's men-of-war being in the vicinity were received, Anson ordered his crews to dismount most of the upper-tier guns on the flagship, *Gloucester*, *Severn* and *Pearle* and to lower them into the holds. This additional weight below, he calculated, should serve to stiffen his vessels against those gigantic seas he expected them to encounter off Cape Horn.

This, Anson fully realized, was taking a calculated risk; with his heavy ships' lower deck guns already useless behind sealed ports, they temporarily were being rendered all but impotent — which fact did not escape the notice of Dom José Silva da Paz, the affable Governor of Santa Catharina.

On an especially humid afternoon while hammers rang and tackle blocks creaked aboard the English squadron, Dom José, ever bland of expression, sought his study, seated himself and, perspiring a trifle more than usual, wrote out in duplicate a detailed description of the weight, appearance and armament of those varicolored men-of-war visible beyond his window's wrought-iron grille.

Dom José Silva da Paz also took care to report to the Portuguese Governor of Maldonado the exact number of white-painted wooden crosses which had been erected in that rough and ready cemetery the English had created on the sandy beach near their hospital. Thus far they numbered fifty-two.

"Therefore, my most esteemed and distinguished Colleague," he wrote in conclusion to his letter, "it is my opinion that these English ships, seriously undermanned and with most of their heavy guns incapacitated, are quite unable to defend themselves. Further, my informants lead me to believe that the English *Comodoro* intends to depart from this port on or about the fifth day of January."

After tossing a peanut to his pet monkey which came gamboling in, Dom José dried hairy, sweaty fingers before rolling his information into neat slim sylinders and then wrapping them into casings of waterproof oiled silk. One report he entrusted to a sergeant sailing that day for Maldonado with still another request for replacements — white troops didn't last long in such a climate.

Just to be on the safe side with information of such signal importance, the Governor then gave the duplicate to one Pedro Terceira, semi-piratical captain of a small but swift barcalonga which might easily arrive in the River Plate before the government sloop conveying the sergeant.

The sergeant's vessel sailed at noon and respectfully dipped her colors when she passed *Centurion*, but Captain Terceira delayed until after dark under the pretext of restowing the scant cargo loaded aboard his rakish, low-hulled craft. Actually, he wished to quit Santa Catharina unobserved by lookouts aboard the English ships.

Shortly after sundown, four cruelly sunburnt figures in European sea clothes slipped furtively into a tumble-down shed which stood sufficiently near the waterfront to permit them to watch a succession of liberty boats pull out for the visiting men-of-war. With even greater interest they watched the restowing of Captain Terceira's cargo.

In a hoarse whisper, Nat Wade stated, "That's her. Will she leave soon?"

"No. They ain't got even the half o' her cargo stowed," muttered Ben Clipperton, leader of the would-be deserters. A tough sailing master's mate out of *Severn*, he wouldn't have been here if he still weren't smarting over recent demotion to the forecastle.

"Maybe she won't sail till tomorrow," grunted a surly, one-eyed ex-convict who called himself Kildare. "Happen so, we'll sure get caught and have our necks stretched." By the half-light he appeared terribly frightened. "Say, mates, maybe we should try to take another boat?"

Clipperton shook his head so hard that gold rings let into his ears flashed faintly. "The hell we will! We'll take that barca tonight. She's just the right size. The four o' us can easy handle her crew if you'll do just as I say. I've marked a dugout canoe down the beach, so easy does it."

Grinning savagely, the ex-sailing master's mate stroked the brass butt of a stolen boarding pistol and turned to his companions.

"Any fainthearts had better quit now. All ye've got to do is to pretend you got drunk and fell asleep. The Bosun will likely let you off wi' week in irons and a few dozen wi' the cat."

With a raging bitterness in his heart Wade stared through a crack at the fading sunset. "I'd tackle a sloop-of-war if it meant starting towards home and — my wife." Vaguely, he wondered again if possibly Peggy might have conceived during those few hours they'd shared so passionately. How might she be faring? Probably she'd gone back to her family in Romsey. What bothered him most was the fear that, if he didn't get back in a hurry, Peggy just might take up with some other man.

"You sure you kin get us to Barbados?" queried Kildare.

"Aye. You can lay to that," snarled Clipperton. "I ain't a sailing master's mate for nothing! I've twice sailed this coast clear down to Rio Janeiro."

In order to turn sidewise and view the other would-be deserter, Wade had to ease the cutlass he'd stolen and now wore at his belt. "What about you, Fox? You going to see this through?"

"Burned if I ain't!" the fourth man snapped and shifted uncomfortably, for, under a canvas shirt, his back still was bleeding from a flogging he'd taken aboard *Tryall* because Captain Cheap had been rendered extra short-tempered by Santa Catharina's humid heat.

"What about you, Kildare?" queried Clipperton tensely.

"I ain't quitting," said the one-eyed man. "I've heard wot that Invalid Cap'n promised us whilst dying. No, mates, I ain't cheated the gallows just to git took by the Spaniards or leave me bones off t' Horn. Besides, some o' the bloody old *Gloucester*'s timbers are so rotten that, come a real storm, she'll crack like a dropped egg."

The group fell silent while a file of barefooted, straw-hatted Portuguese soldiers tramped by and afforded the ex-leather-worker occasion to recall Tom Ramster's refusal to join the desertion.

He'd spat contemptuously through the nearest gunport. "Ye're a pack of precious fools! Bad as things may seem aboard this ship, 'tis

[93]

no worse than usual, and better than some. The Commodore's doing his best for us. No. I'm not minded to risk dancing a hornpipe from the mainyard. Thank ye kindly, but Tom Ramster ain't minded to lie buried below the high-water mark 'thout bell, book or candle to speed his soul to hell."

Hot as it was, Nat Wade shivered on recollection of that conversation.

Later on, the would-be deserters shrank in trembling fear among shadows because a shore patrol of British Marines, sweating under white crossbelts, black tricornes and red jackets, came tramping along with musket barrels aglint under a half-moon and halted squarely before the shack's door. They overheard a Marine grunt, "'Ope t' bloody fools got clear awye. I'd not admire to 'ave to tyke 'em in for 'anging."

"You can fall out," came the corporal's voice. "Rest yer arses and take a smoke, but there'll be no tippling or chasing petticoats. Ye'll come when I call, smart-like, if you know what's good for ye."

White-eyed amid the gloom, the hidden men held their breaths, powerless even to scratch cruelly nipping fleas. From the harbor's edge presently came bursts of Portuguese, the creak of blocks and a slatting of canvas.

"Damn!" breathed Clipperton. "The barca's leaving."

Obviously unwilling to conduct a thorough search for the missing seamen, the Marines lingered until the barca made sail and started to slip smoothly out over the harbor's moonlit water. Only then did they move off in the direction of the Plaza Santa Catharina.

Wade choked. "What'll we do now?"

"Exactly wot I've planned," Clipperton informed grimly. "We'll snitch that canoe and follow. If there ain't more wind further out, we ought to overtake that bloody barca beyond the harbor's entrance."

Silent as hunting owls, the four Englishmen darted across the beach and into a palmetto thicket, then along the refuse-littered shore until they reached the canoe. Quickly, they emptied this crude craft of rainwater, caught up clumsy paddles and shoved off, hearts in mouths. The canoe, fashioned out of a single log, proved terribly crank and threatened to swamp or capsize at any moment.

The deserters fully expected angry shouts and an alarm to be raised, but only a couple of dogs noticed the theft. They set up a furious barking but no one paid them any attention.

To their right they saw a few reddish lights blink sleepily in the forts. To port, clearly limned by the moonlight, loomed the masts and yards of the ships they were deserting. Their hulls were lost against the land.

Deep English voices floated across the water from them as Fox and Clipperton, real seamen, plied paddles in the canoe's bow and stern. Kildare and Wade crouched low on the slimy bottom praying there might be no patrol boats on the lookout for them. They expelled sighs of relief when the first of a series of low clouds obscured the moon.

Soon rain began to fall while the paddlers, shoulders bunching with effort, commenced to overhaul the barca. Amid this gloom she all at once appeared distressingly large. Now rain descended in sheets.

Fat, warm raindrops smelling of decaying vegetation swiftly blotted out shore and squadron alike just as the canoe entered the harbor's mouth.

"Now's our chance!" Clipperton panted. "Paddle harder."

"Can't," wheezed Fox. "Me bloody back's bleeding rivers. Here!" He shoved his paddle to Wade immediately behind him.

The landsman was clumsy but so much stronger than Fox that the log canoe fairly surged forward.

Rain fell so heavily that the barca's helmsman, huddled under a poncho, failed to notice the canoe's approach. In fact, he remained unaware of anything untoward until he felt a horny hand clamped over his mouth. Although he couldn't call out, the helmsman nevertheless managed to kick over a bucket which landed with a resounding *thump!* on the deck and alarmed men taking shelter in a little cabin forward.

Clutching his cutlass in a death grip, Nathaniel Wade lurched forward. Eyes blurred by hard-driven rain, he glimpsed a tall fellow loom into sight and level a pistol at such close range that Wade guessed he was about to die. However, there came no explosion, only a *click!* made by the flint in striking the pistol's iron frizzen.

Forgetting to use his still unfamilar cutlass, Wade butted the Portuguese right back down a short companion ladder and, roaring like a challenging bull, flourished his cutlass and leaped inside, barely aware that Kildare and Clipperton were at his heels.

Captain Terceira and his four compatriots, utterly taken by surprise, promptly raised brown, pink-palmed hands and quavered for quarter.

None of the deserters had dared to dream that this barcalonga could be taken so very easily. With Fox at the helm she continued to sail slowly but steadily on through diminishing rain. Now not

[95]

a single light was to be seen astern. Of course it was too early to celebrate, yet it seemed as if the attempt was off to a promising start.

"Nah then, mates," demanded Kildare, dashing rain from shaggy brows, "wot'll we do with these garlic-destroyers?"

"Knock the buggers on the head and chuck 'em overside," came Clipperton's prompt solution. "As prisoners, they be a hamper."

Wade shook his powerful, blond head. "No. The bodies'd likely be spied come daylight, then everybody'd know this boat's been captured. *And who took her!*"

Clipperton hesitated. "By God, mate, ye've made a strong point. Whilst I tie 'em up, you, Kildare, hold this pistol onto 'em. Wade, you reprime the Cap'n's weapon. Good thing it misfired."

Wade looked about, noticed a powder flask and a wooden box of pistol balls on a shelf above a bunk. While Clipperton used Wade's cutlass to cut a slender rope into convenient lengths, Kildare, wearing a menacing scowl, held Clipperton's pistol on the prisoners — which really wasn't necessary because the Portuguese cowered flat against the cabin's side, liquid jet eyes white-ringed by terror.

Awkwardly, because he'd only just learned how to load a firearm, Wade jerked out a short rammer seated under the pistol's barrel, tilted powder into the muzzle and started to press home a wad when the rammer's horn-capped tip was halted halfway down the tube. Wade worked out the obstruction, which proved to be a short cylinder of paper sewn into a strip of oiled silk.

Yellow brows knitted, Wade using his sailor's clasp knife commenced to slice through the threads.

Over his sodden blue shoulder Clipperton snarled, "Reload that pistol, damn yer eyes! Don't waste time doing that!"

Wade objected while uncurling the sheet of paper, "If that fellow's taken so much trouble to hide this so carefully, it must be something important."

Although the scrawl was in Portuguese, Wade at once recognized the names of Anson's ships; also that, in each case, the correct tonnage and number of guns had been listed.

Clipperton finished tying up the prisoners tightly, then made them lie on the deck. "Now what in hell *is* this?"

"Don't know for sure," admitted the former leather-worker. "But it looks like this may mean treachery on the Governor's part."

" 'Treachery'? Wot's yer meaning, mate?" Kildare demanded.

"Here's a tally of our ships and armament being sent away, secret-like, to Maldonado."

"Maldonado's a port at the mouth of the River Plate," Clipperton said. "But to hell with this. Wade, you stay here. Kildare, you come on deck and help me trim this craft's canvas. We'd better find ourselves out o' sight come sunup."

Big figure swaying to the barcalonga's choppy motion, Wade hesitated. "Undoubtedly. But if the Portuguese are being treacherous the Commodore ought to be warned."

"What the hell's that damn' squadron to us?" raged Clipperton, short gray beard abristle. "Thought we settled that last night. To hell wi' George Anson and all his curs'd ships!"

Unexpectedly Fox spoke up from his seat at the tiller. "I care. My back's still bleeding, but I don't aim to see none of my mates sail south and get their ruddy guts blown out unexpected-like."

The dispute ended when even the ex-convict, Kildare, agreed that the Portuguese must be attempting to furnish their Spanish cousins with a report of the British squadron's strength, state of health and plan of movement.

For the life of him Nathaniel Wade couldn't understand why he'd been the first to suggest turning back. Surely they all risked hanging or, at best, a severe flogging?

By common consent, the deserters decided to lie off and on outside the harbor of Santa Catharina until daylight. During night hours, they appreciated that sentries, English and Portuguese alike, would be given to shooting first and challenging afterwards.

So it came about that, when quartermasters aboard the men-of-war began sounding six bells, the barca bore down to pass slowly under *Centurion*'s stern.

In a shaking voice Wade hailed, "We've news o' great import, sir! Request an immediate interview with the Commodore."

"Damme, 'tis those bastards as deserted last night!" cried the master-at-arms but, removing his hat, he ran over to inform the officer of the deck. "What shall I do, sir?" he demanded.

Snapped Second Lieutenant de Saumarez, "Order the rascals aboard, you idiot, and have Marines to cover 'em with a swivel gun lest they try to change their minds."

When the four attempting deserters, white-faced and trembling, were hustled aboard, it happened that the Captain's ever inscrutable secretary had sought the quarterdeck, there to enjoy the morning's cool which, too soon would end. Accordingly he overheard some of Clipperton's desperate protests to Lieutenant de Saumarez.

"I ask ye fair, sir," he was panting. "What for would we have come back, if we was rogues? For God's sake, believe us."

"We took a spyboat, sir," Wade shouted in a sudden access of terror prompted by the grim faces ringing him in. "We've captured — paper — Commodore ought — see it."

"Silence!" de Saumarez snapped. He turned to the sergeant-at-arms. "Start this impudent rascal!"

Immediately the petty officer whirled up a colt and rained blows on Nat Wade's head and the arms he raised in an effort to protect it. Fixed where he was by bayonet points, the former leather-worker was forced to stand shielding his head as best he might against the colt's vicious, dazing blows.

Presently Wade screamed, "For God's sake, sir, make him stop! We've brought back news of first importance. I swear we've —"

"How dare you address an officer unbidden? D'you want to be flogged through the fleet ere they hang the lot of you?"

All the same, de Saumarez shortly afterward ordered the colting to end and all four prisoners put into bilboes — shackles for wrists and ankles connected by a short length of iron bar.

George Anson, comfortable in shirtsleeves and long linen panta-loons, was about to assault a breakfast of strong black coffee, paw-paws and fried fish when Menzies knocked and entered, thin features taut.

"Well, Andrew," Anson demanded, his pleasant expression evapo-rating, "what brings you here so early?"

When he heard what his secretary had to report the Commodore slowly picked up a spoon. "There's no doubt, then, that these fellows intended to desert?"

"No, sir. Last night they captured a barcalonga in order to further their escape."

Anson helped himself to a mouthful of baked red snapper, then asked, cheeks bulging, "But why in the name of common sense did these deluded fools venture to return?"

"That's why I've come to you, sir," Menzies put in quickly. "They're claiming to have intercepted what appears to be a treacher-ous communication sent by the local Governor to his colleague at Maldonado."

With precision Anson wiped sauce from his lips before straightening on his chair. "Pray present my compliments to Colonel Cratch-erode. Inform him that I wish immediately to interview the deserters."

Menzies started for the door, then paused. "Here, sir?"

"No. I'll see 'em in the steerage."

The steerage, largely sheltered from the weather by the quarter-deck's overhang, was situated on the far side of those flimsy removable partitions which separated the captain's cabin from the rest of the quarterdeck. Here was located the man-of-war's binnacle and her great double steering wheel.

When in due course Anson appeared in the steerage it was to find the prisoners waiting under heavy guard. Bright threads of scarlet from a contusion the sergeant-at-arm's colt had raised on his scalp still were trickling down Wade's cheek.

Anson briefly, dispassionately, ran an eye over the disreputable figures. "Which of you will speak for the rest?"

Kildare cringed in his irons, as he often had in the past, whined, "Let it be Wade, yer Honor. 'Twas him talked us fools into comin' back."

Through lips thickened by a knot on the colt, Wade described the barcalonga's capture and his discovery of the document in the captain's pistol barrel.

"Where is this document?" The morning growing suddenly hot and airless, Anson fished a kerchief from his cuff and blotted away sweat that was springing out all over his broad, red-brown features.

"Still in my breeches' waistband, sir."

Narrowly Anson studied the sweat-dampened scroll, then, without comment, passed it to de Saumarez, who was fluent in both Spanish and Portuguese.

When the second lieutenant had made a translation, Anson said, "Mr. Saunders, please order the barcalonga's original crew brought here."

Judging by the terrified screams which soon arose, the Portuguese must have deemed themselves on their way to immediate execution.

"Well, Captain," de Saumarez queried. "The Commodore wishes to hear what you have to say."

Captain Terceira waved his hands and began an angry outburst that crackled like a brush fire until Anson silenced the dark-faced fellow with a gesture.

"Mr. de Saumarez, instruct this man to speak softly and more re-spectfully."

[99]

"Captain Terceira claims, sir, that he is innocent of wrongdoing. He says merely that he was entrusted by Governor Silva da Paz to deliver this message to the Governor at Maldonado only that he might be prepared suitably to receive you."

Crisply, Lieutenant Saunders interpolated, "If that is so, then why does he feel it necessary to list our tonnage and number of guns?"

De Saumarez briefly conferred with Captain Terceira. "He says he believes that His Excellency mentioned the size of our ships simply in order to enable his colleague to secure sufficient supplies for them."

"Why did our dear host deem it necessary to dwell upon the sickly condition of our crews?"

The barcalonga's captain exposed yellow teeth in a quick smile and seemed rapidly to be regaining confidence. "No doubt, sir, it was with the intention that the Governor farther south should learn of your needs and so have time to collect medicines for your sick and otherwise prepare to care for them."

He jerked a little bow to the expressionless British Commodore. "Your Honor, I swear on my mother's virtue, I believe this to be the truth."

At dinner aboard the flagship later in the day, Governor Dom José Silva da Paz looked pained at the implication of treachery. "I swear by the glory of the Virgin, my one and only motive was to help an old and respected ally."

Icily, Anson observed, "Whilst I will credit your motive, Your Excellency, I find such solicitude most dangerous. Suppose that a Spanish cruiser had intercepted such a messenger?"

The Governor sighed in aggrieved innocence. "That, your Honor, was exactly why I ordered Captain Terceira to seal my message in his pistol."

"Surely that wasn't simply to protect it from spray and salt water?" suggested Lieutenant Colonel Cratcherode from down the table rarely bright with bowls of fruit and flowers.

"That may also have been his reason," smilingly admitted Dom José.

The repast at an end, Governor da Paz was rowed ashore in the Commodore's barge. Sweating with more than the heat, Dom José sought his study and there gulped several drafts of canary wine cooled in a sweating olla of red clay.

Senhor Jesu! That could have been a near thing! He began to chuckle. What gullible fools the English had proved themselves, including their handsome, wooden-faced *Comodoro*. No Spaniard, Italian or Frenchman would have been so easily taken in.

He poured another goblet and bowed to himself before a tarnished mirror. José, are you not the astute one? Imagine having possessed sufficient wit to dispatch a duplicate report by Sergeant Gomes.

"Sir, what do you wish done with the men who sought to desert?" Lieutenant Saunders queried, once the Governor's portly figure had descended *Centurion*'s gangway to a booming of salutes and the shrilling of pipes.

"Return them to their duties. That they mistook the purpose of the Governor's message stands to their credit."

Lieutenant Saunders permitted faint astonishment to enter his tone. " 'Mistook,' sir?"

"That is what I believe I said, Mr. Saunders." George Anson's expression remained as inscrutable as ever.

~~~ 2 2 ~~~

Spanish Squadron, I

SHORTLY AFTER Anson's expedition sailed from Santa Catharina — nearly a fortnight behind schedule due to the necessity of repairing *Tryall*'s masts — Captain Dandy Kidd fell ill of the bloody flux. For a day he tottered bravely about *Pearle*'s quarterdeck before collapsing. Gone a ghastly yellow-white, he lay in his berth unable to eat or drink.

At times he lapsed into a slumber so deep Surgeon James Hall thought he might be in a coma. When, briefly, the Captain waked, he inquired into his ship's progress and the health of her depleted crew.

On February 7, 1741, Dandy Kidd roused to a cannon's roar and sent for Lieutenant Samuel Salt, his grizzled second-in-command.

Standing grim and erect beside the stricken Captain's berth, Salt explained, "Sir, we are entering a blanket of fog denser than any I've seen in the Channel. 'Tis so thick on deck a man can't see the spritsail from the waist. I am firing guns to identify our position."

Kidd's sunken eyes rolled slowly upwards. "We sail — on — larboard tack?"

"Aye, aye, sir," the lieutenant replied, clutching a thick deck beam above to steady himself against *Pearle*'s wild plunging.

"How often — you signaling?" Captain Kidd's feeble voice barely was audible above the constant creak and groan of the old Fifth Rate's fabric.

"Every half an hour, sir; according to orders."

"Good," wheezed the sick man. "You've reduced canvas?"

"Aye, aye, sir." Salt wiped spray from bony, rather sheeplike features. "To tops and gallants. The wind and the sea are increasing."

Kidd struggled a little higher on his sweat-drenched pillows. "Whatever befalls, don't lose contact — other ships." Suffering a sudden griping in his bowels, he gasped, "Odd, Mr. Salt, but I've a very strong presentiment Spaniards are not far off."

"I hope you're wrong in that, sir," Salt said soberly. "We're in no fit state to meet 'em. How are you feeling, sir?"

"Be about tomorrow, damme if I won't."

"I sincerely hope so, sir. We're all most anxious to see you back on the quarterdeck." Mr. Salt was being genuinely solicitous. Everyone, down to the last seasick and half-starved powder monkey, felt a respect for their new Captain bordering on fondness.

The old lieutenant saluted, then went out into the boiling mist, an anxious look on his gray face. No doubt about it. The Old Man was very sick indeed. Too bad. Dandy Kidd, like himself, had been at sea nearly forty years and also had "come in through the hawsehole" to win a commission.

Samuel Salt was very glad for Dandy Kidd that finally he'd won his Captain's pendant. As for himself, he knew better than to expect a similar miracle. Lacking wealth or influence, at the age of fifty he had attained the highest grade possible for such as he. Long since he had conquered his bitterness over seeing arrogant, ignorant popinjays such as Captain the Honorable Edward Legge of *Severn* and Captain the Honorable George Murray buy their promotions.

Striding over *Pearle*'s fog-veiled deck, Lieutenant Salt engaged in yet another struggle with himself. He *mustn't* hope, even surreptitiously, for Dandy Kidd's death, even if his passing meant that, possibly, he might succeed to command of this ship. Besides, there was no need for so disloyal a thought. He'd seen too much of the bloody flux's progress; a plump, middle-aged man like Dandy Kidd could not survive much longer.

This storm, First Lieutenant Salt foresaw, would soon develop into

[102]

a full gale, fog or no fog. He found a measure of comfort in the knowledge that the coast of Brazil, cruel and rock-studded, now lay well to the westward; also that the charts showed no reefs or shoals in the vicinity. On the other hand, who dared to rely on the sort of charts issued to this expedition?

Aware that *Pearle* was making heavier going with every passing moment, he shouted for the gallants to be taken in.

Drenched by successive sheets of icy spray, Mr. Salt clung, shivering, to the mizzen shrouds and watched barefoot topmen work out along wildly swaying yards to furl stiffening canvas.

Men working about the deck also were having a hard time; giant waves had commenced to curl over the weather bulwarks and to sluice across the deck. Half-frozen and drenched, sailors were prevented from being washed overboard only thanks to lifelines rigged along the gundeck.

Anxiously, Mr. Salt and the second lieutenant strained streaming eyes and ears into the impenetrable, whirling fog; despite every change in course, the report of signal guns aboard the other ships were growing fainter.

"Perhaps, sir," shouted the second lieutenant, "we're as close as ever, but the gale's so increased it's carrying the reports away?"

"Let us hope that such is the case."

Footing was dangerous on the forecastle. Several times Nat Wade was forced to clutch the foremast's pin rail. The former leather-worker found himself there because, mysteriously, he'd been promoted to an able seaman's rating and then had been transferred out of *Centurion* on January 17th, the day before the squadron had cleared from the Island of Santa Catharina.

Nat found conditions aboard *Pearle* somewhat better than those prevailing in the flagship. Rations issued aboard this Fifth Rate were better and the crowding below decks was not quite so intolerable.

How cold the weather was turning! Wade's feet, though toughened by so many months at sea, felt like slabs of ice while he worked to furl the furiously flapping fore-staysail; cold seawater kept running down his back and legs. By the time the Afternoon Watch appeared on deck, struggling under vaulting clouds of spray, he was chilled to the bone and able to move only stiffly.

By four bells of the afternoon, Lieutenant Salt and his subordinates no longer could hear signal guns other than *Pearle*'s as she plunged on through dim gloom until, in mid-afternoon, the bitter wind faltered, then died out abruptly. It was as if some gigantic window had been slammed shut.

Almost as quickly, the fog began to burn away. A sudden shout from the maintop of "land ho!" constricted the acting commander's throat.

"Land? Why, there *can't be land out there!*" Salt yelled to Kidd's sailing master.

Yet there, off the port bow, lay a low island, a blue-black streak drawn across the foaming ocean!

Once they had trained telescopes on this barren land and had found it to be indubitably real, Salt and the sailing master sought *Pearle's* great cabin to find Captain Kidd fearfully flushed and babbling nonsense about some long-forgotten court-martial.

"Sir, may we examine your chart of these waters?" demanded Salt's companion.

Kidd stared vacantly. "Verdict? Eh. Well, I vote he's guilty. Guilty as Judas Iscariot."

Samuel Salt wasted no time and fumbled about the Captain's chart locker until he found a scroll of stained paper marked "Ye S. Coast of Ye Brazils, 1693."

"Here it is! A fine new one — fifty years old!" he rasped, then spread the chart on a nearby chest. After studying it a long while — Salt didn't read very readily — he came to a decision.

"Yonder must be Pepys Island," he grunted over his shoulder. "Says here 'twas sighted by a Cap'n Cowley in 1686."

"What position does he give, sir?"

"According to this and to Dr. Halley's 'General Chart' it's 47° 40′ South," Salt muttered. "If my dead reckonings are worth a fart he's got it 'way out of true position."

Both men's heads suddenly lifted from above the chart. A lookout had begun excitedly to hail the deck.

They left the delirious Captain and raced out into a glorious sunset. Immediately, Salt cupped hands and shouted, "Masthead there! What do you see?"

"A sail, sir."

"Where away?"

"A big ship standing out from behind the island, sir! Ho! There's another — and another! Now I spy five ships!"

Salt's leathery lips formed a silent whistle. "Thank God. That'll be the rest of our squadron."

For him it had been, as acting captain, a more than uncomfortable sensation to discover *Pearle* cruising alone with a strong Spanish fleet rumored to be in the vicinity.

Captain Kidd continuing in delirium, Lieutenant Salt ordered gallants and courses reset and instructed the helmsman to bear down on the distant squadron which now had emerged from behind Pepys Island and was steering as if to intercept *Pearle*.

"Beyond any question those are our ships, sir," announced the sailing master, telescope still trained. "I can even make out the Commodore's pendant at the biggest ship's main."

Salt ordered all hands on deck, sent them scurrying about to tidy the deck, brace yards and recoil ropes washed into shapeless tangles. Most certainly he had no desire for Commodore Anson to feel that, because Captain Kidd lay incapacitated, discipline had slacked aboard *Pearle*.

When gold work on the approaching vessels began to flash in the lowering sun, Salt picked up his spyglass and leveled on that tall ship showing the long, bright-red pendant.

"'Tis the *Centurion*," he assured the Fifth Rate's second lieutenant. "I recognize her golden lion figurehead."

With an expert's interest to see how much damage the flagship might have sustained, he next passed his glass over the rigging, then all at once he gasped.

"My God! *That's not an English pendant!*"

The second lieutenant looked startled. "How can you tell, sir? It's swallow-tailed and red."

"To be sure! But that one ain't slung, banner-wise, from a bridle. It's hoisted straight up to the maintop — like a bloody signal flag! They're Spaniards!"

In desperate haste Lieutenant Salt ordered *Pearle* close-hauled on the wind in such thundering tones that Captain Kidd heard and struggled out of bed. Crazily, he tacked across his cabin and had almost gained its door before he collapsed in a moaning heap. Lugged back to his berth, Captain Kidd lay shouting senseless orders until he lapsed into unconsciousness.

Meanwhile, Nat Wade and the other topmen were sent swarming aloft to loosen all reef points. Lying out on the wildly swaying foretopyard he was pleased to discover that he no longer felt sickened by the mast's tremendous swing.

"Cor!" called a topman working alongside. "Blast me if that

bleedin' brown wessel ain't 'e werry spit and image o' our *Centurion!* And yonder green one! I'd have took me Bible oath she's 'e rotten old *Gloucester!*"

Once *Pearle*'s studding sails had been set she fairly surged along before the wind, poor sailer though she was.

From his post in the fore-top, Wade, A.B., was able to obtain a clear view of the pursuers and saw that their hulls varied in color quite as much as the British ships.

Last lingering doubts as to this squadron's identity were removed when red and gold Spanish colors were raised to all mastheads and a great Royal Standard displaying the lions and castles of Castile appeared above the largest man-of-war now racing up over the rough, sunset-tinted ocean.

"Masthead there!" Salt hailed. "Of what rate are they?"

Wade, clinging to the fore-topgallant crossyard, bellowed down, "Two o' them, sir, look like Third Rates of eighty guns or more. Two of 'em look like Fourth Rates and there's one of about our size, forty guns, sir!"

Lieutenant Salt, wooden-faced, watched the squadron astern successively set studding sails which glowed all red-gold in the sunset and felt his heart sink with the realization that General Pizarro's towering men-of-war rapidly were overhauling *Pearle.*

From their stations on deck shaggy-headed crew members stared aft in ever-increasing anxiety.

"God send we somehow get away," growled a heavily tattooed gunner's mate. "Brother o' mine got took by 'em off Cuba last year. They nigh beat and starved him to death before sending him to Hispaniola for exchange."

A nearby gun captain nodded moodily.

"Aye. The Papists be a cruel-mean folk. Cut the nuts off a mate o' mine they captured off Florida, let the poor bugger bleed to death, they did."

"Aye. And they nailed Cap'n Jenkins by the ear to his own foremast. Remember?"

The leading pursuers were coming up so fast that Lieutenant Salt was faced with the unpleasant fact that, long before darkness fell, the Spaniards must come into effective cannon shot; he gave the order to clear for action.

"What's the use?" muttered a gunner's mate with long black hair whipping about his eyes. "Wi' our heavy guns behind sealed ports we can only fight our nine-pounders and there must be near two hundred and eighty cannons coming up astern."

"Sir Richard Grenville gave longer odds than that," reminded a midshipman busy issuing priming quills, "and won eternal glory."

"He jolly well got sunk, too," a passing powder monkey muttered under his breath.

Captain Kidd's delirious outcries meanwhile grew so loud that they could be heard distinctly above the hum of wind in the rigging and the curses of gunners trying frantically to prise free chocks which had been nailed to the deck to immobilize gun-carriage wheels during tempestuous weather off Cape Horn.

On being recalled from the tops, Able Seaman Wade immediately was handed a maul.

"Go for'ard, ye splay-footed swab! Start the middle water butt." The carpenter indicated three great casks clamped to the deck below the forecastle's break. "Hurry! Or do ye want us to rot in a Papist dungeon?"

The expression of men sent to stave in the butts was grim. To a man they foresaw what the loss of this precious water would mean until the squadron rendezvoused at Port St. Julian — if it ever would.

While fresh water was spraying into the scuppers, those men who could caught it in cupped hands and drank until they could hold no more. Others walked through the spouting water, hoping it might wash off some of the salt in their clothing; salt kept raw and angry those ulcers from which nearly every seaman suffered.

The gravity of their situation was borne in on all hands when Lieutenant Salt, in a further desperate effort to lighten the fleeing Fifth Rate, ordered the longboat stove in and cut away.

The ocean now was darkening but it seemed inevitable that the leading Spaniard's bow chasers must begin to play at any minute.

Despite the unbearable tension, Samuel Salt at that moment recalled an unpleasant fact. Before leaving Santa Catharina, to ensure added stability on rounding the Horn, most of the squadron's upper deck guns had been struck down into their holds. So, with their lower gunports sealed, Commodore Anson's ships would be almost helpless should dawn suddenly disclose the enemy.

There was only one thing to be done — draw General Pizarro away, even if it meant lessening *Pearle*'s slim chance for escape by altering the course to the northwest as if she were making for Santa Catharina.

Should darkness enable him to escape he'd immediately change course again and run for St. Julian. With luck he might warn the squadron in time to grant it a chance to get up their guns, jettison impediments and otherwise prepare to engage the incomparably more powerful Spanish vessels.

Just before darkness descended, the leading Spaniard — that ship which so closely resembled *Gloucester* — opened with her bow chasers at about a mile's range and hurled a pair of round shot into the ocean uncomfortably close in *Pearle*'s wake.

The great Spanish ship only had time to fire and miss again before sea and sky became blended amid a starless, Stygian gloom. Almost weeping with relief, Samuel Salt immediately ordered the helm put over and sent *Pearle* speeding through increasingly frigid blackness on her original course.

This accomplished, Lieutenant Salt, eager to break the good news, at once sought the Captain's cabin only to find him unconscious and under treatment by Surgeon's Mate Hall, who, by the light of a carefully hooded lantern, was bleeding Captain Kidd into a pewter basin.

"I think he's resting easier, sir, since I've started bleeding him. His pulse seems stronger. He may pull through yet."

"Let us hope so." And at the same time Salt thought savagely, Aye, Dandy Kidd probably *will* pull through and spoil my last chance for a captain's flag.

~~~ 2 3 ~~~

Spanish Squadron, II

WHEN THE FIRST hint of dawn brightened the sky, Lieutenant Salt, a bit stiffly, climbed to the mizzen truck. He could see the big A.B. called Nat Wade in the maintop with two other men, straining his eyesight over an endless succession of black, white-headed billows which came racing out of the northeast.

First off, the veteran noticed a great herd of seals — "seadogs" the sailors called them — swimming on a course parallel to *Pearle*'s. How human they looked in the water with their bristly mustaches and intelligent, limpid eyes. Then quantities of penguins appeared, headed the same way.

[108]

Simultaneously, lookouts at all three mastheads sighted five ships cruising dead ahead. Commodore Anson's squadron! A ragged cheer arose from the deck. True, the distant vessels numbered five, when six should have been visible, but perhaps, as Salt reasoned, another ship, like *Pearle*, had become detached from the main formation. It was also possible that *Anna* was too small to be discerned at such a distance.

For almost an hour Salt kept *Pearle* steady on her course, then, to his horror, the sun came out and brightened the sky sufficiently to reveal that Spanish, not English, colors were flying from the distant squadron's rigging. This time, to make the situation more ominous, Don Jose Pizarro was in possession of the weather gauge. Enjoying the advantage of an enormous spread of sail, there could be no doubt that he could overhaul *Pearle* at his leisure.

Feeling as if some invisible giant was wringing out his bowels, First Lieutenant Salt ordered the ship put about, ordered more water casks to be stove in, ordered more heavy stores to be hurled overboard.

In a short while everything had been done aboard HBMS *Pearle* that could be done, save cutting away anchors critically important to a vessel navigating all but unknown waters.

Under a dazzling sky the Spaniards bore in pursuit, battle flags standing out straight in the strong, keen wind. Soon martial music plainly could be distinguished playing aboard General Pizarro's huge flagship, *Asia*.

At the end of an anguished half-hour Lieutenant Salt concluded that *Pearle*'s only hope stood in beating to windward on a long slant which just might enable her to skirt the Spanish formation. If she kept running downwind she was doomed, that much was certain.

He was preparing to order the change of course when a lookout screamed, "There's broken water showing dead ahead! A shoal!"

His old sheep's face tightening, Salt swung about his spyglass, then vented a hoarse croak of delight. Sure enough, at right angles to *Pearle*'s bowsprit, showed a long stretch of foaming white water. Perhaps a mile distant the sea seemed to be suffering a convulsion. Lieutenant Salt, amazed, could see countless cones of spray twisting high into the air.

"There's a shoal yonder, make no mistake about it," grunted the Fifth Rate's sailing master. "And God alone knows how deep is the water covering it!"

After making a careful study of the tormented water, Lieutenant Salt snapped, "That well may *be* a shoal, mister, but it also might be only a replin."

"A replin, sir? What's a replin?" queried *Pearle*'s youngish second lieutenant.

"Why, that's the commotion which results when two powerful currents collide off shore. Some people call 'em cross-rips."

The young fellow's voice quivered. "Can you tell for sure, sir, what it is that lies ahead?"

"No. Nor could anybody else."

"But, but — sir, if that's a shoal, aren't we likely to break the ship's back?"

"Very likely." Salt's tone was acid. "Still, 'tis better than rounding to and striking to those bloody Dons.

"Keep her steady as she goes!" he roared at a bull-neck quartermaster who, with a mate, was sweating at the Fifth Rate's huge, brass-bound mahogany wheel.

Samuel Salt went over to grip the mizzen shrouds; grimly, he watched the wild water come closer. Looks like I'm about to lose my first and last command. Always did play in muddy luck, right from the start. My fault for not picking the right family to get born into.

Although the helmsmen rolled their eyes in fright and kept looking at the old lieutenant, he said nothing to keep *Pearle* from charging straight into that fearsome, chaotic strip of water which appeared to be about a quarter of a mile in width.

Nat Wade, for the first time in weeks, thought of Peggy. The few Catholics aboard crossed themselves and many a hard case mumbled a prayer as wild white water began to seethe under *Pearle*'s beak.

"Hold hard!" shouted the sailing master an instant before the man-of-war staggered so violently that a careless topman was snapped overboard. *Pearle* reeled and wallowed, then drove deeper into the frothing area. Like a harpooned whale, she struggled on, yawing crazily in the grip of the tremendous currents grasping her hull.

Lieutenant Salt, nevertheless, began to dance about and pound the rail in hysterical fashion. "By God, it *is* — it *is* a replin!" He whirled on the still pallid and wide-eyed second lieutenant. "And now, sir, let's see what stomach the Dons have for following us."

" 'E Papists will think twice, sir," called the quartermaster, muscles standing out in cords along his leathery neck. "They'll think we've crossed a shoal only because of our slight draft. They know theirs is a damn' sight greater."

The quartermaster's reasoning proved sound. Fearful of venturing too close to what seemed certainly to be a shoal, the Spanish ships, one after another, veered to port and commenced to parallel that menacing froth which seemed to extend to the horizon.

Pearle's company reacted variously at having so narrowly escaped capture or destruction. A few, especially ex-landsmen, knelt on the sunlit deck, joined hands and offered fervent thanks. A majority enjoyed this brief lapse of discipline, went below and, drawing on cleverly secreted supplies of grog, got so royally drunk that the boatswain, his mates and the few Marines remaining soon had their hands full.

Still others stared soberly at the receding enemy sails.

"Wonder," one said, as if to himself, "if maybe this don't mean that Captain Arnand's curse is broke?"

When the good news reached *Pearle*'s noisome 'tween decks even the sick attempted to raise a cheer, for all that death again was striking hard down there. Very few of the Invalid-Pensioners now remained alive and only the youngest and strongest of the Army recruits.

It seemed as if, for once, Surgeon's Mate Hall had been correct in his prediction. When Lieutenant Salt once again quietly entered the Captain's cabin he found Dandy Kidd clearheaded and propped up a little in his berth. He was swallowing gruel spooned to him by a big seaman whose face and neck were dotted by yellow-headed pimples. When, finally, he noticed his First Lieutenant's presence, Kidd attempted a curious drooping smile. He had lost so much weight that the grayish skin of his face fell into unfamiliar folds.

Kidd ordered faintly, "Take away that damn' gruel. Now, Mr. Salt, please report."

Samuel Salt complied, lanky body rocking rhythmically to the Fifth Rate's slow pitch and heave. When his lieutenant had done, the stricken captain nodded painfully.

"You've done well. I'm sure I'd — not have had sufficient temerity — gamble on running over a supposed shoal." He drew a long, shuddering breath before continuing. "I — I'll see — you — credited in the log — preservation of the ship. Recommend a captaincy for you — first opportunity."

Lieutenant Salt's pallid, sheeplike features flushed. "That would

be very handsome of you, sir. I've waited years for my pendant —
God alone knows how many."

Kidd sank back and momentarily closed dreadfully sunken eyes;
then, as if by a tremendous effort he reopened them. "Understand
how you feel, Mr. Salt. I, too, was passed over time and again —
watched noble fools, well-connected fops and carpet knights handed
— captain's pendant." Another seemingly interminable sigh escaped
Dandy Kidd. "Fancy I'd be — lieutenant still, but — but for George
Anson. Sit down, man! You can have had no sleep in days."

He closed his eyes once more, then, without opening them,
queried in a somewhat stronger voice, "Think we've seen the last
of the Spaniards?"

"I doubt that, sir. The fact that they've twice chased a British
man-o'-war must prove to them that an enemy squadron must be
somewhere nearby."

"What — force — Spanish?"

"We counted two Third Rates, sir, two Fourths and one Fifth."

"Sure?"

"Aye, sir. They just now sailed so near there's no doubt of it."

Captain Kidd tried to struggle up on his pillow, but failed and lay
gasping.

"Mr. Salt — ?" His voice had faded so badly that the lieutenant
had to bend low. "Make all haste — rendezvous — warn Commodore
— Pizarro's presence. I — I —"

The surgeon's mate entered and touched Salt's damp and threadbare sleeve. "Sorry, sir, the Captain needs to rest."

Captain Kidd raised a hand, thin and speckled with dark brown
splotches. "One more question. How long before — reach Port St.
Julian?"

"Why, sir," Salt replied uncomfortably, "I can't give a precise answer, not knowing how the tides run or which winds prevail in these
latitudes at this time of year. Offhand I venture we should reach the
rendezvous in around a fortnight."

"Then," Kidd said, "you mus' 'deavor — try — intercept our squadron *above* St. Julian. Know I can rely — your seamanship."

"Thank you, sir." To his considerable surprise Salt felt his eyes fill.
"May I say, sir," said he gruffly, "the entire ship's company is happy
to hear that you are making such fine progress towards recovery."

Captain Kidd's livid lips formed the ghost of a smile. "Thank you,
Mr. Salt. Thank you very much."

That these would prove to be the last rational words to be spoken by Dandy Kidd, Salt, of course, had no way of foreseeing.

That evening, while *Pearle* bucked into a rising sea and sudden snow squalls, Captain Kidd died. It was the last day of January, 1741.

There being no chaplain aboard, it fell to Lieutenant Salt to read the burial service. He did so in a harsh, barking voice. That his best green velvet coat was being ruined by flying spray mattered not at all. His friend, Dandy Kidd, was being buried.

The ensign was dipped, all on deck bared their heads, and a handful of Marines able to be on deck presented arms as a hatch grating was raised and the canvas-shrouded figure disappeared.

"Commodore's going to take this hard," predicted the boatswain. "Him and the Captain was like brothers."

<del>~~~</del> 2 4 <del>~~~</del>

Rendezvous

WHILE *Pearle* fought her lonesome way southward toward bleak and barren Port St. Julian, reported to lie some four hundred miles north of Cape Horn, no ships, friendly or otherwise, were sighted, but the weather grew increasingly bitter. Day and night, sleet stung the men's faces like hungry sandflies. Sail handling became a dangerous misery. Icy ratlines burned the topmen's bare feet like hot irons; canvas, stiff with frost, caused broken fingernails and chilblained fingers.

Ten days after the death of Captain Kidd a series of jagged, snow-capped black mountains, stretching endlessly along the horizon, was sighted. Cautiously Lieutenant Salt navigated *Pearle* past a group of rocky islets which barely showed above the stormy gray ocean.

At first seamen crowded the rails to jeer and vainly threaten herds of sleek and quite unfearful sea lions which, from convenient ledges, stared curiously at the passing ship.

Nat Wade was among those who found amusement in viewing dense ranks of penguins, very solemn in pastoral black and white plumage, congregated on various rocks. By the thousands, these curious birds suddenly would dive into the sea and reappear alongside.

Swimming with arrow-like speed, the comical creatures often disported themselves far ahead of the ship as if in mockery of *Pearle's* blundering progress.

Seized by a strong premonition that the last of Don José Pizarro had not been seen, Lieutenant Salt kept doubled lookouts on duty night and day. The mercury dropped steadily until the wretched, badly dressed seamen, after they'd worked in the rigging for even a short while, became semi-congealed; often they had to be assisted below.

Surgeon's Mate Hall secretly had been hoping that this colder weather might discourage the sickness raging in the 'tween decks; but he soon learned that these lower temperatures in no way affected the fearful mortality rate. Every day anywhere from three to seven cadavers unceremoniously were shoved through a convenient gunport.

"Well," commented a messmate of Nat Wade's, "like my grandsire always was saying, 'No great loss 'thout some small gain.' Every day we're gaining more elbow room."

On the 17th of March *Pearle's* position, by her officers' calculations, lay in latitude 49° 10′ and not far from Port St. Julian. Lieutenant Salt silently rejoiced when, on the 18th, dim clusters of sails were sighted running close under the land.

"Our ships, sir, I'll stake my life on it," gabbled the sailing master.

The Acting Captain laughed harshly. "Mister, that's just what you've done."

"Aye, sir, stands to reason."

"Does it? Think, man. The rest of our squadron must be awaiting us at the rendezvous. *They* haven't been chased far off course."

Lieutenant Salt breathed a silent prayer of gratitude. Despite everything he'd safely brought his ship — *his ship* — safely to the rendezvous.

Salt's alarm mounted when it was noticed that two of the distant vessels had begun to make sail in their direction. *Pearle's* officers crowded the rigging, anxiously studied the approaching vessels.

Suddenly the second lieutenant cried a little hysterically — he'd gone without sleep for over two days, "Sir, sir! Those *aren't* our ships! That one in the lead I recognize. She's the Spanisher who looks just like our *Gloucester!* The other with the black and orange hull is one o' their Fourth Rates."

What should be done? Briefly, a terrible indecision racked Samuel

Salt. With a captaincy almost within his grasp this was no time to make a mistake.

"Prepare to wear ship," he snapped to the sailing master.

"Shall we show our colors, sir?" the second wanted to know.

"No. Damn' Spaniards may have become scattered. Maybe they'll fancy we're one of 'em."

The stranger ships closed in rapidly and again poignant anxiety gripped the chilled wretches working on *Pearle*'s deck and in her rigging.

By midday the leading pursuer had attained broadside range.

"She'll yaw and let fly in a minute," predicted *Pearle*'s gunner an instant before a Royal Jack appeared at the stranger's main. "That's only a dirty, Papist trick! That's wot."

The Acting Captain's voice rang out, harsh and clear. "Show our colors!" He had thought to recognize the stranger's figurehead — a crowned and bearded triton.

Not knowing what to think, Salt kept his spyglass trained on the nearest pursuer, watched a string of bright little flags climb to the stranger's signal yard, then heaved a shuddering sigh.

"Yonder's our recognition signal. Mr. Midshipman, I'll have you display our number!"

Quickly it became evident that the vessels astern were none other than His Britannic Majesty's ships *Gloucester* and *Severn*.

~~~ 2 5 ~~~

Readjustments

DURING THE WEEK his weather-battered squadron lay at Sir Francis Drake's old anchorage in the Bay of St. Julian, George Anson spent many lonely hours before a brazier which only removed the worst of the chill from his cabin. Clearly, it was imperative that he make a number of decisions with regard to a reassignment of officers and a re-arrangement of rigging and guns.

Further, urgent repairs must be effected before the dreaded passage around the Horn could be attempted — work that would have to be done under the greatest of difficulties. Of course, there existed no dockyard of any sort, nor apparently did timber of any useful sort grow on this barren coast. Worst of all, the environs of St. Julian's appeared to be destitute of fresh water.

Although he sent landing parties far inland, nowhere had they discovered sufficient fresh water even to replace that jettisoned by *Pearle* and otherwise exhausted during the long voyage down from Brazil. He therefore, albeit reluctantly, ordered all hands, himself included, rationed to a single quart of water a day.

Because of the now undoubted proximity of a powerful Spanish fleet Anson determined to order all upper-tier guns hoisted from the holds and remounted. To venture out unable to fight General Pizarro's ships without every possible gun ready for action would have been to court annihilation. And how would their lordships of the Admiralty like that?

In order properly to make space in which to fight the cannon, it became necessary to hoist out extra supplies brought from England and to store them, at least temporarily, aboard the little victualer, *Anna*. This caused secret anxiety among the squadron's more thoughtful officers.

Captain Mitchell of *Gloucester* said to Peircy Brett, his first lieutenant, "I don't like this at all. We may not encounter the Spaniards at all, but we surely will meet appalling seas off Cape Horn. How will we fare among them with our guns on deck and much of our stores, which also serve as ballast, removed?"

"God only knows, sir," admitted the long-faced young officer. "This has worried me, too. But I see no remedy."

As a further concern it was reported that *Tryall*'s masts, repaired at Santa Catharina, again had become so unsound that no choice remained but to shorten them by half their length — which proportionately would reduce her speed and that of the entire squadron in consequence. Again, Anson — bitterly but silently — cursed that appalling corruption which had condemned him to risk so many lives in ill-found vessels. If ever he survived this cruise he'd see to it that something was done, even though it might cost him his career.

Meanwhile Lieutenant Samuel Salt pushed repairs to *Pearle* with a veteran's unostentatious thoroughness. While, in compliance with orders, new sails were being bent onto all the Fifth Rate's yards, he couldn't help glancing from time to time over to *Centurion*, lying in the icy gray water only a cable's length distant.

Was the Commodore noticing how smartly his orders were being executed aboard *Pearle*? Of course he must have. Everyone admitted that there wasn't much of significance which escaped George Anson's attention.

The night before the squadron was expected to depart for the Pacific the "All Captains" signal appeared at the flagship's signal yard. Salt deliberated attending, wasn't he at least an *Acting* Captain? But then he thought better of such a move; no, it might seem presumptuous and so prejudice the Commodore against him.

So, smiling, the veteran lieutenant sought his cabin instead. At last, at last! They couldn't help making him a Captain, not after he'd twice saved the *Pearle* from the Dons. From the bottom of his sea chest Mr. Salt brought up a neatly sewn package. It contained a Captain's long, red and white pendant. How long had it rested there? Eight, or was it nine years? Anyhow, it had reposed there ever since that bitter day he'd deluded himself into thinking he was about to be commissioned Captain of HBMS *Minerva*.

While waiting for his Captains' gigs to arrive alongside, George Anson stood, hands locked behind back, staring out of the great, glazed and leaded stern windows. When his eye reached *Tryall*, it lingered there. Then he sighed so profoundly that Andrew Menzies, the cabin's only other occupant, glanced up from the pile of papers he was sorting.

Straight brows merged, he said, "I trust you will forgive me, sir, if I inquire whether you have taken decision in the matter of Mr. Salt? I know I need not remind you that he commanded the *Pearle* with exemplary courage, force and ability during Captain Kidd's illness and after his unfortunate demise."

"You've no need. All you say is quite true," Anson admitted thoughtfully, at the same time massaging chilled hands behind his faded wine-colored boat cloak. Despite heat given off by the brazier it remained so bitterly cold that his breath escaped smokily from his lips. "I appreciate Mr. Salt to be an able, straightforward and experienced officer. What else have you to say, Andrew?"

"Is it not only just that his long years of service should now be rewarded? Mr. Salt is getting on, sir; at best he has only a few years of service left."

"It is that very fact which has caused me so much concern and deliberation," Anson remarked and, as if seeking understanding, turned to face the dark-complexioned Carolinian. "You see, Andrew, there are already too many superannuated officers serving in the Royal Navy afloat, men who have long passed their prime, men who tire readily and have become no longer able to act boldly at a critical moment."

Slowly, the big figure gathered his boat cloak closer before he went over to stand before the glowing brazier. "Believe me, Andrew, I've been confronted by one of the most painful decisions I've ever had to make. If I don't promote Mr. Salt to be captain of the *Tryall*, I know I'll be condemned by every fair-minded man in this squadron and yet —"

Frowning, Anson took a short turn past that uncomfortable chair in which he consumed his meals. "And yet, is not my real duty to the ultimate good of the Navy? Should not promising young officers be granted the opportunity of proving their abilities to the end that when this Navy is called upon to fight the Monsieurs again — which surely it will be and before long — the King will find a corps of tough and well-seasoned young Captains to draw upon?"

The secretary shrugged. "No doubt, sir, in the long view that is entirely true." Wishing he might find words to alleviate George Anson in his unhappy dilemma, Menzies spilled more charcoal onto the brazier.

"Then, sir, I presume you intend to promote Mr. Saunders to be a Captain and, as such, commander and master of the *Tryall*?"

"For the reasons I have given, I believe that will be the wisest course."

"Who then will command the *Pearle*?"

In a toneless voice Anson said, "I will transfer Captain Murray from the *Wager*."

Menzies understood that flat note: Captain the Honorable George Murray had many connections at Court.

In the background could be heard Captain Legge's coxswain hailing for permission to board the flagship; the sound of feet hurrying to man *Centurion*'s side.

"I will then move Captain Cheap up to the *Wager* and send Mr. Saunders to try his hand as captain of the *Tryall*."

"But, sir, is not Mr. Saunders dangerously ill?" Anxiously, Menzies wet dry-looking lips. From a portable writing desk the secretary took out a leaden ink pot and brass pen case and otherwise prepared to record the impending transfers and promotions. How entirely typical of George Anson that he should have waited until this last moment to make known decisions obviously taken some time ago. "Could you not perhaps appoint Mr. Salt? He really deserves such a promotion, sir."

Levelly, the Commodore surveyed his secretary a long moment before speaking with a touch of asperity. "I am well aware of that. Nevertheless, Mr. de Saumarez will act in Mr. Saunders's place until he recovers. Incidentally, I deem Mr. de Saumarez a young officer of singular promise. Upon his return from the *Tryall* I have decided to appoint him first lieutenant of the *Centurion*."

"— And for second, sir?"

"Mr. Peircy Brett out of the *Gloucester*. In my humble estimation there's another young gentleman with good qualifications for command. For third I shall appoint Mr. Peter Denis."

Someone knocked briskly at the great cabin's door.

"Captains Legge and Cheap are here, sir."

While the council of war was being held, Mr. Salt sought a secluded corner of *Pearle*'s quarterdeck from which, unnoticed, he could study *Centurion*'s deck through his glass.

Shrewdly, he suspected that important decisions were being taken.

"While actually rounding the Horn," Anson informed his captains, "all ships must keep station within two miles of *Centurion*. If we succeed in rounding the Horn together, I intend to first attack the port of Valdivia which lies roughly a thousand miles up the West Coast and is the enemy's southernmost port on the western coast of Spanish America."

His gaze circulated the row of intent, cold-nipped officers standing across the table from him. "However, gentlemen, should the ships become separated we will rendezvous at the Island of Nuestra Señora del Socorro. There you will wait for a period of not longer than ten days. After that you will proceed to the Island Juan Fernandez, the same on which Alexander Selkirk spent above five years until rescued by Captain Woodes Rogers in the privateers *Duke* and *Duchess of Bristol*." He couldn't help offering this irrelevant information. For years he'd read *Robinson Crusoe* from end to end.

Although very cold, the day was so bright that Lieutenant Salt was able to recognize the various captains when, finally, they appeared to descend *Centurion*'s side. Anxious beyond description, the veteran watched the Captains step into their gigs: there was saturnine Captain Matthew Mitchell of *Gloucester,* Captain the Honorable Edward Legge of *Severn,* burly Captain Cheap of *Tryall* and, finally, Captain the Honorable George Murray. The gigs shoved off, then started pulling for their respective ships.

Suddenly a sickening apprehension shot through the spare figure standing so alone on *Pearle*'s well-scrubbed quarterdeck. *Wager*'s smallboat was not carrying Captain Murray back to his ship! It was steering straight for *Pearle* — that could mean but one thing.

"Oh, no! They can't — the Commodore's a fair man. Oh, no!" In a miserable daze, Samuel Salt watched *Wager*'s boat approach until he could read smug satisfaction written broad across Captain Murray's bloated, ruddy countenance.

With a snap Salt closed his spyglass cover then, for once ignoring a Marine sentry's salute, clumped down the ladder to seek his cabin mumbling, "Didn't think he'd do it! By God, I just didn't believe I'd be denied again."

He knelt, reached and fumbled in his sea chest until he found the familiar packet. Trembling, the suddenly aged officer twice drew a sharp clasp knife across his Captain's pendant, then tossed the red and white tatters out of the stern port. Laughing harshly, he then uncorked a bottle of fine French cognac he'd saved to "wet" his Captain's pendant and up-ended it.

By the time Captain the Honorable George Murray appeared alongside and began roaring for side-boys, Lieutenant Salt was thoroughly drunk — which by no means endeared him to his new Captain.

BOOK II
The South Sea

"– A Scene of Pleasing Horror"

SIX DAYS SOUTH of Bay St. Julian, Anson's ships sighted a jagged, snow-covered headland. When he heard it was called The Cape of Ten Thousand Virgins, Coxswain King Parmer drawled, "If there ever was so many such females I reckon yonder's about the *only* place they'd be likely to stay that way. Who'd go there to prove if they was or wasn't?"

Then the sea flattened out and everyone wondered: where were those fearsome storms everyone had heard about and had dreaded for weeks? Why, it actually was growing warm down here and the sun shone all day long.

Boats put out from the various ships, conveying their Captains over to *Centurion*, the Commodore having invited all commanding officers to share a decanter of Madeira wine.

Grateful for this unexpected fine weather, the Captains stood about on the flagship's sunlit quarterdeck and discussed, among other subjects, their chances of encountering the fabulous "Prize of All the Oceans."

Young Lieutenant Brett looked puzzled, asked of the Commodore, "Why is it, sir, that sometimes this ship is referred to as the 'Acapulco Galleon' and at others the 'Manila Galleon'?"

Everyone listened for Anson's answer. They'd been wondering themselves.

"Why, Mr. Brett, 'tis simple enough. When outward bound from Manila to Mexico she's known as the 'Acapulco' ship or galleon. On her return voyage she takes the name of her destination — Manila." He raised his glass. "Whichever name she sails under let us hope —"

The sound of a resounding explosion aboard *Gloucester* cut him short.

[123]

"God above! What's happening?" burst out Cheap.

"Permission to leave, sir?" burst out Captain Mitchell, then pelted down to the gangway, roaring all the while for his boat.

Meanwhile Anson and his guests anxiously watched clouds of dense black smoke climb from *Gloucester's* forecastle and form an ominous pall which soon disappeared. The green and white Fourth Rate then signaled "Fire extinguished" and sent scared young Midshipman Hyde Parker to report that the ship had sustained no serious damage.

It appeared that an over-ambitious third lieutenant by the name of Foley — only recently promoted from passed midshipman — had not taken sufficient precautions while experimenting with a hand grenade of his own design and manufacture.

Anson commented, "No doubt a commendable enterprise, Mr. Parker. But what went wrong?"

"Why, sir, Mr. Foley was working in the fore part of the ship. I guess, sir, a spark from the blacksmith's forge landed among some loose powder."

"Was he hurt?"

"No, sir." The youth grinned. "Only got his brows and forelock singed off."

The beautiful weather did not endure, for within the hour such livid black clouds loomed on the horizon that the visiting Captains hurried back to their vessels.

They reached them just before a powerful wind commenced to roar out of the southeast.

Soon George Anson's seven vessels were strung out in an irregular column, struggling along off the forbidding and snow-covered coast of the Tierra del Fuego. Sailing masters ordered soundings taken, consulted the meager charts, checked their position and otherwise prepared to enter the dreaded "Streights le Maire" which, supposedly, separated a large, rocky island called Statenland from the coast of South America.

On the advice of Sailing Master Justinian Nutt, Anson ordered his squadron hove to for the night — there was no advantage, he decided, in approaching this treacherous area in darkness.

All hands, therefore, were afforded ample opportunity to observe this, the southernmost tip of South America.

Mr. Thomas Pascoe, *Centurion's* schoolmaster, having finished his instruction of junior midshipmen in the evening's exercise, used a well-worn penknife to re-point his quill and wrote in his *Journal of a Voyage to the South-Seas:*

The 6th in the Morning we saw the Land of *Terra del Fuego,* consisting of high craggy Hills, towering above each other, mostly covered with Snow, with deep horrid Valleys, some few scattering Trees, no Plains, nor one chearful Green thro' all the dismal Scene; so that the whole may not improperly be termed the *Land of Desolation:* And I much question whether such an Uncomfortable Prospect be to be found in any other Part of the habitable Earth, for some Voyagers say this is inhabited, if so I am morally certain that its Inhabitants must subsist in a very Miserable Manner.

The next day proving fair, the flagship at six in the morning fired a gun, then signaled the squadron to get under way and assume daylight stations.

If the Tierra del Fuego had appeared desolate, Statenland seemed so much more fearful that Mr. Midshipman John Phillips wrote into a journal ambitiously entitled: *An Authentick Journal of Commodore Anson's Expedition:*

Sunday 8. Fresh Gales and fair Weather. At 2 P.M. got thro' the Streights of *Le Mair,* and having the Wind and Tide with us we had a fine Passage through. We had a clear View of the Land on both Sides, which afforded us a very uncomfortable Prospect, being nothing but high craggy Hills and Mountains cover'd with Snow, no Trees nor so much as a Shrub to be seen on it, in short, the whole was a Scene of pleasing Horror.

Chaplain Richard Walter blew on numbed fingers before dutifully making an entry in the diary he was keeping for the Commodore's benefit — and his own; he was hoping someday to write an account of this voyage.

I cannot but Remark, that though *Terra del Fuego* had an Aspect extremely Barren and Desolate, yet this Island of *Staten-land* far surpasses it, in the wildness and Horror of its Appearance: It seeming to be composed of inaccessible Rocks, without the least mixture of Earth and Mould between them. These Rocks terminate in a vast number of ragged Points, which spire up to a prodigious Height, and are all of them covered with Everlasting Snow; the points Themselves are on every side surrounded with Frightful Precipices, and often overhang in a most astonishing manner; and the Hills which bear them, are generally Separated from each other by Narrow Clefts, which appear as if the Country had been rent by Earthquakes; for these

Chasms are nearly perpendicular, and extend through the Substance of the main Rocks, almost to their very Bottoms: So that nothing can be imagined more Savage and Gloomy, than the whole Aspect of this Coast.

The Reverend Mr. Walter felt so depressed that, much later, he continued to describe his sensations on that occasion.

— On the 7th of *March*, in the morning, we opened Streights *Le Maire*, and soon after, or about ten o'clock, the *Pearle* and the *Tryall* being ordered to keep a-head of the Squadron, we entered them with fair Weather and a brisk Gale, and were hurried through by the Rapidity of the Tide in about two Hours, though they are between seven and eight Leagues in Length. As these Streights are often considered as the Boundary between the *Atlantick* and *Pacifick* Oceans, and as we presumed we had Nothing now before us but an open Sea, till we arrived on those Opulent Coasts, where all our Hopes and Wishes centered, we could not help Flattering ourselves, that the greatest Difficulty of our Passage was now at an End, and that our most sanguine Dreams were upon the Point of being Realised; and hence we indulged our Imaginations in those Romantick Schemes, which the fancied possession of the *Chilian* Gold and *Peruvian* Silver might be conceived to inspire. These joyous Ideas were heightened by the brightness of the Sky, and the serenity of the Weather, which was indeed most remarkably pleasing; for tho' the Winter was now advancing apace, yet the Morning of this Day, in its brilliancy and mildness, gave place to None we had seen since our departure from *England*. Thus animated by these Delusions, we travers'd these memorable Streights, ignorant of the dreadful Calamities that were then impending, and just ready to break upon Us; ignorant that the Time drew near, when the Squadron would be separated never to unite again, and that this Day of passage was the last chearful Day that the greatest part of Us would ever live to Enjoy.

The Watch Below was about to be called away to dinner when Nat Wade — once more assigned to the flagship — was startled by a series of shrill and imperative blasts on the boatswain's pipe. A moment later the command was bellowed, "All hands on deck to hear the Captain!"

From the waist, Ramster, Buckle and Parmer agreed that the Commodore was looking uncommonly pleased about something, while the quarterdeck officers grouped to leeward of him all were wearing smiles.

The crew soon grew cheerful too, and cheered an announcement by the first lieutenant that, in celebration of having so easily passed through the dreaded Straits, the Commodore had ordered a double ration of grog served to all hands.

George Anson's wide-shouldered figure drew itself more erect than usual, if that were possible, as he crossed the break of the quarter-deck. Ever since school days he had detested oratory, but conscience dictated that this moment was a proper moment to address his men.

Gripping the white-painted rail, he watched men all over the ship uncover, as was the custom when the Captain was about to speak. He drew a deep, deep breath and hoped that his voice would sound clear and strong.

"My brave lads, let us rejoice, let us praise our Maker, let our hearts beat high! We have left the Atlantic behind and are at this moment sailing the waters of the South Sea — until now the undisputed dominion of the Enemy."

Anson broke off, his voice submerged by cheers so loud that color spread out along his cheekbones. "I am confident that this is the turning point of our voyage. Soon the wide and tranquil Pacific will open before us, bearing on its bosom many rich Spanish ships waiting to become English prizes. Somewhere on this ocean sails the great Manila Galleon." Another shout. "Even if we should not succeed in prizing her, let me assure you that the shores of South America are bordered with opulent colonial towns requiring but a few salvos to make them render up immense treasures of gold, silver and emeralds. Aye, lads, there'll be plenty of prize money for all!"

"Prize money for all!" roared the crew. *"Prize money!* PRIZE MONEY!"

When the tumult subsided the boatswain jumped up onto a gun carriage. "Three cheers for our gallant Commodore!" The color deepened in Anson's broad features as he wondered, How can these poor devils cheer me when they can't help but hold me responsible for so much of their sufferings?

"Prize money for all!"

Once the master-at-arms and the ship's corporals had restored order by a liberal use of colts and canes the Commodore invited and led three cheers for His Gracious Majesty King George II.

Then the eagerly anticipated order was given: "Splice the main brace!" and the crew was dismissed. Thoughtfully, Anson noted that many hands were so weak that companions had to assist them below.

The Watch on Deck, however, seemed to return to duty more light-heartedly than at any time since boarding HBMS *Centurion*.

While clumping down the main companionway with Tom Ramster and his slick-haired "chicken," Ben Canty, Will Pallister queried, "Tell me, Tom, does such a vessel as the Manila Galleon really exist, or is it just another sailor's fable?"

Ramster resettled a faded wool muffler he'd worn on deck, looked a trifle impatient. "Of course there is. Such treasure ships have been crossing the Pacific for nigh on a hundred years — or so I've always heard."

"— And is the treasure she carries really so great?" queried smooth-faced young Canty.

"Aye, Ben. They say that every year, sometime during the month of July, a great ship sails from the Philippine Islands deep laden with costly stuffs, silks, ivories, jewels of all sorts, gold dust and many priceless spices."

"Where are these Phil — Philippines?"

"Dunno 'cept that they lie somewheres off the coast o' Cathay. They say she generally reaches Acapulco in Mexico sometime durin' January."

"You're certain-sure?" demanded Canty, delicately retying a broad red ribbon Ramster had bought to put in his greasy blue-black hair.

"Yes, my pretty. I've it from Joe Bostock, a shipmate who served the John Company."

" 'John Company'?" Pallister demanded as he swabbed out the grog bucket in which Tom presently would draw his mess's share of rum and water.

" 'Tis but a slang name for the Honorable East India Company. Like I was saying, Bostock once sighted this galleon off Macao —"

"— Where's Macao?" young Pallister broke in, ever curious in matters of geography. He needed to know more, at least, than the midshipmen he was helping Mr. Pascoe to instruct.

"A Portuguese port on the south coast o' Cathay. Bostock said this 'Prize of All the Oceans,' as many term her, was bigger than a First Rate line-of-battle ship. Said she was fair plastered with gold leaf. He heard that the ornaments in her Admiral's cabin are of pure gold and that her officers dine off tableware of virgin silver."

More and more sailors crowded about to listen, eyes bright with greed, as Ramster continued. "Aye, and their weapons are all encrusted wi' great rubies, emeralds and pearls."

[128]

That hard-bitten veteran, Clipperton, called, "What sort of cargo does this galleon fetch back from Ac — Ac —"

"Go ahead and sneeze —" somebody laughed.

"Back from Acapulco? Why, she carries payment for treasures fetched out from the Orient."

"In gold?" voices cried amid the creaking gloom of the main gundeck.

"No, in silver mostly. Bostock told me most o' the gold mined in the Americas is shipped straight to Spain. For some reason, the heathen Cathayans value silver almost as high."

Red head brushing beams supporting the upper gundeck, Ramster towered above his rapt listeners.

"It's fetched to Acapulco by long mule trains guarded by whole regiments of European troops."

Clipperton shouted, "Then, b'Gawd, I'm all fer prizing her outward bound from Mexico."

"Why?" challenged Buckle.

Ramster, anxious not to lose the center of attention, replied for Clipperton. "Why, it's plain as the nose on yer face. Silver has a fixed value and don't need to be bargained for like furniture, silks and ivories."

"When does 'e galleon 'ead for 'ome?"

"Generally she sails in March, after she's been refitted, watered and wooded."

Deliberately, Ramster ran shrewd gray-blue eyes over the hairy faces ringing him in, then winked. "I'll tell you something I overheard on the quarterdeck. For sure, the Commodore's going to —" He broke off because, abruptly, the flagship lurched and shuddered as if she had run onto a shoal.

Voices roared down the mainhatch, "All hands on deck! Quick! For your lives!"

Rushing on deck, the Watch Below were amazed to find that the pleasant sunlight had disappeared and an arc of purple-black clouds had appeared in the northwest and was driving before it a wall of towering, white-headed billows.

Although all topmen were ordered to race aloft and furl sail the storm pounced with a weird, howling sound such as no one previously had heard. Every ship in the squadron staggered, and was taken aback before it could turn to flee before the furious blast.

Nat Wade barely missed being blown off the mainyard, but the man on his left was not so fortunate. His body flashed into the sea like a stone flung from a sling.

Topmen, toiling in *Gloucester*'s rigging, barely were able to hang on when the weary old Fourth Rate heeled over so far that men working on deck were spilled as a struggling, half-drowned mass against her lee bulwarks.

The seas became so overpowering that Captain Mitchell and Lieutenants Baird, Scott and Foley could only cling to the rail and bellow orders which could not possibly be executed.

Ominous reports sounded aloft as sail after sail split and then blew out of the buntlines, but, for a miracle, none of her dubious spars broke.

Mountainous gray-black combers drove the helpless squadron back into the Straits le Maire towards the hideous, murderous coast of Statenland.

Gloucester, more top-heavy than her consorts, began to labor painfully when seas, vaulting the bulwarks, buried her gundeck under feet of water. One wave, more tremendous than the rest, carried away the port head gratings and smashed its door. All manner of loose gear washed freely across the deck.

Ordinary Seaman Kildare's empty eye socket ran great tears as he worked doggedly to secure the barge on its booms. He couldn't help yelping after a while because of the icy water nipping at his legs.

Below, Ted Waxter was better off. Having successfully insinuated himself into the favor of Purser Millechamp, it no longer was his duty to freeze on deck with seamen as stupid as they were brutish. Books and ledgers fell off shelves; a snowstorm of papers drifted crazily about the cabin. Although white to the lips Waxter braced his feet against the purser's well-anchored desk and grinned in sardonic amusement at Mr. Millechamp, who, wild-eyed, was clutching its opposite side.

Several times the purser's mate passed an ink-stained hand over blond hair grown satisfactorily long once more. Suddenly he remembered Sophia, who, if she were really bright, must have forgotten all about him. Over the crashing of waves against *Gloucester*'s hull he declaimed, in mock tenderness:

> "If to be absent were to be
> Away from thee;
> Or that when I am gone
> You or I were alone;

Then, my Lucasta, might I crave
Pity from blustering wind or swallowing wave."

Mr. Millechamp stared, tried to retrieve a paste jar rolling about his feet. "Shut up, you loon. Have you gone crazy?"

"Not yet, dear Mr. Millechamp, not yet. Tell me, ain't this touching?

"But I'll not sigh one blast or gale
To swell my sail,
Or pay a tear to 'suage
The foaming blue god's rage;
For whether he will let me pass —"

"— Stop that damn' crazy gibberish!" roared the purser.

" 'Gibberish,' sir? I do but quote from Richard Lovelace, a most sensitive poet."

"Can't you see we're about to sink at any moment? Stow your bloody nonsense!"

"Aye, aye. Stowed is poor Mr. Lovelace."

Water began to cascade down the main companionway and sluice darkly across the deck of the purser's cabin.

"I fancy," observed the Earl of Burfurd, features pallid but set in derision, "that we must have been struck by one of those 'williwaws' — fascinating term, ain't it? — I've heard old salts speak of."

Mr. Millechamp failed to reprove his assistant clerk for not having added "sir" to his observations because he didn't quite dare to. Only yesterday he'd become fairly certain that this clever young fellow had made note of a considerable number of "dead-heads" listed in *Gloucester*'s muster book — sailors who, though long dead, still were drawing pay, imaginary rations and clothing from the ship's slop chest.

Bitterly, Mr. Millechamp lamented that Captain Mitchell, a strict Presbyterian, most likely would not admit that, in His Majesty's Naval Service, such peculation long had been the purser's unofficial perquisite. This wasn't fair; it being for the enjoyment of this, and similar peculations, that a man was forced to pay a high price for a purser's warrant from the Admiralty, aside from furnishing a security of four hundred pounds.

Only when *Gloucester* finally was able to struggle out of the trough of the sea and, like her consorts, begin to run before the storm was it possible to restore a semblance of order on deck. During brief lulls in the wind's roaring terrified cries could plainly be heard rising out of the foul-smelling 'tween decks.

It was no wonder, decided Peter Vesey, struggling to attend the sick assigned to his care. What with every bit of light and air cut off due to the battening down of the main hatch, and the hammocks incessantly swinging and banging against each other, conditions in the berthdeck were more nightmarish than ever.

Surgeon Kerr, his mate and Vesey, now confirmed as chief of loblollies lurched around and struggled to do what they could for moaning men brought below suffering from sanguinary contusions, dislocated joints and broken limbs.

Mr. Kerr yelled at Vesey over the thundering of seas against *Gloucester*'s sides. "Where in hell are your damned loblollies?"

"As fast as I fetch 'em, sir, they run off and hide."

"Then go find the master-at-arms and tell him to bring the first twenty men he can collar!"

Even as Mr. Kerr spoke, *Gloucester* gave such a sickening lurch that he was forced to cling to the pommel of a cannon, the preventer tackles of which were whining like gigantic hounds under the strain.

"Oh, Christ!" a voice wailed. "Help! Me teeth is crumbling." By the light of a lantern Vesey raised a one-armed Invalid who hung his head over the hammock's edge and spat several teeth onto the filthy deck, then sank back groaning. "Oh, God, why can't I die quick-like?"

Shaken by frightful forebodings, the chief loblolly steadied himself against a beam and shone his light directly upon the veteran's face, then felt his stomach turn over. *Scurvy!* There could be no doubt about it. Large, livid, purple-brown patches discolored the Invalid's face and his breath smelt like a cesspool's exhalations.

As quietly as possible, Vesey informed the harassed surgeon.

Mr. Kerr gave him a curious look. "How'd you know it's scurvy? I've thought for some time that you were once a physician. Am I right?"

"Yes, Mr. Kerr, I once studied medicine, sir."

"— And you hold a doctor's degree in medicine. Don't lie to me."

The hawk-nosed chief loblolly nodded grimly.

"Well, Doctor —" Mr. Kerr stressed the title "— although I've said nothing about it thus far I, too, have observed the symptoms in some other patients. God help us all now."

"Maybe the contagion won't spread," suggested Vesey.

[132]

But it did. Scurvy swiftly raged through the storm-racked ships, and every day slew men by the dozen.

～ 2 ～
Nightmare Passage

THE TEMPEST WHICH, on March 24th, 1741, had pounced on the squadron right after it had so easily negotiated the dreaded Straits le Maire proved to be the first of so many terrific gales and glacial hurricanes that everyone, saving George Anson and those who had to keep the ships' logs up to date, soon lost count.

During the first of these battles with Cape Horn weather the seas ran so high that, frequently, they completely concealed all ships and tossed even the Fourth Rates about like pitiful little wherries. How, under such conditions, his Captains managed even approximately to keep station would have baffled Anson had he not selected them, above all other qualifications, for their seamanship.

The first major crisis occurred when *Tryall*'s mainsail blew out; had the sloop not been sailing under jury rig she must inevitably have foundered. As it was, Anson's heart seemed to falter while the stout little vessel lay over on her beam's end with combers washing over her. Terrible, interminable minutes passed before her shortened masts permitted her slowly to right.

There was nothing for it, the Commodore decided, but to signal his struggling vessels to flee under bare poles and pray that they could avoid Statenland's pitiless coast and also a multitude of small icebergs which now had begun to dot the steel-gray seas.

Duty on deck entailed indescribable misery. The icy rain turned into sleet which quickly coated the rigging and rendered footing extremely perilous.

Hour after hour, Anson remained on the quarterdeck sparing himself not at all. He managed this by knotting about his waist a lanyard with an iron hook at one end. By means of the hook, secured to various stays, shrouds and other fixed objects, he remained able to move about the heaving, spray-drenched deck without being swept overboard. For all that, he slipped and fell continually. Sleet beat his face raw and so swelled his eyelids that he could barely see, but

[133]

still he refused Lieutenant Denis's repeated pleas that he go below. It never occurred to him that he should stop, even for a moment, observing the condition and positions of those ships which the Admiralty had entrusted to his care.

Furious snow flurries began to obscure now one and then another of his vessels for longer and longer intervals.

Blue-lipped, Sailing Master Nutt drew near, slipping and sliding over the ice-glazed deck.

"How does *Anna* survive?" he screamed. "She's of only one hundred tons burthen."

Anson, shielding bloodshot eyes from the sleet's needle-sharp blast, shouted, "Perhaps, Mr. Nutt, her very smallness preserves her. See? She slides over the billows one at a time, instead of having to try to straddle two of them."

To the half-frozen Commodore it appeared that *Gloucester* and *Wager* were laboring the worst. They struggled painfully, their bows raising clouds of spray which would freeze on the rigging and so render the ship increasingly top-heavy.

Again and again it appeared inevitable that these ships, the one green, the other blue, must become overwhelmed. The tremendous size of the seas they were battling was what most worried Anson. He'd read many descriptions of the huge billows to be encountered off Cape Horn, but foolishly had ascribed this phenomenon to a mariner's innate readiness to exaggerate.

Stubby, square-faced Third Lieutenant Peter Denis appeared, lurching up to the quarterdeck to stand his watch. Anson saw that already he was shivering violently under a sodden boat cloak.

Philip de Saumarez, Anson realized, should have appeared in Denis's place, but he must be doing his capable best to keep *Tryall* afloat and as near on station as possible. Charles Saunders, *Tryall's* newly designated captain, lay below, recovering from a critical seizure of the bloody flux.

Peering through the darkening storm, he frowned. *Severn* and *Pearle* barely were visible. If only those honorable gentlemen, Edward Legge and George Murray, could prove as successful in maintaining station as young de Saumarez!

Unhappily, Anson wondered whether, if he'd made a captain of Samuel Salt, *Pearle* wouldn't be better handled right now? Poor old fellow. How bitter he must feel — and justifiably. Oh God, he thought, I hope I've not made the blunder of my life.

[134]

"Mr. Denis! Fire a signal gun and show *Pearle* and *Severn*'s numbers. Warn them to stay closer to the flagship."

Next day the storm increased in fury; canvas on all ships was reduced to storm trysails. Colossal seas kept filling *Gloucester*'s longboat as it lay double lashed upon its booms. The weight of water imprisoned in it caused the Fourth Rate to list so heavily that Captain Mitchell, grown gaunt and hollow-eyed, was forced to order it stove in so that it might drain.

The worst conditions in the squadron arose in *Gloucester*. Every day she signaled that more of her company had perished of scurvy. Anson could guess how badly off Captain Mitchell must be; *Centurion* was losing eight to ten men every day.

Soon the number of hands visible on *Gloucester*'s deck became noticeably fewer; her sails were sloppily trimmed and her rigging began, here and there, to sag; but officers on the other vessels hardly noticed it. They had troubles of their own and plenty of them.

At the end of three weeks, marked by incessant squalls, icy gales and howling hurricanes, the weather moderated, livid clouds disappeared and a pale sun appeared, diffidently, as if it were ashamed of having remained so long invisible.

At once every well officer from Commodore to midshipman got out sextants, hurried out on deck to take sights and set about calculating the bedraggled squadron's position.

The consensus of their findings was the appalling fact that the squadron was in the latitude 59° 30′ S., and, by dead reckoning, in the longitude 5° E., which meant that it lay some two hundred miles *southeast* of the tip of Cape Horn!

As bad news always will, the ill tidings swiftly circulated the entire squadron. Incredible though it seemed, during the month which had elapsed since Anson's ships had left Bay St. Julian's behind, they had *not yet rounded the Horn!*

"This can only mean," Captain Mitchell explained to Patrick Baird, his haggard first lieutenant, as they gulped steaming rum in *Gloucester*'s great cabin, "that the current flowing out of the Pacific must be broader and far more powerful than either Dr. Halley or Sir John Narborough have led us to believe."

"D'you know, Ted, I believe I've arrived at a tenable hypothesis," Peter Vesey observed as, with his friend Waxter, he braced against a 24-pounder and struggled to choke down a half-cooked midday meal.

"A tenable hypothesis? If it's that this swill is inedible, I'll willingly concur."

"No. It's that the receipt of ill news adversely affects scurvy-stricken men. Notice how fast they've been dying since they learned that we're not yet in the Pacific? Ever since the disease appeared I've noted how prone scurvied men are to take alarm over even the most trifling incidents. This tendency, I'd say, marks one of the disease's most dangerous symptoms."

"Conditions are worse in the orlop?" Waxter mumbled, his bristle-covered jaws working hard at a chunk of beef stiff with salt crystals.

"They're utterly horrifying. Almost all of the poor old Invalids are either dead or dying. The Lords of Admiralty can congratulate themselves."

"Damn' sleek swine! It's high time those rascals were brought to book. Maybe this will do it." Waxter gulped the last of his cooling grog and glanced sidewise at his disheveled, exhausted companion. "Suppose you know that scurvy's now raging even in the forecastle?"

"Yes, I know. By the bye, where are you berthing now? Haven't lately seen you sleeping in the 'tween decks."

Waxter, while scratching fleas under a coarse brown serge coat, chuckled. "Like you, Peter, I've come up in the world. In fact, I've just been made an acting purser's mate: I'll be confirmed in that rating the minute my predecessor decides to die."

Vesey, re-examining his companion, decided that for all that he was unshaven, Waxter must be doing pretty well. The red jersey he was wearing seemed of good quality, his shoes, canvas breeches and stockings appeared to be of the best quality offered by the purser's slop chest.

After the ship had completed a particularly vicious roll, Vesey said a little enviously, "Wish to God I'd fallen on my feet as squarely as you."

"Haven't you? I'll swear I overhead someone say, 'Vesey's soon to be rated surgeon's mate.' If that's true, I venture we, the Lord Mayor's men ain't doing too badly."

"I guess not, save that I'm being worked half to death. Poor Mr. Kerr isn't much of a physician. They work you hard, too?"

"They try to," Waxter winked, "but I take my time. Damned purser daren't remove me from the storerooms."

"Why?"

"I know too much about his peculations. The blighter's been selling watered vinegar for wine and palming off old salted meat for new; besides, he's carrying at least a hundred 'deadheads' on the muster roll. You'd have died laughing to see him when that precious swine, Robinson —" Waxter's pale brows merged and, as always, he scowled whenever he spoke of the officer who'd ordered him gagged "— came to protest the rottenness of the beef allowances. Old Millechamp looked the bastard square in the eye and said, 'Pray look for yourself, Mr. Robinson. Yonder entry proves that this meat is less than two years old.'" Waxter broke into harsh laughter. "And it did read that way; Millechamp told me to reduce the purchase date by *nine* years!"

Vesey arose and dumped his rations into an overflowing half-barrel. "Small wonder scurvy rages and so many hands are close to dying of starvation! None of my mess could stomach the carrion they've lately been serving out of the galley. 'Fore God, Ted, I'm hollow to my heels, right now."

Waxter fumbled in a side pocket and brought out a grimy piece of cone sugar and sea biscuit which, for a miracle, was not weevil-riddled or of the consistency of cement. "Whyn't you tell me so before, you great ass? Any time you need a treat, Peter, just pass the word."

"On deck, the Watch Below!" The boatswain's whistle sounded, tiredly it seemed. Men crouching in the semidarkness cursed sullenly then, swaying as if half drunk, began to adjust ragged scarves and button up "wrap-rascals" — long-skirted coats of coarse brown frieze — and pull down knitted stocking caps of various hues.

Among the foremost was John Clipperton, eager because he'd been rated gunner's mate again — several of surly Mr. Nuttal's subordinates recently had been shoved overboard.

The new Watch emerged into swirling, clammy fog, a fog so dense that the other ships became completely obscured.

Young Lieutenant Foley's slim figure, looming amid the grayness, called, "Clipperton! Take some men forward and fire the signal gun each half-hour 'til further orders."

"Aye, aye, sir!" Hunched into a damp and sour-smelling jacket, Gunner's Mate Clipperton selected a slow match from a locker and

[137]

groped his way to the ship's galley which he found to be badly crowded, this being the only place on board where, because of its brick floor, seamen were allowed to smoke.

Clipperton nodded to the cook, a beefy and red-faced former gunner who'd lost a leg in battle. He continually was cursing a listless group of helpers, and roaring for a fresh supply of firewood. The new gunner's mate lifted a stove lid and took care to get his match well alight before he went back out into the icy fog.

Shielding the match under his coat, Clipperton climbed the forecastle ladder and bore down on a battery of light signal cannon. Without being told, two ice-dusted gunners on duty promptly removed a lead shield designed to protect the little cannon's touchhole from flying spray.

Despite his caution Clipperton slipped on an ice patch. As he went spinning crazily across the forecastle deck, he heard a gun boom dully somewhere in the opaque silvery gloom off to port. Shortly afterwards another and much fainter-sounding report came from astern. Before Clipperton could prime the signal gun from a flask of extra fine 4-F powder two more reports reverberated close off *Gloucester*'s port beam.

Once the gunner's mate had ground the match's ruby red end into the priming the signal piece, a 9-pounder, roared valiantly and slammed back against its breeching as a cloud of smoke quickly blended with the fog.

The wind nipped Clipperton's ears like icy claws while he helped to clear ice from the gun carriage's wheels that it might be run in for reloading. Next the veteran made sure that the 9-pounder's bore was thoroughly swabbed out and an extra thick wad driven down on top of the cartridge lest seawater seep in and spoil the charge.

Since his duty didn't require him to linger on the spray-clouded forecastle, Clipperton retreated to the galley where, from a rack, he selected a half-hour glass which he reversed, setting its sand to flowing. In this smoky but blessedly warm place there was very little conversation. Off-duty men in steaming clothes just smoked, hugged the galley's sides and watched the cook and his helpers pitchfork pallid chunks of salt meat into great copper cauldrons.

"Pork, b'God!" someone coughed. "I'm near starving, but I'll not try to choke down any more rotten beef."

Presently Clipperton asked, "I say, Cooky, where's 'e ruddy Marine that's supposed to guard yer galley door?"

"Cursed if I know. Hasn't a Guffy showed up since night before last."

Kildare, the one-eyed ex-convict who with him had attempted to desert back in Santa Catharina, called across the steam-filled galley. "Didn't mark no Lobsterbacks near 'e magazine scuttle, neither."

"And you won't," informed a helper. "Them Guffies is mostly down sick or gone to Jones."

Other signs of slackening discipline became evident as, inexorably, the number of able-bodied men decreased. Quarterdeck officers, now performing many duties not their own, commenced to shave only every other day. Watches were called at increasingly irregular intervals and turned out in slovenly fashion.

So many midshipmen and petty officers had died or lay disabled that the log ship was being heaved with increasing irregularity; normally, it would have been dropped from *Gloucester*'s stern every hour and her rate of progress chalked on a small blackboard hung near the wheel.

No longer did a lanky, chin-whiskered Irishman pipe "Drops of Brandy" or "Nancy Dawson" at midday, summoning mess captains to draw their rations from the grog tub.

Blown-out sails sometimes weren't replaced for hours and no attempt whatever was made to cleanse the 'tween decks.

At the end of two days the wind-driven fog became dispersed by another terrific gale out of the southwest. One supremely savage blast struck *Gloucester*'s substandard mainyard and, before the course it supported could be furled, it snapped squarely in the middle and dropped a wildly flapping smother of rigging and sodden canvas onto the deck. Several topmen who'd been feebly working on it were never seen again.

Gloucester, deprived of her mainsail, lost headway and started to roll so sickeningly that Captain Mitchell, gray-faced, shouted for a distress gun to be fired.

The moment George Anson realized that a disaster of the first magnitude had befallen his second most powerful ship, he ordered the squadron to assemble and lie into the wind. Only then was he able to perceive the critical condition of several other vessels.

Wager, he noted in grim anxiety, retained only the jagged stump of her mizzenmast; her main topsail yard also had carried away, leaving only a tangle of snapped halyards and braces to stream in the screaming wind.

Tryall was riding so low and sluggish in the water she must have sprung several serious leaks.

Tiny *Anna,* farthest to leeward of all the battered vessels, now fired two guns drawing attention to the fact that her bowsprit and forestay had carried away.

But of *Severn* and *Pearle* there was neither sight nor sound. Both had vanished! George Anson felt an icy sensation invade the pit of his stomach. Then he rallied. They were somewhere near. *They must be!*

3

Cape Noire

IN SEARCH OF *Pearle* and *Severn,* last seen as gray shapes fading amid a howling, blinding hailstorm, the battered, half-crippled ships fanned out dangerously far apart, risked losing contact with the flagship. Stubbornly, George Anson refused to admit that half of the expedition's fire-power had been lost to him and, in half-frozen sleeplessness, haunted *Centurion's* tiny poopdeck, swinging high above the crashing black waves, for hours on end.

What have I left undone, what wrong decisions have I taken that the squadron should be dogged by so many disasters that even Captain Arnand's vengeful ghost should feel satisfied?

Somehow it never occurred to the haggard-eyed Commander in Chief that the blame lay with those corrupt or inefficient ministers at Whitehall who had condemned him to sail in ill-found, ill-provisioned vessels and had forced him to accept worse than useless pensioners for troops. Then, as if to cap all these injustices, they'd so delayed his departure that now he was losing irreplaceable ships in battering his way around the Horn during the very worst season.

Wearily, the wide-shouldered figure elevated his gaze to watch a few luckless seamen swaying high above the deck; they were attempting, without much success, to replace the main gallant sail which had split and blown out a little earlier. How brave they were to lie out on that wildly swaying yard, clutching ice-coated footropes with toes turned purple by the pitiless cold.

In desperate indecision, the Commodore communed with himself.

How much longer dare I keep my remaining ships fanned out? If a sudden snowstorm breaks, more may get separated. What *can* have happened to *Severn* and *Pearle?*

Anson bit chilled lips, shook his muffled head several times. If they've foundered, God help all the poor souls aboard — and God help me, too; half of my effective guns have been lost. But they *can't* have sunk! Captains Legge and Murray are brave and capable above the average. They'll appear at the rendezvous.

When the tumultuous ocean commenced to darken, Anson reluctantly signaled the remaining five ships to take night stations, never more than a mile distant from the flagship. Only then did he lumber below, his cloak white with frozen spray and his body numb.

To conceal mounting anxiety and also to encourage *Centurion's* senior officers, he said, "Mr. Menzies, please convey my compliments to Colonel Cratcherode, Sailing Master Nutt and such of the lieutenants who are not on duty and invite them to take supper with me."

Menzies looked horrified. "Pardon, sir, but hadn't you better take some rest instead? You've had no sleep in a long time."

While warming frost-nipped hands over a charcoal brazier, Anson said mildly, "Mr. Menzies, I believe I'm the best judge of my condition."

At the moment *Centurion* was sailing a trifle more easily, dipping the chipped and tarnished gilt of her lion figurehead into seas which, in any other latitude, would have been deemed tremendous.

"— And, Andrew, on your way please send my steward to the galley for a pot of hot water — if poor Oldham's still about."

Anson relaxed and, grinning, passed fingers over a brown two-day stubble. "Must shave — must look a disgrace." He loathed appearing frowsy: how else could one inspire subordinates to keep up appearances?

Some little time elapsed before Oldham could twice negotiate the icy deck and fetch a steaming bucket. Meanwhile, Anson gratefully pulled at a bottle of brandy set out by Andrew Menzies.

Never in all his life, thought George Anson, had he felt more thoroughly dispirited than while, continually clutching for hand holds, he braved the great cabin's chill and began to strip off his sodden shirt and pantaloons and so noted that since he'd last been below painful chilblains had formed on his wrists and ankles.

[141]

When he peered into a mirror screwed into the bulkhead above his bunk he grimaced. "You look older than your grandsir." Deep and unfamiliar lines now were scoring his forehead, and deeper ones slanted from the corners of his mouth. "I say, Oldham, have I a dry shirt left?"

"Only one, sir. And will you wear these? They're not very warm, I fear." Oldham offered a pair of white cotton knee breeches.

Before commencing to shave, the Commodore had to hook a wiry knee about a special brace he had devised to steady himself before the mirror. Nevertheless, shaving proved to be an ordeal.

Word must have spread through the officer's country that the Commodore was shaving, for when the guests appeared, chilled and red-eyed from fatigue, all save Lieutenant Saunders had managed, at the cost of sundry nicks and cuts, to scrape away at least a part of their whiskers.

" 'Pon my word, sir," roared Lieutenant Colonel Cratcherode over the boom of seas against *Centurion*'s hull, "while I'd give half a year's pay to sight *Severn* and *Pearle*, I fear we've seen the last of 'em. To disappear like that, they must have sunk like stones."

Major Cowan, commanding the flagship's surviving handful of Marines, eagerly accepted a steaming toddy. "I'd say those aboard were lucky, damn' lucky, to have got this cursed cruise ended so quickly."

"Come, gentlemen, drink up and let us take a brighter view of the situation," Anson invited. "Personally, I am confident. If an old Indiaman like the *Wager* and a half cripple like the *Tryall* can survive, there's every reason to believe such stout men-of-war have only been blown out of sight and will soon rejoin us."

Quickly, drawn-faced Lieutenant Saunders took his cue. "Very likely we'll find both ships awaiting us off Valdivia."

Sailing Master Nutt also followed the trend towards optimism. "Aye, sir, 'tis a vast comfort to know we've rounded the Horn and must be well into the Pacific."

"How far?" intently demanded young Peter Denis, *Centurion*'s newly appointed third lieutenant.

The sailing master looked into his pewter toddy mug. "Why now, that's not easy to determine right now, Mr. Denis. Over a month has gone by since we last saw land and no one's been able to shoot the sun in a week's time. Further, we've no means of telling how strong the currents flow hereabouts — or in what direction." He

[142]

nodded a balding head as if to reassure himself. "What with all these cursed hurricanes out o' the nor'west, I allow we must have made considerable leeway to the south'ard."

In a transparent effort at heartiness, Anson said over the wind's screaming, "I'm confident that your computations will prove accurate, Mr. Nutt. So far, you've never been far wrong. Like Mr. Denis here, I'd be pleased to hear your estimate of our progress into the Pacific."

Mr. Nutt beamed, for all that he too hadn't enjoyed a whole night's sleep since he could remember. "Why, sir, I'll venture that at present we're sailing above three hundred miles off the west coast o' South America!" He turned to Lieutenant Colonel Cratcherode. "Soon, sir, you will be exercising your troops ashore."

Harsh laughter escaped the bony-faced land officer. " 'Exercise my troops?' By God, that's rich! Damme, sir, I doubt whether I've a corporal's guard left that's fit to shoulder a musket!"

Abruptly aware of Anson's level gaze, the commander of the land forces tugged his red-veined and aquiline nose. "Ha-harump! At that, I presume I *should* appear pleased the *Wager* and the *Anna* haven't disappeared."

Lieutenant Saunders, still thin and pale from his almost fatal attack of the bloody flux, inquired, "Why so, Colonel?"

"All my tents, land guns and the ammunition for shore operations are aboard the *Wager* and my reserve rations are in the *Anna*."

Anson dipped his mug into the steaming punch bowl, then raised it, dripping. "Well, gentlemen, here's to a change in the luck! Let us take comfort in the fact that we successfully have weathered the worst storms Cape Horn can offer. If Mr. Nutt's calculations prove correct, we should soon enter an area where mild weather prevails and it will be child's play to run up the coast to Señora del Socorro where, no doubt, the *Severn* and the *Pearle* will already have arrived."

He gestured his weather-beaten officers to seat themselves. After somehow bracing themselves against *Centurion*'s violent plunging, they clutched bowls to their chests and ate like the half-starved men they were.

The instant supper — a miserable affair of lukewarm stew, bread and preserves and "Scotch Coffee" made of scorched ship's biscuit — was over, the guests offered thanks, then lurched away to their quarters.

Once the last of them had departed George Anson extended himself on the stern transom, where he should have sunk immediately into the sleep of near exhaustion. Instead he lay shivering, lost in miserable conjecture over the fate of his missing ships.

Next he became tormented by doubts concerning his failure to promote Lieutenant Salt. Had he been in command could that grim veteran have kept *Pearle* on station?

A fresh worry seized the weary Commander in Chief. What would happen if the Spanish already had entered the Pacific and, having found opportunity to refit during the past five weeks, was lying in wait for his diminished, sea-torn and disease-riddled squadron.

Painfully, he gathered the damp blankets higher, turned over and, characteristically, sought for an encouraging topic to dwell upon. Well, for one thing, young Philip Saumarez was proving able far beyond expectation. The capable way he was handling jury-rigged *Tryall* commanded respect; handled less skillfully, she almost certainly must have foundered.

While his burning eyes stared into the noisy darkness, Anson tried to picture conditions aboard the ill-equipped, leaky old *Gloucester*. There he was blessed with another good Captain. It had been typical of Matthew Mitchell that only when in the direst of straits had he made a distress signal.

David Cheap, too, was proving himself a competent and loyal officer. He should go far if he could teach himself to be less bull-headed and to suppress his occasional furious fits of rage.

And what about Mr. Gerard? Before he could estimate the merchant captain's worth, he sank into that sleep so aptly described by Will Shakespeare as "Death's half-sister."

But not for long. A hand shook his shoulder as violently as a dog worries a rat. "Sir!" came Oldham's frightened voice. "Beg pardon sir, but Mr. Denis says please to hurry on deck. The *Anna's* fired a warning signal."

Shivering violently, Anson threw off his blankets and, all in an instant, became alert. "She's in distress?"

"No, sir. Not rightly so, sir," Oldham's hoarse voice answered out of the gloom. "It's just that the moon's out and land's been sighted."

"Land! Land?" Anson knuckled sleep from his eyes. "Why, that's impossible. No land lies within three hundred miles of our position."

"Aye, aye, sir." Oldham beckoned forward a fellow with ice particles showing on his beard. There were also a few chocolate-hued scurvy patches marking his cheeks. "Better you speak to his Honor."

[144]

"You say land is in sight?"

"Aye, aye, sir. Lookouts can make out a coast by the moonlight, plain as can be."

"What kind of a coast?"

"A long line of high black cliffs, sir."

Helped by Oldham, Anson began struggling into his jacket. "How far off?"

"Close by, sir, maybe half a mile off. 'Too damn' close,' says Mr. Saunders."

A frightening sense of helplessness shook Anson. *What land was this?* Probably an uncharted island; if so, it must be a large one since the seaman had spoken of a coast. Could it be the rendezvous island of Nuestra Señora del Socorro?

On the wind-lashed deck he found Saunders and Denis leaning far over the rail and peering intently past the bows. God above! An icy rivulet coursed down Anson's spine. Considerably less than a mile ahead foamed a long and sable lee shore!

As calmly as if conducting maneuvers off the Isle of Wight, Anson ordered a hoist of lantern signals — all ships to wear immediately. Half-frozen seamen skated to the braces, helms were put over, but deep within him George Anson was aware that if the wind didn't veer in his favor the expedition must be driven onto that ominous black coast.

In agony, Anson gripped the rail until, just when it seemed inevitable that his helplessly wallowing ships must perish amid a welter of surf, the wind faltered momentarily, then shifted, as it so often did in these latitudes, and commenced to blow hard *out of the northeast!*

In a flat voice Anson ordered a course shaped to the southwest.

What land had this been? Shaken to the depths of his being, he went below and sent for Sailing Master Nutt. Perhaps together they could arrive at some conclusion?

The next day dawned — and stayed — fair and warm, the first enjoyed by the expedition since running through the Straits le Maire half an eternity ago, it seemed. At noon every officer, warrant officer and midshipman possessing a sextant hurried on deck to make an observation.

After they had completed their calculations their smiles faded in rapid succession. An awful truth had become inescapable. All calcu-

lations agreed more or less that the squadron now was sailing in the
latitude of 54 degrees, 30 minutes, which meant that, far from
cruising in the boundless Pacific's safe and placid waters, the squadron had narrowly missed being lost on Cape Noire of the Tierra del
Fuego and their actual position was only a hundred miles off Cape
Horn's tip. During five horrible death and tempest-ridden weeks the
expedition had progressed *only two hundred miles* on its journey
towards the west coast of South America!

Despair settled on the decimated, hungry, hopeless and bewildered
crews like a foul and smothering blanket. When the grim tidings
spread, scurvy-stricken men remembered Captain Arnand's prediction and began to die with terrifying rapidity.

A majority of the survivors believed that Anson, having lost half
of the men in his remaining vessels, surely must bow to the inevitable
and run back into the Atlantic.

They had yet to understand George Anson.

At a hastily convened council of war the Commander in Chief informed his Captains, "Gentlemen, we owe our duty to His Majesty
and his Ministers, so must take the good with the bad.

"We shall now stand southward, this time so far that, surely, we
shall enter the Pacific, rendezvous at del Socorro and then proceed
to sack the treasure towns that invite our attention."

~ 4 ~

Mutiny on the *Wager,* I

IN THE ORLOP OF HBMS *Wager,* Joe Utting, ex-farmer, clung doggedly to life for all that the ship was being hurled about by still
another of those violent storms which for successive weeks had
racked the old Indiaman. Again her hull was booming like a beaten
gong, again her ancient timbers protested and groaned like men undergoing torture. Incurable landsman though he was, Utting guessed
how great the danger became when the storeship's mizzen topmast
carried away. But he couldn't appreciate how impossible it was to rig
a jury mast — even though Captain Cheap, haggard but indomitable, drove his strongest men until they fell, utterly exhausted.

Joe had remained alive thanks only to a constitution tough as any billy goat's. He just couldn't figure out why, despite his long bout with the bloody flux, he'd not taken the scurvy and actually was gaining strength. Perhaps his survival was due to a certain low animal cunning he'd acquired? For example, when the rows of swaying, misery-burdened hammocks remained, as usual, neglected by the loblolly boys, Surgeon Elliott and Captain Oakley, physician to the Land Forces, he would ease out of his hammock and skulk about, stuffing an old stocking with food ignored by the dead or dying. It pleased Joe inordinately that he should have thought of this.

Call him a "Jimmy Dux" would they? The ex-farmer grinned to himself even though the storeship just then lurched over the crest of a gigantic comber and began plunging down its anticline with sickening speed. "I'll show 'em! By God, I'll still be drivin' straight furrows when all these seafarin' bastards are fish food."

He also learned to steal extra blankets and pull the clothes off a defunct Pensioner before the loblollies got to him. Soon Joe had hidden, behind a chest of muskets, a good supply of stockings, shoes and shirts he could sell should the scurvy ever let up and a normal routine be re-established. Hee! Hee! He was in a fair way towards becoming a haberdasher.

Presently Joe became aware that no ordinary storm was tossing *Wager* about. Must be a full-force tempest. It blew so bitterly cold he reckoned it must have been honed on the South Pole.

An officer bellowed excitedly down the main companion, "All able men on deck!"

Immediately Utting sought his hammock. Maybe it wasn't so bad being a Jimmy Dux? Furtively, he watched seamen, half-frozen and staggering with fatigue, being herded on deck by the use of canes and colts.

Briefly Joe wondered how his friend, brash Harry Cozens, who'd been newly appointed a midshipman, might be faring. Actually, Cozens, drenched and chilled to the bone, was clinging to the main shrouds, waist deep in frigid water that kept sweeping across the supply ship's deck. Teeth chattering, he saw but could not prevent a pair of men from being swept overboard.

With one hand Cozens attempted to shield his eyes from a sudden squall of hail. The stones stung like so many hornets. By peering between stiff, dripping fingers, the midshipman managed after a bit to make out *Centurion*. She was reeling along a mile ahead, with the tatters of her burst topsails streaming from crazily swaying yards.

Then, causing a report like that of a heavy cannon, *Wager*'s mizzenmast snapped off at the hounds, tottered and then sagged over the starboard rail. By the time Mr. Midshipman Cozens and a handful of ice-covered men succeeded in hacking free a tangle of spare canvas and rigging, neither HBMS *Centurion* — nor any other vessel — remained visible.

To *Wager*'s company the night that followed proved to be the most terrifying of all. Huge seas kept cascading over the bulwarks to boil about the aged Indiaman's decks. They shattered the forecastle doors and again carried away both heads. Three more men were lost overboard, screaming for rescue.

Morning found the Indiaman struggling quite alone among tumultuous and patternless cross seas. To even the stupidest crew member it was evident that *Wager* was now a cripple, a crazy ship in that her mainmast's starboard shrouds, as well as the plates supporting them, had carried away. Gone also were the storeship's main royal and gallant yards. Worst of all, *Wager*'s foremast now sagged ominously towards her bowsprit.

Captain Cheap, having remained on deck all night, cursed furiously when only eight scarecrows appeared to stand the Morning Watch. The usual muster should have turned out at least thirty hands. Only eight! Damnation! This meant that a lot of well men must be malingering.

Thick neck swelling, David Cheap struggled below. "All well officers, men and servants turn out!" he bellowed. "Sick men to the pumps! Goddam it, jump, else we'll founder!"

Harder than anyone else, Captain Cheap drove his ax at the hampering tangles of rigging that encumbered the deck; pitilessly, he ordered blue-faced and semiconscious men to replace essential halyards and braces. Next, he superintended repairs to the steering gear. All the while he damned Cummins, *Wager*'s always surly carpenter, for his lack of initiative.

The men worked slowly, their fingers white and dead-looking through constant soaking.

Back on deck, Cheap snarled at his first lieutenant who was struggling to supplement the longboat's lashings. "Dammit, Mr. Beans, this is no week-end jaunt off Blackpool! Can't you set an example?"

Since he was suffering from a number of broken ribs which caused every breath he drew to stab like a dagger's thrust, Lieutenant Robert Beans, not unnaturally, cast his Captain a murderous look. Fortunately, it went unobserved.

"Get cracking, you lazy dog!" Cheap bellowed up at Midshipman Cozens, who, numbed with cold and fatigue, was working on the main gallant yard. "Hurry those snail-footed swine and secure the mainyard before it carries away!"

As, gradually, the hurricane blew itself out, Captain Cheap restored a semblance of discipline and, presently, *Wager* was able to carry sufficient canvas to regain headway and so facilitate the carrying out of essential repairs. Cheap then ordered several slightly injured seamen into the rigging with orders to keep a sharp lookout for any sign of the squadron.

When by six bells of the first Dog Watch no sail had been reported, Captain Cheap retired to his cabin and, after consulting his charts, but no other officer, he ordered a new course set — due north.

At once Sailing Master Jones protested. "Sir! With all due respect, I feel that we've not made near enough westing from Cape Noire to risk steering due north along a barbarous lee shore."

"'Damn you for an impertinent rascal! Hold your tongue," Cheap rasped. "When I want your opinion, by God, I'll invite it." Less belligerently he added, "I am acting on explicit orders from the Commodore; I mean to follow them to the letter!"

Midshipman Cozens stepped forward, long yellow hair coiling wetly about his throat. "Leave to speak, sir?"

"Granted."

"May I say that I believe Mr. Jones's objection is a sound one? Sailing as blind as we are, it would be hazardous to sail a northerly —"

David Cheap's bulldog's jaw purpled, rendered prominent the strong blond bristles covering it. "Silence! How dare you question my decision?"

Surprisingly, Cozens's hard gray eyes did not waver, a fact noted by Captain Pemberton, who commanded the surviving handful of land forces.

"Damme, Cozens," snapped Cheap, "you talk too big for a snottie. Possibly a return to the fo'castle would likely remind you of your place? How'd you like that?" He wheeled to confront Pemberton and

Marine Lieutenants Campbell and Hamilton. "Surely you must understand why I *must* reach Valdivia with all speed?"

"Valdivia! I thought we were to meet at Socorro," growled the sailing master.

"Valdivia was given me as an alternate rendezvous."

A lieutenant of the land forces who was nursing a broken hand in a sling queried brusquely, "Why such haste to reach Valdivia?"

Cheap glared. "Why? Damme, ain't I got your precious artillery, shot and ammunition on board? Must be ready for operations on land."

"'Operations on land'?" sneered Captain Pemberton. "You're a ruddy optimist, Captain, as well as bull-headed for countering your sailing master's advice."

For a moment it appeared that Cheap would strike Pemberton, but he turned away instead and crossed the quarterdeck, thick body lurching to the storeship's sluggish motion — she was leaking badly thanks to a number of seams which had opened below the waterline.

Tramping below, Cheap, in a fury, ordered the boatswain's mates indiscriminately to dump the sick out of their hammocks and drive them to work at the pump handles.

Joe Utting was not in the least surprised to see a pair of scurvied men whom he'd overheard speaking in strong voices suddenly stagger and pitch onto the deck where they died almost immediately. It now was a well-known fact that even the least exertion would kill a badly scurvied man, no matter how strong he looked.

While making his way below, Captain Pemberton snarled, "Something ought to be done or that arrogant jackass, Cheap, will be the death of us all!"

Cozens cast the Army officer a quick, sidewise glance. "You really believe so, sir?"

"Aye. Although I'm no sailor, thank God, I've an instinct which warns that Captain Cheap is about to venture too near the mainland." Pemberton wrung water from a limp red muffler and coughed hollowly. "Doesn't it stand to reason that this last hurricane's driven us far to eastward?"

"I'd say so, sir. But I'm only a snottie, and who listens to such?"

Lieutenant Beans tramped into the wardroom's frigid gloom and snatched a rum bottle from its rack. He took a big drink before confronting his fellow officers. "Know what I think? I believe that Captain Cheap intends to desert the Commodore and start plundering the Spaniards on his own."

"Why so?" demanded the injured Marine officer.

"Not having to divide prize money, he'd stand to win a great fortune," Cozens answered quickly.

Unexpectedly, Captain Pemberton shook a blunt, iron-gray head. "You're wrong there, Mr. Cozens. In my opinion your precious Captain's a stubborn fool, but, to grant the Devil his due, he's no self-seeking knave; just a blockhead who's determined, at all costs, to carry out what he conceives to be his orders."

While clinging to a stanchion Robert Beans, *Wager*'s only surviving lieutenant, gnawed bluish lips. "Aye, I agree something must be done to persuade the Captain to alter this northerly course."

"That's only common sense," Cozens agreed. "It's plain that Captain Cheap is deluded, but dedicated to his conception of duty. But how many of you gentlemen wish to lose your lives because of that?"

Snapped Captain Pemberton, "Then what's to be done?"

"Tonight, let each one of us try to foresee what steps should be taken and meet tomorrow."

The older officers eyed this bold and muscular midshipman with something less than approval before shuffling off to their duties.

During the night yet another violent gale blew out of the west in white-headed fury and carried away *Wager*'s laboriously replaced topsails. With her canvas blown out, the crippled storeship was driven before the blast, helpless under bare poles. And then the foretopmast fell. Captain Cheap at once was clawing his way forward along the spray-lashed deck bawling, "All hands on deck to clear away the wreckage!"

Less than a dozen men, mostly petty officers, responded. David Cheap worked with a fury. Powerful legs braced, he heaved at a mare's nest of broken yards and running gear. He had lost his hat and his scant pale hair stood out from his scalp, stiff as wire.

"Come on, ye damned spineless jellyfish! Prize up that yard! Heave, you whoresons, heave when I give the word! Am I to do all this by myself?"

Cozens, struggling to replace a snapped halyard, couldn't suppress a sudden, if brief, admiration when he saw the Captain splash through frigid water up to his waist and, at the risk of smashed fingers, cut loose a heavy block that was banging against the bulwarks.

Just then a sea more mountainous than the rest smote the supply ship on her quarter and caused her to reel so violently that the Captain lost his balance and was hurled, with arms and legs flailing, down the forward companionway.

When the ship's surgeon finally reached David Cheap his face was ashen and he was wheezing in his efforts to keep from shrieking over the pains shooting through a grotesquely dislocated shoulder. Despite Mr. Elliott's pleas Captain Cheap struggled back on deck just in time to hear a frightened shout of "Land ho! Land ho!"

"Where away?" Sailing Master Jones screamed over the tumult.

"A lee shore lies off the port bow, sir."

Seeing that *Wager* was being driven straight towards that deadly black streak on the horizon, Cheap, his injured arm slung through a leather belt, somehow worked his way forward to superintend the swaying aloft of a new foreyard.

"Work for your lives, damn you," he panted. "If this ship can't be made to wear, there'll be a lot of new widows in England before night!"

Aided by a few stalwarts, Midshipmen Cozens and Byron managed to cross the yard and bend on a new topsail.

Once *Wager* got under way again, Quartermaster Richard Noble and his mates managed to bear away in a southerly direction, crowding the threatened vessel offshore. Only then would Captain Cheap, semidelirious with pain, consent to go below. However, it proved impossible to get him to his own quarters, so cluttered by debris was the companionway. The sufferer therefore had to be berthed in Mr. Elliott's cabin where the ominous *clank-clank* of the hard-worked pumps was especially audible.

Terrified and cowering in his hammock, Joe Utting joined the really sick in praying aloud when word was passed that the new foresail had blown out and *Wager* again was at the hurricane's mercy.

All night long the leaking, terribly punished storeship pitched, rolled and wallowed until, at four o'clock on the morning of May 14, 1741, she struck.

The first impact was not violent — it seemed only as if yet another titanic wave had struck her — but then followed a series of grinding, crunching noises which ended as *Wager* slid off the reef and, because her rudder had been torn off, staggered blindly on towards her doom.

Badly bilged, *Wager* began to fill so rapidly that Midshipman the

Honorable John Byron little suspected that he might live to become the grandfather of a world-famous poet. This seemed especially unlikely when, out of the confusion, the *boom! boom-m!* of great seas breaking over invisible reefs began to resound on all sides. The staccato snapping of tattered canvas attested that *Wager*, with all sails gone, must be yawing blindly through a veritable maze of reefs.

At his lookout's station in the foreshrouds, Midshipman Byron tightened a line lashed about his slim waist and prayed as he would never pray again. The world no longer retained recognizable aspects: there was no horizon, no sky, no sea to be seen. All was black confusion.

Even the force of gravity seemed no longer to operate. Again and again the deck fell from under Byron's chilled feet so violently that he seemed to linger, unsupported, in mid-air. He guessed that he was about to drown. What would his sensations be? People who'd almost perished in that fashion had claimed that the sensation wasn't at all unpleasant — something like drifting off in a hazy dream.

When *Wager* struck for a second and last time the impact was terrible. Men were knocked flat, weakened topmasts came tumbling down, waves now rushed freely over the bulwarks, air roared up and out of the companions as water rushed into the hull through great holes puncturing her bilges.

Although titanic rollers continued to hammer her, the wrecked storeship no longer moved; she was too firmly wedged between two huge rocks.

From below arose piteous screams. The sick were clamoring for rescue — and the shrieks of cowards in the presence of Death were terrible.

Sailing Master Jones, however, attempted to set an example. Byron later remembered hearing him shout, "Friends, let us not be discouraged. Have you never seen a ship amongst breakers before? Let us try to push her through them. Come, lend a hand! Here is a sheet and here is a brace. Lay hold. I don't doubt that we may yet drive her near enough to the land to save our lives."

The helmsman, too, Byron later wrote in his "Narrative":

Applied himself to his duty with Customary Serenity and could not be persuaded to desert his Post so long as the Ship held together.

The uncertainty was not of long duration. With a crunching roar HBMS *Wager* was driven further up between the two great rocks

[153]

and there remained, let gigantic combers hammer her as they would.

The night of horror dragged on. Towards the end of it the master-at-arms struggled up to Lieutenant Beans and shouted something.

"Can't hear you!" shouted Beans, though his broken ribs hurt horribly from the effort.

"I said — men are breaking into arms chests and are going wild with liquor!"

～ 5 ～
Mutiny on the *Wager*, II

THE COMING OF DAYLIGHT was accompanied by no abating of the wind's force. The only encouragement it brought was the sight of a wide, white sandy beach lying only a couple of hundred yards distant, as a break in that otherwise jagged, black and surf-smothered shore. However, to land on this beach for the moment was quite impossible. Everyone could see enormous combers thundering up its length, hurling sheets of spray over dunes covered by wind-bent sandgrass and into the tops of stunted trees showing beyond them.

Those of the injured and scurvy-stricken who were able struggled out of their hammocks and crawled towards the main companion ladder. Only a few succeeded in reaching the deck so constant were the torrents of sea water pouring into their faces; most of them fell and died a miserable death.

Joe Utting was one who managed to struggle aloft, where he clung to a cannon and listened stupidly to bursts of insane laughter. Wild-eyed men, squalling in utter panic, appeared and began splashing about, often up to their waists in swirling water.

A hairy giant wearing a gentleman's bright green velvet coat burst out of the forecastle and lurched about waving a cutlass at the storm and roaring defiance at the world.

Presently he bore down on the cowering ex-farmer and, whirling up his blade, roared, "Down! Down on yer knees. Kneel to your King, you bloody serf! I'm King Walter the First of this land, by right of discovery!"

Utting, too weak to stand any longer, knelt readily and raised supplicating hands. "Spare me, Yer Gracious Majesty!" he quavered, long gray hair whipping about his eyes.

The madman veered away and began to hack first at the rail and then fell to slashing at loose rope ends. Trembling violently, Joe Utting watched him in the green shirt veer over to a bald old Pensioner who, clinging to a stay, had been praying at the top of his voice.

"Down before your Sovereign Lord! Down I say!"

"I kneel to none save God and my true King," gasped the graybeard. "And be damned to you for a mutinous scoundrel!"

Roaring obscenities, the berserker whirled up his cutlass but Midshipman Cozens, pale gray eyes ablaze, wrenched away the blade and smote the madman across his face with its flat; he dropped, howling and bleeding, onto his knees.

"Go forward, you fool!" Then, unexpectedly, he added, "From now on *I* rule here!"

Meanwhile *Wager*'s deck, as Mr. Midshipman Byron later on described it, "became a scene of horrid confusion."

Some men, when they saw breakers foaming and spouting all around the wrecked storeship, went insane and rushed blindly about until their strength gave out. One fellow became so terrified that he mounted the rail and would have thrown himself overboard had not Sailing Master Jones grabbed him by the waist and hauled him, gibbering, back to precarious safety.

Efforts to restore discipline were made. Captain Cheap, on emerging from a coma, demanded to be carried on deck, roared this and that command — to which no one paid any heed. Lieutenant Beans, gray-faced with the pain, staggered about the deck in company with Captain Pemberton. Both officers were carrying blunderbusses in addition to several pistols stuck into their belts. Next, Midshipman Alexander Campbell appeared carrying an armful of firearms which he shared with the sailing master, Midshipman Byron and Pensioner Officers Fielding and Ewers.

Lieutenant Beans disappeared below and returned almost at once to shout over the ceaseless thundering rush of the waves, "Captain's orders — cut away all masts — ship won't struggle so hard."

Man after man refused duty until, grimly, the officers were forced to club recalcitrants over the head with pistol butts. For nearly exhausted men, toiling in water up to their waists, it was desperately slow work, but somehow the fore- and mainmasts finally were hacked through and sent grinding over the side. The mizzen, of course, long since had carried away, leaving only a jagged stump a few feet high to mark its former position.

Seeing how things were going, Midshipmen Campbell and Byron and Marine officers Hamilton and Campbell jammed their weapons into their belts, grabbed axes and fell to work.

To clear away the tangled mess of shrouds, sodden canvas, snapped rigging and fallen yards took much longer for, the moment they were not threatened with immediate death, the crew ran below, towards the sounds of conflict and of drunken singing.

Some mutineers now broke into the spirit room to secure a fresh supply of liquor. They found plenty since *Wager* was carrying the squadron's reserve supply. Midshipman Byron noted that among the most dangerously drunk were the boatswain, John King and Gunner Bulkley.

Once the storm commenced to abate seamen began to come out, some so drunk that they fell unconscious and soon drowned in water surging about the foredeck.

Although half-smothered in spray, Sailing Master Jones clambered onto the beak and, on the Captain's orders, laboriously chopped through the starboard bower anchor's cable; it had been let go by someone as soon as daylight had disclosed the storeship's situation. Cheap intended that, if the wreck were lifted off the rocks, nothing should prevent her being driven onto the comparative safety of the sandy beach.

Presently inebriated seamen appeared, screaming and grimacing, on the forecastle wearing grotesque bits of stolen finery or swathed in gaudy yard goods intended for trade with the natives of lands which HBMS *Wager* now would never visit.

A moment later Captain Cheap succeeded in reaching the deck. Lips livid and writhing, heavy features scarlet with fever, he fired a pistol into the deck and bellowed, "Return to your duty, you mutinous dogs! Prepare to launch my barge!"

Most of the men on deck scuttled below, but a few, threatened by Campbell's and Byron's pistols, began unlashing the barge. It seemed like a good idea to get off this wreck, so Joe Utting crawled slowly forward and tried to help, but he looked so feeble that Midshipman Campbell sent him off to huddle, disconsolate, under the weather bulwarks.

"— Can't understand it," Byron panted to young Campbell.

"Who'd guess that steady men like Shoreham, Stook and Pitman would mutiny?"

The second midshipman licked a row of skinned knuckles. "They no' mutinous, John — ainly crazed. Small wonder, when ye think back on what they've suffered."

No one paid attention to bodies washing about the deck. They knew by now that, eventually, a sea would roll them over the shattered bulwarks and lose them to sight.

When, finally, the barge lay plunging alongside, Captain Cheap ordered his quartermaster, one Richard Noble, to proceed ashore and reconnoiter the vicinity; this seemed advisable since a peaked roof was discernible among the dunes.

Lieutenant Beans said, "Shouldn't you go yourself, sir? The ship can't hold together very much longer."

"I'll not go — nor you either, you cowardly dog! By God, we'll be the last to leave this vessel!"

Once the barge, manned by a few sober hands, pulled away, plunging and swaying amid the rollers, Cheap sank onto the streaming deck and had to be carried below, again raving in delirium.

Lieutenant Robert Beans, gnawing methodically at a ship's biscuit, announced to the assembled midshipmen and warrant officers, "Soon as the barge returns to report it's safe to go ashore, all hands will leave this wreck. Therefore, you had best go below, gentlemen, and secure warm clothes and other useful gear."

Midshipman Harry Cozens who had been working hard to free the other smallboats was first to descend the main ladder and barely avoided the thrust of a bloody-bladed boarding pike. Cozens at once shot the man down but had no opportunity to ascertain how seriously he was hurt, for at that instant the wreck gave a violent, heart-stilling lurch, whereupon water began to gush through *Wager*'s splintering side with such violence that he and Byron were forced to abandon their search for clothing and hurry back on deck.

The forecastle now was resounding to yells and drunken cater-wauling.

"Listen to those stupid fools!" Cozens snarled. "They'll drown like caged rats come a little while; it'll serve 'em damned well right."

The yellow-haired midshipman's prediction quickly became fulfilled when, abruptly, *Wager*'s center of balance shifted and her bow was plunged under water.

[157]

Now barrels, casks and bales commenced to float up through hatches from which the covers had been ripped to serve as life rafts and began to roll about the debris-littered gun deck. Unfortunately, some of the casks contained spirits, which the more reckless mutineers immediately broached. Ignoring the threats and blows of the officers and a few loyal seamen, they dipped heads into the rum and began to lap, but they howled like starving wolves when the alcohol burned their eyes.

Because Captain Cheap still was raving in the surgeon's cabin Lieutenant Beans and Sailing Master Jones marshaled their followers under the break of the quarterdeck to await the barge's return. There were few sick men among them; most of these had died or had been swept overboard.

When the barge failed to return by noon, Lieutenant Beans grew fearful lest its occupants had been killed or captured, so launched the gig. *Wager*'s lieutenant also took with him Midshipman Byron and Captain Pemberton, both half-dazed with fatigue and a well-armed party of seamen.

Shortly after the smallboat had reached the shore Captain Cheap regained his senses, but when told that neither barge nor gig had returned, he ranted like a madman and in a foaming rage ordered Midshipman Cozens and the boatswain to launch the remaining boats and otherwise prepare to abandon the wreck.

The boatswain, John King, thoroughly but not obviously intoxicated, spat onto the deck, then truculently eyed the Captain. "Who the 'ell are you to give orders any more?"

"What do you mean by that, you insolent dog?"

"Our pay stopped the minute your bloody bull-headedness drove us onto the rocks — and so did our duty. We're free men now and bound by no regulations. So, Mister Cheap," he laughed raucously, "me and the lads ain't goin' ashore 'til we've drunk our fill and are damn' good and ready."

Purple-faced, Captain Cheap attempted to arise but proved able only to sag back onto the surgeon's sweat-sodden pillows wheezing, "I'll see you hanged for this, King, damned if I don't! You know the penalty for mutiny. Mr. Cozens! Arrest this rogue!"

But the blond midshipman had vanished.

Under the direction of Midshipman Isaac Morris and the two Marine lieutenants, loyal seamen and a few soldiers managed with considerable difficulty to lower Captain Cheap, only semiconscious, into the cutter which was rising and falling as much as fifteen feet alongside the shattered storeship.

While preparing to man another smallboat, Cozens growled at King and the gunner, "You're a pair of prize fools! This ain't the way to go about winning our way!"

"Ah-h, go drown yer 'ead in the surf," hiccoughed Gunner Bulkley. "This ship ain't about to break up."

"Stay then and be damned to you," Cozens snapped, then dropped into the second cutter's stern sheets beside Purser John Harvey.

Over his shoulder Cozens counted fifteen men yelling obscene farewells over the rail. How many more were below he'd no notion but became much too occupied in guiding his cutter through the angry, white-headed surf to speculate further.

While steering for a break in the white-headed line of reefs ahead he recognized the outlines of the two boats sent off earlier. They were drawn up on the beach and had men standing, sitting, lying down around them. Good! Evidently there were no enemies to be reckoned with. A few of the men on shore were trying to haul what looked to be bread casks above the waves' reach.

In order to see into the boat next ahead, Harry Cozens braced himself and stood up, holding the tiller between his knees. Captain Cheap appeared to have lost consciousness again, for he lay slumped on the bottom gratings with his head propped against Midshipman Morris's thin knees.

Several half-submerged bodies were overtaken, also sizable pieces of wreckage and items from the cargo.

When he felt solid ground beneath his feet Joe Utting sank flat and, sobbing with relief, dug fingers into the sandy earth. Subconsciously he realized that such soil wouldn't be much good for farming. All the same, he patted the cold ground then caressed a bunch of sand grass just as if it had been a prize pig.

Midshipman Byron came up using a piece of driftwood for a crutch; he'd wrenched his knee while boarding the cutter.

Said he, "My poor fellow, I know you are near the end of your tether but can't you find enough strength to help some of the sick ashore?"

Utting slyly raised red-rimmed eyes, coughed and shook his head. "I fear I be too feeble, sir, but, come the morrow, Joe Utting'll be doing his pore best. Ye can count on that."

Joe, crouching somewhat apart on a dune top, noticed a corpse

[159]

rolling leadenly about in the surf and noted that the dead man still was wearing a brass-hilted cutlass buckled about him.

Quite without forming a plan, the ex-farmer peered cautiously about and, perceiving that everyone's attention seemed to be fixed on the second cutter's struggle to win through the surf, he slunk down the beach.

Although the icy salt water stung cuts on his scrawny legs, Joe waded out to the cadaver and pulled the cutlass free of its sheath. He wished he'd sufficient strength to undo the belt buckle and so salvage the scabbard as well, but he couldn't, so, dripping, he hid behind a hummock topped with coarse, wind-twisted grass.

He barely was able to bury the weapon before overpowering weakness seized him and he truly collapsed onto the sandy ground. Gasping and shivering, he lay still until he heard feet drawing near. Stricken with nameless fears, he opened his eyes a crack, then emitted a slow sigh of relief. Bearing down on him was no drunken mutineer but Private Nathaniel Robinson, a one-armed Pensioner he'd been friendly with.

"You all right, chum?" Robinson hunkered down, rheumy gray eyes narrowing.

"Aye, will be after a bit of rest."

"Hungry? I got a ship's biscuit. 'Tis a mite soaked but yer welcome to it."

"Why, that's main kind o' ye, Nat." Joe glanced quickly at the spot where he had buried the blade and felt reassured to perceive how well he'd concealed it. "I *am* a might peckish, I'll admit." Although his few remaining teeth were loose from incipient scurvy he chewed eagerly. "I'll not forget this," he assured the scrawny figure in the frayed red coat, " 'tis the only kindness anyone's done me since I got 'pressed back o' the Sheaf o' Wheat."

The first chance he got, Midshipman Byron confessed to his journal:

> Getting to Land was the highest Attainment of our Wishes. Yet, all Things considered, our Condition was but little mended by the Change. Which every way We looked, a Scene of Horror presented itself: on one side the Wreck (in which was all We had in the World to Support and Subsist us), together with a Boisterous Sea presented us with the most Dreary Prospect. The Land did not wear much more Favorable Appearance: Desolute and Barren without Sign of Culture, We could hope to receive little other Benefit of it other

than the Preservation which it Afforded us from the Sea. It must be Confessed that this was a Great and Merciful Deliverance from Immediate Destruction; but then We had Wet, Cold and Hunger to Struggle with, and no visible Remedy against these Evils.

~~ 6 ~~

Mutiny on the *Wager,* III

A QUICK COUNT revealed that one hundred and thirty officers and men somehow had made their way to shore, all in deplorable condition. However, soon fresh fish and the eggs of seagulls, plover, ducks and geese — plus plenty of fresh clean water and an abundance of what was termed "scurvy grass" — caused the less badly stricken to start recovering.

The Marine lieutenants took fowling pieces and crawled up to a small brackish pond on which rested hundreds of ducks and geese. At first these proved to be utterly fearless, but they did not long remain so. As the result of four shots, quickly delivered, some eighty birds lay dead or wounded and flapping wildly about.

"What a pack of rogues and ragamuffins we've become," snuffled Captain Pemberton, bending his head so that Mr. Elliott might lance a huge boil on his neck. "Egad, at home I'd order such raffish characters to be shot on sight."

"Including yourself, no doubt," grinned Lieutenant Beans while clumsily braiding his greasy black hair into a queue. He kept grimacing at the pain the effort was costing him.

"Aye. To look at, we're as fine a collection of gallows birds as ever was haled under Tyburn Tree." Sailing Master Jones's teeth gleamed in the depths of a week-old beard. He was wearing a bloodied bandage about his forehead, having had it cracked by a falling spar.

During the second day after the wreck the officers — Captain Cheap still remained delirious with pain — directed the construction of crude shelters from the masses of rigging, sails and spars which began drifting ashore. These, however, accomplished very little towards shielding the soaked and half-famished survivors from a frigid wind which seemed never to falter. The castaways suffered greatly that night because all driftwood in the immediate vicinity quickly was consumed and nobody had thought to send out a wooding party.

[161]

Mr. Elliott, the former horse doctor, insisted — often at the point of a blunderbuss — that the sickest men be put into some Indian's stone and thatch fishing hut. It was the roof of this structure which, sighted from the wreck, had caused so much alarm.

Shortly after reaching shore, Midshipmen Byron, Morris and Campbell took it upon themselves to search the hut and found a large supply of lances, arrows and what appeared to be war clubs. So the inhabitants of this coast were of a warlike disposition?

Campbell looked anxious. "God help us if the savages return and discover us in our present condition. Remember those cannibals that damned old Arnand mentioned?"

"Aye," agreed Morris. "All too well. What do you think?"

"'Tis possible," Byron agreed, "so I fancy we'd better conduct a reconnaissance inland. There may be more dwellings or perhaps even a village somewhere in yonder woods."

The self-appointed scouts, however, discovered nothing alarming, or even of interest, only scrubby trees and coarse grass.

Before returning to the beach, Byron struggled to the top of a high dune and remained there quite a while studying the sea.

"Nice view, eh?" grunted Morris.

"I was hoping to sight one of our ships," Byron explained while wiping streaming eyes.

Spat Alex Campbell vehemently, "There's not a bloody earthly chance we'll ever sight one again. They've all foundered or been wrecked like us — if they were that unlucky."

The food found on shore wasn't nearly sufficient for so many mouths once the wild fowl grew wary and their eggs were consumed. Therefore, everybody went hungry until casks of salted meat washed ashore from the wreck. It lay less than a quarter mile off the long, crescent-shaped beach which at either end terminated in towering rock pinnacles.

By noon of the second day drunken noises subsided aboard *Wager*. The dismasted wreck lay, forlorn and silent, with her bows lost to sight among the reefs that forever boiled about her.

Captain Cheap, sprawled in the salvage tent upon a bale of sodden trade goods, caught up a musketoon when Midshipman Morris burst in.

"Sir, sir!" he cried after belatedly offering a salute, "those men who stayed on the wreck —"

"What of them?"

"They're signaling, sir, that they wish to be taken off."

The Captain's undershot jaw shut with an audible *click!* "Do they so? Well, those precious rogues asked to drown, so by God, I'll accommodate 'em, though for mutineers 'tis too easy a death."

"No doubt, sir," agreed Lieutenant Beans, who had just entered. "But may I remind you, sir, that our carpenter, gunner and boatswain are out there and that we'll soon stand in need of their services?"

"Dammit, hold your tongue! I can see that without being told." Stifling a groan, Cheap arose and swayed over to grip the tent's flap. For a long moment he stared out over the water. "Harumph! Sea's too rough to chance sending out a boat now. Let 'em swill brandy a while longer."

Soon Midshipman Cozens appeared, swaggering over the trampled sand, his yellow hair whipping free in the glacial wind. With half an eye Beans could tell he'd been drinking. Face flushed, Cozens confronted the ghastly pale captain. "What's this? You say you won't send out a boat?"

Cheap stared him full in the face. "Say 'sir' when you address a superior, damn you!"

" 'Sir' or not. Do you refuse to send out a boat — sir?"

"In my opinion it's too dangerous. Remember, Mr. Cozens, my word is law."

"Oh no it's not!" Cozens placed hands akimbo, cocked his head insolently to one side. "Not any more! All the hands know their pay was stopped the instant the ship struck. They all say, 'No pay, no duty.' "

A trace of red began to creep out along the Captain's wax-hued cheekbones. "Do you really credit that, you poor deluded idiot?"

"Aye, sir, and so does every man-jack in the crew."

His attention attracted by angry voices, Joe Utting looked up from a pile of sodden sailcloth which he was exploring to find the makings of a shelter. The Captain, he felt sure, was going to strike Midshipman Cozens, yet he only balled his fists while shouting, "By the Lord Harry! You'll rue this insubordination and so will anyone else who dares to question my orders. Go tell your fellow mutineers they can threaten all they please but I'll send no boat out to save treacherous dogs at the risk of loyal lives. Get out of my sight!"

Next morning the wind still was blowing a gale, so when Lieutenant Beans attempted to launch a cutter it promptly was overturned and its crew only narrowly avoided drowning.

Through a spyglass, Midshipman John Byron watched despair manifest itself aboard the crumbling wreck. Chilled lips compressed, he noticed activity on that small part of the forecastle which yet remained above the surface. He saw *Wager*'s gunner ram a powder charge down the bore of a bow chaser.

His companion, Isaac Morris, while shielding his eyes from stinging sand particles, growled, "Bet they're going to signal 'immediate danger.' "

Morris was proved wrong, for when the gun boomed, a roundshot came screaming over the water and, just missing the Captain's tent, crashed into the scrub woods.

Beside himself with rage, Captain Cheap stormed out of his tent, musket in hand. "Damn their mutinous souls to hell! They'll not intimidate me. No boat shall put out till *I* order so."

By afternoon the weather had moderated a little, so Captain Cheap ordered a cutter sent out because *Wager* obviously was breaking up. It soon returned conveying twelve mutineers.

The rescued men presented a curious sight. Evidently King, Bulkley and the rest had been looting the officers' quarters since many of these hairy fellows were wearing velvet dress coats trimmed with gold or silver lace. Further, they had adorned themselves with brooches, rings and gold watch chains.

Cummins, the carpenter, had jammed an ostrich-trimmed tricorne onto his greasy brown head while his mate wore a clump of ostrich plumes which now drooped like a whipped puppy's tail.

While the cutter was being run up the beach, Midshipman Byron noted an odd frozen expression on Lieutenant Beans's long and somber face, and saw that he hurried off to the Captain's tent which was being guarded by a slovenly Marine.

Those mutineers who had remained on board jumped onto the sand and, apparently by prearrangement, formed into a compact group. They were armed to the teeth and looked ready, even eager, to use their weapons. Boatswain King, clad in a light-blue silk tunic under a baldric of red-gold damask, was ugly-drunk. He swaggered about brandishing a gentleman's dress sword and attempted to form his companions into a column. But they could only reel about clutching muskets and musketoons. Before King could get them under way Captain Cheap bellowed from the crowd's rear.

"Make way! Damn your eyes!" Quite unarmed except for a heavy cane, he plowed through the ragged crowd like a bull through an alder thicket. Somehow, he had urged his horribly swollen shoulder under a scarlet frock coat and wore his hat jammed down over bushy brows.

Amazed, the men fell back. Byron thought at the moment, and later wrote, "Never since have I witnessed a more inspiring example of personal bravery."

Cheap marched over to the boatswain, whirled up his cane and, although Bulkley attempted to parry the blow with his little dress sword, he failed, and was tumbled unconscious onto the trampled sand. The bulldog-faced Captain paid the fallen ringleader not the least attention and instead confronted the rest of the gaudily clad mutineers.

"Drop those weapons this instant! *Drop them,* I say!"

To everyone's amazement the men newly come ashore obeyed, tossing their weapons onto the sand beside Bulkley's sprawled figure.

"Off with those stolen clothes, you filthy thieves!" Although the castaways behind him muttered ominously, Captain Cheap strode about, liberally using his cane. "Now, by the eternal God, you'll return to duty and will draw half rations for a month! Thank your stars that today I feel mercifully disposed!"

Had Captain Cheap known about the terrible scenes encountered by Lieutenant Beans on boarding the wreck, most assuredly he would not have been so lenient. The bodies of several murdered men had been discovered lying about the deck; this was bad enough, but that the mutineers, in their alcoholic frenzy, wantonly had ruined much useful gear was unforgivable.

Midshipman Cozens, on the edge of the crowd, muttered to his crony, Quartermaster Noble, "Seems I've been wrong, Dick, our beloved Captain remains a force to be reckoned with."

Eventually a number of Army tents drifted ashore as a part of a floating island composed of boxes, barrels, broken gun caissons and other wreckage. So at last all survivors were afforded shelter — of a sort. In one of the largest tents the precious food and liquor supplies were stored and, supposedly, guarded night and day by Marines. All the same, it was successfully pillaged time and again, usually with the guards' connivance.

Thanks to Joe Utting's new-found cunning, he, Nat Robinson and another Invalid-Pensioner named Benton fared better than most. On recalling the advantages of a root cellar back on the farm, Joe dug a hole into the lee side of a dune then lined it with old blankets and ruined sails. Once a driftwood fire was kindled before its entrance the shelter proved to be very smoky, but much warmer than a canvas tent, which would admit icy air and threatened to collapse under heavy gusts of wind.

Shortly after the three had set up housekeeping, Benton succumbed to scurvy, but Joe said nothing about it and continued to draw the dead man's ration.

To take Benton's place, Utting, after considerable deliberation, selected a weedy cook's apprentice named Butterfield. Although the pimply youth complained eternally about being hungry, he had been the cook's "chicken" so the latter generally looked the other way when Butterfield stole an extra ration or two.

"Reckon we'll all leave our bones here," Butterfield whined extending clawlike hands to the fire. "Ain't near enough food coming out o' the wreck to feed us all. The best o' what the hunting parties bring in gets took by the officers and the stronger men. I tell 'e, Joe, things will git desperit soon."

"Aye," Utting admitted. "So they will. Me, I'm cruel hungry. In two days I ain't et nothin' but a few shellfishes." He turned to Nat Robinson, last survivor of the Invalid-Pensioners. "How you feeling, gaffer?"

"Heh! Heh!" cackled the veteran. "And to think that before Malplaquet I complained about Army beef and hard bread! Jesus, if only I had some, even only a little, right now!"

"Hell, Nat, you couldn't chaw it," Utting consoled. "Not with hardly no teeth at all."

"Maybe not, but I sure could suck on it." The skeletonic figure sighed. "I'm sure hungrier 'n I've ever been in m'life. Won't they issue us a little somethin' at the provision tent?"

"No," snarled the Butterfield lad. "Account o' somebody's stole a mess o' salt meat last night, Cap'n Cheap says no allowances for two days, if the thief ain't turned in."

A succession of gnawing, weakening gripes wrung the ex-farmer's bowels. Suddenly he decided to get something to eat, somehow, somewhere. The best way, he decided, was to risk stealing it from the provision tent.

True, it was supposed to be kept under guard; but often it wasn't. Discipline had grown so lax that Marines on duty either stole themselves or looked the other way. Was it worth the risk? Captain Cheap

[166]

had punished thefts by marooning seven men on the barren mainland, which was really a death sentence, and had had two Marines, caught red-handed, severely flogged.

"You fellers bide here. I'll get us somethin'. See if I don't."

Furtively, Joe made his way through the ramshackle camp, heard snores and moans arise in all directions. He had almost gained the supply tent's rear when a Marine guard with a shouldered musket loomed into sight. Panic-stricken, Utting shrank, shivering, against the side of a tent shared by *Wager*'s gunner and boatswain.

Because, for a miracle, the wind had dropped, Joe found himself able to hear and to recognize the voices of those within. The carpenter was in there, too, and so was Midshipman Harry Cozens.

"Aye," the carpenter was saying. "I can add fifteen feet to the longboat's length — easy. I'll raise her thwarts six inches and then we'll have us a main seaworthy craft."

Queried Bulkley's hoarse voice, "How many men will she carry then?"

"Maybe eighty. Depends how much water and gear we'll have to take along."

"Could it carry us to Valdivia?" the boatswain queried.

"Aye, and further, provided we don't get caught offshore by a tempest."

"Weather's getting better every day now," Cozens observed. "Mark my words, we'll reach Valdivia all right and sack the place. Then we'll seize a Spanish ship and sail home, all rich as lords."

"Unless savages catch and eat us," growled the carpenter. "I expect they'll be coming along any time. You heard about them arms that was found in the hut?"

Utting overheard Cozens say, "Now listen well. I'll pick seventy or eighty of the strongest. Last night I talked to the sailing master's mate. He's agreeable towards coming along and is ready to help me navigate."

"What about them's as won't join; will they likely try to prevent us?"

"Very likely," Cozens predicted lightly. "So when the time's ripe, we'll seize the arms store and the supply tent. After that, we'll disarm the Captain's party — peaceably if possible. I want no unnecessary bloodshed."

"What about that Army feller, Captain Pemberton?" Cummins's voice demanded.

[167]

"We've no worry in his direction. He hates Cheap's guts; so does the Army surgeon, Oakley. They'll both string along with us."

"What about Cap'n Cheap?" queried the gunner. "He'll be the hardest one to handle."

Cozens vented an ugly laugh. "Leave him to me."

"What d'you aim to do?"

"It's very simple. I'll simply provoke him into attacking me and then shoot him down."

Joe Utting, terrified over the results of his eavesdropping, commenced to crawl away, crab-wise. Should he listen any longer he would feel duty-bound to seek out the Captain.

When Joe regained his shelter, Private Robinson whispered, "Ye found somethin' to eat? Give it me quick, I'm near dead o' hunger."

"Not yet, Nat, but I'll yet find us some food. Where's Butterfield?"

"Dunno. Think mebbe he's gone to hunt oysters," whispered the old man. "Cover me wi' 'nother blanket, will 'e, Joe? I — I'm so turrible cold."

The young fellow's tracks proved easy to follow across the sand because the wind kept erasing earlier footsteps. Butterfield's trail led northward along the beach towards a row of dunes. On the crest of these the ex-farmer halted to swing his arms against the bitter wind. Abruptly he stopped flailing when he noticed two dark outlines merged at the water's edge.

One was Butterfield, the other was that of a corpse which, evidently, had just been washed in from the wreck. The youth was so intent on what he was doing that he never noticed Utting's presence until he was standing right above him.

Butterfield sprang up, leveling a sheath knife. "Lemme alone! Oh! Thank God, it's only you, Joe."

"What you doing? Oh Jesus, my God!" gasped the ex-farmer when the youth knelt and continued a slash he had commenced along the dead man's back. Butterfield rolled up frayed cuffs and began fumbling inside the cadaver.

"You oughtn't to do that, lad," Utting choked. " 'Tain't right."

"Maybe not, but don't you try to hinder me," warned the youth, sunken eyes wild and glittering in the starlight. "I'm terrible hungry so, by God, I aim to eat!"

While Utting hesitated that terrible griping recommenced in his bowels. "This is a awful thing, lad, but I guess God will understand our need and forgive us. Don't go away — wait while I fetch somethin' more useful 'n that knife."

He lumbered back up the dunes and wandered about until he located that hummock under which lay the concealed cutlass. Terrified of discovery, the two worked at frantic speed; they eviscerated and dismembered the cadaver then hid its most useful parts under seaweed in a cleft among the rocks. The rest they tossed back into the ever restless sea. Next, they kindled a small fire — where it couldn't be seen from the camp and in silence roasted and greedily consumed their departed shipmate's heart, liver and kidneys.

As soon as Joe Utting returned to the dugout, Private Robinson awoke and watched him take from his pocket an unidentifiable chunk of flesh which he set about boiling in a kettle of sea water. When the meat felt soft under his knife's point Joe knelt and spooned it between the old man's toothless gums.

The Pensioner was so grateful that tears trickled down his hollow cheeks. "That were mighty tasty," he sighed. "Wherever did ye come across such nice fresh pork?"

Before Joe could invent an explanation the one-armed veteran sank into a slumber from which he never emerged.

As the dreary days dragged by, Midshipman Harry Cozens's truculent arrogance mounted until at last he dared to proclaim himself the disaffected men's leader and representative.

First, he provoked and, to his vast surprise, got worsted in a fist fight with Surgeon Elliott, which brawl he was most tragically to regret.

The imminence of a crisis became unmistakable when, one day, Captain Cheap encountered the mutinous midshipman rolling a cask of dried peas up a steep section of beach. It had proved such hard work that even Cozens, well-fed and powerful as he was, had had to pause and catch his breath. He appeared so flushed and was breathing so hard that Cheap, not unnaturally, assumed that the cask contained liquor to which the midshipman had been helping himself.

"You're drunk," Captain Cheap accused.

Cozens straightened, glaring. "On what would I be getting drunk?"

"You know better than I. Call more hands and roll that cask up to the store tent."

"I need no help."

[169]

"You mutinous scoundrel, don't you dare to answer me back!" roared the Captain and caned Cozens across the face.

The younger man started forward with muscles standing out on his neck and arms, but he just managed to control himself. Said he thickly, "I've not yet decided whether you're a self-seeking rogue or a stubborn stupid fool, but now, by God, I deem you to be both!"

Captain Cheap immediately summoned a Marine and ordered him to march Cozens to the store tent.

"You great tyrant, d'you actually mean to keep me in there all night?" snarled the midshipman.

"Aye, that I do. And for so much longer as pleases me."

"Why damn you for a —"

This time the Captain's cane raised a welt across the midshipman's arm.

Unexpectedly the Marine spoke up. "Sir, you may be our Captain, but even so, you must not strike a prisoner under my guard!"

"What! I — I —" Cheap suddenly turned away, heavy jaw outthrust.

Once in the supply tent, Harry Cozens boldly stove in a brandy puncheon. Smiling, he offered some to the sentry, who soon let him escape.

On discovering that the cask Cozens had been rolling contained only dried peas Captain Cheap suffered second thoughts and made no effort to have the mutinous midshipman re-arrested, but ordered that his liquor allowance should indefinitely be halted.

On hearing of this Cozens, in a towering rage, rushed toward the store tent where Purser Harvey, with meticulous impartiality, was doling out the tiny rations. Well gone in liquor, Cozens began to storm and curse the Captain.

"How dare you stop my grog, you damn' thieving rascal?"

"By God," blazed the purser catching up a pistol, "you're for sure the trouble-making swine everyone says. I'd have stopped your ration if the Captain hadn't. Who the devil d'you fancy yourself?"

"An honest man and not a thieving purser. I'm Captain now, so you'll take orders from me!"

"Like hell I will!"

"You will!" Cozens cocked a boarding pistol and undoubtedly would have used it had not the ship's cooper knocked the weapon aside a split second before it exploded. Mr. Harvey's pistol also was knocked up in time.

Captain Cheap and Marine Lieutenant Hamilton, conferring in the former's tent, heard the shots. Hamilton rushed out, then called breathlessly, "Come quick, sir! Cozens is trying to murder Mr. Harvey!"

Emitting a bellow like that of an enraged bull, David Cheap ran from his tent and saw armed men milling before the store tent. Without an instant's hesitation he fired at Cozens. Shot through the jaw, the midshipman fell and lay writhing on the sand.

Ragged scarlet tunic flapping, Lieutenant Hamilton rushed over to the officers' shelters shouting, "Turn out! Mutiny! Armed mutiny!"

The sailing master, surgeon, Captain Pemberton and Marine Lieutenants Ewers and Fanning at once turned out with weapons ready for use.

Meanwhile seamen came running up from all sides yelling to know what was going on. The Captain calmly was blowing smoke from his weapon's barrel.

Bulkley, the gunner, stepped forward panting, "Sir, why have you shot poor Mr. Cozens?"

"For open mutiny, you insolent dog!" Captain Cheap announced and pulled a fresh pistol from his coat's pocket. "And you will get the same treatment an you dare to threaten me."

"But, Captain, sir, you see I am unarmed," Bulkley pointed out. "No more are the rest of us poor fellows."

Captain Cheap set his jaw and stared about, utterly unafraid. "It is well that you are. Remember, the lot of you, that *I* am still your commander! Now let every man go to his tent."

Surprisingly, the throng dispersed.

~~ 7 ~~

Mutiny on the *Wager,* IV

SOON AFTER Midshipman Harry Cozens had been carried to the sick tent, dripping blood from his shattered jaw, *Wager*'s survivors turned ugly. Fortified by rum, John King, the boatswain, who appeared to have succeeded Cozens as chief of the mutineers, swaggered into the officers' country and called out: "We are placing Captain Cheap under arrest and keeping him prisoner until he can be brought back to England to stand trial for attempted murder! All officers will immediately surrender their arms."

Captain Cheap charged out of his tent. "Get gone, you insolent rogue before I shoot you, too!" Perhaps wisely, he made no demands that the disaffected men turn in their weapons.

Thereafter whenever he went out of his tent two armed seamen always trailed him as "guards." At night, also, guard was mounted over Cheap's tent — along with the Marine regularly designated to protect him.

Two days later the leading mutineers approached Captain Cheap with a request that he send Mr. Elliott to dress the now delirious midshipman's jaw.

"You may all go to hell, singly or collectively," roared the undaunted commander.

The surgeon appeared, swathed in an old blanket. Snarled he, "I'm damned before I'll waste my art on that treacherous bullyboy. I'd sooner pare a corn from the devil's hoof than lift a finger to help Cozens."

He stared hard at Cummins, Bulkley and King who had moved up to confront him. "Decent men have had a bellyful of your truculence and insubordination. You deluded fools had better grasp the right of this matter and return to duty."

"That's as may be," snapped Cummins. "Since you won't go, will you allow your mate to 'tend Mr. Cozens? He's in turrible pain."

"So much the better!" Mr. Elliott snorted, then added, "What Stook does is no concern of mine."

Samuel Stook found the wounded midshipman lying propped on one elbow and with his unwounded right cheek resting on the palm of his hand, in company with Vincent Oakley, the Army surgeon. The latter was saying, "I'd willingly remove the ball from your jaw but the Captain forbids me. However, Stook, here, has received permission to dress your wound."

"Stook?" moaned Cozens. "That cock-eyed butcher? He ain't fit to dress a boil on a dog's ass."

There was no alternative than to allow Stook to do his best. First he bled the patient, then used rum and water to swab out the festering hole. He was so rough and thorough about it that Cozens's handsome features turned a ghastly greenish-white before he fainted.

"I felt the bullet and splinters o' bone," grinned the long-un-

[172]

shaven surgeon's mate. "Can they be dug out, he'll likely survive, him being strong like a young bull."

For a week longer Harry Cozens lay with purplish features framed in tangled yellow hair, his jaw swelled out of all recognition and oozing evil-smelling pus. At length, the midshipman's pitiful condition overcame even Mr. Elliott's antipathy, sent him to interview Captain Cheap. "I feel he has suffered long enough, sir. Shall I now go and remove the ball?"

"No, by God! If he lives, I'll carry him prisoner to the Commodore for hanging."

So ugly grew the temper of the crew when they heard of the Captain's obstinacy that Lieutenant Beans and the other officers urged Cheap to reconsider his decision.

Even so, the actual operation was performed by Sam Stook. A series of frightful screams rang from the sick tent before the surgeon's mate appeared bearing on a pewter plate the flattened bullet and a long segment of bloodied, yellow-white bone set with a couple of teeth. " 'Twere a neat job, if I do say so," Stook explained heartily. "Them's is from his upper jaw."

Following the operation "a decay of humor," as Mr. Elliott described it, set in with the result that, on the twentieth of June, Midshipman the Honorable John Byron blew on chilled and dirty fingers before making an entry in his journal:

> There Died today Mr. Harry Cozens, Midshipman. There have Died, sundry ways, since the Ship struck, forty-five Men, and seven have been Marooned or Deserted.

With Cozens's death the men appeared less insubordinate, but a new controversy arose among the starving survivors. A majority of the officers, commissioned and otherwise, were convinced that their best and only chance of salvation lay in sailing back round the Horn, with the hope of eventually reaching some port in friendly Brazil.

Sailing Master Jones felt confident that to convert *Wager's* longboat into a small schooner would be no trick at all. Such a craft would be less lofty in its masts and much handier to sail. When queried, the carpenter admitted that it would be quite feasible to lengthen *Wager's* thirty-foot longboat by eleven feet and ten inches.

In vain did Captain Cheap, supported by Marine Lieutenant Hamilton, Mr. Elliott and Midshipmen Byron and Campbell, insist that the only right and honorable course was for the entire company to sail north and attempt to rejoin the Commodore, either off Valdivia or at the squadron's third rendezvous at the Island of Juan Fernandez — it being much too late to expect to come up with them off Socorro.

After weeks of bitter wrangling, the majority, headed by Lieutenant Beans and Sailing Master Jones, secured Captain Cheap's permission to leave him, sail south and attempt to reach Brazil.

Joe Utting was one of the eighty officers and seamen who, on the thirteenth of October 1741, crowded into *Speedwell*, as the enlarged and schooner-rigged longboat had been christened. *Speedwell* did not depart alone; ten gaunt and desperate survivors somehow had crowded into *Wager*'s remaining cutter — the other having been lost during an expedition sent to hunt food on the barren mainland.

Just before the two boats raised their sails, Gunner Bulkley who, after Cozens, had caused the most trouble, did a surprising thing. He pulled off his cap and invited three rousing cheers *for brave Captain Cheap!*

"Well, I'll be damned!" burst out Midshipman Byron. "Can you top that?"

Captain David Cheap did just that. "Men," he turned to the eighteen ragged scarecrows who had remained on the beach with him. "Let us return the courtesy! Three cheers for Mr. Beans and his companions! May they enjoy a safe journey home!" He swung a crumbling tricorne. "With a will now. Hip! hip! hurrah!"

Bad weather forced the Captain's party considerably to delay their departure from Wager Island — as they had come to call the place — in fact, until the gusty morning of December 14th, when the last meager supplies were piled into *Wager*'s barge and the yawl. Around midday the jerry-rigged craft started their long voyage northwards along the coast of Chile.

In company with the inflexible Captain were Mr. Robert Elliott, Lieutenant Hamilton, Midshipman the Honorable John Byron, Midshipman Alexander Campbell and fourteen sickly seamen and Marines.

That either boat ever would reach civilization appeared most unlikely; the yawl soon began to leak like a sieve and the barge proved to be the clumsiest sailer since Father Noah had launched his Ark.

8

The Blunder

Sunrise of May 28, 1741, disclosed HBMS *Centurion* cruising alone over a warm and sparkling bright blue sea. Seen from a distance, all would have seemed well with the big Fourth Rate.

But had the observer come closer he quickly would have perceived that this handsomely designed man-of-war with the natural wood sides, white topsides and waterline had suffered cruelly. He would have noticed a distressing number of parted stays and snapped clew lines swaying forlornly across the sky. Some of these rope ends had dangled so long that they had become frayed into brushlike "Irish pennants."

Next, he might have seen that the foremast's port shrouds had carried away and had been only clumsily replaced; the weather-beaten remains of the original shrouds sagged down the side and trailed in the water. Ragged strips of grayed canvas, adhering to the main gallant yard, flapped idly in the gentle breeze, testifying that, although the sail had blown out a long time ago, nothing had been done to replace it. Jagged gaps in *Centurion*'s bulwarks bore silent witness to the terrific impact of those seas which for weeks and months had battered her.

As *Centurion* sailed slowly on her course she trailed long, green banderoles of weed; above her lead sheathing she showed a thick incrustation of gray-white barnacles. The scant canvas she was showing — jibs, fore and main topsails and her mizzen's lateen — all had been frequently patched and were badly weathered. Useless lengths of rope drooped over her side. The main yard braces had not been hauled taut, so the great yard creaked and swayed in a fashion which, normally, would have sent shivers of horror racing down the back of any Royal Navy man.

Had the solitary man-of-war been approached from downwind its company could have recognized, at a mile's distance, a loathsome stench commonly associated with slavers.

On *Centurion*'s quarterdeck stood or sat a listless group of gaunt, sunburned and dull-eyed figures. With a single exception, they wore filthy tatters and rags that fluttered grotesquely in the gentle breeze. Although he worked tirelessly, Commodore George Anson somehow had managed to shave once in a while. No one's linen was clean, because for many days there had been no fresh water to spare for washing; not enough remained to satisfy the sick, lying helpless in the ovenlike temperature prevailing below decks.

Again and again Anson's battered brass spyglass followed the horizon through 360 degrees. He ended by sighing and snapping shut its lens cover.

"Still nothing, sir?" croaked Peircy Brett through sun-cracked lips. "It would encourage the men no end if —"

"There's nothing to be seen — at least not from this deck. I'll try climbing to the foretop later on." Anson turned sunken eyes forward. What appalling disorder prevailed upon *Centurion*'s dirty gundeck!

Only six wraith-like creatures still were on their feet. Listlessly they were doling out to each man a dipper of foul-smelling, greenish water. By the dozen, crew members sat or lay limp upon the deck. A knot of them had collected at the mainmast's foot; others slumped weakly against the hatch coamings and gun carriages. Several new corpses now lay in the scuppers, Anson noted. They'd have soon to be pushed through a break in the bulwarks.

The strongest of the men still able to move about was Nathaniel Wade, but even he swayed with weakness like a drunken man. He offered a dipper to the gaping mouth of a hairy fellow propped against the main hatch's coaming.

"I know this stinks, but try to swallow. Maybe it'll keep you going a while longer."

Red-lined, glazing eyes rolled painfully upwards. "No land yet?"

"Not yet. Come now, drink." Wade lifted the dipper but the fellow's mouth, foul and toothless from scurvy, sagged further open. Sighing, he fell over sidewise and died beside a corpse which had lain there, bloating and smelling dreadfully, for over two days.

Wade beckoned Tom Ramster. "Let's get these things overboard."

"What's — use? Too damn' many," mumbled the scrawny, red-haired giant, then sat down heavily on a length of broken spar. "Besides, I'm about done in — beginning to tremble all over whenever I walk."

After a while, Ramster remembered something, got up, went over to the untended galley and from it took a tin pot in which he'd been soaking a sea-biscuit in wine stolen from the spirit room.

[176]

He found Ben Canty in the forecastle — where he'd no business to be — looking surprisingly well in the new hammock and the clean blanket he'd brought for the boy. Ben's naturally large blue eyes seemed enormous as he complained, "Where you bin, Tom? I bin hungry ever so long. Guess you just don't care 'bout me no more."

"Oh no, Ben, don't ever think such a thing. It's only there's so few of us left fit to bear a hand. Here," gently the wasted giant spooned softened biscuit to the boy's mouth. "Eat it — eat all of it."

Next, he combed Ben's coarse brown hair and wiped his face with a damp cloth.

"Tom? I'm sorry for what I said just now. I — I guess you still love me."

"Sure I do."

"Am I going to die?"

"Hell no! We're going to have plenty more fun together. For sure, we'll be sighting land any time now."

Gingerly, Andrew Menzies rubbed his bristle-covered jaw on which a scurvy spot had appeared. Um. Must be a dozen new corpses among those disheveled figures sprawled about the deck below. Although it had become one of his duties to list fatalities, he felt too weak to do so today. Like everyone else who still was able to stand up, he felt he must conserve ever-diminishing strength for more essential labor.

Lieutenant de Saumarez clung to a brace and, as if mesmerized, kept staring blankly over the dazzling, pitiless sea. His once lively black eyes had retreated so far into their sockets that they appeared shrunk to half their normal size. Actually, he was trying to forget that his young brother, Midshipman Thomas de Saumarez, like Sailing Master Nutt, today was displaying the first symptoms of scurvy.

"We're in for 'nother scorcher," sighed Mr. Pascoe Thomas. Normally, *Centurion's* astronomer and schoolmaster would have no business on the quarterdeck but, as matters now stood, even the lowliest "waister" who remained on his feet was welcomed there. Vaguely, he wondered how his assistant, young Pallister, was faring now that he was too feeble to come on deck any more.

Mr. Thomas massaged a brown and stringy throat and, like Lieutenant Brett, lamented silently that another hour must pass before he would receive his daily water ration — a pint of thick fluid alive with algae and other microscopic plants.

His gaze sought that slate on which, hourly, should be recorded the ship's log reports. There had been but two entries made in twenty-four hours! Both were the work of George Anson, who insisted on heaving the log himself every twelve hours.

Surgeon Ettrick had the helm and could only remain erect by steadying himself against the flagship's seven-foot brass-bound wheel. Because he'd lost his fat belly, Mr. Ettrick's breeches hung baggily from a belt constricted to its last notch. He was glad to be in the shelter of the steerage because, on deck, the sun momentarily was growing hotter.

Fortunately the ship was running free, so he and Midshipman de Saumarez hadn't much of a job to keep the man-of-war on course. Lord knew what would happen if a storm broke; young de Saumarez wasn't really much help.

Later in the day, Anson focused his telescope by sighting at *Centurion*'s foretopmast — and promptly wished that he hadn't; a long crack had appeared on its side! Under even a moderate breeze, it surely would split. If that happened, he knew it couldn't be replaced. He'd not enough able men left to send up a substitute.

Lieutenant Peircy Brett and a few other officers followed the Commodore's example and, dutifully if hopelessly, scanned the horizon for land or a sign of those consorts which had vanished during a furious hurricane on April 24th.

Presently Anson said in a low and quivering tone, "Gentlemen, please study that mass of clouds bearing five points off our larboard bow. Am I daft or do I see land?"

In silence, the officers did as they were told. At length Justinian Nutt heaved a groan so deep that it stirred his ragged walrus mustache. "Sorry, sir, I see no land. Yonder's only a cloud bank."

"Mr. de Saumarez?" Anson queried. "Do you see anything?"

Obediently, the first lieutenant scanned that distant cloud formation with painstaking thoroughness. As well as anyone else he knew the critical importance of sighting land. At length he shook his shaggy black head. "Sir, I regret I see nothing like land."

"Mr. Brett?"

"Sorry, sir, my vision's too clouded to see much."

"Odd. I felt *sure* I noticed a dark streak lying below yonder clouds," Anson insisted. "Don't *you* see anything, Mr. Denis?"

"No, sir," the horribly sunburned third lieutenant confessed. "I spy nothing but clouds. I fear, as Mr. Nutt maintains, that we've made too much westing and have passed Juan Fernandez Island, possibly at night."

Since no one would support his contention, George Anson bowed to the inevitable. Hoarse with thirst and feeling more than a little lightheaded, he called down to the surgeon that he must alter course and steer to the eastward; if anyone survived long enough, the coast of South America eventually must be sighted.

It tore his seaman's heart to see how slowly, sloppily his handful of officers and men wore ship.

Anson knuckled eyes red-rimmed with sleeplessness. They scratched and burned as if they'd been dropped into hot sand and then crammed back into their sockets.

Much as my instinct warns against it, I suppose I'm doing right in turning back. If I keep on westward I may miss Juan Fernandez. If I do, all hands will soon perish of thirst and scurvy.

For once surrendering to a black depression, the haggard Commodore wondered: If conditions are so bad on this ship what can they be suffering aboard *Gloucester*? She's so badly found and so much worse crowded. And what of *Tryall*? She's only two hundred tons of wood and iron sailing under jury rig.

The *Wager*? Ah! He experienced a faint stir of hope. If any ship will appear at the rendezvous it will be David Cheap's; he's a hard, rash man, but a most consummate seaman. He *must* appear at Juan Fernandez. He's got all my land force's equipment.

Of course, there can be no hope for the *Anna*. She can't possibly have survived.

Could that really have been land I believed I saw? Perhaps I should have insisted on keeping to the westward? No. No one else sighted it.

A harrowing thought. By sailing east I'm increasing my chances of meeting Pizarro — provided he's weathered the Horn. If the Don made it, he'll be picking my ships off piecemeal as they enter the Pacific. How many has he sunk?

9

Paradise Gained

THE AWFUL SUSPICION that he should further have investigated that heavy cloud bank loomed large in Anson's mind when, after only two days of running before a westerly half-gale, a long line of jagged, snow-crowned peaks was sighted. The Andes! *Centurion* could not have made too much westing; therefore she had sailed exhausting hundreds of miles *away* from Juan Fernandez — and salvation.

Characteristically, George Anson found no one to blame but himself. Because of my blunder he groaned, how many lives have been and will be lost?

With the possibility of having to fight Pizarro, Anson at once ordered the course reversed — but now *Centurion* was forced to contend with contrary winds which prolonged the agonies suffered by her company. Even the simplest bracing about of a yard became a Herculean task. After a few days, many men were forced to crawl on hands and knees to tail onto the tackle ropes.

"Oi, Tom Ramster! Time for your watch," mumbled scurvy-stricken Will Pallister; the minister's son already had lost half a dozen teeth and was about to lose some more.

"Ain't heard no bell."

"You know bells haven't been sounded in ever so long."

"Aye, Will. I know," Tom growled over the monotonous creak and whine of the ship's timbers. "But my strength's going. Last night my legs swelled something awful. I've tried but, damn it, I — I can't swing 'em out o' the hammock. Reckon the officers and men of the afterguard will have to sail this floating graveyard 'thout me."

"How do they fare?"

"Only a bit better off than the rest of us."

"I wonder why?"

"Dunno. In a long time they ain't et no better nor us, nor do they draw a bigger water allowance — not even the Commodore, let the croakers say what they will."

Surgeon Ettrick also had conjectured on this curious fact. Why should the officers and their servants succumb less readily?

On running up an estimate, Second Lieutenant Brett was appalled to discover that, as a result of that unnecessary run back to South America, seventy-eight irreplaceable men had lost their lives!

Lieutenant Denis, hollow-eyed and looking twice his real age, silently handed to Commodore a roster revealing that *less than* 200 remained alive of the 521 men and boys who had sailed out of Spithead Bay aboard *Centurion*. Worse still, of this number only five seamen remained in any way able to assist in handling this 60-gun ship.

On the ninth of June, 1741, when even tough old Lieutenant Colonel Cratcherode who had worked tirelessly, despite continual grumbling, lay listless and querulous on his narrow bunk, King Parmer, coxswain of the Commodore's barge swayed over to the sunbleached mainshrouds and gazed blankly out over the hot and glittering ocean.

After a minute, his unkempt head tilted backwards until his peeling nose pointed skywards. He sniffed several times then croaked, "B'God, I believe I smell land!"

"Ah — ye've grown batty as the rest," grunted a man lying near the main hatch.

"No, I ain't," Parmer insisted and he was right.

At noon Peter Denis cried feebly, "Land! There's land in sight!" Soon word spread through the ship that a solitary bluish peak had appeared on the horizon.

"Over yonder's 'e rendyvoo," cried William Buckle, A.B.

"How d'you know? We bin navigation blind for weeks."

"I *know* it is! Commodore's finest navigator as ever was."

By mid-afternoon a sizable island had come into view as a series of volcanic peaks and crags. Seen at a distance, these appeared to be quite as forbidding as those of Cape Noire. However, when the battered flagship lay some two miles offshore, telescopes revealed that many small valleys covered with dense woods lay between a series of jagged ridges.

"Do you mark all those waterfalls, sir?" Menzies babbled.

"Aye, Andrew, I expect each of us could drink one dry all by himself," smiled the Commodore, no longer even attempting to conceal his overpowering thankfulness.

Over the rail a few spectral and tatterdemalion figures gazed in unbelieving wonder on broad green savannahs and dense groves of towering palms.

Weaker men crawled over rotting corpses to breaks in the bulwarks and lay gibbering like idiots to see so many cascades of fresh water tumbling, lacelike, to lose themselves in the sea.

"Tom! How soon will they give us fresh food?" Tears were sliding slowly down Pallister's pinched and grimy cheeks.

"Soon, lad, soon. In another day's time for sure."

"Don't know if I can last that long."

"You will. You got plenty of teeth left. Which is more 'n Ben Canty had, the last I saw of him."

"Is he dead?"

"Don't know. Most of the boys are, poor little buggers."

Everywhere the scurvy-stricken brightened; men who had been deemed half-dead roused, weakly pled for fresh food and water.

Anson issued orders that every man might drink his fill from the residue of water taken on board at Santa Catharina and himself carried buckets full of the slimy green stuff to anyone who would ask for it.

Two hours of toil under a torrid sun was required of the exhausted officers and their servants to reduce *Centurion's* canvas to fore and main courses — which might be handled from the deck; no one remained able to climb the rigging.

Mr. Nutt forced sunken eyes into focus and bent over Captain Sharpe's crude, sixty-year-old chart of this thirteen-mile-long island. Desperately, he needed to locate a "broad and peaceful haven" reported to exist somewhere along the northern shore of Juan Fernandez.

No such harbor having been located by nightfall, there was nothing for Anson to do but stand away from those inviting but rock-studded shores until daylight returned. So great was the survivors' disappointment over this necessity that several more gave up the struggle and died.

During that night of torturing frustration, a strong current carried *Centurion* so close inshore that the Commodore, fearing she might strike a reef, ordered the best bower dropped. So, for the first time in over three months, the flagship once more found herself at anchor.

At four o'clock of the following morning, while the sky was still a milky gray, Anson drove himself on deck and sent for Lieutenant Peter Denis.

"I want the yawl lowered as soon as may be. You'll have Mr. Menzies, some midshipmen and servants to help you."

"Aye, aye, sir. And what are my orders?"

"You will explore the shore for signs of recent visitors, bring off some green stuff but, most important of all, you're to discover the harbor indicated on Sharpe's chart. There should be one," said he tensely, "if this really is Juan Fernandez."

From the poopdeck, George Anson, indescribably weary and anxious, watched the yawl pull slowly away and prayed silently that its return would be prompt. With his ship so utterly helpless, he foresaw that all would be lost should one of those fierce squalls, which could so suddenly arise in these latitudes, strike the crippled flagship.

Lieutenant Denis, at the yawl's tiller, began to feel better by the moment. Pulling a feeble stroke oar was the Commodore's own coxswain, that lanky Carolinian named Parmer. The seat next forward was occupied by Midshipman de Saumarez and a newly appointed quartermaster's mate named Wade. A big man, he somehow had retained a measure of strength and alone was rowing strongly. Tugging an oar behind Wade was Midshipman the Honorable Augustus van Keppel. His Dutch ancestry was attested by his round blond head, round red face, stocky body and pale blue eyes. Once he had been plump, but was so no longer.

Forward of van Keppel toiled that enigmatic figure, Andrew Menzies. The Commodore's dark-visaged secretary had become so emaciated Denis wondered that he could even handle an oar.

On nearing the shore, Denis's craft was speeded on its way by a succession of long rollers driving lazily toward a narrow, pebbly beach.

Being ordered to rest on their oars, the rowers were able to peer hungrily over their shoulders at a noisy cascade which came plunging, fresh and clean, onto a jumble of rocks at sea level.

To Quartermaster's Mate Wade the scene was of such magical beauty that his eyes filled.

On its shoreward course to the beach, the yawl passed close to flat-topped reefs on which hundreds of seals lay basking. The few of these sleek brown-black creatures which even bothered to raise doglike heads, only waggled white whiskers and gazed mildly at the passing boat. For the most part they kept right on sleeping.

To Menzies's incredulous astonishment he presently heard a chorus of yelpings and bayings. The yawl was still a hundred yards out when a pack of red-brown mastiff-like dogs raced down to the shore baring their fangs and raising a terrible racket.

"Where there are dogs, there usually are men nearby," Andrew Menzies pointed out in a cracked voice, but he couldn't tear his gaze from the waterfall.

Flushing at the implied reproof, Lieutenant Denis called, "Bow four! Cease rowing and ready your arms. The rest of you pull hard. Won't do to overturn now."

Those in the yawl braced themselves when it slipped up the back of a final glossy roller and was hurled violently towards a graveled bar beyond which showed an expanse of smooth water. By some miracle, the yawl passed unscathed into the calm area.

"God has been good to us at last." Midshipman de Saumarez seemed to express everyone's reaction. "Wouldn't Captain Arnand be disappointed?"

"He would; may his soul fry eternally!" Denis rasped and steered for the base of that wonderful cataract, the soft thundering of which had begun to drown out the sound of surf breaking on the bar.

He'd never expected to see green things grow again, so Nat Wade began to tremble when he beheld broad emerald-hued leaves shimmering just ahead and smelled the long-forgotten odors of vegetation.

Because of weakness, the yawl's crew made a sloppy landing but managed to tug their craft a few feet towards the high-water mark just after the discharge of Denis's musket served to disperse a pack of dogs which had come out onto the beach and were advancing in ominous fashion. Yelping, the brutes faded back into incredibly lush undergrowth.

"Follow me, but don't drink too much all at once," croaked Lieutenant Denis and set off at a lumbering run across a stony beach towards that spot where giant ferns shivered and dripped amid rainbow-hued mist rising at the waterfall's base.

Emitting wheezing grunts, the boat party dropped their weapons and splashed into a pool boiling under the waterfall. Many lay down and, like tired hounds, commenced to gulp long draughts of blessedly cool fresh water.

"Never thought I'd say it, but there ain't no likker in the world half so good!" gasped King Parmer, tilting back his Indian-like head and allowing water to pour between scabby lips.

Young de Saumarez repeatedly dipped bronzed features beneath the surface, made weird bubbling noises like a child in its bath.

Others pulled off their noisome rags and waded further out into the pool where they splashed and whooped to their heart's content.

Peter Denis and Augustus van Keppel also stripped off their garments, then used fine sand from the bottom to scrub their insect-scarred and scurvy spotted skins. So did Andrew Menzies, except that he retained his breeches. Probably he had valuables concealed in them, thought Denis. After that, being the only ones able to swim, the three swam through the translucent pale green water towards the misty waterfall, panicking an army of tiny fishes into silvery flight.

The Commodore's secretary turned onto his back and, staring at the lush vegetation, became reminded of a swimming hole back of his father's big house near Charles Town, South Carolina. There, too, parakeets and other bright birds had twittered, colorful blossoms had glowed, vines had grown in graceful loops and curves. Ah — h — h! It was sheer luxury to feel the salt ingrained in his skin dissolve.

The party's pitiable condition was emphasized when the men began uprooting handfuls of soft, sweet-tasting grass and munching like so many browsing cattle. Painfully visible now were a lot more gurry sores or running boils caused by the pressure of clothing too long laundered in salt water.

For the first time in weeks, Menzies smiled when he noticed gaunt, wide-shouldered Wade tuck a big red and yellow blossom behind his ear, strike an absurd attitude and shout, "Look, Ma! I'm Queen o' the May."

Clothes dried quickly under the hot sun.

"Wonder what makes the air smell so fresh?" remarked young van Keppel, rebuttoning his shirt.

"Damned if I know," mumbled Denis, his mouth full of sweet grass.

Said Midshipman de Saumarez, "Some variety of sandalwood must grow here. I once had a box made of it. Smelt just like this."

Lieutenant Denis suddenly felt guilty of carelessness, so ordered half of the party to resume their arms while the rest scattered in search of fruit or set about filling a hogshead with fresh water. Coxswain Parmer, who had returned to guard the yawl, waded into the ocean, bent, then held up a tremendous and wildly wriggling crayfish or spiny lobster. "Ahoy! Whole shore's alive with 'em!"

A brassy-looking sun having lifted high into the heavens, Lieutenant Denis dropped an armful of coconuts into the yawl and shouted, "All hands come in. Prepare to shove off!"

Once the yawl was under way again, Denis steered westward close under a wildly beautiful coast. The oarsmen stared curiously at *Centurion*, anchored half a mile offshore. How forlorn she looked with her rigging slack and her poorly furled sails drooping from crazily braced yards. Remembering the luckless wretches still dying on board, they plied their oars with renewed energy.

Menzies, narrowing jet eyes against the increasing tropic glare, noted that this island's jagged silhouette was dominated by a tall, anvil-shaped mountain rising from near its center and that, between

[185]

innumerable little canyons, stretched emerald-green savannahs, watered by an abundance of brooks and streams. Many of these verdant areas were shaded by magnificent stands of what appeared to be myrtle, sandalwood and towering feathery-topped trees; later these were identified as cabbage palms.

More than an hour's rowing was required before the yawl's crew sighted what undoubtedly must be the "wide and peaceful haven" described by Captain Sharpe. Certainly there could not be another anchorage so magnificent.

Half a mile in width, and easily a quarter of a mile in depth, this bay, Peter Denis realized, was admirably sheltered from all winds — saving only from the north.

Delighted, he steered among great herds of seals and some much larger, strange-looking sea animals, which seemed to breathe through short, elephant-like trunks, swimming towards a narrow gravel strip which offered an easy landing — nowhere was a sandy beach to be seen.

Once ashore, the lieutenant directed, "Half of you under Mr. van Keppel are to collect more sweet grass, coconuts and fruit. Mr. Menzies, please see that it is efficiently packed in the bow. Coxswain Parmer, Wade and the rest, follow me."

He pointed out a group of seals drowsing on a bird-whitened ledge. "Do any of you know how to kill such creatures?"

The coxswain fingered his lantern jaw. "Sir, I once heard somebody tell a seal dies right easy if you club it 'crost its snoot."

Wide-set gray eyes narrowed, Denis studied the shiny, somnolent beasts a moment then said dubiously, "May as well try clubbing. If we shoot, I fear the others may take alarm. The brutes look as if they might not run off, if we can kill the first ones quietly."

Swaying in their gait — they had not trod solid land in such a long time — the men scattered in search of suitable lengths of driftwood and soon returned, using sheath knives to trim them into usable clubs.

Had Nat Wade not recalled conditions aboard *Centurion*, he might have experienced compunction over clubbing these harmless creatures that only chirruped sleepily or looked trustingly upwards from round and glistening black eyes.

As it was, the seal hunters soon discovered that King Parmer's informant had been entirely correct. When clubbed across the muzzle, the creatures promptly collapsed and lay shuddering with bright scarlet streams gushing from doglike noses.

Care was taken to slaughter only ten half-grown seals — because, as Menzies pointed out, such should furnish tender meat and certainly would prove easier to handle.

Finally the yawl, already deep loaded with greens, was pushed alongside the red-dripping ledge. It proved quite an exhausting task to handle the limp carcasses — half-grown or not, the lightest weighed easily a hundred and fifty pounds.

By the time the yawl had been loaded with still-bleeding brown bodies, only a precarious few inches of freeboard remained.

Lieutenant Denis chuckled wearily, "Curs'd if we don't more resemble a gang of bloody buccaneers than men of His Majesty's Navy."

"If only dear old Canon Walker could see his acolyte" — Midshipman van Keppel sounded more than a trifle hysterical — "he'd take him for the butcher's boy."

To pull back out to *Centurion*, lying mirrored on a glassy sea, proved an exhausting task. Often the yawl's crew were forced to lay on their oars and recover a measure of strength.

A tragically weak cheer arose when Lieutenant Denis steered close enough for the handful of men on deck to see his cargo.

Menzies glimpsed the Commodore's wide, red-brown face peering down from the poop. So long had Naval etiquette been allowed to lapse that Anson called down, "Well done, Mr. Denis! Well done, indeed."

To hoist in the seal carcasses, gutted and headless though they were, was a real problem for *Centurion*'s exhausted survivors; the greens, therefore, were sent aboard first. It was terrible to watch how eagerly the officers and men crammed scurvy grass between bleeding jaws.

Still chewing, the more able-bodied, under Anson's direction, then distributed grass and raw meat to those who lay moaning and helpless about the deck among piles of debris and the double-lashed guns.

For the first time in weeks smoke commenced to climb from the galley's rusted chimney. Schoolmaster Thomas had volunteered to try his hand at cooking.

When darkness fell an atmosphere of renewed hope pervaded the flagship. Even so, several more men died despite the fresh food and water they'd consumed.

Next morning the wind arose and, blowing hard out of the south, rendered it impossible for *Centurion,* in her present condition, to beat into the "haven" discovered by Denis's party, which harbor the Commodore christened "Cumberland Bay," in honor of His Royal Highness, the Duke of Cumberland. He made careful note of this in his log: Costing nothing, this bit of flattery might win the Duke's support when he returned to England to face the inevitable court-martial over having lost ships under his command.

In fact, it blew so hard all that day that not a single water cask could be sent ashore, for all that a number of beautiful cascades were splashing tantalizingly only half a mile away!

Not until the morning of the third day after *Centurion's* arrival off Juan Fernandez did the wind veer and begin to blow towards Cumberland Bay. The moment it steadied the Commodore said, "Mr. de Saumarez, please muster all able men to raise anchor."

Only fifteen rail-thin figures collected around the flagship's great capstan dominating the orlop's nauseous gloom and disorder.

Anson's hope dimmed when not half of the men proved strong enough even to lift the capstan's heavy iron bars. Accordingly, he, Denis, de Saumarez and Marine Lieutenant Gordon fitted the rusting bars into their sockets.

Said de Saumarez in a pathetic attempt at encouragement, "Now if we'd a fiddler to play us 'Tom Bowling,' we'd have the hook up in a trice."

"Save your breath," snapped the Marine officer. "You're going to need it."

Gordon was more than right. The group's united strength could not even revolve the capstan a full turn, even when Sailing Master Nutt and Andrew Menzies, in the steerage, manipulated *Centurion's* wheel in order to ease pressure on the anchor line.

When, after four hours of heartbreaking effort, it proved impossible to raise the anchor, Anson panted, "Everyone go on deck."

"Aye, aye, sir," wheezed de Saumarez. "And now, sir, what do you intend?"

"Trailing our anchor I will take the ship, under fore and main courses, as far as possible into Cumberland Bay."

He forced a smile.

"All hands had better pray that we pass well into the Bay before the anchor engages."

Fortune, who for so long had denied any favor, smiled at last. The flagship had crept well past the center of Cumberland Bay when her anchor, dangling at a depth of fifty-six fathoms, finally grounded. Immediately sheets were let run and, as *Centurion*'s bowsprit gradually swung into the wind, Sailing Master Nutt bawled, "Brail courses!"

The dark-faced de Saumarez brothers at once were sent ashore in the longboat, all the food brought aboard by Denis's party having been consumed long since. Lemons, limes and other fruits were plucked by the sackful. More gory seal carcasses were being tumbled into the longboat when Midshipman de Saumarez uttered a strangled gasp. "My God! Isn't there a sail out yonder?"

"Where away?" snapped his brother.

"On the horizon, nearly in line with the flagship!"

The disheveled, sunburned heads snapped about to follow the direction indicated by young de Saumarez.

Sure enough. A tiny triangle of canvas was glimmering on the horizon to eastward of Juan Fernandez!

10

Rendezvous

ONCE *Centurion*'s longboat pulled away, Anson, the purser, Schoolmaster Pascoe, Denis and several servants laboriously laid out on the main topyard. While working along the foot ropes Anson moved cautiously, thinking, Lord's love! When did I last handle canvas aloft? Not in fifteen, no, nearer twenty years.

Clumsily, the amateur topmen commenced to cut away the blown-out topsail's ragged remains.

From where he swayed, with bare toes hooked over the foot ropes, Anson was pleased to see some of the sick start fishing and meet with considerable success. Silently, he wished he dared set all hands to fishing, but that was not practicable; the flagship must be rendered really maneuverable again — which couldn't be accomplished under bare yards and blown-out sails.

Anson nodded encouragement to Hazeltine, his new steward. Poor Oldham had died — for a miracle, not of scurvy but of gangrene resulting from a leg smashed during one of the endless storms.

Hazeltine was cursing a broken fingernail; his hands weren't sufficiently tough to handle ropes and canvas.

"In another half-hour," promised the Commodore, "you can go below and catch fish for the officers' mess and —"

He got no further; someone working in the foretop suddenly yelled, "Christ above! Ain't that a sail out yonder?"

"Where away?" Anson's deep voice rang through the hot sunlight.

"Over there to — to the —" the amateur topman fumbled. "Oh damn! I don't know what the direction's called — only that it's yonder!"

Like an invigorating tide, sudden wild hopes surged into George Anson's being. Surely, *surely* this must be one of his squadron coming in from the northeast! Fervently he prayed that she might prove to be *Gloucester*. Her presence would double the number of guns at his disposal should he have to engage Pizarro.

Pizarro? PIZARRO? With the force of a blow occurred the awful thought that this unknown vessel might be one of the Spanish Admiral's towering ships-of-the-line; not that a mere sloop couldn't have trounced the flagship in her present condition. As fast as he could, Anson descended to the deck fully determined to fire *Centurion's* magazine should the stranger prove to be Spanish.

He started to shout, "Fire a musket and raise the recall signal!" but remained silent when he saw the longboat hurriedly putting out from shore.

By the time Anson had secured his spyglass and had swarmed up the mizzen crosstrees, the distant vessel's hull was over the horizon. To his overwhelming relief the stranger didn't look sufficiently tall to be a frigate, let alone a ship-of-the-line! No. She seemed more the size of a coasting vessel.

At the end of ten minutes, the Commodore thought to detect orange paint on that far-off hull. Further inspection convinced him that the stranger was not an enemy but *Tryall*, next to the smallest of all his ships!

So short were the little sloop's masts, he deduced she still must be sailing under the same jury rig which had been contrived for her in Port Julian!

With tears in his eyes, Anson choked, "Dear Lord, I, thy humble servant, thank thee. Charles Saunders has proved himself all I deemed him."

Confidence in the expedition's ultimate success returned and banished some of Anson's near exhaustion. The other ships surely must appear in time. No less than Saunders, Matthew Mitchell, David Cheap and Mr. Gerard were uncommonly fine seamen and navigators. He'd made no mistake in selecting and appointing them, of that he was confident. About Messrs. Legge and Murray he wasn't so sure. But, probably, they too would turn up.

Smiles, at first incredulous, appeared on deck. Then Denis voiced the common thought, "If the *Tryall*, nearly the least of us, has safely rounded the Horn then, surely, the rest can be expected to join us."

That the sloop's condition was deplorable became obvious even at a considerable distance. Her foremast was canting drunkenly forward and, in place of a main course, she was carrying only a storm staysail. Since *Tryall*'s bowsprit had disappeared, her only headsail consisted of a trysail crudely rigged to her splintered stem. Most of that gay orange and black paint which had shone so bravely in Southampton Harbor had been worn away; unpainted planks, mending her bulwarks, showed up a raw yellow. Worst of all, only four figures could be discerned on deck.

"Sir!" cried Denis. "Have you noticed? She carries no anchor."

"I have," Anson said quietly. "We shall have to assist Captain Saunders."

By the time *Centurion*'s longboat had brought its precious green and red cargo alongside, *Tryall* still was tacking laboriously inshore. Without even waiting for the seal carcasses to be hoisted in, Anson ordered Lieutenant de Saumarez to proceed to *Tryall*'s assistance.

That the sloop stood in dire need of help swiftly became inescapable when de Saumarez brought his craft alongside and became enveloped by a nauseating stench. A dead man's shriveled head and arm were projecting from a nearby port. To appear so mummified the cadaver must have remained in that position for a considerable time.

"Ahoy, the *Tryall!*" shouted Lieutenant de Saumarez. "Throw us a line!"

Over the sloop's splintered rail peered the dazed and red-rimmed eyes of Captain Charles Saunders. At first Lieutenant de Saumarez quite failed to recognize his old friend. It was no wonder. *Tryall*'s Captain had grown a thick, black-brown beard and his terribly emaciated features were cracked and distorted by a terrible sunburn.

"Pray convey — apologies — Commodore," croaked the apparition. "Tardy reporting — rendezvous. Fear we — in bad case."

"We're little better off," de Saumarez reassured. "Toss us a line, please. We've some fresh meat and fruit."

After considerable delay spectral figures eased a rope over the sloop's side. "Haven't strength to lower — ladder," groaned a tatterdemalion. "For God's sake, hurry."

Lieutenant de Saumarez and Quartermaster's Mate Clipperton grabbed the sloop's forechains and managed to scramble weakly aboard and were halted dead in their tracks by what they saw.

On deck stood only Captain Saunders, two skeletonic seamen and Surgeon Allen, who drooped over the tiller's handle, the rags of his filthy shirt fluttering forlornly in the breeze.

"Sorry, such a bother —" mumbled Saunders. He stood with arms hanging limp and blinked like a man who, long lost in darkness, again finds himself in sunlight. "Lost all — anchors. Orders?"

"Best sit down and rest, sir. The lot of you. We'll take you in and tie you to the flagship."

Although there was really no call for further conversation, de Saumarez encouraged, "Take heart, Charles. I've fruit and raw meat in my boat and a vast abundance ashore. This island's an earthly paradise."

"No doubt, Philip, but I fear this paradise won't be enjoyed by many of my company." *Tryall*'s Captain managed a ghastly smile. "They've already left for the celestial one." Absently, he tested a running sore on his jaw.

"Never did that Italian poet — I forget the fellow's name — describe a hell more terrible than — one we've suffered — I don't know for how long."

Scenes of Santa Catharina became re-enacted on Juan Fernandez, but on a far more painful scale. So few able-bodied men remained in the two vessels that six days passed before the last of the stricken men reached shore. Although many of these died, the less ailing mended rapidly on a diet of purslane, watercress, wild sorrel, scurvy grass, fresh fish and seal meat.

Soon it was discovered that seal steak, or "sea mutton" as the sailors dubbed it, was less tender and tasty than another available kind of meat; but at first they could not eat enough of it. The sailors came to prefer dog meat because, when the first boatload of men landed to rear hospital shelters, they suddenly were assailed by a snarling pack of huge mastiffs such as Denis's party had seen. They had attacked so boldy that several were shot and killed, and since it chanced that no other fresh meat was available, the half-starved sailors skinned one of the mastiffs, then roasted its saddle and haunches.

"B'God, lads, 'tis better nor any veal ye ever tasted," announced the insensitive experimenters. Other dogs quickly were skinned and devoured and the tidings of their tastiness spread so fast that soon dogs were being hunted like deer.

"Wonder where they came from?" remarked Saunders, tearing eagerly at a chop.

Commodore Anson wiped greasy fingers on the soft grass beside him. "Why, I've read in Mr. Defoe's *Robinson Crusoe* that the first of these fierce creatures were brought in by the Spanish authorities to destroy goats established here a century or more ago by Juan Fernandez, who discovered this place."

"But why destroy such an excellent food supply? I don't understand."

"It seems," Anson explained, "that the goats which used to swarm here offered an inexhaustible source of provender for privateers, buccaneers and other enemies of the Spanish Crown. I fancy the vast goat herds described by Alexander Selkirk have largely been destroyed, but no doubt some survivors persist among the crags and cliffs.

"Well, I must be off. Rest yourself, Charles, till you're more recovered."

Disdainful of tradition, Anson himself pulled an oar in his own barge, at present employed in ferrying essential supplies ashore. To set an example to his officers, he often would support one end of the carry-poles of a hammock in which lay some wretched waister or ship's boy.

Not until all the sick had been landed would the Commodore consent to have a tent pitched for his private use. Grateful hands raised it on a beautiful little savannah divided by a purling brook and shaded from the burning sun by a stand of myrtles and fragrant sandalwoods.

Despite every care, seventy men died almost immediately after being brought ashore; after that, however, there were no more casualties and the remaining invalids started to take on weight. When suffi-

[193]

ciently recovered, they shaved off their beards and took to trimming one another's hair.

Once his decimated crews showed signs of recovery, George Anson re-established a measure of discipline and gradually discouraged familiarities. Parties were detailed to slaughter seals and penguins; others were sent to catch cod, cavallies, breams, groupers and snappers, which were incredibly numerous. Any surplus of these was taken aside, split and sun-dried. The stronger men were sent out to work at cleansing and repairing the King's ships.

Schoolmaster Pascoe Thomas, who had been working tirelessly among the sick, seized his first opportunity to seek peace and privacy and bring his journal up to date. Seated under a feathery cabbage palm, he pulled out a brass pen case and cut a new point for his quill.

One Afternoon eleven Days after *Centurion's* Anchor had gone plunging downward a Team of Sea Elephant Hunters set forth to bring down some Sea Beef as Sea Elephant meat was called. Similarly Seal meat was called Sea Lamb. Heading the Party were two of *Centurion's* Midshipmen, Hyde Parker and Lieutenant de Saumarez's young brother, Tom. The Expedition seemed more like a Picnic than a Bloody Search for meat. Most of the Party had been selected from the younger sailors. Gaily they chaffed one another as they scrambled over the Rocks against a Herd of Great Torpid Beasts.

"Where's the biggest one?" grinned Tom de Saumarez, musket dangling at his side.

Freckled and snub-nosed Hyde Parker pointed. "That old bull with the long trunk. Cock's bones! The brute must measure easily twenty-six foot over all."

"Nearer twenty-eight *I'd* say. With all those cows nestling around him don't he look like a Turkish bashaw in his harem?"

"Aye, that's quite a seraglio he rules!"

Although the meat hunters' voices rang out over the ocean's slow rushing, the brown-black marine monsters only gazed mildly at the advancing men. When a sea elephant moved, masses of blubber, fifteen inches thick, rippled like waves below its inch-thick hide.

Midshipman the Honorable Hyde Parker had been sea elephant hunting before and didn't mind flaunting his knowledge. "Watch, Tom. This is the way it's done."

Yelling and waving his arms, the youth ran up to the nearest bull which, with a ponderous effort, heaved itself up on its front flippers;

[194]

its brief trunk writhed up and back exposing a cavernous red mouth. The sea elephant then emitted a roar as terrifying as that of an enraged lion.

Grinning, the tanned young midshipman jerked a boarding pistol from his belt, reached out and thrust it inside the sea elephant's mouth. When Parker pulled the trigger a blast of smoke for a moment enveloped the vast creature, then it rolled over onto its side, gasping burnt powder fumes. The dying bull commenced to jerk spasmodically and to vomit incredible quantities of bright red blood.

Being an inquisitive sort, young de Saumarez later measured blood lost by a similar bull and was astonished to find that it filled two hogsheads!

After four sea elephants had been slaughtered, the meat detail really settled down to work, using specially sharpened cutlasses. For a while the bereaved cows remained looking on dispassionately, then fell asleep.

The hunters took a long while to hack through layer after layer of ivory-hued blubber. When they got down to the meat, they became gruesomely blood-splashed while hewing out gargantuan steaks. These they dropped into slow-match tubs.

Hyde Parker, a slight, cheerful youth a trifle older than his fellow midshipman, went to wash his hands in the sea. "Had enough of this slaughterhouse, Tom? Let the hands finish the job. We'll go climb the heights and maybe shoot a goat. I'm so sick of dog, sea lamb and sea beef I could vomit."

Despite recently regained strength, the midshipmen made slow work of ascending a volcanic peak upon which a band of gray and white goats could be seen browsing. Both youths were red-faced, puffing and sweat-soaked before they reached the edge of a small plateau on which a magnificent billy, sporting a long beard, was standing guard over his followers.

Before Parker could warn his companion to shoot a young nanny, de Saumarez had dropped the patriarch. More by chance than good aim, Hyde Parker knocked over a fleeing nanny.

"Plague take you for a great fool!" snapped Parker. "Why did you have to go and kill an old billy? His meat'll be stronger than a polecat's and tougher than sole leather. By God, you'll have your share out of him!"

They were bending over the fallen patriarch when de Saumarez said, "I say, look at this! There are notches in this old fellow's ears.

Look, in three places. Somebody must have marked him for his own."

"Aye, and judging by his splintery horns that must have happened long since."

Later, they were amazed to be informed by the Commodore that, almost undoubtedly, this must have been a goat marked by Alexander Selkirk, otherwise "Robinson Crusoe," around 1704, thirty-four years ago!

Anson, having reread the tale many times, was able to identify various landmarks; he even found the remains of Crusoe's stockade and a cave inhabited by the famous castaway.

"Faugh!" Parker complained. "This creature stinks like a whore's drawers. I'm going to try for another nanny."

After reloading and repriming, the younger midshipman left Tom de Saumarez to skin his nanny and started climbing again. A few minutes later Tom grabbed for his musket, so violent was young Parker's yell of "Tom! I see a ship on the horizon — looks like a big one!"

"Where?" gasped Tom after pelting up a goat path.

"See? Over there. No, look more to the north! See her? *See her?*"

"Aye. Damn! There she goes." The stranger had become lost amid a bank of pearl-gray mist.

~~ I I ~~

Ghost Ship

TO OCCUPY A hammock chair beside a clear-running brook and to be free, even for brief intervals, to revel in solitude over the varied fragrant beauties of this secluded, wholly enchanting savannah was George Anson's present conception of paradise on earth.

How generously nature had endowed Juan Fernandez! It teemed with gorgeously colored birds and an infinite variety of exotic blossoms, plants and trees. The music of water purling past his tent suggested a soft sonata. Half dozing, the Commodore thought of his flute for the first time in months, wished it were not aboard his flagship.

The moment's iridescence became shattered by the sound of furiously running feet. Smothering resentment, Anson roused to be shaken into quick alarm. Two men in blood-splotched clothing were splashing across that brook which meandered so gently through a natural lawn of brilliantly green grass. Quickly he recognized the runners as Midshipmen Parker and de Saumarez. What could have gone wrong? Mutiny? Murder?

When they drew near, the blood-covered midshipmen pulled off their caps, tried to control their wild breathing and stand to attention. "Permission to speak, sir?"

"Granted."

"Sir," gasped Parker, "we've sighted a ship from the crags!"

"You're sure it *was* a ship?"

"Aye, aye, sir. She was so rigged. Isn't that so, Tom — er — Mr. Saumarez?"

"Aye, sir. She looked to be a very large ship — the little we saw of her."

The calm and penetrating blue eyes shifted to young de Saumarez. "The 'little we saw'?"

"We'd only a glimpse of her, sir, before she lost herself in a bank of mist. She never reappeared."

With the speed of sound, the electrifying news spread throughout the sprawling encampment that a large, unidentified ship had been sighted cruising off the northern coast of Juan Fernandez!

Officers ran up to Anson's tent with anxiety written in varying degrees across their sunburned features.

Lieutenant Colonel Cratcherode, still leaning on a stick, spoke first. "'Pon my word, sir, we must get busy! She's most certainly a Spaniard."

"And why, Colonel, are you so sure of that?" Anson queried evenly.

"Were she one of ours, wouldn't she come straight in?"

"Spoken like a true landsman," snapped Sailing Master Nutt, who didn't in the least admire Mordaunt Cratcherode. "Even if she wanted to, she couldn't come in. Wind's dead against her."

To the group at large, Lieutenant Brett observed, "If she's friendly, she'll probably reappear."

"Well, Captain Saunders, and what is your opinion?" Anson invited.

Because he'd shorn off his beard, the tall young officer's still wasted

[197]

features could be seen contracting. "I fear it's likely she's a Spanisher, sir. Somewheres I've read that, there being so much good food, wood and water on this island, it's frequented by the enemy."

Intense, dark-eyed First Lieutenant de Saumarez cried anxiously, "I believe Mr. Brett's fears are justified. Do you not recall, sir, that freshly broken jars and scarcely decayed fish were discovered shortly after we landed?"

Briskly Anson arose. "Very well, Mr. Brett. You will at once take all the strongest men out to the flagship. We will defend ourselves as best we can."

"Aye. As best we can," bitterly muttered Brett for, at the present moment, *Centurion* lay stripped of rigging and with all yards and topmasts sent down. Worse still, the flagship's guns had been dismounted and their ports sealed to facilitate fumigation of her hull.

As it was, the party from shore reached *Centurion* barely in time to prevent Surgeon Ettrick from igniting smudges of sulphur and gunpowder soaked in vinegar and then dried.

Somehow a battery of 32-pounders were readied and other preparations made to offer the most desperate resistance. If worse came to worst, Anson ordered both ships be blown up.

As anxious hours dragged by and not a glimpse was had of the stranger the midshipmen claimed to have sighted, a conviction grew that they had been deceived by a mirage.

The Commodore, however, was not among these disbelievers. For one thing, Hyde Parker was known to possess excellent vision. For another, he retained bitter memories of what could happen through mistrusting one's eyesight.

So, not for two days was the cleansing of *Tryall* and *Centurion* resumed or that cordage and canvas which had been rushed aboard the flagship returned to shore.

Anson and Chief Surgeon Ettrick both were astonished and delighted by the speed with which men who had appeared on the point of death began to recover amid this idyllic environment. Soon the convalescents found strength to launder their befouled garments. Untidy beards were shaved off and, with the help of friends, they got their hair again dressed into queues.

Although more and more hands were returning to duty, the officers and men were depressed not to see many familiar faces. Only in this grim fashion could they come fully to appreciate how very great had been the loss of life since quitting Port St. Julian. There was no blinking the fact that, from now on, both men-of-war must sail dangerously shorthanded.

Copper ovens and bulk flour for baking a fresh supply of ship's bread were sent ashore and used night and day. Charcoal was burnt for use in a portable forge set up by the blacksmiths and their mates; a small hill of rusty, broken and bent ironwork awaited their attention.

Bill Buckle and John Clipperton were among those detailed to relay worn or damaged cables and hawsers into smaller ropes for running gear, of which there was a serious shortage.

As long as there was light to see by, sailmakers cut and sewed to patch or replace lost or damaged sails.

Will Pallister, having recovered some of his strength with the resilience of youth, was sent to fish for bacalao, a codlike fish which kept migrating in great shoals past Juan Fernandez. It was easy work; a smallboat could be filled in less than an hour. The catch was then gutted and split for drying on rock pans. The Commodore lent the fishermen every encouragement, since the supply of sea stores remaining to the diminished squadron was perilously inadequate.

More sea elephants were slaughtered and their blubber tried out for oil and grease. Their meat was pickled in salt beef barrels, although no one was entirely confident that it would keep well. It did not.

～ I 2 ～

Coffin Ship

ON THE TWENTY-SIXTH OF JUNE, 1741, a few moments after dawn had drawn a red-gold brush across the cloudless horizon, Camp Cumberland became gripped with hysteria. Everyone able to move rushed to the water's edge and stood there yelling and cheering for, five days after Hyde Parker had reported sighting a ship, *Gloucester* had appeared!

Although she was sailing slowly along, all of three miles out, there could be no mistaking her identity. There were the sturdy, if unimaginative, British lines of her dark-green and white hull.

Heart hammering, George Anson trained his glass on her and

noted that the Fourth Rate was limping along under sagging courses and a very ragged main topsail.

His elation faded on making out a bleached and frayed Blue Ensign aflutter inverted among a fantastic tangle of snapped shrouds, braces and halyards. Lord above! *Gloucester's* rigging was drooping like washlines in a poor housekeeper's back yard. That she had become almost unmanageable was evinced by the erratic course she was sailing.

Burst out Captain Saunders, "She looks in even worse case than my *Tryall!*"

George Anson wasted no time in analyzing his sensations: "Mr. Brett, take only the strongest men — I need not warn you to hasten — load the cutter with water and fresh food and shove off."

While with deeply mixed emotions he followed *Gloucester's* uncertain approach Anson thought, "Oh Lord, I thank Thee for having restored another ship to my squadron and to His Majesty's Service."

He turned to Captain Saunders. "When did we last see her?"

"Why, sir, I've no notion of the exact date, but 'twas above two months ago."

Schoolmaster Pascoe Thomas spoke up. "Sir, it was on the twenty-fourth of April that we lost sight of her. Do you think, sir, the rest of the ships will now appear?"

"I see no reason to doubt it, Mr. Thomas. If two ships have found their way here, why not the rest?"

As the heavily laden cutter began to cleave through a succession of bright blue rollers, a pod of cachalot whales surfaced between it and the stricken man-of-war. The leviathans must have been in a playful mood, for they swam in circles about the cutter, blowing and raising enormous dripping tails high into the air before they sounded and disappeared for good.

"It's a mercy she's worked in so close and we can reach her quickly," muttered Lieutenant Denis, still thin and shaken from scurvy. "Those poor devils must be perishing."

Coxswain Parmer, at the cutter's helm, observed to Lieutenant Brett seated in the stern sheets beside him, "I don't spy no one on her quarterdeck nor any heads at her rail. Her people must be in a main bad way, sir."

"Nor do I. Conditions must be worse than they were with us."

Wade, pulling number two oar, risked a glance over his shoulder and caught a crab.

Immediately Coxswain Parmer snapped, "Keep yer eyes inboard, ye bloody mother's mistake!"

The frown deepened on Peircy Brett's rather high brown forehead when he perceived that all of *Gloucester*'s smallboats either were smashed or lay crazily canted across the booms which normally supported them. Long since, it had been noted that the green and white Fourth Rate's mizzen topmast was missing and that her bulwarks gaped in places like lacunae on a printed page.

When the cutter was still half a mile from her goal, the wind suddenly shifted and caused a loud rattling of blocks and slatting in *Gloucester*'s hoary, slatternly canvas.

"Bend to those oars!" Brett yelled, realizing that the breeze had begun to blow *offshore*.

"Damn," growled Lieutenant Denis. "Now we'll have the Devil's own time to fetch her in."

Francis Drake called back from his place in the cutter's bow, "Have you noticed, sir, that the *Gloucester*'s alive with rats?"

What the boat's crew then saw horrified them beyond expression. The loathsome rodents were swarming about the rigging and running along the bulwarks; some even had ventured out on the bowsprit.

Once the cutter passed into the Fourth Rate's lee, her crew started to gag over a stench far worse than ever had been exuded either by *Tryall* or *Centurion*. Like a pestilential miasma it enveloped the boat crew when they pulled under the gangway.

Tom Ramster, rowing beside Nat Wade, gasped, "Christ in His High Heaven! What a charnel house stink!"

Brett cupped his hands, shouted, *"Gloucester* ahoy!"

No answer.

Again the lieutenant hailed. Then a ghastly, mottled and heavily bearded face appeared at the quarterdeck's rail.

"God above!" gasped Denis. *"That* can't be Captain Mitchell!"

Another shaggy caricature of a face appeared beside the first. For Midshipman Drake to recognize Third Lieutenant Foley proved difficult.

"My service to — Commodore," croaked Matthew Mitchell. "Flagship's safe?"

"Aye, sir. We've brought water and fresh food, with the Commodore's compliments. Can you heave us a line?"

"No. Too far gone," came the listless reply. "You'll — get aboard — best you can."

[201]

Lieutenant Foley called down, "Pray God — water. We're dying — thirst."

As the cutter's crew made fast to *Gloucester*'s battered beak they became aware of an unearthly stillness prevailing upon this tall line-of-battle ship.

Myriad rats squeaked and scuttled off the forecastle when Brett and Drake, followed by a couple of seamen, clambered over the bowsprit and paused in frozen horror. The Fourth Rate's broad sunlit deck was littered with partially consumed human bodies and a fantastic tangle of fallen gear. Only four hollow-eyed, rag-clad scarecrows were on their feet and they had to cling to support of some sort.

Automatically, Lieutenant Brett saluted first the quarterdeck and then Captain Mitchell's spectral form.

Foley's legs suddenly gave and his emaciated figure sank onto its knees. Hoarsely he whispered, "For God's sake — water."

At the same time pulling the cork of a canteen, Drake ran over to steady him. Brett gave *Gloucester*'s semidelirious Captain a drink.

Chills of horror raced down the newcomers' backs. There was something unspeakably macabre about these huge and strangely defiant brown rodents which, with scaly, naked tails trailing, swarmed everywhere.

"My God!" choked Wade. "Look yonder!" Catching up a belaying pin he pointed to a sailor lying near the main hatch. Not quite dead, he was feebly trying to ward off a ring of rats which already were attacking his bony bare feet.

More rats were closing in on the dying man when Wade yelled and hurled the belaying pin. Although it killed a couple of the brutes, the rest, squeaking defiance, recoiled only an instant before returning to the attack.

Grisly, half-consumed corpses lay partially concealed under the ship's boats, between the guns and under fallen rigging.

"If you approve, sir, I will make signal to the camp to send out more men and supplies," Brett told Captain Mitchell. "This offshore wind is increasing."

"In Heaven's name, do," mumbled Captain Mitchell, stuffing his mouth with watercress which drooped from between his inflamed and bleeding gums like a verdant waterfall. "I've had no one left fit to pull a rope since currents and the weather carried us away after we'd sighted Juan Fernandez — I — I don't know how long ago."

[202]

1 3

Souvenir of Funchal

A SIGNAL CANNON, hurriedly loaded by Lieutenant Brett's party, boomed twice and brought *Tryall*'s cutter sailing out under the command of brawny and buoyant Lieutenant Hughes. Although she was gunwale-deep with supplies, she was manned by fewer men than Brett had hoped for. As it was, *Tryall*'s men boarded the coffin ship barely in time, for the south wind quickly increased to half-a-gale, which drove the weary old Fourth Rate even farther away from Juan Fernandez. The men from shore were neither sufficiently numerous nor had they fully recovered their strength. To restore a measure of order to *Gloucester*'s crazy top hamper proved such a task that all Brett could do was to keep her from being driven completely out of sight of Juan Fernandez.

Peter Vesey and Ted Waxter were among the very few of *Gloucester*'s men able to move about once their thirst was quenched. Although gaunt, feeble and listless, for some obscure reason neither had taken the scurvy.

"Damned if I understand why we've been spared," Vesey had remarked one evening a month earlier while he and Waxter were munching a delicacy — dried peas filched from the Captain's private stores. They hadn't felt guilty about this theft because many of the peas had sprouted and must soon have spoiled. Fortunately, the supply had been sufficiently ample to last them quite a long time.

For two agonizing days *Gloucester* blundered crazily about, just managing to keep in sight of Juan Fernandez until a favorable slant of wind brought the semi-derelict to within nine miles of the Island.

It was then that Peircy Brett sought the quarterdeck where Captain Mitchell lay, all but helpless, on some old sails. "Sir, reluctant though I am to say so, I deem it my duty to return ashore and report your condition to the Commodore."

"I understand, Mr. Brett. I suppose there is no help for it, though I hate to see a single able man quit my ship. Will you please take with you my official report — and some of the sickest men?"

"Certainly, sir. You may rest assured that I'll return with all possible speed bringing supplies and as many strong hands as the Commodore can spare."

Gloucester's sick literally sobbed with joy when *Tryall*'s cutter conveyed them into Cumberland Bay and they became able again to distinguish waterfalls. Ironically, three of their number quietly died before the cutter's bottom could grind ashore on that island, the sight of which had tantalized them for so long.

Once George Anson received Captain Mitchell's report he retired to his tent and, after reading the first page, he arose and closed its flaps lest someone see tears creeping down his broad, bronzed cheeks.

> I trust your Honor will excuse me for not arriving at the appointed rendezvous more promptly.

Captain Mitchell had written in a spidery hand that kept wandering off the page.

> Alas, that my tardiness has been unavoidable. I regret to report, sir, that of my original Complement of 396 men, 254 have perished and 80 of the remaining 98 are more dead than alive. We are resolved, however, to do our duty to the end.

Through swimming eyes, Anson stared at the grass beneath his shoes. Good God! The poor devil's lost *over two thirds* of his men! What can be done to replace his losses? But something will have to be, or *Gloucester* will become useless to the expedition.

Fingering a quivering chin, Anson read on:

> All the Pensioner troops are dead. I have left one lieutenant and two Marine privates, all far gone in scurvy.

Anson determined that should this favoring wind continue to die out, as it was threatening to do, he would try to tow the crippled man-of-war into Cumberland Bay. But, before he could give the necessary orders, "Captain Arnand's Curse" — as some would have it — sent a contrary wind roaring in from the south which, assisted by unsuspected currents, quickly drove the luckless ship out of sight.

Two days later when everyone save the Commodore had given *Gloucester* up for lost, the coffin ship — which grim name had stuck to her — reappeared, flying-Dutchman-like, ten miles off the eastern end of Juan Fernandez and, quite unnecessarily, fired two guns to announce her distress.

Under the command of Lieutenant de Saumarez, *Centurion's* longboat immediately was sent out carrying water, fresh food and strong men.

But even while the succoring craft was discharging her cargo another terrible tropical storm broke without warning. When it cleared, the luckless man-of-war again was no longer anywhere in sight.

"Loath as I am to say so, sir, this time I fear we've seen the last of her," was Captain Saunders's comment as he and the Commodore glumly consumed a supper of cabbage palm hearts, radishes and broiled dog chops.

"Why so? She had many new hands on board."

"I fear there wasn't sufficient time to set enough sail to pull her through."

"I believe you are wrong, Captain. Mr. Brett and Mr. Hughes are excellent seamen. Somehow, I cannot credit she has been lost."

Anson's quiet confidence proved justified, for on the 23rd of July the coffin ship appeared for the fourth time. On this occasion she was sighted to the westward of Juan Fernandez and was running before a fair wind which should carry her straight into Cumberland Bay.

After twenty-seven days of agonized blundering about offshore, HBMS *Gloucester* finally dropped her hook between *Tryall* and *Centurion*.

Hardly had the long-lost ship rounded to her anchor than Anson had himself rowed out personally to congratulate Captain Mitchell on having reached the rendezvous. Meantime, boats brought out work parties which were to range through the battered Fourth Rate with instructions to separate the sick from the dead and dying.

To guide these temporary loblollies, Captain Mitchell told off Vesey and Waxter. Said he heavily, "It will soon be dark, so you who are familiar with this ship will lead search parties through the 'tween decks. Take every precaution that no one is overlooked; any oversight at this time will have fatal consequences."

Although hardened to the fearful sights and smells to be expected aboard a sea-worn, thirsty and scurvy-stricken ship, the men from *Centurion* and *Tryall* were utterly revolted by the conditions they encountered in *Gloucester's* 'tween decks.

Only after tying handkerchiefs soaked in vinegar over their noses, were they able to brave the horrible stench pervading the Fourth Rate's hull. They unslung and carried on deck every hammock which, in the opinion of Peter Vesey and Chief Surgeon Ettrick, contained a spark of life.

Another rescue party, guided by Purser's Mate Waxter, kicked aside hordes of rats to explore the officers' country. This included the wardroom, various commissioned officers' quarters, the gunroom and the midshipmen's berth. Several midshipmen, warrant and petty officers must have died a long while ago; little more than bones remained in their hammocks. Others were so far gone that they could only moan feebly in answer to shouts that help was at hand.

Because darkness was closing in rapidly, the rescuers, at Waxter's suggestion, scattered to call out and search the various compartments.

With a curious tight smile on his blond-bearded lips, Waxter said to a quartermaster's mate out of *Tryall,* "Suppose you take the purser's quarters while I search the lieutenants' cabins."

Lieutenant Mouton, Waxter knew to be dead, having himself dropped the Marine's scrawny corpse overboard. Lieutenants Foley and Scott he had seen on deck drinking fresh water and eagerly munching melons.

After casting a quick look about and, finding himself momentarily alone, Waxter slipped into Lieutenant Robert Robinson's dark, tiny and ill-ventilated cubicle formed by those sliding wooden partitions which easily could be taken down whenever the ship was prepared for action.

Waxter's strong white teeth glinted in the light of the purser's glim he was carrying as he slapped several rats off the lieutenant's cot. At first he feared that Robert Robinson had died, but when the lamplight illumined the sick man's parchment-hued face the eyelids slowly slid back.

"Thank God," whispered the lieutenant. "Been fearing — I — I — be missed."

Holding the lamp higher, Waxter stared down in cold hatred.

Softly he invited, "Is there anything you'd like, Mr. Robinson?"

"Water. For God's sake, I — dying — thirst."

"Hang on, I'll go fetch you some," Waxter encouraged and hurried on deck.

When he returned the purser's mate, with great gentleness, slid a hand beneath Robinson's scabby shoulders and raised the invalid so that he could push a blanket behind him.

"So you're thirsty, are you? Well then suck on this souvenir of Funchal!" snarled Waxter and shoved an iron belaying pin between Robinson's rotting teeth. Next, he knotted the gag in place with a grimy kerchief. "I hope, sir, 'twill grant you as much comfort as yours did me."

Followed by Robinson's sunken and terrified eyes, Waxter reentered the passageway an instant before Surgeon Ettrick tramped into sight.

"Anyone alive in there?" he mumbled through his vinegar-soaked mask.

"No, sir. The lieutenant's dead. Shall we examine the midshipmen's berth? We may find someone with the breath of life still in him."

Silently Lord Burfurd reminded himself that he must return soon enough to remove evidence of the manner in which Robert Robinson had met his death.

～ I 4 ～
"A Most Fortunate Passage"

AT THE END of two weeks even the most convinced pessimists agreed that Captain Arnand's curse seemed, at long last, to have lost its force; from now on things would, *must*, go better. The ships would be refitted and start "annoying" the Spaniards. Then, of course, men assured each other, the Acapulco Galleon would be taken off Mexico, and everyone would sail home for England, millionaires.

Like a healing tide confidence pervaded tents and cabins arranged in orderly rows beside a deep, fresh-running stream. Hopes that this ill-starred cruise might not prove an unmitigated disaster mounted when, after the first day, not another of Captain Mitchell's men died and his sick began to recuperate with almost incredible rapidity.

Almost the first thing done to rehabilitate *Gloucester* was to fumigate her and get rid of the multitudinous rats. When the noxious fumes of sulphur and brimstone had done their work, thousands of gray and brown carcasses were shoveled overboard in an ebb tide;

it proved a sickening task to locate and dislodge rats which had suffocated in obscure or inaccessible places.

Clipperton, tough as he was, swore he'd never see a rat again without wanting to vomit.

Although harried by secret fears that General Pizarro or some other enemy force sent out from South America might fall upon the squadron in its present defenseless condition, George Anson forced himself not to work newly recovered men too hard; he allowed them ample leisure in which to eat, bathe and sleep to their hearts' content. Formality dispensed with, he relaxed as far as possible the iron discipline of His Majesty's Navy. This, he assured himself, was only right. Had not all ratings suffered the same horrors and faced a ghastly end, together?

This taste of democracy made possible any number of new friendships.

Lieutenant Brett, for instance, was able to make the acquaintance of Will Pallister whom he first discovered laboriously sketching a sea elephant.

"Not bad, not bad at all," he'd observed while hunkering down beside the youth. "Haven't you perhaps rendered the eyes a bit too large? I know I did at first." Smiling, he produced a lively sketch entitled, "A Sea-Lyon and Lyoness."

Later, Peircy Brett, long-faced and sensitive of expression, lent the youth, who had grown a full inch during his illness, a set of water colors, so while others fished, shot or indulged in rough horseplay under the ever-fragrant sandalwood trees, Will kept on painting — and with increasing skill. For subjects he selected unusual beasts and birds, as well as particularly lovely little vales and stretches of seacoast.

One evening Will, in returning late from a sketching expedition, chanced to pass the Commodore's solitary tent. To his astonishment the Marine on duty before it was standing with hands crossed on his musket's muzzle and was listening in rapt attention to the music of a flute and violin being played in harmony. A glance through the open tent flap revealed the fiddler to be Commodore Anson's private secretary, while the flautist was none other than the Commander in Chief himself!

Andrew Menzies smiled while lowering his instrument. "Well, sir, after so long a lay-off I don't think that was too bad."

Shaking spittle from his flute's end, the solid, red-faced figure laughed softly. "Let us hope, Andrew, that from now on we shall find more occasion to woo the fair Calliope."

Tilting back his big, deeply bronzed head, Anson stared at the lamp-gilded canvas. "D'you know something, Andrew? I've a real conviction that we've weathered the worst Captain Arnand could wish us. In a few weeks more we'll be busy taking prizes and sacking towns."

Menzies's heavy black brows climbed a fraction of an inch. "I wonder, George, what kind of town you can capture, lacking shore troops and field artillery?"

"The element of surprise, properly employed, can reduce the strongest city. Surprise is what I must now rely upon. Besides, the *Wager* still may appear." Anson lowered his voice. "Failing that, we can always lie in wait for the treasure ship from Manila which, I'm told, usually appears off Acapulco a few weeks from now."

There was also renewed speculation about "the Prize of All the Oceans" in the tent village where sailors sang and gambled about campfires. Faintly, bonfires kindled on the beach tinted the three men-of-war a lovely rose-gold color.

"Aye. Soon's we're fit for sea," a grizzled boatswain declared, "I trow 'e Commodore will shape a course straight for Mexico where we'll lay in wait for 'e treasure ship."

"Moonshine!" someone called out. "We're to attack the Spanish coast — a port called Valdeveso. Overheard the Old Man say so myself."

It came as an happy augury that, on the morning of August 17th, still another sail appeared off Juan Fernandez. This time no alarm was taken because the stranger was a very small vessel which hesitated not at all in making straight for Cumberland Bay.

"God above!" roared Charles Saunders from a lookout platform built in a towering tree. "It — damme, it can't be! But it *is* the *Anna!*"

Cheer after cheer arose as the tiny storeship came bowling in with Mr. Gerard's crew smartly furling her threadbare canvas.

George Anson felt too moved to speak. Praise the Lord! Now that the spare stores carried in *Anna* would be available much could be accomplished which previously would have been impossible.

True, the pink's paint had become badly worn and blistered, but she betrayed none of those signs of near disaster such as had distinguished *Tryall* and *Gloucester* on arrival.

Before Mr. Gerard, neatly attired in brown, came ashore, *Anna* fired eleven guns in honor of the frayed pendant trailing from the flagship's bare mainmast.

On halting before the Commodore's tent the merchant captain removed his hat and jerked a bow. "Servant, sir."

"Pray accept my heartiest congratulations, Mr. Gerard, on having preserved and brought in your vessel." He hesitated. "— And how many men have you left?"

The civilian's teeth gleamed in a broad grin. "The same seventeen with which I departed from St. Julian's, your Honor."

An incredulous gasp escaped the assembled officers.

"What! You've not lost a man?" burst out Captain Mitchell.

"No, sir. I've not even a sick hand on board."

Captain Saunders, in something like awe, queried, "Then you've had only a little scurvy?"

"Only a bit, sir. No doubt because we touched at an island and were able to refresh ourselves," Gerard replied a trifle smugly. Cock's bones! Time these haughty fellows learned that the Royal Navy had no monopoly on ability.

"Which island?" Anson demanded slowly. "Record of it must be made on the charts, eh Mr. Brett?"

"Why, sir, it was a near uninhabited island called Inchin-mo by the natives, which lies off the coast of Patagonia in the latitude of 45° 15' South."

"— And when did you make this landfall?" the Commander in Chief queried over the quarreling of parrots among some sandal-woods.

"Why, your Honor, 'twas on the sixteenth of May. I were running before a fierce storm out o' the west-sou'west, when the mainland was reported to leeward." Mr. Gerard spoke slowly and carefully that Menzies might take notes. "Whilst attempting to run my vessel out of danger the fore-tops'l split, so, fearing lest the rest of my rigging might carry away, I ran for shelter under some big islands off the coast to the s'uthard. In their lee I hoped to repair the pink and recover my men from the scurvy which had just appeared amongst them. This done, I proposed to continue in search of you," Gerard explained simply.

"Pray continue your account, Mr. Gerard," Anson invited, while indicating a shady spot where a number of felled tree trunks offered seats.

"I lost both anchors in my efforts to avoid the *Anna*'s being driven towards what seemed to be an unbroken line of cliffs." The burly merchant Captain spread expressive hands. "We had commended our souls to God and were preparing for death among the reefs when a narrow break among the cliffs appeared to starboard. I ordered my headsails set and was able to steer through a rough and narrow channel into a sizable bay which was blessed with deep and calm water."

Ringed about by solemn, sunburned Naval officers in ragged but clean garments, the merchant captain continued, "We remained at Inchin-mo for nearly two months whilst my men recovered their health and repaired my vessel. We then came straight here, your Honor, making a most fortunate voyage."

⤙ I 5 ⤚

Retrenchments

SHORTLY AFTER the *Anna*'s arrival Commodore Anson summoned all Captains and senior officers to a council of war. When they assembled only a few were steadying themselves on sticks or canes; for the most part they were barefooted and bare to the waist. They sat under an old trysail rigged between the few cabbage palms remaining in the vicinity, for, thoughtlessly, the survivors had hacked down nearly all of these magnificent seventy and eighty-foot trees to remove a ball of succulent foliage which sprouted at their tops. When cooked this resembled, and tasted like, fresh young cabbage leaves.

Seated on the smooth gray logs were angular Captain Mitchell, swart Charles Saunders and phlegmatic Mr. Gerard. Present also were Sailing Master Nutt and Lieutenants de Saumarez, Denis, Brett, Hughes and Scott.

Somewhat apart, the land officers sat grouped in instinctive isolation. These included tough old Lieutenant Colonel Mordaunt Cratcherode, Lieutenants Ewers, Gordon, Bruce and Captain Crowden, the only surviving Invalid-Pensioner.

Andrew Menzies, his face still splotched with fading scurvy spots, sat on a stump and arranged documents upon a portable mahogany desk which he held balanced on his knees.

For a while Anson's bright blue eyes probed one sunburned face after another. At length he said, "I have summoned you gentlemen because of certain decisions which may no longer be postponed.

"Mr. Menzies, please pass me Mr. Gerard's report on the *Anna*."

After clearing his throat the Commodore read aloud: " 'Damage to the victualer, *Anna*, pink; viz., fourteen knees decayed or broken, twelve deck beams badly decayed, one breasthook cracked, two standards carried away, much ironwork almost rusted through.' Have you anything to add, Mr. Gerard?"

The merchant captain stood up. "I fear so, your Honor. Many of my vessel's timbers and planks are rotten or so worm-eaten that they must be replaced. Further, her whole fabric is badly strained since my little craft never was constructed to endure such buffetings as she suffered off Cape Noire."

"That is an obvious fact, Mr. Gerard," came the Commodore's unruffled agreement. "In your opinion, can she be repaired here?"

Frowning, the merchant captain scratched his newly shaven pate. "I love my brave little craft so well I'm grieved to admit that, in my opinion, she cannot be rendered seaworthy without the services of a proper dockyard." His voice thickened. "I guess my *Anna* ought to be broken up and her sound portions employed in your Honor's other ships."

Saunders nodded agreement, then his eyes sought the Commodore's. "Sir, much of *Tryall*'s side planking will have to be replaced. I'm also very short of spars and running gear."

Captain Mitchell at once spoke up to advance his claims for replacements. When he had finished, Anson, after glancing at his secretary, smiled faintly. "Mr. Gerard, what value do you place upon your vessel in her present condition?"

The merchant captain replied promptly, "Three hundred pounds, your Honor."

The Commodore's big, sun-bleached head inclined. "That is a fair enough price, Mr. Gerard. I will purchase her." Silently, he hoped that the Lord Commissioners of Admiralty would agree.

"While I feel pained to part with my command," Gerard declared a trifle sententiously, "I feel that any sacrifice which will speed your Honor's squadron home to England is worthy."

Anson treated the merchant captain to a level, but not unfriendly glance. "I fear that you are laboring under a misapprehension, Mr. Gerard. It is *not* my intention to turn back. Not in the least."

Under its tan, Mr. Gerard's flat, round face went dark red. "But surely, sir, you have no choice!"

"— And what prompts you to think so?"

"Why! Why, Lor' love your Honor. All your remaining ships are so badly sea-racked and strained they'll leak like bloomin' sieves ere they reach a dockyard. Many of their masts and spars are known to be unsound."

"All of which is unfortunately true, Mr. Gerard. However, I do not deem such handicaps sufficient to justify my abandoning my mission." He could feel all but a few of his officers' dismayed astonishment. As for Mr. Gerard, he goggled in his incredulity that he was hearing aright.

"But, sir, how can you keep on, having lost half of your force in guns and two thirds of your crews?"

"That is also true, alas," came the equable admission.

"To keep on is impossible. Your Honor has not enough men left properly to sail and fight the *Centurion* alone!"

For the first time Anson spoke a little sharply. "I am all too well aware of that. However, it does not alter my determination to carry out the orders given me, to the extreme limit of my capability."

"And so say us all!" called out Saunders, Brett, de Saumarez and Hughes. But Captain Mitchell and Lieutenant Colonel Cratcherode only nodded.

"The moment *Centurion* and *Tryall* are seaworthy I will sail against the Spanish. After a space I shall return here to pick up *Gloucester*." Briskly Anson turned to her commander. "How long do you esteem it will take to complete repairs?"

Captain Mitchell replied after a pause. "Another two weeks, sir, at the very least. I have in all only eighty men left, so I shall have to ask for the *Anna's* entire company and every other man who can be spared from the other ships."

Powerful features aglow under the awning's sun-gilded canvas, Anson nodded. "Captain Mitchell, you will be lent every possible assistance."

He turned to Lieutenant Colonel Cratcherode, who absently was peeling dead skin from his flaming beak of a nose. "You have, I trust, prepared a return on the present state of the land forces?"

Colonel Cratcherode uttered a barking laugh and the scar disfiguring his left cheek reddened. "Sir, there is no need to prepare a return. Of the land forces under my command I have left exactly

[213]

twenty-two of all ranks. Of them, four are commissioned officers."

Sailing Master Nutt gaped. "That means you have only eighteen soldiers?"

"Exactly," came the Colonel's stiff rejoinder. "At present I command fourteen Marines, four recruits and four officers. I am fully prepared, however, to carry out my orders." He smiled wryly at the Commodore. "It must be admitted that an array so magnificent can't be expected to accomplish much against even a small town — especially since I lack field artillery of any description."

Following this implied acceptance of *Wager*'s loss a brief silence ensued in which the singing of birds and the booming roar of amorous sea elephants could be heard above the ringing of hammers and the rasp of saws at work on the ships.

A hummingbird with a cinnamon body, blackish purple wings and a crown of golden red darted under the old sail and briefly hovered above Anson's head, as if appraising these clumsy humans, then, bright as a jewel's flash, it sped back out into the sunlight.

When George Anson dismissed his officers three definite steps had been decided upon. *Anna* was to be broken up and her useless parts burned. *Centurion* and *Tryall* would depart on a short cruise to look for prizes and, if possible, gain intelligence of Pizarro's whereabouts. Lastly, *Gloucester* would remain at Juan Fernandez to complete repairs and be ready to assist any other stragglers from the squadron.

Even yet, Anson, openly at least, refused to admit that *Severn*, *Pearle* and *Wager* might not appear. Weren't all three of these ships much larger than either *Anna* or *Tryall*?

⁓ 1 6 ⁓

Nuestra Señora de Monte Carmelo

DELIGHTEDLY, THE DREAMER watched Pamela Vesey's long and slender legs flash whitely beneath skirts held bunched up before her as she splashed gaily across shallows below the river's bank. Alabaster teeth glimmered amid the exquisite oval of her features while her dark-brown hair gleamed unbound behind her like a silken gonfalon and her huge and heavily lashed gray eyes shone extra bright beneath slim, winged brows.

"Oh, Peter — Peter!" he heard her call. "Isn't it simply enchanting to be by ourselves on so beautiful a day, with no nasty patients waiting to snatch you away?"

He saw himself running to meet his wife over an emerald meadow splashed with patches of buttercups, poppies and daisies. Laughing, he ran her down, caught her into a breathless embrace and rained kisses onto her provocatively heated features.

"Oh, sweet, my darling!" he heard himself pant. "Have you any excuse for appearing so indescribably desirable?" Peter Vesey watched himself glance about the dell all ashimmer under the early summer sun. Persuaded that no one was in sight, he jerked undone her bodice's ribbons, exposed her breasts and kissed them. Next he swung Pamela off her feet and made for a clump of alders.

"Put me down, you great rogue," she squealed, then dealt him playful slaps as he began undoing her petticoats' ties — she was wearing six.

"Aye, in that I'll obey you."

Abruptly the scene became dissolved by a gruff voice saying, "Now then, enough o' that! Wake up afore it's too late."

Peter Vesey turned on his grass bed and only reluctantly regained consciousness. He yawned, turned his head and found his tentmate, a fellow surgeon's mate named Horsefall, looking at him with an amused expression.

"Who's Pamela?"

"A girl I once loved."

"Evidently. Was she that good in bed?"

"Every bit. What's the hour?"

"It's still too early to get up. Hear the seals barking out on the reefs?"

Vesey settled back on his sweet-smelling couch and found himself wondering what had happened to Pamela of late. Probably by now she'd married Sir Paul Markham, a brother of the lover he'd slain. Someone had reported him to have become most attentive after Sir Arthur's funeral.

What had been done about Minden? Sold, in all probability.

Soon coughs and sleepy curses sounded in the cook tents, then chopping noises and the clang of a skillet striking some object. Next, the balmy air of Juan Fernandez became tinctured by the odors of burning sandalwood and of fish and other meats being fried in sea elephant oil.

[215]

Recently appointed Surgeon's Mate Peter Vesey pulled on his shirt and, through the tent's flaps, watched deeply tanned men emerge, yawning and spitting, from their shelters to relieve themselves wherever fancy dictated. He was donning a pair of ragged but clean canvas pantaloons when, out on Cumberland Bay, sounded the *boom! boom!* of alarm guns. Instantly, the camp boiled with activity. Men rushed down to the water's edge and watched twin puffs of smoke drift away from the signal battery on *Centurion*'s forecastle.

Then everyone noticed the faint glimmer of a sail on the northeastern horizon.

"She one of ours?" demanded Purser's Mate Waxter of John Clipperton.

"Aye. Very likely."

"Then I'll lay you a shilling she'll be the *Pearle!*"

"No. She don't look big enough."

"Come on, be a sport. I'll bet it's the *Wager* if you like."

Clipperton stared. "B'God, I think you'd bet on the hour of your own death."

"Granted the right odds, I would," Waxter laughed, then returned his attention to that strange sail gliding along the horizon.

The men forgot all about breakfast, looked expectantly at a knot of officers who, spyglasses in hand, were clambering up a rude ladder to a lookout platform.

"God grant she ain't one of Pizarro's," Lieutenant Colonel Cratcherode grunted. "He still can utterly destroy this expedition."

After leveling his glass a long while, Anson observed in a taut and even voice, "Gentlemen, I am confident this stranger is not one of ours; her rigging has a foreign look."

Peircy Brett also lowered his telescope. "I agree, sir; one has only to view her stern to see that she is not English built."

Crustily, Cratcherode demanded, "What's he mean by that, eh?"

Captain Mitchell explained, "Spanish shipwrights still join the stern and sides at right angles; ours are rounded — have been a long time."

In frantic haste the smallboats began to push off for the flagship, Anson having decided that, in the event of danger, only *Centurion* would be manned. There weren't near enough men to handle the other vessels, even if they'd been ready to fight — which definitely they were not.

Although *Centurion's* batteries were mounted and ready, much needed to be done before the flagship could be got under way; her lower masts stood bare as three dead pines, innocent of shrouds, yards and topmasts. A considerable but unavoidable delay ensued while her hull was ventilated after fumigation with flowers of sulphur, brimstone and vinegar-cooked gunpowder which, for several days, had smoldered to exterminate rats and other vermin.

As soon as possible, shrouds and certain essential stays were rigged and secured. Officers and men, toiling side by side under a broiling sun next sent up topmasts and yards. None worked more devotedly than George Anson, who, sweating like a longshoreman, personally crossed the main gallant yard in company with a brown-faced seaman. At first he failed to recognize John Clipperton as one of those deserters who'd risked their necks to bring back warning of the Governor's treachery in Santa Catharina.

"Sorry you returned, my man?" Anson queried while adjusting a row of parrels across which this all-important yard would soon be swung.

"No, sir," Clipperton admitted, expertly knotting a pulley into place. "And I'm *that* glad to have back me old quartermaster's mate rating."

"You well deserved that promotion. Do you believe we've just sighted an enemy vessel?"

Clipperton's gapped yellow teeth showed in a shy grin. To be talking to the Commodore like this! "No, sir, I think we've sighted our first prize!"

"Correction accepted. That's the spirit! And she'll not be our last, either."

As acting captain of the mizzentop, Nat Wade drove his men hard to bend on sail and reeve tackle. Clipperton thought, to watch that fellow at work one would never suspect that, a year ago, he couldn't have distinguished the mainmast from a backstay.

Tom Ramster, his hard face flaming in the heat, yelled across from the maintop, "By God, we'll soon be earning us a pot o' prize money. Yonder craft's a tall one!"

Despite the survivors' best efforts *Centurion* wasn't ready for sea before six of the evening, by which time the stranger had vanished on a westerly course.

In quiet desperation the Commodore ordered: "All available boats will take the flagship in tow."

Night had fallen and strange constellations were sparkling before a breeze at last arose and, in a well-suppressed frenzy lest the chase be lost, Anson ordered the smallboats to cast off. Exhausted though they were, the oarsmen raised a cheer before commencing their long pull back to Juan Fernandez.

Once the night wind really began to blow, *Centurion* picked up such speed that soon the glow of campfires along Cumberland Bay faded from sight.

Although his flagship was under way once more, George Anson fought down a rare sense of depression because she sailed so sluggishly. Great clusters of barnacles and yards upon yards of weed upon her long uncleaned bottom were holding her back.

His discouragement increased while *Centurion* plowed on, engulfed in the darkness. Was she sailing the right course to overtake the stranger? Why hadn't he had at least a few yards crossed and a few sails bent on? A truly capable commander in chief like Drake or Hawkins undoubtedly would have.

Bitter curses arose when daylight disclosed the flagship sailing quite alone over a placid, dawn-gilded ocean.

Men who, despite grinding fatigue, had been all smiles the day before now glowered as they muttered, "That damn' Cap'n Arnand ain't done wi' us yet!"

Anson summoned his lieutenants and succeeded in appearing confident. "Gentlemen, from the stranger's course when last seen, I am confident that her destination is Valparaiso." He turned to his grimly silent sailing master. "Mr. Nutt, I want all studding sails set. Instruct your quartermaster to steer southeast by south."

After two days and another night had passed with never a glimpse of the chase, Anson silently swallowed his disappointment and ordered *Centurion* on a course that would take her back to Juan Fernandez. What *had* he done, or not done, that this expedition should be so persistently hounded by misfortune?

Characteristically, the Commodore allowed no idleness. Further repairs to the rigging were effected and the flagship's newly assembled crew drilled in duties which, to most of them, were unfamiliar.

George Anson was consuming a solitary meal of cold seal meat, purslane, yams and Sicilian radishes when Midshipman Francis Drake came clattering below to be challenged by a Marine again guarding the Commodore's door.

"We've sighted her, sir!" the youth panted. "I — oh!" Under Anson's expressionless stare Drake remembered his manners, pulled off his hat and stood awaiting permission to speak.

"Proceed, Mr. Drake. How does she sail?"

"Sir, she s-sails about t-ten miles off," the midshipman babbled. "Mr. Denis th-thinks s-she is s-steering straight in our direction!"

"My compliments to Mr. de Saumarez and will he please order the men to quarters? Inform Mr. Nutt that I want all useful sail to be set on a course to intercept the stranger."

Even before Anson could reach his command post on the poop-deck, the only remaining drummer boy had begun to beat to quarters. Everywhere furious activity became evident. Flimsy bulkheads creating officers' cabins hastily were knocked down and stowed or hoisted out of the way against the deckheads. Bare feet pounded down to the magazines as powder was lugged up to supply the guns; roundshot was placed in rope garlands and sand scattered over the deck to ensure steady footing should blood begin to flow.

With difficulty preserving his reputation for unshakable calm, Anson paused on the quarterdeck and smiled to see Lieutenant Colonel Cratcherode, already wearing a spotless scarlet tunic, cursing delightedly while buckling on his sword.

His scarred cheekbone appeared more craggy than ever, and his cold gray eyes shone when he saluted smartly. "Seems at last, sir, that we're in for a bit of sport, eh? Have you any special orders for me?"

"Yes, Colonel. I'm so shorthanded I wish your Marines to handle the mizzen braces till we engage."

Midshipman Tom de Saumarez, in the maintop, noticed the Commodore's presence on the poop and called down, "She's a big one, sir, and making straight for us. Her masts are all in line."

"She must be of at least five hundred tons, sir," Lieutenant Denis interjected excitedly. "She may even be one of General Pizarro's lesser men-of-war."

Pray God she's not! thought Anson. The men are still weak, too few and in dire need of more gun drill. Wonder if I can overawe the enemy without matching broadsides?

Grizzled old Clipperton, in the foretop, so far forgot discipline as to yell across to Wade, busy setting the main royal, "Two to one it's the *Wager!* 'Twould be just our bloody luck."

"I'll take that!" Nat bellowed back. "You be damned for a sour owl."

[219]

One after the other *Centurion's* heavy guns were run out as, successively, portlids were hoisted to reveal their scarlet undersides to the hot and dazzling sun.

"Mr. Keppel, please show Spanish colors at the main."

"Aye, aye, sir."

Immediately after the red-gold-red ensign of Castile and Léon had appeared at *Centurion's* main truck a similar flag climbed into the stranger's rigging.

Anson suddenly put down his spyglass and observed to Menzies who, silent and efficient as always, was noting the time and the wind's direction for subsequent entry in the log, "That is not the same ship we sighted off Juan Fernandez. I imagine the Dons over there are mistaking us for the one we saw, which would explain why she continues to close in so confidently."

A hoist of butterfly-bright flags fluttered to the enemy's mizzen. Undoubtedly they were private signals, which couldn't be read by anyone aboard *Centurion.*

Without an instant's delay Anson directed Midshipman van Keppel, acting signal officer, "Hoist a jumble of flags; may serve to keep the Dons continuing towards us whilst they try to make sense of 'em."

The Commodore's ruse succeeded beyond all expectation; less than a mile of sunny water separated the two ships when the stranger finally, and in frantic haste, wore onto the starboard tack, whereupon Sailing Master Nutt altered course to intercept.

Not until half after noon was the stranger positively identified as the first Spaniard to be sighted by Anson's squadron since *Pearle* had eluded Pizarro's ships off Patagonia — half an age ago, it seemed.

Along with several others told off to form a boarding party, Tom Ramster was sharpening his cutlass at a grindstone in the armorer's room when Wade appeared looking very serious. "Think she'll give us a fight?"

"Hope so, our bloody gun crews need practice. What's the matter? Got the wind up?"

The topman flushed. "We-l-ll, I was wondering what it's like to get hit."

"Depends where and how," came the unconcerned reply. "Just pray you don't cop a spent ball or splinter in your guts; man takes a long time dying that way."

Will Pallister, detailed to run messages down to the main gundeck, experienced wild exhilaration at the prospect of actually coming to grips with the Papists. He kept patting the butt of a clumsy boarding pistol that had been issued to him. Wonder how Hawkins, Drake and Grenville felt when they sighted the Spaniards for the first time? Were they afraid of getting killed? Of course they weren't, so I won't be, either.

At long last, Anson turned to his first lieutenant, ordered crisply, "Mr. Saumarez, I want four blanks fired."

Hearty cheers rang out when the guns spoke, even though harmlessly. Soon the word circulated that this green and yellow painted ship was no man-of-war, but a towering, high-sided merchantman. Better yet, she was riding so deep in the water she must be carrying a very heavy cargo!

After the warning gun's smoke had cleared and the enemy still made no sign of heaving to, Anson ordered Brett, as gunnery officer, to fire roundshot into her rigging.

When a fifth cannonball had smacked through the stranger's canvas, puncturing sails and severing rigging, down fluttered the Spanish flag, a sight which restored to Anson a self-confidence lost off Cape Noire. At the same time the enemy Captain ordered his sheets loosed so that his canvas flapped useless, empty of wind.

Hoarse, triumphant yells burst from the throats of men who still couldn't quite credit that the squadron had taken a prize — and, best of all, without a single casualty!

～ I 7 ～
First Spoils

BECAUSE LIEUTENANT PHILIP DE SAUMAREZ spoke fluent Spanish — as well as French and Portuguese — Commodore Anson sent him to take possession of the big green and yellow merchantman now squattering about on the bright blue Pacific, for all the world like a wounded mallard.

Bare brown torsos swinging in unison, the longboat's oarsmen kept stealing glances over their shoulders while the handful of scarlet-jacketed Marines and cutlass men — one must be on guard against Papist trickery — grinned happily at this foreign-looking ship with its soaring masts, square stern and peat-brown sails.

Never a head showed above the big merchantman's ocher-hued rail and de Saumarez was forced to yell threats before a rope ladder was slipped over the side. De Saumarez then paused on the bulwarks, utterly amazed, for, on the deck immediately below, was kneeling a trio of dark-bearded men. They were holding up hands joined in supplication.

The oldest of them quavered, "*Piedad! Por amor de Dios!* Have mercy upon your miserable servants, most noble *señor*. Grant us quarter. We are no soldiers, but only poor merchants."

Infinitely amused, de Saumarez noticed that a gang of Indian, Negro, mulatto and mestizo sailors had collected about the foremast and feverishly were telling their beads. Obviously they expected immediate torture and death. Around them discarded small arms slid about.

After assuming a severe, military expression, *Centurion's* first lieutenant leaped lightly down onto the untidy, sunlit deck to be immediately followed by Lieutenant Bruce, then big, blond Midshipman van Keppel.

Solemnly, de Saumarez touched a hat trimmed in verdigris-dimmed gold lace in the quarterdeck's direction. To it was secured just such a crucifix as had graced English ships until the eighth Henry had put an end to the practice.

"*Quién es el Capitán?*"

A brown-bearded individual whose spaniel-like eyes were ringed in terror shuffled forward on his knees. "I am that most unfortunate wretch, *Señor Almirante.*"

"Your name?"

"Don Manuel Zamorra, *Ilustre Señor Inglés.*"

"Very well," crisply directed the lieutenant. "Get up and let's have no more of this nonsense."

Then, in a loud voice, he addressed the crew. "Lay aside your fears and know that our *Comodoro* is a most generous enemy; one no less remarkable for his lenity and humanity than for his resolution and courage."

Even the dullest member of that boarding party realized these dark-faced fellows were crediting fantastic lies circulated by the Spanish government about barbarities to be expected at any Englishman's hands.

With hearts lighter than in many a horror-haunted month, the prize crew bound the Spaniards' hands behind them — they numbered fifty-four, but neither the officers nor any of the thirteen passengers aboard were tied up, or even searched for valuables.

Copying George Anson's manner, de Saumarez, standing very straight and reserved in bearing, followed Captain Zamorra below to accept a goblet of sherry from a silver tray passed by a Negro servant who at first trembled so violently he spilled most of the wine.

The swarthy young Prize Captain quickly learned that *Centurion*'s initial prize was the *Nuestra Señora de Monte Carmelo*, of 450 tuns burthen, twenty-seven days out of Callao in the Vice-Royalty of Peru, bound for Valparaiso in the Captaincy-General of Chile; also, that several passengers were men of considerable importance, among them the son of the Vice-President of Chile.

Through *Carmelo*'s stern windows — her captors at once abbreviated her name — de Saumarez was relieved to see *Centurion* cruising only two hundred yards to windward with guns run out and British flags snapping from all three masts.

He remembered Anson's final instructions: "Once you have secured the prize, ascertain the extent and value of her lading and send me the most valuable parts without delay. She may have consorts nearby."

Upon de Saumarez's insistence, all bills of lading, invoices, and the manifest were pondered. While glancing through these documents de Saumarez's sensitive features lit; then he ordered that specified chests and bales of valuable cloth be produced at once and ferried over to the flagship, it being by no means unlikely that, at any moment, Pizarro's royals might lift above the horizon. Accordingly, he signaled that *Centurion*'s longboat and barge should be sent to carry off the loot.

Once these boats arrived, Lieutenant Bruce ordered the dejected and still terrified seamen untied. Next, they were forced to descend a rope ladder and leap into the barge, heaving and lurching below.

Personally, the *Carmelo*'s prizemaster then superintended the lowering, by means of a whip rigged to *Carmelo*'s mainyard, of fourteen iron-bound chests, each weighing over two hundred pounds.

To *Centurion*'s curious and delighted boat crews de Saumarez issued a stern warning: "Look lively down there! Carelessness or pilfering will be punished by severe flogging!"

The lowering sun was staining the broad and placid Pacific with colors suggestive of the Spanish national colors — scarlet and gold

[223]

— when Lieutenant de Saumarez, looking slighter and younger than ever in his simple white shirt and breeches, managed his sword and nimbly ascended the flagship's gangway. Gravely, he saluted the Commodore waiting impassively on the poop.

In honor of the moment, George Anson had turned himself out in a ruffled shirt, lace stock and cuffs and a handsome green velvet frock coat glittering with gold lace and buttons of the same metal.

Lieutenant de Saumarez commenced his report soberly enough. "Sir, I discovered by reading the bills of lading that those ironbound chests contain milled silver to the value of" — then excitement bubbled into his voice — "at least eighteen thousand pounds!"

"That is very gratifying news, Mr. Saumarez."

Anson was finding it increasingly difficult to retain an impassive face but somehow he managed it. Ever appreciative of dramatic effect, the Commodore ordered all hands piped on deck and mustered about the main hatch.

Grinning, the sunburned, half-naked fellows lined up and "toed the mark" by ranging their big toes along an indicated deck seam in which tar remained soft after the day's heat.

Peircy Brett set the ship's armorer to smashing a series of massive padlocks. To the assembled men, the harsh ring and clang of iron on iron played the sweetest of symphonies.

When the chest lids were thrown back, delighted gasps and yells made the flagship's deck resound. The treasure chests were seen to not only contain silver dollars but also in great quantity finely wrought plate, gold rings, chains, bracelets and earrings!

Several chests were packed with the most delicate gold and silver lace imaginable. The greatest shout of all went up when a small bronze coffer was opened to the sunset's glare and gave off the maddening brilliance of unset emeralds, amethysts, turquoises, pearls and sapphires.

For a moment, hunger, thirst, sickness and deaths all were forgotten. A man standing beside Nat Wade chuckled, "Reckon this oughter lay old Arnand's ghost for keeps."

"Don't count on it," muttered someone else. " 'E were a main powerful curser!"

The spirits of all hands soared still higher next day when it became known that the prize had been carrying cargo worth over 20,-000 pounds — not counting the value of *Carmelo* herself. Visions of an easy old age, of riotous living, of revenge or satisfied ambition rose again.

The two ships were steering for Juan Fernandez under a dainty fingernail cutting of a moon when Commodore Anson invited Captain Zamorra to dine — to the latter's vast astonishment.

The Spaniard's perplexity grew further on learning that his officers and passengers were being entertained in the wardroom and the gunroom. The prisoners still seemed unable to credit that they weren't about to be blown from the muzzles of guns, skinned alive or keelhauled by the dreaded *Ingléses.*

In very halting Spanish, Lieutenant Brett reminded these quick-gestured and voluble gentry to thank their respective patron saints that they'd been taken by the Royal Navy and not by buccaneers or pirates.

"It must have been a matter of deep regret to you, Captain," Anson glanced at Andrew Menzies who sat ready to record pertinent items of conversation, "that your vessel was not armed. Certainly, it would have afforded you both pleasure and honor to have exchanged some broadsides with us? For a fact," Anson lied blandly, "I had entertained hope that your vessel might be one of a certain Admiral Pizarro's squadron."

The square-bearded Captain stared. *"Pizarro?* Then you cannot have heard, *Señor Almirante?"*

De Saumarez broke in, *"Señor* Anson is *'Comodoro'* — not *'Almirante.'* " Silently he added, though he ought to be one!

Anson treated his second to a look of mild reproof.

"I have not heard what, Captain?"

While waiting for Zamorra's reply Anson experienced a sudden constriction in his throat; then Pizarro must have taken one or all of his missing ships!

"— That you no longer have cause to fear General Pizarro's squadron."

Anson and de Saumarez sat bolt upright. The latter queried sharply, "And why so, *Señor Capitán?"*

Before replying Don Manuel de Zamorra, in exasperating deliberation, swallowed a draught of Fayal. "Why, *Señor Comodoro,* for many weeks it has been common knowledge in Spanish America that *General Almirante* Don José was forced to retreat to Rio de la

Plata by a number of fearful *huracánes* encountered by his ships off la Tierra del Fuego.

"In fact, *Señores,* the unlucky gentleman never succeeded in passing through the Straits le Maire. It was while attempting to do so that he lost two of his finest ships."

Anyone but Anson would have betrayed overwhelming relief. The Commodore said only, "The weather at that time is not at all agreeable." It never even occurred to him that he might congratulate himself and his captains on having succeeded where the Spaniards had failed.

De Saumarez's lively black eyes began to glitter. "This is most gratifying news, sir. Is it not?"

"Capital!" gravely admitted the Commodore. "Except that I should have preferred to have met Pizarro and beaten him in action. A drop of wine, Don Manuel?"

The captive Captain's reticence, he noticed, was decreasing in direct proportion to the number of times his glass was refilled.

"*Mil gracias,* your wine is indeed admirable." *Carmelo's* former Captain bowed in his chair. "For me it has proved most unfortunate that the Viceroy of Peru should have lifted the embargo on coastwise traffic when he did."

"Why such an embargo, *Señor?*" Anson demanded almost carelessly.

"Even while you were resting in Brazil, it became known to the authorities that a strong English squadron was about to depart for the Pacific." Don Manuel's spaniel-like, brown eyes shifted. "So, was it not sensible for the Viceroy to forbid unarmed merchantmen, like my unhappy ship, to sail and risk being taken?"

"I suppose so," Anson admitted. "What then?"

"When, for many weeks nothing was seen or heard of your ships after they had sailed from Santa Catharina last January, was it not natural, *Señor Comodoro,* to assume that they had all been destroyed off Cape Horn in those very same *huracánes* which ravaged the *flotilla* of *General Almirante* Pizarro?"

"I presume so."

Captain Zamorra pulled from his pocket a handful of thin, black *cigarros* and very diffidently, offered them to this most inscrutable of hosts. "*Ay de mí!* It was that lifting of the Viceroy's embargo which allowed me, and many others, to sail, all unsuspecting of Your Excellency's presence."

[226]

De Saumarez left off translation and, flushed with excitement, addressed his superior. "Therefore, sir, the Spaniards along this coast *must be unaware* of our presence! With any luck, we shall be like wolves in a sheepfold."

"We shall — provided we allow not a single Spaniard to get away."

Dessert was none too adroitly served by Peter O'Brien, Anson's new steward — poor Hazeltine having followed Oldham overboard. Over steaming coffee — the Commodore's supply had been replenished from *Carmelo* — de Saumarez's continued questioning brought forth two more important, but less palatable, items of intelligence.

The first was news of the failure of Lord Cathcart's powerful expedition — it had been sent against Cartagena in Colombia and was then to cross the Isthmus to Panama City expected to effect a junction with Anson's forces. But, Captain Zamorra stated with obvious relish, the noble lord had been repelled before Cartagena with terrible losses and driven off to lick his wounds in Jamaica.

To George Anson, the Spaniard's next piece of news proved even more dismaying. Soul-sick, he learned that, far from having been lost off Cape Noire, Captain the Honorable Edward Legge of *Severn* and Captain the Honorable George Murray of *Pearle*, by secret agreement, had deserted their duty and *had turned back to England!*

Although suffering greatly from scurvy, Zamorra stated, they, nonetheless, had reached Rio de Janeiro in safety and soon afterwards had sailed for home.

For the first time in Anson's memory, Andrew Menzies permitted himself an outburst. "Those utter, unmitigated swine!" snarled the Carolinian. "May God damn those cowardly carpet knights to hell!"

Although feeling ready to vomit with disgust, Anson for once spoke sharply, "Now, now! Vilification accomplishes nothing, Mr. Menzies."

Savagely Anson reproached himself. To think he'd passed over poor old Salt for the Honorable George Murray! Surely Admiral Blake would never have been guilty of such crass stupidity.

Anson found himself wondering if *Wager*, too, had deserted him.

HBMS *Carmelo*

When HBMS *Centurion* and her impressively huge prize entered Cumberland Bay they fired victory guns, which immediately were answered by *Tryall* and *Gloucester*, now armed but incompletely rerigged. Their crews, when they made out a Spanish flag beneath a Royal Jack aboard the *Carmelo*, shouted themselves hoarse. Victory at last! Soon they'd be taking ships on their own.

Once *Centurion* lay at anchor, the Commodore sent for Captains Mitchell and Saunders. After congratulations had been offered in Anson's great cabin, he dispatched Menzies to fetch *Carmelo*'s papers. Not until his secretary had gone, did the Commander in Chief, stony-faced but imperturbable, describe the desertion of Captains Legge and Murray.

Matthew Mitchell, ever religiously minded, was so shocked he exploded with an old Elizabethan oath. "By the gullet of God! Who'd have deemed *them* capable of desertion in the face of the enemy?"

"I fear I did not," Anson admitted. "And, because of that misjudgment of character, I have lost half of my fighting force."

Saunders's usually good-humored expression dissolved into a scarlet mask of fury. He was so angry he started to shake all over. "Pray God I'm on hand to watch them shot! No. Damme, such cowardly curs deserve to be hanged, gentle blood or no gentle blood!"

"At least we've one thing to be thankful for, gentlemen," Anson pointed out. "General Pizarro is not in the Pacific."

"What?" burst out both Captains.

"Yes. He turned back nearly three months ago."

"Thank God," sighed Saunders. "That will simplify matters."

Once Menzies returned, Anson's big, brown hands carefully flattened the papers. Said he, "I have here reports concerning movements of several coastwise merchantmen, some of which are reported to be carrying plate and silver bullion, as well as very rich cargoes. But whether this will prove true is another matter."

Saunders's flush faded and his wide-set brown eyes began to twinkle. "I would be very pleased, sir, to try my luck with them as soon as may be!"

"So you shall, Captain," smiled Anson. "You have earned the right to try for the fattest ship on this list. Tomorrow, you are to make sail for the mainland and attempt to intercept her off Valparaiso, but, mark this well, only *out of sight of land!* The Spanish authorities *must not* learn of our presence any sooner than is inevitable."

By the light of the cabin's great brass lantern he squinted at a paper handed him by his secretary. "Her name is the *Santa María de Aranzazu*. Quite a mouthful, eh, Saunders?"

"Aye, sir. I expect it will prove easier to take her than to pronounce her name."

"Incidentally, should you prove successful, I intend to commission her into His Majesty's service and arm her with the *Anna*'s guns, so try not to shoot her up too badly."

Saunders grimaced. "With the *Anna*'s guns, sir? Why, she mounts but four little six-pounders."

"True. Still, they are better than nothing."

He made no mention of his resolution to restore his squadron to its original number of six men-of-war. The Board of Admiralty might be mollified — even gratified — should he return with the same number of ships entrusted to his command. Well, he had one back already, definitely a step in the right direction. If only *Anna* had not had to be destroyed!

Watched by his Captains, Anson commenced to pace, then paused to view *Carmelo* through the stern windows. She now was surrounded by boats from shore filled with men consumed with curiosity to view, at close quarters, this, the squadron's first prize.

"I know how shorthanded you are, Captain, so tomorrow I will reinforce you with eight prime seamen out of the flagship; also some Indians out of the prize — or would you prefer Negroes?"

Had Captain Saunders possessed a tail he would have wagged it. "Negroes, sir, if it's all the same to you. As a rule they're stronger."

Matthew Mitchell listened dolefully, wished his *Gloucester* were ready for sea. But she wouldn't be, not for a week at the earliest.

With the first light of September 15th, 1741, *Tryall* dutifully saluted the Commodore's long red pendant before standing out of Cumberland Bay.

[229]

To Saunders's keen disappointment, *Tryall*'s departure was by no means dashing; her masts, despite everything done to strengthen them, had remained very tender and could not be depended upon to carry more than normal sail even in fine weather.

Long before *Tryall*'s gallants had disappeared over the southwestern horizon, the Commodore conducted a solemn commissioning service aboard *Carmelo*. At the end of it, Lieutenant Philip de Saumarez was directed to raise a Blue Ensign to her maintop.

Hardly had the delighted Acting Captain complied, than a gang of carpenters began to pierce her sides for guns and otherwise transform this ponderous ex-merchantman into a regularly commissioned man-of-war.

Anson's next action was to increase *Gloucester*'s inadequate complement by twenty-eight prisoner seamen — brown, black or white. Even so, Captain Mitchell would remain shorthanded by nearly a hundred and fifty men.

Four days of furious activity ensued, devoted to completing repairs, taking on water, the salted fish, and sea elephant meat and each ship's share of *Anna*'s sea stores which had not spoiled.

Aboard *Gloucester*, Purser's Assistant Waxter was busy making book on what the Commodore would do next.

"Five shillin's he'll attack Valparaiso," offered a sailmaker's mate.

"Done!" laughed Waxter. "Five shillings say he won't. The place is too strong for our present force. Any other wagers?"

"We'll sail against Panama, soon's the *Tryall* gets back. Ten shillings on it."

"That's a good bet, Tim, so I'll only give you one for two."

"Yer both addled," cut in *Gloucester*'s blacksmith. "I'll lay a month's pay 'e Commodore sails for Mexico to take the great galleon."

"At the first opportunity?" Waxter shrewdly qualified.

"Aye. He's not the sort to dillydally. The wager's made?"

"Made!" Using a sharpened bullet for a pencil, Waxter quickly made an entry in a pocket book he carried. "Thirty-five shillings say we don't head straight for Mexico!"

Wild enthusiasm pervaded the squadron but, all the same, there was occasional trouble. After the free and easy months ashore, the men resented restoration of that rigid discipline essential to the management of a British man-of-war.

On September 19th Anson elected to wait no longer for completion of repairs on *Gloucester* and announced his plans to Captain Mitchell, Acting Captain de Saumarez and Lieutenant Brett.

"The flagship and *Carmelo* will proceed, in company, to the *Tryall's* appointed cruising ground. Once she is found, our three vessels will then fan out and work northwards along the coast — always well out of sight of land. By fanning out," Anson explained, "we gain a double advantage. This will better prevent possible prizes from slipping by unseen. Further, if the Spaniards should sight a single ship they should have no grounds for misgivings; whereas even a glimpse of two or more vessels sailing in company most certainly would excite alarm."

After a while hawk-faced Captain Mitchell inquired, "Where am I to join you; off Valparaiso perhaps?"

The Commodore fixed piercing blue eyes on Mitchell and spoke with grave deliberation. "I prefer you to complete your repairs, then proceed to the vicinity of the Port of Payta in northern Peru. You will remain in the latitude 5° 12′ South until I appear. Now mark this again, gentlemen, *under no circumstances* is any one of you to risk having his ship sighted from the shore."

In terminating the conference Anson offered his hand to Captain Mitchell, thus far luckless. "I am confident, my dear uncomplaining friend, that on your way to meet me you will take several rich prizes. God knows you've earned such."

Some five days after *Centurion* and *Carmelo* had tacked out of beautiful Cumberland Bay for the last time, Will Pallister was enjoying a particularly vivid sunset from his lookout's post in the foretop. Brown-faced and filled out, he, like the rest of the crew, now was discharging multiple duties.

If only he'd thought to bring aloft a little box of water colors recently donated by Peircy Brett! At the same time the youth appreciated how futile it would be for him to attempt reproduction of such gorgeous colors. He might, however, have depicted green and yellow *Carmelo* and white and brown *Centurion* under way with the sunset's glow warming their sails.

Briefly, he followed the playful antics of a herd of seals as they pursued one of their mysterious migrations. Seabirds still shrieked and wheeled astern while tracking the raiders away from Juan Fernandez, as if reluctant to see them go.

A warm current descended Will's back with the sudden realization that Parson Pallister's runaway son now was owed a considerable sum in prize money! No one could guess, of course, what each man's share would amount to. But, as a newly appointed assistant to the Commodore's private secretary, he ought to be able to find out.

With his remaining teeth sound — he'd lost quite a few — and his eyesight restored to normal, Will felt well on his way towards achieving his ambition of becoming a genuine mariner — of the sort described in sailors' ballads.

He was roused from his happy introspection by the creaking of the fore-topsail yard just beneath him, and realized that the Watch was bracing about to catch a new slant of wind. The sound reminded him that the Commodore, recently, had offered the bonus of a pound sterling to whosoever should first report a sail of any sort.

Before resuming his methodical study of the horizon, Will once more feasted his eyes on the sunset and caught his breath with a little click.

Was a small something flashing rose-white on the brass-hued horizon? No. Yes. No. He enjoyed extra sharp vision. Everyone who knew him had commented on it. Yes! There *was* something out there and, what was more, yonder distant sail *was not alone!*

Heart pounding, Will drew a deep breath, tried to make his voice sound deep and manly when he shouted, "Ahoy the deck! Sail ho! Two sails!"

Instantly Lieutenant Denis, Officer of the Deck, yelled back, "Masthead there! Where away?"

Will was so rattled he forgot seamanship and failed to give a compass bearing, only screamed, "Over there! There, just to the left of the sunset."

The ship's company reacted instantly. Presently, the Commodore, himself, swarmed into the mizzen shrouds. For so big and solid a man he was extremely agile.

At once Anson ordered studding sails set and *Centurion* put onto a course straight for the sinking sun's eye, so, thanks to a stiff following breeze, his flagship fairly surged to meet the two strangers. At the same time the lone drummer, for a second time within the month, beat "to quarters" and the boatswain's pipe shrilled incessantly.

Fervently, all hands prayed that the strangers might not escape during the onrushing darkness.

By the deepening twilight *Carmelo* was seen dropping far astern.

To Anson's bitter and unspoken disappointment the prize had proved a very sluggish sailer, despite her considerable spread of canvas and comparatively clean bottom. What mortification it must have cost her new captain to acknowledge his Commodore's signal and obediently stand away from the flagship.

Only Brett and Denis could appreciate how this must have galled ambitious Philip de Saumarez. However, he must have recalled the Commodore's determination never to allow the Spaniards to sight two British ships in company; his *Carmelo,* at present, was sailing so far astern that the enemy might very well thus far have failed to notice her presence.

Soon it became pleasantly apparent that the strange ships were even more sluggish sailers than *Carmelo.* What presently puzzled the little knot of sun-bronzed officers collected on *Centurion's* poop was the fact that, instead of making off at top speed, the larger of the two strangers continued to make for the flagship while her smaller consort spread all possible sail and bore away to the westward.

Why? Wariness seized Anson. Might this unknown commander be contemplating a stratagem? If so, what was it?

At seven o'clock, *Centurion* had arrived within long cannonshot of the larger ship, but complete darkness was near, so Anson ordered the flagship rounded to that she might present her starboard broadside. Quarter-gunners stood ready, blowing on their matches, very eager to fire the expedition's first real broadside. They recalled orders to shoot at the stranger's rigging and spare her hull.

An unfamiliar sense of well-being warmed the Commodore. This looked like another addition to his growing squadron! Soon five ships would be showing his Majesty's Blue Ensign on the Pacific.

The two ships were sailing on parallel courses a musket shot apart, when Anson directed crisply, "Mr. Nutt, pray hail yonder vessel and summon her to show her colors."

Justinian Nutt's great voice carried over the darkening ocean, *"Quién está usted? A Donde está su bandera?"*

Equally clear, an English voice bellowed back, "Belay there, *Centurion!* This is *Tryall's* prize! I've no British flag to show."

Muttered van Keppel to his good friend Midshipman Hyde Parker, "That'll be Big Mouth Hughes. Ten shillings on it."

"When ain't a bloody Dutchman looking for a sure bet?" Midshipman Parker retorted a trifle too loudly and thereby earned a hard stare from Lieutenant Brett.

"Who are you?"

"Lieutenant Hughes of *Tryall*."

Walking to the rail, Anson borrowed Mr. Nutt's trumpet, demanded sharply, "Is that she to leeward?"

"Aye, aye, sir. She's all but disabled aloft. At first we took you for Spanish."

"Well done! My compliments to Captain Saunders!"

With the sea hissing comfortably between them, both ships sailed down to join *Tryall* after the flagship had raised a hoist of lantern signals to bring up *Carmelo*.

Lieutenant Hughes, from the mizzen shrouds, informed that the newest prize was the *Santa María de Aranzazu*, the very ship Commodore Anson so earnestly had hoped would fall prey to gallant little *Tryall!*

The big-voiced Prize Captain informed that *Aranzazu* was of 600 tuns burthen — thrice *Tryall*'s. "We chased her half a day and one night. We'd likely have lost her if a light hadn't showed through a crack in a stern port cover. We'd no trouble in following her course."

Centurion's company strained their hearing to listen when Brett hailed, "What's her cargo?"

"Silver bullion amounting to nearly five thousand pounds sterling! Also some valuable bale goods, sugar and fine leather work."

Once the two ships had neared the victorious sloop and *Carmelo* had come up, Captain Saunders, by the light of a brilliant half-moon, had himself rowed over to the flagship.

Considering that he had taken a large and well-found merchantman carrying a not inconsiderable treasure, Saunders's manner seemed subdued while accepting the Commodore's simple but earnest congratulations.

"Why so glum, Captain?" Anson demanded. "Have you not ample cause to appear pleased?"

"Sir, I regret to report that, during the chase, my command again has sprung her mainmast. You will recall, sir, that, previously, it was the *Anna*'s foremast?"

Anson nodded, dreading what Saunders was about to report.

"Sir, ever since the capture I have been enforced to carry sail on the foremast alone, which has prevented me from intercepting more prizes." He lowered his voice. "In fact, sir, I fear the *Tryall* is no longer seaworthy."

"I had suspected as much when I sighted you sailing under a bare mainmast," Anson admitted.

He was forced to raise his voice, for the wind, which had begun to increase at sundown, now began to blow much harder. "Is there any other bad news, Captain?"

"Aye, sir. Through the *Aranzazu*'s Captain I have ascertained that last spring the Viceroy of Peru fitted out a strong squadron intended to replace Pizarro's. It is still in being, and somewhere at sea."

Only through long practice was Anson able successfully to suppress his alarm. So an enemy fleet still was hunting his sea-weary, undermanned command! "And of what force is this Viceregal squadron?"

Saunders looked his Commander in Chief in the eye. "I shall not attempt to minimize our danger, sir. There have been armed and commissioned four large ships of force. According to the Captain of my prize, one is a ship of fifty guns, two mount forty and one is of twenty-four carriage guns."

"Humm. That means a hundred and fifty-four guns — quite a few more than our present total. Very inconvenient."

"Nevertheless, sir," quickly pointed out Lieutenant Denis, "this squadron may never hinder us since it's still believed throughout South America that none of our ships ever entered the Pacific."

Anson overlooked the impertinence of a junior officer's speaking without leave. "Notwithstanding, the unpleasant fact remains that an enemy squadron *is* in being and cruising these waters. Gentlemen, we must remain vigilant and ready to meet and deal with this enemy."

For two days a strong gale roared out of the southwest and forced *Tryall*, unable to carry even enough sail to run downwind, to wallow about under a storm trysail. Since the sloop could not be left to her own devices, the flagship made signal for all four vessels to heave to and ride out the storm together.

When, finally, the weather moderated, Captain Saunders requested permission to board the flagship and, on receiving an affirmative, hastened to bring on board a report signed by himself and all his officers. In part it read:

> During the recent Tempest HBMS *Tryall* strained her Mainmast for which there is no Replacement. She has become so leaky that, although the Pumps are manned incessantly, Water continues to rise in her hold. Now her Foremast is sprung and very Tender.

It is feared that, should another storm arise, the Sloop will break up entirely and all aboard will lose their Lives.

It being quite impossible to repair *Tryall* on the high seas, Anson reluctantly issued an order which cut him to the quick. After her guns and stores had been removed, *Tryall* must be scuttled — not burnt — lest the resultant smoke and glare alert an enemy invisible beyond the horizon.

In the great cabin George Anson gave no thought to his flute. How could I have deluded myself into fancying that the luck has turned! First I learn of Murray and Legge's desertion, then about Lord Cathcart's failure before Cartagena, then I lose *Anna*, now I hear about the Viceroy of Chile's squadron and am about to lose the *Tryall!*

Finally, through having to stand by the sloop, I've probably lost my chance of snapping some of those fat prizes I've heard about.

What *have* I done to deserve so much misfortune and to fail the Admiralty so utterly?

Once the ocean became sufficiently smooth, the squadron labored five days in the stripping of the sloop of valuables, which were distributed to best advantage.

Long before this complicated operation was completed, George Anson had rechristened *Aranzazu* the *Tryall's Prize* and had commissioned her to be a frigate in the Naval Service of His Britannic Majesty, George II. Charles Saunders would be her Captain; Peircy Brett must wait a while longer for a ship of his own.

Crestfallen, Lieutenant John Hughes returned as second lieutenant to the flagship. Like Captain Saunders and almost everyone else who had served aboard the little sloop, the big officer failed to restrain his tears when *Tryall*, lying loglike in the water and with porpoises and shoals of silvery fish playing about her, settled lower and lower into the dark blue Pacific.

Because holes had been opened aft, she created practically no disturbance in disappearing stern foremost.

Off Payta

ONCE *Tryall* had slipped beneath the surface, the three survivors fanned out again in the general direction of Valparaiso. Until the 2nd of November *Centurion* cruised for almost a month without once raising a sail. So, reluctantly, Anson ordered his flagship put on course that would fetch her to the prearranged rendezvous out of sight of land, where *Carmelo* and *Tryall's Prize* must already have appeared.

There was profound disappointment when it became known that neither Captain Saunders nor Captain de Saumarez had sighted so much as a pirogue.

After considerable self-commuting, Anson ordered the "All Captains Aboard the Flagship" signal. Once the weather-beaten young Captains had paid their respects and had gathered in the cool semidarkness of the Commodore's cabin, Anson's steward, O'Brien, served them Malaga from jeweled silver cups captured in the *Aranzazu*. Not until his goblet had been thrice filled did Anson put it down.

"Gentlemen, since none of us have sighted a sail in a month's time I have reached the conclusion that the ship we sighted first and chased off Juan Ferdandez must have gone on to Valparaiso and reported our presence."

He paused to pour himself a fresh draught of Malaga and then crunch a sea biscuit between large and slightly uneven teeth. "The non-arrival of the *Carmelo* and the *Aranzazu* must have confirmed the Spanish authorities' suspicion that hostile ships are operating along this coast."

He glanced at big, heavy-browed Saunders. "Granted that this is the case, what would you say our enemies will do?"

"Why, sir, the Viceroy will reinstitute last spring's embargo on coastwise travel; next he will dispatch his squadron in search of us." Saunders shrugged. "Necessarily, my thinking is English; a Don might act differently."

Anson nodded and turned to de Saumarez. "If it were left to you,

Captain, what course should we follow?" Long since, he'd made up his mind as to what was going to be done, but felt it important to gauge his young Captains' acumen. Someday, if they survived and assumed command of a squadron, they might be faced with problems of equal gravity.

De Saumarez's slender and sensitive fingers stroked his bluish jaw. "Why, sir, I'd order the squadron to proceed to a cruising ground where it would not be expected." He hesitated, bold black eyes narrowing, "Say, off Callao. Rumors of our presence may not yet have reached that far."

"Very good, Mr. de Saumarez," smiled Anson offering the carafe of Malaga. "A small reward. That is exactly the course I intend to pursue."

Eagerly Saunders reminded, "The *Gloucester* will be operating in that vicinity, so once more you will command an important force; enough to take bold action."

"That earns a drink for you, too," laughed the Commander in Chief. "Well, here's confusion to the King's enemies."

For three days the squadron sailed north-northeast, paralleling the coast of South America with the Andes' snow-capped peaks barely in sight.

To the Commodore's secret disappointment both *Carmelo* and *Tryall's Prize* sailed sluggishly on even a fair wind, or no matter how much canvas was spread.

When, on the third day, a sail was seen northward of the course, Anson at once ordered the squadron put in pursuit. By evening, *Centurion,* for all her foul bottom, had left her lumbering consorts invisible below the horizon.

The flagship, therefore, found herself alone when, during the First Night Watch, her chase was brought into gunshot, broad on the port bow.

Eight nine-pound roundshot fired into the stranger's tophamper sufficed to bring about her surrender.

When a boarding party under Lieutenant Denis scrambled over the newest prize's orange-painted bulwarks, they found only one man on deck. He proved to be Captain Bartolomé Urranaga, a handsome, red-bearded Biscayan who didn't grovel a bit.

"What ship is this?" Denis demanded, with difficulty smothering excitement over having at last been sent to take possession of an enemy vessel.

"Until this moment, *señor*, I have commanded *la Santa Teresa de Jesus,* out of Guayaquil for Callao."

Steadily, the Spaniard eyed this florid-faced, blue-eyed young fellow who stood with bared cutlass ready. *"Señor,* I am not a rich man, but I stand ready to pay a heavy price for the protection of my wife and two young daughters."

"That will not be necessary," Denis announced stiffly. "We are of the Royal Navy and not brigands or buccaneers. Where are they?"

"In my cabin, *Señor Capitán.* May I be permitted to warn them that they need not expect rape and abuse? Otherwise, I fear they will kill themselves the moment the door is opened."

"You may, but I will accompany you to post an armed guard outside their door."

"Santissima María!" Tears welled into the Biscayan's eyes. "Are you indeed in earnest?"

Santa Teresa de Jesus proved to be of 300 tuns burthen and was carrying, or so her master declared, a cargo of coconuts, cacao, tobacco and hides, in addition to planks and cordage.

In the Captain's pay chest was discovered only 175 pounds in Spanish milled dollars — which, by long odds, represented the squadron's poorest capture so far.

When Don Bartolomé was ushered in to dine with the Commodore, he bowed profoundly, swept the deck before him with the scarlet ostrich plume ornamenting his hat.

"Señor Comodoro, may I, with all my heart, thank you for the noble conduct of your men? One is ashamed ever to have listened to lies which are being circulated about the cruelties of *los Ingléses!* Indeed, your Excellency, because of your honorable treatment of my ladies and myself I will —" he broke off and directed a quizzical glance at Sailing Master Nutt, who was translating — de Saumarez being away in command of *Carmelo.*

"Mr. Nutt is entirely discreet. You may proceed," Anson directed.

"— I am about to reward you with certain information which can make you and all your people rich for life!"

Over the monotonous creak and groan of *Centurion's* fabric Don Bartolomé mentioned a port in Peru called Payta. "It lies, *Señor Comodoro,* at no great distance from your present position — less than four hundred miles away."

"I've heard of the place," admitted Anson in rising interest. "But it is not marked on any chart in my possession."

[239]

"That is not surprising, *Señor Comodoro*. Payta is but an ugly little town situated on a barren and rocky coast. Nevertheless, it is very rich; vessels sailing along the coast, in either direction, must pause there to take on water and fresh food."

"You are most kind, Captain," Anson observed, struggling with an increasing excitement.

Justinian Nutt retained his impassive manner. "Unfortunately, sir, I have no accurate chart of those waters."

"You will have no need of one, *señor*." The Spaniard's short square-cut beard glowed like copper in the sunset beating through the flagship's stern windows. "Not only will I, myself, pilot you to the vicinity but I will also draw a map of the port." Almost too eagerly, he added, "If you wish, I will guide your landing party."

Anson permitted himself to look incredulous. "And why should you do all this, Don Bartolomé?"

"As I have said, it is because of your humanity towards me, my family and my crew." Briefly, the Biscayan's leathery lips compressed themselves. "It is also because I do not very much admire the Governor there. Don Julio is a pompous windbag, a braggart and, I suspect, a miserable coward as well."

"Most braggarts are," smiled Anson.

To Nutt, Don Bartolomé's contempt seemed entirely genuine, but Anson was not quite sure.

Not until early the next morning did His Britannic Majesty's Ships, *Carmelo* and *Tryall's Prize,* finally come up with the waiting flagship and her most recent capture.

Joyfully, Captains Saunders and de Saumarez saluted Anson's long red pendant, then acknowledged signals ordering them to rendezvous at latitude 50° 123' — some thirty miles off the coast of Peru.

All four ships were setting sail on the new course when a strange thing happened. Imperceptibly, the Pacific's color commenced to change from dark blue to purple and then shone such a vivid red that it seemed the squadron was sailing on an ocean of blood!

In vain did the flagship's astronomer and schoolmaster, Mr. Pascoe Thomas, attempt to reassure the superstitious that this phenomenon was easily explicable. Once a bucket of the amazing scarlet fluid was drawn, he poured some of it into a wineglass. When he held it up, it was seen that a multitude of tiny and very slimy red globules were floating about on the surface of otherwise clear sea water.

Square-lensed spectacles flashing, Mr. Thomas addressed the officers on Watch: "Gentlemen, please observe, the coloring we perceive is due to nothing more than spawn, or fish eggs, which we see floating about on the top of this glass. From which species of fish it originates I have as yet no idea." He nodded gravely. "I intend to inquire into the matter."

Superstitious pessimists, nevertheless, continued to take the phenomenon as an augury that, one and all, they were headed for a bloody end. A few amateur soothsayers took the water's redness to be a sign that *Gloucester* had met with a final disaster.

George Anson's secret apprehensions concerning the fate of Matthew Mitchell's ill-starred man-of-war increased until, when *Centurion* was cruising roughly one hundred and twenty miles south of Payta, the gallants of a full-rigged ship were sighted.

Ha! Here at last was *Gloucester* with her 50 guns and a stout, largely English crew.

However, Anson's relief proved to be tragically short-lived. The apparition proved not to be *Gloucester* after all, but a very large Spanish merchantman, so Anson signaled his consorts to follow him in pursuit. As expected, Saunders's *Carmelo* and Denis's *Teresa* soon began to lag, but, as if to buoy the Commodore's always sanguine nature, *Tryall's Prize*, which must have been sailing a course better suited to her design, kept up with the flagship.

Everything seemed to point towards another easy capture when suddenly the wind died out and left the black and orange painted stranger and her pursuers two cannon shots apart and rocking helplessly upon an endless succession of oily swells.

Fearing that with the onset of darkness a wind might spring up and enable the chase to escape, Anson recalled that the squadron's more important smallboats recently had had swivel gun stocks built into their bows. He sent for the first lieutenant.

Peircy Brett's expressive dark brown eyes narrowed as the Commodore directed briskly, "Have the pinnace and barge lowered at once. Arm them with swivel guns and for your boarding party select whomever you please."

He turned to Midshipman Hyde Parker, for the moment acting as signal officer. "Signal *Tryall's Prize* to call away boarders and send them into her pinnace."

"You may encounter trouble," Anson warned Brett. "She's big and uncommonly high-sided. However, Mr. Brett, I've no doubt you'll take her handsomely. Good luck to you."

"Thank you, sir. We shall do our best."

Among those tugging at the barge's oars were Tom Ramster and John Clipperton — for all they both were petty officers. Like their companions, they were grinning and eager to use the heavy boarding pistols they'd just been issued. Less veteran seamen, as they rowed, noticed the tug of heavy, brass-hilted cutlasses slung to their belts.

"Jesus God! That damn' ship's a sight bigger nor I deemed," growled Clipperton. "Don't like the look o' her. Don't spy no open gunports, do you?"

"No. Reckon her skipper's waiting till the last minute. Then he'll run out and blast us." From the corner of his mouth Tom added, "If there's wenches aboard, I hope the Old Man will let us at 'em. I'm fair bustin' me britches for a tumble."

In silence broken only by the dull *clunk-clunk* of oars against tholepins, all three boats pulled through the dusk until they came within pistol shot. Brett then hailed but received no reply, so, to the boarding party's huge delight, he ordered the swivel guns to open fire.

Even while acrid smoke clouds still obscured the boats, he roared, "Close in! Smartly now, before they can open!"

Ordinarily levelheaded, Peircy Brett found himself standing, waving his hat and yelling at the top of his lungs over the brisk rattle of small arms fire. Suddenly the ship's side was looming blackly above him. Lord! It seemed to tower to the very stars.

"All hands, up and over!" roared Brett and brandished his service sword, whereupon a dark, milling crowd of boarders swarmed aboard, howling for blood and the long-denied privilege of indulging in a cut-and-thrust melee.

They were doomed to disappointment. Not one man was visible on the stranger's shadowy deck! An explanation soon became evident; the *Nuestra Señora del Carmine,* aside from the officers, was manned by only forty-three mulattoes, mestizos and Indians who long ago had dropped their weapons. On their knees, they began yammering for quarter.

One of the Spaniard's petty officers startled Midshipman Drake by crawling down from his hiding place in the maintop, calling, "Praise God and the Holy Virgin! 'Tis saved at last I am!"

[242]

"Bring that man up here!" Brett called down from *Carmine's* quarterdeck.

The speaker proved to be a squat, bandy-legged and very hairy individual with a long upper lip and a button nose. He advanced warily, touching his red bandanna head scarf at every few paces. "An it please yer Honor, sor, I've a bit of information that will play sweet music in yer Honor's ear."

"I'll listen to you later," Brett snapped, then roared an order to start loading prisoners into the boats.

The Irishman, however, ran up pleading, "What I have to tell yez, sor, loses value every instant ye delay listening to me."

The lieutenant was curt. He didn't like or trust the Irish one little bit.

"Your name?"

"John Williams, yer Honor, who wishes he'd never quit County Sligo."

There was something in the gap-toothed Irishman's expression which carried conviction, so, briefly transferring direction of the boarding party to Passed Midshipman John Campbell, Brett crossed to the quarterdeck's windward rail. "Well, what is it that's so confounded important?"

Williams was completing his story when a light breeze sprang up. Accordingly, Brett cut him short and, after taking prisoner-laden boats in tow, braced the prize's yards about and started the *Nuestra Señora del Carmine* creeping towards *Centurion*.

By the time she arrived within hail, Peircy Brett had routed her captain, Don Marco Marino, disheveled and slime-covered, from his refuge in the cable tier and had forced him to produce bills of lading which made very pleasant reading indeed.

"Good God, sir," cried Midshipman de Saumarez, "she's got two hundred thousand Spanish dollars below!"

"Capital! What's the rest of her cargo?"

"Mostly iron and bales of cloth, sir, that I reckon will never reach Callao now."

Once the *Carmine* arrived within hailing distance, Passed Midshipman Campbell shouted, "Request permission to come aboard!"

"Permission granted!" Denis presently called back.

To the Commodore's astonishment, his barge began thrashing across the star-spangled ocean towards the flagship at a furious clip.

Sensing a vast excitement underlying Lieutenant Brett's impassive manner, George Anson abbreviated congratulations to consider the prisoner, John Williams. Repeatedly, he knuckled a limp auburn forelock while awaiting permission to address so lofty a personage as the Commodore of a British squadron.

"Speak up, man!" Brett ordered. "Repeat to the Commodore what you have told me, and be quick about it."

"Aye, aye, sor. Me name, yer Excellency, is John Williams. Like I told this gentleman here, I hail from County Sligo which — "

"Skip that," cut in the long-faced lieutenant. "Tell the Commodore how you came to be aboard the prize."

"Why, yer Excellency, I worked me way across the Atlantic, before the mast, from Cadiz to Santa Cruz, which lies in the Audiencia of Mexico." He grinned. "For, bein' o' the True Faith, 'twas no trick at all. From Santa Cruz I peddled rosaries across Mexico to a stinkin' little port called Acapulco."

At Williams's mention of Acapulco everyone within earshot listened hard.

"There I tried to make a livin' as a wine dealer, yer Excellency." Williams winked a bloodshot brown eye. "But I soon drunk up me stock and had to ship afore the mast again — this time down to Payta."

The sunburned Commodore's features tensed imperceptibly, "Payta, eh?"

"Aye, yer Excellency. 'Twas there I wuz thrown into chokey because of a wee Donnybrook some champion liars claimed I provoked. Ye see, sor, the girl's father —"

"— Never mind that. Proceed with your tale."

"Sure and I will, yer Excellency. 'Twas many weeks I languished in durance vile. — Then, through the kindness of a poor whore I'd once favored, I escaped two days ago and fled aboard yonder vessel which, the Virgin be praised, ye've just took."

"*Will* you come to the point?" snapped Brett. "Tell the Commodore what's just happened in Payta."

"Well, yer Excellency, the very day before I escaped, in comes a coaster claiming she's been chased by a great foreign man-o'-war."

Brett put in, "From this fellow's description, sir, she must have been the *Gloucester!*"

"Let us hope so."

"Well, yer Excellency, like I wuz sayin', this coaster's skipper legs it straight to the *Gobernador* with his news. So, quicker than a wee

[244]

man can blink, Don Julio starts moving the King's treasure twenty miles inland to a place called Piura."

"When did this occur?"

"Like I said, yer Excellency, 'twas only two days ago."

"How large is this treasure?"

"Some say one thing, some say another, yer Excellency." Williams paused to heighten this moment of personal importance. "But this I do know for *certain:* there's four hundred thousand dollars in private-owned silver still in the customs house! 'Tis waitin' transportation to Panama in a ship which even now is bein' readied, sor. They wuz still cleanin' and tallowin' her bottom the day we cleared Payta!"

The silence of profound speculation descended on the quarterdeck and ended when Anson demanded succinctly, "Is there a fort there?"

The Irishman bobbed his auburn head. "Aye, yer Excellency. 'Tis a stone affair mountin' eight cannon and garrisoned by at least three hundred soldiers."

"Thank you very much, Williams. If what you say is so, you will be generously rewarded. Mr. Denis, please see that this prisoner is given food from the regular mess and send him to my cabin in an hour's time."

When Williams, his flat, semi-humorous features wreathed in smiles, returned to Anson, he found that deceptively impassive gentleman dictating to Andrew Menzies a further entry in his "Letter of Proceedings."

He terminated with — "Because of Captain Don Bartolomé Urrunaga's offer to guide a landing party and the Irishman Williams's presumed truthfulness, I have, therefore, my lords, concluded to attempt the capture of Payta with all possible speed."

Having arrived at this decision, George Anson would have felt more satisfied with the present state of affairs had he been able to rid himself of nagging doubts concerning *Gloucester's* position and welfare.

∼ 2 0 ∼

Land Operations

TOWARDS SUNDOWN, Anson's expanded squadron, under reduced canvas, approached the coast of Peru. With betraying royals and gallants furled, it felt its way inshore some fifteen miles southeast of Payta. From the Commodore down to the least powder monkey everyone prayed that their arrival had remained undetected. On that point hinged success, or sanguinary failure — the fainthearted still were recalling that blood-red area over which the ships had sailed.

At ten o'clock, Anson's ships came into the wind and lowered three selected smallboats with a minimum of noise. Soon their suddenly sobered crews started pulling along a rocky coast only dimly revealed by starlight, which was sufficient, nevertheless, to draw faint glints from dripping oar blades, musket barrels and pike heads.

Alone on *Centurion's* poopdeck, George Anson watched the little landing party lose itself in the gloom. Bitterly, he reflected: how different this venture would be if only I'd been given the 500 seasoned, disciplined troops they promised me! Why did I have to lose *Wager* and the land artillery in her? What can have happened to her? Probably she's been lost with all hands. With all his faults, David Cheap would never have turned back.

If only I'd been given adequate land troops and not delayed until I had to round the Horn in midwinter, I might now be about to assault some great port like Valparaiso or Callao instead of this insignificant little town.

All the same, it may mean much if I can carry out their lordships' orders to "annoy and distress the Spaniards either at sea *or on land*" and "to seize, surprise, or take any of the towns or places I shall find it practicable."

Silently, the brooding figure reviewed orders he had come to know by heart, and tried not to worry over what was about to take place in Payta.

Commanding the shore party was tall and quick-witted Peircy Brett. At the moment he was sitting, erect and tense, in the stern sheets of *Centurion's* big, eighteen-oared barge.

[246]

Lieutenant Denis had charge of the flagship's ten-oared longboat, while bumptious, big-voiced Lieutenant Hughes was responsible for the longboat from *Tryall's Prize*. The little flotilla was manned by a contingent of fifty-eight hand-picked officers and men.

At Lieutenant Brett's side sat red-bearded Captain Bartolomé Urranaga; continually, he fingered his pistol's butt and appeared dreadfully anxious. Brett's eyes, therefore, seldom left the Biscayan.

Carmine's pilot accompanied Lieutenant Denis who was wearing a Royal Jack twisted about his lean middle. He intended soon to raise it over the fort when, and if, the landing party captured Payta.

The foremost of the shadowy landing craft was *Tryall's Prize*'s longboat, steered by that loquacious Irishman, John Williams.

Midshipman van Keppel, through some caprice, had donned a jockey's peaked cap and had set it at a rakish angle on his round blond head. The other midshipmen, Campbell, Hyde Parker and Tom de Saumarez, were in a stew of excitement and kept fiddling with cutlass grips and boarding pike hafts as if they'd never before handled such.

King Parmer, the Carolinian coxswain, found his skill taxed to the fullest when, as silently as possible, Brett's party started to row parallel to the shore; the deep-laden boats began to roll dangerously among long, very deep swells described by Don Bartolomé as characteristic of this coast. These rollers shattered themselves in noisy white fury upon a shore as barren as it was jagged.

The men, although pulling strongly, spat nervously and enouraged themselves by boasting about what they'd do to the Papists once they got into Payta.

Tom Ramster's solid body, clad in ragged canvas pantaloons and a striped jersey, swayed rhythmically to his oar's strokes. His seatmate, one-eyed Paddy Kildare, voiced the general anxiety. "D'you think, Tom, we can *really* take the town by surprise or is this Spanish Captain leading us into a trap?"

"Surprise or not, we'll take the place and swing our cutlasses 'mongst the Papists!"

John Williams growled, "Ye'd best quit bragging and pray instead, for 'tis eight whacking great cannons the Dons have mounted in their *fortaleza* and above three hundred soljers to our fifty-seven men and three swivels."

"How's that?" queried Kildare. "Only fifty-seven of us?"

[247]

"Aye. Four officers, seven snotties an' forty-six of us," Ramster informed.

By prearrangement, the three boats attempted to maintain a close line-ahead, but briefly lost sight of each other among the long, black swells.

"Once you round that promontory, *Señor Teniente*," Don Bartolomé hoarsely predicted, "we will find ourselves in the roadstead of Payta."

Terrific suspense silenced further conversation while the boats were being rowed around a high, rocky headland. Then the invaders began to make out a line of low, white houses beyond a scattering of anchored merchantmen.

Since very few lights were showing, the landing party reasoned that Payta was not on guard — unless it was the Governor's intent to trick the hated *heréticos* into coming so close in that escape would be impossible.

Once the boats entered quieter waters, the oarsmen responded to their coxswain's profane but low-pitched urgings and raised the beat until they fairly raced across the harbor's southern end. Fervently, they were hoping to remain invisible under the loom of the coast.

Lieutenant Brett was beginning to breathe more easily when, aboard the nearest of the anchored merchantmen, arose a sudden high-pitched yell of, "*Alerta! Alerta! Los Ingléses! Los perros Inglés estan aqui!*" — The English! The English dogs are here!

Immediately, unintelligible commands sounded aboard the sleeping merchantmen, feet raced about and lights flared into being.

"Tell your men to pull hard! Harder!" pleaded Don Bartolomé, teeth aglint in the starlight. "The beach is not far ahead."

In a savage undertone Brett warned, "For your sake, I hope you're not lying."

The British oarsmen need no urging. Ahead, more and more lights were beginning to glow; lanterns could be seen bobbing along the beach and among houses lying ghostly white under the stars.

"*Ay de mi*," groaned the pilot in Lieutenant Denis's boat. "That accursed fort is taking alarm!"

The fort fired its first shot just as the boats mounted a great roller and were flung violently towards a little beach which, if Don Bartolomé's map had been accurate, lay at Payta's southern end.

Whether by good luck or good gunnery, a cannonball screamed by, just missing the heads of the straining, sweat-blinded oarsmen.

Involuntarily, everyone ducked and swore, shaken by the knowledge that had the cannon's muzzle been depressed an inch or so, *Centurion*'s barge would have been cut in two.

Midshipman the Honorable Augustus van Keppel felt an unpleasant writhing and plucking in his bowels. "Hear that?" he yelled to Tom de Saumarez. "Damn' Dons nearly bowled our pins that time!"

"Buggers didn't, which is what counts! Suppose we'll find more of us on the beach?"

Having acquired a smattering of Spanish while privateering in the Caribbean, King Parmer was able to follow Don Bartolomé's instructions while steering through a smother of foam towards the beach.

"Keep pulling till we touch!" he bellowed. "Then back your oars. Steady now. Steady, damn you!"

Brett, half standing, steadied himself against a thwart. He glimpsed the outlines of other boats which, properly, had fanned out on either beam and approximately abreast.

"Prepare to land! Remember now. Keep together!"

Boom-m! A second shot from the fort screamed by, happily farther out to sea. Van Keppel's heart began pounding like a red Indian's drum when he made out, just above the beach, the outline of a solid-looking two-story structure. That must be the Customs House where the treasure lay, he decided, visualizing a plan of Payta drawn by Don Bartolomé. To orient everyone, it had been shown to all members of the landing party.

Heart in mouth, young Hyde Parker strained his vision for a glimpse of Spanish troops lined up and ready to repel a landing.

In another boat, Passed Midshipman Campbell pulled out and cocked one of the three heavy pistols he'd somehow managed to jam into his belt.

The first thing Brett knew he was leading his men, hip deep, in surging warm water and up a steep incline of coarse gravel. Among the first to reach dry land were two drummers — one very young, the other a toothless oldster.

"All right, you two," panted Brett. "Beat fit to raise the dead — and don't dare to stop!"

The raiders didn't need prompting to make all the noise they could and so confuse the enemy into believing that many more than fifty-seven men were attacking them.

[249]

Tom de Saumarez scrambled over the thwarts and felt the under-tow tug viciously at his legs when a roller hissed back down the beach. All around him he saw stumbling dark figures, pike points and cut-lass blades dully agleam.

"Yah-h" he screamed, attempting to make noise enough for five. "Come along, the First Company!"

When the fort fired again, de Saumarez, from the corner of his eye, watched a lance of red-gold fire briefly probe the darkness. On this occasion, a near miss doused the men lining up on the beach with flying spray.

"Follow me!" shouted Brett, waving an officer's espantoon — a short-shafted spear. "Beat those drums! And yell, all of you!"

"At them!" yelled Denis. "Rendezvous in the market place fast as you can!"

"Keep together!" Lieutenant Hughes's tremendous voice rang out like a brazen trumpet. "Keep together! Stop for nothing!"

At a jolting dogtrot, Peircy Brett led his landing party into the sec-ond street back from the waterfront. He tried to look in all directions at once but saw nothing more alarming than the vision of terrified citizens half-dressed, or wholly naked, scurrying towards a row of low and barren hills looming not far behind Payta A few of these fugi-tives were carrying valuables but abandoned them the moment they heard drums and English yells advancing along the street.

Pounding along behind Lieutenant Brett and Captain Urrunaga, young van Keppel tightened his already spasmodic grip on a brace of pistols, but, although he glimpsed frightened faces behind a long succession of heavily barred windows he didn't shoot — much as he yearned to fire a shot in anger; small point in warning the fort just where the raiders were.

More and more articles dropped by fleeing inhabitants littered the streets' dry and rutted mud.

The houses, young van Keppel noted, almost uniformly were of one story, constructed of whitewashed mud bricks and roofed with frayed-looking palm thatch.

Shrieks, shouts and wails arose from all sides. Tom Ramster, pounding along near the short column's middle, sought a target for his blunderbuss. But he saw nothing except a naked girl peering fearfully down from a window. He made mental note of a fancy double dolphin painted above her door.

Peircy Brett simply couldn't credit his luck, for by the time the breathless landing party debouched into the *plaza mayor,* or market place, not a single shot had been fired!

The panting, perspiring sailors and a handful of Marines under Lieutenant Bruce — Lieutenant Colonel Cratcherode had pled to lead them, but the Commodore had decided, with wry humor, it would be beneath a Colonel's dignity to lead six men — were checking their flints. They kept looking at *Centurion's* first lieutenant in expectation of orders.

All at once giant fireflies seemed to dance along a gallery running around the Governor's square, two-story mansion. Reports rattled through the empty streets, reverberated against the hills and brought deep anxiety to George Anson and his squadron waiting, invisible, down the coast.

"*Dios salvame!*" yelped Don Bartolomé. "I have been wounded in the wrist!"

At the same moment Midshipman de Saumarez realized that the man at his side — Peter O'Brien, the Commodore's steward — had dropped his musketoon and had collapsed to lie sprawled and dreadfully limp on the plaza's dusty flagstones.

"Fire at will!" Brett shouted and set an example by leveling a pistol at dark figures swarming about the gallery.

Joyfully, the raiders opened fire. At last! At last they had found an enemy willing to fight back! Meanwhile, the drummers added to the racket by banging away for dear life. The plaza became streaked by bright brief bursts of flame and resounded to the deep *boom-m!* of muskets and blunderbusses. The lighter reports of pistols seemed almost frivolous, thought Tom Ramster while hurriedly reloading.

Having discharged his pistol, Tom de Saumarez didn't wait to reload but snatched up poor O'Brien's blunderbuss and took aim at a group of men silhouetted behind the gallery's iron grillwork. When he pulled the trigger the midshipman's shoulder was jarred so savagely he was knocked back onto his heels. Hell! The steward had been so all-fired keen to come along he must have overloaded his piece.

John Clipperton fired, raised an eldritch screech of triumph on watching his target spin crazily about and topple over the gallery's railing. He landed almost on Lieutenant Denis, who was leading a party towards the mansion's entrance.

Abruptly all resistance ended and it became so still in the plaza that the patter of retreating feet could easily be heard. Was this retreat

[251]

genuine? Brett had no desire to send the men inside the mansion only to have them mowed down at close range.

Amid clouds of dust and pungent-smelling gunsmoke, he deliberated long enough to reprime his pistols, then called out, "Mr. Denis! Take your party in, secure the mansion and then stand ready to repel attack. The Papists must soon return. The rest close up in column and follow me!"

~ 2 1 ~

The Fort and the Mansion

LONG AFTERWARDS, when he'd become First Lord of the Admiralty, Augustus van Keppel could recall his sensations as, amid a throng of yelling seamen, he pelted over the hard and dusty ground towards the fort's dim silhouette. Somewhere, the drums were beating and creating enough noise for ten times their number. The drumming proved inspiring, so the raiders yelled until their throats grew raw.

Soon he saw that the *fortaleza's* crenelated battlements were crowded with soldiers carrying muskets. Whew! Just one ball from any of those hundreds of pieces could blast the life from his body! To dispel a sudden sharp sense of fright, the midshipman waved his pike above his head and began to whoop like a Red Indian — or the way Coxswain Parmer once had told him they whooped.

Along the parapets ahead shone brief, dazzling spurts of fire and the night reverberated to musketry fire. Balls began to whistle — fortunately too high to do the attackers any harm.

Lieutenant Hughes pointed his blunderbuss at a row of heads outlined against the stars and fired. To his left young van Keppel shot at a pair of white crossbelts above, then felt something rap his jockey cap's bill. When, instinctively, he reached up to test it he found that a bullet had blown it off close to his forehead.

Someone cackled from amid the dark confusion, "Now yer a monk, sir, 'stead of a jockey."

"Get over that wall! Quick! Quick!" shouted Brett and dashed forward, waving his espantoon.

"Bleedin' swine are makin' off, sir," yelled someone to Brett's right.

"Aye," shouted Ramster. "Look at 'em scamper, just like monkeys with bees up their arses."

[252]

By the dozen, members of the garrison began to throw away their weapons and leap down from the *fortaleza's* ten-foot battlements. Shrilling terror, the defenders ran off along the shore towards a second rocky promontory which, to the north, completed the perimeter of Payta's harbor.

"Seems 'e bloody cowards won't stand either hot lead or a cold steel. Cock's bones! Keep that bleedin' muzzle outer me eye!"

"Bet there's a treasure in this fort. Hey! Give us a boost up!"

Peircy Brett's voice rang out, taut with excitement. "Five of you get through that embrasure!"

Hughes's booming roar beat through the swirled dust and smoke. "Follow me through the gate; look alive!"

Incredible though it seemed after all that shooting, Payta had been won with the loss of only one man, the Commodore's steward. Later, it became known that Don Bartolomé had been wounded only slightly.

On gaining the fort's interior Brett wiped smoke, dust and sweat from his face. "I say, Hughes, where are you?"

"Here, sir!" Hughes was posting dependable men to guard the magazine.

"Where's that flag you brought along?" Anxiously, "You haven't lost it?"

The begrimed lieutenant's mouth curved in a wide grin. "No, sir. It's wrapped around me, so's to leave my hands free."

The two officers clattered up a wooden ladder-stair leading to the watchtower's top. Laughing a trifle hysterically now that the tension was lessening, Brett jerked down a frayed Spanish ensign which was hanging limp and unrecognizable.

"Reckon the Old Man'll be pleased to see this, come daylight," remarked Hughes while bending on a Royal Jack.

Red-haired Lieutenant Peter Denis quickly deployed his powder-blackened party and reconnoitered the mansion's cool first floor. A candle lantern, kindled by the raiders, presently disclosed a number of terrified Indian maidservants cowering in a sort of dormitory. Some of them, half-dressed or stark-naked, knelt wailing and raised joined hands in supplication. Others tore their long black hair and literally beat brown breasts in the depth of their despair.

Because the mansion's ground floor windows were barred by ornate iron grillwork typical of Spanish countries, these unfortunates had been unable to escape.

"Come off it!" Laughing uproariously, Nat Wade and his detachment slapped the tearful servants on their bare bottoms, then locked them, squealing, into a pantry.

"Enough of that!" snapped Denis. "Make sure there are no armed men around."

A torch in one hand, pistol in the other, Wade led a party of four cutlass men towards the mansion's rear. The torch's smoky glare revealed a spacious salon, library and dining room in which glowed gilded silver, rich brocades and tapestries. At the moment, Peggy and Romsey seemed very far removed.

Peter Denis, mindful of his Commodore's injunction that, at all costs, the Governor's person must be secured, followed Captain Urrunaga up a wide mahogany staircase with Midshipmen Hyde Parker, Tom de Saumarez and a dozen eager seamen at his heels.

"There is Don Julio's private apartment!" panted Don Bartolomé, tightening the bloody rags about his wrist.

Everyone held ready his weapon when Denis, with his pike's butt, began to hammer on an ornately carved door.

"Open up! Open up!" Then, a trifle grandiloquently, he added, "In His Britannic Majesty's name! Surrender, and you have nothing to fear."

All the reply he received was a series of hysterical screams. When Lieutenant Denis turned an engraved bronze doorknob the portal, to his astonishment, swung smoothly inward. Pike leveled, he glimpsed a scrawny naked and gray-haired figure straddling a window sill.

"Halt! Where you are! Halt, damn you!"

But the gray-haired man slid out of sight down a rope improvised from silken bell-pulls. Denis reached the window barely in time to see the figure lose itself among some shrubs in the garden below.

"Halt him! Halt him!" Denis yelled down, although it wasn't at all likely there'd be any English below.

Sobs from behind him made the breathless young lieutenant wheel about — to remain transfixed. The weeping came from an exquisitely lovely — and quite naked — young girl cowering in the center of a great, canopied bed.

Breathless and excited as he was, Denis perceived the extreme youth and beauty of this nude young female who was compressing her cheeks between the palms of her hands. The nipples of immature breasts peeped through luxuriant black hair cascading over her slim shoulders and bosom. The child's huge dark eyes became enormous and her lips quivered piteously when Denis panted, in English, of course, "Beg pardon, Mistress. Where's the Governor?"

"*N-no esta aquí!*" quavered the pitiful figure. "*Por amor de Dios, no — no me maté!*"

From the door Wade called, "Sir, shall I search the rest o' this floor?"

"No, the Governor's slid down a rope. Follow me."

The whole party in vain searched a small, dried-up garden.

To make matters worse, when Peter Denis returned upstairs, the naked girl, whom he learned later was the Governor's very new bride, somehow had disappeared.

～ 2 2 ～
Plunder Galore

HIS JERSEY DARK with sweat, Gunner's Mate Ramster found Lieutenant Denis supervising the stowage of silver and other valuables into bags improvised from ripped-down hangings.

"Mr. Brett's compliments, sir," he panted, knuckling his forelock, "and will you please come to the fort at once!"

"Was there trouble in carrying the place? I heard shooting."

Ramster grinned. "No, sir. 'Twould ha' been harder to break into a girls' school at home. Cowardly bastards gave us no trouble at all, turned tail and ran after one volley."

Recalling that pretty face he'd noticed peering out of the house with two dolphins above its entrance, the burly gunner's mate lurked in a doorway until Denis and his men had trotted out onto the plaza and disappeared into the dark. Only then did he start back along that street on which the landing party had advanced.

He knew he was about to disobey a very strict order of the Commodore's, but he didn't care. He'd about forgotten what a woman felt and smelt like. Poor Ben Canty, dead these many weeks, had offered only a miserable substitute.

When Denis regained the shadowy plaza he found, under guard, a growing group of inhabitants, mostly women and children, who had not been able to run away. Sullen, or weeping in noisy despair, but never defiant, these sad creatures were about to be marched to an extemporized prison suggested by the Irishman, John Williams — a stone church belonging to the Order of Mercenarians which was situated just beyond the town's limits.

"Come along!" bellowed King Parmer from the head of the prisoners' column. "Let's get these sniveling scutts under lock and key!"

"'Ere goes our last 'opes o' a good rousing," bitterly commented a half-naked seaman when the weeping women were hustled away.

"— Which will probably spare somebody from a hanging," grunted a Marine. "When 'e Commodore ordered 'no raping' 'e bloody well meant it!"

In this the speaker was entirely correct. George Anson had foreseen an inevitable and perilous breakdown of discipline and, more important, of self-respect, were the captured town sacked, buccaneerstyle. He'd even gone further and with grimness rare in him had promised a severe flogging to anyone found drunk and incapable.

Sounds from the plaza and the *fortaleza* lying beyond it gradually faded as Tom Ramster hurried back towards the landing place. Occasionally he glimpsed figures flitting between houses on their way to safety among the hills. Everywhere lay valuables dropped by fugitives in their frantic haste.

While it was tempting to stop and examine the more promising of these, Tom never once checked his rolling stride. What he prized more than jewels or fine gold lay farther down this street — he hoped. Maybe the woman had run off? No. She hadn't looked half as scared as the rest — or was he imagining things?

Without difficulty he identified the doorway which had two leaping dolphins painted on it. He paused with his hand on a dolphinshaped brass knocker, then looked carefully down the street both ways. His heart began to hammer. What if he got caught at this?

As if to make up his mind for him, the door opened slowly inwards until he could recognize the woman he'd noticed. She was wearing a long black gown and, surprisingly, had a jeweled comb tucked in her dark, neatly braided hair.

Almost deliberately she smiled and crooked a white finger. "Come in," she whispered in excellent English. "You will not let the others know?"

"Ye can stake yer life on that," came Tom's fervent assurance. Then, hurriedly, he stepped inside, but, all the same, kept his boarding pistol ready. For a while he surveyed surroundings revealed by the light of a shaded oil lamp.

"Do not fear, *Monsieur l'Anglais.* I am alone. My servants have fled. My name is Madeleine. I am French — from the Island of Guernsey. That is why I speak English."

Tom grinned, lowered his pistol's barrel. "Now ain't that dandy? I'm called Tom — 'Rowley Red' by some."

"It pleasures me, M'sieu Tom, that you have red hair and are so big and powerful." Her squarish mouth parted in a slow, insinuating fashion. "I like such a man."

Madeline's loose black gown billowed when she crossed to a little sideboard and removed from it a silver bottle and cup of the same metal.

Utterly incapable of understanding this perfectly self-possessed female — and his own good luck — Tom noticed that the room was well, if not richly appointed; in better style than the simple façade of the house would have indicated. He noticed something else. In turning, the woman's gown rippled briefly apart; if she was wearing anything under it, it wasn't in the least apparent.

"This is rum. I know the English prefer rum to wine."

"Ye're right there! C'mon, lass, give us a buss!" He granted her just time to set down the bottle before he caught her in a bear-hug and lost no time in ascertaining that Madeleine indeed was garbed only in green velvet slippers and a black silk robe.

The soft, heavily perfumed creature winced and gasped under the crushing she was suffering, but she made no effort to free herself, only to ground her mouth the more fiercely against his.

A roar like that made by a waterfall on Juan Fernandez began to sound in Tom's ears as his breeches grew tight about the groin. Let the Commodore hang him tomorrow, but nobody was going to prevent "Rowley Red" from taking his pleasure tonight.

Staring into Madeleine's strong round face he noted an almost imperceptible line of fuzz on her short and sensual upper lip but it only served to inflame him further. Once he'd managed to unclasp a brooch at her throat the gown slipped to form a Stygian pool on the red-tiled floor. He said, thickly, "Where d'you sleep?"

Because he was kissing her so hard the young woman could only point to a nearby door. Without even bothering to unbuckle his cutlass belt, he swung Madeleine off her feet, kicked open the door and carried his delicious burden into a narrow, surprisingly severe little room. There was a small red bed on its far side with a heap of feminine clothing flung across it.

Madeleine wriggled in his arms and uttered a muffled laugh. "Not in here, *stupide!* Put me down, and I will show something to you."

Flushed, eyes flashing, the nude ran over to what appeared to be a tall wooden wardrobe and parted a row of gowns hung within and revealed a door let into the wardrobe's back.

Aflame, Tom lurched through powerfully perfumed garments to find himself in a small apartment containing no furniture whatsoever beyond a nightstand and a huge couch. Lacking head or footboards it was upholstered in flame-colored velvet.

As in a dream Tom saw that the walls were almost completely covered with mirrors of varying size and design; there was even a big one affixed to the ceiling.

"Alors!" Madeleine slid onto the vast couch and flung wide her arms. "Hurry, *mon brave,* but, for heaven's sake, remove that ugly cutlass! You may hurt me with it."

"I may hurt you," Tom chuckled, "but 'twon't be with any damn' issue cutlass!"

Somewhat later Madeleine gasped, "Enough! I can no more. But," she reached up with both hands to tousle his tangled red hair, "believe me, it is so very fine indeed to enjoy a vigorous man again."

"Again? What d'you mean by that?"

Languidly, Madeleine rolled over, pulled a comb from under the mattress and commenced to untangle her tresses. "It is all very simple," she explained in suddenly harsh tones. "Don Julio, the Governor, brought me from Callao two years ago to this stink-pot of a port. He swore that when his whining old bitch of a wife died he would marry me."

Using short, angry strokes that made her opulent breasts undulate, she continued to comb her brown hair. "Like a fool, I allowed him to install me in this miserable hutch. Julio proved generous, I will admit that, but, God knows, I deserved the best of everything in return for consenting to exist in this horrible place with only that silly old goat for a bedfellow! I should have my sanity questioned."

"Ah! That explains this room!"

"Precisely. But what a waste of good money! The old fellow's nearly impotent." She sat up, pointed with her comb. "Behind the long mirror there is another door constructed for Don Julio's convenience."

Angrily, Madeleine commenced to rebraid her hair. "Imagine my indignation when, a week ago — after the wife of Don Julio had

[258]

been dead a year, that miserable old beast confessed that he was about to marry — not me, but a silly, sniveling child from Panama!"

The woman's black button eyes hardened. "Can you wonder that I despise Don Julio as the thought of Hell? That you should have appeared when you did is as a gift from Heaven."

Tom couldn't help but grin over the idea of Heaven having had anything to do with his present situation. "That's as may be, but I'll be going straight back to Heaven in a hurry if I get caught with you."

By now his head had cleared sufficiently for him to see, in his mind's eye, an ugly, dangling noose.

"Sorry, my pet, but I must leave." He commenced to pull on dusty pantaloons.

"What! I would not have thought you so easily satisfied, my brave red-haired one." Madeleine pouted, then gave him a calculating and not especially tender smile. "Oh, so you were forbidden to — to make love? In that case, we shall make a little arrangement. I will not make complaint to your Commander if you will advise and protect me. Also you are free to use the Governor's door so long as you remain in Payta. *Entendu?*"

Chuckling, Tom leaned over and kissed her moist lips. "I'd say your best bet, ducky, is to hide your best things in here; dress sloppy-like, put dirt on your face and, if anybody tries to plunder, yell like hell that you're French and will tell the Commodore about it."

"*Bien sûr.* You seem a most sensible fellow." Madeleine arose, stretched lazily, then went out and returned wearing her black robe. "You will bring me food when you return?"

"You c'n bet your pretty arse on that!"

"When?" she blinked like a drowsy cat.

"Soon's I can. Don't know when that will be, though."

The Governor's door, it turned out, was small and cleverly masked by a shallow shed designed to hold garden tools.

Issuing into a pre-dawn grayness Tom heard loud voices — English voices — at the front of Madeleine's house, so ran quietly along the third street from the ocean and reached the plaza unnoticed.

On arriving in the *fortaleza* Lieutenant Denis was astonished to see a long line of well-guarded Negro slaves trot up lugging sacks, boxes and bales of valuable loot. There could be no doubt that the Commodore had been right in selecting Peircy Brett to lead this raid.

That brisk young officer had done everything expected of him, and was not losing an instant's time in securing the wealth of Payta.

"Ah, there you are," Brett greeted, once more calm and apparently all-seeing. "Catch the Governor?"

"We were just a minute too late. Sorry, sir."

"Too bad. The Commodore will be greatly disappointed; now, he'll have one hell of a time bargaining for the town's ransom."

Denis nodded. "What about the merchants' treasure in the customs house, sir? Hope the Dons haven't lugged it away."

Midshipman Parker, red-faced, appeared with a short keg under each arm. "The treasure's safe in the customs, sir," he panted. "Heaps and heaps of it! Here's the first of it," he informed as a red-coated Marine appeared at the head of column of slaves, each of whom carried a small but intriguingly heavy wooden keg. "These, sir, are full of milled silver dollars!"

Throughout the captured town delighted yells and shouts began to arise. So great was the raiders' preoccupation with their delightful task that only a few of them noticed the approach of dawn which was revealing the outlines of rounded bare brown hills rising some three hundred yards behind Payta.

Lieutenant Brett was one of these. Once he'd glanced seaward and still saw no sign of the squadron, he dispatched a number of scouting parties with orders to keep a sharp lookout against a return of the enemy. Surely the Governor must soon reappear heading a small army.

Leaving Hughes in command at the *fortaleza*, Brett sought the customs house in order to speed the treasure's transfer. Like many others, the breathless young officer then gaped in wondering delight at the lofty tiers of coin kegs rising along three sides of a large strong-room. Besides the money casks he noted many ironbound wooden chests which the officer in charge described as being full of Oriental silks, carved ivory and jeweled gold altar ornaments.

Hoarse through yelling most of the night, Peter Denis added glee-fully, "Those smallest caskets, sir, are brimming with jewelry, loose pearls, emeralds, sapphires and other precious stones."

~~ 2 3 ~~
The Ransacking

ONLY WHEN THE CUSTOMS HOUSE had been emptied of its last valuable did the landing party's weary commander permit a general ransacking of private establishments — warehouses and dwellings alike.

Clipperton was excused from guarding prisoners in the church just in time to participate. On the plaza he encountered his friend, Nat Wade, also off duty, who hailed him saying, "I've marked a fine large house on the edge of town. Let's see if it's been rummaged yet."

"Hell yes! Plunder's what I signed Articles to get."

Coxswain King Parmer appeared, swinging down a side street, so Wade signaled him to come along. He'd always liked the lanky, lantern-jawed Carolinian very well; besides, at the back of Wade's mind was a recollection that Parmer was reputed to wield considerable influence with the Commodore, which, in case of misunderstanding, might prove useful.

Wade led his companions over a low wall at the rear of a better than average-looking dwelling in time to seize a pair of well-built young Negroes who had selected that moment to emerge from hiding. Both blacks fell on their knees and rolled terror-stricken eyes, but they began to grin when Clipperton, laughing, kicked them to a standing position. Said he, "They'll come in handy to lug the loot."

Meanwhile, Wade and Parmer readied their weapons and pushed open the rear door; so far, there'd been no resistance, but one never could tell, as Parmer recalled from his privateering days.

The first thing the three did was to help themselves to a strange variety of food lying about the kitchen. Still champing greedily, Clipperton closed a tattooed fist on the handle of a wicker-covered jug.

Wade warned, "Go easy! Commodore meant what he said. He'll have the skin off yer back an ye get drunk."

"Damn' right," Parmer agreed, snatching away the jug. "But he didn't say a feller can't have a drink or two, so long's he don't get drunk."

Clipperton drove one of the slaves at his cutlass point towards the front of the house. Pretty soon he entered a room in which a big wardrobe stood open and uttered a crow of delight; it was full of rich wearing apparel. Watched by the owl-eyed slave, he selected a particularly gaudy suit from a double armful of clothing. To get it on he was forced to undo his cutlass belt but, being an old hand, kept the unsheathed weapon handy while pulling on a pair of scarlet pantaloons over his greasy petticoat breeches. Next he slid a shirt of purple silk over the tatters which covered him.

"Hey, lads, this way fer yer coronation robes!"

The others helped themselves, chortling with delight.

"Cock's bones!" cackled Parmer. "This day, at least, we'll dress like bloody Admirals."

Ludicrous in their finery, the plunderers then set about ransacking every chest, closet or wardrobe they came across. Choice items such as laces, gold chains, rings and bracelets, silver ornaments, embroidered vests and garters were tossed into the center of the floor to be stowed by the slave into sacks improvised from blankets and bed sheets.

After once more referring to the wine jug — but with caution — the trio set about the exhilarating, if strenuous, business of breaking the massive padlock on an iron strongbox cleverly hidden under a four-poster bed. When, finally, the lock clattered off Wade raised the lid.

Parmer burst out, *"Will you look at that!"*

Before them glowed a maddening jumble of gold and silver coins, of reliquaries, dinner plates and goblets of gilded silver, jeweled rosaries and several daggers with gem-encrusted hilts. Most provocative of all were four leather bags which were found to contain pearls, but they were so irregular that Parmer claimed they were of doubtful value.

They went on looting until an impressive pile of bags, clothing and chests arose on the long kitchen table.

"Let's lug this stuff to the fort," Parmer opined. "Damn' Papists ought to be coming back now it's light and they can count how few of us there are."

Wade nodded. "Aye, we'd best turn this stuff in for listing!"

Slyly, all three plunderers crammed their pockets with rings, brooches and other small items of jewelry — all the while pretending not to notice that the others were doing the same.

A flaming crescent of sun was peeping over the hills behind Payta when, driving the loot-laden slaves before them, the ransackers finally started back to the plaza. Clipperton was the last to leave, being hampered as he was by the weight of the sacked doubloons. The bag wig he'd pulled askew over oily gray locks lent him a grotesque air as he staggered along with the ends of a pair of gilded silver candlesticks protruding from his pockets.

Payta's dry and shadeless streets gradually filled with parties of garish, ludicrously attired seamen. Some minced along in ladies' finery, flapped limp wrists at one another and, in high falsettos, offered lewd invitations.

That not a single man was palpably drunk spoke volumes for George Anson's application of discipline.

Some raiders were hugging whole bolts of gold and silver embroidered damask to sweating, hairy chests; others shouldered make-do bags from which peered silver chalices, candlesticks and other items of plate. A Marine private had opened his sodden red jacket to flaunt a number of jeweled necklaces, rosaries and ivory crucifixes slung about his neck.

Halfway to the fort, the bag of doubloons Clipperton was lugging grew so heavy under the torrid sun that, cursing, he halted and used a sheath knife to cut a small slit in the sack's bottom so, when he heaved it back onto his shoulder and swayed onwards to the fort, it began to leak gleaming silver coins onto the bone-dry ground. Shouting, men and boys less fortunate snatched up and quickly pocketed the cash.

A heterogeneous, but awe-inspiring, mound of plundered goods grew steadily higher in the fort's courtyard. Grinning guards, ridiculous in looted garments, watched shiny-skinned Negroes roughly sort the plunder as it arrived. Under Lieutenant Denis's vigilant eye, cases of specie and bullion from the customs house already had been stacked in the shade of a colonnade.

"Cor! Wi' my share o' this I'll buy me a pub," panted a gap-toothed topman. "Wot will you do, chum?"

"Me, I'll climb into bed with a pair o' the prettiest whores in Lunnon, drink French wines, and stay there till me share's all spent."

As the sun rose, Lieutenants Brett and Hughes took care to make sure that patrols guarding the town's perimeter remained on the alert, and saw to it that sailors, reluctantly on guard over the despairing dark-faced residents crowded into the Mercenarian's Church, were relieved regularly.

Sentries, growing drowsy through reaction to the night's excitement, roused and shouted an alarm when a dense crowd of lancers appeared to line the crest of the low hills behind Payta.

Brett estimated that, by noon, fully two hundred men in brilliant uniforms were riding about flaunting banners and pennons. Also they brandished glittering swords — but always from a safe distance. To the landing party it came as a sobering realization that, after poor O'Brien's death, they numbered but fifty-six tired men.

"Mr. Hughes, please run to the fort and learn whether our ships are in sight," Brett directed. "If they are, make signal that I stand in urgent need of reinforcements."

When *Tryall's Prize's* lieutenant reached the watchtower's summit he found Denis already there.

"There they are!" he yelled, grinning.

Anson's four ships, with battle colors flying, indeed had appeared, but were still far offshore.

"Damn! They're away far off and the Papists are swarming like bees on the heights."

"I know. We've been watching 'em. What shall I do?"

"Fire alarm guns. Two pieces at three-minute intervals until you get acknowledgment."

"Yes, sir, but I fear the Commodore won't stand in very close," confessed the younger officer.

"Why not?" snapped Hughes, grown short-tempered with fatigue.

"I don't believe he'll risk getting pinned by the Viceroy's squadron against the coastline."

"Damned if you ain't right at that!"

Hughes then sent a runner pelting back to the long-nosed Peircy Brett with the news that the Commodore was in sight. He found him scarlet of face and wearing a wide-brimmed straw hat, for the sun was approaching its zenith and blasting Payta with heat rays which normally would have driven its inhabitants to seeking coolness and repose in a long siesta.

"Good, good!" He turned to Midshipman de Saumarez. "Now run back and present my compliments to Mr. Denis. Tell him to load Mr. Hughes's boat with the choicest plunder and go out to the flagship to report our situation." Brett paused long enough to mop streaming features with an already sodden kerchief. "You will assure the Commodore that while our situation here is satisfactory for the moment I need to be reinforced; I am convinced the enemy will soon attempt to recapture this place." Brett's expression hardened, "You will also convey my regrets that, despite our best efforts, the Governor and his bride succeeded in escaping into the interior."

Secretly, Peircy Brett was relieved that he wouldn't personally have to report this failure. At certain times George Anson's blue eyes could penetrate a man like bayonet points.

Once the squadron had reduced canvas and had commenced working inshore, Lieutenant Hughes felt it mightn't be a bad idea to salute the Commodore's pendant with eleven guns. Such a move might please him and, at the same time, discourage the enemy.

Guns, acknowledging this courtesy, boomed aboard *Centurion* as the "well done" signal rose into her rigging.

Immediately on receiving Brett's order, Peter Denis lost no time in complying, and was now on his way out to the flagship in Hughes's pinnance. Despite the oarsmen's best efforts, progress was slow, so deep did the smallboat ride under its cargo of treasure.

When the burden of Lieutenant Denis's report became known, men long deprived of comfort, hope and health cheered their throats raw; some even wept with delight. Nevertheless, discontent soon manifested itself among those who felt themselves unfairly denied the pleasures of plundering. Why had they been condemned to stay aboard these stinking ships when, very likely, no enemy squadron was going to appear?

A number of malcontents were mollified, however, when landing parties were told off and sent in to reinforce Brett's tiny expedition; for the first time they rejoiced that almost no land troops had survived. Other boats were dispatched to seize and cut out the masts of five coasters found at anchor in Payta harbor.

With joy filling his heart for the first time since his expedition had set out, Anson ordered the sixth captive ship, a large, fast-appearing vessel, to be secured but not crippled. If a survey found her to be sound, he intended to commission her and thereby augment his squadron to six well-found ships — always provided the absent *Gloucester* was safe.

Without confessing his ambition to anyone, he intended to take two more prizes and so restore the squadron's original number. Of course it was going to be difficult to find enough Englishmen to man them adequately; already among his crews there was a dangerous number of unpredictable foreigners.

Despite a number of threatening maneuvers by the Spaniards, the first day of the Occupation of Payta ended with no attempt made to drive off the raiders.

George Anson paced his quarterdeck thinking, What I'd give to be able to go ashore and see for myself what Brett has accomplished. But I can't. No Commander ever should quit his flagship while operating on a hostile coast. Still, I really would like, for once, to walk through a conquered town. Never have yet. Maybe I never will.

The impassive figure, however, found a measure of satisfaction in watching boat after boat come threshing out to lie alongside the flagship and disgorge a precious cargo. If only so many English corpses weren't strewing the ocean's floor, he'd have enjoyed the sight a great deal more. Still, he couldn't deny a certain sense of satisfaction. His three consorts, with their guns run out, yards tightly braced and sails neatly furled, offered reasonably good counterfeits of real British men-of-war.

Anson then leveled his glass and studied HBMS *Carmine* patroling well offshore and prepared to fire a warning the instant she sighted a sail of any description.

That evening Anson sat down to celebrate the victory with fine wine and a meager repast, but it came to an abrupt end when Lieutenant Brett sent out the ill news that very few fresh supplies had been found in Payta.

In a scribbled report Brett had written:

— The Coast being very arid hereabouts the usual source of Meat and Vegetables for the Inhabitants is Paiura, a large Town lying above twenty miles inland. It is at this place that some Negroes, who have deserted their Masters, report that the Governor is assembling a Formidable Army.

~~~ 2 4 ~~~

The Fate of Payta

THE ORIGINAL LANDING PARTY was able to snatch a little sleep while the reinforcements were burying William O'Brien — a Roman Catholic — in the local cemetery.

By lantern light the new arrivals then continued a systematic ransacking of Payta, but Brett's command had done such a thorough job they had to hunt long and hard before coming across plunder of any value. When the reinforcements did discover a *cache* they generally made a very rich haul, it being only natural that the inhabitants should have secreted their most valuable possessions, usually jewelry, in places very difficult to find.

On coming off picket duty, Tom Ramster joined those expert plunderers, King Parmer and John Clipperton — Wade having been sent out to the flagship. The trio ranged the town with such good results that, aside from valuables they turned in to *Centurion*'s purser at the fort, they carried an inconspicuous but impressive collection of loose gems, small jeweled brooches, buckles, rings and necklaces in wash leather bags concealed under their voluminous petticoat breeches.

While they were stowing the last of their private loot in the shelter of a ramshackle stable Clipperton said uneasily, "Wonder wot 'e Commodore will do if 'e finds we've 'eld out these 'ere trinkets?"

"I ain't worrying," Parmer grunted. "There's too many of us in the same boat — officers included."

Ramster nodded. "Aye. Just now I saw a snotty slippin' a gold cross under his shirt." He grinned. "If all the landing party was made to stand on their heads there'd be enough treasure fall out to ransom an earl." Naturally, he made no mention of a sizable hoard secreted in Madeleine's house, and added to whenever he succeeded in slipping through the Governor's door.

The partners in crime were asleep on a heap of soft but smelly llama pelts found in a private warehouse, when a boatswain's mate thrust his sun-bleached head inside and yelled, "Turn out! Turn out! 'E bloody Dons are marshaling for battle!"

"It's about time the bastards give us a bicker," Ramster yawned, then buckled on his cutlass.

"Me, I aim to capture a officer and hold him to ransom," announced Parmer while in the distance sounded the rolling of drums and the braying of many trumpets.

On the plaza the English began to form irregular ranks. In pillaged finery they presented so ludicrous an appearance that Lieutenants Brett and Hughes couldn't help laughing aloud. But their merriment was brief, because, on the hilltops back of Payta, a lot of cavalry was milling about and collecting near the base of a huge wooden cross. To estimate their actual number proved difficult; riders kept appearing, then disappearing below the skyline.

[267]

Separated from the enemy's main body was a detachment of lancers which Marine Lieutenant Gordon estimated at two hundred. These stood in their stirrups to wave weapons, shout defiance and flourish brightly colored standards. The faint flash and sparkle of their swords reminded Brett of waves breaking on a moonlit beach. That black-clad officer who, astride a handsome white horse, kept riding back and forth before the cavalry must be the Governor, he decided. But it soon appeared that Don Julio was not yet ready to attack, and would content himself with this noisy show of force.

In the meantime Anson, in response to signals shown on the *fortaleza's* tower, ordered *Tryall's Prize* and *Carmelo* towed inshore and anchored where their guns could command the town at short range.

Even while the Spaniards were threatening to attack, the English calmly continued to ferry loot out to *Centurion*.

Later in the day, Anson finally sent Lieutenant Colonel Cratcherode ashore with further reinforcements and orders to erect barricades at the landward end of all streets running towards the bald, brown hills behind Payta, and to keep them well-manned at all times.

Along with Cratcherode, the Commander in Chief sent one Don Gonzalo, a prisoner of sufficiently high rank that he might parley with the Governor on terms approaching equality. Anson's terms were most reasonable: all he wanted was a herd of beef cattle, water and vegetables. In return he would promise not to burn Payta or destroy any valuables which were too bulky to be carried off.

Towards sundown Don Gonzalo returned looking both frightened and angry.

"Well?" Anson demanded sharply.

"Your Honor, I tremble to report that that pompous ass of a Governor refuses to parley. He would not even listen to your Honor's most courteous and general proposals. In fact, Don Julio was most arrogant and swears that, with nightfall, he will storm Payta and drive your men into the sea."

"How large a force would you say he commands?"

The envoy hesitated, licked thin, brown lips. "Alas, your Honor, he must have gathered above a thousand followers."

At dusk of the second day a number of Negro slaves filtered down from the hills and, approaching the barricades, held up empty hands and begged piteously for water. Once their thirst was quenched, they mostly volunteered for service in the squadron, but a few attempted, unsuccessfully, to steal away with jars of water intended for their masters on the heights. Evidently these must have become very thristy indeed.

Lieutenant Denis was in consultation with Lieutenant Hughes behind one of the principal barricades when a straight-backed Negro drew near and, in an elaborate bow, swept the ground with his shapeless straw hat. "Good evening, sars," he greeted. "I am most delightful to see English gentlemens again. I am wery unhappy here."

Denis noted the fellow's finely formed features and bronze-black complexion. "Where in God's name did you learn to speak English?"

"Sar, I were born originally on Jamaica."

"Were you indeed?" Hughes on narrowly observing the speaker decided that he must have more than a trace of Indian blood in him. "Tell me, fellow, what's your name and how do you come to be here?"

"Sar, me name is Michael Despeda," said he with a flash of strong yellow teeth. "I got cotched by Spanish buccaneers and was sold for a slave in Porto Bello, Panama. There I was bought by wery fine, kind gent who made I be body servant. I were so 'cute to learn and to please, pretty soon he set free."

"Panama's a long way from Payta," Denis grunted with one eye on the hills where drums and bugles again were sounding ominously loud.

"Aye, sar, that it are!" Despeda agreed and anxiously revolved his frayed hat before him. "When I freed I hire me to new gent who took I to Lima where that vicked willain re-enslave me. Last month he bring I to Payta." The slave shook a powerful brown fist at the distant cavalry. "He up there now ready to die of thirst."

Struck by a recollection, Denis regarded this straight-backed apparition with sudden interest. "You say you are a gentleman's body servant?"

Michael Despeda ducked his narrow head. "Aye, sar, and a wery fine one, too. Yes, sar."

Denis laughed, "Then you'd better ask to see the Commodore. His steward was stupid enough to get himself killed the other night."

"Oh, thank you, sar! Thank you wery kindly, sar."

At the first opportunity the Jamaican made application and, on creating a favorable impression, was taken on and remained George Anson's devoted body servant to the end of that gentleman's life.

[269]

The next day was devoted to ferrying plunder out to the flagship and to spoiling the captured vessels with the exception of one named *Soledad*. She was that same big bark which was being readied when Brett landed to carry away the silver found in the customs house.

On that same day the Commodore appointed Lieutenant Hughes of *Tryall's Prize* to be *Soledad*'s Prize Captain and also lent him ten English sailors to form the nucleus of a crew otherwise composed of unpredictable Indians, Negroes and mestizos.

Perhaps for the hundredth time since arriving off Payta, George Anson scanned the seaward horizon. What *could* have happened to *Gloucester?* True, she'd been sighted by that vessel which had brought the alarm to Payta, but that had been a good while back.

It was not like steady and loyal Matthew Mitchell to delay appearing at a rendezvous if he could possibly help it. Um. Could he have encountered the Viceroy's squadron and, at the cost of his ship, made possible this encouraging success?

Poor Mitchell, what ill star had doomed him and his command to such unbroken bad fortune? For instance, his not having been in sight of Payta at any time precluded *Gloucester*'s crew from winning a share of this impressive loot.

Later on, eighty-three prisoners were landed — much against their will, so kindly had they been treated — and confined in the Church of the Mercenarians. To Chaplain William Walter it was significant that a Jesuit priest, Señora Urrunaga, and her two daughters positively refused to be set ashore until they had been permitted, in person, to kneel and kiss the Commodore's bronzed hand.

Raising swimming black eyes, Señora Urrunaga held out a magnificent rosary of ivory and ebony. "*Señor Comodoro,* I am aware that you are not of the Faith, but I beg you to accept this trifle. May the Virgin and all the Saints ever reward your noble nature. May they keep you safe from harm and send you safely home to those whom you love and who love you."

Deeply touched, Anson hurriedly helped the ladies to rise. "I ask only, Señora, that when you are again among your people, you will inform them that they can never expect harsh or cruel treatment at the hands of His Britannic Majesty's Navy."

Able-bodied seamen among the prisoners, however, were allowed to volunteer for service in His Britannic Majesty's ships — which they did, almost to a man. This was a step Anson deplored; yet the alternative was to sail on with a critically undermanned squadron.

Anson wrote to Brett:

> Since the Governor persists in his refusal to treat, you are to burn
> the Place; leave standing only the Churches.

On the afternoon of the third day, hitherto weary seamen responded to the vandal instinct inherent in most men, and gloated over
the prospect of burning down a whole town. Consequently, they
worked hard distributing pitch, tar and other combustibles in most
of the 124 structures composing the doomed town.

"We'll be a crew o' blinkin' Neroes," chortled Buckle. "Wot price a
bloomin' fiddle?"

"T' hell wi' fiddles!" roared a big gunner. "We'll just kindle such a
bonfire as will singe the Papist King's whiskers over in Spain!"

Once purple-blue shadows again commenced to deepen along the
coast, Anson ordered his landing parties to commence embarking.
Special details lit the first fires at the town's southern end.

Once the clouds of blue-black smoke began to billow along Payta's
dusty streets, howls of rage rose among the troops still riding futilely
along the skyline. Several times parties of cavalry started to descend
the slope, but always they reined about when they saw the barricades
still defended.

"Ain't our bleedin' Commodore the foxy one?" commented a
brawny coxswain in a boat drawn up and waiting on the beach.

"Wot for?"

"Why, 'e's ordered so many fires set 'e bloody Papists can't save
nothink after we've cleared out."

By some fortunate circumstance, Payta's two red-tile-roofed churches
had been erected close together and at a fair distance outside the
town's northernmost limit, so the guards there were afforded a fine
view of the spreading conflagration. Encouraged by a strong breeze
out of the southwest, the flames soared even higher and brighter. As
the flames advanced the English successively abandoned their barricades.

Of the impending evacuation, Tom Ramster remained blissfully
unaware, lying, as he was, in Madeleine's vast bed and eager arms.

"Give another dram, ducky," he directed drowsily — he'd been
absent without leave for a considerable time and, what with all the
rum and frolic, he'd fallen asleep.

Lazily, Madeleine stretched, then scratched Tom's red head a
while, she having discovered that he loved this attention. "One

[271]

more, *mon amour*, but no more. You have had much already. See?" Smiling, she held up a nearly empty bottle. "Your Commodore punishes drunkenness, no?" She held a goblet to his lips. "Besides, we still have a little time left to us, so let us not spoil it through drinking too much. Ah, *mon amour*," she wound sweaty arms about him, "I do not know what I shall do when you go." Wistfully, "When will that be?"

"Dunno. Tomorrow, or maybe the day after. Come here."

Coughing in the thickening smoke and slapping out sparks that landed on their bedraggled finery, Anson's men collected in the plaza, then, by sections, were marched down to boats waiting on a stretch of beach beside the now defenseless fort — its guns had been taken out to arm *Soledad*. Midshipmen and petty officers tallied their arrival with strict attention.

The tumult of flames crackled towards an awesome crescendo. Sailors standing guard over the prisoners in the churches had to shield their faces from the scorching heat. The captives within began to wail and scream that the *heréticos* had condemned them to be burnt alive.

Above the conflagration's roar, Lieutenant Brett, leading the last of the landing party towards their boats, heard a new sound. Down the firelit slopes was galloping a dense mass of screaming, shouting lancers.

As calmly as Anson himself, Peircy Brett, although coughing hard, deployed his garishly garbed rear guard into a double rank. "You're not to fire," he warned, "until I give the word. Understand?"

Eagerly the men checked flints and musket pans. For too long a while they'd been denied the opportunity of mixing it up, hand-to-hand.

They were due for another disappointment. When the enemy found the raiders standing drawn up with firearms ready, they reined aside at the last minute and retreated headlong through clouds of smoke, sparks and dust.

As soon as the men guarding the churches had been relieved, the last boats prepared to shove off by the light of huge, yellow-red sheets of flame, some of which were soaring half a mile high. Palm-thatched roofs, long sun-dried, burned so brightly that the entire squadron as well as the harbor, hills and rocky promontories all were revealed in sharp detail.

In the final moments Lieutenant Gordon ignited a powder train leading into the fort's magazine and a minute later there followed a deafening explosion which would render that defense useless for a long time.

"Lor', we'll never see the likes o' this again!" panted an awe-struck seaman.

"Like hell! This 'ere's only a beginning!" Buckle exulted. "We'll sack Callao and Panama City, too, afore we starts fer Acapulco to take 'e bloody Galleon!"

When Coxswain King Parmer scrambled into the last boat Midshipman Hyde Parker counted heads for the last time. "Hold on! Don't shove off! One's man missing," he announced sharply. "Who is he?"

"Ramster, sir!" yelled someone over the infernal roar of the flames. "Tom Ramster's missing!"

Midshipman Parker wiped streaming eyes, then peered once more through the smoke drifting low along the beach. "I shall count to fifty. If that man is not here by then, we'll shove off."

Fanned by a stiff land breeze, roaring, crackling flames rolled along the beach while sparks and flaming brands rained onto boats already pulling out to the ships.

"— Forty-three, forty-four —"

"Please, sir, let me go fetch him," Parmer pleaded between fits of coughing. "I'm sure I can find him."

"No! Stay where you are! Forty-seven, forty-eight — forty-nine, fifty. Shove off!"

Suddenly someone shouted, "There he comes!"

A dimly seen figure lurched out of the gloom. Ramster yelled, apparently half-blinded by the acrid smoke, "Oi there! Wait! Wait for me!"

The big gunner's mate started to wade out to the boat, but had to pause long enough to rip off his shirt which had begun to smoulder. Singed, half-naked and obviously drunk, he was hauled aboard. "By God, boys, I thought I was in hell!"

Midshipman Parker grimly predicted, "You'll wish you were there when the Commodore learns you got drunk. You've earned yourself a hundred lashes at the least!"

In scrambling forward, Ramster snapped a hurriedly tied string which had been supporting that wash leather sack under his wide-legged breeches whereupon gems and jewelry clattered onto the bottom grating right at Midshipman Parker's feet.

[273]

"Now, you damn' toss-pot," snarled Parmer, "ye've really pissed in the beer!"

It was sunset by the time Anson's boats had rowed the five dismasted Spanish coasters out to be scuttled in deep water.

The Commander in Chief, ever apprehensive that the Viceroy's squadron might appear and pin him against the coast, ordered a signal gun fired and his flag officer to display the "up anchors" number.

Despite her crew's best efforts to achieve order, the flagship's decks remained in considerable confusion. Bale goods and casks, waiting to be struck into the holds, stood in the way; the handful of pigs and goats found in Payta were frightened by smoke drifting out over the water and squealed and blatted dismally from pens contrived of boarding netting. Nor had the flagship's boats been fully secured onto their booms.

To Will Pallister, always sensitive to color and movement, the scene presented such a painter's delight, that he hurried to record it. A vast smoke cloud, dyed purple by an especially brilliant sunset, hung over the doomed port from which dazzling sheets of flame were soaring high into the sky.

Lieutenant Brett also felt so impressed that, although on the brink of exhaustion, he dug out his sketch pad and hurriedly reproduced the burning of Payta as best he might.

On *Centurion*'s lofty poop, George Anson's anxiety commenced to abate as his six ships shook out gallants and topsails which immediately became encrimsoned by the glare.

Um. Now, if *Gloucester*'s still afloat I need to take but a single ship to number my original command, mused the Commodore. Of course, on leaving England, my squadron consisted of six regular men-of-war, not slow-sailing converted merchantmen. And, without *Gloucester*, my weight of guns is miserably unimpressive, so, if I meet the Viceregal squadron, an engagement will likely prove a touch-and-go affair.

Moodily, the broad-shouldered figure studied his ships as they squared away from the coast and fanned out in search of *Gloucester*.

Nevertheless, he found it reassuring to feel the deck — which, he noted subconsciously, stood in need of a good holystoning — begin to heave and roll as *Centurion* left Payta flaming and crumbling astern.

[274]

Well, at least this venture had proved worthy of the risks entailed, and at the cost of but a single life. Their Lordships *should* be pleased with the treasure — ah, the treasure!

As usual, when confronted by an unpleasant duty, George Anson commenced to pace about the poop.

〜 2 5 〜

The Disgorging

ANDREW MENZIES, while making entries in the Commodore's "Official Letter of Proceedings," took time to conjecture upon George Anson's preoccupied manner at breakfast. The dark and delicately featured Carolinian had come to understand the Commander in Chief so intimately he guessed that a grave problem must be confronting him.

It didn't take Menzies long to discover what was wrong. Through Midshipman Haldane, the Commodore's compliments were conveyed to Lieutenant Peircy Brett, and would the first lieutenant please report to the great cabin at once?

"Mr. Brett," said he seriously, "at eight bells I wish the entire ship's company paraded on deck. All officers and men who at any time went ashore during our visit to Payta will stand in the first rank."

The lieutenant's bold and close-set dark eyes narrowed momentarily. "Aye, aye, sir. At eight bells."

While proceeding below, Brett wondered how the Commodore should have learned so swiftly about the furious dissension raging between members of the landing parties and those who had remained aboard ship throughout the occupation of Payta.

The trouble, Brett knew, had arisen when it was discovered that almost every member of the shore party had kept some plunder to himself. During the Morning Watch fist fights and a knifing or two had occurred in the 'tween decks since it became known that Gunner's Mate Ramster had spilled jewelry, secreted on his person, all over the longboat's bottom.

A hot sun was shining when Commodore Anson, impassive as usual, briskly descended to the upper gundeck upon which the entire ship's company stood aligned in three ranks. When his foot touched the quarterdeck's starboard ladder the boatswain's pipe shrilled, all heads were bared and the few Marines presented arms.

From his position at the towering mainmast's base, the Commodore deliberately surveyed the silent and increasingly uneasy ranks. Then, over the gentle humming of wind in the rigging, he began to speak in a voice which, though low-pitched, carried to both ends of the deck.

"Men, recently we have achieved a success which redounds to the honor of His Majesty the King and that Service in which we are privileged to serve."

He raised his voice a trifle and continued to traverse his gaze along the multi-complexioned ranks. "I doubt if ever before in the annals of the Royal Navy only three boat crews have surprised and taken so large a town protected by a fort and several hundred soldiers.

"As I have stated in my report to the Lords Commisioners of Admiralty, the shore party sent aboard a treasure of enormous value." He paused and made no effort to check an involuntary ripple of satisfaction, then continued.

"Through your efforts this squadron also has now rewatered and has been supplied with a few live animals and some fresh food. Because of this, when we rendezvous with the *Gloucester,* we will be able to continue visiting terror and confusion to His Majesty's enemies whilst enriching ourselves!"

Despite his deep-seated aversion to public speaking, Anson had grown sufficiently skilled to wait until a loud shout had rung out and had died away. Then he stiffened and allowed his piercing, bright blue eyes inexorably to travel along the foremost rank.

"Now hear this: I have learned with sorrow that many members of the landing party have brought off plunder from the shore which you consider to be your private property. This is not the custom of His Majesty's Service; not even among pirates are men so selfish.

"In the taking of Payta those who were ordered to remain aboard ship had duties to perform quite as important as those of the boat crews who were ordered to land. The ships supported that successful landing with their guns and kept a patrol offshore lest we be surprised in a dangerous position.

"Those who had to remain offshore," he permitted himself a grim smile, "much against their inclination, also had to keep guard over the Spanish prisoners in this ship while the looting of the town went on.

"Now hear this: I order that every man in the *Centurion* and the *Tryall's Prize* and the other vessels, whether landed or not, has a just claim on *all* that was taken."

Standing a few paces behind the Commodore, Andrew Menzies watched frowns and anxious scowls appear on the faces of those standing in the front rank — nor was it seamen and petty officers alone who displayed uneasiness. Several officers had flushed and had flattened their lips.

In suddenly ringing tones Anson ordered, "The landing party standing in front of me will now, every officer and man of them, go below and — so that all will be open and above-board — bring up to me on the quarterdeck all the articles they each brought off from shore, that they may be put with the remainder of the booty in the ship's treasure locker, to be delivered later through the Admiralty for division amongst us, according to every officer's rank and man's rating, as laid down in Prize Law."

Lieutenant Brett drew breath to order the shore party below, but remained silent on perceiving that the Commodore had not finished.

"In order to encourage everyone in the future to perform his duty whatever it might be, and to carry it out in the same gallant fashion as these men standing before me have done, I will donate my entire share of prize money from Payta to be divided among the men who did not go ashore, as a compensation.

"I hope I shall never hear again of dissensions among you on the lower deck such as has come to my knowledge this morning. May Fortune send us plenty more opportunities for sharing."

~~ 26 ~~

A Course for Acapulco

THAT *Gloucester* should have failed to rendezvous off Payta on time was entirely typical of her, decided the victorious crews. Beyond a doubt the old Fourth Rate was doomed to cruise forever under a malign star.

At twilight of the first day after his squadron's departure from

Payta, George Anson, fearful of losing his only remaining British-built man-of-war in the dark, ordered the squadron hove to at night stations. He didn't dare to risk missing *Gloucester*, which mounted more guns than all these converted merchantmen put together.

The wisdom of the Commodore's decision was proved next morning when, with daylight, two sails were sighted to the northwest — and not very far off, either. The larger vessel's identity was established barely in time to obviate the necessity of clearing for action.

Gloucester came bearing smartly down on the squadron, for all she was towing a snow which Justinian Nutt estimated to about 400 tons burthen.

"Thank God!" muttered the sailing master. "At last poor Matt Mitchell's won a prize!"

Within an hour, *Gloucester* and the snow had sailed close enough to dip her ensign and salute the pendant with the customary eleven guns. Thoroughly delighted, Anson made an exception and quitted his quarterdeck in order to greet his senior Captain at *Centurion*'s gangway.

Once Mitchell had saluted the quarterdeck and Anson's pendant the Commodore gripped his hand. "I can't tell you, Captain, how pleased I am to observe that you've met with some luck!"

"Aye, sir, but only in a small way," Mitchell admitted sourly. "Since leaving Juan Fernandez I've taken only two unimportant prizes."

In silence the two, clad in salt-stained coats, together traversed *Centurion*'s once more snowy deck, between lines of polyglot seamen. At the foot of the quarterdeck ladder, Colonel Cratcherode and his handful of land troops presented arms; their scarlet jackets and freshly pipe-clayed white crossbelts showed bright under a radiant sun.

"My dear fellow, I hope you'll sample this Madeira and think well of it," the Commodore said while his new steward, Michael Despeda, decanted a vintage captured in Payta.

Mitchell drank and, sighing, wiped his mouth on a ragged cuff. "Capital, sir, this is capital stuff."

"Good. Rather fancy it myself. I'll have a barrel sent aboard of you. Now, if you please, tell me about your cruise."

"Sir, after quitting Cumberland Bay I searched for almost a month without sighting anything beyond seals, sea elephants and sea birds until, on the twenty-first of October, I raised and ran down a barcalonga. She couldn't have been above four tons burthen and had on board only four men and a boy."

Poor Mitchell! Anson recalled his own first capture, the fine, large *Carmelo*.

"At first I feared we had only wasted our time in chase," the Senior Captain continued, his dour expression lightening. "However, Mr. Scott, who is now my second lieutenant, boarded the barcalonga and, although her captain pled to be liberated on the grounds that he possessed nothing of value, Scott saw a pigeon pie on the table and noticed that it was being served from a bowl of pure silver!

"Next, he discovered that the plates also were of the same metal. Scott then rummaged the boat, which, apparently, was laden with nothing more valuable than baled cotton."

Mitchell's gaunt features brightened still further. "Under a pile of rags, his men discovered a number of earthernware jars stuffed with rags. It was noticed, however, that when lifted they proved uncommon heavy. You may imagine our delight, sir, when said jars were found to contain dollars and double doubloons to the value of twelve thousand pounds sterling, in the opinion of Mr. Millechamp, my purser."

"Twelve thousand pounds? Good! Good!" Brett clapped Mitchell's sloping shoulder.

Anson observed, smiling, "You deserve this bit of fortune which I trust will prove only the first of many successes. Whither was your prize bound?"

"For Payta, sir," *Gloucester*'s Captain replied with a wry grin. "Had she escaped me you would undoubtedly have added her to the spoils of that place. May I inquire how well the in-taking rewarded?"

"Thanks to Mr. Brett's industry and the sobriety of his subordinates" — Anson didn't feel called upon to mention either Ramster's lapse or the fifty lashes it had earned him — "we took some thirty-one thousand pounds in silver and gold alone. How much the unset gems, baled cloth, brocade, leather and other trade goods eventually will fetch there's no saying."

Ever tactful, Anson then diverted the talk from Payta by inquiring about the vessel *Gloucester* had in tow.

"Sir, she is the *Nuestra Señora de los Dolores*, a snow of 400 tons burthen. She'd a crew of only thirty men and boys. Mr. Gerard, my Prize Captain, discovered something in her cargo, sir, which I think will please you." A thin smile appeared on Matthew Mitchell's

[279]

lean features. "Extra choice wines and spirits, of which I will send you an assortment."

"They will prove most welcome, Captain. Had you further luck with the snow's cargo?"

"Only middling fair, sir. Mr. Gerard found in her loose silver plate to the value of about seven thousand pounds."

"Again, my earnest congratulations. I hope your run of bad luck has ended."

That night, for the first time since leaving Juan Fernandez, George Anson carried his flute out on his stern walk and tootled happily for quite a while.

On a beautiful evening late in November, the flagship signaled, "All Captains."

When they appeared in *Centurion's* great cabin, Menzies was struck by their changed appearance. In only a few ways did they resemble those officers who had attended the council of war in Fayal Harbor. All these hard-bitten Captains were grave of mien and looked easily five years older than their actual ages. How odd to reflect that only Matthew Mitchell had held a Post Captain's rank on that occasion!

Yes, they presented a colorful group, Menzies decided, as the Anson-appointed Captains gathered about the Commodore's scarred oak dinner table gravely to sip Madeira from heavy silver goblets. All were wearing captured velvet or brocade frock coats liberally laced or frogged in gleaming silver and gold. Captain Mitchell was no less resplendent than the younger captains, because the Commander in Chief, with typical consideration, had sent over to *Gloucester* a chest of captured finery.

As for George Anson, he was enjoying his highest spirits since that hideous night when, off Cape Noire, his squadron had become dispersed. Praise the Lord, once more he was commanding a squadron of *eight* sail! For all that only two of his vessels were genuine ships-of-war, it meant much for him to see eight Blue Ensigns aflutter in that fine breeze which had been blowing ever since Payta had been left behind.

"I have summoned you, gentlemen," Anson announced, his big frame swaying to *Centurion's* easy roll, "for the purpose of disclosing to you my intentions at this point in our voyage.

"No doubt you all are aware that, by now, the Spanish authorities along this coast have learned of our presence, so are keeping their coastwise traffic in port. Because of this, I have decided it would be wise to shift our field of activity northward, where the enemy still may remain unalarmed."

By the light of the afternoon sun beating through his flagship's stern windows, Anson, on considering his Captains' bronzed and vital faces, became gripped by a premonition that, among these varying types, were several men who someday would fly an Admiral's flag; a few might even become Peers of the Realm; one might even rise to become First Sea Lord. Saunders, de Saumarez and Brett he felt convinced might win such high honors; also some of his midshipmen: Drake, Parker, van Keppel, Campbell and the younger de Saumarez, maybe more.

"Mr. Menzies, the copy of my General Orders if you please."

When the document had been passed into his hand, Anson turned his back towards the leaded windows that more light might fall on the closely written foolscap. He read a moment or two, then looked quickly up at his guests.

"Thus far I have confided nothing to you gentlemen concerning that part of my instructions which I am about to reveal, so I shall now read, exactly, the last paragraph of his Royal Majesty's orders:

" 'If you shall find no occasion for staying longer in those seas, that is, the South Seas, and should judge it best to go to the north as far as Acapulco, in Mexico, or to look for the Acapulco ship which sails from that place to Manila in the Philippine Islands at a certain time of the year, and generally returns at a certain time, you may possibly, in that case, think it more desirable to return home by way of China, which you are hereby authorized to do.' "

Acapulco? China? The assembled officers stiffened on their seats.

Blue eyes twinkling, Anson paused for effect.

"To encourage you that this is not an impossible project may I speak of what some of you probably already know about? On November fourth, 1587, Sir Thomas Cavendish, of Trimly in Suffolk, captured, off Acapulco, a treasure ship called the *Santa Ana* and that, not far from there — in fact off Puerto Seguro in Lower California — Captains Woodes Rogers and William Dampier took another such vessel, the *Encarnacion*, in 1709. So you see, gentlemen, it's clearly up to us to make it three in a row!"

A roar went up that made the Marine on duty hurriedly open the great cabin's door and peer inside.

"I propose to sail north and take the Acapulco ship, called by some the 'Prize of All the Oceans.'

"Gentlemen, I am now open to question. I shall endeavor to satisfy your curiosity within the limits of discretion. Mr. Brett?"

"Sir, what, if anything, is known concerning the size and armament of this great ship from Manila?"

"By the latest report available at the Admiralty, she is generally a merchant ship of never less than twelve hundred tons burthen. Usually she mounts seventy carriage guns and is officered and manned by over five hundred men from the Spanish Royal Navy."

The Commander in Chief's prompt reply argued that, over many long and dreary months, George Anson had memorized his information.

Slight, dark-faced Lieutenant de Saumarez arose. "Sir, of what does the galleon's cargo usually consist?"

"On the eastward voyage, I am given to understand, she is laden with pearls, emeralds, rubies, sapphires and such other precious stones as are found in the East Indies. Also she carries valuable spices such as cinnamon, cloves, mace, nutmeg and pepper, in addition to rich carpets from China and Persia, camphire from Borneo, benjamin and carved ivory from Pegu and Cambodia, as well as the silks, muslins and calicuts of East India.

"She also is reputed to transport tea, chinaware, silk, inlaid cabinets and such from China and Japan. Finally," Anson's voice deepened, "this ship's strong room should contain a considerable treasure in gold dust. You will therefore see, gentlemen, that all of this must amount to a prodigious sum."

Over the sibilant *hiss-hiss* of seas under *Centurion*'s stern and the gentle knocking of the rudder against its pintles arose a babble of irrepressible excitement.

Captain Saunders fixed large and vivid brown eyes on the Commodore as he stood with his head all but brushing the beams above him. "Sir, on this galleon's return voyage to Manila from Acapulco what is likely to be her lading?"

Succinctly, Anson replied, "An my information is correct, her most valuable cargo will consist of quantities of minted dollars and silver plate — which I understand is the main product of South America. It is sent east in payment for those Oriental luxuries which I have just described."

"And — and, sir," tensely queried de Saumarez, "what would be the value of this silver?"

"That is not an easy question to satisfy with any exactitude," smiled Anson, "but it has been reported to the Admiralty that the value of the cargo carried on the galleon's eastward voyage is limited by Royal Edict to the sum of six hundred thousand dollars — it being that government's policy not to risk, as we say, too many eggs in one basket."

Secretly, Anson was amused to watch consternation appear in varying degrees on his Captains' deeply sunburned faces. He erased these glum expressions by quickly adding, "However, it is also reliably reported that this limitation is seldom observed; in fact, almost never does the ship sail with a cargo valued at less than three million dollars. Incidentally, may I point out that, on her Asian voyage, she is known as the 'Manila Galleon' and as the 'Acapulco Galleon' when proceeding towards Mexico, but no matter under which name she sails it is indisputable that she deserves her common designation of the 'Prize of All the Oceans.' "

Wide cheeks speckled by sunlight glancing off the Pacific, Anson watched enthusiasm flood the faces about him. "What do you say, gentlemen, shall we drink to the day on which we'll find, and take, this 'Prize of All the Oceans'?"

Once they had done so, Anson resumed in a graver tone. "Because our English hands have become so reduced in number and we have lost both the equipment and the troops necessary for the extensive shore operations I had contemplated, I feel that I have, within the limits of our capability, obeyed that part of my orders which directs that I shall 'harass and annoy the Spaniards ashore and on the sea.' "

He drew a deep breath, then said simply, "Therefore, I feel that I may, with clear conscience, devote my attention to a single purpose — that of capturing the great galleon. Are you agreed?"

"That we are, sir!" burst out Peircy Brett.

"Should we succeed in this adventure, there's not a Briton amongst us but can look forward to the enjoyment of comfort, if not luxury, for the rest of his life."

[283]

Subtractions

IT WAS ENCOURAGING THAT, for a few days more, the wind continued fresh and strong out of the west-southwest and drove George Anson's once more impressive-appearing squadron steadily on its course towards Acapulco, distant by some seventeen hundred miles. However, it would have to put in somewhere to take on wood, water and fresh food; the water taken on at Payta had proved to be of very poor quality and the supply of fresh food was running out so rapidly that soon salted meats and other sea rations must be substituted. The very possibility that scurvy might reappear set Anson to tramping his stern gallery in an agony of apprehension.

After making another survey of his charts, dour Sailing Master Nutt observed, "If, sir, the squadron's present course in maintained, it would come very close to the coast of Ecuador."

With a black-nailed forefinger, Nutt indicated a shapeless dot. "This here's Quibo Island, sir, which, according to Captain Dampier's journal, is uninhabited and offers a secure deep-water anchorage. He states further that it is plentifully supplied with accessible wood and an abundance of pure water."

Soon Andean peaks once more showed as a jagged silvery line along the horizon, so when Nutt's calculations placed the insignificant port of Manta abeam, Anson ordered the squadron hove to. Then *Gloucester's* number was hoisted and Captain Mitchell was instructed to send his non-seafaring prisoners ashore in that same little barcalonga which had carried such a surprising treasure.

Peter Vesey remarked, while leaning on *Gloucester's* sun-bleached rail and watching the jabbering, gesticulating prisoners being herded towards the gangway, "Thank God I'm not going off in such a cockleboat; must be all of ninety miles to the mainland."

Ted Waxter laughed easily. "Don't waste your pity on 'em. They've a few old sailors along and water and food enough for a fortnight. Besides, the wind stands fair for the mainland."

"All the same," Vesey observed, "that's a mighty small craft; the poor devils will be fearfully crowded."

"Nothing like we were at the beginning of this blasted voyage, or have you forgotten? I hope the damn' thing sinks." The purser's mate spat over the side. "There'll be that many less Papists to worry about."

"All the same, I wish they'd at least one real navigator among 'em. If the wind turns foul and blows out to sea they'll die a horrible death."

"I repeat, 'Good riddance.' Can you blame Captain Mitchell for not risking a single useful man when he's still short ninety hands? And even if we get that ninety, we still won't be able to sail and fight this ship with a mongrel crew such as this. Just look." He indicated the Watch on Deck. Only one man in three was English, the rest were mestizos and mulattos or full-blooded Indians and Negroes.

Subconsciously, Vesey noticed how easily these foreigners moved about their work, compared to the heavier-built Englishmen. He felt curious, too, to learn how they would fare should another epidemic of scurvy sweep the squadron — which God forbid!

Off the entrance to the Gulf of Panama, the wind died out so, for several days, the squadron was forced to drift about with sails slack and useless. The water taken on in Payta grew so indescribably foul that it could hardly be swallowed.

However no idleness was permitted Anson's crews. He ordered them drilled until they fainted beside guns which had become so sun-heated that their metal raised blisters on any skin that even brushed it. New topmen were sent aloft time and again to spread, clew-up, reef and then take in canvas.

With a view to more effectively attacking the treasure ship, which certainly would be both high-sided and tall-masted, Anson ordered sturdy swivel stocks built into the fighting tops of both *Gloucester* and *Centurion*.

As they paced the quarterdeck together, he explained to Brett, "To fight a galleon carrying so big a crew we will have to keep raking her decks from aloft. Swivels charged with langrage and musket balls should do the trick."

"Aye, sir, especially since we've so few trained hands left to fight the guns."

Bleak lines formed about the Commodore's wide mouth. "On that score, Mr. Brett, I've been doing considerable thinking and have reached a most disagreeable decision."

"I'm sorry for that, sir. What is it?"

[285]

"I can no longer blink the fact the *Teresa*, the *Soledad* and the *Dolores* are such hopelessly sluggish sailers that, on entering dangerous waters, the entire squadron might be jeopardized through not being able to keep together.

"In other words, I would be forced to fight my squadron at the speed of the slowest ship. So I must destroy the slow ships and send their crews to reinforce the faster ones."

Although he didn't say so, Brett knew that to reduce his squadron from its original number must have come as a terrible wrench but the Commodore had never been one to deceive himself, least of all on a point of personal pride.

As if to strengthen Anson's resolve, Sailing Master Nutt came up and stood to leeward, quietly awaiting permission to speak. "Sir, we must make every effort to reach Quibo without delay. Our water, bad as it is, is running out fast. Today I have had to ration all hands to a quart and a half per day."

Once everything of value had been removed from the condemned ships, Prize Captains Denis, Hughes, Gerard and the Englishmen in their crews were returned to their original ships, while non-British seamen were assigned where most needed.

For a while *Dolores*, *Soledad* and *Teresa* created an unforgettable picture as, already scuttled, they blundered crazily about, spouting flames.

That night George Anson felt much too depressed even to think of playing music. Instead, he ordered a second bottle of brandy and summoned his secretary for a game of piquet. Andrew Menzies, he knew, could be trusted to sense his mood and to respect his silent misery.

Despite determined efforts to concentrate, the Commodore played badly and lost a round sum, for the Carolinian was no opponent to be careless with. Finally, disgusted with his lack of self-discipline, he put away the well-fingered cards and offered a thin *cigarro* from Don Julio's choicest stock.

Relaxed by a third goblet of brandy, Anson experienced, and resisted, a rare temptation to probe into certain aspects of his companion's past. Why did Andrew so often retire to his stuffy little cabin when he might have enjoyed the meager comforts of the wardroom? Why should he stand solitary by the rail, of a moonlit night, and gaze fixedly, almost mournfully, out over the ocean?

[286]

What could have happened to him between the time he'd forfeited his plantation and when he'd appeared in Wilmington, pallid, drawn and haunted-looking? Another matter vaguely piqued Anson's curiosity; why was it that when his secretary visited the stern head he invariably made sure that he would be alone? Was it because Andrew had ever been supremely sensitive and modest?

The temptation to yield to curiosity was removed when Menzies commented, "It must have been a vast disappointment to order your slow prizes destroyed. You've my especial admiration — for whatever that's worth — for having done so."

"Thank you, Andrew," Anson said a trifle thickly, "for an understatement equaled by few and excelled by none." He managed a bleak smile. "And why do you think I was wise in what I did?"

Before replying the secretary drew a long puff on his seegar, set its end glowing jewel-like amid the cabin's half-light. He spoke softly, almost soothingly. "First, for the obvious reason, our water is so low that your squadron must reach Captain Dampier's Island at its very best speed."

"Correct," Anson admitted, flicking his ash out of a stern gallery window. "And my second reason?"

The Carolinian's somber eyes suddenly commenced to gleam. "The galleon from Manila customarily appears off Acapulco about the middle of January. Does it not?"

"— And so?"

"Should you delay too long about taking on wood, water and fresh food, you'll risk finding the treasure ship already safe in Acapulco."

"You are astute, Andrew. If you held the King's commission, I most certainly would promote you tomorrow when I intend to reward young van Keppel and a few others who have earned advancement."

"I am sensitive to the honor all the same, sir," came the grave acknowledgment. "May I refill your cup?"

~~~ 2 8 ~~~

The Turtles of Quibo

ON THE 6th day of December, 1741, *Tryall's Prize*, sailing far out in the van — as had her namesake — made signal that land had been

[287]

sighted. Thanks to Mr. Nutt's skilled navigation this proved to be the Island of Quibo, where, true to Dampier's report, penned some thirty-four years ago, an excellent anchorage protected from nearly all points of the compass did exist.

Compared to mountainous Juan Fernandez, Quibo seemed almost flat, for all that several respectable hills loomed in its interior. Like Juan Fernandez, this island was clothed with fine tall trees growing just above a wide sand beach which was bisected by a clear, fast-running stream. As Acting Lieutenant van Keppel pointed out, a more convenient watering place would have been hard to imagine.

"It would appear," observed Lieutenant de Saumarez, "that we've stumbled upon a second Eden."

"Aye, it would appear so," agreed Peircy Brett, slowly traversing his spyglass along a green shore all a-shimmer in the tropic heat, "for I see no signs of inhabitation."

Up on *Centurion*'s poopdeck, Anson kept glancing anxiously out to sea, for while his squadron was beating inshore, *Gloucester* suddenly had come about and, when last seen, was heading out to sea. Apparently, she had been unable to weather the last of several long and rock-studded peninsulas.

Hardly had the anchors gone seething bottomwards than landing parties were piped away, the Commodore having made it clear that the halt at Quibo must be as brief as possible — in fact only long enough to replenish the ships at top speed.

Quartermaster's Mate Wade and Will Pallister, assigned to *Centurion*'s landing party, soon discovered that Lieutenant de Saumarez's Eden was not quite what it purported to be. The jungle, although flower-festooned and sweet-smelling, proved to be discouragingly dense.

Wade and his party of sharpshooters several times sighted herds of deer, but the dainty creatures evidently had been hunted before. After staring at the intruders a moment, they would abruptly spin about to vanish amid the lush tangles.

Although the hunters swung cutlasses to hack a passage through lianas draped in a beautiful but infuriating network, they soon had to give up and return to the beach, purple-faced, insect bitten and bathed in sweat.

Suddenly a mestizo yelled, *"Alerta! Tigre! Un tigre!"*

"What's that yellow monkey yammering about?" panted Wade, thumbing bark dust from his eyes.

Will Pallister, having learned something of their language from Spanish prisoners, yelled, "He says there's a tiger somewhere nearby."

"Tiger!" The hunters closed in together and readied their weapons. "Where's he at?"

Following the line of the mestizo's index finger, Pallister made out a large black and yellow spotted member of the cat family flattened and poised to spring from a heavy branch. Startled as he was, the youth couldn't help noticing how very pink the beast's nose appeared and how white its muzzle. What savage beauty was expressed in those clear, topaz-hued eyes. How soft and silky were the beast's almost perfectly rounded ears.

Wade took hasty aim, but before he could fire, the *tigre* had merged with the background.

An Indian behind Pallister hissed, "Puma!"

"Puma or tiger," Wade snapped, " 'twas a nasty-looking brute."

Will delighted in brilliant flashes of color caused by flocks of many-hued parakeets, green and red parrots and scarlet or vividly blue macaws in rocketing about the treetops. A few macaws and parrots were shot, but proved to be so tough that thereafter they were ignored.

There were other dangers in de Saumarez's Eden; a pretty tree-shaded stream proved to be infested with huge, yellow-eyed alligators which did not hesitate to charge a man or to attack a smallboat. Several of these hideous, surprisingly fleet-footed saurians were shot down only a few feet short of an intended victim.

To grimy men who, for many a week, had looked forward to a wash and a swim in fresh water, the presence of those alligators proved a bitter disappointment. Then, too, a good many snakes were seen undulating through head-high grass or lying wrapped around a tree limb, waiting for some victim to pass below.

Keeping a sharp lookout, the hunting party returned, crestfallen and empty-handed, to the beach and joined in felling trees for firewood.

The crews of several smallboats, sent out to fish, also came in disappointed. They had been forced to abandon their efforts because of swarms of enormous, evil-looking manta rays. Some of these frightening creatures Lieutenant Hughes reported to be above eight feet square; by the hundred, these kept jumping, almost vertically, some six feet out of the water, then falling back making a tremendous splash.

Said he, "If one of those brutes were to fall on a boat it would be utterly destroyed." Efforts were made to drive the rays away by harpooning some of them, but their numbers were too great; fishing had to be abandoned for the time being, at least.

"Ah, *señores*," said a skinny mestizo who, supposedly, was familiar with the coast, "you had better remain near the beach. The forests here are infested with swarms of flying serpents."

Fearfully, the half-Indian rolled yellowish eyes. "They dart out of trees with the speed of arrows and sting an unwary person with a poison so potent he soon dies in the most dreadful agony."

"Yes! I heard one o' Dampier's men speak o' such fearsome reptiles," solemnly averred a gray-bearded gunner.

Despite all dangers, real and imaginary, the wooding and watering proceeded at a satisfactory rate of speed, thanks to the abundance of pure water and various acid fruits.

When, towards sundown, there still was no sign of *Gloucester*, a lugubrious fellow out of *Tryall's Prize* growled, "By grabs, if ever a vessel were meant for Old Man Jones's Navy, *Gloucester's* her!"

For the benefit of the Admiralty's chartmakers, Peircy Brett made another of those fine elevations he'd methodically been rendering whenever land was sighted during the voyage. Later, on a rough chart, he would compare Captain Dampier's few soundings with those reported by various officers detailed by the Commodore to this duty.

Will Pallister, perched on *Centurion's* cutwater, happily recorded his impression of the puma and the plumage of a dead macaw.

After consuming a half-bottle of a very excellent vintage presented by Captain Mitchell, Anson felt so confident that *Gloucester* must appear at any moment that he sought the privacy of his stern gallery and sent flute music to drifting softly over the star-spangled waters of Quibo Bay.

Early the next day boats were dispatched to explore a number of sandy, palm-dotted cays lying a short distance down the coast. About noon they returned, jubilant, their craft deep in the water under cargoes of giant, sadly sighing sea turtles.

"Some of these moss-backs," Clipperton exulted, "must weigh nigh two hundred pounds!"

When native-born seamen beheld the feebly squirming, flapping turtles, they grew wildly excited, cried, *"No! No comé, venenoso! No eat! Poison!"*

Even after the Jamaican, Michael Despeda, explained how delicious such meat really was, the foreign sailors threatened to mutiny if required even to taste it. Only after they'd several times watched their British shipmates eat hugely and remain quite unharmed did they also fall to.

The cays were reported by Lieutenant Scott to be alive with these succulent reptiles which had come ashore to lay eggs. Buckets, nets and tubs soon overflowed with pale, leathery-looking ovals which were pronounced by hungry men to be in no way inferior to the barnyard product.

"This is positively providential!" exulted Chief Surgeon Ettrick. "No need now to eat salted meat."

"How long can these creatures survive out of their natural element?" primly inquired the Reverend Mr. Richard Walter. "I must make a note on the point."

"For several veeks, sar, all depending on de heat," Michael Despeda informed him with an ivory grin. "Which is good, 'cause seldom man tires of turkle meat."

For two days Anson's men, despite infernal heat, wooded, watered and netted great rafts of turtles which were discovered asleep on the surface. It proved no trick at all to capture as many as a boat could hold and then stack them upside down, often three deep, in pens hurriedly knocked together by the ships' carpenters.

<hr>

29
A Light High in the Night

ON THE MORNING OF DECEMBER 9th — three days after the squadron's arrival in Quibo Bay — Anson carefully suppressed bitter anxiety and ordered up the "Heave Anchor" signal.

In succession, Anson's other four ships followed *Centurion*'s weather-beaten sails out of Quibo Bay and into the terrifying vastness of the Pacific.

If only *Gloucester* had been along everyone would have felt supremely confident as the five bowsprits swung towards Acapulco — and the great galleon due from Asia.

Hopes brightened when, during the First Dog Watch, a sail was sighted. But they soon dimmed. The stranger's canvas was too slight to be *Gloucester*'s.

Anson ordered *Tryall's Prize* in chase. In command of the squadron's speediest vessel, Captain Saunders had no trouble in running down a small barque which turned out to be the *Jesu Nazareno*, Captain Antonio Navarro. She was found to be carrying a prosaic, but most welcome cargo: rock salt and oakum, both of which were badly needed.

Since the *Nazareno* was much too small and slow to keep up with the rest of his ships, Anson ordered her crew taken to round out *Tryall's Prize* complement and, as soon as her cargo plus some forty pounds in silver money discovered in the bilges, had been unloaded, she was scuttled and sunk.

With dawn, the expedition's spirits soared. *Gloucester* had appeared dead ahead! However, Anson's elation faltered almost at once. For some reason his second largest ship was carrying not a shred of canvas on her foremast!

Adam Hayes, *Centurion's* carpenter, spat disgust over the rail. "I'll wager me last penny that rotten stick they put into her at Portsmouth has sprung again. 'Twere cracking even afore we cleared the Isle o' Wight."

"Aye," snarled a Scottish shipmate, "and may auld Clootie forever burn those plundering Commissioners o' Supply in the hottest corner o' Hell!"

Hayes's diagnosis of the cause for *Gloucester's* absence proved to be entirely accurate.

Disgustedly, long-faced Captain Mitchell reported, "Sir, whilst I was attempting to weather that last cape off Quibo, my foremast suddenly began to groan. Chips investigated and reported that a great crack had appeared at the deck line and was opened halfway up to the crosstrees.

"My only course was to strike all canvas supported by the threatened mast which, of course, included my headsails. Therefore, I was left powerless to tack and had to run downwind and away from the rendezvous."

"You have my sincere sympathy, Captain," came the Commodore's brisk assurance.

Although deploring the consequent delay in arriving off Acapulco, Anson hesitated not at all about ordering *Gloucester* into the Quibo Bay for wood, water and turtles. Also he sent *Centurion's* carpenter and his mates over to inspect the damage.

While the weather-racked Fourth Rate was supplying herself, they fished the tender foremast.

Three days were required to repair the half-rotten foremast, but when *Gloucester* ran out to join Anson's flag it looked most ungainly and clumsy yet capable of supporting *Gloucester*'s headsails and a little upper canvas.

Gloomily, Justinian Nutt noted that an arrival off Acapulco now had been delayed by nine, instead of four, days. This boded no good if the Galleon had made even the normal four month's passage from Manila.

So it was not until December 12th that Anson's five ships squared away on a northwesterly course. *Centurion* had taken *Carmelo* in tow and *Gloucester, Carmine* in an almost pathetic attempt to increase the squadron's speed.

"It will never do," Anson had warned his captains, "to allow the ships to straggle whilst we sail in Mexican waters. Above all, you must at all times maintain your proper stations. For all we know, the Viceroy's squadron may appear at any moment; were I the enemy's admiral I most certainly would lie in wait for us below Acapulco — perhaps off Puerto Seguro where Cavendish and Dampier waited before taking their galleons."

New Year's Day 1742 was celebrated by all crews with much rum and genuine enthusiasm. Why not celebrate? Were they not still living? Had not the worst storms the Horn could offer been weathered? Best of all, down in *Centurion*'s treasure room lay silver coin, bullion and plate conservatively valued at 147,900 pounds — and this did not include jewelry, fine cloths, pearls, precious stones and other booty of almost equal value.

When Anson ordered figgy duff served and the main brace to be spliced, not once but twice, the hairy, sun-darkened crews cheered him to the echo. Later, the Commodore entertained his Captains and senior lieutenants with a rum punch brewed, in honor of the day, by his Jamaican steward. Despeda's concoction proved deceptively bland to the taste but soon took such effect that, in the great cabin, faces grew flushed and voices were raised in song. When Andrew Menzies produced his violin and struck up a lively reel the younger officers, brave in captured finery, lined up and capered about as best they could to the flagship's slow lift and roll.

"To your very good health, sir!" Matthew Mitchell, smiling for once, lifted a jeweled cup in Anson's direction. "God send 1742 atones for the losses and disappointments we've suffered this last year and a half."

After a while the Reverend Mr. Walter called for silence. "Please, gentlemen, let us not on this joyous occasion forget those of our brave companions who will never again see England. May God grant their souls eternal peace."

In silence the panting dancers refilled their punch cups and toasted the dead. It came as a sobering thought to realize that of every three men who'd sailed from St. Helen's on that rainy September afternoon of 1740, two were no longer living.

Favoring winds drove the squadron north so rapidly that, despite the delay due to *Gloucester*'s misfortune, Anson felt justified in believing that the Manila Galleon might not have yet reached Acapulco. He could even conjure up a dozen sound reasons why she might have been delayed.

At dusk on January 6th, while the squadron was preparing to assume night stations, *Tryall's Prize,* sailing in advance of her consorts, signaled that she had in sight a light which burned so high above the water that it would only be shining in the rigging of some great ship!

With the speed of burning gunpowder the good news flashed from ship to ship, sped from quarterdeck to forecastle and down to the sweltering 'tween decks. For once never a starter, colt or cane was used to hurry topmen into the rigging.

Passionate curses sounded aboard *Carmelo* and *Carmine* when their tow lines were cast off. They knew there wouldn't be much chance now of their being in sight when *Tryall's Prize* and the two Fourth Rates brought to action what *surely* must be the Manila Galleon; what other ship of such size would be found cruising these waters?

His voice vibrant with tension, Sailing Master Nutt ordered out studding sails and set every stitch of canvas which might increase *Centurion*'s speed by even a fraction of a knot.

"Looks like Old Man Mitchell's set to gamble his foremast!" remarked Tom Ramster when *Gloucester*'s big forecourse billowed, ghost-like, into being.

After an hour's time, hands working about the flagship's upper rigging could see for themselves that light reported by *Tryall's Prize.*

"B' God, there she shines!" exulted Buckle. "Steady and bright like a jool in a angel's crown!"

Further encouragement was given when Captain Saunders's signal lanterns reported that he could now glimpse the stranger's topsails.

Lieutenant Brett, burning with excitement under a coldly correct manner, couldn't help inquiring of Denis, "But why should she show so bright a light?"

"I've not the least notion, sir. Except that her master knows of no enemies in this ocean and imagines himself quite safe."

"Yes. But why show any light at all?"

Unexpectedly, Anson's voice issued from among a patch of shadow at the weather rail. "Possibly I have an explanation."

Both lieutenants stiffened and took off their hats.

"It has been reported to me that on occasions when the galleon cannot accommodate all the cargo destined for Mexico, a *capitana*, or overflow ship, is provided to sail in consort with the galleon which, under such conditions, is called the *almirante* or admiral.

"That brilliant light is designed, I imagine, to keep the *capitana* ship informed of the *almirante*'s position. So, with any luck, I believe we are about to secure two prizes instead of one."

Thuds and rumblings below, irritated voices and loud cursing testified that *Centurion* was being cleared for action. Long before the Mid-Watch appeared on deck at midnight swivel guns had been swayed aloft and their well-greased pivot shanks eased into those stocks which had been built into the fighting tops at Juan Fernandez.

To the secret chagrin of all hands serving in the Fourth Rates it was observed that, in this light breeze, *Carmine* and *Carmelo*, sailing on their best point of wind, far from lagging, were almost maintaining station. Damn! Now they'd likely qualify for shares in the plunder, provided they could see the Acapulco Galleon and her *capitana* brought to action.

Few of the Watch Below closed their eyes, no matter how weary.

"Hell's roaring bells," rasped Clipperton, "won't daylight *ever* come?"

Dreaming of those fabulous riches almost within reach, the men dozed beside their guns. Matches, lit much too early, continued to glow sleepily on sand in the match tubs.

Ceaselessly, Lieutenant de Saumarez who, in action, would command the main gundeck, strode about restless as a fox terrier; repeatedly he inspected the cannons and their gear.

Several times, quite pointlessly, he reminded his gun captains,

"For the first broadside all great guns are to be loaded with two roundshot each. You understand?"

"Aye, aye, sir."

Under battle lanterns dully aglow, his gaze flitted from one sweaty face to the next — as usual it was stiflingly hot below decks. "For the second broadside you will fire a single roundshot."

"Aye, aye, sir!"

"For the third and subsequent broadsides — if more are required — you will load with grape. Now, each of you repeat the sequence of loading."

While they were doing so, de Saumarez swabbed his features; although he'd opened his shirt down to his belt it was sopping as if he'd fallen overboard. "Finally, no gun is to be fired without *direct orders* from me."

"Question, sir?" demanded a hairy, stoop-shouldered individual. "How soon ought we to be in range?"

"Within an hour, if the lookouts are not mistaken. We are fast coming up with the enemy."

Lieutenant Brett, taut as a guitar string, instructed the quarterdeck gunners and those handling 16-pounders mounted on the forecastle to fire but one round of solid shot before raking the enemy decks with cannister — a deadly charge containing a triple handful of musket balls — which could mow down a crew as thickly packed as the one expected to be found defending the Prize of All the Oceans.

By the time a quartermaster's mate had sounded three bells of the Morning Watch, dawn was more than a presentiment.

Soon there was sufficient light to bring home two appalling facts: one was that the only ships in sight were British, the other was that the light they had chased all night was caused by flames flaring from one of two curiously rounded volcanoes, which were thrusting above the horizon like the breasts of some gargantuan female.

The sun appeared and gilded flying fishes were skimming under *Centurion*'s lion figurehead as, sullenly, the guns were run in and the ships otherwise were restored to normal cruising conditions.

Sailing Master Nutt appeared on the quarterdeck seeming quite excited. "Sir, may I offer a word of encouragement?"

"You may, Mr. Nutt," Anson said. "I'll snatch at even a crumb of hope."

"Well, sir, I've just been rereading Captain Dampier's sailing directions for this coast. Those two burning mountains we see he calls 'the

Paps of Acapulco'; I've also heard them mentioned by a pilot captured by the *Gloucester*. He swore that the port we seek lies at their base; so have several other prisoners."

Slowly, Anson's broad, red-brown features kindled. "How far away would you say are yonder peaks?"

"About twenty-five leagues, sir."

"Seventy-five miles? Hum. Do you know where Acapulco lies in relation to these 'Paps'?"

"No, sir, but I'll soon find out."

"Good. Now, the next and most important question is this, has the galleon already arrived?"

"There is no way of telling about that, sir, without sending in a spy boat, is there?"

"Correct. But it will be difficult to do so without surrendering our advantage of remaining undetected. 'Twould be folly to send even the *Tryall's Prize* any closer."

Anson thought to solve this problem by sending perceptive Peter Denis in to reconnoiter, along with Lieutenant Scott of *Gloucester*, Acting Lieutenant van Keppel and the *Jesu Nazareno*'s dreadfully pockmarked pilot. He, and two of the Negroes toiling at the oars, all had sworn that they knew this coast intimately. How intimately? Peter Denis wondered.

～ 3 0 ～

Lieutenant Denis Reconnoiters

LIEUTENANT DENIS, timing his approach with care, kept the barge invisible from the shore until nightfall, then hoisted his craft's little leg-of-mutton sails and steered towards the volcano's glare.

Triangular sails star-silvered, the barge for hours ran parallel to what seemed an unbroken line of breakers while all three officers, through night glasses, studied the coast. They agreed that there were no signs of habitation; only a succession of bare, rocky points separated by sandy beaches which could not possibly be landed upon because of the murderous surf. Nor had they detected any opening to that bay upon which Acapulco was supposed to lie.

With the approach of daylight, Denis grimly ordered the barge

[297]

turned about and cruised well off shore for nearly one hundred and forty miles to the eastward. Then, to the Spanish pilot's obvious confusion, a *second* pair of rounded mountains, remarkably similar to those which had led to the squadron's disappointment, appeared upon the horizon.

"Por Dios! Those must be the true 'Paps of Acapulco!' "

To Acting Lieutenant van Keppel, Denis announced, "We will continue this course until I am satisfied about the truth of this matter. Only then will we return to the Commodore."

"Not a bad idea," came Scott's dry comment, "since our food and water's about gone."

Once Denis's discovery was made known, enthusiasm flared white-hot among the crews.

Never less than sixty miles offshore, Anson sailed his ships eastward until the second set of "paps" was sighted. Then, for a second time, his barge was sent in after nightfall.

Quartermaster's Mate Wade, who, because of his excellent vision at night, this time had been posted as lookout on the barge's bow, finally announced, "I spy a light! A lot of 'em."

Van Keppel's grin spread all over his rounded visage. "Ah! Acapulco at last!" A short time later he was proved mistaken; the lights came only from grass fires.

Denis snapped to Parmer, "Lower the sails, then get out the oars and muffle them; we'll run less risk of being noticed."

Near midnight of February 17th, those in *Centurion's* barge approached the harbor's mouth and noted that, nearly in the center of it, loomed a low and rocky islet. The pilot whispered, "That is called la Roqueta. It is a huge rock which divides the entrance into two channels. The wider passage, *Señor Teniente,* is known as 'la Boca Grande,' the smaller 'la Boca Chica.' "

"On which side of the bay is the town?" Denis queried over the rhythmic *clunk-clunk* of the oars against tholepins.

The fellow's eyes and teeth glinted in the starlight. *"Señor Teniente,* Acapulco lies on the northwest side, across the bay."

"Which channel should I follow?" Assuming a fierce expression, he glowered at the ugly little Spaniard's smallpox-ravaged visage. "For your sake, *piloto,* you'd better not ill-advise us!"

The pilot commenced to tremble and the two native Negroes looked anxious before he muttered, "Most certainly Acapulco should be approached through la Boca Chica. If there still are guards on la Roqueta they will be not so likely to notice you."

Nat Wade felt his excitement soar once the rocky shoreline loomed closer, higher overhead, and the surf's thunder grew so loud as almost to preclude conversation. It was a good thing that the tide was flooding, otherwise the shadowy smallboat would not be carried so rapidly towards the entrance of the Boca Chica, which Wade guessed to be about four hundred feet across.

Once the barge nosed into the channel, Denis ordered his men to lay on their oars; when they obeyed, red-gold phosphorus dripped prettily from blades held parallel to the surface. Soon the smallboat entered smoother water and the roaring of the surf diminished rapidly.

Ramster strained his vision ahead, then asked Parmer, "How far off d'ye figger is the ruddy town?"

"Quite a ways, I allow. They say it's a big harbor."

Faster and faster still, the spy boat rode the tide through the Boca Chica into a bay which Lieutenant Scott later described as being broad and roughly oval in shape.

Suddenly Wade grabbed the shoulder of the man behind him and hissed, "Pass the word aft. I see a weak light dead ahead."

Without being told, the rowers readied their oars, while those in the bow cocked their firearms.

Presently, one of the Negro oarsmen said he was almost certain that the faint light was originating in some fisherman's boat. He was right. Before long, a low black smear appeared which proved to be a dugout canoe. Its occupants were either half asleep or so preoccupied in fishing that the barge was able to drift within fifty yards of them before someone uttered a startled yelp.

Instantly the three fishermen — all Negroes — dived overboard and struck out strongly towards Roqueta.

"Out oars!" rasped Denis, then to Parmer, "Steer to cut off the fastest one."

There ensued an anxious ten minutes, for in this jet-hued water the frightened Negroes proved to be almost invisible, and elusive as fishes. However, when blunderbusses were aimed at close range the fugitives surrendered and were hauled inboard, dripping and chattering their teeth in abject fear.

Denis whispered, "Now, Parmer, make for the canoe; I want it taken in tow."

Scott supervised the binding and gagging of the three all but naked blacks while van Keppel prepared the crude dugout for towing.

"All secure, sir."

"Very good, Mr. Keppel. We will now return to the squadron."

The rowers bent to their oars with a will; every man was fearful that daylight might catch them in sight of the guards on Roqueta Island.

Ramster, Wade and the rest pulled until their tendons crackled and sweat streamed down their faces in acid trickles; Parmer nevertheless kept on calling, "One, two, *stroke!* One, two, *stroke!* Come on, ye jelly-backs! Put yer thews into it! Want to lose us our chance at that damned galleon?"

Not until the barge again was riding the long swells far beyond the entrance to the Boca Chica did Denis order the canoe let go, despite a suggestion from Lieutenant Scott. "Wouldn't it be better, sir, to bring this craft along with us? It just might drift back inshore and spill the beans."

Denis's reply was immediate and decisive. "No. It would slow us too much; besides, it's bound to be smashed to flinders by the surf. The Dons will imagine that the dugout capsized and these niggers got carried out to sea or were killed among the rocks."

Everything proved so well-timed that when dawn broke and long lines of pelicans, flapping in ragged formations, started out for their fishing grounds, Roqueta Island was safely out of sight and only the Paps of Acapulco remained to identify the port's location.

Because the pilot could speak a little English, Peter Denis ordered the most intelligent-looking of the prisoners to be ungagged. He was a beautifully muscled, black-brown young fellow distinguished by a long, pinkish scar running from one eye all the way down to his chin.

Summoning a savage expression, Denis told the pilot, "Warn this man that if he tells the truth he'll be rich for life; if he lies by even so much as a single word he'll be skinned alive, rubbed with salt and eaten!"

When the pilot translated, the prisoner's eyes, lemon-tinted by the sunrise, rolled in terror.

"Ask him whether the galleon has made port."

"*Sí, señor,* she came in, unharmed, on the ninth day of January."

"Then she's in already!" groaned Scott. "Oh, blast the bloody luck!"

Ramster snarled, "There's Arnand's ghost at work! Will we ever win clear of it?"

"Not likely," Wade muttered. "Like a lot of us, Arnand was done the dirty, so, by God, he ain't going to let us off easy-like."

After digesting the unwelcome news, Lieutenant Denis brightened. "I say, let's not be so glum. Our prospects mayn't be so bad after all."

"How so?" Scott queried wearily. "I'd like to know."

"Why, now we've the opportunity of prizing the galleon when she *leaves* Acapulco."

"What's so fine about that, sir?" asked Acting Lieutenant van Keppel.

"She'll then be laden with silver and mayhap some gold, both of which are a deal easier to sell than the fancy junk she fetches in from the East."

"Why, that's so!" chuckled Scott. Then, as if having made a profound discovery, he added, "Now that we know where she is, all we have to do is go in and take her!"

As the barge heeled under a brief squall and sped out to sea, Tom Ramster inquired, "Sir, if I may make so bold, how much does the Commodore say she'll bring?"

"Not less than three million Spanish dollars," stated Scott, grinning from ear to ear.

"Three million bloody pieces of silver!"

The ragged and sunburned men shook hands and laughed so uproariously that the prisoners lying, loosely bound on the bottom gratings, stared in wonderment.

Silently, each of the rowers then attempted to guess what his share in this enormous sum might amount to — if he were still alive at the end of this fantastic voyage.

Van Keppel, hunching forward on his seat, overheard Denis ask the pilot, "Do these fellows know if the Spanish are aware of our presence?"

When questioned, the eldest fisherman shook a fuzzy head frosted with gray, then broke into a flood of broken Spanish. Several times Scott thought to recognize a familiar word — Payta.

When the pilot had done translating, everyone in the barge learned that no sooner had the English ships disappeared than the valiant Governor of Payta had dispatched gallopers to spread an alarm that *Ingléses heréticos* had appeared and were ravaging and burning ports all along the coast.

The officers, however, found a measure of encouragement on hearing that His Excellency the Governor of Acapulco was unaware that the dreaded British were hovering just over the horizon beyond his bailiwick.

The wrinkled old man continued, "For a while after the news arrived, His Excellency posted lookouts along the southern shore of the island called Roqueta with orders to signal sight of a strange sail. But three days ago, *Señor Capitán*," the Negro went on, "these lookouts were recalled because His Excellency believed the *heréticos'* ships had departed from Payta in a different direction, perhaps towards la Tierra del Fuego and their homeland."

At this, murmurs of satisfaction circulated the barge, which now was making such good speed that flirts of spray kept dousing men near the bow.

How curious, Wade reflected, as he settled back against the thwarts and watched the land lower astern. This last-minute withdrawal of enemy lookouts had happened thrice before — off Madeira, off Saint Julian's and again at Juan Fernandez!

Questioned separately, the fishermen divulged that the *Santa Pilar*, this year's treasure ship, was new and unusually large, that she carried sixty-six guns and was manned by half a thousand officers and men out of the Regular Spanish Navy.

But what pleased the English most was the information that, at this very moment, *Santa Pilar* was taking on water and supplies in expectation of sailing for Manila on the third of March.

"The third of March!" Denis repeated softly. "The third of March!"

The muscular young Negro added, "To protect *la Santa Pilar* until she departs, *el Gobernador* has caused six batteries to be built in addition to thirteen others already raised about the bay of Acapulco."

Denis instructed the pilot, "Ask him about the weight of the cannon in them."

"*Señor,* he says he does not know, but he says he has heard that they are of weight. He says also that the Governor recently has received from Mexico City a reinforcement of two hundred veteran troops from Old Spain."

"How many soldiers does he command altogether?"

"He says one thousand militia and a great army of Indians armed with lances, bows and arrows."

Acting Lieutenant van Keppel started when a flying fish burst out of a foaming roller and landed *plop!* at his feet. Then he laughed. "I say, Acapulco seems to promise even more fun than Payta."

"Rather," Denis admitted. "Maybe this time the Dons will really show fight."

～ 3 1 ～

Blockade, I

DIRECTLY HE RECEIVED Lieutenant Denis's report, Commodore Anson initiated a series of moves evolved long ago but which, as usual, he had kept to himself.

He at once strung his ships out in a long line so that if the *Santa Pilar* sailed in advance of the expected date at least one of the squadron could not fail to sight her.

The squadron, therefore, was ordered to fan out opposite Acapulco — out of sight of land — leaving an interval of ten miles between ships. Anson posted speedy *Tryall's Prize* on the extreme left of the line, next sailed *Gloucester* and *Carmine,* then the flagship and, finally, *Carmelo* on the right.

As a further precaution, the Commodore ordered two swift-sailing cutters to patrol the coast at a distance of ten miles, but with orders to remain unobserved at all times. At nightfall these spy boats must creep in close enough to observe the harbor's twin exits and make assurance doubly sure that this Prize of All the Oceans did not slip out unseen.

Just before the vessels dispersed, Anson ordered all trained and healthy hands aboard *Gloucester* and *Centurion* and left only skeleton crews to navigate his prize ships.

As day followed day the sturdier volunteers — mostly Negroes, who as a rule proved more powerful and enduring than either the Indians or mestizos — none too gently were introduced to the art of serving broadside cannon. For hours on end gun carriages rumbled in and out, in and out. Others were instructed how, with every shot, to raise and lower the heavy, red-painted port lids, and how to employ ladles, spongers and rammers.

Lightly built mestizos and Indians were trained as powder monkeys to replace English lads who, with a few exceptions, had perished long ago. Theirs would be the dangerous, if less exhausting, task of racing below to fetch powder, shot and wads from the magazines.

If gun drill was weary work, the topmen found toiling about the rigging under a broiling sun no less wearisome. Time after time the new men, cursed and beaten by veterans, swarmed aloft to spread and then take in, to clew up and reef, canvas. Royals, gallants and topgallants were unbent and sent down on the pretense that they'd become damaged in action and needed to be replaced.

As permanent captain of the maintop, Nat Wade came into his own and efficiently used his new-found knowledge. Fingers which had been cunning in sewing leather proved even more adept at contriving those often intricate knots which controlled *Centurion*'s weather-worn canvas.

Wade grew increasingly concerned over the standing rigging, most of which was seriously worn, chafed and gray. Without that cordage taken from the captured ships, the top hampers of both Fourth Rates couldn't possibly be trusted in a hard blow. About the soundness of the Fourth Rates' yards and topmasts, as Carpenter Hayes growled, "the less said the better."

On a fly-blown calendar, Will Pallister — shifted from Schoolmaster's Mate to act as Andrew Menzies's assistant — ticked off the number of days since the blockade had been imposed. Even ordinary seamen and foreigners had taken to tallying the passage of time on blunt, tarry fingers till the second of March. Tomorrow, by God, should see the great *Santa Pilar* come sailing out of Acapulco!

Sailing Masters Nutt and Lambert of *Gloucester* also were keeping track of time, but for another and less exciting reason. Because over two months had elapsed since Quibo had been left astern the last turtles had been consumed and salted meat again was being issued. Also, the water casks were sounding increasingly hollow. True, another month's supply remained, if severely rationed, but suppose the treasure ship delayed her sortie or proved fast enough to require a long chase out to sea? What then?

~~~ 3 2 ~~~

Blockade, II

LONG BEFORE DAWN could be expected to gild the twin peaks behind Acapulco almost every man in the squadron was on deck and straining his eyes to glimpse a spy boat's sail racing out to report the great galleon under way. Would the *Santa Pilar* venture out early in the day — or later on? Wind and tide undoubtedly would decide that.

Dawn proved to be uncommon beautiful, with delicate gold, salmon, emerald and sapphire clouds draped across the sky, but the brightening day revealed neither spy boats nor a more imposing flash of sails; only the dorsal fins of sharks and gigantic fishes called merlin by the Spanish.

The Forenoon Watch was called and the men of the Morning Watch reluctantly went to breakfast on noisome porridge and burnt-biscuit "coffee." Even so, no one appeared in the least downhearted. Surely the treasure ship must soon appear.

"After a'," remarked Kipps, the flagship's gunner, while cooling boiling hot coffee, "d'ye no' ken the way of them cursed Papists? 'Never do today what ye can put off tae tomorrow.' They've a single word for yon philosophy, but I've mislaid it."

"*Mañana,*" sang out one of the men eating between the ready cannon.

"She'll most likely come out at sundown," opined Ramster, leaning forward because his back was yet tender from the flogging he'd earned in Payta. "Tide'll be right then, too, or so they say on the quarterdeck."

Although never a signal light was shown that night by either cutter, there was no slacking of vigilance. Men slept about the deck and among the gun carriages while the stars, blazing bright as miniature beacons, wheeled slowly over head. After all, were not three million dollars about due to come in reach? Not until the seventh of March did some men admit, but only to themselves, that something must have gone wrong.

[305]

After General Inspection, Lieutenant Philip de Saumarez, accompanied by the captured pilot, appeared on the quarterdeck and stood respectfully to leeward of the Commodore.

"Well, Mr. Saumarez, what is it?"

"Sir, this fellow tells me that next week comes Palm Sunday."

"Well, what of that?"

"He swears, sir," de Saumarez reported unhappily, "that, under no circumstances would a Spanish ship leave port during Holy Week. I've questioned the volunteers, sir. One and all say that the Governor will not allow the galleon to depart before the fourteenth or fifteenth of this month."

If, indeed, she's not already slipped by unseen, thought Lieutenant Brett.

"In that case," Anson admitted with deceptive imperturbability, "I fear we must consider further delay as an unpleasant necessity."

He and all the crews waited impatiently until, on Palm Sunday, the cutters came scudding out to report the *Santa Pilar* still in Acapulco.

Holy Week was passed in hot and tedious gun drill and sail-handling. Faced with a rapidly dwindling water supply, the squadron for the first time since reaching Juan Fernandez, was placed on short water rations, which prompted a familiar plaint, "Cap'n Arnand ain't done wi' us — not by a long shot."

"Ah-h, come off it!" snapped a gunner's mate. "Bloody galleon's still in there, ain't she? If she don't come out, our Commodore will damn well go in and take her!"

"The 'ell 'e will! 'E ain't forgetting about all them batteries which can blow us right out o' the drink."

On Easter Monday evening the cutters which, two days earlier, again had been posted inshore made no signal of the *Santa Pilar*'s departure, so George Anson summoned to his cabin Saunders, Brett, the elder de Saumarez, Sailing Master Nutt and, of course, the inscrutable Andrew Menzies.

He invited them to sit upon a long locker running under the stern windows where they might benefit from a breeze beginning to blow off the distant land. They were grateful. All day it had been so fearfully hot that tar payed into the deck seams had bubbled.

While using a palm leaf fan, Anson fixed his gaze on the sun-darkened faces before him. "I fear, gentlemen, I must voice an unpleasant conclusion which no doubt already has been reached by you.

I am now convinced that the cutter I first sent to reconnoiter the approaches to Acapulco were seen, despite all Mr. Denis's precautions."

Brett gazed with compassion at his grim-faced superior as he continued.

"I have since heard that the fishermen's canoe was found which, coupled with the disappearance of the Negroes in it, could only have brought the Spaniards conviction that a hostile force must be somewhere in the vicinity. Eh, Mr. Nutt?"

The sailing master inclined his cruelly sunburned bald head. "That, sir, undoubtedly must be the case. Further, I've been given to understand that, under no conditions do the local fishermen ever venture out to sea *beyond* the Boca Chica — which is where the canoe was discovered. Also, it is known that all three prisoners are excellent swimmers and could have had no difficulty in reaching safety if their canoe had overturned. Failure to recover even a single body must have clinched the matter for the Spanish authorities."

Anson's sturdy legs, concealed under blue and white striped cotton pantaloons, twice carried him the length of the great cabin's beam before he halted and faced the officers perspiring on the stern locker.

"Since beyond a doubt the enemy has taken alarm, it goes without saying that the Governor in Acapulco will not authorize the departure of so valuable a ship whilst he believes us in the vicinity."

Brett blotted at sweat dripping from his long and narrow jaw then said, "In that case, sir, is it not possible that the authorities will not permit the galleon to sail at all and send out two treasure ships next year instead? I believe once you stated that such was their practice when Thomas Cavendish was harrying this coast."

Anson quickened the motions of his fan. "That is true, so I will now disclose the scheme I have decided upon; but, before I explain it, you will raise your right hands and solemnly swear that, neither by inference nor direct speech, will you disclose my intention."

When they had done so the Commodore instructed Menzies to spread out a chart of Acapulco harbor recently drawn by Brett on information gained from various prisoners. It depicted the location of all batteries, old and new, and also gave a few soundings which might or might not prove to be accurate.

The Commodore's voice swelled suddenly. "In simple, gentlemen, it is my intention, together with the *Gloucester,* to sail in at night and bombard the forts into submission, then to seize the galleon as she lies at anchor. If this venture is brought off handsomely enough, I feel it stands every chance of success, especially if the Dons display no more vigor than they did at Payta."

"A question, sir?" Saunders put in eagerly. "Might it not be better to make this attack with a landing force carried in the boats?"

Anson shook his head. "No, Captain. So many boats would have to be employed in such an enterprise that, undoubtedly, they would be detected even before they could enter the Boca Grande; also, they would be unable to reply effectively. It is my belief that our gun crews are now sufficiently well trained to reduce the Spanish batteries to rubble."

Amid a penetrating silence, he turned to the sailing master. "Mr. Nutt, I invite your opinion, but please deliberate with care before replying, for it is your advice that I value the most."

Nutt blinked like an owl in daylight, scratched at his shiny red scalp.

"What manner of winds and currents can we expect to encounter during a night attack?"

The sailing master frowned and nervously cleared his throat. "Although I agree with your scheme in spirit, sir, yet I fear that the maneuver you contemplate must end in disaster."

"— And why?"

"Because, sir, from my own observations and those of officers serving in the spy boats the following unfavorable conditions must be expected: The sea breeze which, at dawn, starts to blow strongly in from the ocean, dies out during the afternoon, and is followed by a flat calm which usually endures throughout the night." Nutt paused and glanced about, as if seeking support. "Then the land breeze springs up, and, as you undoubtedly have observed, sir, blows out to sea until near noontime, at which time it fails and the sea breeze commences."

"In other words," Anson said, fingering his powerful, bronzed jaw, "the prevailing winds flow from exactly the wrong direction favorable to a night attack? Is that what you mean to say?"

"I fear so, sir."

For several minutes the council, most of them frowning, stared in silence out of the stern windows while assimilating the sailing master's remarks. Finally Anson faced about. "Such being the case, it would be sheer folly to attempt the attack I had contemplated. However, on the odd chance that the Governor may change his mind, we will continue patroling until a shortage of water and fresh supplies forces us to move on. How much water have we left, Mr. Brett?"

The first lieutenant's reply came with distressing promptness. "Sir, not a ship in this squadron has more than a scant ten days' supply."

Briefly, Anson gnawed at his upper lip. "I hadn't imagined us to be quite that short. Since this is so, we cannot linger here any longer." The Commodore's manner altered, became brisk and his speech succinct. "Mr. Nutt, pray fetch me Captain Dampier's charts of this coast. I wish to determine the most advantageous point at which we can supply ourselves for a long journey."

" 'A long journey,' sir?" de Saumarez burst out.

"Home?" queried Justinian Nutt.

Anson nodded. "Aye, Mr. Nutt, home — by way of China. The crazy conditions of our fighting ships makes it imperative that, without the loss of a single day, we secure the services of a dockyard in some friendly port."

In the bewilderment the perspiring officers eyed one another.

One of Brett's ever-expressive brows climbed a trifle. "And where, sir, is such a port to be found, short of Brazil?"

"The Portuguese colony of Macao lies on an island very near to Canton on the Chinese mainland. I am told that the East India Company's ships frequently refit there. So, after watering and replenishing our stores of fresh food, we will sail for China."

For a moment utter astonishment kept everyone silent. What the Commodore had so casually proposed meant a voyage of seven thousand miles across the vast and largely unknown Pacific, in crazy half-wrecks which had been at sea for almost two years and now were manned to a great degree by undependable foreigners!

⟞ 3 3 ⟝

Chequetan

ALL THE OFFICERS and most of the men foresaw that circumstances soon would force a momentous decision upon their Commander in Chief. In their present condition neither *Gloucester* nor *Centurion* could hope to weather such frightful storms as had been encountered off Cape Noire and Statenland; nor did either man-of-war retain sea stores sufficient to complete such a voyage. It came as a clinching argument that nowhere near enough English seamen now survived to handle the ships in heavy weather; moreover, a high percentage of the foreign sailors were dying off, unable to stand up under the harsh routine of life aboard a British man-of-war.

Clinging obstinately to an admittedly slender hope, George Anson therefore provisioned *Centurion's* cutter for a month's cruise and ordered Lieutenant Hughes, of the stentorian voice, and six picked men to maintain the patrol off Acapulco. If, at the end of twenty-four days, the *Santa Pilar* had not been sighted, Hughes was instructed to make for the squadron's projected watering place at Chequetan — a harbor described by Captain Dampier as lying some ninety miles north of Acapulco.

Many of those watching the battered little cutter standing away towards those twin peaks which for so long had been symbolic of dazzling hopes wondered if she had not been too heavily laden with supplies for her long and lonely patrol. Only six inches of freeboard remained.

"I wouldn't worry too much," observed Lieutenant Scott of *Gloucester*. "If anyone can bring her through it'll be Johnny Hughes. He's the tough one!"

Waking at midnight, Andrew Menzies heard the Commodore endlessly traversing his private gallery — an indication that he was arriving at yet another critical decision, the nature of which became evident when, next day, he ordered *Centurion* to take *Carmine* in tow and *Gloucester* to assist *Carmelo*. Next, during the thirsty and heat-plagued passage to Chequetan, everything of value gradually was transferred from the prizes — which on the open ocean proved a most difficult and exhausting maneuver.

Over the prospect of reducing his command to only three vessels bitter lines reappeared about George Anson's wide, good-humored mouth, but there could be no denying the fact that *Carmelo* and *Carmine* were such poor sailers that they would dangerously delay the squadron in its contemplated voyage across the Pacific. Further, their crews were badly needed elsewhere, especially in weary old *Gloucester*, still showing splints bound about her tender foremast.

"Arnand again!" groaned Ramster when the wind remained so contrary that a whole week was lost making a passage which should not have required three days.

Several deaths by sunstroke were recorded in the Muster Books before land was sighted and cutters, under Lieutenants Scott and Denis were sent in to investigate the harbor of Chequetan. Four days later they returned with the welcome information that William Dampier's information once more had proved essentially correct. At Chequetan, on the Mexican coast, they had discovered a deep harbor with a fresh water lake nearby.

Accordingly, on April 7th the squadron prepared to enter a beautiful little bay and the sad duty of destroying *Carmine* and *Carmelo* had to be discharged.

Tears filled many eyes when the prizes were towed into shallow water and there set afire.

For many weeks dried out by the fierce sun, they burned like gigantic torches. Tongues of flame, like agile topmen, scurried up the remains of the standing rigging and curled about the bare masts.

Furious clouds of steam erupted when flames reached the waterlines; masts toppled, sides crumbled until, raising volcanoes of smoke and steam, HBMS *Carmine* and HBMS *Carmelo* vanished from sight for all time.

Scenes reminiscent of Juan Fernandez and Quibo became reenacted, except that this time the ships were hauled close to shore and emptied of cannon, ammunition and all manner of heavy gear. After that, the men-of-war, by means of tackles rigged from great stumps on shore to the crosstrees, were hove down to have their bottoms scraped as well as possible.

Under the pitiless sun and without benefit of a breeze, fearful efforts were made. After a mixture of tar, pitch and brimstone had been prepared in huge kettles, all seams requiring attention — and they were legion — were caulked to the ring and bang of heavy mallets.

At Chequetan the expedition became confronted by an unfamiliar problem. It was discovered that, since Dampier's visit, fifty-seven years earlier, the vicinity had become inhabited! Lieutenant Brett, while on a chart-making expedition, spied a troop of some two hundred horsemen galloping parallel to his course.

Said Midshipmen Haldane to Hyde Parker, "One wonders whether the Dons in these latitudes feed on stronger meat than they did at Payta."

Brett overheard, said, "Suppose we find out," and ordered his coxswain to steer inshore.

Haldane, a cheerful, sparrow-faced youth, checked the priming of a handsomely ornamented musketoon — his pride and joy since *Carmelo's* capture. "I've been wanting to try this out."

When they saw the cutter heading towards land, the cavalry yelled defiance and, through shimmering heat waves, rode down to the water's edge. There they dismounted and tethered skinny little horses to lances driven into the ground. Next, the enemy pulled carbines from holsters slung to their saddles and, forming in line abreast, ran forward among slimy rocks littering the beach.

"By God, this affair seems to have promise," laughed Brett. "Bow oars stop rowing and ready your muskets!"

Buckle narrowed red-rimmed eyes when the Spaniards fired a ragged fusillade which sent bullets singing over the water. All of these raised miniature waterspouts considerably short of the target.

Happily, Nat Wade cuddled a musket to his cheek and felt the heat of its stock burn his skin. Confident through months of firing at a mark suspended in the rigging, he aimed at a cluster of green, red and white figures. As the cutter again mounted the back of a long roller Brett yelled "Fire!" for all he guessed that nothing could be accomplished beyond possibly disconcerting the Spaniards.

Before the smoke cleared away — there was not a breath of air to move it — the boat's crew had reloaded. Wade looked up from priming his pan, then swore feelingly because the horsemen were in full retreat. Sabers banging against their legs, they were running back to where their frightened mounts were snorting and plunging, trying to break the reins.

Chorused the English: "Come back, ye bloody cowards! C'mon back, let's enjoy a bicker." "We won't hurt ye — much! Promise, honor-bright!" "Hell, ain't one o' you garlic-eaters got the heart of a hen rabbit?"

Brett couldn't help laughing when Midshipman Parker stood up, bowed. "Don't go away, dear friends. Please tarry. Look! There are fifteen of us; we'd have the Devil's own time making a landing! You could shoot a lot of us."

But the dark-faced horsemen only flung themselves into their saddles and spurred out of sight amid the depths of a tropical forest.

Ludicrous though the incident was, it served, nevertheless, to warn the intruders that enemies *were* present and at a time when the ships would be helpless to defend themselves. Anson, therefore, caused trees to be felled across every trail leading towards the careening place and posted strong pickets behind every barricade.

A chore, necessitating all manner of precautions, was the emptying of the powder magazines. This had to be done by work parties stripped to loin cloths and wearing not even rings or buckled belts; even a tiny spark might have ended the expedition then and there.

Brought ashore, the precious gunpowder was sifted by the use of copper ladles, then spread thin over flat rocks to dry, it having become exceedingly damp. Finally, with infinite care, it had to be ladled back into kegs, barrels and chests.

Since *Gloucester* was in much worse disrepair, work on her went forward so slowly that Captain Mitchell, in desperation, sent the Commander in Chief a Service Letter in which he explained that this slowness was not due to lack of industry on his part but rather because *Gloucester*'s crew was so disproportionately short of Englishmen.

He took occasion to remind his superior that, since leaving England, he had lost 314 out of 396 seamen and concluded his communication by pointing out that the increment received from *Carmelo* and *Carmine* had done little to remedy his problems because most of the replacements had been clumsy foreigners.

George Anson, spending a few nights ashore, again was forced to wrestle with his ambition to restore his squadron to its original number. As he sat in the starlight before his tent, staring out at the helpless hulks of his two Fourth Rates and listening to the cries of owls and howler monkeys, one especially stark fact confronted him: a recent examination of the Muster Books revealed that only 381 white sailors remained under his command!

A further bitter probability was that during the long voyage across the Pacific the normal loss of seamen dying through accident or disease must be allowed for. Hardly a week elapsed aboard a large man-of-war when less than three or four lives were lost.

Three hundred and eighty-one men, Anson mused, are not enough to fully man even one of my big ships. This being so, *Tryall's Prize* will have to be sacrificed. Oh Lord, it's a crying shame. She's so swift and perpetuates such a brave name. Oh, Damn! *Damn! DAMN!* This will come close to breaking Charlie Saunders's heart.

The 14th day of April, 1742, marked the lowest ebb of the men's spirits since they had struggled ashore on Juan Fernandez, rotten with scurvy.

For one thing, everyone was growing concerned because Lieutenant Hughes, who had been left to patrol off Acapulco, had yet not put in an appearance and was now six days overdue. For another, they felt dreadfully depressed after seeing *Tryall's Prize* burned in shallow water. Usually unemotional, Captain Saunders turned away, stony-faced, and sought his tent, there to hide his tears and grieve in private.

As he watched his scout ship burn, Anson quoted to himself a childhood jingle:

> Eight little, seven little,
> Six little Indians,
> Five little, four little
> Three little Indians,
> Two little —

How soon would there be but one, or no 'little Indians'? Resolutely, he terminated this morbid train of thought and sat down to pen a report to the Lords Commissioner of Admiralty.

Only gradually did George Anson's buoyant nature reassert itself as he began to perceive rays of light in this murky situation. Through his sacrifice of the consorts, both Fourth Rates now were almost fully manned and better than a third of their complement were English, veterans toughened by adversity and once more in reasonably good health. The Fourth Rates' bottoms had been fairly well cleaned and many leaks had been stopped; abundant supplies of fresh food and sweet water now lay in the storeroom and water tiers.

Although the natives had failed to bring in cattle — despite the posting of lavish offers along well-traveled trails — fresh meat had been supplied by sea turtles which, by the hundreds, were found asleep on the sea. The food supply was increased also by an abundance of fish resembling cod. These readily were seined and, for as long as possible, consumed fresh. The rest were dried or salted down against the tremendous voyage in prospect.

Surgeon's Mate Peter Vesey grew anxious. "Nowhere on this section of the coast have any acidulous fruits been found; in fact, very little fruit of any kind except for hog plums, pawpaws and a few wild limes."

"I don't like it, either," said Mr. Allen, *Tyrall's Prize*'s surgeon who had come aboard *Gloucester*. "But I fancy we ought to make out all right with the wild onions, yams and coconuts, of which we've a plenty."

The day before his squadron sailed, the Commodore ordered Andrew Menzies to prepare a message for Lieutenant Hughes — he not having appeared as yet — stating that the ships had returned to Acapulco in search of him. Should it fail to find him, the squadron would then sail southward to join the "rest of the fleet." This last was intended to mislead the enemy should he come across the message before Hughes found it; that astute lieutenant, of course, would be aware that there was no "rest of the fleet."

Finally, the message was put into a tightly corked bottle and placed in an old boat belonging to *Carmine* which was left moored in the center of the anchorage.

3 4
The Fate of the Cutter

No HINT OF THE FATE of Lieutenant John Hughes or his men was found when the familiar Paps of Acapulco again gleamed white upon the horizon.

Post Captain Charles Saunders, reduced to the role of an unhappy supernumerary aboard the flagship, expressed the general concern when he dined with Anson that evening. "Seems almost certain that poor Hughes either has been taken prisoner or driven out to sea and lost."

With deliberation, the Commander in Chief lifted his glass of sherry and absently admired its hue by the light of a candelabrum before observing, "I fear it is much more likely that he has suffered capture. Mr. Hughes is far too competent an officer ever to get driven out to sea." The Commodore sipped. "If that is the case, I intend ransoming him and his men."

Consequently, one of *Tyrall's Prize's* smallboats was lowered and manned by certain prisoners who carried along a letter signed by all the Spanish captives saying that they were being kindly treated and petitioning the Governor at least to enter into negotiation with *el Comodoro Inglés.*

Propelled by a fine slant of wind, the launch scudded off towards the Paps, thus committing the diminished squadron to a period of anxious waiting, which proved to be of short duration for, early next morning, lookouts reported news that a smallboat was in sight to the southeast.

"Capital!" Saunders burst out. "I was fearing the Governor here would prove as haughty and unapproachable as that valiant poltroon in Payta."

Doubts that this really was the emissary boat returning began to form as soon as the two Fourth Rates had sailed close enough for spyglasses to reveal that this little craft was neither under sail nor had any oars out; in fact, she seemed to be drifting aimlessly amid a ring of huge sharks.

To Anson's consternation, the derelict swiftly became identified as the missing cutter. He experienced a measure of relief when an arm appeared above the thwarts and feebly waved a rag in proof that her crew had not all perished.

Lieutenant Peter Denis and the longboat's crew would be a long while in forgetting the ghastly sight which greeted them when they pulled alongside the drifting cutter.

Apparently about to die from exposure, hunger and thirst, Hughes and his six men, all horribly sunburned, lay sprawled and helpless upon the bottom. Not one of them could speak above a whisper, and they proved so very weak that, aboard the flagship, a boatswain's chair hurriedly had to be rigged in order to hoist these gaunt wrecks of men onto *Centurion's* deck.

Almost tenderly, the rescued men were put to bed and, under Chief Surgeon Ettrick's supervision, afforded the best possible care. Typically, the Commodore at once sent to the cockpit a supply of his choicest brandy as well as delicacies from his private larder.

Although consumed with anxiety to hear Hughes's report, Anson, out of consideration, waited until evening before sending ex-Prize Captain de Saumarez down to obtain an account of the cutter's cruise. He found the rescued officer lying, bush-bearded and skeleton-thin but smiling, upon a cot rigged in a corner of the wardroom.

By the light of a yellow-burning lantern, de Saumarez only then realized how seriously his friend had suffered from the sun; great raw patches showed all over his face, shoulders and arms. Some of these had suppurated and created an appalling smell.

Thanks to stimulants and food, John Hughes recovered some of his big voice and a degree of strength; his bony fingers closed over the visitor's with surprising energy.

"Well, old friend," de Saumarez began, dropping onto a stool, "seems you've cheated the Dons and the hangman once again."

"— Not by much of a margin," Hughes admitted, then grimaced

[316]

because his sun-cracked lips were hurting. A loblolly quickly brushed them with fingertips dipped into a pannikin of sea elephant oil. "Several times I felt sure I was smelling hell's own smoke. How're my men?"

"Doing well. Ettrick vows they'll all pull through."

"Good of you to come."

"Wanted to. Feel up to making a report? The Old Man's anxious to hear what happened to you. Here —" He held a goblet of Canary wine to Hughes's mouth. "Try this. I warrant 'tis better than elephant oil."

"Aye, that it is," sighed the invalid. "Prop me higher, there's a good fellow. Dear God, how often haven't I dreamt of cool liquids and a full belly." Once the pillows had been rearranged, Hughes settled back with sunken eyes half shut. "As you know, Philip, I was ordered to cruise about outside Acapulco, which blasted port I hope never to hear mentioned again! When, at the end of the twenty-fourth day, there still was no sign of the galleon's getting ready to sail, I shaped a course for the rendezvous at Cheq — Cheq —"

"Chequetan."

"From that moment on we ran in foul luck. If there was any wind at all it blew dead in our faces; then the cutter became gripped by a very strong eastward current." The recumbent figure slowly shook his raw and peeling head. "Even though we trimmed the sails to best advantage and rowed our hearts out, we still lost ground. Finally, the wind died and it grew so hot I thought we'd stifle. Was it hot at Chequetan?"

"Hotter than Hell's own hinges, but at least we spent a lot of time ashore. Hate to imagine what it must have been like in an open boat."

"No one who wasn't with us could imagine what we suffered. While being carried far to the eastward we finished our last drop of water, for all I'd been most sparing of it. Worst of it was, sometimes we sailed so close to land that we could see green hills and waterfalls and streams. Often they weren't half a mile away, but for all the good they did us they might as well have been back in Wales."

De Saumarez said in a low voice, "I presume surf prevented you from landing?"

"Aye," came the bitter assurance. "To have attempted to run through it would have been sheer suicide."

"— In the end, you found a way through?"

[317]

"No. Nowhere along that whole damned coast did we sight a possible landing place — there wasn't even a slight break in that accursed surf. God's love, pass me some water, Phil — no, to hell with wine." He drank deeply. "Ah-h, that's better. Well, as I was saying, we were on our last legs and practically broiled alive when we chanced on a big turtle asleep on the surface."

The hollow eyes closed momentarily. "You can imagine how carefully we went about getting it. Well, first we drank the creature's blood, which somewhat relieved our thirst, then ate every last shred of its flesh, even its guts and eyes."

A lantern slung over Hughes's cot swung lazily as *Centurion* plowed through another of those immensely long rollers which kept driving in towards the Mexican coast.

"We were about to die of thirst again when, barely in time, a heavy rain squall struck us. We roused in a hurry, flattened our sail across the boat and channeled most of the water into our cask. My God, Philip, you'll never know how sweet that rain felt on our poor parched bodies! I swear 'twas like the touch of fairy fingers, like — like, oh, I don't know — like anything that's sweet and tender. But for that squall, you'd have found only bones and rawhide in the cutter."

"What fetched you to where we found you?"

"Remember to report this for record on Peircy Brett's charts," Hughes directed weakly. "On the day after the rain fell, damned if the current didn't suddenly veer about and carry us just as strongly *back towards Acapulco!* Some days later, I don't know how many, we sighted the smoking Paps — the first pair that fooled us when we came up from Quibo."

"What course did you follow when you found yourselves off Acapulco?"

"We decided, if it rained again, we'd run down the coast to the Bay of Panama and somehow capture a ship big enough to carry us to Macao."

De Saumarez stared at the casual way Hughes mentioned what he had proposed to do. It was as if seven men seized an enemy ship and sailed over seven thousand miles every day. "Good God, John, you didn't!"

"Surely we did. What else was there to do? You, Saunders, Scott — all would have decided to do the same."

[318]

"Maybe, maybe not. You're uncommon hardy, John. I gather no more rain fell?"

"Correct. We squeezed our cask dry three eternal days ago."

"Why didn't you sail into Acapulco and surrender when you were about to die of thirst?"

"Surrender?" Hughes gaunt body stiffened on the cot. "If I didn't know you better, Philip, I might take that question seriously amiss. Surrender? Hell, no! In fact, my men and I made a pact that we'd never surrender to the damn' murdering Papists!" Then he added almost irrelevantly, "They'd probably have done us in anyway."

Somewhat later, the Reverend Walter commented in his Journal:

> It was a Pity that Mr. Hughes and his Companions in the Cutter could not have Known that, as soon as the Boat bearing the Spanish Prisoners' Petition arrived in Acapulco, the Governor, on reading Commodore Anson's Proposal, immediately prepared a Most Courteous Reply. Apparently, he had been greatly Moved by the Prisoners' Accounts of the Courteous and Humane Treatment received at our Hands. This Petition only served to Substantiate Reports from Payta that never, in any way, had Our noble Commander-in-Chief allowed even the least of his Captives to be ill-used.
>
> As an Earnest of his Appreciation at once the Governor dispatched for our use two Boats charged with the very Choicest Refreshments and Provisions to be Procured in Acapulco.
>
> On the day following the Rescue of Lieutenant Hughes our Commodore honor'd a Promise made to every Foreigner in his Crews which was not to carry him away from America unless he was Entirely Willing. Therefore, two captured Launches were equipped with Masts, Sails and Oars and Provisions for Fourteen Days (for all that Acapulco lay not over Fifty Miles Distant). Into these were transferr'd eighteen Prisoners out of the *Gloucester* and thirty-nine from the Flagship.

When *Gloucester* and *Centurion* went about and pointed their battered figureheads towards the Ladrone Islands, lying some six thousand miles away, the liberated captives cheered, waved their hats and yelled, *"Buen viaje! Váyan con Dios!"*

Sailing Master Nutt predicted, "If we encounter the trade winds where they are said to blow, we should sight the Ladrone or Thief Islands in about ten weeks' time."

BOOK III

In Far Cathay

I

An Arrow from the Almighty's Bow

IN *GLOUCESTER'S* great cabin, Lieutenant Hughes, thin but otherwise recovered from his ghastly experience off the coast of Mexico, merged heavy brows as he joined Captain Mitchell and Sailing Master Robert Lambert in bending over a stained and sadly incomplete "Chart of the Pacifick Ocean."

"— As you gentlemen will observe," Matthew Mitchell commented in his dry, precise way, "little is shown here about winds prevailing in these latitudes, or their direction. Nor is there any indication as to the presence of currents — let alone how they may flow."

"My firm opinion, sir," Master Lambert remarked heavily, "is that we should have encountered the trade winds at least a week ago. Instead, we've been making barely forty miles in a day — near to drifting."

The cast in Captain Mitchell's left eye seemed extra apparent when he queried, "Have you any theory as to what can have gone wrong?"

"No, sir. — Well, that is, yes, sir." The sailing master obviously was hesitant to cast reflections on the ability of *Centurion's* navigators; he glanced out of the stern windows at the flagship sailing slowly along at her accustomed daytime station.

Captain Mitchell said sharply, "Well, Mr. Lambert, and what is your idea?"

"Very well, sir. The other day I overheard one of our mulatto helmsmen say, that while it's all right to sail southwards from Acapulco to pick up the trades during the spring, later on, as summer approaches, the trades shift northward."

"Um. And we are now near the end of June," Mitchell commented. "I could wish that you'd mentioned this before."

[323]

All three officers remained bent over the chart, sweat-soaked bodies shifting in unison to *Gloucester's* sluggish roll.

Finally, Hughes straightened and looked hard at his Captain. "May I suggest, sir, that Mr. Lambert should communicate this information to Mr. Nutt?"

Mitchell wiped a drop of sweat from the tip of his beaklike nose. "I concur. Mr. Lambert shall go along in the boat conveying my daily report to the flagship."

It proved most unfortunate that, on this particular afternoon, Justinian Nutt should be feeling uncommonly out of sorts due to the reappearance of pains in his legs. His reception of his fellow sailing master, therefore, proved something less than cordial.

"Stuff and nonsense!" he snarled. "Everyone knows the trades blow to the s'uthard of Acapulco; we'll keep on south!"

"Everyone?" Chunky, round-bellied Robert Lambert with difficulty ruled his temper. "Aye. You mean everyone except the Spaniards who've been sailing these waters for over two hundred years!"

"Bosh! The fellow said so only to deceive us."

"I don't agree."

"Why?"

"Because I *overheard,* and did not invite, his opinion on the subject."

At any other time Mr. Nutt, usually cautious and entirely reasonable, might have listened. As it was, with a wave of nausea engulfing him, he cut his colleague short, with the result that for seven blazingly hot and airless weeks both men-of-war continued to wallow helplessly about on a glassy sea, or to be propelled for a short while by light puffs of wind which, whimsically, blew from any and all points of the compass.

Finally, a strong wind sprang up and blew steadily out of the northeast, so *Gloucester* and *Centurion* loosened sheets and, at long last, made real progress towards their far-off destination.

Ted Waxter sat in the purser's room daintily sipping from a flask of Spanish brandy he'd managed to purloin after *Gloucester's* capture of *Nuestra Señora de los Dolores.* The purser's mate savored a mouthful before swallowing, then sighed in purely Sybaritic pleasure.

If things keep on as they are, he reflected, I ought to be damned well off by the time I get back to England. How absurdly easy it's been while inventorying loot not to list an occasional ring, pearl or gold piece which no one will miss anyhow.

On his paper-strewn desk Waxter idly shuffled a greasy deck of Spanish tarot cards which should serve his purpose, for all they bore unfamiliar markings. Again and again his supple fingers dealt and redealt the pasteboards until he felt reassured that they'd lost little of their dexterity since that horrendous afternoon at White's. In fact, he'd regained his skill to such good effect that, with his winnings piling up so rapidly, he guessed he'd have to find another strongbox to join the other he kept chained beneath his bunk.

For a convict once condemned to death I've not done badly at all in His Majesty's Service, have I? With my gains and the prize money due me, I can, if I so choose, again cut a fashionable figure around St. James's.

Silently, Lord Burfurd debated upon which booters, hatters and tailors he might reward with his patronage. Several dazzling coats should be cut from a certain bale skillfully secreted among the purser's stores; it was small, to be sure, but it contained unique pink brocade, shot with pure gold that Princes of the Blood Royal easily might envy.

Waxter again sampled his brandy, then sat watching the lantern above his head swing to *Gloucester's* endless motion. He wondered: *What can have gone wrong with the Old Man's navigation? Something has, or he'd not have lost seven weeks blundering about to find the trades.*

Some smelly foreigner long ago said we ought to have encountered them ten days after leaving Mexico. No. The Old Man can't be happy over having wasted seven weeks' supply of food and water while we're still thousands of miles short of China.

A large wave smote *Gloucester,* made her strained fabric complain louder than usual. *How heartily everyone who's ever served aboard her hates this rotten old ship! By God, I do! She'll always be unlucky; sensed that the minute I came aboard.*

The instant a knock sounded on the purser's door Waxter swept his cards into a drawer and substituted a ledger.

"Come in."

A pinched-faced ship's boy in ragged pantaloons and a red jersey several sizes too large appeared. "Mr. Kerr's compliments, sir, and would you care to stop by his cabin fer a drop of wine?"

Waxter smiled pleasantly. "Thank you, my boy. Pray inform Mr. Kerr that I'll be along directly."

Once the lad had gone Waxter locked his playing cards into a drawer to which not even Purser Millechamp held a key.

The assistant paymaster's spirits rose while he groped along a series of dimly lit passages towards the surgeon's cabin. Why not? With the possible exception of Commodore Anson, Mr. Kerr knew his wine better than anyone else in the squadron.

Peter Vesey, seated in the surgeon's stuffy little cabin, appeared more than a little jingled. To judge by their flushed faces and flat lips so did Mr. Kerr.

"Damn it!" Kerr was shouting. "I insist that that pompous ass, Ettrick, is all wrong! If you've even half-read his 'Treatise on Scurvies' you can tell that, or you've not the wit of a louse! Scurvy ain't caused or aggravated by prolonged cold weather alone!"

"I didn't say so!" Vesey snapped, pale brown eyes narrowing. "What I maintain is that too much salted food, bad air and water are contributing factors."

"Bad air? Crowding? How utterly ridiculous! And *I* say salt meat has nothing to do with it."

"In case you're interested, you damn' horse doctor, I'm positive that overcrowding plays a most important part in causing the disease!"

The doctor's nose, red and misshapen by acne rosacea, flared brighter still. "Damn it, don't you dare to 'horse doctor' me! For a blasted ex-convict you lend yourself too many airs!"

The surgeon's mate flung aside his cup, sprang and, had not Waxter restrained him, he undoubtedly would have earned hanging for striking a superior. "Ex-convict!" A hideous kaleidoscope of memories spun about his head. There was Lady Pamela testifying against him, the judge donning his black cap, the condemned men's cell —

He ceased struggling when Waxter began to laugh, saying, " 'Ex-convict' said you, Mr. Kerr? Odd, but I take that appellation as something of an honor. What a pity that so many petty and warrant officers now serving in this squadron haven't been caught! Especially those who falsify their records and sell medicines which should be freely dispensed."

Now it was Kerr who sprang up, fists balled. "Curse you for an impudent rogue! How dare you — you gallow's-bait?"

In a calm, supercilious voice Waxter replied, "I dare, Mr. Kerr, because I've noted and *written down* how cleverly you and certain other physickers sell cinchona bark to fever-stricken wretches who should have it at no cost!"

Kerr glared. "And you, you snotty pen-pusher, no doubt have dutifully listed *every* single costly item that's been fetched into the treasure room? Bah! This is a sheer case of the pot calling the kettle black!"

The surgeon's manner changed. "Speaking of pots, I've some fine Oporto in yonder jug."

Vesey sat down, pulled at his enormous nose, and began to laugh while retrieving his cup. "Why bicker? Haven't we other worries — and to spare? I say, Mr. Kerr, I presume you've noticed how listless some of the hands have grown of late? I hate to mention it, but I've noticed a few livid spots on them." Vesey offered a Spanish silver mug to the newcomer, then, still shaking from his recent outburst, he refilled the surgeon's cup.

Said Mr. Kerr thickly, "If yer hinting that those spots presage a return of scurvy, then I deem you, doctor or no doctor, as daft as I've just said."

As if inviting confirmation, he glanced at Ted Waxter, who, beginning to sweat in the evil-smelling heat, had opened his shirt and exposed a lean chest densely covered with curly blond hair.

"I'll wager my bottom shilling there'll be no recurrence of scurvy! None of the scurvy causes you've named now exist! Look you, we've still masses of coconuts. Moreover, there's a good many sea turtles still alive in the pens; besides that, the men are catching all the fresh fish they can eat. Salted food's not to blame if scurvy returns!"

Owlishly, Kerr stared at his hawk-nosed mate. "Nor is overcrowding; that's been a thing of the past since we rounded the Horn. There's plenty of space below decks with no Invalids and Recruits puking and lying about in their own shit. Five pounds says the scurvy will not reappear — for a long while, at least."

Waxter grinned across the little cabin. "If I were you, I'd hedge that bet, Mr. Kerr, or at least copper it."

"Why?"

"In the past few days I've heard a dozen men complaining of swollen gums and loosening teeth."

"Nonsense! They're only suffering from the bad teeth they've always had."

Peter Vesey won the bet — and all too quickly; next morning nearly a dozen men answered sick call complaining of dull pains in the chest or legs and, most ominous of all, about an increasing shortness of breath.

After Surgeon's Mate Vesey had handed him the sick list Captain Mitchell joined bony hands, knelt on the well-holystoned cabin's deck. "Why, O Lord," he groaned, "dost Thou continue so to persecute Thy unworthy servant? Wherein have I sinned that Thou should remain so wroth? Spare us, I beseech Thee, this further affliction. Spare us another arrow from thy bow!"

Matthew Mitchell's deeply lined features quivered and his mal-aligned eyes filled. This just wasn't fair! Hadn't he always tried to act as a good and loyal officer? And now the scurvy had reappeared! It was almost too much for a man to bear.

From the quarterdeck lithe young Lieutenant Sam Scott glowered out over the bright blue and seemingly limitless ocean; bitterly he cursed his luck. Why, when *Tryall's Prize* had been destroyed and her crew dispersed, couldn't he have been sent to *Centurion*?

Yearning, he watched her bowling along under full sail, a froth of foam agleam under her famous lion figurehead. Scott might have felt better had he known that scurvy had suddenly broken out aboard the flagship also; that men were faltering and falling about her decks as well. But he didn't.

Peter Vesey, a few days later, sighed and made a grim entry in the journal he'd kept since the capture of Payta:

> It is Impossible to set down on Paper the Depth of that Horror and Despair which Seizes All. We, who had Thought to have left the Scurvy behind for Good and All, are Appalled. This Morning had my very Bowels wrung out while Attending the last Hours of Mr. Gerard, late Master of the *Anna*.
>
> His Despair was overwhelming when he Realized that he would never Enjoy the Spending of his Prize Money. He raved and cursed the Deity and poor Captain Mitchell as though Either was responsible for his Miserable Fate. Many others of the sick take the same Attitude although because of their Winnings they struggle to repel the Grim Reaper far harder than they did off Cape Horn, yet they perish like Lice in a Fire.
>
> Why, *why*, WHY should the Scurvy thus return? Present are none of the various Conditions to which we Physicians & Surgeons have attributed the first Outbreak. We are Utterly Baffled to Explain. Privately, I can only Conclude that the Constitution of our men was irremediably Impaired by the First Seizure and that the Poison has never truly deserted their Systems.

[328]

Mr. Henry Ettrick, our Chief Surgeon, is again dispensing Ward's Pills and Drops to those who will take them: though their Effect is violent, to my mind they cause no Perceptible or lasting Benefit.

Yesterday night Mr. Kerr and I secretly opened a Number of Cadavers but could discover nothing indicative of the Cause of this Malady.

If only some remedy could be Devised that could Alleviate this Horrible Plague. I must Study and Reason without Pause until I arrive at some Result.

Later the same day Vesey wiped a drop of sweat from his beak-like nose, then dipped into a leaden ink bottle and wrote:

Have just helped with the Burial of Seventeen Seamen, a sad solemn Duty. Many more have been Stricken. Poor Captain Mitchell appears utterly Distraught. God help us all.

That night he was struck by an idea and went in search of Waxter. "Do you think you could find some dried peas?"

"Why? Are you drunk, or have you gone out of your head?"

"D'you recall how we fed upon sprouted dried peas on the way to Juan Fernandez?"

Waxter roused up on his bunk. "Aye. But what of that?"

"Were we not among the very few who escaped the contagion?"

"True," yawned the Purser's Mate. "But what can the eating of sprouted peas have to do with that?"

"Nothing at all, perhaps," admitted the hollow-eyed visitor. "Still, mayhap some unknown virtue lies in such."

Aboard *Gloucester* death, this time, struck harder among the officers. Shortly after Mr. Gerard's body had been dropped overboard, Lieutenant Patrick Baird died, leaving a somber and silent Welshman by the name of Jelfs to take his place aboard the sea-worn Fourth Rate on her tortured, seemingly endless voyage.

Only a few days after the scurvy had made its reappearance a serious crack opened in *Centurion*'s foremast. Then, just after it had been fished in rough-and-ready fashion, *Gloucester* was seen suddenly to take in all canvas on her main. Soon a boat came over to report that her mainmast had rotted within for almost its entire length and was in momentary danger of collapse.

Anson at once dispatched to the consort his flagship's entire gang of carpenters, who, to Mitchell's utter dismay, were forced to shorten the main by twenty-six feet. This left a stump barely tall enough to support a jury fashioned from an old topmast.

As a result of her jury rig, *Gloucester*'s speed became so severely reduced that Justinian Nutt was forced to shorten *Centurion*'s sail in order not to leave her consort behind.

Luckily, the trades continued to blow steady and strong for another month and a half; both ships made fair progress towards the Ladrones.

Then, as if to pile the Pelion of bad luck upon the Ossa of misfortune, the wind faltered and failed so far that both ships lost headway and were forced to roll helplessly among immensely long and oily rollers which rocked them with relentless savagery.

~ 2 ~

Death Blow

AFTER THE TRADES died out completely the two men-of-war made no progress except for the influence of an uncharted current which, flowing strongly, bore the flagship and her lone consort in God only knew what direction.

Somber expressions deepened on the faces of *Centurion*'s afterguard when all calculations agreed that the Ladrone group of the Mariana Islands still lay over a thousand weary miles away! Meanwhile, scurvy continued to rage through both sun-baked Fourth Rates, even more deadly and violent than it had off icy Cape Noire and Patagonia.

Deprived of steerage way, *Gloucester* and *Centurion*, day after blazing day, rolled sickeningly in the trough of towering, glassy rollers which, for all there was no wind to drive them, kept tumbling over the horizon.

Without respite, the men-of-war creaked, groaned and resounded to the thump and slatting of slack sheets and idle canvas. Loose gear kept rolling or sliding back and forth, but nothing could be done about securing it. The few men remaining healthy were forced to conserve their energy for labor at the pumps.

The fearful rolling reopened seam after seam, especially in *Gloucester,* and threatened to rock out the masts.

The dead and dying rolled helpless about filthy decks and the violent motion pitched many sick out of their hammocks.

Most active among *Gloucester*'s crew were Surgeon's Mate Peter Vesey and Purser's Mate Waxter. The latter, to everyone's surprise, took to busying himself among the sick, especially those who seemed about ready to perish. With a mysterious air he would exhibit a small bottle containing a purplish liquid of some sort.

"Here, my lad, I have something can save your life."

"Wot is it?" the dying man would gasp.

"*Aqua vitae,* which is a secret specific 'gainst the scurvy. One swallow of this and I guarantee you'll live to spend your prize money and part many an ivory thigh before you're through."

"How do I know it's wot you sye?"

"Don't I appear healthful?"

"Aye, that ye do, so for the dear Lord's sake, gi' us a swig. I be close to death."

"Gladly, my lad, but, since *aqua vitae* is among the costliest of remedies known to medicine, 'twill have to be for a small consideration."

"Gi' us —" Clawlike hands would appear out of the gloom. "Quick!"

Waxter would raise his lantern so that the stricken man could stare hungrily at his bottle of purple-dyed water. "I'd give it you freely, but, as I've said, this is a most costly compound."

"But —" the stricken wretch would sob. "I've no money — not a farthing."

"Aye, but you've something better than cash. You've a fat sum in prize money due you."

"Aye — but that ain't coin, sir." Staring, glassy eyes would peer up into Waxter's lantern. "Please, kind sir, gi'e us a sip — just a tiny sip."

"You shall have one, my poor fellow, in just a moment." Waxter would reach into his shirt's bosom and bring out a slip of paper. "I'll not cozen you, my lad; this assigns your prize money to me. Make your mark on this and you shall have a swallow of this priceless elixir which will soon restore you to rosy health."

"God bless ye, sir. I — Gimme." A grubby hand tipped with yellow broken nails would snatch for the document. Once the scarecrow had signed his name, or made his mark, he'd be given a mouthful of purple water tinctured with peppermint and oil of cloves and settle happily back — to die within a few hours.

Soon the soft-spoken purser's mate had nearly a hundred such assignments tucked into his strongbox.

One sweltering afternoon a seaman came stumbling up to *Glouces-ter*'s quarterdeck as fast as the ocean's endless roll and his swollen legs would permit, and found Lieutenant Scott clinging weakly to the mizzen shrouds.

"Sir," he mumbled, slowly knuckling a lank forelock. "Carpenter reports a bad leak somewhere i' the port bow! Mr. Baird says there's five foot o' water in the for'rad well already and it's gainin' fast."

Scott nodded dazedly. "What can I do about it?"

"First Lieutenant says please to send some hands below to pump — immedijit-like, sir."

"I can't. There isn't anyone left fit to go. He ought to know that." Scott glanced at his own hands and hardly recognized them they were so blistered from another all-night session at the pump handles. "Hold on. Inform Mr. Baird that I'll look about below and see if I can find anyone strong enough to send."

As the second lieutenant had foreseen, in the 'tween decks no help was to be found. Most of the men were lying inert in their hammocks, loudly delirious, comatose or dead.

Scott had just succeeded in relieving a quartermaster who appeared ready to collapse at the Fourth Rate's bucking but useless wheel when he heard a faint shout from the forecastle. Next, he was shaken to hear an ominous, groaning, screeching noise which hadn't been audible previously, so he descended to the upper gundeck and lurched forward over half-decomposed corpses that slid uglily about.

He passed the crazy jury mast rigged to the mainmast's stump and, growing dizzier by the minute, clawed his way along a lifeline run-ning fore and aft. Without such even a healthy man couldn't have hoped to keep his footing, so violent was the rolling.

While ascending the forecastle ladder, Scott gasped to see those long and rusty bolts which secured the starboard foremast shrouds to the ship's side pull out farther with each agonized roll. The wood, he saw, had become so rotted that it could no longer resist the strain.

Scott tried to shout, but was too late: the foreshrouds' dead-eyes jerked loose, then the shrouds themselves began to flail crazily about. Deprived of support, the doomed foremast swung far out over the port side, then, responding to the reverse roll, pulled out of the port shroud ends.

Scott found his voice, yelled, "Stand clear!" then jumped aft a second before the fore-topmast snapped and buried the bow under a crazy welter of cordage, broken yards and mildewed canvas. *Glouces-*

ter's jibs and fore-staysail, which had been flapping uselessly in the sunlight, also fell to float soggily upon the Pacific's warm and bright-blue water.

From below staggered First Lieutenant Baird to inform Captain Mitchell that water was gushing through *Gloucester*'s strained seams so fast that a handful of moderately healthy men, borrowed the day before from the flagship, had to quit clearing away the wrecked foremast and go to work at the pumps.

"Christ! Ain't there never going to be no end of this?" wheezed Clipperton as he and Buckle bent over the handles.

"Dunno. But I'm ready to drop." And a few minutes later he did and his unconscious form joined those already tumbling about the slimy deck.

Since there remained on board no spar capable of replacing *Gloucester*'s foremast, George Anson ordered his helpless consort taken in tow and a spare mainyard of *Centurion*'s sent over.

So, during ten terrible days, *Centurion* stood off and on while her ever more sickly carpenters made heroic efforts to contrive a jury foremast for the luckless Fourth Rate.

The carpenters hardly had finished their Herculean task than Peircy Brett, showing an anxious double V between his bold, close-set eyes, approached the Commodore.

"Sir, Mr. Nutt reports the barometer is sinking like a sounding lead."

Anson spoke as easily as if a summer thundershower were about to threaten a lawn party. "Very well, Mr. Brett, we shall have to see that all possible precautions are taken."

Soon inky clouds darkened the horizon, the wind arose and blew hard, harder. Finally it exploded into a screaming gale which shrieked in the rigging like a banshee chorus; in no time at all mountainous seas began to leap at the struggling men-of-war.

A Spanish volunteer explained that this was one of those violent cyclonic storms which, during the summer months, must be expected in these waters.

Justinian Nutt, although badly afflicted by scurvy, roused sufficiently to order canvas reduced to storm trysails. He had now to be especially solicitous of *Centurion*'s cracked mainmast, since nothing remained with which to rig a jury should it carry away.

It seemed to *Gloucester*'s haggard survivors that the cry of "All hands to the pumps!" was never-ending. Like victims of a prolonged nightmare, the sixteen officers and men yet able to walk would struggle down into the noisome, nearly lightless lower decks and heave endlessly at the handle bars.

There was only one mitigating circumstance; on this occasion there were no swarms of savage rats to intensify the horror. The fumigation undertaken at Juan Fernandez had been most effective.

So loud grew the splash and slosh of water in the holds that Peter Vesey several times guessed the weary old semi-wreck was about to founder.

A carpenter's mate, sounding the main well, watched Captain Michell, like an embodied ghost, surge near, lantern in hand.

"What water d'you find?"

"Above seven foot, sir," came the doleful reply. "It gains so fast ye'd think we ain't pumped a stroke."

"Gaining by how much?"

"Near six inches the hour, sir."

For three days the cyclonic storm flailed Anson's ships without mercy, then finally it passed on, leaving but seventy-six souls still breathing aboard *Gloucester,* which now was riding very low in the sea. All the same, Matthew Mitchell refused to appeal for help until the jury mainmast toppled over the rail and created a dismal, hampering tangle of halyards, yards and braces.

When George Anson saw this fresh disaster he drew a slow, deep breath and observed to Peircy Brett, "Doesn't she look exactly like a ship beaten in battle?"

"Aye, sir. She does. Shall I —"

"Yes. Call away a boat and conduct a strict survey of *Gloucester's* condition."

The Commodore's voice was impassive, but there was pain such as the lieutenant never before had seen in Anson's eyes.

To assist in the survey, Quartermaster's Mate Wade was sent along, *Centurion's* carpenter being much too ill to attempt such a trip.

If Peircy Brett had deemed conditions bad aboard *Centurion* he was appalled by what he found after he'd gripped *Gloucester's* mizzen chains and swung himself aboard. For a long instant he could only stare in stark disbelief on fallen spars, sagging canvas, parted and dangling ropes, corpses and all.

Yes. The Commander in Chief had been right. Peircy Brett might as well be boarding a surrendered enemy. When he drew near and saluted Captain Mitchell, wraith-like and long unshaven, propped against the side near the idly spinning wheel, he couldn't trust himself to speak.

"By your expression, Mr. Brett," Captain Mitchell commented faintly, "I judge you find us in a parlous state. Please inform the Commodore that those of us who are left have done our best, but I fear there no longer remains a hope" — his reddened eyes wavered to the deck — "a hope of keeping my poor, brave ship afloat."

No more than a most perfunctory examination forced Brett to agree that the old Fourth Rate had degenerated into a helpless wreck which could not be kept afloat very much longer.

Wade muttered to another of the boarding party, " 'Tis a shining miracle she ain't gone down long ago."

<hr style="border:none;text-align:center">

 ~~~ 3 ~~~

"One Little Indian"

IT WAS WELL that the seas moderated and flattened sufficiently to permit the *Gloucester*'s nearly dismasted hulk to be brought alongside *Centurion*. She arrived barely in time to save her survivors from starvation and the agonies of thirst; her water casks and sea stores had been inaccessible, submerged by the water steadily rising within her.

But to keep the two ships lashed together for long proved impossible; giant swells kept grinding them together and damaging the flagship's hull; therefore, two days of back-breaking toil ensued while boats manned by sick and failing oarsmen plied between the two men-of-war.

To begin with, *Gloucester*'s sick were helped aboard or hoisted to her deck on stretchers when incapable of riding a boatswain's chair.

Next, the Commodore ordered that all ammunition, spare sails and every yard of cordage which could be salvaged should be transferred. Stripped to the waist, sunburned and streaked with sweat, George Anson worked harder than anyone in striking down transshipped supplies. Although grown gaunt and hollow-cheeked, it was seldom that an encouraging smile was absent from his lips.

Among the first to arrive aboard *Centurion*, very solicitous about his heavy seabag, was Purser's Mate Waxter. Farsighted as usual, Lord Burfurd had been at pains, during the refitting at Juan Fernandez, to

[335]

make friends with Will Pallister, his opposite number in the flagship. Accordingly, Waxter encountered little difficulty having his bag locked away in a closet in Purser Weldon's office.

This accomplished, he promptly volunteered for labor aboard *Gloucester* where his zeal won considerable commendation because he declared himself ready to toil in the doomed ship's incredibly foul 'tween decks. True, of course, he also was free to search mouldering corpses and ransack ownerless seabags and ditty boxes without risk of discovery.

It was only to be expected that Gunner's Mate Tom Ramster, known to have become a most proficient swimmer and diver, should go along with that party from *Centurion* which was ordered to empty *Gloucester*'s treasure locker before she sank. The trouble was, the loot now had become submerged under several feet of foul-smelling bilge-water and drifting debris.

By the uncertain glare of several battle lanterns the malodorous leakage looked, and was, as opaque as ink.

"Can't see a blasted thing down here," gasped Lieutenant Scott after making several dives with the intention of fitting keys into a pair of huge padlocks which secured bars across the strongroom's wrought-iron door.

The lieutenant was forced to call quits after being half-stunned by a piece of debris drifting, unseen, about the hold. In fact, he was saved only by being pulled to the surface by means of a rope tied about his waist.

As he lay, ghastly white and bleeding from the mouth, he wheezed, "Can't — more. Someone else try."

"Shall I have a shot at it, sir?"

"Aye, but watch out for a nasty tangle of rope shifting about down there."

Ramster dropped greasy trousers and stood naked since, in the stifling heat prevailing below decks, no one wore anything else.

The problem appeared simple at first, for Ramster soon found the upper padlock and succeeded in unlocking it, but things went differently when he started groping down through the foul and lightless water in search of the lower lock. He nearly was drowned when a mess of blankets drifted first between his arms and then his legs and clung to them as tenaciously as the tentacles of an octopus.

For an interminable period he struggled to free himself, then tugged frantically at the rope about his middle. Before the men above could haul him up fiery spirals were writhing about in his eyeballs and his lungs felt ready to explode. At length he succeeded in tearing aside the hampering fabric and shot to the surface.

"Thought you were done for," said Lieutenant Scott gravely. "I've never seen anyone stay under half so long."

Still bug-eyed, wheezing and panting, Ramster explained, "Sir, even if we do get that door unlocked 'twon't be possible, what with all that cultch adrift down there, to tie ropes to all them heavy chests and drag 'em out." He turned to a carpenter for confirmation. "That so?"

"That's sure enough so."

"What do you suggest?" Scott wanted to know, testing the great bruise on his forehead.

"Why, sir, we'll have to chop a hole through the orlop deck; maybe we can rig block and tackle."

"Sound idea, but we've got to hurry, this deck is tilting worse every minute."

When, after a jagged hole had been hewed, a full day passed before all the boxed silver and chests of treasure were rescued.

"Seems a blasted pity to abandon all those fine bale goods," grunted Lieutenant Hughes, while heaving yet another keg of silver coin onto a skinned and bleeding shoulder. "Must be easy five thousand pounds' worth down there. I know, because I stowed it myself."

"No use trying for it?" queried Lieutenant Baird, who, along with Midshipman Haldane and Campbell, was tailing onto the hoisting tackle rope's bight.

"No," replied Hughes. "Those brocades are in the lowest section of the hold — under ten or more feet of water by now."

And although the party sent over from *Centurion* worked ceaselessly at *Gloucester*'s pumps, water in her hull kept rising until it began to slosh over the orlop deck.

To all hands it came as a serious blow when the discovery was made that only *five* casks of biscuit flour remained unspoiled and, worse still, that forty casks of brandy could not be salvaged.

Nevertheless, as sailors will, they came across a cask of rum in an unsuspected place and promptly got roaring drunk.

Although seeming to move in the grip of a miserable trance, Captain Mitchell nonetheless supervised salvage operations to the bitter end.

On the afternoon of August 15, 1742, he broke down briefly and

[337]

sobbed like a child when Peircy Brett said, "I loathe having to give you this, sir, but it is my duty."

The order read:

> Since We do not know how far We lie from Spanish Islands, also that Ships seeming ready to Sink have remained Afloat for a long time, I require you to Burn the Wreck that she may not possibly fall into Enemy Hands still bearing those Guns we have not been able to Remove.
>
> You will order all Guns double-loaded with Tompions driven Home so that they must surely Burst when the Charge becomes Ignited. Combustibles are to be Collected and placed in Various Strategic Positions with long lengths of Slow Matches leading to them. The Wind being light, Considerable Time must be allowed to permit the Flagship to proceed to a Safe Distance.

One by one, all smallboats were pulled back to *Centurion* where as many as possible were hoisted inboard; the rest, for the time being, were towed astern.

On the doomed man-of-war's quarterdeck stood three gaunt and disheveled figures: Matthew Mitchell and his surviving lieutenants, Scott and Jelfs. In silence, they watched Kipps and Bargecroft, gunners of the two Fourth Rates, lay the last powder train. It was the largest and longest of all and led to the magazines.

Mitchell, his face ghastly, stood rigidly erect beneath the sagging mizzenmast. "Mr. Scott, you may strike my pendant."

Once his Captain's red and white pendant had fluttered to the deck and his lieutenants had dropped into a cutter bobbing alongside, Matthew Mitchell paused bareheaded in the gangway and, for the last time, saluted the quarterdeck.

Then, in muffled voice, he said to Gunner Bargecroft, "You may ignite the fuses."

When the fuse sputtered and a small gray cloud arose, something died within Matthew Mitchell. Here was the end of his ship which he had so long preserved in defiance to the worst Man and Nature could do to her.

For all she rode low in the water, HBMS *Gloucester* blazed furiously, gave off tall, lazy clouds of orange-tinted black smoke. Men still able to stand lined *Centurion*'s rails, their haunted, hairy faces reddened by the glare.

From the poopdeck, George Anson, a silent, wooden-faced figure, watched all that went on. What his present sensations might be not even Andrew Menzies could guess, especially when, at irregular intervals, the doomed Fourth Rate's guns began to blow up.

Matthew Mitchell proved unable to bear the sight and stumbled below, stony-eyed and trembling as with a palsy.

Toward midnight Lieutenant de Saumarez also sought his quarters and, despite overwhelming fatigue, took time to note in his private log:

> Soon after, our People who had been Employed in Firing her returned on Board. The Confusion of four or five Boats towing alongside in a great Swell in the Night-time, their crews most of them Drunk with Liquor they had Rummaged on board the *Gloucester*, the Apprehension of a Squall which Threatened to take us Aback; the hurry of hauling down our Sails, which the Weakness of our People rendered Slow and Dangerous, all this joined to the Incumbrances we had on Deck, of Sick and Dying Men which our Hurry and shortness of Time had not permitted us to take care of; the Chests, Casks, and Lumber received from the other Ships which filled up the Decks and Entangled all our running Ropes; all these different Accidents, still Aggravated with the last Ship of our Squadron Blazing within two Miles of us, Combined to make as Melancholy a Scene as I ever Observed since I have been in the Navy.
>
> The Remainder of the Night proving Tolerably Moderate, we saved all our Boats, with the Exception of the *Gloucester*'s Barge, which broke Adrift and Sunk soon after, being deeply laden, and our People too much Fatigued to hoist her in.

Thought long-faced Charles Saunders, standing beside Lieutenant Colonel Cratcherode near the main shrouds, It's really incredible the old girl can burn so long without a spark having reached one of her magazines.

Bom-m-m!

"There goes another!" the Army officer muttered. "B'God, it's as if she were firing minute guns for her own funeral."

"Yes, Colonel. It would seem so. She's dying hard."

Miraculously, when daylight returned, *Gloucester* lay with decks nearly awash, but still afloat and giving off tremendous clouds of Stygian smoke.

Anson sighed and said wearily to himself, "The fire has reached her store of pitch and brimstone."

Diffidently, Michael Despeda padded near on broad, pink-soled feet. "Breakfast hot and ready, sar."

Without turning his head, Anson said, "Later, Steward. I feel not in the least hungry," and remained where he was, aloof and silent, until, at precisely six o'clock, a terrific explosion took place. Witnesses watched a tremendous shaft of dazzling fire shoot vertically half a mile into the rosy sky.

When a great bank of smoke cleared away, only widely scattered debris remained to mark the last resting place of HBMS *Gloucester*.

～ 4 ～

Rocks in a Weary Ocean

CAPTAIN CHARLES SAUNDERS, R.N., returning from a backbreaking spell at *Centurion*'s after pump, sank gratefully onto the wardroom's mildewed stern locker and called for Michael Despeda. Because all the regular wardroom stewards were either sick or dead, the Jamaican no longer remained the Commodore's private servant. The big Negro pattered in, gold earring flashing and actually managed an ivory smile.

"Sar?"

"Steward, I'm near perishing of thirst." He frowned while adjusting rags about his badly blistered hands. "What is today's water ration?"

"Only a pint, sar," the Jamaican informed, liver-colored lower lip petulantly outthrust. "An iffen a breeze don't come along pretty pert, sar, 'twill soon be less."

The big Captain blinked. "So it's that bad, eh? Well, then get a bottle of Canary out of my store and mix it with the ration. I'm hellish dry."

Lieutenant Peter Denis presently clumped in, features seared and peeling with sunburn, and collapsed, rather than seated himself, beside his superior. "Beats me how the Commodore can remain patient and so calm-spoken for all he must be near crazed with anxiety and disappointment."

Saunders let his head fall back and panted in the heat like a hard-run hound. "Aye. He's incredible. Sometimes I think the man hasn't a nerve in him. Think back on what he's suffered: two of his best fighting ships deserted and the *Wager* vanished without a trace."

Denis used a penknife to dig a splinter from under a fingernail. "I think it must have been more difficult to have ordered the *Tryall*, the *Anna* and the *Gloucester* destroyed — let alone the prizes."

The steward reappeared carrying two pint pots and Saunders's wine, which he used to increase the water ration.

Denis made a wry face after sipping a mug of wine and water. "Thanks for the wine, but the stuff still stinks." He surveyed his shaggy, thin-faced superior's drawn expression. "Why so downcast?"

Saunders indicated a Strength Return lying neglected on the wardroom's mess table. "Read that, and you'll wince when you recall that when we left the Isle of Wight the squadron carried one thousand nine hundred and fifty-five officers and men of the Royal Navy — which ain't including those Recruits and poor Invalids. How many do you think were alive at noon today? Make a guess."

Denis's flaming features contracted. "I've no idea."

"Surgeon reports three hundred and forty-eight of us are still breathing and we're dying at the rate of ten and twelve a day. Another 'arrow from the Almighty's bow' and there won't be sufficient hands to man the pumps. When that happens we'll sink — quickly, too, if that new leak ain't found in a hurry. Ah, Samuel — welcome to our post-mortem."

Lieutenant Scott, late of HBMS *Gloucester*, swayed across the wardroom and sagged into an armchair. All the same, he managed a faint grin. "Post-mortem, hell! We've located that infernal leak for-'ard."

"Thank God. Where was it?" Saunders demanded.

Scott passed a grimy hand over sun-cracked lips. "Chips claims a brace of breast-hooks have pulled out and let go."

Denis glanced up. " 'Breast-hooks'? What in God's name are breast-hooks?"

Saunders grinned. "Ignorant bugger, aren't you?"

"Guess so. Must have been asleep when the schoolmaster was explaining 'em to us snotties."

"Well, they're a series of iron hooks, sharp at both ends, which bridge the stem and are driven in to secure beam-ends to form the bow."

Saunders yawned cavernously, "It's all very well that the leak's been found, but what in hell can be done about it?"

Scott frowned, "Precious little till we reach land, I reckon."

"Why?"

"Because that damn' leak's below the waterline, so Chips can make only makeshift repairs from inside the hull."

"Do any real good?" Saunders drawled.

"May reduce the flow somewhat, but not enough to save us from pumping till we reach a proper dockyard — if we ever do."

"Aye — if we ever do," Saunders repeated slowly. "A while back I overheard one of the men say 'We've sailed so bloody far we've left all the land in the world astern.' "

"He mayn't be so wrong at that." Eyelids sagging, Denis yawned, too. "What's supposed to be our last position?"

The stocky Captain shrugged, drained the last of his wine and water. "Nutt assumes we were cruising somewhere between the thirteenth and seventeenth latitudes. Very exact, eh?"

"Very. What's our longitude?"

"God alone knows. No one else does."

Scott made a pathetic attempt to appear confident. "Everything will turn out all right once we find a breeze." Disgustedly, he reversed his empty pot. "Damn. I'm so curs'd thirsty I'm about ready to copy Mark Antony."

"What did he do?"

"One of Shakespeare's characters says that once, when Mark was near death through thirst, 'Antony did drink of the gilded puddle.' "

Slowly Saunders shook his shaggy black head. "That won't do, either. I've been so dry I ain't pissed in a week."

Denis arose, it being nearly his time for a trick at the pumps. "Aye, wind's what we need — but *not too much!* If the hull suffers strain just once more it'll open up like a dropped market basket — which will mean the end for certain future admirals I could name."

"— Not to mention the prize money that's owing 'em." Scott managed a grin. "Well, my trick at the wheel's coming up. Have fun at the pumps, Peter." He left the wardroom moving with a peculiar dragging gait which prompted his companions to exchange glances.

"Notice that?" Saunders queried. "Poor devil must be coming down with the goddam scurvy."

"And so, I greatly fear, is the Commodore," Denis informed in an undertone."

"The hell you say!"

"This morning, whilst we were handling the braces, I noticed that a number of small brown splotches have appeared on his face."

"God, that's bad! What about you?"

Unexpectedly Denis nodded. "I fear I've taken it, too. During the past three days my teeth have grown looser and looser and my breath's begun to stink like an old outhouse. God send we raise the Ladrones before long."

Next day a wind sprang up and commenced to blow hard out of the southwest — from the very direction in which Mr. Nutt insisted the Ladrone Islands lay — and drove *Centurion* ever farther from her destination.

Under this unfriendly blast the solitary man-of-war commenced to creak, groan and protest. Very soon, just as Captain Saunders had predicted, the leaks increased and the death rate soared.

Mr. Walbank, a surgeon's mate out of *Tryall's Prize* who recently had succeeded to the late Mr. Kerr's appointment, stared fixedly into Peter Vesey's face. "I'm dying and glad of it. I've my belly full of suffering and disappointment. Maybe you'll be lucky, too, and come along. Eh, Doctor?

" 'Doctor'?" Vesey started. Three years had passed since he'd been so addressed. "What makes you think I'm a physician?"

"Don't pretend you ain't been a physician — and a graduate from Oxford at that. Many's the time I've heard you talking — in your sleep. Why didn't you admit it? You've forgotten more about real medicine than the rest of us surgeon-barbers put together."

Vesey glanced about the nearly deserted gun room. "I'll try to explain; being an ex-convict, I'd no desire to cast disrepute on my profession — even less on my University. Besides, I've learned a great deal about surgery which I wouldn't have, had any of you known that I am, or rather was, a licensed physician." Vesey frowned. "Dear God, why do you surgeons feel you must stand in awe and envy of physicians?"

Mr. Walbank fetched a deep sigh amid the fetid gloom. "It's because we can't read Latin, I suppose. Anyhow, Doctor, I want you to have my share of prize money — you're both kind and very able."

"Oh, I couldn't accept — surely you must have family —?"

"None. None at all. If you won't have it, then bestow it on some promising young surgeon or physician who will devote his life towards determining what causes this accursed plague of which I lie a-dying and why it has reoccurred under such contrasting conditions."

Bony fingers plucked feebly at a vomit-stained blanket. "Should you survive this awful passage, Dr. Vesey, will you promise someday to assemble and set down the sum of our findings? For instance, why do Indians and Negroes die so much quicker than half-breeds or whites?"

"I promise," Vesey assured softly. "Now, Mr. Walbank, please try to swallow some of this wine. 'Twas sent by the Commodore himself. For a fact, he's caused almost his entire private store to be distributed."

"No," Walbank said huskily. "Save it for someone who can benefit. I'm sped, my friend, and know it."

Gently, Peter Vesey pressed the older man's cold, skeletonic hand. "I fear I must leave you for a while. Midshipmen Haldane and Phillips are in serious condition. Poor lads, they were so grand and gay over what they were going to do with their prize shares."

A mounting despair pervaded the stinking, leaking flagship while the gale continued to scream out of the southwest and relentlessly drove *Centurion* away from those islands which she must reach soon — or not at all.

Strangely enough, considering their previous disinterest in such matters, Lieutenant Colonel Cratcherode, Captain Crowden and Marine Lieutenant Gordon offered to do loblolly duty. Probably it was George Anson's tireless efforts and undaunted bearing which shamed the Army men into doing such loathsome work.

Conscientiously, the irascible old officer and his scarcely younger juniors inspected the shortening rows of hammocks. To the living they offered ribald jokes, scraps of food and watered brandy. The dead they merely shoved through the nearest open gunport.

On the night of August the 22nd, Andrew Menzies perceived a faint crack in George Anson's air of confident composure when he straightened above the chart over which he had been at work and shoved aside his reckoning of position.

"God damn it! If *only* I could be sure about the longitude! Why wouldn't those pompous asses at the Admiralty let me have even one chronometer of Mr. Harrison's invention?" Face working strangely, he turned to his secretary, "But they wouldn't lend me one, Andrew, saying that, as yet, there were only three or four such time pieces in existence — all were reserved for the use of Vice-Admirals who, damn it, won't stir far beyond the Channel!"

Absently, the harassed Commander in Chief rubbed at a livid lump which, during the day, had appeared on his forehead. "I fear, Andrew, that we rest in God's hands more than ever." He squared

[344]

broad shoulders. "'Tis time for another spell at the pumps; pray steady me to the door."

"*Must* you go, sir? Since you are the heart and soul of this expedition, is it not your truer duty to husband your strength? Some of us are in better case than you."

"You shameless toady!" Anson accused with a faint grin. "No, I'll take my turn. Every man must, if God means us to win though."

Only after the Commodore had departed did his secretary test a painful swelling which was forming on his groin. His heart sank on finding it to be so much larger; it was difficult not to limp when he sought the steerage to relieve a quartermaster's mate who stood, sagging, at *Centurion's* wheel.

To Andrew Menzies it appeared that God must have heard George Anson's unique admission, for towards nightfall the wind died out, then came about and blew as strongly out of the northeast to drive *Centurion* onto a strong current which, all unsuspected, greatly accelerated her progress towards that place where the Ladrones were presumed to lie.

When the 23rd of August dawned, bright and clear, three dark specks were sighted.

"Land! Oh, my God, there's land yonder!" yelled the lookout.

Some men broke into uncontrollable sobs, some stood silent as if pertrified; others, Captain Michell among them, dropped onto their knees and mumbled thanks to God.

Said Captain Saunders dully, "Well, sir, we've done it."

Anson turned slowly. "Not yet, Charles, not yet. We've no notion what that land is — whether there's food and water to be found on it. For all we know, the enemy may occupy it in force."

Nevertheless, the word "land" proved as a magic elixir. Men and boys on the point of death struggled back towards life, wailed to be carried on deck so that they might see dry land.

This febrile elation, however, commenced to evaporate as a shattering fact became apparent; no more than three great surf-ringed rocks were thrusting above the Pacific's dazzling blue.

Only one, said by Sailing Master Nutt to be "Antacan," displayed even a trace of vegetation. The other two, Paxaros and Serigan, were utterly devoid of life except for huge, shifting clouds of seabirds which must nest there by the hundreds of thousands.

"Why don't we land?" moaned Will Pallister from his hammock, once more reduced to skin and bone. "I — I must taste fresh water — chew something green. I-I'll die if I don't."

Even Tom Ramster gave way, ranted like a madman. "It's that old bastard Arnand again! Ah-h! Curse on those rotten self-servers what sent him and the other Invalids to Portsmouth!"

Towards sundown *Centurion,* under reduced canvas, lay in the lee of Antacan Rock. Everyone able to level a glass probed the shore, but sighted only ramparts of sheer, bird-whitened cliffs, never a trace of fresh water.

At length, Captain Saunders declared he'd detected a tiny beach so, with the help of Schoolmaster Thomas, Michael Despeda, Wade and King Parmer and a few others, he managed to lower a gig and pull towards this overgrown reef. Around nine of the evening, when the boat returned, one look at Saunders warned Anson to expect the worst.

"There's not even a puddle of fresh water and no fuel beyond driftwood; there isn't even a safe landing place. We were so feeble at the oars we were hard put to avoid swamping before I got ashore."

While Saunders continued, Anson studied the few notations on his water-stained chart. "We managed, however, to collect a few eggs and drift-coconuts for benefit of our sick."

"That's good, Captain. Very good. In the morning we will endeavor to discover some more."

But it was not to be; for, around midnight, the wind commenced to blow strongly offshore. It being impracticable to drop anchor Anson, struggling against a miserable semi-daze, ordered the gig taken in tow and told Mr. Nutt to shape a southerly course which, he hoped and prayed, might bring *Centurion* in sight of some larger islands.

〜 5 〜

The Thief Islands

ONCE THE ROCK OF ANTACAN had been left behind several men suddenly died, of acute disappointment, said Peter Vesey. Among the casualties was Dennis Crowley, *Centurion's* experienced and hard-driving boatswain, unlamented by the many who had suffered flogging by him and his mates.

Someone rapped softly at Lieutenant Peircy Brett's door. So nearly exhausted was the first lieutenant that he only half-roused, mumbling, "Wha? My turn — pump a'ready? Can't be —"

"No, sir, 'tain't that," Acting Gunner Ramster's speech was blurred because, lately, his gums had become so terribly infected and his teeth so loose that his enunciation was distorted.

"Well, then?"

"Begging your pardon, sir, 'tis about young Pallister, sir. He's bad off." Because of an unfamiliar weakness in his legs Ramster had to grip the door frame to keep from falling.

"Pallister? Curse you, who's Pallister?" Brett demanded, slowly raising himself on an elbow.

"Why, sir, he's the lad you've been teachin' to paint."

"Oh. He asked to see me? Of all the —"

"— Oh no, sir," Ramster said hurriedly. "'Tis only that he fair worships you for being so great a artist — and officer," he added quickly. "Please don't go blaming him for impudence, sir. 'Tis only — well, just now I was thinkin' that maybe, if you was to drop him a kind word — well, he might last till we reach land."

Swinging long, thin legs over the edge of his bunk, Brett uttered a croaking grunt. "— If we ever do. Where is he?"

"In Mr. Weldon's cabin, sir. Pallister's the purser's mate you know, sir."

What prompted Brett to pull a few sketches from his sea chest he couldn't have said, but he did.

It was fortunate that the wind was so light that *Centurion* cruised on an even keel, otherwise the lieutenant might have fallen on his way below, he had so little strength left.

"Now then, Pallister," said Brett in a gentle tone, "what's this I hear about you dipping your colors?"

"He weren't really, sir," Ramster hurriedly interpolated, then turned up the wick of a purser's glim until its flame glinted off the youth's barely parted eyelids. "He ain't never complained."

"You must have been misinformed, sir," Pallister said in that surprisingly strong voice which often remained to men near death from scurvy. "I'll be all right, sir — in a day or two; you'll see." Then, weakly, he shook his head. "That was a lie, sir. I'm going to die, Mr. Brett. I feel it in my heart."

The lieutenant dropped onto a stool at the bunkside, with hair awry and soiled shirt unbuttoned. "You're not going to die, Will, be-

[347]

cause, sure as I'm sitting here, someday you'll become a famous painter. I'll prove what I say. Where d'you keep your work?"

"Top of my chest, sir. But they're not worth your bother."

"Allow me to be the judge of that." Once the lieutenant had scanned a handful of water colors he muttered, "Hum. Remarkable. Really remarkable. You've improved a good deal since you began back there on Juan Fernandez."

Pallister's sunken eyes widened and he managed to struggle higher on his moldy-smelling blanket. "You think so, sir? You *really* think so?"

"I wouldn't say so otherwise," came the quiet assurance. "Now take your sketch, 'The Burning of Payta.' I find it first rate, but the sketches you made at Quibo and at Chequetan are superior. Wish I could work as you do with color. Pen and ink, I fear, will remain my best medium."

"Made any drawings of late, sir?" The glim's flame revealed a touch of color entering the stricken youth's splotched and bony cheeks.

"Not since we destroyed poor old *Gloucester*." He delved into the portfolio he had brought along. "Here's my impression of that melancholy event. And see, I also sketched the burning of Payta. It's quite different from yours. Odd, that two artists will observe the same scene at the same time and depict it so differently —"

"Artists?" Will actually grinned. Mr. Brett had called him an artist!

"I presume we emphasize that in a scene which interests us the most." Said he in leaving, "Now, if you'll keep on planning an artist's career I, well, maybe I'll help you get started when we return to England. Incidentally, I'll bet you my sketch of Cape Noire that land will be sighted tomorrow."

To Peircy Brett's vast astonishment, with the first light of day, his prediction became fulfilled and land was reported.

"Masthead there!" bawled Officer of the Deck Hughes. "Where away and what does it look like?"

"An island — a big island, sir, lying dead ahead!"

"Land! Where?" called de Saumarez running from below, his ragged pantaloons half-unbuttoned.

"Dead ahead," Hughes told him.

The lookout hailed again, voice hoarse with tension. "'Tain't just one island, sir — 'tis three of 'em, all strung out in a row! Middle one's 'e biggest."

To everyone's disappointment, Justinian Nutt estimated this group of islands distant by at least forty miles. Therefore it was an excruciating experience to have the wind die out when only half the distance to those verdant isles had been covered.

"So near — and yet so God-damnably far!" groaned Lieutenant Colonel Cratcherode, pounding softly on the rail. "Court-martial me if I ever quit dry land again!"

"To think on all that clean water and good fruits waitin' yonder," mumbled King Parmer. His tongue had grown so badly swollen he could hardly speak.

When darkness fell, the semi-derelict flagship remained too far offshore for Anson to risk sending in a smallboat so, the half-delirious survivors, for another night, had to make out on a scant half-pint of slimy green water.

When Peter Vesey was called to take his turn at the pumps he wasn't able to descend from his cot. He simply couldn't muster sufficient strength. Badly shaken because, somehow, it had never occurred to him that when his supply of sprouted peas gave out he would take the disease so badly, Vesey slumped back onto the fetid blanket deciding that he was about to lapse into that stupor from which so few emerged.

Why not drift off? He was tired, oh so tired and his memories were so bitter. Wouldn't it be fine, once and for all, to forget that tragedy enacted at Henley; to erase his recollections of Pamela's cool air of triumph on hearing him sentenced; of Sir Paul Markham's sneering smile which said as plainly as though he had spoken, "This is a fine riddance, my dear Dr. Vesey. You never belonged in our society."

Then, surprisingly, the familiar sensation of burning outrage returned to sear Peter Vesey's soul. No, by God! I'll go back to Henley a free man and a very rich one! I'll spoil their wicked marriage. Aye, I'll live and make 'em pay, somehow. Then I'll resume my practice, but not in Henley. I'll go to Reading, perhaps, or maybe Oxford. Or Lincoln?

All night George Anson lay sprawled on the poopdeck, almost helpless, on a mattress Despeda had fetched up for him. He wished he could sleep but he couldn't, so, hour after hour he stared up at the dark tangle made by *Centurion's* rigging, tattered gallants and topmasts. Endlessly it swayed across the purple-black heavens.

Maybe some of those most brilliant constellations weren't stars at all?

[349]

Maybe, in reality, they were only more of those spots such as had begun to swim about his eyeballs. He couldn't be sure.

He heard the Watch clump painfully on deck and then de Saumarez's tired voice giving orders. Without pause the hollow *thump-bump! thump-bump!* of chain pumps played an ominous obligato far, far below. How relentlessly those pumps were draining the survivors' last pitiful measure of strength.

With daylight a fair wind sprang up which quickly drove *Centurion* towards the most beautiful-appearing islands ever seen by the expedition.

What lent fresh vigor to the emaciated Commodore and his handful of mobile survivors was the sight of a slim canoe with a triangular brown sail coming up from the north. Presently it steered a course paralleling the flagship's, then the swift little craft went ahead and seemed to be piloting the man-of-war towards a wide sandy beach which glowed all pink and gold in the early morning sunlight.

Heavily, Anson beckoned Saunders over to the wheel. "What d'you make of that?"

"Either they think us friendly, sir, or are hurrying in to alarm a garrison."

He uttered a low, mirthless laugh. "As if we could harm even a little canoe like that."

Anson then called to Lieutenant Scott, sitting listless on the flag locker, "Try to find Spanish colors and break them out at once." Meanwhile the Commodore tilted back his shaggy, lean head and bit his lip over *Centurion*'s hoary rigging, flapping buntlines, ragged sails, sagging sheets and braces.

"Aye, sir. Who'd ever take this for a King's ship?" croaked Justinian Nutt. "We more resemble a buccaneer."

Anson snapped his fingers. "Go forward as quickly as possible, Mr. Keppel, and hoist a large red flag to the forepeak." At the Acting Lieutenant's startled look, he explained. "I've heard that, on her return voyage from Acapulco, the galleon identifies herself with a bright red flag."

Then, recalling Lieutenant Salt's experience in *Pearle*, half a lifetime ago it seemed, he added, "I reckon my pendant's similar enough to a Spanish Flag Officer's to serve — tattered and bleached as it is."

"Aye, aye, sir."

After van Keppel shuffled away, Anson began to pant with that shortness of breath typical of the scurvy-stricken. "Despeda! My compliments to Colonel Cratcherode and Mr. Hughes — they're at the pumps — I believe. Inform them — desire every man — who can even crawl — hurry on deck. Mr. Brett, see if you can man — few light guns on — fo'c'sle. Gunner must — issue cutlasses and blunderbusses to — anyone who can hold one." The Commodore swayed so violently he had to grip the rail. "If — Spaniards want to fight — must give 'em — warm reception."

"All hands on deck!" Boatswain Adams croaked down the main companion and his voice reverberated strangely through the silent hall. "Out, down — and up, you whoresons. Don't ye want to get ashore?"

Quartermaster's Mate Wade staggered over to that hammock in which John Clipperton for several days had lain vacant-eyed and inert. "Can't you make it on deck?"

"No, Nat, I fear not."

"Nonsense! The enemy's been sighted."

"Enemy d'you say? Dammit, Nat, can you lift my legs out o' this pigsty of a hammock? I'll somehow get on deck." Bits of fecal matter pattered onto the deck when Clipperton struggled to stand; largely supported by Wade's scurvy-spotted arm, he started for the companion ladder. "Don't let go, mate, I aim — to disappoint them thieving pursers and draw me prize money someday."

Presently, the wind died out, so it was not until the afternoon that *Centurion*, with a red flag flying, arrived within two miles of the island which, according to Justinian Nutt, was called Buena Vista by the Spaniards and Tinian by its original inhabitants.

Never, as long as he lived, would Midshipman Tom de Saumarez forget the ghostly appearance of the fifty-odd physical wrecks who struggled on deck and crawled on hands and knees towards their action stations. Without exception, they were gaunt and hairy; their bodies and clothing were unspeakably fouled. Several men collapsed on the deck and died; others hung weakly to the gun carriages.

Meanwhile, a cutter under the command of hollow-eyed Lieutenant Peter Denis was slowly rowed inshore. With bated breath those in the flagship watched the little, white-painted craft disappear behind a point of land barring what appeared to be the entrance to a harbor.

Clinging to guns they were far too weak to serve, the ragged apparitions blinked and stared in dazed disbelief on gently rolling emerald-hued hills crowned with towering hardwoods, at dense groves of

[351]

feathery coconut palms marching down to the water's edge across beaches of glistening sand.

Several small streams could be seen splashing down to the shore in a series of miniature cascades which set dry throats to closing and burning anew. Juan Fernandez all over again! They tried to forget their pangs by anticipating that moment when the first shots would ring out on shore.

Desperately, Quartermaster's Mate John Clipperton attempted to get his eyes into focus, and was succeeding, when someone handed him a rammer. Its weight proved too much; when he collapsed the iron staff caused a resounding clatter.

By the time Wade had staggered over to his friend the veteran lay as dead as if he'd been struck down by a bullet. Hardly anyone even turned his head at the sound of Clipperton's fall — it was too ordinary an occurrence.

Other men who had succumbed to the exertion of reaching the guns lay about the long unholystoned deck and, in no time at all, attracted flies which swarmed aboard by the millions.

Still no gunfire sounded from behind that shimmering, palm-studded point. *Centurion's* men were growing anxious when the cutter reappeared under sail and with the pirogue in tow!

Croaked Scott, "Looks like her crew were taken in by the red flag and the Commodore's pendant."

What puzzled the gaunt wretches aboard the flagship was the fact that none of the prisoners appeared to be tied up and that an olive-complexioned European sat chatting animatedly in the cutter's stern sheets beside Peter Denis.

Uniformly, the captives — pale brown and well-built South Sea Islanders, saving their officer — on reaching *Centurion's* deck recoiled from the grisly sights and smells upon it.

Once the Spaniard, who turned out to be a noncommissioned officer or a *sargento-major,* was brought before the Commodore he bowed profoundly. "Welcome to Buena Vista, *Señor Comodoro!*"

"Why should he welcome an enemy?" Anson demanded in painful deliberation and de Saumarez quickly translated.

The sergeant-major's teeth gleamed yellow in the depths of a black spade beard. "Because of that accursed Governor — I piss on his heart!"

"— What Governor, *señor?*" interpolated de Saumarez.

"The one who rules in Guam, *Señor Capitán.*"

"How near is that island?" Nutt broke in, aware that Guam was the Capitol and seat of Spanish power over the far-flung Mariana Archipelago, of which the Ladrone Islands formed but a small component.

"— It lies a scant forty leagues distant, *Señores*."

"And why do you so hate this Governor?"

The Spaniard spat furiously and glowered at a long V of rusty-black cormorants flapping by on their way to fishing grounds beyond the reefs. "That lecherous dog ordered me on this voyage in order that he may at his leisure seduce a daughter of mine who is to be married this week."

"Sounds a most unpleasant fellow. But tell me, why do your 'Indians' also appear overjoyed?" De Saumarez described these South Sea Islanders by that term which, throughout the cruise, was used to describe any native other than Negro.

"It is because, *señores,* their people originated on this island."

Anson grabbed a rail and steadied himself, "Why did they desert so lovely a spot?"

"Sixty or seventy years ago, *Señor Comodoro*, a terrible plague swept the Marianas. On Guam it proved especially severe, sparing only a few of the *Indios*. The then Governor was hard-put to man our fortifications, so he ordered the entire population of Tinian — which we call Buena Vista — transported to Guam. So, for many years, there have been no regular inhabitants on this beautiful island. It is visited only by those who, like us, from time to time come to kill cattle."

"— To kill cattle?" Anson demanded, sinking onto a stool unobtrusively thrust forward by Despeda.

The ragged and scurvy-stricken officers now listened with renewed attention. "Cattle" meant fresh beef in the offing!

"*Sí, Señor Comodoro*. At that time the *Indios* were removed so swiftly that they were forced to leave behind all their domestic animals." The sergeant-major waved expressive hands. "You will not credit the vastness of the herds of cattle, swine and burros you will see grazing in the interior, where lie many lush savannahs.

"All these animals have grown so fat, lazy and unafraid that they can be run down and slaughtered without the least effort; in short, *señores,* such beasts are to be had for the taking — and as many as you want."

The Spaniard then hesitated, surveying the gaunt and evil-smelling apparitions about him, added a trifle uncomfortably, "But possibly not by you, until you have somewhat recovered your strength." His gapped yellow teeth gleamed in a grin intended to be encouraging. "However, *amigos míos,* there are on Tinian quantities of fowl — pigeons, chickens, ducks and geese which allow you to pick them up."

Chief Surgeon Ettrick drew near, supporting himself against the bulwarks and queried, "Is there fruit?"

"Plenty of all varieties, *señor.* Indeed, you could not have encountered an island more suitable to satisfy your needs." He shrugged. "Buena Vista — or Tinian, as *los Indios* name it, is a paradise on earth. Gladly would I fetch my family and live out my days here, as would many others, if that rutting boar of a Governor would allow it."

With the sergeant-major and the South Sea Islanders at her helm, *Centurion* was worked inshore along a channel already sounded, despite near exhaustion, by Lieutenant Denis. At twilight, the sea-worn man-of-war, her pumps still clanking ceaselessly, dropped an anchor twenty fathoms deep in a lovely, fairly well-sheltered bay, already tenanted by a European-designed bark of about fifteen tons burthen.

Significantly, fully five hours were required to furl and snug down *Centurion*'s canvas, a task which under normal conditions, would not have required fifteen minutes' time.

⚅ 6 ⚅

Tinian Island

COMMODORE ANSON, thoroughly infuriated over feeling so weak and uncertain of his movements, was forced either to occupy a chair or to lie under an awning on a mattress, although his will remained inflexible as ever. Instead of being able personally to observe and to direct proceedings, he was forced to rely upon the services of Saunders, de Saumarez and Peircy Brett.

To his surprise he also found himself often acting upon suggestions made by Acting Lieutenant Augustus van Keppel, who, though barely turned nineteen, was proving sagacious far beyond his years. To him Anson, therefore, assigned the duty of making certain that none of the prisoners were given opportunity of escaping and so warning the Governor of Guam that a helpless enemy lay nearby. True, the handsome, light-brown natives appeared to be friendly, but who could be sure?

Curiously enough, none of *Gloucester*'s ex-officers, with the exception of raw-boned Lieutenant Hughes, proved overly efficient in the discharge of assignments; it seemed to Anson that, while Captain Mitchell and his officers were doing their best, the destruction of their ship had deprived them of a subtle but irreplaceable *élan*.

The encampment which grew on Tinian Island in many respects proved to be quite dissimilar from previous landings. Here, instead of seals, sea elephants or turtles, roamed fat and friendly hogs, goats and great herds of cattle; these last were uniformly white save for black or brown ears.

Instead of virgin territory, evidences of previous habitation were found everywhere, among them several aisles of tall and beautifully fashioned stone pillars which, arranged in double ranks, challenged the viewers to divine their purpose.

Also there were found a number of palm-thatched stone huts in which the sick could immediately find shelter. Cold and fresh water was abundant and, to begin with, bananas, lemons and oranges could be picked all along the beach.

In the late afternoon, Lieutenant Brett returned to the ship and, removing his hat, approached Anson's awning.

"Are the worst of the sick ashore?" the Commodore demanded, licking orange juice from still red and raw fingers. Because Despeda had combed his hair and shaved him before fetching a clean shirt, Anson, despite his scurvy, felt a trifle more himself.

"Aye, aye, sir, but eleven more men died before we reached land."

"There's plenty of food?"

Brett's lean, tanned features lit. "Aye, sir. In a short while we came upon great groves of limes, lemons and sour oranges; there are also guavas, wild plums and cabbage palms. As to vegetables, sir, we have recognized dandelions, mint, sorrel and an abundance of scurvy grass — also more watermelons than can possibly be consumed."

"What about water?"

"Alas, sir, many of those pretty streams we spied are brackish; nevertheless, we have found a number of fresh-water ponds convenient to our needs."

Presently, Captain Saunders appeared from below, sweating and red-faced. He didn't speak without invitation which, Anson felt, was the first indication of reviving discipline. "Well, Captain?"

"Sir, in my opinon one of the first things to be done is to stop the leak in our bow. Even at anchor, our pumps are barely able to keep the water in check."

Accordingly, after the last of the sick and some essential supplies had been put ashore, Anson ordered the prisoners and the well men to trundle all forward guns as far aft as possible — a task which required several days of accomplishment.

Next, from the forward magazine, 130 powder barrels were lowered into the Spanish bark, brought alongside for the purpose. Heavy gear was then shifted towards the stern until, gradually, the flagship's weed-encrusted bow, beak and lion figurehead became lifted out of the water.

Supported by two canes, the Commodore, still denying himself the luxury of going ashore, remained to inspire his sun-scorched crew. One thing he found to be most encouraging; officers and men who had recovered even a measure of strength willingly came out from shore to bear a hand.

Not until carpenters had stripped away the sheet-lead covering *Centurion*'s bows were they able to locate that all but disastrous leak. During some convulsive struggle against the sea a bolt near the cutwater had pulled out, leaving its seat unstopped.

Only then would the Commodore consent to go ashore and occupy a tent pitched in the shade of a clump of towering *rima* trees. Despeda had caused it to be pitched on one of those natural lawns which, in many places, lent to the island a park-like aspect.

Midshipmen Francis Drake, Tom de Saumarez and John Campbell led a party detailed to catch poultry, or to shoot game — which was not really encouraged; only a little gunpowder as yet had been fetched ashore.

The fifteen Chamorros, as the Spaniards called the islanders, demonstrated, laughingly, that one had only to chase ducks, geese and chickens until they took off on unwilling flight. These were so fat they could fly but a short distance before they fell so exhausted that they could be picked up and have their necks wrung.

While the foragers rested before starting back to camp, John Campbell grinned and fell to stroking a plump rooster. "How d'ye aim to cook yours?"

"Fried. And you, Drake?"

"Going to roast mine, provided I can fight off these pesky flies long enough."

"To hell with fowls!" grinned young de Saumarez. "All I want is beef, beef and more beef!"

On their way out to hunt upon the savannahs they had passed a shed near which were penned a number of white cattle; wide-eyed, they placidly were waiting their turn to be butchered and skinned.

The one serious flaw in this South Sea Eden, the men found, was its multitudinous insects. There were also voracious ticks which buried their heads under a man's skin and, if pulled off too quickly, later caused painful, suppurating boils. If unnoticed, these grew as large as small purple plums. There was also a scourge of flies of many varieties. When a man attempted to eat he had to fan aside these insects with one hand while trying to feed with the other. Even so, flies often flew into a diner's mouth were he to open it ever so briefly to receive a morsel.

"'Fore God," grumbled Ramster, "a bugger can't tell *what* he's eating."

During the first week on Tinian thirty-three of the sick continued to languish; they died despite the best efforts of Messrs. Ettrick, Allen, Keating and Dr. Vesey. But after their demise no more casualties ensued, thanks to the abundance of acid fruits. Soon all remaining invalids were better; even the worst affected became able to move about on sticks or crude crutches.

The Commodore, to all intents and purposes once more hale, took especial pleasure in watching his crew at mess. He remarked to the Reverend Mr. Walter, "Isn't it incredible how much they can eat? Thank the Lord there's plenty for everybody."

"I expect, sir, that their gluttony is stimulated by the availability of such familiar viands as fresh beef, pork and domestic fowl."

"Whatever the cause," smiled Anson, "I note that all hands gorge themselves three times a day and hang about the cooking fires between meals."

"Sir," the Chaplain queried, "can you tell me the name of that vegetable which is being substituted for bread?"

"Mr. Thomas tells me 'tis the *rima*, which the Chamorros describe as most palatable. When baked and broken open, the *rima* is found to contain tasty and nutritious kernels which have a breadlike consistency. The men, therefore, have taken to calling it 'breadfruit.' "

[357]

After considerable deliberation, the Commodore decided to announce some reassignments among his officers. With so many supernumeraries of superior rank present, such as Captains Saunders and Mitchell, *Centurion's* regular officers continually found themselves in equivocal positions.

Accordingly, Anson appointed Philip de Saumarez to be the flagship's first lieutenant — after returning him to his permanent rank from Prize Captain. Ever tactful, Anson felt that by doing so he would not be forced to deprive Charles Saunders of his Post Captain's commission. By retaining a Captain's pendant, Saunders, on his return to England, almost certainly would obtain a ship of his own.

Peircy Brett was made *Centurion's* second lieutenant and Peter Denis, third; then, to the surprise of everyone and the disappointment of some, beardless young Augustus van Keppel was appointed a full lieutenant and Anson's flag officer.

"I assure you gentlemen," Anson explained gravely, "I am deeply grieved that I have no choice but to list as 'supernumerary' such capable officers as Captains Mitchell and Saunders and Lieutenants Samuel Scott, Patrick Baird and John Hughes.

"Also carried as supernumerary is Surgeon Joseph Allen of *Tryall's Prize.*"

Menzies, although still gaunt and pale, was taking down reassignments among the warrant and petty officers when Peircy Brett halted before the tent in which the Commodore sat fighting off myriad buzzing flies. "Sir, in compliance with your instructions, I have had the roll called and regret to report that our company is now reduced to two hundred and twenty-four men of all ranks and ratings."

Thoughtfully, the Commodore's vivid blue eyes stared across the verdant savannah, then came to rest on Brett's thin, red-brown features. "How many of these are English?"

"Only about two thirds, sir. For some reason, many Indians and volunteers of mixed blood have died off; most of the foreigners surviving are half-bred Negroes."

From half a coconut Anson took a sip of rum, lemon juice and coconut water. "Hum. In that case, each of us must do the work of three men. Pray seat yourself, Mr. Brett."

For a while the approaching end of the rainy season was discussed. "The Spanish sergeant tells me," informed Anson's junior, "that, after the new moon in September — which this year is expected on the eighteenth — hurricanes, which in these latitudes are called typhoons, may strike at any time before the northeast trade winds set in again."

"In that case every conceivable precaution must be taken to ensure the safety of our ship, and also of the Spanish bark."

Centurion's angular sailing master came tramping up and pulled off the kerchief with which he had been shielding his nearly hairless scalp from the sun. "Sir, may I point out something?"

"Pray speak, Mr. Nutt."

"Well, I feel, sir, that immediate steps must be taken to protect the ship's cables. While the anchorage is a good one, it is exposed to storms out of the east. Also" — *Centurion*'s sailing master lowered his voice for emphasis — "the anchors rest on a dangerous bottom."

"Dangerous? How so?"

"Sir, I have surveyed it and find that this harbor's bottom is studded with sharp coral ledges which readily could sever a cable were it to saw against them for any length of time."

"Mr. Brett also has reported this. Therefore, I wish you to have a hundred feet of chain attached next to the anchor. You will also cackle the cables above that point as high as you deem necessary."

"Aye, aye, sir. And what weight of rope shall be employed in fashioning this chafing gear?"

"Use the thickest you can find in that pile of canvas and cordage down on the beach."

"Aye, aye, sir. Are there any further precautions you wish to have taken?"

Calmly the Commodore's clear eyes rested upon his sailing master's anxious features. "You had best send down all yards and topmasts, then put out the second best bower and ready the sheet anchor for instant use."

∼ 7 ∼

Typhoon

A FEW TWILIGHTS LATER, the one hundred and thirteen men and officers camping ashore noted the appearance of a dainty new moon;

but, new moon or no new moon, the weather remained so wonderfully fair that they forgot to worry.

"Take comfort, *señores*," advised the Spanish sergeant-major while drawing his evening ration, "hurricanes do not always strike here; very possibly there will be none this year."

He was proved to be very wrong, for towards noon of September 23rd, the sky lost its customary azure hue to assume a sickly yellow-gray color. The Chamorros tilted flat noses into the wind, sniffed, then excitedly declared that there was a typhoon somewhere in the vicinity.

Presently an unearthly, breathless stillness descended upon Tinian; birds fell silent, wild cattle, goats and hogs disappeared into deep woods, while the men, under Anson's personal supervision, cast ropes over the palm-thatched huts and anchored them to trees or stakes driven deep into the ground.

Often they looked out at *Centurion*, appearing more forlorn than ever without her topmasts or a single yard crossed. When the sky darkened, Lieutenant de Saumarez hurried about, with meticulous care checking preparations to withstand a blow.

Around four of the afternoon a few uneasy puffs of wind commenced to stir the palm fronds and seabirds hastened inshore in search of shelter among the rocks.

"Damned if the wind don't sigh like a passionate maiden," drawled Paymaster's Mate Waxter to his friend Lieutenant Gordon of the Marines.

"That's maybe so, Ted, but it's so goddam long since I've bedded a wench I can't be sure," Gordon laughed as they stood at the water's edge and watched silvery little squalls, like playful kittens, chase each other around the anchorage.

In inarticulate anxiety the men on shore watched the Pacific, under clouds of fast-flying spindrift, change in color from emerald to a cloudy dark-blue and then to yellow-gray.

Masses of livid-black rain clouds hurtled over the horizon, while, to windward, the ocean began angrily to froth and boil. Flash after flash of jagged white lightning lanced through the lowering sky and a weird whining noise swelled in volume until, with a screaming roar, the typhoon pounced out of the east — the one direction from which the anchorage was not protected. Its violence bent thick palm trees into deep arcs, tore off large boughs and, in rapid succession, uprooted scores of trees.

A sort of vacuum was created which seemed to suck the breath out of men's chests. Then, wild, blinding rain drummed down obscuring everything beyond the radius of a few feet.

George Anson attempted to shield his eyes sufficiently to determine how his flagship was faring, but the effort was in vain. Hard-driven raindrops stung his eyes so viciously he could not bear to keep their lids parted.

Poor young de Saumarez! Wonder how many men he's got aboard? Thank God, it's he who's in command. He'll surely do what's expected of him.

When, quite inexplicably, the rain abated for a few minutes, the Commodore perceived that short, but very steep waves were riding in the harbor. They were breaking against *Centurion*'s hull just as they might upon a reef.

The wind, screaming like a thousand tormented banshees, deluged the scourged island with rain. Palm fronds, branches, land birds and all manner of debris flashed through the air as if propelled by a Titan's sling. Soon the thatching of several roofs was wrenched off and the men in those huts were forced to cling to trees or lie flat to avoid being blown into the harbor.

Clinging to a backstay aboard *Centurion*, Lieutenant Philip de Saumarez felt half-smothered by the furious rain and salt spindrift. His only encouragement at the moment was a realization that Lieutenants Brett, Baird, Hughes and van Keppel happened to be aboard.

Including midshipmen, he guessed he had with him some ninety white seamen and a dozen Negroes — in all, about 115 men to handle a Fourth Rate which normally would require three times that number.

Fervently, he wished himself ashore with the Commodore but managed to laugh when a parrot, blown out from shore, clung to the mizzen shrouds upside down and squalled its fright until an especially vicious gust wrenched the bird away to destruction at sea.

The new first lieutenant's chief concern was for the longboat which had brought out a work party just before the typhoon struck. He seemed to recall that a man had been left in it to replace a splintered section of thwart.

De Saumarez fought his way aft and, on peering over the taffrail, saw the longboat bucking and pitching like an unbroken stallion at the end of a longe. The workman he recognized as Tom Ramster; the

[361]

big, red-headed fellow had crouched under the weather thwart and was bailing frantically.

Then, from forward, sounded a sharp report. Although he could see absolutely nothing beyond a few feet, instinct warned de Saumarez that an anchor cable had parted — and the ship without a yard crossed or a sail bent on!

Confused shouts and yells faintly penetrated the wind's tumult while de Saumarez, buffeted and half-blinded by rain, fought his way forward, hand over hand. His heart seemed to fail when the flagship, deprived of one of her bow anchors, slewed violently about until her dismantled bowsprit pointed shorewards and her stern towards the black and raging ocean.

All might still have gone well with the wallowing Fourth Rate had not the tide just then turned. With the wind howling across the anchorage, this fresh force swiftly created tumultuous cross-seas which tossed the sail-less flagship in all directions.

When it seemed impossible for the typhoon to rage any more fiercely, it did just that. Tossed hither and yon by mounting cross-seas, *Centurion* tugged and tore at her remaining anchor line like a scared goat at its tether.

In the dim 'tween decks, Nat Wade struggled to secure a gunport's lid, but had the breath knocked out of him time and again by the impact of unseen objects that were tumbling about. To the bewildered quartermaster's mate water seemed to be spouting into *Centurion* from all directions.

After managing to shoot home the lid's bolts, Wade struggled back onto the rain-lashed deck but found that it had grown so dark that he could see nothing of the island; in fact, he couldn't tell whether anyone else was on the quarterdeck or not.

Staggered by the wind's vicious force, Wade had the curious sensation of his body's being hollow, of feeling that he was about to smother. Branches, palm fronds, flowers, leaves and all manner of small birds fell onto the deck only to be whirled away again.

Finally, he sighted a cluster of dim figures and joined a party under Lieutenant Peircy Brett which was attempting to double-lash a 24-pounder that had shown signs of breaking loose and running wild.

The breechings had barely been secured when once again sounded that heart-stopping *crack!*

"Other cable's parted!" screamed Boatswain Adams, his cheeks blown out like balloons by the wind's force. "God help us! We'll be driven out to sea under bare masts!"

When de Saumarez heard *Centurion*'s second cable break he yelled for Lieutenant Baird to hack through that catting which, until now, had been holding a sheet anchor ready to be dropped in just such an emergency.

The men on deck dashed water from their eyes and sobbed in relief when they felt the hook scrape along the bottom and seem to take hold. Leadenly, *Centurion* swung about until her stern was presented to the wind. But would her sheet anchor, lightest of all the flagship's ground tackle, really serve?

Although his cheeks were inflated by the tearing blast, de Saumarez cupped hands and shouted at van Keppel, flattened white-eyed against the lee bulwarks, "Fire distress signal!"

One after another four guns were touched off, but the reports were muffled by the wind's violence.

Only through supreme efforts did the high-strung first lieutenant cling to his composure — which, thanks to his Spanish ancestry, was a difficult feat.

To Chaplain Walters he yelled, "Pass word — light flares — and pray like hell!"

Clinging to the mizzen, de Saumarez became half drowned by the solid sheets of water which came cascading over the poop. He watched a flare sputter and die almost immediately. Another and another were ignited, but only one burned for more than a few instants.

What should be done now?

The first lieutenant's indecision was terminated by a terrific crash almost beneath his feet. The longboat, which had been towing astern, had begun to batter into the flagship's stern with the force of a pile-driver. Four times, to a vicious crackle of smashing wood, the longboat crunched into *Centurion*'s gilded stern.

De Saumarez became dreadfully certain that, in so doing, it could not have avoided damaging the rudder. Finally, the longboat's painter snapped; it bumped along the port side until, badly crushed, it drifted clear and became lost to sight amid whirling spindrift.

Lieutenant Baird fought his way up to the quarterdeck with wet hair streaming and shirt billowing above his broad belt. "Dragging, sir! Anchor's bumping along the bottom!"

De Saumarez nodded and took a fresh grip on his quivering nerves. He'd already foreseen that the flagship's light sheet anchor wouldn't

[363]

be enough; if it dragged across the harbor without snagging, it would drop into such deep water that it would find nothing to hook onto. Ever more violently *Centurion* plunged towards the open Pacific with waves breaking across her quarterdeck.

What would the Commodore do under such conditions?

The situation clarified itself when the dragging and scraping sensation ceased as the sheet anchor dropped into the deep. There wasn't any chance now, de Saumarez knew, of getting some yards crossed and sails bent onto them, because night had fallen and the ship was plunging so crazily that it would have been sheer, pointless murder to order men aloft.

～ 8 ～

Nil Desperandum

FOR THREE WHOLE DAYS the typhoon raged; sudden, vicious squalls blasted Tinian from almost every point of the compass. At last on the third night the wind's howling slackened, but torrential rains continued to lash the chilled, exhausted and hungry castaways.

Next morning's dawn was brilliant and brought perfect peace, but some time passed before the men remembered to speak in anything less than a shout.

In dazed fashion, Anson and his men began to search for missing property among great windfalls of overturned trees, roofless or blown-down huts. Twisted palm fronds, ragged branches and hundreds of green coconuts and fruits of all kinds strewed the sodden ground. Pools and puddles gleamed everywhere; in some dead birds and small animals floated among vivid blossoms.

Everyone tried to avoid looking out at the anchorage; it was empty now except for that little bark which had brought the meat hunters over from Guam. Of *Centurion* there remained no trace except for the wreckage of her longboat which was detected floating, mostly submerged, amid a huge bed of golden-brown seaweed. Apparently some vagary of wind or current had propelled its remains inshore.

Arms folded, George Anson stood on a small knoll and steadily regarded the sea, his broad, red-brown features devoid of expression.

Behind him Lieutenant Denis muttered, "Seems hardly possible to realize that our gallant old ship's been done for at last."

"— And all those poor fellows who were in her," added Lieutenant Scott, biting his lip.

Anson turned, said steadily, "Gentlemen, let us not mourn prematurely. I am far from convinced that she has indeed been lost."

The officers, uncomfortable in their still damp clothing, exchanged glances. They felt deeply for this big, apparently unshaken gentleman whose courage seemed so boundless.

"I cannot bring myself to believe that, after having preserved us through so many trials and misfortunes, God intends our expedition to end here."

Abruptly, Lieutenant Scott said, "Whatever for are they launching a boat?"

Under a cloud of returning seabirds a cutter, rowed by four oarsmen and steered by Midshipman Hyde Parker was moving toward the longboat's wreck.

Anson snapped, "Lend me a spyglass, someone." Focusing the wreckage, he soon saw why the cutter had put out. What appeared to be a man's head and arm was protruding from a splintered section of the bow.

The boat's crew became so curious as to what they would find, that their stroke became uneven, and so earned them a tongue-lashing from the midshipman.

When they pulled close the bowman called out, "Sir! Sir! That there's 'Rowley Red' Ramster, or wot's left of 'im."

The big gunner's mate was unconscious and lay, lashed by one wrist, to a section of thwart in such a fashion that, even after he'd lost consciousness, his battered head had remained above water. They found a gash across his long-unshaven chin and a huge, purple-red bruise on his right side.

Once Hyde Parker tilted a little brandy into his mouth, Ramster stirred, swallowed and then coughed and mumbled, "More — I'll have 'nother, Miss," as he lay staring blankly into the midshipman's wide eyes.

"Good Lord," Parker remarked, "you ought to have been fishfood days ago."

"Hullo, sir," Ramster gasped. "Reckoned I'd stick 'round long enough to draw me prize pay — I've got plans —" Then the terribly bruised petty officer relapsed into an unconsciousness from which he did not emerge until long after he'd been placed on a pallet in the now roofless hospital shed.

[365]

"He's suffered some cracked ribs, sir, and a pair of broken fingers," Peter Vesey informed Saunders who'd been sent by the Commodore. "All the same he ought to be up and about in a short while; such hurts hardly feaze a hard-shell like Tom. I'll warrant he's hungry already."

Ramster roused and grinned. "Aye, that I am. I could eat a cow and chase its calf."

Black gloom settled upon the encampment when, after twenty-four hours, there came not the least hint that *Centurion* might have survived. Men sat on the beach and stared mournfully at the anchorage, empty except for masses of storm-wrack that still were drifting about the placid, emerald-blue harbor.

Observed a shaggy seaman as he sat emptying his mess kit beside a campfire, " 'Tis certain-sure she's been lost with all hands. Most likely, she were driven onto a reef and broke up into little pieces."

"Sure," agreed a messmate, moodily employing his forefinger to dislodge shreds of beef from between broken and discolored teeth. "She were helpless, wi' not a single yard crossed when 'e ruddy storm broke."

One-eyed Paddy Kildare nodded. " 'Twould be better they drowned then be blown down to Guam and get took by the murdering Dons and hanged for pirates."

"Hanged?" The mess captain belched. "Why so, Paddy?"

"Faith and yer a great fool to forget that Mr. Saumarez ain't got his King's commission along, which would prove the *Centurion*'s an honest ship of war. His Honor ordered all such fetched ashore fer safekeeping."

Kildare's mess captain angrily tossed a stick onto the fire, sent sparks whirling up among the ragged palm fronds. "Damned if ye ain't right, for all yer only a blasted Roman Catholic harp! That's the hell of not havin' uniforms like the soljers. Uniforms would force 'e Dons to believe us are of 'e Royal Navy, commission or no commission."

"Aye. The officers have been complaining over that ever since we left Funchal. Heard Cap'n Saunders say that the Commodore means to do something about it when we get home."

"*If* we get home, you mean," sneered one of the mess. "Wot odds we'll ever see England again?"

No one answered him.

Curiously enough, George Anson, at the moment consuming a

lonely supper in his tent, also was deploring the lack of naval uniforms. Especially he resented that his able, but less well-to-do, officers must constantly remain outshone by their wealthier associates. Officers and men of the Royal Navy, he told himself for the hundredth time, should *not* be forced to go about dressed like merchantmen or privateers.

Further and more immediate concerns then harassed the unhappy Commander in Chief. Worst of these was the fact that an examination of the supplies on hand had revealed only a few stands of small arms and *only three pounds* of gunpowder! As if to compound this disaster, it turned out that all the expedition's charts and navigating instruments had been aboard the flagship, as well as all the hard-won spoils of Payta and the prizes.

Still, we'll manage, he assured himself grimly. We always have. We must not falter in our duty.

Later, as Anson ranged the encampment in an attempt to inspire confidence, he was encouraged to hear that three chests of carpenter's tools had been found on the beach, as well as a portable forge and a considerable pile of damaged canvas and cordage.

Early next morning Anson summoned Captains Mitchell and Saunders. "Gentlemen, I feel that I should more closely examine the Spanish bark. Be good enough to accompany me."

As a cutter rounded under the grubby little vessel's counter, the Commodore remarked, "Gentlemen, may I invite you to inspect the *Centurion's* successor?"

Mitchell reddened. "Surely you jest, sir. A craft of this burthen could never accommodate us all, let alone sail to China!"

"True enough. As she is, this over-grown shallop could not transport even the half of our number."

Captain Saunders, foreseeing what impended, smiled to himself when Anson said briskly, "You've been aboard before. Tell me what you can, Captain, about this vessel."

"Sir, she is of about thirty tons burthen, fifty feet in length and exactly fifteen feet in the beam. I found her sails, gear and finish crude but reasonably sound."

"Good. Then, when lengthened and decked over, she can serve our purpose."

Upon his return ashore, Anson at once summoned all officers and midshipmen and addressed them saying, "Gentlemen, before I speak on another matter, I wish you not to conclude that our gallant old

Centurion has been lost. Although undermanned, she is in the most capable of hands. Also, I invite you to recall that only open water lies to the west of this island; according to my calculations, our ship probably has not been driven into the vicinity of Guam.

"However, it would be folly not to admit that the trade winds have begun to blow once more so, to return to Tinian, she must find the wind in her teeth.

"I conclude that if Mr. Saumarez decides that he cannot beat back to Tinian, due to his shortage of sails and of men to manage them, he undoubtedly will make for Macao on the coast of China; in doing so he would benefit from a fair wind. Barring capture, he should gain the mainland without undue difficulty.

"You will now accompany me to the beach where I shall cause all hands to assemble, as near to the hospital as possible, in order that the sick also may hear what I have to say."

In groups of varying size men appeared from various directions: the red-handed butchers from their gory task, the fishermen left off contriving nets out of odds and ends of rigging and hunters came up carrying their guns and gear.

Once all heads had been bared out of respect a profound silence descended broken only by the raucous chatter of parrots, the plaintive cries of seabirds and the ravings of Tom Ramster, who, after gorging himself, had relapsed into a delirium.

Squaring his shoulders, George Anson spoke in a big, hearty voice. "My brave fellows, I have a plan by which all of us on the island may get away to Macao while the trade wind blows, as it should for several months. I have consulted with our carpenters. They consider my plan to be possible of execution, but it will require the united industry of us *all* alike to accomplish it.

"My plan is to haul up on the beach the Spanish bark we have here, to saw her in two halves amidships, and then to lengthen her by twelve feet. This will convert her into a vessel of near forty tons burthen, large enough to convey all hands in safety to the China coast, though the voyage there is one of over fifteen hundred miles."

A rising undertone of excitement commenced to circulate as, gradually, the listeners lost their grim expressions.

"We must all set to work at once, so as to be certain of being able to get away while the fair winds blow. This will not be a quick nor an easy job; further, we must prepare our minds to accept the probability that the *Centurion* will not be able to beat back to Tinian for us to rejoin her. If, through some happy chance, she should get back, we shall then only have thrown away a few days of wholesome work."

Anson paused, looked levelly about, then raised his voice to a confident pitch. "So now, my hearties, let us fall to at once! We are all of us rats on the same raft, and for my own part, I am entirely prepared to share with my own arms and strength in the necessary work; I shall expect no more from any man I see here before me than I am myself prepared to do. Unless we wish to end our days here in this wild place, we must put our backs into the work before us, and each labor as much for himself as for his shipmates."

He broke off, surveyed the hairy, bronzed and black faces around him, then concluded, "I think, men, that ere we start to work we should give the new vessel a name. Shall it be *Nil Desperandum* — Never Despair?"

"Hear! Hear!" shouted the officers and the cheers of the crew reverberated in the forest beyond the beach. Even the sick joined in when, quite unexpectedly, Lieutenant Colonel Cratcherode called for a cheer for the Commodore.

"We're wi' ye, Gov'nor! Lead us where ye will, we'll follow!"

Never despair, thought Peter Vesey as he turned away; if the Commodore ever attains a coat of arms he should adopt that for its motto.

The project began at once with George Anson setting an example by himself felling and trimming a coconut tree to be used as a roller upon which the bark eventually would be hauled up onto the beach.

Three carpenters who had chanced to be ashore when the typhoon struck, yellow-bearded Hayes of *Centurion*, one-eyed Winter of *Gloucester* and dark-visaged Shepherd of *Tryall* were sent into the woods to blaze such trees as they deemed suitable for timbers and planking.

The blacksmith, a burly, swarthy-bearded fellow who, as Peter Denis remarked, suggested Vulcan himself, set up the portable forge only to discover that the bellows for it had not been brought ashore!

It was then that acidulous Lieutenant Colonel Cratcherode displayed an unsuspected degree of ingenuity. "Bellows?" he snorted. "Easiest thing in the world to make. First off, select a pair of prime bullock hides and coat 'em thick with lime."

"Lime, sir? We ain't got none," growled the smith.

"Then burn coral rock, you dolt, and make some," snapped the veteran. "Seen it done in India. Fact. You can use that broken firelock's barrel yonder for your air pipe and nozzle. Damme, don't just stand there gawping. Get busy!"

The doughty Colonel then retired to his tent and designed the bellows' frames — neatly and to a precise scale. Lieutenant Gordon, with the help of a cooper, had them made before midday, so, in the late afternoon, a pair of great, clumsy bellows was in operation, driving into the forge powerful blasts of air which smelt abominably because the leather had been incompletely tanned.

After the first few days it became noticeable to even the least observant midshipman that by no means all the men had their hearts in the work. Under one pretext or another, they would excuse themselves from labor on the *Nil Desperandum* and slip off to climb the nearest height and remain there, hopefully scanning the horizon.

In Saunders's opinion these slackers not only distrusted the new vessel but were clinging to a forlorn hope that *Centurion* might reappear. Wrathful, *Tryall*'s ex-Captain warned the halfhearted, "I'd not like to be around when the Spaniards on Guam learn of our presence and dispatch an expedition to seize us. What will you do then?"

"Why, sir, we'd just fight 'em off," mumbled a sullen seaman.

"Aye, 'fight them off' and with what, pray? You know, or ought to, that we've among us less than a dozen useful muskets, which couldn't possibly save your precious hide from the Dons' tender mercies."

Men, slow in recovering from the scurvy, were put to smoking wild cattle meat into jerky or *boucan* — it having been discovered that, for some obscure reason, the local beef did not salt well. So, under Michael Despeda's direction, the beef was cut into very thin slices in the Jamaican fashion, and then smoked on green wood racks over slow fires until it was cured to *boucan,* such as was made by the buccaneers on Hispaniola in the West Indies.

Gradually great piles of coconuts, citrus fruits and root vegetables were accumulated and stored in one of the Spanish-built stone warehouses.

Under Mr. Justinian Nutt's supervision sailmakers made careful calculations before recutting *Centurion*'s and *Gloucester*'s old sails to suit the bark while boatswains superintended the manufacture of braces, shrouds and running gear from serpentine tangles of cordage piled along the beach. The weakest men were set to picking worn-out hawsers to contrive a caulking material which, with beef tallow used in lieu of tar, would be payed into the *Nil Desperandum*'s seams.

Everyone, from Anson down, was hard at work when one morning a lookout posted in a crow's-nest constructed on one of the tallest trees suddenly shouted, "A sail! A sail, by God!"

Exultant shouts arose but soon faded and the alarm was given when it was reported that those distant sails could not possibly be *Centurion's* but those of another large ship.

Presently the lookout yelled down, " 'Tain't just one ship, sir. Them sails is too far apart. It's two vessels!"

Captain Mitchell sighed. "I knew all along that that couldn't be the flagship; she's surely been lost with all hands."

"Nevertheless I remain hopeful," Anson insisted. "Those sails may very well be those of Mr. de Saumarez and his men returning in the smallboats."

Nothing in the Commander in Chief's tone betrayed his bitter disappointment. Since it wasn't his flagship sailing out there, small chance remained of ever capturing the Prize of All the Oceans.

Angrily, the Commodore snapped shut his telescope's lens shield and shouted down, "Those are not the *Centurion's* boats; they're proas! Everyone get into the woods!"

Mordaunt Cratcherode commented a bit caustically, "Those boats are sure to have been sent from Guam to discover what's happened to the meat-hunters' bark."

Taut with apprehension, *Centurion's* survivors watched two sailing canoes come speeding inshore until, just outside the harbor's entrance, they lowered and furled triangular brown sails. Then their crews got out paddles and started for the landing place but, for some reason, the visitors soon quit paddling and allowed their long, low and rakish craft to float motionless, faithfully reflected by the harbor's turquoise surface.

For over two hours the lurking English and Negroes peered through the underbrush until, without betraying what had aroused their suspicions, the visitors suddenly upped sail and sped away on a southerly course — towards Guam!

"Now that," laughed Purser's Assistant Waxter, "really throws the fat in the fire! Those proas will speed back to Guam and give the alarm."

"And then, God 'elp us!" grunted Bill Buckle. "The Papists will hunt us down like rats!"

With that possibility in mind, previously halfhearted laborers applied themselves so effectively that soon the bark was ready to be hauled out of the water by means of rollers and a crude but effective windlass and then sawed in halves.

The *Nil Desperandum*'s alteration progressed so rapidly that George Anson would have felt truly confident of the future but for the complete lack of charts and navigational instruments. What irked him especially was, that on the morning of the typhoon, he'd lent a fine pocket compass to Peircy Brett.

Midshipman Francis Drake ran to the Commodore's tent, panting, "Sir! Sir! I've found it!"

"Found what?" smiled Anson — formality again was in abeyance. "A bar of gold?"

"No, sir, something better than that, I believe, sir. Whilst I was working on the bark I just now found this in her bilge!" He held out a small compass, crude and no larger than a toy, but its needle, nonetheless, seemed to point steadily northwards.

"You are entirely correct, Mr. Drake. What you've brought me *is* more precious to us than many bars of gold!"

Later that same day, Ted Waxter, while rummaging a pile of rubbish emptied onto the beach in hopes of coming across some "unconsidered trifle" of value, noticed a bit of brass gleaming underwater a few feet out from shore. Investigation proved it to be the frame of an old-fashioned octant which, since his name was engraved upon it, must have belonged to the late Midshipman Haldane.

"All very fine," grunted Lieutenant Scott when the supernumerary Purser's Mate brought him the instrument, "but where are its vanes?"

"Vanes, sir? Are they important?"

"Important? Hell, yes! This instrument's useless without 'em."

"Why is that, sir?" Waxter appeared properly abashed at his ignorance.

"An octant's vanes are two small brass plates, each of which is pierced with a tiny hole through which a sight is taken. As I've said, without such, this instrument's of no use at all."

The redesigned vessel commenced to take shape when roughly finished planks were pegged into place with hardwood treenails in place of nonexistent iron spikes, then tallow and frayed cable fibers were payed into the seams for caulking.

Will Pallister, thin as a rail and still pinched about the mouth, was wandering along the shore of a pretty little cove when he noticed a broken-legged table floating upside down. He hobbled down to the water and deliberated a long moment on whether he should draw on his slender store of strength sufficiently to pull the table out.

Curiosity won. The purser's mate noticed a drawer and when he succeeded in worrying it free he found, to his disappointment, it contained only a mass of pulpy papers; most of this seemed to be letters addressed by the late Midshipman Haldane to his family and friends.

Poor Haldane! The intended recipients of these missives wouldn't learn for quite a while that his body, like that of Shakespeare's hero, lay "full fathom five" and that eventually his bones would be of "corals made."

The drawer also contained odds and ends of writing material, a blackened stub of sealing wax, a rusty penknife, a lead ink bottle and even a few bedraggled quills.

In exploring the drawer — it would not come out all the way — Pallister's fingertips encountered two hard, flat objects which he recognized to be the missing vanes of Haldane's octant.

Almost lovingly, Captain Saunders, into whose freckled brown hands Pallister passed the treasure trove, caressed the vanes before slipping them into place and sighting at the sun.

"It will serve," he chuckled. "By God, the Commodore will go daft with pleasure!"

Exactly two weeks after *Centurion* had been driven out to sea, the bark lay on rude stocks, lengthened and re-decked; her masts, freshly scraped and oiled, lay ready to be stepped and crossed with a set of sturdy yards. In the shade of a clump of cabbage palms a party of riggers sang bawdy ballads while knotting shrouds destined to support the *Nil Desperandum*'s masts.

On October 12th work was proceeding as usual when one of *Gloucester*'s men, hunting goats on high ground, spied something which sent him leaping downhill until he blundered into a party of coconut gatherers led by Marine Lieutenant Gordon.

"What is it, man? You look like you've seen a ghost."

"M-Maybe I have, sir, or else *I've seen the ship!*"

"The *Centurion?*"

"As God's my judge, I believe so, sir!"

Gordon wheeled, bounded down to the beach yelling, "The ship! The ship!" at the top of his lungs.

Purple-faced, he dashed up to the Commodore, who was planing a crosstree. "Sir! Sir! The flagship's in sight!"

Deliberately, Anson set down his plane, demanded, "Where away, Mr. Gordon?"

The Marine could only gasp, "— Haven't sighted her myself, sir, so I don't know where. But I know she's been reported."

Although everyone else pelted up the nearest height, George Anson forced himself to ascend to the crow's-nest in calm dignity — for all his heart was thumping like some of the Indian drums he'd once heard beating among the swamps behind Charles Town, South Carolina.

"If this is indeed so, dear God, I thank Thee in the name of my poor followers," he whispered.

Centurion, when she came into sight, was wearing no top canvas whatever, only jibs and courses, so her progress towards her former anchorage was painfully deliberate.

All at once George Anson gave way to emotion, something which he'd never before done publicly. Snatching off his weather-beaten hat, he swung it on high. "Come, lads, I want three rousing cheers for His Majesty, then three more for Mr. Saumarez and his valiant crew!"

~ 9 ~
The Lost Day

STILL LEAKING BADLY, with her paint and gold-work dimmed and flaked, with her lion figurehead canting to one side, HBMS *Centurion* sailed away from the beautiful island called Tinian on the 21st of October, 1742.

The Spanish sergeant-major and his Chamorros paid the departing Fourth Rate no heed, only scowled on smoldering remains of that bark upon which the English had wasted so much labor and ingenuity. What would the Governor of Guam say, and do, about its loss?

George Anson enjoyed a rare sense of elation when, with the trade wind driving her steadily along, his flagship pointed her bowsprit towards the coast of China, 1500 long miles away. If only her rigging were not so gray and weathered, her thin canvas so patched, her masts and hull so badly strained, he would have felt like singing.

Sighing, he turned his attention to Midshipman Francis Drake, who was about to heave the log, a triangular wooden frame weighted on two of its corners in order that the third might float with its top level to the surface. At each angle of the log ship a hole was drilled, through which a length of cod line could be passed and secured. Two of these were lashed to the log ship itself, but the third was attached to an ivory peg — which could not swell and therefore fail to come free.

The ends of all three cod lines were joined and spliced into the end of a long, light rope called the "log line" which was wound on a wooden reel that revolved about an axle supported at either end by the reel man's hands.

Once the log ship had been heaved over the stern it would lie where it had fallen with its weighted corners down; meanwhile the reel would spin free, paying out the log line as the ship sailed on.

A heavily freckled ship's boy stood ready holding a small hourglass designed to empty itself in exactly twenty-eight seconds.

"Get ready!" ordered Mr. Midshipman Drake in a gruff voice intended to disguise its immaturity.

By its handles a tall, squint-eyed Negro raised his reel to shoulder height. Drake then stripped off the log line till he came to a "stay mark" which told him that the line was long enough to clear *Centurion's* rudder and stern galleries.

"Get ready," barked Drake then, with a practiced heave, sent the log ship flying. The instant the stay mark of dark blue worsted had flashed over the rail Drake barked, "Turn!" whereupon the freckled boy reversed his hourglass and watched the flow of sand through it as if his life were at stake. When, at the end of twenty-eight seconds, the last grain had dropped through the neck the time-boy shrilled, "Stop!"

The Negro then applied a brake to his reel which stopped it and so pulled free the log-ship's ivory peg and allowed it to skip horizontally along in the flagship's wake.

In silent amusement, Anson watched Midshipman Drake, lips pursed in concentration, commence to count the number of knots — actually bits of cod line woven into the log line — which had flashed over the stern before the reel had been stopped.

Drake then approached Lieutenant van Keppel, Officer of the Watch, and, forgetting that he was now a commissioned officer, winked. "Five knots, sir!"

"Damn your impertinence, Mr. Drake! Report properly and let

me have no more of your childish nonsense." This afforded the Commodore considerable amusement; Francis Drake was several years the elder of the two.

Stiffly, Lieutenant van Keppel stalked over to a slate set into the taffrail, stooped and chalked on it the hour and a large figure 5.

Even the most pessimistic agreed that, at long last, Captain Arnand's malevolence seemed to have spent itself when HBMS *Centurion* continued to speed along her course despite that heavy growth of weeds and barnacles which had formed upon her bottom since her rough and ready careening at Chequetan.

The sun continued to shine and there remained plenty of good water, fresh fruit and smoked meat for the messes, which also enjoyed a variety of fish caught by men off-duty. As a further good omen, porpoises, dolphins and flying fish continued to disport themselves about the lonely Fourth Rate.

Because the Commodore made no mention of seeking the Manila Galleon it gradually became assumed by the ship's company that he must be satisfied with the considerable treasure already stowed below and would linger in China only long enough to refit for the voyage home.

"That's what he'll do!" boomed John Hughes, formerly of *Tryall's Prize*. "He's got sense, and is content with what we've won."

"Surely he is," agreed Matthew Mitchell. "Besides, he knows that, with his ship not even half manned, it would be the sheerest folly to attack a larger vessel crammed with well-trained men of the Spanish Regular Navy."

Said Tom Ramster, now entirely recovered and unmarked except for the dull red scar running across his chin, "Now that we've got a fine, fat bird safe in our larder, why risk losing it by chasing another which mayn't even let itself get took?"

As, under an effulgent moon, *Centurion* neared the coast of China, George Anson, for the first time in months, sought his stern walk and put together his flute.

Phweet-phweet! Phloo.

What conditions will I find in China, which the older men still call "Cathay"? What sort of life do its inhabitants lead? What can be their notion of law, decency and good music? Some stupid people claim that the Chinese are really half monkeys whose tails grow out of their heads instead out of their rumps. Wish I'd talked longer with the

East India Company's officers I've met. I'd know better how to approach their officials.

Hum. By appearing so weak it won't be easy to command respect. I've no squadron, only the half-wreck of a man-of-war. How can I, under such conditions, hope to impress the Celestials and uphold His Majesty's dignity and puissance? Too bad that neither Drake nor Dampier even mention China in their journals. They might spare me mistakes in policy.

Phfwee, faloo — phootle.

Too bad Matt Mitchell's become only a supernumerary; he deserves so much more. Charles Saunders, too, is without a ship.

Ought I to send them home? War with France is bound to break out again — and soon. Possibly it's already begun. Once they're back in England they'll each be given a ship of their own again, always provided the Admiralty heeds the dispatches I'll write the moment we reach Macao.

Given opportunity, they both ought to go far. So ought Brett, Saumarez, Denis, Keppel and those promising youngsters, Campbell, Drake, Parker and Tom Saumarez. Nathaniel Wade, too, ought to be given a chance. Yes. Think I'll appoint him a midshipman before long.

The night was so fine that Peircy Brett and certain other officers felt moved to add half forgotten details to the personal logs they were required to keep. Chaplain Richard Walter and Schoolmaster Pascoe Thomas worked especially hard on journals they proposed to rush into print the moment they reached home.

As for Will Pallister, he felt so restored he got out water colors and took to sketching bright and weird-looking fish caught by men fishing from *Centurion*'s beak. Often the catch was wondrously beautiful, but it grieved Will no little to see the glorious colors fade on a dying dolphin.

Nobody could quite credit the fact that, only twelve days after quitting Tinian, a dim blue streak was sighted in this boundless and eternally empty ocean.

When, grinning widely, Tom de Saumarez hurried up to report, Anson characteristically accepted the good news without change of expression, but Andrew Menzies could not keep from observing, "Well, sir, it seems that you have plotted the correct course."

" 'Even a broken clock is right twice a day,' as the French say. I wonder, Andrew, what is going to happen to us in China? I really do."

On the morrow, the southern end of a great island was sighted which Sailing Master Nutt tentatively identified.

"It is called 'Formosa' by the Portuguese and 'Taiwan' by its inhabitants," said he.

On the forecastle, the Commodore and his sailing master watched leadsmen heave steadily from the forechains, once soundings revealed that, beyond a doubt, *Centurion* was entering shallower waters.

Soon a long, harsh-appearing coastline materialized, then thousands of gulls, terns and cormorants appeared to circle curiously about the solitary man-of-war.

Everyone's spirits soared to the highest pitch since the capture of Payta. Concertina and fiddle music resounded from the 'tween deck and on the forecastle voices could be heard bawling out "Betty Martin," "Spanish Ladies" and much less circumspect ballads.

When Officer of the Deck de Saumarez discovered a hornpipe in progress outside the gallery he turned a resolutely blind eye and felt so lighthearted he wished he dared to join in.

In the wardroom toasts were offered in honor of every conceivable subject. Even Andrew Menzies for once got a little drunk and brought out his violin and played so vigorously that Captain Saunders executed an Irish jig.

After rounding the southern tip of Formosa, *Centurion* continued on her southwesterly course until, just as a huge full moon arose, so many small and rocky islands loomed into sight as to shatter Mr. Nutt's peace of mind. He ordered all lookouts doubled; then, when the risk of running onto a shoal or some submerged reef became too great, he ordered in all sail and caused the sheet anchor to be dropped, which was the only one left.

It was as well that Mr. Nutt had taken such precautions, for with the coming of daylight, a strange sight greeted the Watch on Deck. As if by magic, dawn revealed hundreds of weird-looking fishing boats nearby. All were propelled by brown or black bat-winged sails, had absurdly high poops and showed great human eyes painted on both sides of their prows.

Since none of this amazing flotilla had displayed night lights of any description, some of them must have been run down had *Centurion* been kept under way.

The Watch Below rushed to the nearest gunport and gawped excitedly at swarms of half-naked, yellow-skinned men working about these gaily painted fishing junks.

Presently *Centurion,* proceeding once more under gallants and topsails, passed within hailing distance of a sizable junk.

"Oi, there!" bellowed Paddy Kildare. "Got any wimmen along? I'll trade ye a fine Spanish comb for a little tumble with anything in skirts."

"Hell, I don't spy no wimmen nowheres."

"Ah-h! Look again. They *have* got cunnies aboard, but they're all wearing pantaloons."

"Yer crazy!"

"Like hell! Don't yer see that wench nursing her brat by the main hatch?"

The fishermen who, without exception, wore shallow, conical straw hats, paid the man-of-war not the least attention, even when she narrowly missed several craft while picking a course through this veritable floating city. It seemed as if this great foreign vessel, for them, simply did not exist.

To Anson and his officers this proved more than a little disconcerting. "One begins to wonder," remarked the Commodore, "whether they are not under orders to ignore foreign ships."

All the same, his need of a pilot was so pressing that Anson invited his officers to keep on hailing in English, French, Spanish, Portuguese and even in Latin. Foreign crew members then attempted various native dialects, but to no effect. Even when silver ornaments, lengths of rich brocade and bags of coins were held up, the fishermen ignored such usually effective temptation and went on fishing.

Grown hoarse, Saunders drew a gourd dipperful of water from the quarterdeck's scuttle butt and observed to Peircy Brett, "The Commodore's right; these people *must* have orders to ignore us."

"It would seem so. What a strange people; they appear neither hostile nor friendly, not even curious. I'm beginning to wonder how we're going to deal with them — and God knows we must!"

Cautiously, *Centurion* groped her way through a network of reefs and rocky, almost barren islands with her afterguard dreadfully anxious and on the *qui vive.*

At last, on November 8th, the ocean turned an opaque yellow-gray which Mr. Nutt felt sure indicated that the flagship was entering the estuary of some great river.

He said he hoped it would prove to be the one upon which lay the famed City of Canton, but he would make no promises, his always unreliable charts being now quite useless.

When a leadsman announced a depth of eighteen fathoms and details of the shore had become recognizable, Anson ordered the sails furled and the anchor dropped.

"And where do you think we lie, Mr. Nutt?"

"With any luck, sir, we are lying in the mouth of the Pearl River, about twenty-five miles north of a Portuguese settlement called Macao, which colony is situated, according to East India Company reports, some seventy miles downstream from Canton."

Since darkness was falling there was nothing to do save post extra guards and to remain at anchor.

"I don't like this at all," Second Lieutenant Brett said, pointing to a dozen or more junks which, considerably larger than the fishing boats, were seen to be hovering upstream. "Some of them mount cannon. Wonder if the beggars mean to close in and try to rush us during the night?"

"They might at that, sir," agreed Denis, new Officer of the Deck. "I'll have boarding nets rigged and see that all swivels are readied and the light guns charged with grape."

"Very good. Instruct all gun captains to keep lighted matches handy. I'm going below now, but call me if those junks come any closer."

Peircy Brett was entering the day's events in his personal logbook when Senior Midshipman Campbell knocked. "Sir-r, I ha'e just completed today's entry in my journal. May I make bold to draw yer-r attention tae a curious fact — which ye may well have already noticed," he added tactfully.

Brett's wide, rule-straight mouth relaxed slightly. "What fact, Mr. Campbell?" Increasingly, he had come to admire this dependable, slow-spoken Scot.

"Sir, 'tis ainly that, since leaving the Americas, we've lost eighteen hours or more, so —"

"— So what?"

"Today is really tomorrow. In ither wur-rds, instead of tomorrow being Saturday, the fifteenth, 'tis in fact Sunday, the sixteenth."

"That's an astute observation, Mr. Campbell, which I believe has escaped most of us. Please be so kind as to pass your sad news among the officers; tell them that they've lost a whole day out of their lives."

Chuckling, he dipped his quill. "Which to my mind is a damn' sight better than having lost them altogether. Eh, Mr. Campbell?"

To George Anson's surprise and relief, the next morning a junk showing a bright yellow flag marked with a solid black circle came sailing alongside. A scrawny Chinese, whose wispy gray beard fluttered in the wind, leaned over the rail to hail in Portuguese and inquire whether a pilot's services were required.

Although the Commodore later realized that he'd made a mistake to employ the fellow without dickering, he hired him for a fee of thirty Spanish dollars.

Presently, the pilot appeared in the gangway wearing a coat of faded blue quilted cotton which was so long that its ragged hem brushed the vamps of thick-soled felt slippers.

Briefly, Captain Arnand's ghost returned and so persecuted the flagship with contrary currents and headwinds that four days passed before, on November 12th, *Centurion* at last dropped anchor in the roadstead of Macao.

∼ 1 0 ∼
Macao Roads

ON THE FORECASTLE, Purser's Assistant Waxter abandoned his faintly bored expression as Midshipman Nathaniel Wade, recently confirmed in that rating to replace the unfortunate John Haldane, drew near. Through the latter's telescope they scanned *Centurion*'s surroundings and beheld a succession of jagged, gray-green hills descending from the mainland to form a peninsula on the tip of which the small but thriving settlement of Macao was situated.

Wade lowered Haldane's spyglass. "Quite a sight, eh? I must say it lends me a thrill to see European flags flying once more. Tell me, to what country would that blue one bearing the yellow cross belong?"

"Sweden," Waxter replied. "That tall Indiaman beyond the Swede is flying the red and white ensign of Denmark. Further inshore I think to recognize Portuguese, English, Dutch and French flags, but I can't be sure till the wind straightens 'em out."

"Why so grim of expression?" queried the new midshipman.

"I was just wondering whether or not our fatuous Prime Minister has got us into war with the French yet."

Before Wade could venture an opinion, a small fishing sampan sailed by so close the two could see on its poopdeck a black-haired woman weaving a fish trap out of rattan while steering by means of bare toes hooked over the tiller's handle. Several fat and stark naked yellow-brown children were romping about the deck while their elders mended nets.

In the sampan's waist another young woman squatted beside a sand-box fireplace busy cooking. She went bare down to her blue cotton trousers and wore her hair braided into a thick blue-black queue.

Waxter caressed his chin with a delicate finger.

"Now *there,* my lad, is what I stand in grave need of. Damme, it's so long since I've bedded a wench I've near forgotten how they're constructed."

"Aye. I'm in even worse case," muttered Midshipman Wade as his thoughts flashed back to the Sheaf of Wheat and to the bride from whom he'd been dragged. Um. What would Peggy look like nowadays? Would she still be slim and pretty? Could he possibly have got her with child during their all too brief intercourse? It was possible, he concluded, but hardly probable.

Most likely Peggy long since had forgotten him as, in truth, he'd all but forgotten about her. How disconcerting to realize that he no longer was able to visualize Peggy with any degree of accuracy. Most likely she'd have married again, if she hadn't taken to whoring — she'd been such a passionate, full-blooded creature.

From the 'tween decks crude invitations were shouted at a flotilla of bumboats which, bearing fruit and more exotic cargoes, began to swarm about the man-of-war. The boatswain and his mates with colts and canes soon silenced these comments.

As Anson had anticipated, it was proving no easy matter to restore normal discipline after having shared so many perils and sufferings. To run a taut ship once more was going to be extra difficult because of the foreigners in his crew; yet, cost what it might in floggings, gagging, fines and lesser punishments, *Centurion* again would be run in accordance with the Admiralty's rules and regulations.

The hands had been piped to their midday meal when the Officer of the Deck reported that a whaleboat flying an English flag had put out from the *Princess Mary,* a smallish, bluff-bowed East Indiaman anchored closer inshore, and was heading for the flagship.

The squat, florid man in the smallboat's stern had a colorful, bulbous nose and boiled-looking blue eyes. He hailed the man-of-war so

[382]

arrogantly and demanded permission to come aboard that de Saumarez concluded he must be the Indiaman's Captain.

At a nod from de Saumarez, the boatswain piped "the side," whereupon side-boys, awkward through lack of practice, and the Watch on Deck formed a double rank facing inwards. Midshipmen on duty, who happened to be Campbell, Parker and Drake, stiffened as Lieutenant de Saumarez moved over to meet the visitor at the gangway.

All hands obeyed the barked command of "Off hats!" and the boatswain's "Southampton nightingale" twittered a greeting to the visitor when he appeared, puffing and red-faced, at the ladder's head.

After saluting the quarterdeck clumsily enough, the caller looked deliberately about and said a bit pompously, "Damme, sir, if 'tain't fine to see the old flag so far from home."

"Is it indeed, sir?" de Saumarez observed coolly. "— And who are you, may I ask?"

At the lieutenant's acid tone the visitor blinked and lost some of his patronizing manner. "Why, sir, I'm Captain Jacob Slaughter, sir, commanding the East India Company's ship *Princess Mary*, forty guns."

"Indeed? Please to follow me, Captain." Walking stiffly and still outraged that a mere merchant captain could have attempted to assume equality with a naval officer, de Saumarez then led Slaughter up to the quarterdeck where, in pretended preoccupation, the Commodore stood in consultation with Captains Mitchell and Saunders.

After an exchange of courtesies, Anson offered his hand and smiled that warm, ingenuous smile which had gained him so many friends and a measure of influence among his superiors. He further thawed the visitor's resentment of de Saumarez's icy civility by saying, "You are most welcome aboard, Captain Slaughter."

" 'Pon my word, sir," wheezed the corpulent visitor, "when I spied your pendant and a Blue Ensign I could scarce credit my vision." Puff-puff. "Couldn't believe that a real man-of-war" — puff, puff — "and a British one at that, was coming to anchor in China!"

Anson repressed his surprise. "Then it is unusual for European ships-of-war to touch at Macao?"

Captain Slaughter's bloodshot and slightly yellowish blue eyes rounded themselves. "Unusual? Why, damme, sir, don't you know that yours is the *first* European man-of-war ever to appear in Chinese waters?"

[383]

Pleasantly, Anson admitted, "Until now I was not aware of the fact."

"Even the Portuguese authorities are flabbergasted — don't quite know what steps to take. Believe me, sir, your arrival has thrown Macao into a turmoil which I hope will not result in unpleasantness."

"Let us hope not," came the equable reply. "Shall we seek my cabin where we may converse in greater comfort?"

He was pleased that Michael Despeda, with his usual foresight, already had set out a magnificent carafe of gilded silver and had surrounded it with a set of jeweled goblets taken at Payta.

"Pray make yourself comfortable, Captain," Anson was quick to suggest. "And let us dispense with formality." In America he'd learned, as early as possible, to reassure civilian officials that he'd no intention of patronizing them — a tendency he'd found all too prevalent among officers of the Royal Navy.

The Commodore made sure that a generous amount of Spanish brandy should be warming the vicinity of Captain Slaughter's scarlet and green waistcoat before, very casually, he inquired, "What manner of reception can I expect from the Portuguese authorities?"

Slaughter deliberated, twirling his goblet between grimy fingers. "Well, sir, before I attempt to answer that I'd best explain the situation here in Macao. First off, you must understand that this port ain't actually *owned* by the bloody 'Geese.' 'Tis only rented by them from the Chinese on a long lease; therefore the Portuguese Governor in Macao rules only by consent of the Chantuck or Viceroy of Canton; he, in turn, acts in the Emperor's name."

"I must confess ignorance, Captain, but who is the present Emperor of China?"

"Why, sir, they claim he's quite a great man, even for a Chinese. His name is K'ien-Lung."

"K'ien-Lung? My word, what a language!"

"Here, I'll spell it, sir —" Slaughter's sausage-like fingers seemed to engulf a quill passed him by the Commodore's secretary.

"Aye, sir, he's a great soldier is this K'ien-Lung, and a haughty one, too. His armies have conquered vast territories in the north — all the way up to a river called the Amur." A trifle unsteadily the Indiaman's Captain nodded several times. "Only a short while ago his generals defeated the Emperor of Cambodia, then overran his rich empire."

"Cambodia? Where is that?"

"Why, sir, it lies somewhere to the south of here, near Laos and Tongking."

The crew of a big junk which came sailing by must have been celebrating an occasion of importance, for over the water came the incessant roar of gongs, the agonizing, off-key squeals of flutes and pipes accompanied by the shivering clash of cymbals and the boom of drums. Just as the gaudily painted and gilded craft came abreast, *Centurion's* company was startled by musket-like reports.

"She's a war junk, exploding a setting of firecrackers," Slaughter explained. "Shouldn't wonder but her captain is trying to see if he can frighten you into leaving."

Laughing, Anson diverted his attention to watch this high-pooped craft sail by and noted the great almond-shaped eyes painted on her bows. Many curiously decorated cannon protruded from among her brilliantly painted woodwork — all of small caliber, Anson was relieved to note.

From the top of the war junk's three masts writhed dragon-shaped pendants which, fashioned of scarlet and black silk stretched over light bamboo frames, looked surprisingly fierce and lifelike.

When a series of still louder reports on board the junk argued that firecrackers of larger size were being set off Anson was much amused. "Are such tactics ever effective?"

"Yes, sir," belched Slaughter, "they'd scare pirates and Japanese warships over the horizon."

"Not really!"

"Aye. It'll take you some time to grow accustomed to the Chinese way of thinking. Out here, everything's different from home: food, drink, sports, war" — the Indiaman's Captain grinned suddenly "— but not a woman's private anatomy, no matter what you've heard."

"Ah. Glad to be correctly informed on that point. I had, er — heard rumors to the contrary. Am I mistaken, or have I not observed a great number of dead bodies floating by?"

"You have, sir! Look out of your stern windows a while and you'll count plenty of corpses — the most of 'em girl babies on their way to feed sharks off the Bogue — called the 'Bocca Tigris' or 'Tiger's Mouth' by us Europeans. Otherwise, it's the main entrance to the Pearl River."

"You just now said 'girl babies' not just 'babies.' Why?"

Before making reply, Captain Slaughter treated himself to another swig of brandy then smacked his lips and sighed enjoyment. "You see,

[385]

sir, the heathens don't set much value on human life under any conditions, but girl babies are considered worthless since they can never perform heavy labor and have to be fed just as much as a boy who someday will work harder than any white man. You have no idea, yer Honor, how very poor most Chinese are; trouble is, there's too many of 'em."

Anson summoned Despeda and ordered pipes and tobacco before reminding his guest, "You were about to inform me concerning the government of Macao?"

"Well, sir, like I said, the Portuguese *Gobernador* is hardly more than a figurehead; the real power in Macao lies with the Hoppo, or *Hupu* in the heathen's tongue. This Hoppo, in fact, is an Imperial Chief Customs Officer who obeys the Viceroy and high mandarins in Canton."

" 'Mandarins?' " Anson squared broad shoulders which seemed ready to burst the seams of an overly snug Spanish coat of green and gold, pursed his lips, then sent a great cloud of pipe smoke whirling across the cabin. "Mandarins? What are mandarins?"

" 'Tis a word derived from the 'Geese.' With them *mandar* is to command, hence Chinese officials of exalted rank are called *'mandarinos'* by them, 'mandarins' by the rest of us Europeans."

"I see. What is the nature of the defenses maintained by the Portuguese?"

"They have garrisons in two of the forts commanding Macao Harbor; each of them mounts about one hundred guns. But they're nothing to fear; most of 'em are so old and ill cared for I doubt if the half of them could be fired to any effect."

Captain Slaughter paused, scratched at a flea busy under his waistcoat. "Sir, I expect you ought to know straightaway that the Emperor hates all foreigners or 'foreign devils' as he terms us. He only tolerates us because he has to have certain items of our trade — chiefly munitions of war.

"Macao and Canton are the only ports allowed to receive foreign ships and merchants. Attempt to do business elsewhere, and you'll find your vessel seized and yourself shorter by a head." Slaughter hiccoughed while Despeda was refilling his goblet. "Take care never to get wrecked or castaway on the coast of China — means the end for all hands."

"An intolerable state of affairs," Anson commented.

"Yes. They're a tricky lot, these heathen; one never can count on

[386]

what they'll do. Glad I'm not standing in your shoes; you're in for a hard time, I fear."

"Why so optimistic, Captain?"

"Because, as I've already said, yours is the first European man-of-war ever to visit Cathay. I fear the Emperor will be far from pleased to learn that a foreign devil warship has appeared in his territorial waters."

Said the Commodore briskly, "I don't propose to worry until hostile action is taken. I shall then adopt appropriate measures. Captain, pray inform me as to what steps I should take in order to secure provisions and obtain permission to heave down my ship. Also I need to purchase bar iron, anchors, canvas and cordage."

Jacob Slaughter's plump hand crept up to fondle a shiny double chin covered with blond bristles. "Were I in your place, sir, I'd do my best to win over the *Gobernador*. He'll be the only person able to persuade the Hoppo to allow you to heave down and replenish your stores."

Anson wondered whether there was not a certain uneasiness in his guest's tone. "Granting that the Hoppo will prove amenable, what should be my next step?"

Captain Slaughter glanced hopefully into his empty goblet and was rewarded by having it refilled. "You should request his *chop*, or official signature, granting permission for you to sail up the Pearl to as near Canton as possible."

"Possible? What do you mean by that?"

"Why, your Honor, foreign ships are never allowed closer to Canton than Whampoa, which lies three miles below the city. There are four English Indiamen there now."

"Thank you, Captain. I presume we have a consul in Macao? I should like to fire a salute in the King's name."

"Consul!" Slaughter threw back his blunt head and laughed until tears started slipping over his cheeks. "Consul? Ho! Ho! His Majesty ain't got a consulate nearer than Batavia!"

For the first time Commodore Anson permitted himself to appear stiff. "I see small humor in a fact which may complicate matters for me."

"It will, sir — and more than you now realize. For one thing, the Hoppo will demand payment of port dues."

"*What!*" Anson's blue eyes flashed. "A regular man-of-war expected to pay port dues? Who ever heard of such nonsense?"

"You'll be told to pay — and none too politely, either."

"In that case the Hoppo is in for a disappointment. I refuse to break a convention respected for centuries by all civilized Powers."

"You may be offered no choice," Captain Slaughter predicted suddenly serious. "Well, I must be on my way." The *Princess Mary*'s Captain heaved his bulk onto white-stockinged legs thick as a pinnace's mainmast. "Were I you, sir, I'd waste no time in approaching the *Gobernador*; I suspect the unprecedented arrival of a foreign man-of-war already has presented serious problems for him."

Slaughter bowed ponderously. "May I thank you, sir, for this most cordial reception. The brandy was excellent. If I can be of service, pray don't hesitate to make me a signal."

On his way to the great cabin's door Captain Slaughter paused. "Oh, by the bye, somewhere I've heard that the *Augusta,* one of our ships which lies upriver, has mail and dispatches for you."

〜 I I 〜

Deputations

As USUAL, Commodore George Anson took immediate action. Philip de Saumarez, dressed in his glittering best, was sent into Macao with a Blue Ensign snapping bravely from his barge's stern staff.

The first lieutenant's lively black eyes scrutinized an odd assortment of craft occupying the harbor proper and soon recognized the flags of no less than eight European Powers.

On its way inshore *Centurion*'s barge passed several sampans laden with melons on their way out to the flagship to join bumboats already clustering about her.

De Saumarez, after resetting a heavy tricorne edged in mildewed scarlet ostrich plumes, fell to considering his responsibilities. So I'm to present the Commodore's most distinguished compliments and ascertain, without seeming to, what honors will be accorded a man-of-war in His Majesty's service. Um. I'm also supposed, tactfully, of course, to feel out the Portuguese Governor's attitude regarding a demand for the payment of port dues and estimate our chances of obtaining a *chop* which will permit us to refit at Canton.

Coxswain Parmer, still rail-thin from that second bout with scurvy which had robbed him of most of his teeth, found it difficult to keep his oarsmen from gawping at the strange sights all about.

"*Will* you keep yer blasted deadlights in the boat!" he snapped. "B'God, d'you want the 'Geese' and the heathens should take us for a pack of merchantmen?"

When Parmer's warning proved ineffective, Lieutenant de Saumarez warned in a softly dangerous tone, "The next man misses the beat will suffer two dozen lashes when we return to the ship!"

Philip de Saumarez felt a trifle encouraged to see the green and red flag of friendly Portugal fluttering above two great, brownstone forts occupying strategic heights.

While his barge was threshing up to a set of slimy water-steps he became aware that Macao differed from any port he had ever visited. For one thing, it reeked of strange odors, and then one received impressions of vast antiquity, of weird architecture, of strange writing on the warehouses, and of teeming humanity clad in outlandish garments.

Centurion's first lieutenant returned at nightfall accompanied by a pair of animated Portuguese officials who commanded a droll smattering of English. Like the majority of their compatriots these visitors were dark-complexioned and wore gaudy but beautifully tailored uniforms.

Although instinct warned that neither visitor was sufficiently high ranking to rate a formal reception, Anson deemed it expedient to order them piped aboard in style. Having digested Captain Slaughter's comments about the importance of appearances, he had, as soon as his barge was reported, donned a wine-red satin frock coat and bottle-green pantaloons. Further, he allowed Despeda to knot a fresh grosgrain ribbon about his unruly hair, which certainly needed the attention of a competent *friseur*.

Bows offered by the two Portuguese were profound enough to be somewhat reassuring; it would seem that they had been impressed by the temerity of this straight-backed English *Comodoro*.

Declared the elder of the two Portuguese, "His Most Illustrious Excellency Dom Luis da Carvalho extends to the *Comodoro* from England his most ultimate, distinguished compliments."

Anson smiled cautiously. "I trust you will be good enough, upon your return, to convey my deep respects to His Excellency."

[389]

He glanced in de Saumarez's direction and elevated one brow a quizzical fraction of an inch.

"Sir, His Excellency received me most courteously," the lieutenant reported. "He declares himself ready to present you to the Hoppo in a most favorable light."

The older official, who affected a dagger-sharp beard and spike sharp mustachios, again bowed profoundly. "This is no less than the truth, *Senhor Comodoro*. You are most welcome in Macao.

"Dom Luis suggests that, following a courtesy visit to the town, your ship should then proceed to our dockyard on the Island of Taypa where there are facilities to accomplish even the most difficult of repairs."

A row of dazzling teeth glistened beneath the visitor's bayonet-like mustachios. "Tomorrow morning a dependable *piloto* will be sent to guide you in to the shipyard. By repairing your vessel in Portuguese waters the question of paying port dues will not arise."

With this some of George Anson's inner tensions relaxed until Experience warned that fortune so swiftly arrived at would likely prove too good to be true.

"Please convey my sincere thanks to the Governor, sir."

De Saumarez stepped forward. "Further, sir, the Portuguese Governor indicated he will be pleased to return a salute to his flag and will receive you at his palace."

Although he didn't immediately say so, it occurred to Andrew Menzies, standing somber and unnoticed in the background, that this unexpected cooperation just might be a ruse to lure the obstreperous man-of-war into a trap. Um. The Viceroy of the Philippines and his agents in Macao must long since have learned about the squadron's depredations along the South American coast. In that case, would not the idea of seizing, under one pretext or another, the far from inconsiderable treasure carried in *Centurion* have entered Portuguese minds?

The more Andrew Menzies reflected along this line, the sharper grew his misgivings.

1 2

Démarches Diplomatiques

THE MOMENT *Centurion* sailed in from the roadstead, let fly her sheets and dropped anchor off Macao, eleven guns boomed from a fort to the right of the harbor and a green and red Portuguese ensign on its watchtower dipped three times.

"Smartly! By the numbers!" snapped Midshipman Tom De Saumarez in command of the saluting battery. "Number One, fire! Number Three — fire —"

Eleven times the forts' moldy walls reverberated before the reports caromed off to lose themselves among the rugged, gray hills behind Macao. Then the Blue Ensign was dipped thrice.

Once this exchange of amenities had come to an end, *Centurion*'s barge was piped away and, pulled by eighteen of the brawniest and best-looking men in his ship, George Anson set out to call on the Governor.

As a first feeble gesture towards creating a uniform for seamen, the Commodore had ordered his men into black-painted straw hats, white shirts and pantaloons of black or some dark shade of blue. Also they were given red kerchiefs to knot about their throats.

When the barge passed under the counter of a tall Dutch Indiaman Anson, sitting very straight and stiff on his sun-bleached blue canvas cushions, found that she mounted more guns than *Centurion*. For all this armament, the great *Anneke van Edam* remained essentially a merchantman; her bows were bulbous, her beam ample and her sturdy masts much shorter than those commonly found in a man-of-war. Otherwise, the *Anneke* had been generously supplied with ornate gilt carvings at stem and stern; her beautifully carved figurehead represented a club-bearing Titan with staring, sea-blue eyes.

From the rail, her crew yelled down raucous comments in broken English; so did the men in various lofty Portuguese Indiamen.

Governor Dom Luis da Carvalho proved to be wizened and short with a scant gray-white goatee. Obviously, he was suffering from a complicity of diseases. Bald as any billiard ball, he had bony, parchment-hued features and the whites of his eyes were as yellow as lemon peel.

While solemn civilities were being exchanged, Anson kept a hand on the diamond-and-emerald-studded hilt of a sword captured in the *Aranzazu.*

"And now, my friend," the Governor's bloodless lips formed the ghost of a smile, "how may I be of assistance?"

"Your Excellency, the food I took on at Tinian Island is almost exhausted; therefore I must immediately replenish my supply. I do not deem it advisable to draw on my sea stores."

"As a former naval officer, I can appreciate your unwillingness to do so."

"I wish also to make arrangements for careening my ship and for effecting certain repairs." Anson took care to speak casually, as if the repairs were of minor importance; no point in allowing this withered old fellow to suspect how utterly unseaworthy HBMS *Centurion* had become.

The Governor's bony shoulders rose while his liberally beringed fingers drummed on the arms of a gilded chair. "We have heard and have been much impressed, your Honor, by your remarkable feat of rounding Cape Horn in midwinter. As few others, we Portuguese are able to appreciate such a triumph of navigation and seamanship."

"A generous compliment, sir, which I do not deserve," Anson protested, "especially since it comes from the distinguished representative of that nation whose sailors were the first to encircle the globe."

Dom Luis's staff, gathered behind his thronelike seat, smiled broadly and a cordial air pervaded the dimly lit and mildew-smelling audience chamber.

"Now, your Excellency, what will be done about the supplies I have mentioned?"

Dom Luis lifted a frail, blue-veined hand. "*Senhor Comodoro,* we shall deliver all the food you require the moment the Hoppo grants permission for you to receive it."

So what Captain Slaughter had said was all too true! This functionary, however glittering and dignified, possessed no real power and was, in fact, only a pompous puppet activated by the Hoppo and his superiors in suddenly inaccessible Canton.

That de Saumarez and Brett also had sensed Dom Luis's impotence no one would have guessed, so well had Anson trained his subordinates.

"However," the Governor hastened to add, "I shall deem it a privilege to forward an application to the Hoppo in your name." He made a deprecatory gesture. "One happens to be familiar with the procedure — which, unfortunately, is most complicated."

Brett noticed a tinge of color creep out of his chief's wide cheekbones. "I thank your Excellency for your solicitude, however, in representing His Britannic Majesty as I do, I propose to deal *directly* with the Viceroy of Canton and not through intermediaries or underlings."

A horrified expression stiffened Dom Luis's wrinkled features. "*Senhor Comodoro!* You do not understand the Chinese! Such a move is quite unthinkable. No foreigner has ever dared directly to address the Emperor's Viceroy; an attempt to do so would invite immediate disaster."

"I must risk that," Anson declared evenly. "It appears that the difference between the courtesies due a warship, as distinct from a merchantman, have yet to be imparted to the Chinese authorities."

In obvious agitation, the Governor took snuff and sneezed twice before saying quite coldly, "Be that as it may, you must first obtain the Hoppo's *chop* allowing you to enter the Pearl River. Otherwise, forts guarding the entrances will certainly sink your ship."

Anson smiled. "I doubt that, sir; however, to avoid unpleasantness, you may inform the Hoppo I intend to charter a junk large enough to carry myself and certain of my officers up to Canton to confer with the Viceroy. Please tell this Hoppo that he had better not try to prevent me."

The real cause for Dom Luis's agitation now came to the surface. "If you defy the Hoppo you will cause licenses for all foreigners trading with the Empire to be revoked forever."

"That is your concern, sir, and not mine."

None would have suspected the true depth of George Anson's anxiety when, followed by his staff, he unconcernedly took leave of his host and exchanged the audience chamber's cool dimness for the hot sunshine of squalid and very narrow streets.

Sufficiently shrewd to anticipate difficulties with the Chinese authorities, young Lieutenant Denis, during the Commodore's absence, had encouraged a lively trade with bumboats which swarmed about the flagship. When the side was manned in honor of the Commodore's return, the boatswain's pipe was almost drowned out by the cackling and quacking of poultry and even the grunting of pigs.

Denis uncovered, looked apprehensive. "I trust, sir, I've done the

[393]

right thing in buying out every bumboat that's appeared alongside?"

"You have, Mr. Denis, you have. Always strike whilst the iron's hot, especially with regard to love, food and fighting. Pass the word that all victuals offered alongside are to be purchased, regardless of cost."

Denis's gaze followed his superior's broad figure as he swung across the sunlit quarterdeck towards the steerage and the great cabin which lay beyond. Hum. So matters *hadn't* progressed favorably ashore!

Around noon of the next day a launch flying Portuguese colors pulled out to the anchorage. From the quarterdeck Lieutenant van Keppel guessed that a fat officer seated in the stern must be fetching out bad news. He was scowling at the garbage-littered gray water as if smarting under some personal insult.

When received by First Lieutenant de Saumarez, the caller, a small-pox-scarred captain of artillery, stated that when the Hoppo had received the *Gobernador's* request for permission to supply an English warship the said official had replied with curt, contemptuous and final refusal.

De Saumarez managed a wooden smile. "Thank you, *Senhor Capitano,* for your courtesy in reporting this matter. Will you take some wine in the wardroom whilst I inform the Commodore?"

Leaving his guest to be entertained by Lieutenant Colonel Cratcherode and Captain Crowden, the last surviving Invalid, de Saumarez hurried to the great cabin.

"Quite frankly," Anson commented, "I was in expectation of such an action. Mr. Menzies, pray prepare to take a letter."

Once his secretary was ready, Anson commenced to stride quickly back and forth.

" 'To His August Excellency the Hoppo of Macao' — add the usual greetings of course —"

Menzies's pen scratched briefly. When it fell silent Anson resumed, large bright blue eyes intent and narrowed in thought.

"Since your Excellency has seen fit to disallow my perfectly proper request for permission to purchase essential supplies and have also refused to grant permission for me to proceed on a peaceful mission to Canton in a chartered junk, ordinary requests to which the Governor of any civilized Power —"

Menzies held up his free hand. "A moment, sir. May I suggest that such a word as 'civilized' might affront the Hoppo? Shall I substitute 'European Power?' "

"Very well, Andrew.

"— Any European Power would accede without hesitation I regret to inform your Excellency that I propose to proceed to Canton, with or without your consent. Further, I shall arm my smallboats and proceed to Canton where I shall inform the Viceroy, directly, what an incompetent subordinate he has appointed to this important post."

Menzies's pen scratched faster.

"As Commander of a Squadron of His British Majesty's ships-of-war, I wonder who will dare to question this action which has been forced upon me? You are herewith requested to inform the officer who shall present this letter, to reconsider your decisions."

He broke off. "I believe I'll send de Saumarez. After all, he's second-in-command and is best qualified to cope with an affair of such delicacy."

Hands clasped behind back, Anson then stood looking blankly through the stern windows, several panes of which had been knocked out during the longboat's battering at Tinian. At length he turned to confront his secretary.

"Andrew, although I have deliberated certain risks at considerable length, I remain convinced that firmness is what the situation requires. While this letter may not represent a masterpiece of diplomatic correspondence it's high time that the Chinese authorities learn the difference between greedy and spineless merchants and one of His Majesty's ships-of-war."

"I am sure you are correct in your hypothesis, sir," agreed Menzies. "However, I trust that you are not undertaking more than can be safely accomplished. I am confident there's no need to remind you that this ship is a half-wreck and that you have only sixty undermanned guns with which to defy the Emperor of China."

A snorting laugh escaped Anson. " 'Sufficient unto the day is the evil thereof.' Kindly prepare my communication with all dispatch."

While reaching for a sheet of foolscap the Carolinian hesitated. "Sir, might it not be wise to — er — placate this Hoppo person with a few gifts of value?"

"I've already considered such a move, Andrew, but feel that, by so doing, I might establish a precedent which might cause embarrassment to commanders of subsequent vessels of war. It may be all very well for Captains of the various East India Companies to offer bribes, but I deem it unbecoming in the Commander of a King's ship to do so."

To the bewilderment of the Portuguese Colonial authorities and to Anson's unspoken satisfaction, the very boldness of this move was rewarded by the arrival alongside of an official sampan bearing on its stern cushions a moon-faced Chinese official who only gazed in contempt at *Centurion*'s splintered gangway and refused to come on board.

Without interrupting the movements of a peacock feather fan, he ordered a parchment scroll secured with a profusion of red and yellow wax seals passed up to the Officer of the Deck, and then ordered his sampan to shove off.

"By God, sir!" Lieutenant Colonel Cratcherode burst out, bony features peeling more than ever. "Gad, sir, d'you note the impudent sneer on that fellow's greasy yellow face?"

"Yes, he was an impudent swine," agreed somber Captain Mitchell. "I'd like to have seen him approach the *Gloucester* like this. I'd have ordered a ten-pound shot dropped through his bottom."

All the same, the document thus unceremoniously delivered granted permission, under the Hoppo's personal *chop*, for HBMS *Centurion* to purchase fresh supplies, but no sea stores; also, and much more important, the Foreign Admiral was authorized to proceed by junk up the Pearl River to Canton.

"Which is all very well," remarked Captain Mitchell, "but I fear our gallant Commodore is going to find himself being right royally snubbed up there."

To every Englishman aboard the high-sided chartered junk their voyage upriver proved a succession of surprises. First off, the native craft's bat-wing sails of brown-cotton reinforced with fingerlike battens of bamboo, intrigued them; also the balanced rudders, enormously high poops, blunt bows — all slavishly copied from Portuguese caravels of a past age.

The mission sailing, so outwardly confident, under a Royal Jack was headed by the Commodore, Lieutenant de Saumarez and Lieutenant Colonel Cratcherode; the latter had been included largely because of his bristling white mustache and impressive gold and scarlet tunic. Also present were Passed Midshipman Campbell, Midshipman Hyde Parker, Ordinary Midshipman Nathaniel Wade and the crew of *Centurion*'s barge, which was being towed astern.

Curiously, all hands viewed and commented upon a succession of forts, castles and batteries; they found strangely beautiful the many-tiered pagodas and yellow-roofed mansions, many of which looked capacious enough to be deemed palaces. These last, as a rule, were guarded by high walls and turrets.

Along the Pearl's banks lay hundreds of squalid villages, rickety piers and miserable hovels, excrescences upon the gray-green shores.

In almost every backwater the foreigners noticed floating villages composed of sampans and junks huddled under a pall of thin, grayish woodsmoke. Almost everywhere kites formed like serpents, fish, birds and dragons floated about the brazen sky.

Will Pallister, sent along through the good offices of Lieutenant Brett, who had remained in acting command of *Centurion*, filled page after page of his sketchbook with brilliant and not too badly composed impressions. He was working so assiduously that often he had to stop and rinse out his water pot in the Pearl's tea-colored current.

On rounding a bend some three miles below the walls of Canton, those on the chartered junk sighted seven great high-sided vessels of European construction. They were swinging lazily in the current, surrounded by lighters.

"Well, gentlemen," Commodore Anson remarked, "yonder lie our friends the Indiamen. I wonder how many nations are represented?"

De Saumarez informed, "Sir, aside from our own I recognized French, Swedish, Portuguese, Dutch and Danish flags."

"There's a Spaniard among 'em, too," added Cratcherode.

"The biggest ship at the anchorage," de Saumarez remarked after lowering a spyglass, "appears to be the *Augusta*."

"Sir-r-r, is she no' reported tae be carrying mails for us?" anxiously queried Passed Midshipman Campbell.

"She is." The Commander in Chief overheard, smiled. "Mr. Saumarez, pray direct our pilot to steer in the *Augusta*'s direction."

As the junk veered to port, the mission was inordinately pleased to read *Onslow* and *Defence* written across the elaborately ornamented sterns of two other Indiamen.

Surgeon's Mate Peter Vesey, attached as medical officer to the mission, noted that once the chartered junk's Royal Jack had been recognized, a gig put out from a French Indiaman and disappeared upstream at top speed. At almost the same moment a smallboat trailing from a boom at the *Augusta*'s side was manned. Promptly it made for the chartered junk.

[397]

"Ahoy, there!" shouted its coxswain. "You from the HBMS *Centurion?*"

On being informed that this was so, the grubby fellow pointed to a number of fat sacks piled on the smallboat's bottom gratings.

"Stand by to receive mail!" he bellowed, then held up a small, red-sealed bag. "This 'ere's the official pouch."

"Then be more careful with it, you oaf!" snapped de Saumarez and himself supervised the handing over.

Since considerable time must elapse before the junk could tack up to the dim and smoky city upstream, Anson in silence accepted the dispatch bag, then retired below after ordering his midshipmen and warrant officers to start sorting the post.

Soon it became borne in on the sorters how great had been the squadron's loss of life. Four out of five missives, it seemed, were addressed to men whose bones lay somewhere along that tortured route from Spithead to Tinian.

Midshipman Hyde Parker's mouth tightened when he came across a thick packet of letters intended for Midshipman Haldane. How many hearts would break when these were returned unopened?

Despite himself, George Anson's fingers quivered when he broke heavy blue Admiralty seals securing the neck of the official pouch. Would the pleasure of their lordships prove sane, or more inane than usual, or would these softly rustling papers express approval of what he had done? Would he be ordered home, or permitted to carry out his original instructions?

While unknotting a cord of scarlet silk, Anson drew a deep breath.

To the Commander in Chief's vast relief the dispatches contained no significant change in plan or policy; in fact they confirmed his orders to return home by the route originally decided upon. Nothing beyond that. No time limit, nor any warning of imminent hostilities with the French.

On scanning a second dispatch he was further informed concerning the return of *Pearle* and *Severn.* Suddenly George Anson did something rare with him; he commenced to curse fluently and wholeheartedly.

"God damn it! They *can't* have!" But they had. Captain the Honorable George Murray had been given command of a new 50-gun man-of-war, the Fourth Rate *Hampshire.* As for his fellow deserter, Captain the Honorable Edward Legge was soon to command *Strafford,* another 50-gun ship.

[398]

So they never even court-martialed those cowardly swine! Shows what miracles influence can accomplish. What in God's name *is* this Navy coming to?

But of *Wager* there was no mention; she must indeed have gone down with all hands off Cape Noire.

For himself there was little mail. Not that he expected much, being unmarried, of a small family, and with both parents long dead and buried. There was, however, a long, tedious letter from Brother Thomas and several bills from importunate tailors.

But his bronzed features lit on recognizing the precise, carefully formed calligraphy of Elizabeth Yorke. A friend from childhood, Lord Hardwicke's plain but lively daughter said she gloried in his tremendous achievements of bringing a majority of his ships around the tempestuous Horn. What adventures he must have to recount; she felt confident that the Spanish must dread even the sound of his name. What sufferings had he and his poor crews not endured? Had he heard that his great good friend Sir George Brooke had died of a neck broken in the hunting field? Cousin Phyllis had been safely delivered of twin boys, etc., etc., etc. In conclusion Elizabeth begged to remain his true friend and neighbor. And would he please hurry home?

Anson reread the letter — typically neat and precise, just like Betts, as he'd always called her. Would she have changed much since they'd parted in Shugborough? Probably she'd have grown less animated now that, definitely, she had attained spinsterhood and would devote most of her time to good works.

Philip de Saumarez, on the other hand, received a pleasingly plump package of letters, as did Midshipman Hyde Parker, who also was well connected at home.

"Here's one for you —" called out one of the sorters and handed over a letter to Peter Vesey. To his utter astonishment the address was penned in his former wife's handwriting.

Minden; Henley-on-Thames
November 11, 1742

My Dear Peter:

Strange as it may appear to you, you have been greatly in my Thoughts of late and, I may add, in my Prayers as well. First, you must know that I am now a Widow. Sir Paul is Dead. He died of a shooting accident on the Duke of Bedford's moor shortly after he and I had agreed to Separate. Please Believe that I have been harshly and justly punished for my Fearful Behavior toward you.

[399]

Soon after I Married Paul he quickly proved himself to be utterly devoid of True Affection, Honor or of even Common Courtesy. Had he not Perished I most certainly would have Divorced him.

By using a Connection — my Uncle, Sir John Norris — at the Admiralty I was able to Discover that you had shipped —

A bitter twist contorted Vesey's lips. "Shipped," indeed! Briefly, he stared out over the heat-shimmering river down which a war junk, with gongs wildly booming, was attempting to overhaul a fleeing sampan.

— in Commodore Anson's ship, the *Gloucester*. I therefore write, most humbly, to Implore your Forgiveness for the Hideous Wrong I did you. I fear that this Plea will probably fall before Blind Eyes, but nevertheless I feel impelled to throw myself upon the Goodness of your always Generous Heart. You have ever been among the most Compassionate of men, so I pray on bended knee that you have not Changed and will forgive the Wretched Creature you once Loved and who Loved you no less.

Please, Peter, will you not at least send Word that you are Well and do not Hate me as truly as I Deserve? If, on your Return, you feel moved to look in upon our Old Home you will discover Everything restored almost as it was before that Awful Night. I have put your Study in order, hung your Cloathes to our Wardrobe and keep your Miniature ever close to my Heart.

Please credit that I am as Truly Penitent as any Human being could be and do again Earnestly Beseech your Forgiveness.

Your Distracted Former Wife,
PAMELA

For many minutes Vesey brooded, then sighed and slowly folded the letter away.

When at last the vast, strange-appearing port of Canton hove into sight a blood-red sun was swinging low and staining rose-red a stratum of smoky haze drifting above tall battlements, watchtowers and innumerable tiered pagodas. A faint breeze beating downstream brought a host of unfamiliar odors — most of them sour and reeking of age and decay.

A half-caste interpreter pointed to a vast structure, the yellow roofs of which were glowing in the sunset like molten gold. "Over there, sir, lies the palace of the Chantuck, or Viceroy, as you term him. Does your Honor recognize the Imperial banner above it?"

"No. Which is it?"

"It is the one, sir, which is shaped like a long yellow triangle with scalloped edges — on it a black dragon is swallowing a scarlet sun."

"And where do the East India Company people transact their business?" queried the Commodore.

"The foreign factories — which are also called *hongs* — are located further upstream and are so placed that foreign devil ships must pass under the guns of forts which you will soon be able to see."

"And who is the principal English merchant?"

"A Mr. Shepherd, sir. He is a factor who has lived here for almost twenty years."

"He's to be trusted?"

Several times the interpreter ducked his narrow, brass-tinted head. "Oh, yes, sir. Certainly, sir. Mr. Shepherd will give you excellent advice regarding the formalities which must be observed in order to obtain an audience with His Exalted Highness, the Viceroy."

~~ 13 ~~
A Touch of Machiavelli

AFTER CONSULTING MR. SHEPHERD, a large, deceptively straightforward individual, and other factors administering the British *hong*, which turned out to be a capacious compound complete with offices, living quarters for the officers, and docks and godowns, or warehouses, Anson succeeded in composing a letter to the Chantuck. In it he politely, but not subserviently, requested an interview and permission to move his flagship upstream, at least as far as Whampoa, where the Indiamen had been seen at anchor.

Smoothly, Mr. Shepherd's native secretary then translated into ideographs the British Commodore's further request for a permit to careen, thoroughly repair and refit HBMS *Centurion*. In conclusion Anson said, as tactfully as he might, that he assumed he would not be asked to pay harbor dues; his was a regular ship-of-war and not an East Indiaman, which, for all the guns they mounted, could only be considered merchantmen.

Mr. Shepherd frowned a little over this, but ended by saying, genially enough, "Now, sir, all that remains to be done now is to forward your letter to Mr. Li Ho-tsung."

"And who might he be?" the Commodore demanded brusquely. He hadn't missed that fleeting frown of Shepherd's.

"Mr. Tsung, sir, is one of the cleverest and richest merchants in Canton. Still more important is the fact that my friend enjoys excellent relations with certain mandarins important at the Viceregal court. He can be trusted to channel your communication through to the proper officials."

"Why cannot my letter be presented directly into the Viceroy's own hands? To beat about the bush, as you propose, seems beneath the dignity of an officer of His Majesty's Navy."

Mr. Shepherd raised hands in delicate dismay. "Please believe, my dear Commodore, that these Celestials are a curiously devious folk. The course I have outlined is the *only one* likely to ensure the success of your mission. Please trust me. Mr. Tsung and I know the ropes so well that we've accomplished the seemingly impossible time and again; any of our colleagues will tell you so."

Members of Anson's party were more than a little disconcerted on being informed that no European might quit the Foreign Concessions without carrying a special *chop* from a certain mandarin.

For widely divergent reasons this restriction fell particularly hard on Cratcherode and Will Pallister: the former because now he'd be allowed no opportunity of locating the city's defenses and of estimating their strength; the latter because he would be denied the privilege of studying and painting colorful aspects of this great port.

So, in mounting disgust, Anson's mission was forced, day after stiflingly hot day, to idle behind high walls enclosing the British compound. There was nothing more exciting to do than sleep, eat and watch activities aboard the jumble of shipping tied up to the shore or lying out on the Pearl.

Whenever the fretting Commodore questioned Li Ho-tsung — he who had undertaken to deliver his letter — that Buddha-faced worthy remained bland and pleasant, but also most skillfully evasive.

At the end of three boring weeks even George Anson's monumental patience wore thin. Lieutenant de Saumarez thought he had never beheld his chief in such a frozen rage as when, unannounced, they stalked into Mr. Shepherd's noisy office.

"Sir, I have had more than enough of this shilly-shally. I now intend to confront that trickster who promised to deliver my letter. Be good enough, sir, to secure three sedan chairs and permission for us to quit this compound."

When confronted by three thoroughly angry British officers, Anson, de Saumarez, and Cratcherode, the inscrutable Mr. Li Ho-tsung, clad in a long shimmering gown of turquoise buttoned with pearls, looked pained. He sighed profoundly, then reached into his desk and, to Anson's furious astonishment, brought out his letter to the Viceroy!

Said he, bowing over hands clasped above his belly, "Honorable sir. All this time your most unworthy servant has been attempting to discover sufficient courage to present your petition to His Highness the Viceroy. Alas, that this miserable worm must confess himself still unable to approach so exalted a personage."

From the corner of his eye Philip de Saumarez noticed a nerve commence to tick in Anson's broad, red-brown cheek as he stared into the Oriental's oblique obsidian eyes unblinking behind enormous horn-rimmed glasses. Whereas any other man under the circumstances would have exploded into invectives, roared or beaten the desk, George Anson merely stared on Mr. Li Ho-tsung in withering contempt.

"Very well," said he in edged, even tones. "You may inform your so-called connections at the Viceregal Court that I shall return at once to Macao, ready my ship for action and, permission or no permission, sail her upriver with guns run out."

In a flash the merchant's Buddha-like calm vanished; he appeared utterly horrified. "But, Honorable Commodore, you must not, *cannot* take such an action! To attempt it would mean the utter ruin of all foreign merchants — of all Chinese in the international trade!"

"You should have weighed such a possibility."

"But, sir, the august Chantuck's wrath will be terrible! It is even possible the Emperor will order the execution of every foreigner found within his realm; certainly, if you were to bombard his forts all would die. I beseech you to reconsider such folly."

"What he says is only too true!" burst out Mr. Shepherd, who had turned a sickly gray.

The Commodore made a show of considering the situation, kept his hosts on tenterhooks a full minute before he said, "I cannot very well jeopardize the lives — and fortunes," he added drily, "of so many fellow Europeans. Therefore I will take other steps."

De Saumarez realized, as Cratcherode did not, that his Commander in Chief was in the process of evolving an adroit maneuver.

"Very well. I shall propose an alternative; if, on my return to Macao, you undertake to send me adequate sea stores and arrange to have imperative repairs made to my flagship, I'd be surprised if I didn't set sail for Batavia instead of coming to call on the Viceroy."

De Saumarez's jaw dropped. This was the last move he'd expected on George Anson's part. "*Batavia*, sir!"

"Yes. I believe that port lies on our route towards home. We can complete our refit there." Anson almost smiled, so overwhelming was the relief of Messrs. Shepherd and Li Ho-tsung. "Well, Mr. Shepherd, what do you say to that?"

"Why — why," spluttered the factor, "I am confident that — that this is a most sensible and equitable solution of — of your — I mean of our difficulties."

Said Mr. Li Ho-tsung, his calm restored, "This unworthy person ventures to predict that your Honor's requirements will soon be satisfied. I trust you gentlemen will enjoy a swift and most comfortable return to Macao."

On his return to the British *hong*, Mr. Shepherd without loss of time summoned various Chinese and English merchants with whom he entered into earnest consultation.

At the conference's end, Mr. Shepherd emerged wreathed in smiles. "I believe, sir, that my colleagues and I have found the means of satisfying your requirements."

"I shall be pleased to hear of it," Anson said crisply. "What do you propose?"

"In a short while one of our Indiamen will sail for home. We will undertake to sufficiently overstock the *Onslow* with sea stores and certain other necessities to supply your ship. When the Indiaman reaches the Bocca Tigris she will anchor. You will have only to send your smallboats out at night and none will be the wiser."

With an inscrutable smile Anson nodded. "Let us hope that indeed, 'No one will be the wiser.' Now, concerning the repairs?"

"They also are being quietly arranged for. Rest assured His Majesty's ship will be repaired to your satisfaction."

At anchor near Taypa Island Anson did what he should have done in the first place. He wrote another courteous but firm letter to the Chantuck, then informed the Hoppo that he was sending this missive upstream in one of *Centurion*'s smallboats.

When the Hoppo refused permission for it to depart, Anson, having learned his lesson about dealing with the Chinese, stated that the boat would depart filled, if necessary, with armed men; let anyone molest it who dared to risk affronting His Majesty of England!

Meanwhile the news was disseminated aboard *Centurion*, and on shore, that the Commodore was determined to sail for Batavia at the first practicable moment. The flagship's officers, therefore, wrote letters to friends resident in Java. When the *Onslow* touched there on her long voyage home she could drop them off.

To Menzies, the Commodore admitted, "I was deliberately and badly advised by Mr. Shepherd and the other factors."

"I regret to hear it, sir."

"Yes, I acted stupidly in Canton. After the first few days I should have sensed what Shepherd and the rest were up to."

"— And what was that, sir?" softly demanded the Carolinian.

"Why, that it stood to their interest to make sure that no man-of-war would be granted exemptions and privileges not accorded the East India Company."

"I must be slow, sir, but I can't quite follow your line of reasoning."

Over the racket made by cymbals and gongs aboard a passing junk, Anson said, "They'd lose prestige or 'face,' as I believe they call it hereabouts; by consequence they'd lose certain privileges they've long enjoyed. Bah, Andrew! You've no notion what humiliation those factors endure for the sake of trade."

Only two days after *Centurion*'s barge departed for Canton and before it returned, an Imperial dispatch boat arrived bearing a courier who politely warned the Commodore that he should make preparations to receive in the near future a party of high-ranking Imperial officials.

Next morning, sailors laboriously holystoning *Centurion*'s splintery decks were startled to hear a shivering boom of gongs and the rattle of drums gradually grow louder. Lookouts, on peering upstream, announced that a flotilla of Chinese war junks under a forest of vari-colored banners and flags was bearing down upon the anchorage off Taypa.

Lieutenant Denis pounded up to the quarterdeck and reported, "Sir! Sir! 'Tis a mission from the Viceroy!"

Anson calmly directed, "Until a properly accredited envoy wishes to come aboard you may carry on with routine tasks."

Led by a huge war junk wearing Emperor Kien-L'ung's yellow and black dragon banner, the flotilla came sailing grandly into Taypa Harbor. Midshipman Nat Wade, among many others, counted no less than eighteen war vessels — all mounting cannon and flying colorful banners.

Presently the new arrivals lowered bat-wing sails and dropped curiously designed anchors. Through their spyglasses Captains Mitchell and Saunders watched a sampan being lowered from what undoubtedly must be the flagship. Presently it brought a tall and very gorgeously attired officer alongside who called up something.

"Sir," an interpreter advised, "this official says he is of such low rank that he should not be received with salutes or side boys."

Acting Lieutenant van Keppel, therefore, was deemed of sufficiently humble rank to greet the messenger at the gangway.

On climbing aboard the visitor at once fell onto hands and knees and touched the deck with his forehead in a ceremonious kowtow to officers grouped about the quarterdeck.

Through an interpreter the messenger stated that on the flotilla's flagship were three mandarins, all of very exalted rank, who had been sent by His Highness the Chantuck of Canton.

"He says one is of Jade Button rank and two of the Coral Button, sir. They have come to convey the Chantuck's greetings and salutations."

"Damn' decent of him, after all this time," muttered Midshipman Drake, then fell silent when Lieutenant Brett gave him a hard look.

"They have brought with them carpenters from the Imperial dockyard, your Honor, and are to survey your ship so as to ascertain the exact extent of the repairs necessary to ensure her safe passage to Batavia. Further, the Taotai, or chief mandarin, who also is Governor of a nearby city, requests that the foreign devil warship dispatch a boat to fetch him aboard."

Once the messenger had departed after again kowtowing before him, Anson, grinning broadly, implemented various measures long ago decided upon. All visible brasswork was to be polished until it shone gold-bright; standing rigging was to be tarred as well as possible and clean white covers placed on all boats still inboard.

To Denis he said, "Please see that my barge crew don the same rig they wore during my trip to Canton last month, but on this occasion their shirts must be really white and clean."

Next he sent for Lieutenant Colonel Cratcherode, briskly informed him, "I wish broken out one hundred good sets of Marine uniform, complete with gaiters, caps and crossbelts. Mr. Brett will select as many sturdy and handsome seamen to wear these uniforms. I have observed the extreme importance of color, pomp and noise in impressing the Celestials."

Considerable merriment arose while the selected seamen struggled to find scarlet tunics, white breeches and black gaiters which would come anywhere near to fitting them. Meanwhile their mates polished the breast buckles of crossbelts and those low, brass plates which decorated Marine caps. Others dusted mold off the badly wrinkled red tunics and sought to cold-press them into some degree of presentability.

Sniggering, the counterfeit Marines, under the despairing direction of Captain Crowden and Marine Lieutenant Gordon, at last stood lined up on the upper gundeck.

"God's love," snapped Crowden, turned out in his best dress uniform, "they look like the ultimate defaulters' parade!"

This undoubtedly was true, but to an inexperienced eye these brawny, red-faced fellows appeared deceptively martial, drawn up under gleaming bayonets and wearing varnished black leather caps, the brass ornaments of which now glittered bravely.

From his station on the quarterdeck Lieutenant Colonel Cratcherode glared about like an angry bull while securing a baldric of red velvet to support his slender dress sword.

"God's codpiece! Never, in all my service, have I seen the King's scarlet disgraced by such a pack of mangy whoresons! 'Pon my word, Crowden, I could die of shame!"

Still cursing under his breath, Cratcherode nevertheless descended to the main deck and did his best to render the imitation troops a trifle more presentable.

Rust-pitted muskets were replaced by ones in better condition; dull buttons were ordered buffed and done up, every one; finally, with surprising patience, the purple-faced Colonel demonstrated how stocks and heavy black cloth gaiters should be secured.

Next, Cratcherode literally drove sixty gawping seamen into forming double ranks facing the gangway; then he ordered forty additional red-jacketed louts up to line the quarterdeck on three sides. They slouched there looking sheepish and sweating like fury under these heavy and constricting garments.

When, to a storm of discordant music and the roaring of many kettledrums and gongs, Centurion's barge was seen pushing off from the flag junk the visiting man-of-war commenced a salute of fifteen guns. For some reason, Portuguese forts on Taypa also felt it necessary to honor the Taotai's presence with an equal number of shots.

When the Chinese fired only three guns in acknowledgment furrows appeared on Anson's smooth brow and he turned to his favorite interpreter, a sad-eyed Scot named Charles MacPherson who, although he operated a *hong* in Macao, had been persuaded to remain on board after the Commodore's return from Canton.

"They returned only three; what's the meaning of such a discourtesy?"

Hurriedly, MacPherson murmured, "Please don't take offense, sir. The Chinese always salute with three guns; even their Emperor receives no more."

"How very interesting — and different." Displaying a rare touch of nervousness, Anson resettled a jabot of delicate lace cascading downwards between the yellow satin lapels of a peacock blue dress-coat heavy with a profusion of gold buttons and embroidery.

For the occasion he had selected knee breeches of Turkey-red silk and heavily embroidered stockings of canary yellow. For once acceding to Michael Despeda's almost desperate entreaties, he consented to wear a sparkling white wig — for all he loathed such hot and uncomfortable headgear.

Further, he had slung a splendid dress sword, the hilt and scabbard of which sparkled with diamonds, rubies and emeralds, to a baldric of cloth-of-gold and scarlet brocade — all of which caused George Anson to feel extremely foolish and yearn for a proper naval uniform. If the Army enjoyed such, why not the Senior Service?

While watching his repainted white barge thresh nearer, Anson found reason for pride. King Parmer, standing rigid over the tiller in a gaudy red, white and blue uniform, seemed to tower above a rainbow of flowing gowns seated in the stern. Boathook in hand, the bow man remained motionless as a wooden figurehead.

Lieutenant Brett, waiting in the gangway, stole a glance at the quarterdeck and found occasion to admire the fine figures presented by *Centurion*'s afterguard and supernumerary officers.

Matthew Mitchell was wearing a knee-length frock coat of emerald green; Captain Saunders had selected one of purple and black; Lieutenant Colonel Cratcherode stood straight as a gold, scarlet and white ramrod. The flagship's lieutenants presented an array no less colorful — thanks to the loot of Payta and the prizes.

Centurion's final salute was so well timed that its smoke was yet drifting over the water when the boatswain's pipes began to shrill as the Taotai's head appeared in the gangway. Clad in an ankle-length gown of shimmering turquoise-hued silk, the dignitary clasped hands over his stomach and thrice bowed in the direction of the quarterdeck;

a vivid peacock feather, secured to the Taotai's conical black hat by a green jade button, fluttered sedately.

A barked command from Captain Crowden caused the "troops" to present arms as best they knew how while every drum in the flagship was pounded with delighted energy. Men who knew less than nothing about music puffed out their cheeks and blew bugles as hard as they could.

The resultant cacaphony proved a torture to European ears, but the Chinese appeared both pleased and impressed, especially when, in the 'tween decks, "Cookie," his helpers and the ship's boys banged kettles and pans to swell the fearful racket.

One after another the Chantuck's three emissaries, all gorgeously arrayed and with long queues asway, padded over towards the quarter-deck ladder on embroidered slippers the felt soles of which must have been easily four inches thick.

At the same moment Cratcherode ordered his "Marines" on the quarterdeck to present arms; this they did to the shrilling of fifes that screamed, as Andrew Menzies later said, like fifty bellyaches.

Ten paces short of the spot where Commodore Anson waited, utterly impassive, the Taotai and his companions again clasped hands over stomach and thrice bowed profoundly. This courtesy the Commodore acknowledged by removing his hat and making a stiff half bow, quite unaware that a moment of vast significance had become history. For the first time, ever, a high-ranking Chinese had deigned to appear on a foreign devil vessel!

While the balance of the Taotai's retinue appeared, MacPherson, *sotto voce,* identified certain Eurasians as spies and/or interpreters.

"Ask the Taotai," Anson instructed, "whether he and his fellow mandarins care to descend to my cabin where we may converse in greater comfort and privacy."

Once the expressionless trio, official fans in hand, had grouped themselves about Anson's long, plain table, the Taotai explained through his interpreter: "This worthless personage has received instructions from His Highness the Viceroy to determine the exact extent of repairs required by your Honor's vessel, so, among my retinue, there are some shipwrights. Where shall they commence their survey?"

"Well, Mr. Saumarez, and what is your opinion?"

"Sir, may I suggest they start by examining that leak in the bow which has caused us so much anxiety. In fact, sir, it has grown considerably worse since our arrival here in Taypa."

"Honorable sirs, that leak has already been listed." Gravely, a monkey-faced secretary with a tremendously long queue produced a scroll on which were entered the repairs listed in Anson's letter. To Andrew Menzies's astonishment, Chinese scribes had taken the precaution of leaving lacunae in which figures might be entered by the examiners.

"Mr. Saumarez, pray instruct the carpenter to conduct the shipwrights below; make sure that he misses none of the bulkheads, planks, braces and beams which have become rotten."

After a while the Commodore, not without guile, pressed his principal guests to inspect the gundecks and undertook personally to guide the wooden-faced mandarins. He took especial care to emphasize the caliber, range and destructive possibilities of *Centurion*'s great guns.

Taking his cue, Peircy Brett, in minute detail, described the weight of the roundshot that lay dully glistening, ready in their rope garlands. Further, he explained the murderous uses of cannister, chain and grapeshot.

In turn, de Saumarez enlarged upon the great accuracy of his gun crews and caused the mandarins to inspect, with care, each of the many racks of muskets, pikes and chests of pistols and cutlasses in the armory.

When the Taotai and his companions returned to the great cabin it was obvious that they now comprehended that this was no mere armed merchantman, but a powerful fighting ship, built and equipped for no other purpose than the waging of war.

The moment seemed opportune, Anson decided, to insert a spoke in the wheel of the haughty and uncooperative Hoppo. Said he through the ubiquitous Mr. MacPherson, "I am sure His Highness the Chantuck of Canton will be distressed to learn that his subordinate, the Hoppo of Macao, has attempted to deny me even the least courtesy or assistance, but in every way possible has hampered my efforts to communicate with the Chantuck. At first he even refused me the right to purchase fresh food of which my men, sickly through so long a voyage, stood in the greatest need."

"His Highness shall be informed of this discourtesy," declared Taotai, bowing so low that his pigtail and peacock feather swayed forward. "No doubt he will bestow suitable punishment."

"You now must have perceived," Anson went on to say, speaking slowly in order that MacPherson might have plenty of time to select the exact Chinese equivalent of his words, "that it was not through fear, or want of power to supply myself by force that I have submitted to the Hoppo's persistent contempt. This ship is capable of destroying not only the port of Macao, but also Canton or any other port in China."

The Scot's sallow features reddened as he gasped. "Sir — is it wise thus to threaten —"

Again the quintessence of easy good humor, Anson smiled. "I do not threaten, Mr. MacPherson, I merely state fact. Pray tell him just what I've said — as inoffensively as possible, of course.

"You might also enlarge on the point that, though our distresses have increased daily, my people and I always have conducted ourselves with the greatest of restraint. Also make it abundantly clear to these, our honored guests, that it is not the custom among European Powers to attempt to starve the crew of a friendly warship which enters their ports in distress or to refuse essential repairs."

Menzies sensed that the Commodore was about to indulge in a bit of pawky humor.

"This failure to supply us cannot continue; famine is at hand with us." In grave speculation he considered one well-fleshed mandarin after another. "I am convinced that Your Excellencies will understand that my men cannot be expected willingly to perish of starvation. Before that I fear my crew will soon turn cannibal. In such an event on whom would they be likely to prey? On their bony fellows? Certainly not. I fear they would seek out, seize and devour a number of plump Chinese."

A horrified gabble exploded among the Chinese once the interpreters had translated Anson's prediction.

The Taotai's anguished expression testified he had taken the suggestion quite literally. He spoke hurriedly to MacPherson.

"His Excellency declares, sir, that no such dreadful contingency will ever arise. He promises, personally, to present a written report on your needs to the Chantuck and swears that, without doubt, your every request will be fulfilled — on the one condition that you do not attempt to approach Canton but depart for Batavia as soon as your flagship is rendered seaworthy."

"Very well," the Commodore stated pleasantly, "I shall not insist on proceeding to Canton."

Centurion's bell having struck to summon the Afternoon Watch,

[411]

Anson, as though on sudden inspiration, invited his guests to dine on board — for all that Despeda and his underlings long since had prepared ample food for service in the wardroom.

To the flagship's officers the repast which followed was as funny as it was significant, for the steward's menu included several beef courses — roast, stewed or in pies. The mandarins sampled each offering then, smiling, ignored their plates.

"Chinese don't like beef," whispered MacPherson. "Prefer pork or chicken."

"Onliest pork I got sar," groaned Despeda, darkly resplendent in a Marine's jacket, "is salted and eight year' in de cask. But I got ready-cooked four roast chickens from Tinian."

"Bring 'em in a hurry," pleaded the Scot.

But a fresh contretemps arose when the fowls were served cut in halves. To Anson's embarrassment it turned out that his exalted guests never before had consumed anything without the use of chopsticks. Knives and forks they simply did not understand.

This difficulty, however, was overcome when Mr. MacPherson told the wardroom stewards to cut the fowls into little pieces — much as do grownups for small children. Spoons the mandarins could, and did, manage expertly, so consumption of the viands no longer presented a problem.

When it came to drink, the Taotai and his bronze-faced companions made up for lost time. In rapid succession they drained a bottle apiece of the Commodore's precious Frontignac. Somehow Anson managed a stoic's smile as the last of those wines laid down in England disappeared to a loud smacking of lips. To his astonishment so much strong white wine affected his guests no more than tea.

When the meal came to an end the guests emitted polite belches of appreciation, then bowed and announced that they must return to their ships and start back to Canton.

Again pipes twittered, side boys lined up, the awkward "Marines" presented muskets and officers doffed their headgear.

Eyes wide with excitement, Despeda hurried up behind the Commodore and hovered there in a fever of excitement while Anson, ever impassive, watched his departing guests' brilliant gowns traverse the upper gundeck.

Once the barge had shoved off, Despeda burst out in a great stage whisper. "Sar! Sar! Your gold snuffbox and six silver spoons ain't nowheres to be found!"

"Say nothing about it!" Anson warned sharply; then he grinned. "I presume their Excellencies were expecting presents. It was careless of me to — er — force them in selecting gifts."

<h2 style="text-align:center">～ 1 4 ～
"I Will Fit Out for Batavia"</h2>

GEORGE ANSON WAS ASTOUNDED that, following the Taotai's visit, eighteen days should pass without the arrival of either sea stores or shipwrights, carpenters and supplies to make the promised repairs. How fatuous to flatter himself that the mandarins had been so impressed by HBMS *Centurion* that there would be no more delay. It was becoming increasingly difficult to wait and postpone the threatened attack on Canton. The end of May was now in sight and the success of certain plans laid for June were in jeopardy.

All the same, the Taotai's visitation had had at least one beneficial result; the chastened Hoppo at once had allowed bumboats and fishermen to traffic openly with the flagship. No longer was it necessary for a few bold sampan owners to sneak out under the cover of darkness and attempt to relieve *Centurion*'s distress with small amounts of food and water.

One evening the Commodore reached a decision and summoned Captain Charles Saunders to the great cabin where that worthy was surprised to find Anson alone, for once without his inscrutable Carolinian secretary in attendance.

The Commodore lost no time in coming to his point: "Captain, how would you like to sail for home soon?"

"*Home* soon, sir?" Saunders's strong jaw sagged in astonishment.

"Yes. I hear that tomorrow a Swedish India Company ship will descend the Pearl and pass Macao on her homeward voyage."

Color flooded Charles Saunders's face. "I would *not*, sir! I departed on this voyage aboard *Centurion* and I would greatly prefer to complete it in her — even if she's not to try for the Manila Galleon." The speaker's steady, always bloodshot brown eyes asked a question.

"Captain, for what I deem to be good and sufficient reasons, as soon as supplies arrive, I will fit out for Batavia."

"Nevertheless, sir, I prefer to remain with you."

"Then I'm afraid I shall have to *order* your departure in the Swede and to convey these." He held up a fat envelope taped in linen and carefully sealed with blue wax. "These are my 'Letters of Proceedings' up to today. They must reach the Admiralty with all speed."

Anson relaxed his stiff manner. "You can see for yourself that with conditions as they are here several weeks must elapse before I can hope to continue on the voyage."

"Cannot someone else carry your dispatches, sir?" Saunders pleaded, looking steadily into the other's calm features.

"My dear friend, do I have to remind you that in this ship you are only supernumerary? To remain such will not advance your naval career on the eve of great events in Europe. Your share in the prize money, of course, remains unaffected and will be sent to you upon my arrival in England."

"Hang my prize money!" Saunders burst out. "I love this old ship, sir, and —" He started to say "and you," but didn't quite dare, so blurted, "— To have served under you, sir, is an ample reward."

Anson, although smiling, shook his head. "I foresee, my friend, that when you return home bearing intelligence of the considerable treasure we have taken and present a report I have prepared concerning your conduct and ability, the Lords Commissioners not only will confirm my promotion of you to Post Captain, but will also grant you a man-of-war for your own."

Even so, Saunders only reluctantly bowed to the inevitable. "Very well, sir. I have observed that the advancement of your officers and men is ever foremost in your thoughts."

"I try to reward merit where recognition is due."

When, on the following day, Charles Saunders departed for the Swedish Indiaman, lying under backed topsails off Taypa, the Commodore had a Captain's nine-gun salute fired and, as an added honor, ordered *Centurion*'s weather-bleached yards to be manned.

Shortly after Saunders's departure, Anson determined also to send home certain other supernumeraries; therefore, passages were arranged aboard the Indiaman *Augusta* for Lieutenant Colonel Cratcherode — who no longer had any troops to command — and Captain Mitchell, who still was mourning his beloved *Gloucester* and chafing under enforced idleness.

With them went Chaplain Richard Walter on a plea of having "urgent private business" at home. Anson suspected that this "business" was really to publish — in advance of anyone else — an account of the voyage.

Having reviewed Walter's *A Voyage around the World* and having found it to be reasonably accurate and impartial, Anson decided that it might not be a bad idea for this journal to appear in print as soon as possible. It might explain much which he, personally, could not and place responsibility for the wretched condition of the land troops where it belonged — at the Prime Minister's door.

While the departing officers' chests and boxes were being passed into the longboat, Matthew Mitchell's long jaw began to quiver and his mismated eyes filled. "I am grieved to leave you, sir. To have served so long under your command has been a rare privilege and a great honor."

"Captain — Matthew, I fear you exaggerate my abilities as much as you depreciate you own. Let me say, rather, that your loyalty, indomitable courage and persistence in the face of so many undeserved misfortunes should serve as an everlasting example to all who shall serve in the Royal Navy. May God, and the Government, suitably reward your constancy and ability."

For a moment George Anson came perilously close to betraying emotion while he wrung the departing Captain's hand.

Mordaunt Cratcherode, his scarred face redder than usual, shook hands and rasped, " 'Pon my word, Commodore, the greatest regret of my career is that the troops sent us were of such wretched quality. Had I had seasoned men to command I — why, damme, with your example, I'd have made all England proud of us!"

"Colonel, I know what bitter disappointments you have suffered, through no fault of yours — or of mine," the Commodore replied. "May I observe, sir, that we of the Naval Service have greatly appreciated the stalwart manner in which you have borne your trials? I have stated as much in my 'Letter of Proceeding.' I am sure that all my officers join me in hoping that your next command will prove worthier of so capable an officer."

When the Indiaman sailed by with Mitchell, Cratcherode and the others standing a little apart from the merchantman's officers, Commodore Anson, alone on the poopdeck, solemnly lifted his tricorne and bowed to them lower than ever he had before the Taotai.

At long last beetle-browed Mr. MacPherson received a message from agents in Canton which, in a measure, accounted for the harassing delays. It appeared, his secret agents had reported, that the French East India Company was insisting that their ships also were men-of-war and was protesting the exemption of harbor dues about to be accorded to HBMS *Centurion*.

"It is with considerable shame, sir," wrote MacPherson, "that I confess that Mr. Shepherd and the British East India Company's other factors also are jealous of seeing privileges extended you and have consistently opposed the dispatching to you of the promised supplies and carpenters."

On the receipt of this information Anson announced that, unless the supplies were immediately forthcoming, he would, if necessary, fight his way upriver and bring Canton under his guns.

Whether this threat had anything to do with it or not, a swarm of work junks appeared the next day and anchored near the flagship as she lay near the shore in Taypa Harbor.

Soon she became overrun by gangs of chattering carpenters, smiths, riggers and sailmakers. Labor crews assisted the man-of-war's men to shift ballast, gun, ammunition and all manner of ponderous gear first to one side and then back in order that her bilges might be rolled high enough out of the water to permit inspection by officers from the Imperial Dockyard at Canton.

The bulk of *Centurion*'s crew — much to their disgust — then was sent to camp on a barren island unpleasantly remote from the flesh-pots and temptations of Macao. For amusements they were reduced to gambling, bare knuckle boxing and to watching native fishermen work at night. This business was especially fascinating to Will Pallis-ter and Ted Waxter, by no means an inexperienced angler.

On long poles set athwart a fishing sampan's beam perched rows of brown-black cormorants. As the boat drifted along with iron basket torches burning low over the surface at bow and stern, birds who spied fish attracted by the glare would dive and reappear with silvery prey struggling in their beaks. These birds, the English were told, were prevented from swallowing their captures because of a copper ring secured about their long and snakelike necks. The Chinese would force their pets to surrender their prey five times and then unclasp the restricting band and reward the bird with a fish.

The chartered sheering hulks still did not appear, which caused acute misgivings among *Centurion*'s officers. Mr. MacPherson al-ready had sent out word that Spanish spies long since had departed to warn the Viceroy of the Philippines — ruling less than seven hundred miles away — that the "scourge of South America" lay defenseless in Taypa Harbor.

Even the least intelligent midshipman was aware that if the Spaniards, for once, acted boldly and violated Portuguese neutrality, there was nothing to prevent their looting and then destroying the hated English man-of-war.

The last week in February, 1743, was drawing to a close before the rigging junks arrived alongside; but then Chinese carpenters went promptly and efficiently to work. They swarmed all over the sea-worn Fourth Rate and, to George Anson's surprise and relief, proved to be very competent artisans by anybody's standards.

By the 3rd of March, Centurion's company were breathing more easily because the flagship's hull once more was sound; all leaks had been located and stopped; rotten timbers and planking had been replaced and lead sheathing nailed back in place.

As soon as Centurion rode once more on an even keel, guns and ammunition were rushed back aboard and the ship otherwise rendered capable of a purely static defense; she still could not be fought efficiently, being destitute of rigging.

Chinese laborers had just restepped the lower masts when a seagoing merchant junk came speeding into Taypa Harbor bearing alarming news. A reliable source reported that the Viceroy in Manila, some time ago, had sent out a squadron consisting of two 40-gun ships and two sloops of unknown armament with the sole purpose of catching Centurion unable to defend herself. The trading junk's half-caste master calculated that these ships might be expected to appear at any time.

Accordingly, combined crews of Europeans and Chinese sent up the topmasts in a frenzy of haste; new shrouds were rigged and yards on all three masts crossed in short order. At the same time Anson saw to it that plenty of water, sea stores and fresh food were purchased by his new Purser, Andrew Rule, and his mates, Waxter and Millechamp.

Carrying bags of Spanish silver dollars, the three explored Macao's pungent-smelling waterfront and, when necessary, bribed *compradores* into producing hard-to-get articles which were sent aboard with all haste.

Andrew Menzies also spent much time in replenishing the Commodore's private stock of delicacies, tobacco and fine wines. Among other things, the Carolinian had been instructed to purchase a collection of Chinese instruments — with special attention to any and all kinds of flutes.

In discharging this mission Menzies explored many remote *impressas* — alleys as dark, narrow and foul-smelling as any to be found bordering the Mediterranean. Through that cheerful and adroit Jamaican, Michael Despeda, Anson's secretary purchased a fine stock of Portuguese wines and brandies, Dutch gin, French champagnes and *fines*, also many barrels of stout Jamaica rum for the crew.

It being George Anson's pleasure to sample the Orient's most exotic dishes, he also bought a supply of Chinese ginger, East Indian curries, Bombay duck and chutneys, plus an ample supply of spices. Further, the pair invested in the ingredients for such local delicacies as *bêche-de-mer*, birds' nests, ancient eggs, pickled eels' eggs and dried sharks' fins.

On one of his last foraging expeditions, Andrew Menzies chanced to enter a crowded *impressa* which seemed rather wider and a bit less malodorous than the average.

He was hesitating before an ivory carver's window when a soft voice said, "Good afternoon, honorable sir. Possibly you might care to escape this noise and heat and drink some tea? After that, sir, you may feel inspired to try your luck at fan-tan, mah-jongg or some European game of chance?"

The speaker, Menzies realized, was an Eurasian who carried a fan of scintillating kingfisher feathers and wore a long and very handsome Chinese gown. He had the liquid black eyes, high cheekbones and a thin, hooked nose of a well-bred Portuguese; in fact, his Chinese ancestry was noticeable only in his pale bronze complexion and the faint thickening of his eyelids at their inward corners.

"Why not dismiss dull care for a little while? My name is Joseph Pierce. May I assure you that my little gambling establishment is an honest one? Anyone in Macao will bear witness to that."

Gamble? It seemed as if a trickle of ice water had begun to trace the length of Andrew Menzies's spine.

"I don't gamble," said he gruffly and started on.

Smiling, the Eurasian pattered along beside him. "Please reconsider, sir. I also have to offer beautiful girls, well-trained in the arts of love; they are very washed, very clean, almost white."

Without realizing it, Anson's secretary paused. "Girls don't interest me," he announced. "Nor do I understand Chinese games of chance."

"Sir," the Macaese clasped hands over his middle, bowed ceremoniously, "it is not required that your Honor should. You have to select the game of your choice and you will be cheerfully accommodated. Shall it be loo, écarté or Newmarket, perhaps?"

Almost savagely Menzies shook his dark and well-formed head. "No! No! Years ago I gave up gambling in any form."

"Newmarket, sir, is very fashionable," the young man called Pierce persisted. "Surely your Honor must be ready, for a little while, to forget the tedium of naval service through wooing the Goddess of Chance?"

Menzies didn't reply, only shouldered his way down the *impressa*. However, he soon halted, thinking, dear God, wouldn't it be Heaven to handle cards once again — if for only a few minutes? No. You mustn't even consider it!

Remember, you damned idiot, the night you lost Chartwell to Captain George Anson, who was too magnanimous to accept it? Then to Legaré Daingerfield who wasn't? How ready Legaré was to take advantage of you, a drunken, stupid rake. You'd not a penny left when the game had ended. Remember what it was like to be a pauper living on the bounty of your young brother, forced to accept the pity of Caroline, more divinely beautiful than Aurora in all her glory?

Recollections raced through Menzies's brain as he hesitated in the hot and noisy *impressa*. After all these years what would it be like to cut and deal again? Why not? You can't lose much dealing a few hands of Newmarket because you haven't much money on you, nor any credit either, thank God.

The young Eurasian who still was standing where he'd been, bowed politely when he saw the Carolinian turn back and dodge a wheelbarrow piled high with crated pottery. He saw the slender, dark-faced European halt again, saw his lips form words. No. You swore you wouldn't. Never, ever again. You're not going to!

Eyes shining, he hurried up to Joseph Pierce and allowed himself to be guided through the gambling den's gilded and fantastically carved portals.

Something like a stifled moan escaped Anson's secretary on entering a long room the ceiling of which was supported by elegantly carved and gilded beams. Its walls were hung with some of the richest and most beautifully embroidered silk screens he had ever beheld.

The air was cool and lightly tinctured by a subtle incense rising in a slender blue-green spiral from the back of a bronze Fô dog to dissipate itself among great crimson chrysanthemums arranged in a

[419]

yellow cloisonné vase. Another bronze censer, smoldering in a far corner, amused Menzies; it was the figure of a very fat old man lying, grinning, on a couch of bulging rice sacks and climbed upon by many plump children.

"That, sir, is the god, Hotai," the young Eurasian explained, smiling thinly. "He loves children and is so very rich that he not only feeds them all, but even permits rats to eat grain at his feet. Do you not notice them? May one hope that when you leave the House of the Fifth Pleasure your Honor will be quite as rich."

Perhaps twenty Spanish dollars of Anson's money remained in Menzies's pocket — which, if his luck ran foul, could readily be replaced from a certain strongbox he kept hidden and chained to the bulkhead behind his bunk.

After Mr. Pierce had disappeared for a moment, a pretty little Chinese servant girl fetched a tea tray and dispensed hot towels with which the guest might cleanse his hands.

One after another players entered and bowed ceremoniously to the startled Carolinian, who, hurriedly recalling his manners, returned the courtesy. All four were full-blooded Chinese wearing long, drooping mustaches and grave, inscrutable expressions.

"These gentlemen I have summoned agreed to play Newmarket with you, honored sir. I give you my solemn word there will be no collusion among them. They are all respectable merchants of this quarter."

It came as a shock to Menzies that he found himself subconsciously flexing and otherwise limbering his fingers while the beat of his heart quickened until it almost drummed. How easy it was to substitute familiar faces about the table: Billy Calhoun's, Charlie Ravenel's, Legaré Daingerfield's and Captain Anson's.

Funny. Saving for Anson, he'd no idea what might have happened to those boon companions of other days. Probably they all had married by now and had sired a host of children. Boys among them certainly would be fashionably brought up to drink, shoot, hunt, wench and gamble — also, to care for their properties far more shrewdly than a casual stranger might suspect.

With sharp claws, conscience struck at Menzies's peace of mind; nevertheless, he played so skillfully that, at the end of an hour, he was flushed with excitement and richer by nearly a hundred doubloons. Since he'd been sufficiently experienced to state, at the inception of this game, that he could play for only an hour — win, lose or draw — the other players bowed courteously when he begged to be excused.

"Please assure these gentlemen," he told Mr. Pierce, "that I regret leaving the game while enjoying so much good fortune; also please make them understand that, as I told them, I cannot miss my boat which leaves in only a few minutes."

"They understand, Mr. Menzies," assured Joseph Pierce after translating. "They hope you will stop by on your next visit ashore."

"I'm afraid that will be impossible," smiled Menzies; but all the same knew he would, if it were in any way possible.

~ 1 5 ~

The House of the Fifth Pleasure

IT CHANCED that, at the very moment Andrew Menzies quitted the House of the Fifth Pleasure, he found himself face to face with supernumerary Purser's Mate Waxter. Handsome and debonair, he was strolling along arm-in-arm with a slender, heavily painted and very young Eurasian girl. Something in Waxter's flushed features and the girl's lubricous gait suggested that recently they'd been doing considerably more than just drinking and holding hands.

"Why, my dear fellow, fancy meeting *you* in such a haunt of vice!" Waxter drawled in the supercilious accents of Lord Lawrence Burfurd. "Damme, I'd no notion that our Commodore's sedate secretary was — or is — a fellow gamester."

Menzies flushed, stammered. "Why — why, I'm not really; I — I merely stopped in for only a little while."

Waxter made a mock half bow. "I trust that good fortune has smiled upon you as broadly as she has on this, your humble servant."

With a sudden return of his Tidewater gentry manner, Menzies bowed in return. "I have done well, but not nearly as well as you, it seems."

"That may well be so," grinned the purser's mate and pinched his small companion's plump bottom as it jiggled under tight silken trousers of peacock blue. "In fact, it *is* so; ain't it, O Foremost-of-the-Pear-Orchard?"

The Eurasian squealed and stuck out her tongue. "Oh, you are so naughty! But so nice, too. Good-by." Quick as a frightened rabbit, the girl darted across the street and became lost to sight beyond a file of gaunt straw-hatted coolies bent under cases of supplies destined for HBMS *Centurion*.

"Tasty little thing, that. Should try one before we sail. They're experienced. Wonderfully experienced. So you've won?"

"Why, yes. Just luck, you know."

Something in this must have struck Waxter as inordinately funny, for he laughed so loudly that passers-by stared at him. " 'Just luck' — and playing the Chinese? Cursed if I'd ever thought you'd defiled your ink-stained fingers with dice — or was it that odd Chinese tile game?"

At the other's patronizing tone Menzies's sharp, olive-tinted features contracted. Only with difficulty did the former master of Chartwell succeed in restraining a naturally hot temper. "You are quite wrong, Mr. Waxter; I played at Newmarket."

"Indeed? Odd, that's a favorite game of mine; I usually win at it." Not unnaturally, Lord Burfurd failed to add that this was so only because of a certain skill in improving upon the laws of chance.

Next afternoon, while Andrew Menzies was playing his careful game of Newmarket, Ted Waxter's spruce figure momentarily darkened the entrance to the House of the Fifth Pleasure. Ever since the purser's mate had appeared on *Centurion*, following *Gloucester*'s destruction, Menzies subconsciously had mistrusted this too well-spoken and easy-mannered individual. It also was disconcerting that he again should discover the Commodore's secretary in a gaming house.

"Ah! A rare pleasure, Mr. Menzies, indeed it is. No. Please don't interrupt your play. I shall look for a bit and then decide whether to risk a flurry or not."

The purser's mate drifted off among tables where long-robed Chinese were sipping tea and playing fan-tan or mah-jongg. Finally, he sauntered up to a *cambio valuta* counter presided over by an ancient Chinese who wore a benign expression, a stringy white beard and a pair of enormous horn-rimmed spectacles.

From the corner of his eye, Menzies presently watched Waxter toss onto the exchange broker's scales an assortment of heavy gold rings and chains, such as could have come only from Payta or from one of the prizes.

Waxter's taste must have been selective, for, after the lightning quick use of his abacus, the banker pushed three stacks of golden escudos across his counter, which coins Waxter pocketed with perfect nonchalance. Presently, he dropped into a seat vacated by a gambler in obedience to a signal from Joseph Pierce.

Winking at Menzies he said, "I want a fresh deck of cards. I say, Mr. Menzies, won't you play here? Might learn something, y'know."

The Commodore's secretary shook his head, said stiffly, "Thank you all the same. My boat is due to leave very soon."

"Rest easy, friend Menzies, you have plenty of time left for play."

"How so?"

"Because, not long ago, I instructed your coxswain to leave. You will be returning in my boat, so I have assured us three more hours of play. Besides, I can spot the natural-born gambler on sight. Come now, Mr. Menzies, let's not bicker and rather teach these yellow boys how Newmarket is played in London clubs."

If Andrew Menzies imagined he had ever encountered a reckless player back in Carolina he soon became disabused. Ted Waxter's overbred, undeniably handsome face assumed a derisive expression which betrayed nothing whatever concerning the nature of his cards.

At first the boldness of his play must have disconcerted the Chinese players. Waxter won so often that soon a tea table at his side was stacked high with gleaming gold pieces.

Seized by the contagion of recklessness, Menzies yielded to an overwhelming impulse and plunged, too. Nevertheless, he retained sufficient self-control to refuse brandy offered by Mr. Pierce's petite waitresses.

Eurasians and Chinese quit their tables, came over silently to watch the play. Although the purser's mate continued to win, Menzies's luck faltered, faded and died.

When he retained no more than his initial stake, the Carolinian, much to his own surprise, announced that he felt hungry — which was true, he hadn't eaten since sunup — and would sit out long enough to refresh himself.

"But of course, sir. I, myself, will fill your place," smoothly assured Mr. Pierce.

Somehow, Andrew Menzies's departure influenced the run of cards for Waxter commenced to lose so extravagantly that, in the space of half an hour, his winnings had been reduced to a lone escudo.

"Give me that, damn you!" He grabbed a brandy bottle from a

tray held by a moon-faced waitress, tilted back his head and gulped a draught which, Menzies guessed, would have felled an ordinary man.

During the next turn of cards Waxter lost his ultimate gold piece, whereupon he surged to his feet and, swaying a little, tacked over to Menzies, who was finishing a serving of that Macaese favorite, *xilicote cus-cus* — a pork and rice casserole.

"I'm sure, m'dear fellow," he began in exaggerated politeness, "y'don't mind trusting a shipmate for a few doubloons?"

In unnecessary deliberation Menzies wiped his mouth. "Under ordinary circumstances, Waxter, I would not. But I am not convinced that, at present, you remain in command of your judgment."

Devils glared out of Waxter's large eyes, his neck swelled and he started to clench his fists. "Damn you, you beastly Colonial, don't you dare to lecture me! If I lose, you'll be paid the instant we return aboard."

"Of that I have no doubt, sir, nevertheless I —"

"God damn it! If you wish, I'll pay interest on your bloody loan. How about — ten per cent?" sneered Waxter. "The cards are bound to change. I sense it."

Menzies became aware that the House of the Fifth Pleasure's gambling room was growing deathly still — just as on the occasion when George Anson had won Chartwell.

"About interest, I do not care a fig, sir. However, since I understand your feeling of urgency, you are welcome to this." He counted out fifty doubloons. "It should serve to prove your conviction."

The secretary then poured himself a tiny cup of hot rice wine and returned to his meal. "By the bye, may I remind you that your, our, boat leaves within the hour?"

"Thank you. You won't regret this kindness," Waxter snarled and flung himself back into his chair.

Softly, Menzies asked Mr. Pierce, "I prefer to play at another table. May I? The stakes at the former are running too high for my taste."

"Certainly, sir. Will this do?"

"Of course, and thank you."

With care Menzies selected a chair facing his former fellow player, anxious to observe whether Waxter's premonition of winning again would prove valid. Having won the deal, he dealt and played so shrewdly that soon gold commenced once more to mount on his tea table.

Presently, the purser's mate called out. "How much more time have we?"

Menzies pulled a watch out of his breeches' waistband, but his fingers had grown so sweaty in this humid atmosphere that it slipped and fell onto a sculptured jade-green rug.

In stooping to recover his timepiece, Menzies observed something which should not have happened. His shipmate's hand appeared below the table's top and, in a flash, tucked a card into one of his stocking's top and plucked out another.

A frigid tide seemed to chill Menzies's being. How could a gentleman, or, at least, a former gentleman, stoop to such tactics? He almost cried out, but checked himself in time. Let the Chinese detect the trickery if they could; it would never do to expose a compatriot.

The shock was so great that Anson's secretary lost three hands he might have won; then, recouping, he arose and cashed in his Portuguese escudos for Spanish doubloons.

"We have only ten minutes left, *Mr.* Waxter." He tried to speak naturally. "You must finish your game."

"I am ready." Waxter stood up and, as he was shoveling his winnings into his pockets, cried in a loud voice, "Fancy! I've just taught these heathens how Newmarket is played at the Cocoa Tree."

"You seem to have," observed the Carolinian in glacial politeness. "And since you are ahead, I'll thank you to return my loan."

"Don't you trust me?"

"Should I?" Menzies said, slowly and distinctly.

"Damme, if I don't resent your tone! Understand me, scribbler, I'll repay you when we return to the ship. Not a moment before. An if you don't like it, I'll undertake right now to smack that sneer from your face!"

"If you weren't drunk, I'd invite you to try, you — disgusting jailbird. Now behave yourself and come along."

There was that in the deadly calm of Andrew Menzies's voice which, barely in time, came to Lord Burfurd's rescue and checked his infuriated rush.

All was quiet in the House of the Fifth Pleasure when Anson's secretary solemnly shook hands with Mr. Pierce, then bowed to the men he'd played against. Next, he gripped Waxter by the elbow, hissing, "*Will* you come along, you drunken fool? If you want to spend the night ashore, *I* don't."

The purser's mate looked about in sodden gravity. "Then don't. I'm goin' find me a wench."

"No, you won't!" Menzies warned. "Come along — and don't you dare cause trouble or it'll go hard for you with the Commodore."

Seizing Waxter by an arm, he guided him along the dimly lit Impressa Dom Pedro until they reached the entrance to a narrow and ill-smelling passage which Menzies thought might lead them to the waterfront and that slip at which he hoped *Centurion's* cutter still might be waiting.

The footing became treacherous, thanks to the cobbles having been rendered slippery by slime and refuse upon which feasted hordes of rats as big as cats. There were no streetlamps, so their way was illumined only by an occasional beam escaping some badly fitted shutter.

Waxter suddenly attempted to wrench free, snarling, "Let go my arm, ye blasted quill-driver! Curse you for a spoil-sport! If you'd not dragged me off, I'd have made my eternal fortune."

"No doubt! Damn it, you're making a spectacle of yourself — and the King's Navy. If you don't —"

He got no further. Into the alley sprang a number of shadowy figures. Powerful hands pulled Menzies into a doorway. There, his eyes and mouth were muffled by a cloth, through which he heard the sound of blows and a piercing scream.

It being useless to struggle, Menzies stood still and braced himself against the stinging bite of a blade or the impact of a club.

Instead, Mr. Pierce's soft voice said, "Please accept my most sincere apologies, sir, for your being manhandled. Believe me, it was unavoidable."

A weight fell into the secretary's side pocket. "Here, *Honorable* sir, are the fifty doubloons you lent to your slightly less than honest shipmate. May one wish you a swift and safe and prosperous return to England?"

By the time Menzies had freed his head of cloth, the alley appeared empty save for himself, a few gaunt cats and Lord Lawrence Burfurd's bleeding corpse.

Anchor Aweigh

To *Centurion*'s company, recently reinforced through recruiting undertaken in Macao and aboard passing Indiamen, it seemed hardly possible that their ship once again was sound from truck to keel-son; that all her spars and rigging had been replaced. Furthermore, she sported a new set of sails beautifully cut by the Chinese from top-grade Dutch canvas.

Fresh white paint gleamed along her topsides and gunport streaks and her famous figurehead of a rampant lion had been re-covered with gold leaf, while her handsome natural wood sides glowed a rich gold-brown thanks to the application of several coats of varnish.

Under the boatswain's critical eye the flagship's smallboats had been repaired, repainted and furnished with new oars and sails.

Anson, placidly pacing his stern gallery, thought: the Admiralty *should* be grateful, since all this overhaul hasn't cost them a copper; every bit of it has been met out of the prize money. If only I hadn't had to waste five whole months to accomplish what a British dock-yard could have done in as many weeks!

He interrupted his pacing long enough to consider the Chinese mainland for nearly the last time. How many unprecedented problems had confronted him yonder! Had he solved them all without cost to the Treasury or prejudice to the Crown's dignity? He wasn't at all convinced that he had.

One comforting thought was, everybody aboard seemed positive that *Centurion*'s next port of call would be Batavia; but did the European factors, the Spanish spies, the Chinese and Portuguese government officials feel as sure of his destination?

Smiling inwardly, Anson climbed to the poopdeck and made a show of admiring his new Commodore's pendant. Now that a stiff offshore breeze was driving away a bank of rain clouds, the swallow-tailed scarlet bunting was straining straight out from its bridle.

From *Centurion*'s regilded stern staff a Blue Ensign nearly as big as the foregallant sail streamed as if eager to be away; forward, a Royal Jack snapped bravely.

Anson's critical gaze traveled methodically over his flagship's spotless decks and noted that members of the Watch were neatly dressed and moving briskly in the performance of their duties.

With particular care he observed the activities of that broad-shouldered ex-harness-maker who, increasingly, had attracted favorable attention. He recalled Schoolmaster Pascoe Thomas's remarking that, during off-hours, he'd often been pestered by the hulking midshipman; Nat Wade had appeared genuinely eager for instruction in the art of navigation.

At nine o'clock on the morning of April 19, 1743, *Centurion's* anchor was heaved in the time-honored fashion — to fiddle music and a discordant rendition of "Spanish Ladies." It sounded fine, even though sung by Lascars, Dutch, French, Portuguese and even Spanish voices.

"Anchor's aweigh, sir!" The call came ringing aft when the best bower appeared fouled with mud which promptly was hosed off.

Aloft, top captains responding to Mr. Nutt's barked commands, sent their men scurrying out on the footropes to loose topsails, then gallants and, finally, courses. Everyone felt cheered when a burst of sunshine illumined the new sails and made them shine like well-washed china.

Once *Centurion* really had commenced to gather speed, she began to fire salutes in reply to those offered by the Portuguese forts and by vessels lying in Taypa Harbor.

Gunsmoke from the flagship was whirled out to sea ahead of the Fourth Rate as if to warn all and sundry that His Britannic Majesty's ship *Centurion* had resumed her voyage.

To all who beheld her, she presented a beautiful picture as, with all plain canvas set from courses to royals, she overtook a scattering of decorated seagoing junks, and headed for the Bocca Tigris.

Swiftly, the bare gray-green islands off Macao merged themselves with the coast of China.

The Commodore had to exert his celebrated self-control to the fullest in order to delay an announcement until after the crew had consumed their dinner. At last he summoned his first lieutenant. "Mr. Saumarez, please have all hands piped on deck."

Even while the boatswain's "Southampton nightingale" was still trilling, men tumbled out of the forecastle onto the upper gundeck and gathered below the quarterdeck's break. By the dozen, white, black, brown and yellow bare feet padded up companionway ladders.

Off-duty officers, some still yawning and blinking, lined up on the quarterdeck, their vari-hued coats swaying in unison to *Centurion's* easy motion.

The Commodore, wearing a black tricorne, a simple gray frock coat and breeches, canary yellow waistcoat and bright red stockings, appeared at the break of the poopdeck and lingered there.

Expressionless, Anson gazed down on the many-complexioned faces lifted in his direction and discovered that he'd no difficulty whatever in picking out the round pinkish faces of the few Dutchmen who'd been encouraged to desert a newly arrived Indiaman under the illusion that they would reach home quicker in this fashion.

Gradually stillness settled over the flagship in which could be heard the creak and whine of yards straining against parrels, the strumming of wind in the rigging and the steady *hiss-hiss* of waves alongside.

First, Anson bowed to the assembled officers; they at once whipped off hats and tucked them under their left arms. Next he nodded to the men crowding together below, bareheaded.

He drew a deep breath, then said in loud and ringing tones, "Gentlemen and my brave lads, now that we have left the coast out of sight I have summoned you to inform you about your destination.

"We are not now bound for England; not even for Batavia — but instead for Cape Espiritu Santo, which lies in the Philippine Islands, where I hope we shall intercept and *take the Manila galleon!*"

A resounding yell rolled out over the sparkling blue and white ocean, beat high above the Commodore's pendant. De Saumarez, Brett and the other officers sufficiently forgot their dignity to execute impromptu jigs of joy. The ship's boys — the few who were left — squealed like pigs caught under a gate.

"Aye. I'll take you to the Prize of All the Oceans!"

Tom Ramster cupped hands and roared above the tumult, "Just show her to us, sir, and we'll do the rest!"

Once the uproar had lessened, Anson continued, "In China I learned that it is for this Cape Espiritu Santo that the galleon invariably makes for after clearing from Guam. Apparently she touches there to pick up the latest intelligence before standing north for Manila.

"Also," he paused for effect, "I hear that, this year, there may be *two* galleons because, through our unsuccessful blockade off Acapulco,

[429]

we caused last year's ship to be held in port so long that she missed her return voyage. Perhaps that was all to the good; in any case, I know you will agree with me in feeling that two lots of prize money are better than one."

"The more the merrier!" roared a deep-voiced chorus. "Aye, sir, that's the word!"

"True, it will be stout, full-manned ships we must fight; but we have a stout vessel, too, our beloved old *Centurion!* Men, I am fully confident that the spirit which has carried us all so far, that has weathered the gales of Cape Horn, that has taken prize after prize, has captured Payta, blockaded Acapulco, and crossed the Pacific Ocean in the face of death and disaster lies stronger in you than ever, my lads! It burns hot enough to take two or even more companies of Spaniards — though our numbers are not all they might be.

"Never believe the lies told you at Macao, that the sides of these treasure ships are built so thick that no cannonball can penetrate them — those are the reports of cowards who never have gone near enough to try!

"For my part, I promise you, on my word of honor, that when we meet with these galleons — as surely we shall — I will take our ship so close to them that our balls, instead of being stopped, shall go through *both* their sides and fall into the sea beyond!"

Anson paused, long, light-brown hair whipping in the breeze. "What is your answer to this, my gallant lads?"

A few seagulls which, in hopes of scavenging, had followed *Centurion* out from the coast, veered away in terror at the great, throat-tearing shout that went up.

"We'll have them, your Honor!" yelled the hairy fellows below, "or go down with you and the ship!"

"*On les aura! Vámos tomarlos!*" shouted the foreigners and, in a dozen other languages and dialects, begged to be led against the galleon.

All hands flourished headgear with such enthusiasm that several caps flew over the rail. Young Lieutenant Denis threw arms about even younger Augustus van Keppel and the two executed a crazy dance of some minutes' duration; it was as if the flagship were sailing through a belt of some wildly exhilarating atmosphere.

"How could we have been such fools as to imagine the Commodore wouldn't sail against the galleon?" Scott queried of Marine Lieutenants Bruce and Craig.

"We were taken in, the same as you," Gordon admitted, still, flushed and hoarse from cheering. "It's to our lasting shame that we proved such unsuspecting gulls."

That evening *Centurion*'s course was altered from south to east-southeast in order to pass through the Bashi Channel, south of Formosa.

Anson then directed his self-effacing secretary to fetch the muster and paybooks. After studying them a while he sighed. "I observe, Andrew, that our Muster Roll now lists two hundred twenty-seven Europeans — of which twenty-seven are boys — and fifty Negroes, Chinese and Lascars — all completely untrained. Hum. We shall have to get busy and make do. Please send for the lieutenants."

When they arrived in the great cabin he said gravely, "Gentlemen, as you probably are aware, we have on board under three hundred men, many of whom are completely unfamiliar with the business of fighting a warship."

He eyed de Saumarez, his gunnery officer. "Since we mount sixty guns it will be manifestly impossible to assign the usual six men to each piece; four will have to suffice.

"More serious yet is the fact that I can find but one experienced gun captain for each four pieces. I regret to inform you that of the officers and men who sailed with us from Southampton *only one hundred twenty-seven* remain. This necessitates continuous training and much hard work on the part of us all."

The Commodore's bright blue eyes sought his olive-complexioned first lieutenant. "Mr. Saumarez, you will command the main gun-deck. You, Mr. Brett, will be in charge of the upper deck guns, while you, Mr. Denis, will train selected men as marksmen to be posted in the fighting tops. Mr. Nutt and the supernumerary lieutenants will instruct new topmen in sail-handling. Is that clear?"

"Aye, aye, sir."

"Commencing tomorrow, I expect you, tirelessly, to exercise your men in their several duties. I know you well enough by now —" the ghost of a smile relaxed Anson's expression — "to feel confident that you will recognize and reward the able and the industrious, and punish the lazy and frivolous. Nor shall I, without good cause, disapprove any appointment you choose to make — you may rely on that."

Around noon of May 20, 1743, a midshipman on duty in the fore-topmast reported land in sight.

"That will be Cape Espiritu Santo, sir," declared Justinian Nutt. "I'll stake my reputation on it."

"In that case, Mr. Nutt, I'll thank you to order the upper canvas taken in and alter our course so that we may keep the land under the horizon. Until further orders, we will cruise under courses alone, in order to avoid possible detection from Palapa, where I understand the enemy maintains a lookout station."

～ 17 ～
Off Cape Espiritu Santo

Centurion BEGAN HER PATROL off Cape Espiritu Santo with the crew in high spirits; the new members proved especially keen to engage the enemy — probably because they had no claim on booty previously won. Old hands, having survived so much, were burning to increase shares already due and so assure a lifetime of luxury.

Once the patient patrolling began, painfully reminiscent of those weeks off the Mexican coast, days and nights were devoted to interminable gun drills and sail-handling exercises.

Often *Centurion* was able to run, with sheets loosed, over a placid ocean dotted with wandering rain clouds which, for a while, could reduce visibility to nil, a fact which was causing Anson's men considerable anxiety. Suppose one such obscured the galleon during a brief appearance on the horizon?

Following a recently adopted routine, the Commander in Chief first would visit the poopdeck from which supernumerary officers such as Patrick Baird, Thomas Foley and Sam Scott, were firing at a keg that had been tossed overboard. Together with such noncombatants as Schoolmaster Pascoe Thomas, Purser Millechamp and Andrew Menzies, they had been specially detailed to pick off the galleon's officers.

On noticing the Commodore approaching, Lieutenant Baird stiffened and pulled off a frayed straw hat.

"Well, and how does it go today?"

"Doing a bit better, sir, but I fear we can't properly be called sharpshooters for a while yet. Will you try a shot, sir?" Baird offered a musket.

"I will, but, if I hit, set it down to sheer good luck." The Commodore quickly shouldered the piece, fired and uttered a pleased grunt when yellow splinters and spray flew about the target.

His tour then took him to the quarterdeck on which tough old Captain Crowden and the two Marine lieutenants were instructing a group of sunburned recruits in the arts of loading, pointing and then recharging pedereros — small swivel guns which, eventually, would be placed in the fighting tops. They weren't having an easy time, it being traditional that seamen should detest handling landlubber weapons.

Third Lieutenant Denis came hurrying over from another group he was training in the use of small arms.

"How are you faring, Mr. Denis?"

Although naked to the waist and perspiring heavily, the young officer removed his hat and spoke respectfully, "They're making progress, sir — at least I hope so. I have assigned four men to each of the tops. It's a pity there can't be more."

"It's all of that. Therefore, it is essential that your men shall learn to shoot well and pick off as many gun captains as possible. Have you thus far discovered a real marksman?"

"Only one, sir. The purser's mate, name of Pallister. He's developing into a fine shot."

"Let us see what he can do."

Denis cupped hands, shouted up to a boy perched, monkey-like, near the mainyard's end, "Ahoy up there! Set your target to swinging."

A two-foot square of board upon which a white circle had been painted was set in motion; with the ship's roll added, it presented a far from easy target.

"Whose notion is this?" Anson demanded, hugely interested.

"Why, mine, sir." Denis admitted. "I figured our marksmen will seldom be offered a stationary mark. Now then, Pallister, go aloft and try to give the Commodore an example of your skill."

Upon reaching the fore-fighting-top, Will Pallister hooked a knee over its rail and brought his musket to bear. He waited until *Centurion* hesitated in mid-roll, then fired. Smoke whipped by the lithe

[433]

young fellow's head as splinters flew from the painted circle's edge.

Delighted as always when one of his officers proved himself ingenious, Anson said, "Capital, Mr. Denis! My compliments to young Pallister. Every one of your sharpshooters who becomes as proficient shall receive an extra rum ration. Meanwhile, I shall send you a small reward from my wine locker."

After a week's fruitless patrolling, the Commodore one day was puzzled by the sound of many feet racing back and forth about the main gundeck. On investigation he discovered the usually dapper de Saumarez, disheveled and clad only in a soiled sweat-soaked shirt and breeches.

Anson said, "Be good enough to explain to me this — er — odd form of gun drill you are conducting. It resembles nothing prescribed by Admiralty regulations."

Seen by strong sunlight reflected off the ocean through an open gunport, the young officer's dark features intensified their serious expression.

"With pleasure, sir. As the Commodore knows, on this deck we mount twenty-four twenty-four-pounders — twelve to a side. Aloft, Mr. Brett commands twenty-six nine-pounders — or thirteen guns to a broadside."

A thin smile curved Anson's sun-cracked lips. "I believe that is so."

"In action, sir, a minimum of four men — not including powder monkeys — are required to serve each piece." De Saumarez struggled to even his breathing. "This, sir, would call for the services of two hundred ten hands while the ship's company, at present, totals two hundred seventy-seven — many of whom are boys or ignorant foreigners."

"I believe I understand your point. If all our guns are to be manned, even by the absolute minimum of four men to a piece, only sixty-seven hands would be left over to handle sail, steer, pass ammunition and attend the wounded; an impossible situation, of course. Now then, what have you and Mr. Brett accomplished towards this problem?"

Watched all the while by his barefooted, ill-smelling gunners who improved on this respite by mopping faces or retying handkerchiefs bound about their brows, de Saumarez replied, "— By stationing only two men permanently at each piece. Their sole duties will be to sponge out, load and prime. Meanwhile, gangs of twelve strong men each will, after the initial broadside, commence running along our

[434]

beam to haul in pieces as rapidly as possible — which is all that will be expected of them."

Intensely interested, Anson nodded. "And then what?"

"Once a gun has been reloaded, sir, a second gang composed of trained gun captains will run out, train and fire it." De Saumarez looked anxious. "This, of course, means, sir, that after the first broadside each gun will have to be fired independently."

"Capital! That's all to the good," came the Commodore's unexpected assurance.

"May I ask why, sir?"

"Because Spanish gunners, when an enemy broadside is anticipated, usually throw themselves flat onto the deck to avoid the risk of getting hurt. By firing successive shots, we shall thus keep many of the enemy lying flat a good part of the time; consequently, their guns cannot be served."

A delighted grin spread over the first lieutenant's glistening features. "A third gang, composed of less intelligent foreigners and ship's boys, will supply each piece with ammunition as required."

"Mr. Saumarez, yours is a most original and workable solution to the problem, which I shall mention in my next Letter of Proceedings. However, I fear that if certain Admirals learn of what you contemplate, their bowels would writhe over so practical departure from the procedure prescribed by them."

Many days, some sunny, some calm, some stormy, succeeded each other while *Centurion,* remaining invisible from Espiritu Santo, maintained her dogged patrol. On occasion the dim, blue outline of the Cape itself briefly was brought into sight, but only long enough to check navigational findings.

Gradually, hot hopes began to cool and doubts arose as to whether the Prize of All the Oceans and her hoped-for consort might not have passed in the night or have been obscured by one of the many blinding rainstorms which kept descending.

Augustus van Keppel had written in his journal:

June 5, 1743. Keeping our Station and looking out for the Galleons in great expectation.

June 11. Begin to grow Impatient at not Seeing the Galleons.

June 13. The Wind, having blown fresh Easterly for the forty-eight Hours past, gives us Great Expectations of seeing the Galleons soon.

June 15. Cruising Off and On and Looking out most Stricktly.

June 19. This Nearing the end of June finds us yet Apprehensive. The Galleons, if they arrive at all, must Appear soon. All Hands Apprehensive and Displeased.

Keppel's diary, to say the least, was a monument of understatement. From the lowliest ship's boy to the Commodore, a fear was burgeoning that, somehow, the treasure ships had passed them by. Had they departed from Acapulco earlier than was customary? Perhaps, on learning that the pestiferous English man-of-war still was prowling the Pacific with the express purpose of attacking them, the treasure ships were following a new route to Manila?

For a fortnight Anson's flute remained in its case. Brett and his protégé forgot to use their paintboxes. Survivors of the original ship's company muttered darkly that Captain Arnand's curse had lost none of its virulence.

The twentieth day of June commenced no differently than any of the other thirty-one passed since HBMS *Centurion* had arrived off Cape Espiritu Santo. When the Morning Watch was called at four bells, newly appointed Midshipman Charles Proby yawned and knuckled his eyes before toiling up a seemingly endless succession of ratlines to his lookout's post astride the foreroyal yard.

Since it remained dark, he found difficulty in staying awake and not falling off his perch. Eternities seemed to elapse before dawn broke with unusual suddenness. A moment ago the sky had been dark and starlit, now there was a golden glory in the east which revealed, near its center, a towering pile of sail.

In a shaking voice, Proby hailed the maindeck on which Lieutenant Peircy Brett had the duty.

"A sail, sir! A *sail!*"

"Where away?" Brett's voice soared from far below.

"To the eastward, sir!" shrieked the midshipman. "There may be more than one vessel!"

"How many?"

"Two, I think, and sailing in line, sir. There's too much canvas showing for a single vessel!"

"Clear for Action!"

INFORMATION THAT that cloud of sail growing on the horizon was not being created by two ships, but by one very large one, came as only a passing disappointment. Everyone was obsessed with the joyous realization that this lofty vessel was steering straight for *Centurion* and that, almost certainly, she must be one of the Manila galleons — if, indeed, two really *had* set sail.

The galleon! Anson muttered pulling a sleep-drenched nightshirt away from thick and hairy legs. There she is. At last! *At last!*

He closed his eyes and lifted unshaven features to heavens all aflame with dawn. "Oh, Great God, I most humbly thank Thee. Please, O Lord, grant us Thy favor in this mortal hour. Lend us sufficient strength and good fortune to make a prize of her."

Throughout the flagship, veterans silently were running back over the years, trying to recall when first they'd heard mentioned the Prize of All the Oceans.

Nat Wade, now a passed midshipman, was able to remember that he'd first heard the galleon discussed during that overcrowded, nightmarish passage from England to Funchal. Purser's Mate Pallister had heard, or rather overheard, tall tales told by drunken sailors reveling in a tavern near Stewkey.

Peter Vesey, M.D., was sure he'd not heard of her until *Gloucester* lay, fever-ridden, at anchor off Santa Catharina.

As for George Anson, his memory ran back to a rainy afternoon on which he had sat, rather awed, in a club on St. James's Street in company with Admiral Sir Charles Wager, then First Lord of the Admiralty, the Lord Chancellor, Lord Hardwicke and the Duke of Newcastle.

He was almost sure it had been Sir Charles who'd drawled, "D'ye know, Anson, an you take the Manila Galleon you'll be richer than any of us for the rest of your days."

The expedition's Commander in Chief then recalled another afternoon, that bitter one on which he'd seen the "Seasoned, disciplined regiment" he'd been promised appear, staggering and limping along the quay.

Other memories returned; the deaths of Captains Arnand and Colley and of countless other burials at sea; hot, fever-haunted Santa Catharina; frigid, bleak and barren Saint Julian; and, worst of all, those agonized days and nights off Statenland, Cape Horn and Cape Noire while the scurvy raged with no less fury than the hurricanes, and Death took no time off.

He found that, without difficulty, he could visualize *Centurion*, limping, all but disabled, into Juan Fernandez, decks littered with decomposing bodies; then there was that ghastly arrival of *Gloucester*.

Finally, the Commodore recalled the acute disillusionment which had followed the discovery that that bright light sighted off the coast of Mexico was only a smoldering volcano.

The voice of Sailing Master Nutt directing all sail to be made, roused Anson from his solemn retrospection. Before hurrying below to dress for battle, he swept the horizon through a glass in hopes of sighting the other galleon which, he felt, must certainly be somewhere nearby. But, strain his eyesight as he would, there was nothing to be seen except that tremendous galleon still heading straight in *Centurion*'s direction.

Right after breakfast — Anson insisted on its being served, although almost everyone proved too excited to eat — drums rolled briskly and all hands hurried to clear for action now that the enemy had become visible from both poop and forecastle.

"She's keeping straight for us like a whore on payday!" Tom Ramster exulted to the other gun captains when they sought the galley to light slow matches before its fire was extinguished.

Chortled Gunner's Mate Buckle, "If she don't turn tail and try to run, we'll all be dead or rich as lords come sundown."

In orderly fashion preparations for battle continued to be made; the carpenter and his mates unshipped those light wooden screens which set off and divided the officers' cabins and with them sent below the Commodore's and the wardroom's furniture.

Below decks, mess captains ordered their mates to clear away crockery, to stow chests and ditty bags into the wings, out of the way.

Aloft, sailors stopped all topsail sheets that those sails might not accidentally be lowered during the engagement, then slung light, bullet-proof chains to the lower yards and prepared spare blocks and coils of rope to deal with emergencies. Men in the fighting tops mounted their swivel guns and loaded them with grapeshot.

Next, hammocks filled with bedding were lashed along the rail as

[438]

a protection from splinters; others were used to protect vital dead-eyes and lanyards.

The lieutenants, regular and supernumerary alike, moved quietly supervising the rigging of rope nets over the upper gundeck to catch broken spars, severed tackle or men falling from the tops.

Gunners Nuttall, Bargecroft and their mates saw to the wetting of swabs to be placed behind each gun, the draping of soaked cloths along the mouths of magazines and scuttles; also that dripping frieze blankets were slung to screen magazine entrances so that no spark could possibly get past.

Gun captains, meanwhile, congregated at the gunner's storeroom to draw cartouche boxes containing quills filled with fine 4F powder which should ensure quick and efficient priming. After that, they helped the skeleton gun crews to strike open port lids before inspecting all breeching, preventers and side tackles.

They also removed tampions and those lead aprons which customarily protected touch-holes before laying out the handspikes and crowbars with which the guns would be trained.

Lieutenant Hughes, acting as master-at-arms, issued cutlasses, pikes and pistols to men told off to act as boarders should the ships grapple; muskets, powder horns and bullet bags to the marksmen who would snipe from the forecastle, the poop and from the tops.

Comparative silence continued until an order was given to run out the double-shotted guns; then the hollow rumble of many heavy wooden wheels made *Centurion*'s hull resound dully.

Powder monkeys, mostly boys and hopelessly stupid foreigners, drew leather cases which, normally, they would display to Marine guards posted about the magazines. But today there would be no guards stationed anywhere aboard the flagship, not even by the companionways, where they were supposed to restrain frightened men from running below.

A sobering moment came when wet sand was sprinkled on the deck to inhibit slipping on the gore which would probably flow before long.

Quietly, Peter Vesey passed along both gundecks issuing tourniquets and pledgets for first attentions, then returned to the cockpit to assist the surgeons in rigging an operating table which would consist of an old sail folded over a number of mess tables supported by stacked sea chests. Tubs were set out to receive severed limbs, battle lanterns lit, ligatures readied and surgical instruments placed handy.

[439]

After *Centurion* had been prepared for action — a surprisingly short period considering how undermanned she was — her officers went about, offered elaborately casual reassurances. Expressions were serious now, for not a man but was aware that yonder lofty ship carried not less than six hundred soldiers and sailors of the regular Spanish establishment; also that she mounted many more guns than their own vessel — all of them fully manned.

Andrew Menzies, busying himself about the quarterdeck on which he'd been posted as a sharpshooter, wondered just how he would react once the battle was joined — as a Carolinian gentleman should, he hoped. But — but, he wasn't too sure just what he'd do were Death to look him squarely in the face.

Somehow, he couldn't quite bring himself to realize that, after the passage of so many weary months and years, the Manila Galleon was not over eight miles distant! With her tremendous spread of sail gleaming in the rising sun, she looked to be the most impressive ship he'd ever beheld.

It was a pity that so many former companions couldn't see her, too. Waxter, for instance; if only he hadn't proved such an ignoble rogue.

Rushing along with studding sails set, the flagship showed her giant Blue Ensign at the stern, Anson's fifty-yard-long red pendant at her main; a brand new Royal Jack snapped at her foretop.

A subdued shout arose when the red and yellow painted galleon was seen to take in her topgallants and fire a gun to leeward.

"These cheeky swine are daring us to engage them," tensely muttered de Saumarez.

"On the other hand, perhaps she's signaling her consort to come up," was the sailing master's unexpected suggestion.

Anson, just then arriving at the quarterdeck's lee rail, smiled, said quietly, "Let us hope you are correct in that, Mr. Nutt. 'Twould be a real pleasure to fight the both of them."

⟆ 1 9 ⟆

Battle, I

CAPTAIN CROWDEN, CLAD in a brilliant red tunic braided in yellow, spat over the rail, thinking, Dear God, what absurd confidence we're showing — and us unable even to fire two whole broadsides!

[440]

On watching that contemptuous twist of gunsmoke drift away from the Spaniard, Anson called to Denis, commanding the quarter-deck batteries, "Pray fire a gun to leeward. Yonder gentlemen must not find us wanting in courtesy."

Up in the main fighting top, Acting Corporal Will Pallister discovered that, among other things, his post afforded a most excellent vantage point. Situated almost directly above the quarterdeck, he could see the Commodore pacing about the poop, clad in a simple black cocked hat, sky-blue breeches and a scarlet and black frock coat.

Today he was wearing no jewel-hilted dress sword but a sturdy cut-and-thrust weapon supplemented by two pairs of slim, silver-mounted dueling pistols thrust into his belt.

Will watched the black latticework patterns cast by the shrouds cross and recross the quarterdeck in front of the steerage in which Sailing Master Nutt and the quartermaster stood taut beside *Centurion's* great wheel.

The acting corporal then recognized Lieutenant de Saumarez moving about, terrier-nervous, before descending to direct the main gun-deck. A stride behind the first lieutenant walked Tom Ramster, his whip-scarred body bared to his belt. Tom, Pallister knew, was captain of a gang which would aim and fire the 24-pounders.

To disguise a sudden and most uncomfortable sense of apprehension, Will inspected once more the nearest swivel gun's priming.

One of the three other sharpshooters who shared the fighting top pointed at the galleon. "I can't believe it's really her, can you?"

"Only just."

The seaman nodded while feeding a brace of musket balls into his piece.

"How far away d'you figure she is now?"

"Near a mile," supplied another marksman wearing a small gold ring in his left ear. "Cock's bones, mate! To think there's a fine farm in Norfolk sailing straight towards me; which farm will lay so far from the sea that I'll carry an oar inland until someone asks, 'Wot's that thing?' Wot about you, 'Arry?"

"Me, farm? Nah. I'm minding me of the Blue Bull, which is a tidy pub hard by Winchester; 'ad me eye on the place since I was a little nipper."

To the dismay of *Centurion's* anxious company, a heavy rain squall suddenly came racing over the sea. It dulled the Pacific's deep blue, swiftly drew an opaque veil across the horizon and effectively concealed the great galleon.

"Cover your musket's lock!" ordered Acting Corporal Pallister, amazed that his voice should sound so deep and authoritative. "Stopper your powder horns and cover the swivels!"

On the gundeck below, gunners shielded glowing slow matches, while others replaced lead aprons on the touch-holes. Raising a triumphant howl, the squall struck and dumped cascades of rain upon *Centurion*'s deck as she reeled under the blast.

All of an instant, Will felt chilled to his marrow; cold water streamed down his back and into his baggy canvas breeches. Through the driving rain he couldn't even make out the foremast.

"Lucifer's balls!" growled he with the earring. "Behind such cover the Dons can turn and run, leaving us to whistle for her treasure!"

For forty eternal minutes the squall obscured the scene, then, as abruptly as it had appeared, it cleared away. A hoarse shout arose from the dripping Fourth Rate when the Spaniard was seen, some two miles off, sailing off the flagship's beam and almost abreast.

More impassive than ever, Anson waited until 11:30 A.M., then called down to the quarterdeck, "Quartermaster! Steer across her wake, then bear up along her larboard beam!"

To Acting Lieutenant van Keppel he remarked, "We must get between her and the land for, if she gets hurt too badly, she may try to run for Palapa on Samar Island."

"Yes, sir. Let us pray that, this time, the enemy will not refuse us a battle!"

On the forecastle a badly sunburned powder monkey suddenly queried, "Wot are 'e bloomin' Papists up to? Looks like they're dumping something overboard."

A grizzled gunner shook his head. "They're only now getting rid of their livestock."

"Bloody brutes!"

"Aye, that they are; but not on this account. Everybody does so in prospect of hard action. Can't have wounded critters rampaging about scattering guts and blood about the decks."

Soon a good many cattle, sheep and pigs were pushed into the sea; they swam about, bawling or bleating in despair until they were drowned or were killed by swarms of sharks.

In an effort to bring confusion to the enemy when they commenced to jettison a deck load of lumber, Anson hailed the upper gundeck, "Mr. Brett! You may open with your bow chasers; but do not fire your broadside until we are within pistol-shot."

A ringing shout went up when both bow chasers boomed and a pair of brief silvery splashes showed half a gunshot short of the galleon's ornate stern.

Red-headed Tom Ramster and King Parmer grinned, but Will Pallister went a little pale when the Spaniard fired her stern chasers in reply and two cannonballs raised lazy water spouts from the surface *ahead* of *Centurion's* freshly gilded figurehead.

More suggestive of a high-strung terrier than ever, Philip de Saumarez, armed with boarding pistols, ranged along the main gundeck with narrow dark eyes agleam and all-seeing. Although of less than medium height, the first lieutenant nevertheless had to bend his head in order to avoid banging it against the red-painted beams above.

Since all hatch covers were raised and twenty-four open gunports admitted sunlight, the rows of cannon dully gleaming along the main gundeck were brilliantly illumined.

On the upper gundeck, Second Lieutenant Brett, ever eager to emulate his hero, paced slowly about while managing to maintain a serene expression. Try as he would, though, Brett couldn't suppress a series of yawns, engendered by accelerated heart action, as he moved among the first division's guns.

Midshipman Hyde Parker inquired eagerly, "How soon d'you think we'll fire our broadside, sir?"

"Not until we reach pistol range," Brett replied sharply. "The Commodore wishes our shot to pierce both of the enemy's sides."

Once the flagship arrived within easy gunshot, Anson ordered the spritsail yard to be swung fore and aft, in order to facilitate boarding over the bows — should the opportunity present itself.

When, very slowly, *Centurion* drew abreast of the enemy, Anson called to Midshipman Drake, "The time, please?"

"A half after mid-day, sir," the youth's thin voice replied.

"Very well." Noting that a certain confusion was visible upon the Spaniard's deck and that *Centurion* was beginning to draw ahead, George Anson revised his decision to wait for pistol-shot range — fifty yards — and, in a deep and ringing voice, issued that command for which all hands had been waiting three hours to hear.

"You may open fire; continue to do so at will!"

At half a mile's range *Centurion's* first and only broadside was loosed. When the heavy guns of her starboard battery roared in unison

[443]

she heeled perceptibly to port under their recoil and her all but idle canvas fluttered from the concussion.

Because there was so little wind, whirling, choking clouds of burnt powder fumes drifted back through the gunports and into the gunners' faces; it made their eyes run and sent them into paroxysms of coughing.

"Oh God, why can't we get into musket-shot?" complained one of Pallister's companions. "It cuts me 'ard to bide up 'ere, so bloody useless-like."

Soon an encouraging fact became apparent; due to the narrowness of their gunports, the Spaniards could not traverse very far and so could bring only a part of their broadside guns into play while Brett's and de Saumarez's sweating gunners could, and did, employ all their cannon through *Centurion*'s wider gunports.

All at once Lieutenant Hughes's huge voice boomed above the guns' crashing roar, "Look, sir! They're afire!"

Anson turned and was appalled to see smoke and flames whirling up to the enemy's mizzentop. Barely in time, he smothered an anxious oath. What profit would there be in capturing a burnt-out wreck?

A moment later he relaxed on becoming aware that the blaze was caused by hammocks and nettings which had been ignited by flaming wads from the flagship's guns. Once the enemy had cut away the flaming nettings and let them fall into the sea the smoke abated and soon disappeared.

It was noticed, however, that this brief conflagration had set fire to the ship's huge red and yellow stern colors; presently they were consumed and so left only the Royal Ensign of Spain flying from the maintop.

"How's *that* for a good sign?" bellowed Nat Wade, dashing sweat from his powder-blackened forehead.

Trailed by burnt smoke, and spouting fire all the while, *Centurion* continued to overhaul her lofty adversary and, in so doing, passed through an area in which a few brown and white cattle still were floundering forlornly about.

"Bloody boogers!" snarled one of Ramster's quarter-gunners who, like Joe Utting, had been a farmer until the pressgang had grabbed him. "Granted a chance, I'll send some Papists in to keep 'em company."

"Reduce sail," Anson curtly instructed his sailing master. "Since

[444]

we're unable to fire broadsides, I wish to cut up her rigging before we cross her bow and rake."

Gradually *Centurion* closed in, firing individual shots in rapid succession at the galleon's towering yellow side and now disorganized top hamper.

The fight, however, remained far from one-sided; Spanish guns continued to thunder whenever their gunners could bring cannon to bear; in fact, the enemy's fire became alarmingly effective. *Centurion*'s mainmast was struck so heavily that Pallister and his companions almost were flung over the rail on which their swivel guns were mounted.

"We *must* be in range now," he managed to shout at his companions, furious to find himself shaking like a frightened colt. At the same time he assured himself savagely, "I am not afraid! I *will not* be afraid!" But he was.

Sections of *Centurion*'s bulwarks flew through the air and a series of heart-stilling crashes bespoke Spanish roundshot ripping through her side. Magically, ragged holes appeared in the lower sails, braces were severed and several yards swung uselessly. Walls of choking, gray-white smoke formed, then billowed up to conceal the enemy below her topmasts, her blue, yellow and red Royal Standard and a religious banner at her forepeak.

Will could hear, but could not see, those gangs which must be aiming and loading the pieces thundering below. In his ears also rang the hoarse shouts of gun captains which often were drowned out by the deafening roar of battle.

When briefly a puff of wind dispersed the baffling gloom, Pallister and his fellow marksmen manned the starboard swivel gun and peered through rotten-smelling smoke for a glimpse of the enemy's deck.

Presently, the acting corporal glimpsed a group of brilliantly dressed figures collected upon the enemy's slowly heaving quarterdeck, so slewed his piece to bear.

To Pallister's vast surprise he remembered to select one man for a target, as Lieutenant Denis repeatedly had warned him to. He trained his swivel gun on a brilliant yellow jacket that was traversed by a wide scarlet sash.

Once Will's finger crooked over the trigger's cool and oily surface his nervousness evaporated and he remembered to squint his eyes against that spurt of flame which, inevitably, would escape the pan.

[445]

When he reopened his eyes it was to see not only the yellow-clad officer fallen with his sword gleaming beside him but also three others of the group reeling about the deck and clutching spurting wounds.

"Ha! That's for all the friends I've lost!" Will snatched a loaded musket from its rack — he reckoned there wouldn't be time to reload the swivel before the ships drew apart — and pointed at another richly dressed officer, but forgot to hold the stock tight enough to his shoulder so the piece kicked him like a curried horse with a ticklish belly.

Since everybody else seemed to be yelling, he joined in the deafening tumult while reloading with the sure deftness of long practice. *Bam! Bam!* Only vaguely was he aware that his companions, too, were shooting at the Spaniards' crowded deck.

So many invisible demons screeched, whistled and screamed past his ears Will concluded that the enemy must be aiming high with a view of crippling the flagship's rigging.

"Hurry, you snail-footed bastards!" gasped Tom Ramster, leading his loading gang from Number 3 to Number 5 starboard gun where its two permanent gunners, bug-eyed with exertion, were ramming home a fresh charge.

In leaping over a discarded handspike, Tom bumped squarely into a Lascar powder monkey running through drifting smoke with eyes huge and white in his dark face. He was carrying a leather cartridge case under either arm.

"Out o' my way, ye bloody, black heathen!" Ramster snarled and, with his helpers, flung himself at Number 5's training tackle.

Once the piece had been pointed at a row of gunports, reeking amid the galleon's splintered yellow and red side, he snatched up a slow match burning on a nearby sand tub, then blew on it until it glowed before jamming it into the touch-hole.

Barely in time, the big gunner's mate leaped aside and so avoided the 24-pounder's recoil. Already his men were pounding on through choking gloom towards a glow wrought by sunlight flooding in Number 7's port.

"Hell'll be a holiday to this!" wheezed Bill Buckle. "I'm ready to fall!"

"I'll say! Me throat's burnt out!" panted the huge Negro behind him.

Now and then men on the main gundeck were forced to halt and dig with grimy knuckles at red and streaming eyes.

On the poopdeck George Anson, a bared sword in one hand, was forced to clutch the taffrail with the other to keep from falling, so violent was a sudden paroxysm of coughing, but when a puff of wind momentarily cleared the smoke he continued to survey the battle's progress as calmly as if walking *Centurion*'s stern gallery in a friendly port.

When, almost imperceptibly, the ships sailed closer together, the action swelled towards a deafening, sense-numbing crescendo. The sharp crackle of musketry in the fighting tops increased. One of Pallister's companions, although wounded in the side, leveled his piece and sang out, "Watch me drop that fellow in the fancy green suit!" And he did.

Centurion's fire must be very effective, Anson decided, were one to judge by the almost continual crackle and crash of timbers being smashed and the increasing number of shrieks and screams rising aboard the galleon.

When, through a rift in the swirling smoke, he glimpsed the enemy's upper gundeck swarming with men he called for van Keppel, who ran up hatless and with his face streaked by rivulets of sweat which had poured over a mask of burnt powder grains.

"My compliments to Mr. Brett!" he bellowed above the appalling thunder of guns. "Tell him to load with grape and order his gunners to sweep their deck before the enemy can attempt to board. Then go find Mr. Saumarez and instruct him to cease firing into the hull; he is to use chainshot on the Spaniard's spars!"

Bleeding from a splinter graze across his forehead, van Keppel was shaken to see a seaman named Richmond decapitated by a cannonball not five feet before him. Nevertheless, he found Peircy Brett stalking coolly about amid the suffocating smoke for all that a red stain was spreading across his light blue shirt and dripping onto his pantaloons. His long features had been turned black as those of any Negro in the crew.

A descent into the Infernal Regions could not be very different, decided young van Keppel while fighting his way past a stream of powder monkeys to the main gundeck.

What with the screaming of wounded men and the thunderous discharge of big guns van Keppel's eardrums ached, felt ready to burst as he blundered about in this noisy confusion, barely able to find his way. Continually, he kept tripping over rammer staffs, abandoned cartridge cases, loose cannonballs or other gear. Again and again he collided with, and got knocked down by, loaders and pointers running from gun to gun.

At last *Centurion*'s shortage of manpower began to tell; her rate of fire slackened as her hard-pressed loading gangs neared exhaustion. She was able, however, to maintain a sporadic fire which kept many Spaniards cowering on deck.

Bitterly, the Commander in Chief lamented that another broadside, which well might have terminated the engagement, could not be fired unless the ready, but idle guns of the flagship's port battery could be used.

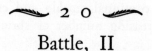

2 0

Battle, II

A STRONG PUFF of wind came out of nowhere and restored enough visibility for Anson to perceive that *Centurion* now was leading her gigantic enemy by at least three ship's lengths.

"Mr. Nutt! Starboard your helm!" Anson rasped over a renewed crackle of musketry from the fighting tops.

Quartermaster's Mate Pack's eyes rolled and his teeth flashed in his blackened face, when in obedience to the sailing master's curt command, he and his mate ground down *Centurion*'s helm so as to put the flagship across the enemy's bow and enjoy the luxury of raking an opponent which could only reply with her bow chasers.

Soon the air became clear enough to permit the men in her tops to see their opposite numbers reloading *pedereroes* — those light swivel guns which, loaded with stones, nails, old flints and chopped-up musket balls, had been raising hob with the flagship's rigging and topmen.

Joyously, therefore, Pallister and his mates diverted their attention to the Spaniard's fighting tops and chortled whenever one of them fell, spinning, into the sea, or crashed onto their fellows below.

Once the flagship lay square across the galleon's bow Anson told Midshipman Campbell, "I want grape from the main battery and cannister from Mr. Brett's upper deck guns."

Centurion, taking advantage of her position, then poured a hail of small arms fire from tops, poop and forecastle and lashed the Spaniard's deck with ghastly effect. Nat Wade, busy among the forecastle guns, watched men fall, limp or writhing all over the galleon's cluttered decks. As if from another planet, he watched Spanish officers' swords flash when they attempted, with some success, to stem a general rush below.

"Merciful God!" choked Schoolmaster Thomas, utterly horrified. "Are they throwing overboard their wounded and dead?"

"So they are," grunted Lieutenant Scott. " 'Tis customary during an action as brisk as this one."

Andrew Menzies, busy among the begrimed sharpshooters stationed on *Centurion's* lofty poopdeck, noticed a splendidly dressed officer ranging about the enemy's quarterdeck and guessed that he might be the enemy's commanding officer.

Recalling certain chill, still mornings when he'd hunted turkeys among the vast swamps behind Chartwell, Anson's secretary cuddled his musket's stock against his cheek and waited for *Centurion* to hesitate at the top of a gentle roll.

When the moment came, he drew a deep breath and squeezed the trigger by tightening his whole hand. *Click!* went his flint against the frizzen's steel plane; then his piece went off with a tooth-rattling roar.

He knew he hadn't missed even before his musket's smoke cleared away because a tremendous outcry arose on the galleon's quarterdeck. When Menzies was able to see again a knot of officers were bending over the man he'd shot at.

Ears ringing, George Anson leaned far out over the poop rail to watch a Spanish seaman climb into the main shrouds and start upwards with the obvious intention of hauling down the Royal Standard of Spain, the halyards of which had been severed.

Snatching up a speaking trumpet, Anson shouted, "Nobody shoot that man! Pass the word! Don't shoot him, or the one starting out towards their jackstaff!"

Even as his voice died away, overwhelming emotion gripped George Anson. They were trying to surrender! The Manila Galleon had been beaten.

No. *It couldn't be true!* Not after all these years of planning, striving and disappointment. Tears welled into Anson's smarting eyes; hurriedly, he dashed them away, thankful that they must be undistinguishable from sweat coursing down his broad cheeks.

Cheer on cheer arose when, jerkily, the brilliant Royal Standard

[449]

fluttered downwards, then fell limp onto the galleon's deck to admit that the Prize of All the Oceans had been captured.

～～～ 2 1 ～～～

Nuestra Señora de Cobadonga

A ROUNDSHOT from the galleon's last salvo plowed through the quarterdeck bulwarks and sent Andrew Menzies staggering as if some invisible giant had pushed him. He spun about several times before collapsing onto the debris-strewn deck with a long, whitish-yellow splinter protruding from the base of his abdomen.

Powder-streaked seamen who had been shouting with the realization of victory quieted and carried Anson's white-faced secretary below before almost anyone knew that he'd been hit.

Anson was accepting breathless congratulations when he heard a muffled explosion. For a moment he imagined that one of *Centurion's* guns had been belatedly discharged by a crew unaware of the galleon's surrender. Then, to his horror, the Commodore noticed a thin column of smoke beginning to whirl up from his flagship's forehold.

Lieutenant Denis appeared on the poop ladder loudly calling congratulations on the victory; he then drew Anson aside and gasped in an anguished undertone, "Sir! The ship has taken fire near the forward magazine!"

"Indeed, Mr. Denis?" Anson's calm remained unshakable. "Then call away the fire brigade and put it out."

Even as the Commodore spoke, there followed several more explosions, each as loud as that of a cannon being discharged. The column of smoke from below decks grew denser.

"Fire! Fire!"

Victorious shouts faded as *Centurion's* company hesitated in frozen fear. Should those flames reach the magazine they'd all die — cheated of victory at the last moment.

Directed by Lieutenant Scott and Thomas Adams, quartermaster since Tinian, the fire brigade formed up and, being well-trained, extinguished the flames just as they commenced to singe those wet blankets which screened the magazine's scuttle.

Investigation revealed that a powder monkey's bare foot had trod

[450]

on a burning slow match; not unnaturally, the boy had dropped his cartridge and spilled its contents upon another cartridge ready for use in the lower deck portside guns.

When the loose powder flared, it had touched off three cannon which had not been fired during the battle. However, since all lids along the port side had been kept triced up in anticipation of action, little damage had been done.

Soon it was ascertained that, for all the enemy's cannonading, only two men had been killed in *Centurion:* Seaman Richmond who'd been decapitated and a hand called Walton who'd been shot through the heart.

Fifteen men had been more or less severely wounded, among them Lieutenant Brett, whose right side had been painfully scored by a musket ball.

To red-splashed Surgeon Ettrick it was evident that only Andrew Menzies and a seaman named Romford, who'd had his leg smashed by a falling block, were in critical condition.

Peter Vesey's professionally impassive expression vanished when the Commodore's secretary was lugged, insensible, down to the dimly lit cockpit where he and Mr. Allen, formerly *Tryall*'s surgeon, were cutting out splinters and dressing the ghastly wounds that resulted.

"Considering the angle of that splinter, 'tis lucky Mr. Menzies is unconscious," observed Vesey, elbowing aside Mr. Allen. "Kindly allow me to attend him, sir, we've been friendly for some time."

"It's as you please," Allen grunted and turned away wiping encrimsoned hands on a wad of rags. "There are plenty of others."

Vesey saw to it that Menzies was placed on a mattress and carried over to a comparatively secluded corner of the cockpit.

Assisted by Keating, a fellow surgeon's mate, Vesey bent over the spare, huddled form and commenced to cut away the bloodied breeches from around that thick, foot-long splinter which had transfixed the unconscious man. Deftly, his scalpel's bright blade severed the sodden cloth down to the knee. Keating then lifted Menzies, enabling Vesey to strip away the fabric.

When the wounded man's small clothes parted, Keating gasped, "Good God, what's this?"

"What's what?" snapped Vesey, while reaching for his instrument case. Something in Keating's tone prompted him to turn and, by a battle lantern's glow, he noted his assistant's round eyes and horrified expression.

[451]

"Did you know Mr. Menzies *is a eunuch?*"

"A eun —! No. I didn't. But," he added fiercely, "we will keep this to ourselves. Understand?"

"Never fear, sir, I'll not say a word to anyone."

"See that you don't! Now hand me those forceps and let's see what can be done about extracting the splinter. Provided it hasn't punctured the bowel, Mr. Menzies may recover."

Vesey ordered another battle lantern brought and held over the patient before, tentatively, he tugged to ascertain how firmly the wood was buried.

"It's fast, I fear," he announced keeping one eye on the patient's sweaty, ashen features. If only Menzies would remain unconscious! "Now pull the flesh aside whilst I cut to widen the point of entry."

The operation briefly was interrupted because, all at once, the flagship shuddered and an ominous grinding noise caused *Centurion's* hull to reverberate.

It soon appeared that the galleon, with her sails untended, had fouled her conqueror with her port bow and was scraping along the flagship's starboard quarter. However, a swell carried the prize clear of *Centurion* and allowed Dr. Vesey to return to his sanguinary task.

Half an hour passed before the jagged piece of wood could be removed and Andrew Menzies lay tightly bandaged and breathing stertorously on his mattress.

Meanwhile, George Anson had issued orders for Lieutenant de Saumarez to take possession of the prize which, by now, had drifted some distance astern. Since the other galleon might appear at any moment he was to send the Spaniard's principal officers aboard *Centurion* with all speed.

A cutter was lowered, whereupon the first lieutenant, Lieutenant Hughes, Mr. Pascoe Thomas, Midshipmen Parker and Proby — he who had first sighted the galleon — dropped into the smallboat as it swayed and lifted under the gangway.

Soon, the victors' cutter was bobbing about under the prize's towering, carved and heavily gilded stern. On it, Parker noted, were sculptured two Roman knights in armor who supported a large escutcheon upon which had been rendered — and very handsomely, too — an image of the Virgin as the Queen of Heaven.

A scroll, flowing below it, bore the treasure ship's name: *Nuestra Señora de Cobadonga.* So this was not the *Santa Pilar,* that galleon which had been so futilely blockaded in Acapulco!

Even as the cutter drew near, more dead or feebly struggling bodies were tumbled over the prize's bulwarks to streak her red and yellow side with blood.

Parker noticed how uselessly the *Cobadonga*'s shot-torn sails flapped and fluttered on masts which seemed to tower incredibly high into the bright blue heavens.

When the cutter approached the gangway, its crew — grinning with anticipation — tossed oars. De Saumarez hailed the deck, but on receiving no reply beyond a medley of groans and wails, scaled a series of wooden battens nailed to *Cobadonga*'s side. He had to climb past a gaping hole torn by some 24-pounder's shot.

When his head reached the upper deck's level, de Saumarez clung to the battens, utterly horrified.

Under overturned cannon and fallen rigging, *Cobadonga*'s deck was running as red as the floor of a slaughterhouse.

Later he wrote:

> Their Decks afforded such a Scene as may be Supposed after a sharp Dispute, being Promiscuously covered with Carcasses, Entrails, and Dismembered Limbs. The main hatchway, likewise, contained Severall of the Dead, which had been thrown into it.

Gagging, Philip de Saumarez stepped on deck, then ordered the boarding party to follow.

Almost at once it was noticed that, of the fallen, a high proportion were richly, if not splendidly dressed — a grim testimonial to the ability of *Centurion*'s sharpshooters.

Elements of the boarding party at once were posted by the main and forward hatchways, ready to beat back any attempt of the Spanish crews to return on deck.

On the gore-splotched quarterdeck a dark-faced officer wearing a red sash and yellow tunic lay half-propped against an overturned gun carriage. He was unconscious and dying from a great wound in his thigh.

"*Señor Capitán?*" An officer, with staring eyes and carrying a mass of scarlet rags twisted about his shattered right arm, staggered out into the sunshine while making futile efforts to draw his sword with his left hand.

"*Señor*, stay where you are!" called de Saumarez. "You are badly hurt."

[453]

"It is nothing. I am Don Juan de Pinero," gasped the wounded officer. "Until now, pilot of this unlucky ship."

De Saumarez nodded, aware that the pilot of a Spanish man-of-war was an important officer, corresponding roughly to a British man-of-war's sailing master.

"Where is your Admiral?"

"Sir, General de Montero lies gravely wounded by a ball through his chest. He has done all that a brave officer could." The pilot swayed, adding, "We had not expected to meet you with a complete crew, *Señor Teniente*. Our friends in Macao sent word to Guam that you had lost three quarters of your company through disease."

"That is accurate — up to a point," de Saumarez admitted, then shot a look at *Centurion* and was vastly relieved to note that her long-boat was putting off, crammed with men. "We lost many men through scurvy and were unable to recruit sufficient useful men in Macao. In fact, *señor,* when we closed for action today our company numbered only two hundred and twenty-seven of all ranks."

"*Señor Jesu!*" The pilot's bluish jaw dropped — and so did blood from his mangled arm. "But surely you err. For two hundred and twenty-seven men to fight a ship of our size is — is impossible!"

"Nevertheless, *señor,* that is what has been done. Please tell me, how many men have you — or perhaps I should say 'had' you on board?"

Clinging to a stay, the pilot hung his head. "When we opened fire we counted six hundred and forty-four — sufficient, we believed, to protect our treasure from the largest man-of-war ever to sail the Pacific."

When de Pinero's knees suddenly buckled, the Englishman stepped forward and flung an arm about his waist. "Let me tighten the cloths about your arm; you'll bleed to death."

While de Saumarez was employing a discharged pistol's barrel as the lever for a tourniquet, de Pinero explained that two treasure ships indeed had sailed from Acapulco; the *Santa Pilar,* however, had sailed a month before the *Cobadonga.* So, if she had not come to grief en route, the pilot thought that she must have reached Manila while the flagship was refitting at Taypa.

To de Saumarez's considerable relief, *Centurion's* longboat now bumped alongside and discharged a swarm of reinforcements, among whom was a preponderance of carpenters, riggers and quartermaster's mates, in addition to Surgeons Allen and Kerr.

The new arrivals went to work immediately, collecting abandoned weapons, extinguishing such slow matches as still burned and carrying the wounded below for treatment. Others made repairs to the sails and rigging sufficient for getting the prize under way again.

That night de Saumarez wrote in his diary:

> The Spanish officers were most Fearful for their Safety. They were Impressed with no great Opinion of our Humanity, they having Represented Us to Themselves as a set of Cannibals. Having Complimented Them on their Behavior and Resolute Resistance, I assured them of such Quarter and Usage as their Bravery Deserved.
>
> I sent the Officers on Board the *Centurion* as fast as I could. The Weather was beginning to look very Windy. By eight in the Evening I sent away over Three Hundred Prisoners in the Longboat and Cutter having been in the meantime Reinforced from the Commodore with Fifty men and Officers. The General in Command, having been Twice Wounded, once severely in the Breast, could not be Moved. He is a Portuguese with a Reputation for Seaman ship and Courage. His full name is General Don Geronimo de Montero. It is said that he has been very Brutal to any of our Compatriots unlucky enough to fall into his Power.

On the following day both ships proceeded over a sea so moderate that the pleasurable task of transferring *Cobadonga*'s vast treasure to *Centurion* was begun.

For all his serene expression, George Anson remained beset by fears no less intense for remaining unspoken. First, he worried lest the prisoners who outnumbered his crew by almost three to one might attempt to rise. Second, he feared that the squadron equipped by the Viceroy of Manila might catch him lacking sufficient men properly to defend either vessel. Third, and most important, he entertained lively apprehensions that hostilities might have begun between France and England.

If war *had* been declared then, certainly, powerful French men-of-war must be expected to appear off the coast of China; indeed, they might already have appeared to pick off a number of British Indiamen.

For all these reasons it appeared wise to transfer *Cobadonga*'s treasure to *Centurion* with all possible speed — not an easy matter on the open ocean.

Anson, nevertheless, took time to perform certain agreeable acts. First, in his capacity of Commander in Chief, he formally commissioned the capture as HBMS *Centurion's Prize*, then made Philip de Saumarez, soberly exultant, a Post Captain in order that he might command her.

Also, he commissioned Augustus van Keppel a full-fledged lieutenant and promoted Midshipman Wade to be acting lieutenant; an unexpected honor which left the former leather-worker in speechless delight.

On the evening of the first day following the action, Commodore Anson found time to make — laboriously, because he hated writing of any description — a new entry in his current Letter of Proceedings. Only then did he fully appreciate how much he had grown to depend upon the quiet efficiency of Andrew Menzies. He was hoping that, at any moment, Dr. Vesey would arrive to report the Carolinian improving.

Frowning, Anson dipped his quill and, in large, well-shaped letters wrote:

> The Galeon's Masts and Rigging were badly Wounded and one hundred and fifty Shott passed her Hull, many of which were between Wood and Water, which has Rendered her very Leaky.
>
> I am Sensible of Occupying a Dangerous Position in Navigating two such Large Ships in a Dangerous and Unknown Sea and to Guard Five Hundred and Eighty Prisoners in them. There being no Ports where I could harbor the Ships, saving Macao, I think it Proper for the Safety of the Great Treasure in the Galeon, which cannot further be Removed at Present because the Weather is becoming very Tempestuous, I have given my First Lieutenant a Commission to Command her and Appointing her Proper Officers to Accompany him, being Apprehensive of losing Company with the Prize.
>
> In the Action we Expended 341 Roundshot and about 24 barrels of Powder. Thus far we have taken Aboard 112 Bags and 6 Chests of Dollars containing over 130,000 Dollars, but this is only a Beginning.
>
> During the Action Fifty-Six Spaniards lost their Lives and Eighty-Three were Wounded of whom Eight since have Perished.
>
> Because of the promotion of Mr. Saumarez, Mr. Brett now becomes my First Lieutenant, Mr. Denis my Second, and Mr. Keppel, I have now confirmed in his Rank as Third.

It did not seem necessary to add, Anson decided, that his new third lieutenant only recently had attained the age of nineteen.

A knock sounded at the door. It was Midshipman Tom de Saumarez.

"Sir, Mr. Menzies has taken a bad turn, sir. Dr. Vesey says that if you care to speak with him you had best come at once."

～ 2 2 ～

Seven Bells, Then the Dark

Darkness had descended over the broad Pacific when George Anson appeared on deck and conferred briefly with Officer-of-the-Deck van Keppel, vastly sedate because of his new responsibilities.

"Ah, Mr. Keppel. I presume you have doubled all lookouts?"

"Aye, aye, sir. The Viceroy's squadron ain't to surprise us in the dark."

For a moment Anson paused by the main hatch down which four swivel guns, loaded to the muzzle with musket balls, had been trained. Guards holding lighted matches seemed reassuringly alert. From below arose the gabble of Spaniards imprisoned and half-suffocated in the orlop.

Of all the enemy's seamen only fifty Spanish Negroes and Indians and about a hundred Spanish convicts — who certainly owed no loyalty to Spain — had been left aboard *Centurion's Prize* to help the prize crew repair and handle her great mass of canvas.

Only upon arrival in the cockpit, two decks below the great cabin, did Anson learn that his secretary had been transferred to Surgeon Allen's empty cabin. He seized the opportunity personally to encourage every man in sick bay.

Peter Vesey met his Commander in Chief outside the door of Mr. Allen's stuffy little cabin. "Thank you for coming so promptly." Then, in an undertone, he added, "I — I regret to report, sir, that your secretary is close to dying."

George Anson's mouth tightened. "But this very noon you reported him on the mend."

"Yes, sir, but during the afternoon he was taken of a high fever for all I don't believe that the splinter actually penetrated his intestines." Vesey's aquiline nose seemed extra prominent as he continued, "What puzzles and grieves me most, sir, is that Mr. Menzies doesn't appear to wish to recover. I have had to force medicines upon him."

"He is conscious?"

[457]

"Yes, sir, and has been all day."

The golden glow of several battle lanterns illumined Mr. Allen's bunk sufficiently to reveal the stricken man's features.

Vesey hesitated. "Shall I — ?"

"Yes. Pray attend the other patients. If necessary, I will send for you."

George Anson dropped onto a stool and then fumbled about his coat's side pocket until he found a silver flask which he unstopped and held so that Menzies could see it.

"Andrew, to celebrate our long-delayed victory I wish you to share the last of my French brandy with me. Besides, it will strengthen you so that we can speak for a while of the famous good times we enjoyed in Carolina."

The Carolinian's paper-white eyelids slid slowly back. "Captain Anson? Sir, why are you here? You shouldn't be wasting time on me."

"Nonsense! Drink this." Gently, the visitor slipped a hand under Menzies's dark head and, raising his flask, allowed a little liquor to slip between the livid lips. Next, he raised the flask to a level with his mouth. "To our ancient friendship, Andrew! Long may it prosper."

Feebly, Menzies shook his head. "No, George, its days are numbered. I know."

"Nonsense," chuckled the big man at the bunkside. "We'll ride to hounds and shoot ducks around Charles Town many times again."

"No, Capt — George, delightful as that prospect appears, I know that Death draws near." The Carolinian heaved a shallow sigh. "I wish I could meet him with a life untarnished by dishonor and foul treachery."

" 'Dishonor'? 'Treachery'? Such words can never be associated with your name!" Wonderingly, Anson took a long-fingered hand that was resting on the blanket and clasped it between both of his. "Now then, when we return to England the first thing we'll do is to —"

Haunted dark eyes bored into Anson's. "Please, George, don't attempt to deceive me." Menzies's voice faltered. "There is a mission I must entrust to you — and to no one else. Will you undertake it?"

"Need you ask?"

"I suppose not, but it is a — well, a most delicate mission —"

"What shall I do?"

"Will you undertake to see that my share in the prize money — whatever it amounts to — is sent to —"

Anson made a final attempt. "Come, come, Andrew! You mustn't talk this way. You will recover. I'm convinced of that; rid yourself of any notion that your life hasn't been anything but honorable."

A silence settled in which the slow creak and whine of *Centurion's* hull became almost unbearably poignant.

"No, George. You aren't aware of what happened once upon a time. Has that clever fellow Vesey mentioned" — momentarily, Menzies's voice faded away — "that the day I boarded your ship — the *Scarborough*, wasn't it — in Wilmington I was no longer a — a whole man?"

"No, Andrew, Vesey has reported nothing to that effect."

"— Which is no more than I would expect of so true a gentleman — who, I suspect, also has had his sorrows. Nevertheless, his discovery is — is true."

For once George Anson appeared disconcerted. "How did so terrible an accident happen?"

" 'Twas no accident, George," came the reedy voice. "In an absurd effort to atone for the horrible crime I had committed against my own flesh and blood I — I castrated myself."

"You were very brave to have done so, but please, Andrew, don't dwell on it. Have a bit more brandy."

The secretary's hand twitched between Anson's. "No. George, I — I must. 'Twill ease my conscience to confess to you — if to no other man."

Menzies's sunken eyes closed, then reopened slowly as if their lids were heavily weighted.

"You recall the time I lost Chartwell and you refused to accept a deed to the property?"

"That incident slipped my memory long ago. Believe me, Andrew, it did."

"I was furious with myself and shamed to the bottom of my soul that I should have acted so great a fool. All the same, George, in those days the gambling fever held me in so firm a grip that, no sooner had you returned the deed, than I recommenced gaming — even more insanely than before. The next time I lost Chartwell the winner was not as absurdly magnanimous as you."

Out in the sick bay a wounded man began to whimper, "Water! For God's sake, somebody give me water!"

Peter Vesey's voice could be heard saying gently, "Drink all you please."

"— Please don't go on," Anson begged, placing a hand on Men-

[459]

zies's forehead. "You are distraught, dear friend; be assured that I shall not remember anything of what you have said."

"I beg of you, dear George, please to hear me out," sighed the Carolinian, his voice faint as the whisper of blackducks' wings in a dark sky. "I must speak whilst I retain at least a measure of reason."

"Very well."

"The second time I lost my property I had nothing left saving the clothes in which I stood. I was as destitute as any of those poor felons they dragged aboard your ship in Southampton. They all turned away — acquaintances, friends and relatives. Everyone scorned me — with one exception.

"— Richard, my youngest brother. He and his bride took me in, sick, discouraged and despised. I had been drinking like a fish for days when I reeled into their home, a filthy derelict. All the same, Richard and Caroline welcomed me and restored me to health and reason, or so I thought.

"Then one day" — Menzies's voice failed so greatly that Anson was forced to bend low over the bunk — "my brother rode away to inspect some property he'd acquired not very far from Ansonville — the village they named after you.

"For the space of three days, I was left with my sister-in-law — beautiful, warmhearted Caroline. Sickened over the loss of Chartwell, I began to drink so much that I must have gone mad — at least, I hope I did, for it was then that I committed my unforgivable crime."

"Don't speak of it!" pleaded Anson. "Please *don't!*"

"No. I must. I — I forced my way into Caroline's bedroom and raped her, for all that she struggled to the limit of her endurance."

With astonishing strength Menzies's other hand, trembling and ice-cold, closed over Anson's.

"Poor Andrew," Anson muttered over the rushing of waves alongside.

"When I came to the next morning and realized what I had done," the faint voice continued out of the gloom, "I snatched up a razor and made ready to cut my throat, but then it occurred that such a punishment would be inadequate, too easy. All day I wandered blindly through strange woods and fields, then, as the sun was lowering, I used the razor — you know how."

"I should never have found the courage —"

"— Nor have committed so dreadful a crime. As it was, I would

[460]

have bled to death — which might have been just as well — had not a field hand discovered me and carried me to his cabin. The physician at a nearby plantation must have been clever; I was so nearly drained of blood that only a very able man could have pulled me through."

Anson murmured softly, "I can only hope, Andrew, that you have regained some peace of mind."

"A measure of it, George, but only a little. Later, I heard that Caroline had borne a male child, which could have been either Richard's or mine." Under the lantern light Menzies's dark-ringed eyes opened wider, clung to Anson's. "I wish this child to inherit my share in the prize money."

"So help me God, he will — if we see England again."

"God bless you," Menzies whispered. "And bless you again also for having given me so great and generous a friendship. My one regret is that — that I shan't be able to witness your triumph. What honors won't they accord you? Some day you will be ranked with Grenville, Frobisher, Hawke and Drake."

Anson shook his bronzed head. "Such recognition would be beyond my deserts. Let me tell you something; I will accept no honor that does not acknowledge the valor of those who have suffered and died at my side. Besides, England is far away and, frankly, I am apprehensive."

"Why? Haven't you won the great treasure?" The skin suddenly seemed to tighten about Menzies's mouth.

"Because, Andrew, at this moment we lie half the way around the world from England. A Spanish squadron is somewhere nearby and, mark you, once news of the galleon's capture becomes known, pirates, Spanish and French men-of-war will try to take us."

Anson was so preoccupied that he failed to notice how shallowly the Carolinian had begun to breathe.

"Remember, also, that we can expect no protection from our countrymen until we reach the Cape of Good Hope. No, I fear the true victory still lies far away. I had —"

Menzies suddenly sat up, hair in wild disorder. "No! No! For God's sake, Caroline — I didn't mean — I'll double the wager. Come, sir, where's yer sporting blood — Sir — I — I pledge — Richard? So good of you — dear Caroline — how positively ravishing you look tonight. Ravishing? Ha! ha! ha! That's it! Come with me into the dell — tra-la-la, tra-la!"

[461]

From Mr. Allen's door Anson called, "Dr. Vesey! Please come here."

Just as the seven bells of the First Watch were being sounded a darkness gathered before Andrew Menzies's eyes; then he achieved that peace for which he had so long sought in vain.

⚓ 2 3 ⚓
Mysterious Man-of-War

FOLLOWING TWO DAYS of stormy weather, the sea flattened and *Centurion's Prize* was taken in tow to facilitate the transfer of her treasure. *Centurion's* crew, as if still unable to believe what had happened, reassured themselves of victory by watching what seemed to be an endless succession of smallboats ply between the two ships.

It seemed as if there was always a smallboat riding alongside the flagship. A block and tackle, rigged to the mainyard, was designed to swing inboard cask after cask of silver dollars. How cheerfully these clinked when a cargo net would lower them into the main hold!

Because a steep swell kept running, it proved no easy matter for Boatswain Adams and his mates to calculate the cargo net's swing so that its precious cargo would be deposited below decks rather than smashed against the mast or entangled with the rigging.

Among those detailed to the pleasurable task of breaking out treasure aboard the captured galleon were Tom Ramster, Bill Buckle and other trusted veterans.

To Purser Millechamp, late of *Gloucester*, and Will Pallister was given the duty of listing the plunder as it was removed. Seated on oak chests containing silver bars, they worked just outside the ex-*Cobadonga's* treasure room to prepare independent tallies of this seemingly inexhaustible flow of wealth.

Meanwhile, on *Centurion*, Purser John Rule and his mate, George Farmer, recently promoted from the forecastle, carefully double-checked the breath-taking succession of ironbound boxes and casks arriving on board.

Like Justinian Nutt, Acting First Lieutenant, Thomas Summers, his second, and Nathaniel Wade, his third, Captain de Saumarez often found an excuse to go below and watch an armorer either pick, or force off, padlocks securing the treasure chests.

"Is there no end to it?" exulted Acting Lieutenant Nutt one warm afternoon while the two ships were plowing slowly but steadily back towards the coast of China.

"I hope not!" grinned Summers and, dropping onto his heels, scooped up a double handful of doubloons waiting to be counted by the pursers and allowed them to clatter back into the chest.

He turned to Pallister. "What's the tally so far?"

The young fellow, standing half a head taller than he had off Acapulco, riffled through a calfskin-bound account book. "Sir, by rough calculation, over seven hundred thousand Spanish dollars already have been transferred to the flagship; also two thousand pounds sterling in platework and bars of virgin silver."

Acting First Lieutenant Nutt licked lean, leathery lips and grinned like a friendly wolfhound. "That's the sweetest of music your words play to my ears. How much more will there be, d'you calculate?"

"That's very difficult to predict, sir," replied the purser, curling an ink-stained finger about his chin, "but I'll hazard there's as much again to be transferred."

"You appear to be working at speed," Lieutenant Summers drily observed to Ramster. "Why hurry over so enjoyable a task?"

"Orders, sir; the Commodore's fair burning to complete the transfer. 'Tis said he fears some stout man-of-war may catch us with our crew spread thin between two big ships."

Aware of an ever-present threat that the multitude of prisoners might suddenly arise and attempt to free themselves, *Centurion's* company slept in their clothes, went about always armed and ready for trouble.

Precautions were redoubled once General Don Geronimo de Montero was judged sufficiently recovered to be brought aboard the flagship, where as Schoolmaster Thomas recorded, "He almost wept for shame when he discovered the insignificant force that had subdued him."

It was no wonder. De Montero's 644 men had been decisively and bloodily defeated by *Centurion's* 227, many of whom were either foreigners or mere lads.

"I regret to inform you, sir," Anson warned the captive General and his eighteen surviving officers, "that, at the first hint of an uprising being contemplated, you will all be shot without any hesitation."

After ten days' easy sailing, victor and vanquished entered the blue-

[463]

green waters of Balintang Channel at the northern end of Luzon Island. By now most of the ex-*Cobadonga*'s dazzling treasure had been stowed in *Centurion*'s capacious treasure room to join, under heavy and continuous guard, the loot of Payta and plunder from the South American prizes. In fact, the treasure room became so jam-packed it was necessary to remove bales of precious brocades, silks and other bulky plunder to one end of the officers' wardroom.

With her prize in tow, HBMS *Centurion* was nearing the Lema Islands, some eighty miles off the Asiatic mainland when, on the rainy 8th of July, 1743, her crew was sent to quarters. A large and unmistakably European-rigged ship had been sighted sailing a parallel course.

Once the stranger drew near enough to be inspected in some detail, Anson ordered the tow cast off. He then turned to Peircy Brett, now the flagship's first lieutenant. "Well, Mr. Brett, and what do you make of her?"

"I'd hazard, sir, that she's very likely a French ship-of-war."

"— And you, Mr. Denis?"

"I think so too, sir. But, on the other hand, she may as well be a Spaniard lying in wait for us."

No one on *Centurion*'s rain-swept quarterdeck even faintly suspected George Anson's anxiety. If this indeed was a French man-of-war, it was entirely possible that the fruits of his hard-won victory might be snatched away. To engage a heavy and vigorously handled French man-of-war must prove a very different matter from fighting a Spaniard of the same size.

However, it was with untroubled mien that he sought his cabin and, mourning Andrew Menzies for the hundredth time, scribbled a message to Captain de Saumarez:

> Having Reason to Apprehend by Letters found in the Spanish Galeon that we may have a War with France and imagining the Ship now in sight to be a Ship-of-Warr belonging to the Crown of France you are hereby Requested and Directed (as soon as you find me Engaged) to Embarque Yourself in the Pinnace and come on Board of me, and for so Doing this shall be your Warrant. Given under my Hand and Dated aboard His Majesty's Ship, the *Centurion*, at sea, this 8th of July, 1743. George Anson to Captain Philip de Saumarez of His Majesty's Ship, the *Centurion's Prize*.

Further, he issued verbal instructions to be transmitted by Midshipman de Saumarez. The Prize Captain was to send over to *Centurion* as many men as he could spare; then, should an action appear imminent, he must abandon the prize after spiking all her guns and proceed aboard the flagship with the balance of his crew.

When all but six of ex-*Cobadonga*'s English crew had appeared and preliminary steps in clearing for action initiated, Anson ordered both ships to set all sail and stand towards this ominous-appearing stranger.

That their Commander in Chief should have adopted so risky a maneuver surprised his officers not at all. Certainly his best chance lay in bearing boldly down on this powerful-looking stranger with two large ships which apparently were ready and able to give battle.

A lesser man, reflected Acting Lieutenant Wade, would likely have turned tail and run, hoping to elude under the cover of night the unidentified man-of-war which now looked big enough to be a Second Rate.

Soon after nightfall the wind failed completely so, when dawn broke, the great ship lay not even four miles away, but near enough to disclose the fact that she was not a French man-of-war after all, although everyone agreed that she suggested one in almost every detail.

Hoping to make a prize of her, the Commodore at six o'clock ordered French colors to be flown, so at *Centurion*'s main truck appeared an ensign showing a white field liberally dotted with large golden fleurs-de-lis.

Said he quietly, "Mr. Brett, now let us attempt to further reassure the stranger. Pray order a gun fired to leeward."

Then, to Acting Sailing Master Jelff, "Strike your mainsail. We must offer every evidence of friendliness."

Despite these amicable gestures, the stranger changed course, set studding sails and ran downwind with such superior speed that, by two of the afternoon, her upper canvas showed only as a faint white speck on the horizon; by three it had vanished.

That evening Peircy Brett made a terse, but significant, entry in his log:

It is well that the Chase was given up. With all these Prisoners Aboard our Water Supply is near Exhausted. Indeed, it is Reported that but Three Days Supply remains. Everyone now on Short Rations. God send that we Encounter no Storms or Contrary Winds on the Remaining Distance to Macao. In order to Proceed at better

[465]

Speed we have once again taken the Prize in Tow and have restored our English Sailors into her.

No one was more relieved than the new first lieutenant when, three days later, the mainland of China again lifted blue-gray above the horizon.

On this occasion Chinese pilots, for some reason, proved quite willing, if not eager, to cooperate, so by sundown both ships lay anchored in Macao Roads — to the complete amazement of all ashore. Not only the Hoppo, but the Portuguese Governor as well, had been convinced that, at this very moment, that troublesome English man-of-war called *Centurion* must be quitting Java.

Profiting from experience, George Anson delayed off Macao barely long enough to take on water and fresh supplies before proceeding to the Bocca Tigris and sailing boldly past the powerful forts at the Pearl River's entrance.

On arriving at the Indiamen's anchorage three miles below Canton, both victor and vanquished hoisted British ensigns to all mastheads before dropping anchor.

~ 2 4 ~

News from the Far East

ON THE MORNING OF JUNE 15, 1744, southern England would have appeared lovely to anyone, but, to the 124 gaunt and weather-beaten survivors of the 2139 men who, almost four years earlier, had sailed under George Anson's command, Hampshire in the spring seemed glorious beyond all description.

While tacking into Portsmouth Harbor, HBMS *Centurion* dutifully fired well-spaced salutes to a Rear Admiral's flag floating above *Frederick*, a trim Third Rate. Next she saluted the port, bathed at this hour in fresh morning sunlight.

Various men-of-war moored or at anchor in Portsmouth Harbor, one after another acknowledged the courtesies and saluted Commodore Anson's scarlet pendant.

From all decks batteries of spyglasses soon were leveled, first in normal curiosity and then in incredulous astonishment. By God, here was *Centurion,* which, far from having been lost — as almost every-one believed — was returning safely to her base!

Aloof on the poopdeck, George Anson was staring about as if he'd never before beheld those grim forts, the towers and steeples of the town, the mewing, dirty-white gulls, the sheering hulks, the graving yard, the King's warehouses and dockyard itself. Yet there they were, much as he'd pictured them off the Horn, on Juan Fernandez and during that anguished voyage to Tinian.

Smartly reducing canvas, the sea-worn flagship picked a course through a mass of shipping composed of fishermen, coasters, supply ships, merchantmen, and ships-of-war lying in ordinary.

At first Anson had been surprised to find so dense a concentration in port but then he recalled that, with war having broken out so recently, they must be fitting out, or sheltering from those French privateers which were swarming about the Channel and in the Bay of Biscay.

"A grand sight, sir," Peircy Brett remarked when Anson descended to the quarterdeck and joined a knot of officers collected by the rail. "One which I'll confess I often thought never to see again."

"— And so did I, *Captain* —" Anson smiled, emphasizing the rank he had bestowed on his favorite lieutenant during the long voyage home.

Privately, the Commodore had been wondering just what the Admiralty might say about Brett's promotion to be *Centurion's* Cap-tain. Possibly he'd exceeded his authority in this matter? Although it was unusual for a flag officer like himself to act as Post Captain as well, he had never been promised one by his superiors, yet certainly Peircy Brett, like Philip de Saumarez and Charles Saunders, had de-served promotion.

Um. Would their Lordships agree that he'd been wise in making captains of men so young while passing over a veteran like poor old Lieutenant Salt? Undoubtedly time would tell.

Brett's promotion, of course, had made it possible to move Peter Denis, barely nineteen years of age, up to first lieutenant, Augustus van Keppel to second, and Justinian Nutt to third. At the same time he'd commissioned Senior Midshipmen John Campbell and Tom Foley as Acting Lieutenants and had made Nathaniel Wade sailing master, in place of Justinian Nutt. He'd figured Wade would get ahead faster that way than as a very junior supernumerary lieutenant.

Eyes traveling slowly over *Centurion's* snowy deck, Anson continued his self-communing. Believe their lordships will agree that I've "annoyed and harassed" the Spaniards to the limit of my ability; always provided politics don't enter into the matter.

What probably won't escape criticism is the fact that they entrusted me with eight ships and I've returned with only one. Then there may be objection raised to my having sold *Centurion's Prize* in Macao for a paltry 1500 pounds; can I make them see that I had to hasten the treasure home before the French War should break out? Wonder what Lord Winchelsea will do when he reads my final "Letter of Proceedings"? He ought to be pleased that he will be the one to inform His Majesty and the Court of St. James's that I've brought home treasure worth 3,000,000 Spanish dollars — at the very lowest estimate.

The tremendous news that HBMS *Centurion* had captured the famous Prize of All the Oceans spread over southern England with lightning speed. Church bells began joyously to clang in hundreds of sleepy towns and villages; cannon roared and bonfires blazed along the coast from Dover Castle to the Lizard.

After post-riders had foundered many a mount in their haste to reach London, the penny press vied in finding the most fulsome eulogies with which to shower Commodore George Anson.

Here was the modern Drake! A new Hawkins! Sir Richard Grenville's peer! Somehow, all the newspapers missed a priceless coincidence — that another Francis Drake — albeit only a midshipman — like his illustrious ancestor, *had* circumnavigated the globe and had returned in a ship laden with booty of enormous value wrested from the hated Papists.

Amid these frantic rejoicings, Peter Vesey and a few others of sensibility noted somber undertones. In sad little groups appeared the friends and relations of those whose earthly remains reposed thousands of miles from England. Tight-lipped, these people inspected the Pay and Muster Rolls and were shown the dreaded initials, "D.D." — discharged, dead — written after their loved ones' names.

Four days after *Centurion's* return, the portly Vice-Admiral who commanded in Portsmouth climbed aboard his barge and was rowed out to Anson's flagship, once more as taut and trim as any man-of-war in sight.

Piped aboard in style, the old man ignored Anson's politely lifted hat and waddled up to offer his hand instead. "Congratulations, m' dear fellow!" he boomed. "I'm delighted, positively delighted, over being the first to address you as 'Rear Admiral Anson!' "

On that same day, the new Rear Admiral, flushed with pleasurable anticipation, departed to be received in private by His Majesty, George II. Shortly after Anson had gone ashore a wherry put out from Gosport and made for *Centurion*, swinging tall and stately to her moorings. In the wherry's stern sheets sat a tall young man wearing the cocked hat, dark blue frock coat and white trousers recently coming into favor among junior naval officers.

Since the flagship's senior officers had found, or manufactured, excuses for going ashore, it was Acting Lieutenant Foley and Purser's Mate Will Pallister who received the visitor at the gangway. The former then burst out, "John Byron, by God! Thought you'd gone down in the *Wager!*"

After saluting the quarterdeck the tall young fellow laughed, "I almost did. Make no mistake about that!"

"Come to the wardroom." To Pallister he said, "Be a good chap and ask Mr. Wade to join us."

" 'Mister' Wade? That — that countryman?" Byron's large and clear gray eyes widened. "Why, he was *'pressed!'*"

"He was, but he's such a natural-born navigator and seaman that the Commodore's warranted him a sailing master."

Presently Wade entered, somewhat diffidently, since to him the 'officers' country' remained unfamiliar. Nevertheless, he wrung the visiting midshipman's hand heartily. "You're looking fine, sir, but a bit older, if I may say so." Then he flushed because it wasn't necessary for him to 'sir' a midshipman any longer.

A brief silence prevailed while a wardroom steward set out port, biscuit and cheese. When Wade picked up a goblet his big brown fingers seemed to engulf its slender stem.

Grinning, Byron raised a glass to his hosts. "Well, here's to you! Once the prize money's divided you'll all be richer than cream."

"We'll do well enough," Foley admitted modestly. "I say, Byron, wish you were going to draw a share; you must have had rather a thin time."

" 'Thin' is putting it rather mildly."

While munching cheese and a biscuit, Pallister mumbled, "D'you mind telling what happened to the *Wager?* Up till we got home we had deemed her lost with all hands."

[469]

"The *Wager* was lost all right; drove right onto a reef and broke up," grunted the future poet's grandfather. "Only thirty-four of all her company are still alive."

"Only thirty-four?" Wade echoed.

"Aye. Rest of us died from bullets, hunger, thirst, cold or drowning. Oh, it's a grim tale I'll tell you."

Staring with unseeing eyes on the bottle before him, the Honorable John Byron then described the loss of *Wager,* the ensuing mutiny and Midshipman Cozens's dreadful end. More briefly, he mentioned murder and evidences of cannibalism among the starving survivors.

"After we had been cast away on Wager Island, as we named that accursed place, for five months, a party of eighty mutineers led by Gunner Bulkley sailed away in the longboat which had been lengthened, on the fourteenth of October, 1741 — abandoning Captain Cheap, Marine Lieutenant Hamilton, Midshipman Alex Campbell, Surgeon Elliott and I, and a few loyal hands — a queer old farmer named Utting was among 'em — to make out with the barge and yawl — the last being so leaky that it soon sank while at anchor.

"I shan't tire you with a strict account of all the hardships endured by Captain Cheap and ourselves after we started, two months later, working our way northwards up that horrible, bleak coast.

"Only Captain Cheap, Hamilton, Campbell, Joe Utting and I were left alive — and only just alive at that — when, finally, we were captured by the Spaniards at a place called 'Castro' in the Captaincy-General of Chile."

Byron's sensitively shaped hands shook a little as he refilled his glass. "We expected the worst but, thanks to the Commodore's humane treatment of prisoners captured off the South American coast, we were decently, even kindly, handled.

"Eventually, the Dons sent us home in a French ship, all except Midshipman Alexander Campbell, who, being of their Faith, seemed in no great hurry to return home and face a Court of Inquiry which, I understand, is to precede the court-martial of Captain Cheap. He, I'm told, is being held at present *sub judice.*" Midshipman the Honorable Byron sighed. "A hardheaded, irascible man that, but loyal, determined, brave as a lion and a most excellent seaman."

"In that case, let us hope Captain Cheap will not fare too ill at his trial," Will Pallister commented while clumsily loading a clay pipe — he'd recently acquired the habit, along with the necessity of shaving every morning. "Pray tell us, if you can, Mr. Byron, what happened to Bulkley and his mutineers?"

"As I've said, eighty of 'em shoved off in the longboat. Recently it was reported that they suffered such horrible privations only thirty of the rascals managed to round the Horn and find refuge in a Brazilian port."

"What!" Wade exclaimed. "They got around the Horn *in a long-boat?*"

"I'll admit it does seem incredible after what we all experienced off Cape Noire, but they did reach Brazil, for all they must have been more dead than alive."

"What since has happened to the mutineers?"

"They're held in prison in Southampton, where I presume they'll remain until called to testify at Captain Cheap's court-martial. After that, they'll have their own fate to worry over."

A burst of drunken shouts from the 'tween decks attested the fact the victorious crew was making the most of a privilege customarily granted to crews fresh in from a long cruise — that of drinking all they could buy and of carousing with the shrill-voiced and crudely painted trulls who flocked aboard, brazenly eager, one way or another, to lay hands on any bauble the returned sailors might have fetched home from abroad.

Wade, in grim amusement, reflected that that detachment of Marines which had appeared on arrival day, must be finding their hands full; curses, feminine laughter and occasional high-pitched screams continued to beat in through the wardroom's open stern windows.

When the tumult subsided, Foley said, "Can you tell us, Mr. Byron, what has become of Captain Mitchell and Captain Saunders, who went home from China?"

Byron's mobile, rather delicate features lit. "I am happy to tell you that when they reached England, bearing the Commodore's second 'Letter of Proceedings,' they were very well received by Lord Winchelsea and other Lords of the Admiralty. I believe both of them are now at sea; Captain Mitchell is commanding the *Worcester* — a new Fourth Rate."

"Which is good and right!" Wade broke in. "If ever an able Captain was cursed with an unlucky ship, Matthew Mitchell's the one."

"And what of Captain Saunders?"

"I've heard he's been given the *Sapphire;* she's old, but a Third

Rate, nevertheless. I expect he, too, is chasing the dancing masters somewhere off the coast of North America."

Foley's squarish features contracted. "Do you by any chance know what's become of those valiant gentlemen, Captains Legge and Murray?"

Before making reply, the guest tapped several fat weevils out of his biscuit then helped himself to a piece of ripe Stilton sent over by some friendly ship. "Wish I could say that they've met their just deserts and been shot for deserting the Commodore's flag in the face of the enemy," Byron said in suddenly metallic tones. "Unfortunately, both of those valiant gentlemen are too damn' well-connected, carry too much influence with the Ministry, which, of course, controls the Admiralty. So Captain Legge is now a commodore commanding a squadron in the West Indies. As for that shining paladin, George Murray, he's quit the Navy to enter politics, which is fit wallow for such a swine."

Another outburst of raucous merriment rang through the flagship above which now was floating George Anson's broad blue Rear Admiral's pendant.

When he had done, handsome John Byron took another pull of his wine, then, using the back of his hand, wiped a frosting of cracker crumbs from his lips.

"Forgive me, friends, for running on like a granny; I've talked too long. Now 'tis your turn. Tell me how you captured the galleon — and what followed."

Will Pallister obliged with a brief but colorful description of the action and a sensitive description of Andrew Menzies's death.

"Sorry to hear of it," stated the visitor. "Mr. Menzies seemed to be such a quiet gentleman. I've often wondered about his past."

Foley then described the victorious flagship's five months in the river below Canton. "The various East India Companies saw to it that the Commodore had to wait that long in order to meet the Chantuck face to face and settle, for good and all, the matter of honors and privileges to be accorded a visiting British man-of-war."

Foley grew animated, ignored outbursts of ribald song from the main gundeck. "I'll never forget that day! There must have been all of ten thousand archers and armored halbardiers on guard all tricked out with flags, banners, lacquered shields and the weirdest collection of helmets and weapons you ever saw.

"Of course from the Commodore on down, we were in our Sun-

[472]

day best; even so, we looked like jackdaws amongst pheasants and pea-cocks."

"How did the Admiral fare?"

"To start with, the Viceroy was difficult, but our Commodore stuck to his guns, in more senses than one, so the interview ended with the Chantuck granting us and any other European man-of-war immunity from harbor dues and the right to re-fit and have access to supplies.

"Naturally, the India Company's factors got hopping mad be-cause they still must pay port dues and can't, like us, go wherever we please in Chinese waters.

"So you see, the Commodore — the Admiral, I mean — won a sec-ond victory, which, Captain Brett claims, in the end will mean more for England than taking the galleon. Now, Mr. Wade, suppose you finish the account."

The big, slow-moving man across the wardroom's table spread his hands. "Well-l, Mr. Byron, the rest's pretty dull telling. After quit-ting Canton, we ran in luck; a steady monsoon wind drove us through the Straits of Sunda and across the Indian Ocean in jig time.

"We reached the Cape of Good Hope on March eleventh of this year and, after restoring our water and fresh provisions, set sail from Cape Town on the third of April. The Commodore — the Admiral, I mean — was almighty worried because he'd learned that war against the frog-eaters could be expected anytime."

Wade, experimenting with a new and painfully acquired vocabu-lary, spoke with deliberation. "Had we not, on June tenth, fallen in with an English vessel bound from Amsterdam to Philadelphia in America, which gave us news of the French war, we mightn't have been so well on our guard." *Centurion's* new sailing master nodded solemnly. "When we were almost home, we stayed lucky and struck so thick a fog off Ushant that we sailed, sight unseen, straight through a great fleet of French men-of-war cruising off Cape Finisterre."

Wade showed scurvy-gapped teeth in a wide grin. " 'Twas on the twelfth we sighted the Lizard, on the thirteenth we passed Plym-outh and on the fourteenth we cast anchor overnight off the Isle of Wight and, like you know, sir" — Wade had forgotten again — "we returned to Portsmouth the next day."

Eyes shining, the Honorable John Byron turned to Anson's acting secretary. "And when do you expect to get paid off?"

"Soon, we all hope. All hands are fairly itching to draw their prize money and pay and get discharged."

[473]

"— After four years at sea, I shouldn't be surprised. I say, Mr. Foley, have you already decided what to do with your share?"

The former midshipman shrugged. "Take some of it home; I've a mess of young brothers and sisters and my parents are aged and ain't by any means well off. Whatever's left I'll bank, and continue on in His Majesty's Service."

"— And you, Mr. Pallister?" The elegant young visitor no longer attempted to disguise his envy of these suddenly affluent junior officers. Why had *Wager* had to end her voyage so painfully, so ingloriously on that icy reef off Patagonia?

The Admiral's acting secretary hesitated. "Well, for one thing, I intend returning to Woking and, if my Father still lives, beg his forgiveness for running away. Next, I'll relieve him of certain debts which have always beset him." With a wry smile he added, "Was there ever in the history of England a well-to-do country parson?"

"No. And then?"

"I shall attempt to study under a court painter, some great artist like Sir Joshua Reynolds, Mr. George Romney or Mr. Thomas Gainsborough."

"And you, Mr. Wade?" Byron queried. "How will you invest your share?"

Anson's new sailing master scratched his head, made no immediate reply. "Why, as to that, I really don't know. Much will depend on what's chanced in Romsey."

No one knew what the big fellow meant by this because, when impressed, his sorrow had been so acute that he'd made no mention of Peggy, his lost bride and, later on, she'd faded so completely from his thoughts that it had never occurred to him to mention her.

At length he said, "Reckon I'll try for a regular lieutenant's commission. Plenty of officers, and some of the best I've noticed, have 'come in through the hawsehole.' Maybe I've enough wit in me to win on merit alone. If not, why then I figger my prize money will buy me a privateer — and with this new French war my chances of success ought to be reasonably good."

Captain Peircy Brett, on returning to *Centurion*, experienced a strange depression. The Admiralty, while satisfied with Anson's accomplishments, had proved unexpectedly diffident about confirming the new Admiral's action in promoting him to the rank of Post Captain. This, to Brett, came as an especially shrewd blow, because their lordships hadn't hesitated about confirming his old shipmates, Charles Saunders and Philip de Saumarez as Captains.

An unfamiliar midshipman appeared to report that Sailing Master Wade was requesting shore-leave for a space of forty-eight hours on an urgent private matter.

Brett at once granted the application and then, to relieve his anxiety, sought his cabin and from a waterproof case pulled a folio of drawings.

Until a late hour, Brett arranged and rearranged his water colors and pen and ink renderings in chronological order. Some were smudged, some were stained by sweat or sea water or had suffered through cockroaches or rats.

Lord! he reflected, how they served to carry a man back and make him recall some things better left forgotten. Not a few sketches required titling, so, after making reference to penciled inscriptions on their reverse side, he deliberated awhile, then commenced to caption them with a graceful, flowing script: "A View of the N.E. End of the Island St. CATHERINS on the Coast of BRASIL." He recognized the ships he'd depicted at anchor there: *Centurion, Gloucester, Wager, Tryall, Industry* and *Anna.*

After trimming the lantern above him, he scanned one of his favorites: "Cape BLANCO on the Coast of PATAGONIA." "The East Prospect of the Island of Iuan Fernandes in the South Sea." Yes. He had to admit to having executed some rather clever penwork on this one. Below lay "A Sea-Lyon and Lyoness." What absurd-looking creatures! Momentarily, Brett forgot his anxiety over what the Admiralty might do.

Presently, he came across an unusually elaborate sketch entitled: "The Burning of the TOWN of PAYTA on the Coast of SANTA FEE in the SOUTH SEA" and wondered what could have happened to Will Pallister's rendering of the same subject. How earnest, how eager the youth had been, how readily he had learned. Would he keep on? He ought to, he'd had a very real talent.

While half listening to Marines relieve the sentry outside the great cabin's door, he flipped over his drawings until he came to "A View of the Entrance of the Port of Acapulco." Lord, would anyone ever forget the sickening disappointment after chasing that bright light all night?

Then came lively sketches entitled: "A View of the Water Place at TENIAN" and "Chinese Vefsels." And, finally, there was the most meticulously rendered drawing of them all: "A View of CAPE ESPIRITU SANTO on SAMAL one of the Phillipine Islands in the latitude of 12.40 m N°. Bearing W.S.W. distant 6 leagues. In the Position here represented his Majesty's Ship the CENTURION engag'd and took the Spanish Galeon call'd NOSTRA SEIGNORA DE CABADONGA from ACAPULCO bound to MANILA."

Was the Admiralty about to disallow his Post Captain's commission? Wearily, Peircy Brett sorted a huge stack of charts laboriously drawn throughout the voyage and addressed them to the Hydrographic Office. Finally, he undid his stock and otherwise prepared to retire.

～ 2 5 ～
Home Is the Sailor

CLAD IN A SUIT of slops so ill-fitting they certainly should not attract attention, Sailing Master Nathaniel Wade caught a stage coach in Portsmouth which, on its way to Salisbury, passed fairly near by Romsey, the village Peggy Trusdale had deserted to marry him, half a lifetime ago it seemed.

Without undue curiosity, his fellow passengers eyed him, a silent, bronze-featured and powerfully built fellow with neatly clubbed and tied reddish-brown hair. His dark-blue eyes were wide set and perceptive travelers recognized in them that far-seeing look peculiar to seafaring men and to dwellers on great plains.

Around noon, the Salisbury coach rattled up to a crossroads just outside of Romsey and halted before a thatched, half-timbered relay house before which that vehicle changed horses.

After dismounting, Wade untied his hair and allowed it to stream untidily over his forehead then knotted his neckerchief high enough to muffle his powerful and distinctive jaw line.

Of course it really wasn't likely that anybody would recognize him around Romsey; he'd only been there long enough to court Peggy, but with what he had to do, he didn't want to take chances. No one in the dusty, untidy and sun-drenched village square paid him the least attention when he entered the Turk's Head.

To play safe, Wade remained in the tavern's taproom until the stage rolled away towards Salisbury, painfully spelling out an article in a discarded copy of the London *Daily Post* for June 17, 1744. His manufactured interest all at once became real as he read:

> Yesterday Morning, about Eight o'Clock, Mr. Dennis, First Lieutenant of the *Centurion* Man-of-War, arriv'd at the Admiralty Office, Whitehall; who brought an Account that Commodore Anson was safely arriv'd at Spithead from the South-Seas, but last from the East-Indies; and, as we are inform'd, has on Board, in Specie and Goods to the Value of two Millions Sterling. In their passage they took an Acapulco Ship, which had on board 1,400,000 pieces of eight.
>
> The Commodore is in good Health, and is speedily expected in Town. In the same Ship arriv'd the Hon Van Keppel, Esq; Second Son to the Right Hon, the Earl of Albemarle, who has been all the Voyage with the Commodore.

Aware that the publican was noticing his interest in Anson's triumphs, the new sailing master hurriedly counterfeited absorption in an article which reported that settlers in the Massachusetts Bay Colony, having become incensed by repeated Indian incursions incited by the French in Canada, were contemplating the recruitment of a military and naval force.

It was stated their objective would be a great fortress maintained by the French near the mouth of the St. Lawrence River in Canada. This place, Wade read with purely simulated interest, was called Louisburg.

The innkeeper came shuffling over with a rotund belly riding under his stained leather apron. "Them colonials in America may be right as all get out," he rumbled, "but they'll certain-sure get their noses bloody if they try to besiege such a place as that 'thout the help of the King's own troops."

"No doubt," Wade agreed from the depth of his tankard. "Everyone knows 'tis folly for unseasoned troops to assail any sort of fortified position. Another, if you please." Then, before the publican could turn away, he added carefully, "A shipmate o' mine hailed from near here. 'Fore he died he asked would I inquire about a miller name of" — he appeared to stumble — "Goodman — is it Goodman Trusdale?"

"Dunno. Let me ask Jennie." The publican waddled out to refill the tankard, his fat bottom jiggling like the breasts of an overweight dancer.

"Jennie's 'minded me of a feller that name uster live on the

Winchester highroad. If he's the one you want, he's been dead going on three year'."

"A pity; he leave any children?"

"Let's see. Um. I mind me of two. One were a lad wot run off to London or maybe to sea; any case, he ain't been heard of since. T'other was a lass, sir."

Below the table Nat Wade's big, calloused hands tightened. "What was she called?"

" 'Peggy' it was and is, sir," the innkeeper informed, wiping froth from the table's worn boards.

"— And what of her?"

"Why, sir, some long time ago she married a harness-maker name of — well now, guess I disremember it. Must be getting old. Anyhow, folks said a pressgang took him up soon after they was wed." The publican suddenly snapped his fingers, "— Wade! Nat Wade, that wuz his name!"

"He came back?"

"Not bloody likely! They say 'e were lost wi' many others in the wreck of a ship called the *Wager*, one o' them vessels wot started around the world wi' Georgie Anson, our new 'ero. Now *there's* a man for you, b'God! Run out o' the very same mold as Frobisher, Hawkins and Drake!"

"Aye! They claim Anson's a real tiger," Wade admitted. "Reckon I'd like to see him sometime." It required considerable self-restraint to abandon the subject of Peggy until the innkeeper returned to it of his own accord. Fortunately, he soon did so.

"Yes, pore Peggy was fair distracted when she came back to her Pa's mill, even wore widow's weeds for a year 'cause a gypsy who read her hand told her her man was dead."

"Very clever, those gypsy women."

"Then happen' Peggy Wade marries young Justin Meade, the feller from around here who bought her Pa's mill after he died."

"This — this Polly — I mean Peggy — seems content?" he demanded, heart beating like a Marine's drum.

"Very, sir. 'Specially since she's bore young Justin a pair o' brats — uncommon lusty, so I hear."

"A happy ending, I'm sure." Then Nat committed an error. "Too bad poor Wade can't know of it."

The innkeeper's eyes widened. "You was shipmates wi' Nat Wade?"

"Aye," the Sailing Master admitted, then added hurriedly, "but I transferred out of *Wager* long before she sailed for the South Seas." Nat groped for a sixpence and stood up. "Well, landlord, reckon I'll be on my way to Fording Bridge."

"Then you wasn't along of Admiral Anson?"

"No, I wasn't, curse the luck! or I'd be rich. I got sent to the Carolinas in North America. A good day to you."

In the warm sunlight, Wade forced himself not to hurry along an alley leading back to the Winchester turnpike, but once he reached it he moved on with a rolling gait which somehow he couldn't get rid of, no matter how hard he tried.

A good mile out of Romsey he recognized Trusdale's mill. Its brown-sailed arms were revolving leisurely with a flock of gray-white pigeons rioting about them. Fortunately, there was no need to risk a close approach, for from behind a hedge of flowering hawthorn he could see Peggy, considerably stouter than he'd remembered her, come out of doors carrying a hamper of what undoubtedly were swaddling cloths.

Humming, she unconcernedly commenced to hang a long row of dripping diapers to a line. Then she dried her hands on an apron and went to hunt for eggs in a henhouse. She found some and then disappeared into the millhouse.

For a long moment Wade remained listening to the mill's mechanism bump and creak on and on.

So this was Peggy? To his relieved astonishment, Sailing Master Wade experienced no pain, no yearning, nor did he experience the slightest sense of loss.

~~ 2 6 ~~

Rewards

THROUGH THE ANCIENT leaded and diapered windows of his lodgings in Spring Garden, Rear Admiral of the Blue George Anson considered a small but pleasant garden just below. The beds down there were gay with many roses, heliotropes, Canterbury bells, larkspur and a profusion of other blooms he couldn't recognize and, on the garden wall opposite, which was shrouded by a flowering espalier pear tree, an enormous black and white cat sat primly washing herself in the warm sunshine.

His solid frame enveloped in a flowing banyan of red and blue silk, the new Admiral wriggled bare toes within a pair of Turkey-red kid slippers and conceded that on this fine morning he had every right to feel pleased with the world. Was he not back in England in perfect health, successful and surrounded by familiar sights, sounds and smells?

He also was cheered to have received word from Shugborough that all was well with Brother Tom and their sisters. Even better, the night before he'd received a long missive from Elizabeth Yorke, so tenderly expressed that, more and more, Betts was beginning to occupy his thoughts.

Hugely, George Anson yawned, then stretched and listened to street calls rising in the distance. "Fish! Here's fine fish, fresh in from the sea!" "Cockles and mussels, O!" Then a female's voice shrilling, "Lavender! Who'll buy my lavender?"

A knock at the door and a flash of gold earrings preluded the appearance of Michael Despeda, inordinately proud of his brand-new chocolate and yellow livery. With his usual silent tread, the Jamaican fetched in a silver tray upon which rested Anson's breakfast, several letters and today's copy of the *Daily Post*.

"A werry fine day, sar," observed the steward. "I only hopes, sar, she ends fair as she's begun."

"Let us indeed hope so, Michael," Anson smiled and had reached towards a heaping plate of kippers and scrambled eggs when he recognized an Admiralty seal securing the topmost missive.

Lips pursed, he employed a fruit knife to slit the letter's end.

Sir: You are herewith informed that the Board of Admiralty has been pleased to appoint Lieutenant Peter Denis to be Captain of the sloop *Spence*, 16 guns.

Anson's face lit and he glanced into his servant's copper-black and Indian-like features. "Mr. Denis is to have a ship of his own. What do you think of that, Michael?"

Despeda ducked his close-cropped head. "That is most agreeable news indeed, sar. He's a fine young officer, is Mr. Denis."

There was a second communication from the Admiralty which Anson opened with considerable trepidation, he having recently threatened to refuse his promotion to Rear Admiral if Peircy Brett were not confirmed as a Post Captain. Um. The contents of this slim, blue-tinted envelope might well decide his future in the Royal Navy.

With a rare, hurried gesture, he broke the seal then read and presently began to chuckle.

"More good news, Michael. It would seem that I've won my little skirmish with the Lords of Admiralty. Listen to this: 'Their Lordships are pleased to appoint Mr. Peircy Brett, late First Lieutenant of HBMS *Centurion*, in the rank of Captain. He is to command the *Mary*, galley, a new ship of 20 guns.'"

The Jamaican beamed. "That, sar is the bestest news I've heard since that ol' galleon throw in the towel. I know you was feared they was going to turn down Mister Brett an' then accept your resignation."

His already keen appetite sharpened by relief, Anson fell eagerly upon his breakfast; at the same time he scanned the newspaper now propped against a silver chocolate pot. Suddenly his hand shot out and picked up the *Daily Post*. He read:

> On Wednesday next the Treasure taken from the Spaniards by Commodore Anson, guarded by the Whole Crew, is to be brought to Town in about forty Waggons; the People are to Breakfast at Mr. Parry's, the Bowling-Green House on Putney Common, between Nine and Ten in the Morning, after which they will come over Fulham Bridge, pass along Piccadilly, St. James's Street, Pall Mall, the Strand, and so to the Bank about Twelve.

Absently, Anson wiped cocoa from his lips and stood up. "Michael, I expect you had best look over my best frock coat, satin breeches and silk stockings."

"Yes, sar."

"And also polish my dress sword. It would appear that, on the day after tomorrow, my crew and I are to be fêted."

～ 2 7 ～

England's Glory

THE 2ND OF JULY, 1744, dawned as an open-and-shut sort of day; sunshine and showers alternately illumined and drenched those Royal

Jacks which flapped above turrets guarding the four corners of that lofty keep which dominates the Tower of London.

From its tallest flagpole, the one which rose from the keep's center, floated a huge Royal Standard which indicated that the Duke of Cumberland, King George's second son, at present was within those grim walls about which fluttered clouds of cawing rooks and a few huge and glossy ravens.

On the Thames — off the Tower's Water Gate — had assembled a motley flotilla of merchantmen, river boats and barges which seemed dwarfed alongside frigates and sloops flying the colors of the Royal Navy. All craft had been decorated with a multitude of ensigns, flags, banners and bunting. Not a few bright-hued female petticoats flapped brazenly above some of the barges.

The Lord Mayor having proclaimed July 2nd a holiday, only taverns, inns and brothels were busy. Crowds of idle apprentices, bound servants, soldiers, sailors and mechanics roamed London's dark and narrow streets. Many already were more than a little drunk. Grimy urchins sought points of vantage along the route by which Admiral Anson's treasure would be conveyed for surrender to the Royal Treasurers.

Trees, roofs and windows along Fulham Road, Piccadilly, Pall Mall and the Strand grew black with eager and noisy spectators. Bunting, gay shawls and bright streamers of all sorts fluttered from every conceivable point; flags were numerous but often incorrectly displayed. Brass-throated balladiers hawked broadsides of inspired doggrel such as:

> Ulysses' Voyage lives by Honour's Pen,
> Who many Cities saw, and many men.
> Ye Muse Inventive, dropped to barren Theme,
> With gentle Circe, and dire Polypheme.

> Shipwrecks and Suffering, Fancy could Display
> In a small Portion of the Midland Sea.
> But what to Anson's work Ulysses' Toils?
> Or what to Indie's Wealth were Illion's Spoils?

> The World Surrounded, all her Nature viewed,
> Each Climate tried, each Danger now subdued.
> Our second Drake, arrived on British Ground,
> Requires no Pope his Honour to Resound.

In upper-story windows along the route, wildly excited women and girls giggled and called out, impatient to shower blossoms on the conquerors of the Manila Galleon.

By midmorning the flower stalls of Covent Garden and Shepherd's Market had been sold out to fashion garlands which soon would festoon houses fronting "the Victory Way." Dogs and children raced about and added effectively to the mounting excitement.

At half past eleven a horde of newsboys appeared, flourishing a new broadside the ink on which still was so wet it smeared.

> Less shall Proud ROME her ancient trophies boast
> The Conquer'd Country and the Captive Host.
> Her Fierce Dominion ASIA, AFRIC knew,
> But 'round the Globe her Eagles ne'er flew
> Thro' ev'ry Clime is ALBION'S Thunder hurl'd,
> And ANSON'S spoils are from a tribute World.

Shortly before noon, an artillery piece in the Tower boomed, reverberated through the humid air; then another and another. Out on the Thames, warships replied by firing minute guns. Church bells clanged and pealed as they had not since the Invincible Armada had been reported dispersed.

In the distance, near Fulham Bridge, could be heard a braying of military bands, the penetrating trill of fifes, the squeal of bagpipes and the blood-quickening flam and roll of many drums which, passing through the narrow streets, produced a deafening racket.

Midshipman the Honorable John Byron, perched on a wall fronting Pall Mall, at last heard a great burst of shouting, "Hurrah! Hurrah! Yonder they come!"

A roof-shaking shout arose when out of St. James's Street turned a troop of scarlet-jacketed dragoons whose burnished breastplates flashed bravely in the watery sunlight. A band playing "Rule Britannia" next entered the Mall, then a battalion of Guards wearing black tricorne hats, white breeches and well-pipe-clayed cross-belts over red tunics.

Presently, Byron made out a rank of Army officers wearing full dress uniform; they were waving glittering swords at the onlookers and riding aside those who lined the curb and were reluctant to fall back for fear of losing places occupied since daybreak.

Following the infantry appeared a company from Colonel Lowther's newly formed Regiment of Marines. Thought Byron, how jauntily they swing their arms — not in the least like those poor, superannuated scarecrows sent to serve in Anson's squadron!

Another band appeared to advance smartly over the Strand's muddy, refuse-littered cobbles before another column of infantry.

The head of the procession was approaching the Tower's Iron Gate when into the Strand jogged a double rank of un-uniformed horsemen wearing enormous cocked hats and gold-laced, long-skirted frock coats of varying hues.

"Anson! *Anson!* Our new Drake!" The cry rolled along the street, reverberated like artillery caissons crossing a wooden bridge.

"Anson! ANSON! God bless you, sir!"

Riding slightly in advance of *Centurion*'s commissioned officers, Rear Admiral George Anson, sedate of bearing, was forced continually to uncover his carefully powdered head and, with his hat, salute this window or that balcony from which clouds of flower petals came raining down in such profusion that for a while they alarmed his charger, a handsome gray stallion presented by a group of admirers.

Yells of "Anson! Anson! Long live Admiral Anson, our new Drake!" arose all along the line of march.

The irrepressible van Keppel, riding in the second rank of officers behind Captains de Saumarez and Brett turned and, grinning like a schoolboy, called to Lieutenant Nutt, "Cock's bones! Isn't this *a show!* I wonder, though, how they'd cheer us had they seen us on Juan Fernandez and Tinian?"

"I was wondering on it, too," the ex-sailing master admitted with a faint smile. "I'd like to believe that some of those cheers are for the poor devils who died to make this possible."

Yet another company of infantry, marching under rows of burnished bayonets, tramped by Byron's perch to the music of fifes and drums just before the crowd again yelled themselves hoarse and waved scarfs so frantically that several men and boys fell out of trees.

Into the Strand had rolled a huge wagon drawn by beribboned dray horses and guarded by half a dozen grinning, leather-faced sailors. These, with cutlasses drawn, were swaggering along inside a double file of infantry.

The wagon's cover had been thrown back, permitting a flagstaff, supported by boys and men from *Centurion*, to rise from among a pile of ironbound treasure chests. From it floated the weather-beaten

[484]

red and yellow ensign of *Nuestra Señora de Monte Carmelo,* first of the prizes to be taken.

"The Treasure! *There's the treasure!*" chanted the throng. "Long live Anson and his brave fellows!"

Another wagon creaked into sight, guarded and decorated like the first; above it flapped a threadbare flag found aboard the *Santa María de Aranzazu.* Then, in succession, appeared the ensigns of the *Nuestra Señora de los Dolores,* the *Santa Teresa de Jesu,* the *Nuestra Señora del Carmine* and the *Jesu Nazareno.*

A plethora of flags and banners, captured in Payta, flew above carts, wagons and wains escorted by every last member of *Centurion's* original company, down to the lowliest ship's boy.

By military standards, the crew members' attitude was deplorable; whenever they sighted a pretty wench they blew elaborate kisses and shouted obscene comments and invitations.

Coxswain King Parmer, clad in the same improvised uniform he'd worn during the trip to Canton, was roaring drunk; so was Tom Ramster, who lolled among barrels of coin like some Roman emperor enjoying a triumph.

He was wearing a crown of daisies askew on his bright red hair and had slung a necklace of cornflowers across the shirt he'd opened to expose his broad and hairy chest.

The crowd yelled delightedly when the big fellow, on spying a group of giggling trollops, pointed to his bulging cod-piece and yelled, "Look, girls! The real treasure is in here! After the show's over come and see for yourselves if it ain't."

Every time an axle groaned under the treasure's weight, excited cries arose. The onlookers were especially pleased that so many examples of captured plate had been exposed: salvers, pitchers, goblets, tureens, chains and church ornaments glittered before their hungry eyes.

"Cor! Must be a prince's ransom in that one wagon!"

"And, will yer look at all them great platters, bowls an' jugs?"

When the final treasure-laden cart, bearing the *Nuestra Señora de Cobadonga's* Royal Standard, had vanished behind the Tower's Iron Gate, a squadron of cavalry reined to a halt under the battlements; meanwhile Anson and his staff dismounted, albeit somewhat stiffly, in the courtyard.

A solemn moment ensued when the gray-bearded Governor of the

Tower advanced, escorted by a file of halbert-bearing Beefeaters, stalwarts wearing Elizabeth the First's livery.

Called the Governor, saluting, "You are most welcome, your Honor. His Grace the Duke of Cumberland will be pleased to receive you and your officers at once."

Inside the Tower it was so dark that, at first, Captain Peircy Brett found himself hard put to see anything, so kept his gaze riveted on George Anson's broad, emerald and gold brocaded back.

Presently, he made out a dais at the far end of a great armor-hung hall; above it four, gilded Grecian columns were supporting a canopy of purple velvet.

Beneath it, on an ornate, high-backed armchair, sat the King's second son, eyes bright and alert. To his right stood Lord Winchelsea, the First Lord of the Admiralty, to his left lounged the Duke of Newcastle, dissipated and hopelessly corrupt, but nevertheless Prime Minister of the Realm.

As *Centurion*'s officers drew near, the Duke of Newcastle, always ready with a neat-turned phrase, bent and murmured into the young Duke of Cumberland's ear, "Your Royal Highness, I believe that this is, indeed, a supreme moment. It is England's glory."

Epilogue

B Y THE BRIEF, UNEARTHLY GLARE of lightning flashes which, momentarily, were becoming more vivid, Peter Vesey — Doctor of Medicine by virtue of degrees hard-earned at Oxford and Edinburgh Universities — could glimpse, through a ragged black pattern of trees, the faint sheen of the Upper Thames. Although riffled by the storm's first warning puffs, it yet wound serenely past the village of Henley and the home which he'd constructed on its southern bank.

The young physician — he was only thrity-three — felt sure that rain must begin to fall at any moment. The fitful wind stirred a clump of weeping willows, made their feathery boughs sway and flutter over the rutted road like palms waved at some triumphant general.

His mount, a weary old nag rented in Reading, seemed to sense the impending downpour as well as he, for, of its own account, it took up a jolting trot towards a scattering of lights in Henley-on-Thames.

Now thunder began to reverberate along the river valley creating a rumble like that of bowling balls rolling along some Titan's alley. The rhythmic *clink-clinking* of the new instruments and medicine bottles in Peter Vesey's saddlebags quickened when, riding with the ease of one reared in a hunting saddle, he spurred his mount into a ponderous canter.

The time, on this hot, early July night, Vesey judged to be near eleven, so the houses he passed without exception were shuttered and dark. Watchdogs, however, clamored fiercely at the nag's heavy hoofbeats. A bit of luck that he'd been able to hire the livery stable's last horse.

On recalling the last time he had followed this road, his mouth tightened. On that occasion he'd been riding home because Granny Swinden, badly shaken by calentures, had taken a wholly unexpected turn for the better. The tough old woman had begun to rally the moment he'd entered her cottage prepared to ease her passing.

A sudden crack of thunder caused the nag to shy clumsily and then come to a quivering halt. Reassuring pressure on its reins and a few soothing words served to set his mount moving on an instant before the night became filled with a wet confusion which, all in an instant, drenched Peter Vesey to his smallclothes.

The wind blew so hard that a succession of twigs, wet leaves and even small branches were dashed into his face and the dirt road degenerated into a quagmire intermittently revealed by the lightning's blue-white throbbing.

He glimpsed a family of swans, ghostly-looking, cowering amid a reed bed on the Thames's farther bank. When the thundering approached a crescendo, the nag, stung by hard-driven raindrops, began to plunge and snort, so, to steady it, Dr. Vesey reined to a walk.

Splashing on through the downpour, Vesey wished the hour weren't so advanced, but he encouraged himself by thinking that Pamela probably would not have gone to bed. She wasn't in the least frightened of lightning. On the contrary, she'd always enjoyed a thunderstorm's noise and vivid majesty.

Raindrops began to pelt his eyelids so hard he had to shield them behind a raised forearm.

The worst of the storm's fury seemed to have exhausted itself when, with cold trickles running down his back and chest, ex-Surgeon's Mate Vesey splashed into a long avenue of the majestic oaks at the end of which lay Minden — once his home.

For all the house was small, it was comfortable and smart architecturally. How fortunate he'd been able to construct this dwelling for his then bride on the site of an ancient manor house which had burned down a few years earlier; otherwise, he never could have boasted such splendid trees to line Minden's driveway.

Through a pelting rain he glimpsed a light in one of Minden's downstairs windows — if, indeed, the property's name had remained the same.

Lord! How weary he felt. No wonder. Since descending from the stagecoach at Reading, he'd ridden many miles and that on top of a long and tiresome journey up from London.

The stable looked just as it had four years ago. Peter Vesey went inside and took time to rub down his mount after he'd unsaddled and unbridled it. He looked for, and found, grain in the feedbox, then pitchforked hay into the manger.

Slinging his sodden saddlebags over one shoulder, Dr. Vesey splashed through a succession of puddles up to Minden's front door. He knocked briefly, then, on receiving no reply, gripped its silvered glass knob. Entering, he called several times, but received no response.

With the tides of memory beginning to run ever more strongly, Vesey hung the saddlebags to a familiar staghorn rack, then without result hailed the servants' quarters. He now felt sure Pamela was still in residence, but his former wife was not in the library, so he hesitated, listening to the crackle of nearby lightning and the crash of thunder. At length, to warm himself, he poured sherry from a decanter standing on a table near the fireplace.

The storm seemed to be gathering fresh fury; lightning blazed near at hand and heart-stilling claps of thunder caused windowpanes and shutters to rattle.

Dripping dark spots along the carpets, Vesey sought the upper floor and again called, "Pamela? Pamela!" But there was no trace of her.

Grimly, he decided that, if she were anywhere about, she must once more have sought the summerhouse.

His muddied boots crunched loudly upon the driveway's wet gravel, but the thunder concealed their progress.

Urged on by an especially vicious squall, Vesey covered the last few yards to the summerhouse at a run and dashed inside.

As he was flinging open the door a very brilliant flash of lightning illuminated the interior in such detail that he could have read titles on a series of flower prints gracing a far wall.

The sudden glare also revealed, in vivid clarity, a single figure occupying that rattan settee upon which Pamela so often had reposed during pleasant weather.

She was sitting hunched forward a little, as though very weary. One slim hand drooped from her lap; the other supported her chin as, fixedly, she stared out upon the tormented landscape.

"Pamela —"

Very slowly she turned her lovely dark head and saw him framed in the doorway. Uncertainly, Pamela arose, full skirt billowing.

"Oh, no! No! It can't be," she faltered, eyes enormous and charged

[489]

with unbreakable suspense. "Oh, Peter! Peter! Have you really come home?"

"I have."

"To me?"

He made no reply, only strode forward to encircle her with sodden arms. Many times he kissed Pamela's mouth, her brow, her eyes.

At last he said very softly, "D'you know? I really needn't have gone out after all, my dear. Granny Swinden was not nearly so sick as they reported. Since I'm cold and wet, shan't we go in and brew some tea?"

THE END

Appendix A

The subsequent careers of:

George Anson

1744 Rear Admiral of the Blue
1744 Rear Admiral of the Red
1745 Rear Admiral of the White
1745 Board of Admiralty
1746 Vice-Admiral of the Blue
1747 Defeated Marquis de la Jonquière off Finisterre
1747 Created Baron Anson of Soberton
1748 Married Lady Elizabeth Yorke
1749 Vice-Admiral of Great Britain
1751 First Lord of the Admiralty, Privy Councillor, and Admiral
1762 Died

Peircy Brett

1747 In Command of HBMS *Centurion* in action against Marquis
     de la Jonquière
1753 Knighted
1760 Rear Admiral of the Red
1760 Colonel of Marines
1760 Lord Commissioner of the Admiralty
1778 Admiral of the Blue
1781 Died

Peter Denis

1744 Captain
1747 Distinguished in action against Marquis de la Jonquière

1761	Captain of Royal Yacht
1767	Made Baronet
1770	Rear Admiral of the Blue
1777	Vice-Admiral of the Red
1778	Died

Augustus van Keppel

1744	Captain
1762	Rear Admiral of the Red
1778	Admiral of the Blue
1782	Made Viscount van Keppel
1782	First Lord of the Admiralty
1786	Died

John Campbell

1747	Captain
1778	Rear Admiral of the White
1782	Governor of Newfoundland
1787	Vice-Admiral of the Red
1790	Died

Charles Saunders

1741	Captain
1752	Knighted
1752	Rear Admiral of the Red
1759	Commanded Naval Forces at Siege of Quebec
1766	Admiral of the Blue
1766	Lieutenant General of the Marines
1766	First Lord of the Admiralty and Privy Councillor
1775	Died

Hyde Parker

1748	Captain
1762	Captured Manila Galleon *Santissima Trinidad*
1778	Rear Admiral of the Red
1779	Vice-Admiral of the Red
1781	Succeeded to Baronetcy
1782	Died, lost at sea

Philip de Saumarez

1743 Captain
1747 In battle against Marquis de la Jonquière
1747 Died, killed in Action off Brest

Thomas de Saumarez

1748 Captain
1758 Captured *Belliqueux* in brilliant action
1766 Died

Francis William Drake

1759 Captain
1781 Rear Admiral of the Blue

John Byron

1758 Commodore at the 2nd Siege of Louisburg, Cape Breton Island
1775 Rear Admiral
1779 Vice-Admiral of the Blue
1786 Died

Appendix B

Principal Fictional Characters

Peter Vesey	Tom Ramster*
Andrew Menzies	Will Pallister*
Ted Waxter	Nathaniel Wade*
Joseph Utting*	King Parmer*
John Clipperton*	Peter Dobey*
Robert Robinson*	Paddy Kildare*
	William Buckle*

* These are the names of men who actually served in the expedition, but that is all that is known about them.

NORTH
&
AMERICA

North of Galapagos label area:

Chequetan
March~May 1742   Acapulco

Quibo I.

Galapagos
Ilands

Guayaquil
Payta~Nov.
1741
Callao
Lima

SOUTH
AMERICA

Rio de Janeiro

PACIFIC

OCEAN

TROPIC OF CAPRICORN

Juan Fernandez I.
Cumberland Bay
June~Sept. 1741

Valparaiso   Rio Grande
R. PLATE

Santa Catharina~Dec. 1740

Centurion nearly lost
in heavy gale   Chiloe I.
Socorro I.

May
14th
Wager wrecked

St. Julian's Port
Cape Virgins

CAPE NOIRE
April 14

PATAGONIA

Le Maire Straits

April
3   CAPE HORN

Severn and Pearle
turned back here
Anna and Wager disabled

March 23, Centurion disabled

April 24   April 22   March 28
Gloucester disabled
Lost sight of Gloucester,
Tryall, Wager and Anna

SOUTH

ATLANTIC

OCEAN

ANTARCTIC CIRCLE

Spithead
Arrived~June 10th
1744

Portsmouth
Departed
Sept 17

Azores
Fayal

Funchal Madeira

Canary Island

NORTH

Bermuda

ATLANTIC

OCEAN

Cape Verde
Islands

St Paul
Rocks

St Helena
April 1744

130° 120° 110° 100° 90° 80° 70° 60° 50° 40° 30° 20° 10° W 0°